SELECTED WRITINGS

HEINRICH VON KLEIST

SELECTED
WRITINGS

Edited and translated by
DAVID CONSTANTINE
University of Oxford

Hackett Publishing Company, Inc.
Indianapolis/Cambridge

10 09 08 07 06 05 04 1 2 3 4 5 6 7

For further information, please address:

> Hackett Publishing Company, Inc.
> P.O. Box 44937
> Indianapolis, IN 46244-0937
>
> www.hackettpublishing.com

Cover illustration: *The Broken Jug*, 1772–1773 by Jean-Baptiste Greuze (1725–1805). Louvre, Paris. Photo credit: Erich Lessing/Art Resource, NY. Printed at Sheridan Books, Inc.

Library of Congress Cataloging-in-Publication Data

Kleist, Heinrich von, 1777–1811.
  [Selections. English. 2004]
  Selected writings / Heinrich Von Kleist ; edited and translated by David Constantine.
    p. cm.
  Originally published: London : J. M. Dent, 1997.
  Includes bibliographical references.
  ISBN 0-87220-744-7 (cloth) — ISBN 0-87220-743-9 (paper)
    I. Constantine, David, 1944– II. Title.

PT2378.A14 2004
838'.609—dc22

                                                    2004054378

CONTENTS

SELECTED WRITINGS

CHRONOLOGY OF KLEIST'S LIFE

Year	Age	Life
1777		10 (or 18) October: born in Frankfurt an der Oder Schooling at home
1788	11	18 June, death of father Schooling in Berlin
1792	14	1 June, joins the army

CHRONOLOGY OF HIS TIMES

Year	Artistic Context	Historical Events
1778	Voltaire and Rousseau die	
1781	Schiller, *Die Räuber* Kant, *Kritik der reinen Vernunft*	
1783		Frederick the Great dies;
1786	Mozart, *Nozze di Figaro* Burns, *Poems*, chiefly in Scottish dialect Goethe, *Iphigenie*	
1787	Schiller, *Don Carlos* Mozart, *Don Giovanni*	
1788	Goethe, *Tasso* Kant, *Kritik der praktischen Vernunft*	
1789	Blake, *Songs of Innocence*	Fall of Bastille (14 July); French Revolution; Declaration of the Rights of Man
1790	Kant, *Kritik der Urteilskraft* Burke, *Reflections on the Revolution in France*	
1791	Paine, *Rights of Man* Mozart, *Zauberflöte* Mozart dies	
1792	Wollstonecraft, *Rights of Woman*	France declares war on the Coalition; the September Massacres; Battle of Valmy, Mainz besieged and taken

Year	Age	Life
1793	15	3 February, death of mother March, at the siege of Mainz
1794	16	Sees action in the Pfalz
1795	17	With the army on the Main, in Westphalia and back to Potsdam
1796	18	Friendship with Ludwig von Brockes
1797	19	Friendship with Ernst von Pfuel
1798	20	Friendship with Rühle von Lilienstern; mathematics and music together in Potsdam Excursion to the Harz Mountains Friendship with Marie von Kleist Essay, *On the surest Way of finding Happiness*
1799	21	April, leaves the army, matriculates at the University of Frankfurt an der Oder
1800	22	Engagement to Wilhelmine von Zenge August, reading *Wallenstein*, keeping a diary; August–October, journey with Brockes via Leipzig and Dresden to Würzburg Preparing himself for 'the literary profession' but also for the civil service; keeping a 'magazine of ideas' With Brockes in Berlin
1801	23	March, 'Kant-Crisis' April–May, journey with Ulrike via Dresden, the Harz, Main, Rhine, Strasburg to Paris; reading Rousseau and Montesquieu November, with Ulrike as far as Frankfurt a. Main, then on to Bern; friends there: Zschokke, Geβner, Ludwig Wieland

Year	Artistic Context	Historical Events
1793		Louis XVI executed (January); Britain enters the war (February) Reign of Terror begins (June); Marie Antoinette executed; the Girondists executed
1794	Paine, *Age of Reason* Fichte, *Wissenschaftslehre* Blake, *Songs of Experience, Europe, Book of Urizen*	Danton executed (April); Robespierre executed (July) End of Terror
1795	Goethe, *Wilhelm Meister* and *Römische Elegien* Schiller, *Über naïve und sentimentalische Dichtung* and *Briefe über die ästhetische Erziehung* Keats born (31 October)	
1796	Goethe, *Hermann und Dorothea*	Jenner performs first smallpox vaccination Napoleon's campaigns in Italy
1797	The 'Balladenjahr' of Goethe and Schiller	Treaty of Campo Formio
1798	Schlegel, *Athenäum*, Novalis a contributor Wordsworth and Coleridge, *Lyrical Ballads*	Napoleon invades Egypt (July); Battle of the Nile (August) The French in Switzerland
1799	Hölderlin, *Hyperion* Schiller, *Piccolomini* and *Wallensteins Tod*	Napoleon First Consul under new constitution
1800	Schiller, *Maria Stuart* Novalis, *Hymnen an die Nacht*	
1801	Hölderlin, great hymns and elegies Novalis dies	Battle of Copenhagen; Peace of Lunéville; French gains in Germany

Year	Age	Life
1802	24	On foot with Zschokke and Wieland to Aarau April–July, Delosea Island near Thun, work on *Schroffenstein, Guiskard, Jug* July–August, ill in Bern; Ulrike comes for him October, with her and Wieland to Jena and Weimar; Christmas with the Wieland family
1803	25	With the Wielands until 24 February; work on *Guiskard*; reading Richardson March–April, in Leipzig; *Schroffenstein* published anonymously in Bern April–July, in Dresden with Pfuel and others; reading Aristophanes and Sophocles; work on *Guiskard, Jug, Amphitryon* July–October, travels with Pfuel and others in Switzerland, northern Italy and to Paris; quarrel with Pfuel, burns *Guiskard*, tries to enlist with the French army in Boulogne Winter, ill in Mainz; speaks of becoming a carpenter
1804	26	*Schroffenstein* performed in Graz June, back to Berlin; applying to join the civil service; seeing Pfuel, Rühle and Marie von Kleist
1805	27	Work in the ministry of finance May, to Königsberg to study economics and politics; Ulrike joins him *On the gradual Production of Thoughts whilst Speaking* Autumn, often unwell
1806	28	August, given six months' leave Sends *Jug* to Marie von Kleist; working hard at his dramas
1807	29	January, with Pfuel and others to Berlin; then, heading for Dresden, arrested by the French as a spy and conveyed to Fort de Joux near Pontarlier 3 April, Ulrike writes to General Clarke on his behalf; he is taken to Châlons sur Marne Early May, *Amphitryon* published in Dresden 12 July released; to Berlin and Dresden September, *Chilean Earthquake* published; December, finishes *Penthesilea* and, with Adam Müller, founds the journal *Phöbus*.

Year	Artistic Context	Historical Events
1802	Novalis, *Heinrich von Ofterdingen*	Peace of Amiens; Napoleon Consul for life
1803	Schiller, *Braut von Messina* Klopstock dies	
1804		Napoleon crowned Emperor
1805	Schiller dies Beethoven, *Fidelio*	Napoleon becomes King of Italy; Napoleon's victory at Ulm Battle of Trafalgar; Battle of Austerlitz
1806		Battle of Jena (14 October), defeat and collapse of Prussia; Prussian court flees to Königsberg End of the Holy Roman Empire
1807		Peace of Tilsit (July) Reforms in Prussia (1807–14) Abolition of the slave trade Peninsular War begins

Year	Age	Life
1808	30	Eleven issues of *Phöbus*, in which he places fragments of *Penthesilea*, *Jug*, *Guiskard*, *Käthchen* and *Kohlhaas*, as well as the whole of *The Marquise of O.*
		March, Goethe stages *Jug* in Weimar; July, meets Tieck in Dresden and *Penthesilea* is published entire; finishes *Käthchen* and (December) *Arminius*; active in patriotic and nationalist politics
1809	31	End of February, twelfth and last issue of *Phöbus*
		Patriotic articles and verses
		Violent quarrel with Müller; May, journey to Prague, via Aspern; by November back in Berlin, via Dresden and Frankfurt
1810	32	January–February, journey to Frankfurt a. Main, continuing efforts to get *Käthchen* staged; March, *Käthchen* staged in Vienna
		May, work on *Kohlhaas* and the first volume of stories: these published in September, also *Käthchen*. 1 October, first issue of the *Berliner Abendblätter*, Müller, Arnim, Brentano, Fouqué, Grimm involved
		Marie von Kleist in Berlin and Potsdam, October–May 1811; Müller, at odds with the authorities, is a difficult colleague
1811	33/34	Moving in Romantic and patriotic society
		February, *Jug* published; ever greater difficulties, financial and political, with the *Abendblätter*: last issue, 30 March
		Betrothal in San Domingo published in a literary magazine; April onwards, efforts to find employment or financial support; May, Müller and Marie von Kleist leave Berlin
		End of June, finishing *Homburg*, working on a two-volume novel; early August, second volume of the stories published
		Marie, back in Berlin till early September, doing her best on his behalf; 3 September she presents Princess Marianne with a copy of *Homburg*
		November, friendship with Henriette Vogel, last arrangements and last letters
		21 November, about four in the afternoon, shoots her and himself on the banks of the Wannsee outside Berlin

Year	Artistic Context	Historical Events
1808	Beethoven, *Fifth Symphony*	Napoleon invades Spain
1809	Goethe, *Die Wahlverwandtschaften* Edgar Allan Poe born	Austrians invade Bavaria (April); Prussia mobilizes; Napoleon captures Vienna (May) Battle of Aspern; defeat of Austrians at Wagram (6 July) Peace of Schönbronn (October); the Prussian court returns to Berlin (December) Darwin born
1810	Napoleon prohibits the publication of Mme de Staël's *De l'Allemagne* (published 1813)	Death of the Prussian Queen, Luise (19 July) English King George III generally recognized as insane Wellington's successful campaigns against France in Spain and Portugal
1811	Jane Austen, *Sense and Sensibility* Shelley, *Necessity of Atheism*	All Germany under the French Napoleon prepares to invade Russia

INTRODUCTION

Kleist was born, according to his own account, on 10 October 1777; but on the 18th according to official records. He was born in Frankfurt an der Oder, into a very ancient, originally Slav, Prussian aristocratic family that had produced by then eighteen generals but also, in Ewald von Kleist (1715–59), one reputable poet. Kleist shot himself and Henriette Vogel in a suicide pact on the Wannsee, Berlin, 21 November 1811. He left seven finished plays, the fragment of another, eight stories, a few poems, some important essays, anecdotes, letters. Other writings, probably including a novel, he destroyed in the sorting out of his affairs before his death. His writing career only lasted eight or nine years and he was productive in a sustained fashion for only the last four or five.

Born into a military family he joined the army before he was fifteen. That autumn, 1792, the revolutionary wars got under way and there was no lasting peace in Europe again until four years after his death. War and the foundering of the old order (the Holy Roman Empire ended in 1806) were the real context for his literary works in which dissolution, collapse and chaos are so predominant. His intellectual context and origins were also mixed. When he began to write Romanticism (Novalis, Tieck, Friedrich Schlegel) was Germany's modern dominant mode, but Goethe and Schiller had established their classicism in Weimar. And in his cast of mind at least Kleist came from an optimistic, rationalistic Age of Enlightenment, which quickly failed him. His personal life was characterized by a terrible restlessness, the utter failure to find for more than a few weeks at a time any abiding stay. He seems flung to and fro in the ferment of the age itself.

Kleist's father died when he was eleven, his mother when he was fifteen. In the army he saw action against the French in the Rhine campaigns. He was a second lieutenant when he got his release in April 1799. He gave up that career because he wanted to shape his own life, and first tried study — physics, maths, the law — at the university of Frankfurt an der Oder. He got engaged early the following year, to Wilhelmine von Zenge, the daughter of a Prussian general, which increased the obligation on him to do something sensible with his life. He gave up his studies, to try the civil service. That same year however, with his friend Brockes, he took a trip via Potsdam, Leipzig, Dresden, to Würzburg, for some purpose which, he said, was to be decisive in his life, but which remains today as mysterious as it ever was. Perhaps he went as a spy or emissary, in the interests of Prussian trade; or perhaps he needed some medical attention, in preparation for marriage.

Back home he had pressure put on him to convert his tentative association with the civil service into a real employment. In a very dubious frame of mind he made some gestures towards this, but was always about to take flight. He did after his so-called Kant-Crisis of March 1801, and arrived, after some wandering with his half-sister Ulrike, in Paris, where he was deeply unhappy. But he conceived a plan for his own salvation. He would buy a small farm in Switzerland, and live there simply. He wrote to Wilhelmine. Would she join him? She had grave doubts. For one thing, the sun gave her headaches. Alone then he rented a house on an island in the River Aare, near Thun, and that spring and summer (1802) made the first sustained effort to prove to himself that he could write. In May he broke off his engagement. The French interfered increasingly in Switzerland, and Kleist felt obliged to leave. He moved to Ossmannstedt, near Weimar, and stayed that winter in the house of Christian Martin Wieland, a grand old man of German letters, who thought him, having been shown his dramatic fragments, as great as Aeschylus and Shakespeare combined.

The Schroffenstein Family, Kleist's first play, appeared anonymously in Leipzig early in 1803. Its author, no more settled in his vocation, spent the year on hectic journeys in eastern Germany, Switzerland and northern Italy and finally to Paris where, losing all faith, he burned what he had done of his tragedy *Robert Guiskard*, and walked to the coast to join Napoleon's army there preparing to invade England. The French would not have him. Indeed, he was fortunate, as a former Prussian officer, not to be taken as a spy and shot. By June 1804 he was back in Berlin, eating humble pie, asking if the civil service would employ him after all. They set him to work in the Ministry of Finance and he did well enough to seem worth investing in. They sent him to Königsberg, to study political science and economics. He worked at his dramas and stories. The strain was great, his health deteriorated, and in August 1806 he was given six months' sick leave. He finished *The Broken Jug* and wrote hard at other things. Then France crushed Prussia at Jena, 14 October 1806. The Prussian court fled to Königsberg. Kleist, always contrary, set off for Dresden via Berlin early in January; was arrested as a spy, transported to France, imprisoned in Fort de Joux, near Pontarlier, then in Châlons sur Marne, until July.

In prison he got on with his writing. *Amphitryon* was published in Dresden. When he came home, at the end of July, having committed himself to literature, his chief problem, the usual one for a man of letters, was how to earn enough to live. He finished *Penthesilea* and in December 1807, with Adam Müller, he founded the periodical *Phöbus*, which ran for twelve issues, until February 1809, and brought several items of his own work to the public. In March 1808 Goethe staged *The Broken Jug* in Weimar, very unsuccessfully, for which Kleist blamed him. In 1809, as the French and the Austrians fought it out, Kleist wandered through the war zone as far as Prague and Vienna. There was a ceasefire in July, after Wagram; and peace in October. Kleist hated the French and wished Prussia would move against them.

By now he had a good number of literary works to his name, but still no livelihood. *Käthchen of Heilbronn* and the first volume of his stories came out in September 1810. With Adam Müller, in many ways a dangerous friend, he edited Berlin's first daily paper, the *Berliner Abendblätter*, and when that foundered on 30 March 1811, his chances were all but exhausted. He petitioned the state, for financial support or for a post in the civil service or the military. He finished *The Prince of Homburg*, saw the publication of the second volume of his stories, but viewed his future hopelessly. Then he met the ecstatic and terminally ill Henriette Vogel and together, 21 November 1811, they ended it.

*

Kleist had an eye for emblems. He spotted a very apt one early on and in the first of his surviving letters (see p. 417) communicated it to his aunt (his parents were dead by then). A man is left howling in the darkness and the mountains. Was he a robber? Perhaps he wanted help? One of Kleist's last letters, written the day before he shot himself, contains this observation: 'The world is a strange set-up.' And we are not at home in it. God, if he exists, is incomprehensible. Speechlessly (in *The Chilean Earthquake*) a victim raises his trembling hands to heaven. And to heaven likewise, in the silence after the lynching, Don Fernando lifts his eyes, full of a nameless pain. No help there, no explanation. There seems to be some mismatch between the way we are and the way the universe is constituted (see p. 422). Human beings, as Büchner's Danton also thought, seem to lack some vital ingredient or faculty. We are not properly equipped. Kleist's famous Kant-Crisis (described — see p. 421 — in suitably simple terms to his long-suffering fiancée Wilhelmine) is only the best-known instance of his fundamental unease. He had been reading Kant for some time by then. Nor is it the case that he was at home in the world before reading Kant and not at home in the world after reading him. Also this desperate utterance occurs in the middle of a long letter dealing at times quite cheerfully with many things. Still, it is a clear statement of the unease he felt more or less acutely all his life. That our faculties are inadequate. Most of his characters suffer from precisely that.

Naturally Kleist's view of how *we* are in the world derived immediately from how he felt himself to be in it. He felt himself to be at odds, he felt embarrassed and uncomfortable, he was not understood. He was known as somebody who muttered to himself at the dinner table in company. People supposed, because of his difficulties in communication, that he must have some speech impediment. Ordinary dealings, ordinary efforts at communication, were bad enough; but to utter the truth of the heart, which he longed to do, this was a nightmare of impossibility. It makes an unhappy leitmotiv in his letters. For example: 'Occasionally I should like to be at least *understood*, if not encouraged and praised, by *one* soul at least I should occasionally like to be understood, even if all the others get me wrong (cf. p. 420). His characters, who (especially in the dialogue of his dramas) speak *past* one another, suffer misunderstandings both laughable and fatal. Kleist's common relations with his fellow human beings were mostly embarrassing. He writes: 'I am sometimes seized by an anxiety, an inhibitedness, which I do strive with all my strength to suppress, but which has nevertheless on more than one occasion placed me in the most ridiculous situations.' In fact 'an inexplicable embarrassment' (as he called it) afflicted him in most of his social intercourse. He says it again and again: 'I don't fit in with people'; 'I am not suited for any usual dealings'. He was, in a word, 'unähnlich' — very unlike the thing people call the world and for that reason 'wholly incapable' of fitting into any of the world's conventional relationships.

His life was rich in instances of being *unlike*. He was perpetually in the wrong place: in the army, to start with, required to be either an officer or a human being (see p. 418); in Customs and Excise; in the Ministry of Finance. All his dealings with Authority — with the King, for example, or with ministers, asking to be let out or to be let back in

— were embarrassing in the highest degree. The tone of his letters was always untoward — too serious and truthful, or parodistically, contortedly self-abasing and obsequious. He seems to be operating according to the criteria of some other and quite incommensurate order. With the Literary Authorities, chiefly Goethe, he got on no better. He came at everyone from an odd angle. He was fundamentally uneasy in the circumstances he was obliged to try to manage in. His family, his fiancée's family, the King, generals and ministers were perplexed by him. He was uniquely unsuitable for any of their purposes.

The times Kleist lived in were chaotic; from end to end of Europe armies went to and fro. He seems to wander through the battlefields in a private trance. Now and then he and the times collide: they intrude on him in retreat in Switzerland; they take him up as a spy and transport him into France. Or he suddenly looks to them to end his misery and tries to force himself on Napoleon (whom he detested) at Boulogne. Persons in authority meeting him ask to see his papers, demand that he legitimate himself, and the reason is always the same: wherever he is, doing whatever, he does not look as though he belongs there. On the battlefield at Aspern, the dead and the wreckage still lying around, Kleist, en route for Vienna on private business, *legitimated* himself to Austrian officers, who thought him highly suspicious, by reading aloud to them some of his own (bad) patriotic verses. He, a former soldier, a bad one, read them his bad verses. Loving emblems, Kleist had an extraordinary flair for appearing as one.

How much was the world's fault, how much his? He acknowledged that he was himself riven with contradictions. He wondered that there could be so many dwelling in the small space of one human heart (his). He acknowledged that he was himself very often the source of his own unease. On the island in the Aare, with the girl Mädeli looking after him and his vocation as a writer becoming clearer in the practice day by day, still he was not at peace. He commented ruefully: 'I should be quite without any unpleasant feelings were I not, after a lifetime's habit, condemned to create them myself' (see p. 423). He inhabits a confusion, or it him. His journeys to and fro across Europe, many of them, I should say, as mysterious to him as they have been to the experts ever since, are the persistent demonstration of an incurable restlessness. Where was he heading? Towards his own abyss, he said. The perpetual uneasiness and tribulation and the search for some abiding stay in the world exhausted him. Aged only twenty-one, again and again in his letters he says that what he needs is rest.

Much of the above characterization of the man may be applied to his literary personae and their predicaments. How often what they do is odd and incommensurate! Homburg, the soldier, babbles 'a sleepy language' in the garden; Eve, reproaching Ruprecht, appeals to values nobody around her knows anything about. And how, in that 'comedy', the paradigms so blatantly offered — Oedipus, Adam and Eve — do not properly fit. Kleist said of himself, 'everything in me is in confusion'. His characters say the same. Their confusion is legendary. Their patterns fail them; playing familiar roles they discover that the lines no longer make much sense. The usual categories collapse. Things it would be comfortable to keep apart — tenderness and sadism, filial and sexual love, chivalry and rape, angels and devils — run into one another. Kleist's characters surprise themselves and everyone else. Their common epitaph might be: 'I never knew I had it in me.' Could Piachi have foretold he would insist on going to hell? Kohlhaas that he would preoccupy Luther, two Electors and the Emperor himself?

Another emblem, to go with the man howling among the mountains in the night. Kleist suddenly noticed — in Würzburg — that an arch is held in place because all of its constituent stones are striving to collapse. He drew a little diagram and sent it to Wilhelmine. Lives hold together in Kleist's world by the tension of their destructive forces. Often in his plays and stories the keystone of the arch of a person's life is removed.

Kleist struggled hard against his own apprehension that man and the cosmos he inhabits are incommensurable. He made every effort to gainsay his own experience. But the efforts themselves, and the cast of mind behind them, were so extreme that they called up almost inevitably their own violent contradiction.

Kleist was forever drawing up plans for his life. No human being worthy the name, he said, could exist without a *Lebensplan*. Against the feeling that the world cannot be understood or managed he insisted that it might be, that it *ought* to be (see pp. 418–19). A man must shape his own life and direct it; decide his purpose and adhere to it; fortify himself against the intrusions of chance; acknowledge no authority but reason; work hopefully and systematically at his own self-improvement. Kleist's letters, until he became a writer, are laced with such assertions. He sounds like the *Aufklärung* in person, except that he insists too much. His affirmation is itself extreme, as extreme as are the doubt and anxiety breeding it. When he advocates self-improvement he uses a naïvely concrete imagery of collecting, constructing, building — as though the world were a treasure house of tangible *pieces of knowledge* which any diligent collector could acquire. As though a satisfactory life could be pieced together. He encouraged his correspondents, notably his half-sister Ulrike and his fiancée Wilhelmine, in the same endeavour. Shaping himself he thought it his duty to shape them as well. He set Wilhelmine little essay-questions. For example: 'A woman who is worthy of esteem is not thereby made interesting. How may a woman win and retain her husband's interest?' Or: 'Which is preferable: to have been happy briefly or never to have been happy at all?' Or: 'Must a woman please nobody but her husband?' He urged her when out walking always to be on the look-out for phenomena that might be used to make some moral point. In that spirit he gave her the arch in Würzburg. She should collect her own such sources of 'moral revenue', and so enrich herself. Thus in his letters (since he was mostly away and their relationship was conducted like a correspondence course) he educated her towards her purpose in life, which was, he told her, to be a wife and mother. Kleist the pedagogue is an embarrassing figure; but poignant too, since he knew all along, by the simple contemplation of his own predicament, that the language of mastery was quite inappropriate. The world was never at his disposal; not its phenomena nor the people in it. The pieties he handed down were of no use to him. The large words 'duty', 'purpose', 'happiness', the oftener and more assertively he used them, the less self-evident their sense, in his particular case, became. He preached decisiveness but could never make up his mind.

In his early years, when letters were what he chiefly wrote, Kleist overrode his own doubt and confusion by insisting, loudly, that a reasonable man, if he exerts himself, can manage the world and be happy in it. But he claimed too much for the rational mind's resources. Reality contradicted him again and again.

Kleist could not be cured of his fundamental apprehension that the world we inhabit is unintelligible and unmanageable. He could not cure himself. Experience delivered him all the wrong proofs. But the question remained, lifelong: How shall we manage in this world? Even whilst asserting, if never wholly believing in, the effective power of the mind and the will, Kleist kept open another and contradictory (because irrational) option, as a last resort when the world confronts us unintelligibly and the mind admits defeat. That option is trust (*Vertrauen*), blind faith, a thing which passeth all understanding. Trust and the lack or failure of it is a central issue in the stories and the plays but long before writing them Kleist made a leitmotiv of it in his letters too, especially in those to Wilhelmine. She had to promise she would trust him eternally. Love entailed, so he believed, an unconditional trust. Perhaps that goes without saying between two people engaged to be married but, very characteristically, Kleist, whilst insisting on it, presented himself to her again and again as someone deeply untrustworthy. Insisting that she trust him he was actually insisting that she go against all appearance and all common sense. In truth — as a soldier, university student, civil servant, bridegroom-to-be — he *was* untrustworthy. He let people make demands on him which by his innermost nature he was not permitted to fulfil. And said: Trust me. Often in the stories and the plays there are grounds for trust but appearances obscure them and the faith required is superhuman. Eve tells Ruprecht he should have trusted her, despite the evidence; so does Toni Gustav. Friedrich begs Littegarde to trust herself, though God Himself seems to have testified against her. It is an extreme appeal. The rational mind is set aside and something other is relied on. Then Kleist, desperately honest, devises situations in which that something other itself proves unreliable. Piachi, Gustav at first, Jeronimo and Josephe at the last are all culpably credulous. Homburg's self-confidence and his faith in the Elector's leniency are quite misplaced. The question is always: How shall we manage? Kleist, the writer, tested the rational precepts of the *Aufklärung*, precepts he had entertained himself to an extreme degree, and proved them in his fictions to be illusory. They fail, the structures raised on them come crashing down, his characters have to begin again, on trust. But often that irrational or supra-rational faculty has been lost or muddled; the circumstances in which it must now be awakened and applied are unpropitious. It is the last resort and would be the best but people being the way they are (confused) often they cannot discover it in a sufficient strength and purity.

Kleist, who doubted whether human beings could ever fully understand one another and whose characters excel in every form of *malentendu*, laid a vast responsibility on human relationships. His own never gave him the secure ground he needed. Though he inspired great love and loyalty in women and in men they could not or he would not let them save him. He seems to have had some ordinary human happiness with the girl on the Delosea Island and with his cousin Marie a true sympathy. But his unsuitability for marriage to Wilhelmine is tragi-comically obvious in every letter he wrote her. Ulrike — eccentric herself, more male than female in dress and manners — was brave and resourceful and did her best for him. But he far outdid her in strangeness and went his own way. And so he slipped from the care of all who loved him. But he was not, I think, a naturally solitary person, nor in the least arid emotionally. Rather, as in everything else, he seemed in his relationships to be out of place. One always wonders what his loved ones made of him. Page after page, for example, he wrote to Wilhelmine in effusive praise of his travelling-companion Brockes, holding him up as a paragon beyond her emulation: 'If you were among girls what he is among men ...' And to Ernst von Pfuel, eighteen months after the occasion, he dwelled lasciviously on the sensations he had experienced — 'truly girlish sensations' — when watching him bathe. Not that the sentiments expressed in that letter, overtly, passionately homoerotic, are in themselves reprehensible or untoward; only they come as a shock and are unlike anything else that survives to Pfuel or to any other man. That letter, and the eulogy of Brockes, read like a venture, a bit literary, a bit embarrassing, into areas of the author's personality still unmapped. He engaged his correspondents in his own experiments and explorations. In the stories and the plays he did that with his characters, ever more riskily.

Kleist associated with people, passionately, intimately, but always, as it seems, somewhat at odds, in a sort of disjuncture. When he did meet his match or his anti-type, in Henriette Vogel, it was fatal. He regularly asked new acquaintances, who might become friends, whether they would be willing to die with him. He seems to have sought that in his relationships, as a premise. With Henriette it was premise and all in all.

Kleist is odd in many respects and not least in this: that it took him so long to settle on his real vocation. When he wrote, in November 1799, aged twenty-two, 'I have set myself a goal that will require, if I am to achieve it, the constant application of all my energies and every minute of my time' he had not then decided to be a writer but was still referring to the more general but none the less serious purpose of educating himself and shaping his life. It cannot be proved that the mysterious journey to Würzburg (August–October 1800) had becoming a writer as its purpose, but that was perhaps an unintended or unenvisaged result. His letters whilst travelling became more writerly, and by November of that year he was telling his fiancée: 'It seems to me that I have abilities, and I mean rather uncommon abilities ... For the future then the whole literary profession would be open to me. I feel I should be very happy to do such work' and, a few days later: 'As you know, I am now preparing myself for the literary profession.' Probably this still does not mean the sort of writing that he did go on to do, but rather something philosophical, scientific, socio-political. A visit in May 1801 to the aged poet Gleim, in Halberstadt, who had known his ancestor Ewald von Kleist, may have had some determining effect on him, but not until he set up house on the Delosea Island in the River Aare in the spring of the following year can we be sure that his career as a writer, first as a dramatist, was definitely if not happily begun. His agonies over *Robert Guiskard* show his seriousness. Very likely he began the play (along with *The Schroffenstein Family* and *The Broken Jug*) in those encouraging circumstances, read some of it to Wieland, with great effect, in the winter of 1802–3, and in March 1803 he was taking declamation lessons so as to be able to recite it yet more effectively. In July he reports that it is dragging on and Wieland urges him to finish it come what may. On 5 October he tells his sister he has laboured five hundred days over it (and most of the nights) but it exceeds him, perhaps it *cannot* be done, and on the 26th, writing from St-Omer, he tells her he has burned it and that he looks forward to dying fighting for the French. But by then he had finished and published *Schroffenstein*, had begun work on *Amphitryon* and although at a loss as to how he should earn a living and turning back to the Prussian state for help, still in his fitful and distracted fashion he had committed himself to the thing he was born to do. Thereafter, in all the chaos of the times and of his practical life, he was a writer and, as editor of *Phöbus* and the *Berliner Abendblätter*, a public man of letters. Once under way he was productive. He was not, unlike, say, Kafka, a chronic non-finisher of things. *Guiskard* is the only fragment among his surviving works. Once he got going as a writer he finished one play after another and story after story, reckoned he could do a play every few months, and had realistic hopes of making a living in his profession. All the sadder then, in the autumn of 1811, is the sudden closure of his future and his final loss of faith.

NOTE ON THE TRANSLATION

True style — the shape and rhythm of a poetic line or of a prose sentence — is never an extra. It is integral and essential. Style is not the embellisher of an author's meaning, but its actual vehicle and maker. Style — in Kleist's case pre-eminently his syntax — is that by which the meaning is engendered and brought home into the heart and mind of the reader.

Translating Kleist, his sentences have to be conveyed in some shape and form capable of producing in English effects at least analogous to those produced by the German. Thus — to make an obvious point — though you might get across the lexical meaning of one of his long and complicated sentences by translating it into several shorter and simpler, doing so you would reduce and travesty the total sense, which consists not only (and often not mainly) in lexical meaning but in the long and complicated workings of the sentence itself. Kleist *makes sense*. He arrives at and holds on to sense through the difficult process of composing sentences. Syntax — a fitting-together — is the expression of his will to make the world make sense.

So my aim in this translation was not to arrive at unexceptionable English; but at an English haunted and affected by the strangeness of the original. All good writing defamiliarizes our world, makes us feel strange in it. Bearing that in mind, the translator's responsibility is clear — and impossibly difficult.

In translating the plays I thought it worth trying to put them into English verse. In the length and scansion of the lines I allowed myself about as much liberty as Kleist did himself. The pitfalls are innumerable and I fell into many. But I never allowed myself to suppose that merely getting a line to scan would do.

The gap between conception and execution is as evident and dispiriting in translating as it is in any other form of literary writing. But translation has to be attempted. English as much as any other living language needs these imports. There are writers we cannot do without and Kleist is one of them. I realized that ever more keenly, doing my best with him.

I used Helmut Sembdner's four-volume edition of Kleist's *Sämtliche Werke und Briefe* (Hanser Verlag, Munich, 1982).

I am grateful to my friend and colleague Jim Reed who discussed much of my typescript with me in a very clarifying way; also to my students and my family who have had a good deal of Kleist, perhaps even a surfeit, for some while now.

SELECT BIBLIOGRAPHY

Joachim Maas's *Kleist. A Biography* (London: Secker & Warburg, 1983), though greatly in need of revision (the German came out in 1977), is a good starting point for any study of Kleist. As are also, if you can get hold of them, the editions of *Homburg* (by Richard Samuel, 1957) and *Amphitryon* (by Keith Dickson, 1966) in the old Harrap's German Classics series. The introduction written by David Luke and Nigel Reeves for their Penguin translation of the stories (1978) is ample and informative. Michael Hamburger, in *Reason and Energy* (London: Weidenfeld & Nicolson, 1970), locates Kleist among the most exciting German authors, and writes very well on him. Walter Silz, *Heinrich von Kleist. Studies in his works and literary character* (Pennsylvania: University of Pennsylvania Press, 1961) and Ilse Graham, *Heinrich von Kleist. Word into Flesh: A poet's quest for the symbol* (Berlin: Walter de Gruyber, 1977), give interesting and idiosyncratic readings of much of the oeuvre. The stories are dealt with in a lively and forthright fashion by Denys Dyer (London: Duckworth, 1977), and Mark Ward's *Laughter, Comedy and Aesthetics* (Durham: Durham University Modern Languages Series, 1989) is a helpful discussion of *Der zerbrochne Krug*. John Ellis's *Heinrich von Kleist. Studies in the character and meaning of his writings* (North Carolina: University of North Carolina Press, 1979) and Anthony Stephens's *Heinrich von Kleist. The dramas and the stories* (Oxford: Berg, 1994) are especially good. The most recent work I know of in English is Seán Allan's *The Plays of Heinrich von Kleist* (Cambridge: Cambridge University Press, 1996).

PLAYS

THE BROKEN JUG
A Comedy

Note: This comedy may well have a basis in a real occurrence; but if so, I have not been able to find out more about it. My starting point was an engraving I saw in Switzerland some years ago. It showed, first, a judge seated on the bench with all solemnity. Before him stood an old woman holding a broken jug and seeming to demonstrate the wrong that had been done to it. The accused, a young farmhand, as though already found guilty, was suffering a fearful telling-off from the judge but was still defending himself, albeit feebly. A girl, very likely a witness in the case (for who knows in what circumstances the offence had been committed) there between her mother and her betrothed was clutching at her skirts — had she just committed perjury she could not have looked more troubled. And the clerk of the court, having no doubt a moment since had his eyes on the girl, was looking from the side suspiciously at the judge, as Creon did, on a similar occasion, at Oedipus. The caption read: The Broken Jug. The painter of the original was Dutch, if I am not mistaken.*

Dramatis Personae*

WALTER	the Assessor
ADAM	the Village Judge
LICHT	Clerk of the Court
FRAU MARTHE RULL	
EVE	her daughter
VEIT TÜMPEL	a countryman
RUPRECHT	his son
FRAU BRIGITTE	
A SERVANT, USHERS, MAIDS etc.	

The action takes place in a Dutch village near Utrecht.

Scene: The courtroom

Scene 1

ADAM *seated, bandaging his leg. Enter* LICHT

LICHT: Now what in hell's name, tell me, brother Adam
  Has happened to you? Look what a sight you look.
ADAM: Yes, look. All a man needs for slipping up
  Is feet. Everything's level here
  But here I tripped, for every man carries
  The cursed stumbling block in him himself.
LICHT: Pardon me, brother? Every man carries ...
ADAM: The stumbling block in him.
LICHT: The devil he does.
ADAM: I beg your pardon?
LICHT: Your first forefather was
  An unsteady man who at the outset fell
  And for his fall was famous ever after.
  You wouldn't yourself ...?
ADAM: Well?
LICHT: Likewise?
ADAM: Wouldn't what?
  I fell down here, I tell you — fell down flat.
LICHT: And only literally?
ADAM: Just so. The figure I cut
  Was not a pretty one. We needn't dwell on it.
LICHT: And this befell you when?
ADAM: A moment since,
  Climbing out of bed. I had my mouth still full
  Of the day's first hymn and was getting on
  Shakily into the morning and before the course
  Was well begun the Good Lord turned my foot.
LICHT: The left, no doubt?
ADAM: The left?
LICHT: This one,
  The weighty one?
ADAM: Indeed.
LICHT: Lord thou art just!
  The one already heavily bent on sinning.
ADAM: The foot! What? Heavily! Why so?
LICHT: The clubfoot?*
ADAM: Clubfoot!
  One foot's much like the other: a club, a lump.

LICHT: Forgive me: there you do your right foot wrong
Your right boasts no such — *growth* and where
A foot might slip would risk it first.

ADAM: No odds.
Where one dares the other follows soon enough.

LICHT: And what brought such disfigurement on your face?

ADAM: My face?

LICHT: Your face. You don't know what your face ...?

ADAM: Or I'm a liar. What does it look like?

LICHT: What
It looks like?

ADAM: Yes, my dear fellow.

LICHT: Vile.

ADAM: Be more exact.

LICHT: It's had a battering.
Looks grisly. You've lost some cheek. How much
I couldn't say without a scales.

ADAM: The devil
I have.

LICHT: (*fetches a mirror*) See for yourself. A sheep that dogs
Are worrying and shoves itself
Through thorn leaves no more wool behind than you,
But God knows where, have left behind of flesh.

ADAM: Dear me. True enough. I'm not a pretty sight.
The nose has copped it too.

LICHT: So has the eye.

ADAM: The eye, brother? Not so.

LICHT: Not so? God strike me dead!
Here's one great bloody blow diagonally
As if, beside himself, the headman did it.

ADAM: Only the bone. — And would you credit it,
All that and I felt nothing, not a thing.

LICHT: Always the way of it in the heat of battle.

ADAM: Battle! What battle? — You might say I battled
With that damned billy goat. I remember now:
Losing my balance and like someone drowning
I'm flailing at the air and grab a hold
On what I hung up yesterday evening
Wet through, on the stove,* my trousers, on the rail,
I grab them hold, do you follow me? and thinking,
Fool that I am, to keep upright, the belt

Rips off and down we go, the belt, the trousers, me
Headfirst and smash my conk, full front,
Against the stove just where the edge pokes out,
For decoration, in a billy goat.

LICHT: (*laughing*) Well, well.

ADAM: Damnation!

LICHT: Adam fell
And you did likewise: rose from your bed and fell.

ADAM: Upon my soul. — But tell me: What's the news?

LICHT: The news! Hang, draw and quarter me
If I'd not clean forgotten.

ADAM: Well?

LICHT: Prepare
Yourself for an unexpected visitor
From Utrecht.

ADAM: Oh really?

LICHT: The Assessor's coming.

ADAM: Who's coming?

LICHT: Walter, the Assessor's coming, from Utrecht.
Court after court receives his visitation.
We shall today.

ADAM: Today! Have you gone mad?

LICHT: God's truth. He was in Holla on the border
And did the court there. That was yesterday.
A local saw them harnessing extra horses
To his carriage, for the road to Huisum.

ADAM: Today, the Assessor, coming from Utrecht, here,
To inspect us, him, a decent sort who knows
What side his bread is buttered on and hates such games,
Coming to Huisum, him, to bugger us about!

LICHT: He came to Holla, he'll surely come to Huisum.
Beware.

ADAM: Pull the other one.

LICHT: I'm telling you.

ADAM: Tell me another. Tell it the marines.

LICHT: Hang me! The man saw him with his own eyes.

ADAM: Who knows who it was he saw with his runny eyes,
The clown. His sort can't tell a face
From the back of a bald head. You put a hat,
A tricorn, on my walking stick
And hang a coat on it and boots beneath

A dolt like that will think it's who you like.
LICHT: Then carry on disbelieving in the devil's name
Till he walks through the door.
ADAM: Him, through the door,
And never tipping us off before he comes?
LICHT: How blind can you be? This isn't the old
Inspector still, Assessor Hooch.
Assessor Walter does the inspecting now.
ADAM: So what if it is Assessor Walter, so what?
The man has sworn his oath of office, has he not?
And practises as we do as the law
And usage of the day and age require.
LICHT: Let me be clear with you. Assessor Walter
Appeared in Holla yesterday unannounced,
Went through the accounts and through the registries
And from their offices, don't ask me why,
Removed the judge and clerk.
ADAM: The devil he did.
Was that in the bumpkin's tale?
LICHT: Among other things.
ADAM: Such as?
LICHT: Do you want to know? This morning
Early they went to find the judge
Who was under house arrest and found him
In the barn behind the house high up
Under the roof from one of the rafters hanging.
ADAM: I beg your pardon?
LICHT: Help arrived meanwhile.
They cut him down, they rubbed and sluiced him
And brought him back, more or less, to life again.
ADAM: They brought him, pardon me?
LICHT: But his house
Is sealed and shut and under oath
As though he were the corpse of himself already
And bench and office are already handed on.
ADAM: Be damned. — Look here, he was a sleazy rat
But decent otherwise, true as I live,
Good company, but bent,
I'm bound to say it, terribly bent,
And if the Assessor was in Holla today
He'll not have had an easy time, poor devil.

LICHT: But for that incident, says the local man,
 The Assessor would be here by now
 And he'll be here by noon, no doubt about it.
ADAM: By noon! Well, brother, now's the time for friendship.
 You cover my back, I'll scratch yours etc.
 Being a judge like me would suit you, I know that,
 And you deserve it, by God, as well as any.
 Only today thine hour has not yet come,
 Today still let this cup pass from thee.*
LICHT: What me, a judge? What do you take me for?
ADAM: You are a lover of the well-turned phrase
 And know your Cicero as well as any do
 Who study in the schools of Amsterdam.
 But hold your ambition down today, d'you hear?
 Other occasions will present themselves
 No doubt for showing us your tricks.
LICHT: We two, thick as we are. How could you think ...?
ADAM: You know, even the great Demosthenes*
 Knew when to hold his peace. Do as he did
 And though I'm not the King of Macedonia
 I still have ways of showing gratitude.
LICHT: I tell you, that's enough mistrusting me.
 When did I ever ...?
ADAM: And see, for my part I
 Will likewise emulate the noble Greek.
 One might, I suppose, also work up a speech
 On sums deposited and where the interest went
 But who wants troubling with rhetoric like that?
LICHT: Well then.
ADAM: I'm clean as far as that goes
 Or string me up. And where there might be something
 Was only fun and games and, born at night,
 It hates the nosy daylight.
LICHT: I know.
ADAM: Be damned. I see no reason why a judge
 During his time off from the seat of judgment
 Should be as solemn as a polar bear.
LICHT: My view exactly.
ADAM: Well then, old friend.
 Come with me to the registry a while.
 I'll pile the piles of papers up again

That lie in ruins like the Tower of Babel.

Scene 2

Enter a SERVANT

SERVANT: God bless, Judge Adam, sir, Assessor Walter
Sends you his compliments. Expect him soon.
ADAM: God serve us right! Has he already done
With Holla?
SERVANT: He's in Huisum already.
ADAM: Ho, Liese! Grete!
LICHT: Easy now, easy.
ADAM: Oh brother of mine!
LICHT: Send him your grateful thanks.
SERVANT: Tomorrow we move on to Hussahe.
ADAM: What shall I do? What not?
(He reaches for his clothes)
Enter FIRST MAID
FIRST MAID: Sir, here I am.
LICHT: Come now — what madness — get your trousers on.
Enter SECOND MAID
SECOND MAID: Your worship, here I am.
LICHT: And now your coat.
ADAM: *(looking round)* Who's here? The Assessor?
LICHT: The maid, only the maid.
ADAM: My bands, my robe, my collar!
FIRST MAID: First your weskit.
ADAM: What? — Coat off! Quick!
LICHT: *(to the servant)* His worship the Assessor
Is very welcome here. One moment more
And we are ready to receive him. Tell him so.
ADAM: The devil he is. Judge Adam sends him his
Apologies.
LICHT: Apologies!
ADAM: Apologies.
Not left has he? Not coming here?
SERVANT: He's still
At the inn. He sent round for the blacksmith.
The carriage broke.
ADAM: Oh good. My compliments.
The smith's an idle wretch. Send my excuses.

Tell him as near as dammit I broke my neck.
See for yourself the frightful sight I look.
And shocks like that loosen my system, tell him.
Tell him I'm sick.

LICHT: Have you gone mad? —
His worship the Assessor is most kind.
    — Shall you?

ADAM: God string me up!

LICHT: What?

ADAM: Devil take me!
You'd think I'd drunk a quart of syrup of figs.

LICHT: Showing him the door before he shows his face!

ADAM: Margrete, hoi! Old bag of bones! Liese!

BOTH MAIDS: We're here. What is it you want?

ADAM: Be off!
The cheese, the hams, the butter, sausage, bottles
Out of the registry, and quick!
Not you, you dimwit. The other one. Yes you.
God blast, Margrete, her, the milkmaid, Liese,
Get to the registry.

                   [*Exit the* FIRST MAID]

SECOND MAID: Can't make your meaning out.

ADAM: You shut your trap for one thing. Fetch my wig.
Quick march! In the book cupboard. Be on your way!

                  [*Exit the* SECOND MAID]

LICHT: (*to the* SERVANT) I trust the Assessor did not meet with
Any unhappy accident along the way?

SERVANT: We overturned, that's all, where the road comes down.

ADAM: Rot it! My buggered foot. My boots won't ...

LICHT: Merciful heavens! Overturned, you say?
But no harm done besides?

SERVANT: Nothing to speak of.
His worship wrenched his arm a little.
The axle broke.

ADAM: A pity it wasn't his neck.

LICHT: He wrenched his arm! And has the blacksmith been?

SERVANT: Yes, for the axle.

LICHT: What?

ADAM: You mean the doctor.

LICHT: What?

SERVANT: For the axle?

ADAM: No, no. For his wrist.
SERVANT: Gentlemen, good day. — This pair are raving mad.
                                                    [*Exit*]

LICHT: I meant the blacksmith.
ADAM: You're giving yourself away.
LICHT: I beg your pardon?
ADAM: You're in a pother.
LICHT: What?
                    Enter FIRST MAID
ADAM: Hey, Liese!
   What's that you've got?
FIRST MAID: Braunschweiger sausages, your worship.
ADAM: They're wards of court.
LICHT: In a pother, me?
ADAM: You take them back. Back to the registry.
FIRST MAID: The sausages?
ADAM: The sausages! What they're wrapped up in!
LICHT: Our wires were crossed.
                    Enter SECOND MAID
SECOND MAID: Your worship's wig,
   Your worship, isn't in the book cupboard.
ADAM: Why isn't it?
SECOND MAID: Because ...
ADAM: Because?
SECOND MAID: Because last night
   Eleven o'clock ...
ADAM: Well? Out with it.
SECOND MAID: Your worship came,
   Remember, home without your wig.
ADAM: Me home without my wig?
SECOND MAID: You did indeed
   And Liese here will swear to it.
   Your other wig is at the wigmaker's.
ADAM: You are saying I ...?
FIRST MAID: No word of a lie, Judge Adam.
   Baldheaded is what you were when you came home
   And said you'd fallen down. Don't you remember?
   I had to wash your head. It still had blood on.
ADAM: The brazen baggage!
FIRST MAID: My word of honour.
ADAM: You'll shut your trap. Not a word of it is true.

LICHT: You've had the injury since yesterday?
ADAM: Not so.
   Today, had it today. And yesterday my wig.
   Wore it white powdered on my head
   And took it off by accident, God's honour,
   Inside my hat when I walked in the door.
   Don't ask me what she washed, I've no idea.
   — Go to the devil, you, where you belong.
   Back in the registry.

                                    [*Exit* FIRST MAID]
                       Now Margarete
   Ask my good friend the sexton to lend me his.
   Tell him that mine the cat this morning early
   Had kittens in, the bitch. Tell him it's lying,
   Fouled, under the bed. I remember now.
LICHT: The cat? What? Are you ...?
ADAM: True as I'm standing here.
   Five kittens, ginger, black, and one a white one.
   The black, I'll drown them in the Vecht.
   What else? Unless you'd like one, would you?
LICHT: In your wig?
ADAM: The devil carry me off to hell!
   I hung my wig up on a chair
   When I retired to bed and in the night
   I knock against that chair, over it goes ...
LICHT: The cat then takes the said wig in her mouth ...
ADAM: God's truth!
LICHT: And carries it under the bed and kittens in it.
ADAM: In her mouth? Not so.
LICHT: Not so? How else?
ADAM: The cat? Never.
LICHT: Never? Or you yourself?
ADAM: In her mouth! I expect,
   Seeing that sight, I kicked it under there
   Myself this morning.
LICHT: Very like.
ADAM: The trollops,
   At it and having 'em everywhere you look.
SECOND MAID: (*giggling*) So I'm to go?
ADAM: And give my compliments
   To Aunty Blackjacket, the sexton's wife.

Tell her she'll have the wig back in good shape
Later today — no need for himself to know.
You understand?

SECOND MAID: I'll see to it.

[*Exit*]

Scene 3

ADAM: Today looks very ill to me, old friend.

LICHT: Why so?

ADAM: Things coming at me every which way.
And don't we sit today?

LICHT: Indeed we do.
The plaintiffs are already at the door.

ADAM: — I dreamed a plaintiff had seized hold of me
And hauled me up before the bench, and I
None the less I was seated on that bench
And homilied, lambasted and badmouthed me
And handed down the iron on my own neck.

LICHT: What! You did that to you?

ADAM: True as I'm honest.
Then both of us were one and ran away
And had to hole up in the woods all night.

LICHT: Well? And the dream, you think ...?

ADAM: The devil take it.
If it's not the dream there's some damn jinx or other
Has got it in for me.

LICHT: These are foolish fears.
But follow the rules while the Assessor's present
And from the bench give those before you justice
Or else the dream of the lambasted judge
Might come true in another way.

Scene 4

Enter Assessor WALTER

WALTER: God's blessing on you, Judge Adam.

ADAM: Your worship, welcome,
Ah, welcome here in our beloved Huisum.
Dear God of justice, who would have thought that we
Might ever be visited so agreeably?
Even this morning when the clock struck eight

Who would have dared to dream of bliss like this?
WALTER: I come abruptly, I'm aware of that,
   And on my travels in the service of our state
   Must be content if those receiving me
   Give me an honest blessing when I leave.
   As for my own, meanwhile, my own blessing,
   It comes, on my arrival, from the heart.
   The High Court in Utrecht is minded
   To mend judicial practice in the country
   Which seems in certain aspects less than perfect
   And all abuse must count on harsh correction.
   But my own business on these travels is not
   A harsh one yet. I'm here to observe, not punish
   And if not everything is as it should be
   Still I'll be pleased if it is tolerable.
ADAM: Such generous sentiments no man can quarrel with.
   I do not doubt your worship will not find
   All of our old ways quite beyond reproof
   And though they be how they have been in Holland
   Since Charles the Fifth was Emperor
   The human mind will always dream up better.
   The world, we are told, gets wiser day by day
   And everyone reads Puffendorf,* I know,
   But Huisum is a little part of the world
   And neither more nor less will come to it
   Than its own portion of the general wisdom.
   Be good enough, your worship, to enlighten
   Our Lady Justice here in Huisum
   And rest assured the moment you turn your back
   She'll be of a kind to satisfy you completely.
   Were she already in our court today
   After your heart's desire I'd be amazed
   Since what your heart desires she only dimly knows.
WALTER: We lack rules, that is true. Or rather
   We have too many. We ought to sift them through.
ADAM: A sieve, a large one. Chaff! So much is chaff.
WALTER: Our clerk of the court, no doubt?
LICHT: Just so, your worship,
   And at your worship's service, Licht by name,
   Nine years in office come next Whitsuntide.
ADAM: (*fetches a chair*) Be seated.

WALTER: Thank you, no.
ADAM: You came from Holla.
WALTER: Eight or nine miles at most. How did you know?
ADAM: How did ...? Your worship's servant —
LICHT: A local man,
   Arrived from Holla this minute, told us.
WALTER: A local man?
ADAM: Just so. Just so.
WALTER: — Indeed
   An unhappy incident in that place
   Caused me to lose the equanimity
   So needful for the conduct of our business. —
   Doubtless the matter is known to you already?
ADAM: Can it be true, your excellency? Judge Graft
   Put under house arrest
   And desperation seizing hold of him, the fool,
   He hanged himself?
WALTER: And made a bad thing worse.
   What seemed untidiness and muddle merely
   Begins to look more like embezzlement
   Which, as you know, the law cannot let pass. —
   How many funds do you have?
ADAM: Five, at your service.
WALTER: Five? But how so? I understood ... In use?
   I understood no more than four ...
ADAM: Forgive me.
   Counting the appeal fund for the Rhine floods?
WALTER: Counting the appeal fund for the Rhine floods?
   But at the present time there are no floods
   And no appeal and nothing coming in.
   — But tell me: is it true you sit today?
ADAM: Is it true —?
WALTER: Is what?
LICHT: First session of the week.
WALTER: So, and the crowd of folk I saw outside
   Along your corridor, those are ...
ADAM: Those will be ...
LICHT: Those are the plaintiffs, already assembled.
WALTER: Ah, very good. Gentlemen, I'm glad of it.
   Be kind enough to let these people in.

I'll witness the procedure. I shall see
How you go about things here in Huisum.
We'll take the registry, the accounts, later
After this present business.

ADAM: As
Your worship wishes. Usher! Ho! Hanfriede!

Scene 5

Enter SECOND MAID

SECOND MAID: Compliments from the sexton's wife, Judge Adam,
  Much as she'd like to ...

ADAM: What? Can't? Won't?

SECOND MAID: She says this morning is a sermon morning
  And one of his himself is wearing it
  And says his other one's not fit to wear
  And has to send it to the mender's.

ADAM: Damnation!

SECOND MAID: Soon as the sexton's back, she says,
  She'll send you round his good one right away.

ADAM: God's honour, your worship, would you credit it?

WALTER: What?

ADAM: By chance, a damned ill chance, I'm robbed
  Of both my wigs. And now the third
  I sent to borrow I can't get hold of either.
  We'll have to sit with me with my bald head.

WALTER: Bald head!

ADAM: Dear everlasting God, yes bald,
  Much as I fear for my authority in court
  Without the reinforcement of a wig.
  — I could try sending to the grange
  Whether the tenant might not ...

WALTER: To the grange!
  There's no one hereabouts who might not ...?

ADAM: No one, for sure.

WALTER: The parson perhaps.

ADAM: The parson, him!

WALTER: Or else the schoolmaster.

ADAM: Your worship, since we did away with tithes
  And I in my capacity had a hand in it

I can't ask favours of either one of them.

WALTER: Well, Judge, well now? What of the day's proceedings?
Have you a mind to wait until your hair grows?

ADAM: If you'll permit I'll send word to the grange.

WALTER: How far might that be?

ADAM: Oh the merest
Half hour or so.

WALTER: What! Half an hour!
And the hour your session starts has struck already.
Come now, proceed. I have to get to Hussahe.

ADAM: Indeed! Proceed!

WALTER: Powder your head instead.
Where in the devil's name did you lose your wigs?
— Manage the best you can. I'm pressed for time.

ADAM: That too.

                    Enter the USHER

USHER: The usher is here.

ADAM: May I meanwhile ...
A bite to eat, sausage from Braunschweig,
A dram of Danzig goldwasser ...

WALTER: No, thank you.

ADAM: Come, come.

WALTER: Thank you, I said. I've breakfasted already.
That saves us time. Proceed. I need it
To make a note of something in my little book.

ADAM: Well, well, just as you wish. Come, Margarete.

WALTER: — You have a fearful injury, Judge Adam.
A fall?

ADAM: — This morning early, such a knock,
As I rose from my bed, a murderous knock,
See here, your worship, flat on the floor
It knocked me, I thought my grave had opened up.

WALTER: I'm sorry to hear it. — There'll be no ill effects,
I hope.

ADAM: I think not. Nor, of course, will it
Hinder me in the doing of my duty. —
Allow me.

WALTER: Proceed, proceed.

ADAM: (*to the usher*)   Call in the plaintiffs, smartly.
                    [*Exit* ADAM, *the* MAID, *the* USHER]

Scene 6

Enter FRAU MARTHE, EVE, VEIT *and* RUPRECHT. WALTER
and LICHT *at the back of the stage*

FRAU MARTHE: Rabble, I say, rabble and jug-smashers,
  You'll pay for this.
VEIT: Easy, Frau Marthe, easy.
  We'll get a judgment on the matter here.
FRAU MARTHE: Easy, he says! A judgment! Listen to him.
  A judgment on my jug, my broken jug.
  Easy to judge it back together again?
  They'll judge my broken jug can stay in bits
  And what's that judgment worth? Less than
  The bits themselves.
VEIT: Listen, will you?
  If you can get the judge to decide your way
  Then I'll replace your jug.
FRAU MARTHE: Replace it, will you?
  Replace it if the judge decides my way?
  Replace it in its proper place, try that,
  Back on the window sill where it belongs,
  My jug that's lost its bottom and can't stand up
  And can't lie on its side and can't sit right.
VEIT: You hear? Stop mouthing! What more can I do?
  If you've had your jug smashed by one of us
  We'll make amends.
FRAU MARTHE: You'll make amends, will you?
  I've heard my cows talk better sense than that.
  We're in a courtroom not a pottery
  And if their High and Mighty Worships came themselves,
  Put on their smocks and fired my pot again
  They'd just as soon do you know what in it
  As make amends. I ask you, make amends!
RUPRECHT: Leave her be, Father. Come along. The witch.
  It's not her broken jug working her up.
  What's wrong's the wedding that has gone to bits.
  She thinks she'll mend it in this place by force
  But I've a mind to put my boot on it.
  Damn me to hell if ever I take the trollop.
FRAU MARTHE: The lout! Conceit! Me mend the wedding here!
  Not worth my thread! Not worth, all in one piece,

One of the broken pieces of my jug.
And if that wedding stood there shining bright
As did my jug on the sill only yesterday
I'd take it by the handle with these very hands
And break it, so they rang, around your ears.
No, what's in bits I don't want mending here.
Me mend it!

EVE: Ruprecht!

RUPRECHT: Off, you ...

EVE: Dearest Ruprecht!

RUPRECHT: Off!

EVE: I beg you, listen to me, Ruprecht.

RUPRECHT: The common good-for-nothing I won't say what.

EVE: Give me one word with you alone.

RUPRECHT: Not one.

EVE: — Oh Ruprecht you must join your regiment
  And once you carry a gun who knows
  If I will see you in this life again.
  Think what war is, and you are going to war.
  Will you go from me now so full of anger?

RUPRECHT: No, God forbid. In anger? No, I shan't.
  God give you all the happiness that He
  Can spare. But me, if I come from the war
  Whole with a body like the iron man
  And live in Huisum to be eighty
  My dying word to you would still be: trollop!
  You're here in court to swear the same yourself.

FRAU MARTHE: (to EVE) What did I tell you? Come away. Why let
                                                          him
  Go on insulting you? The Corporal is
  More what you want, the honourable pegleg
  Who gave some stick in his day
  And not this nincompoop who'll have to take
  Stick from everyone. Now is the time
  For vows and marriages, and a christening
  Would suit me too and even a funeral, my own,
  Once I have trodden down their impudence
  That raised its head against my jugs.

EVE: Oh Mother
  Forget your jug. Let me try in the town
  If there's some mender skilled enough to fit

The bits together again the way you'd like
And if it's had its day take all
My moneybox and buy yourself a new one.
What sense is there for just an earthen jug
Even one come down to us from Herod's time
In making such a fuss and so much trouble?
FRAU MARTHE: That's all you know. Eva, my child, would you
Next Sunday have the parson call you out
And fit you up for chastening in church?
Your good name lay there in that pot
And in the world's eyes it was injured with it
If not in God's eyes nor in yours or mine.
The judge will be my mender, and his beadle.
We need the block and lashes of the whip
And all this rabble on a fire
If we're to burn our honour white again
And glaze the jug the way it used to be.

Scene 7

Enter ADAM *robed but without his wig*
ADAM: (*aside*) Eva, what's this, the darling. And that great lout
Ruprecht! The devil! See here. The whole damn tribe.
— They'll not bring me to court in my own court?
EVE: Oh my dear mother, come away, I beg you
Escape this place, there's only bad luck in it.
ADAM: Brother, a word. Why are these people here?
LICHT: How should I know? Fuss about nothing, nonsense.
A jug, from what I hear, a jug broken.
ADAM: A jug! Ah, ha! — Who was it broke the jug?
LICHT: Who broke it?
ADAM: Who? Yes, brother, who it was.
LICHT: Be damned, sit yourself down, you'll soon find out.
ADAM: (*aside*) Eva!
EVE: (*aside*) Keep off!
ADAM: One word.
EVE: I will not listen.
ADAM: What do you want with me?
EVE: I said keep off.
ADAM: Eva, my chuck, what does this mean? I beg you.
EVE: This minute, or I'll ... I'm telling you, let me be.

ADAM: (*to* LICHT) Friend, listen, damn me, I can't go on with it.
  I have a nausea from my wounded shin.
  You manage here. I shall retire to bed.
LICHT: To bed? Have you ...? Retire? Have you gone mad?
ADAM: God gibbet me. My guts are coming up.
LICHT: Truly now, raving mad. You only rose ...
  — Just as you like. Tell the Assessor there.
  He may allow it. — I wish I knew what ails you.
ADAM: (*to* EVE *again*) Eva, I beg you. By all the wounds
  What is it you want with me?
EVE: You'll see.
ADAM: Is it the jug your mother's holding, only the jug
  That I, if I ...?
EVE: Only the broken jug.
ADAM: And nothing else?
EVE: Nothing.
ADAM: Nothing? You promise, nothing?
EVE: Keep off, I'm telling you. Leave me in peace.
ADAM: By God you, listen here, be sensible,
  I warn you.
EVE: Shameless!
ADAM: I have filled him in.
  It's down in black and white now: Ruprecht Tümpel.
  All signed and sealed the paper's in my pocket.
  Listen how it rustles, Eva. A year from now,
  God's honour, you can come and get it off me
  And clothe yourself in black
  When you read there that Ruprecht, in Batavia,*
  Has croaked — on some fever or other,
  Yellow, it might be, scarlet or the putrid.
WALTER: No conversation with the parties, Judge,
  Before the trial. Be seated. Hear their case.
ADAM: What's that he says? What are your worship's orders?
WALTER: My orders? I told you plainly
  That you must not have secret dubious talk
  Before the session with the parties.
  This is the place appropriate to your office
  And we expect the hearing to be public.
ADAM: (*aside*) Be damned. I'm very disinclined to start.
  — There was a noise of breakage when I left.
LICHT: (*startling him*) Judge Adam, are you ...?

ADAM: Am I? God's honour, no.
   I hung it on it carefully but whether
   My bulk perhaps ...
LICHT: What?
ADAM: What?
LICHT: I asked ...
ADAM: You asked was I ...?
LICHT: I asked you are you deaf?
   His excellency over there addressed you.
ADAM: I thought ... Who did?
LICHT: His worship there, the Assessor.
ADAM: (aside) Oh string me up! Two things can happen:
   I sink or swim. So what? — At once!
   At once! At once! What are your worship's orders?
   Shall we commence proceedings?
WALTER: You seem strangely distracted, sir. What ails you?
ADAM: — Indeed. Forgive me. A guinea fowl of mine
   That I had off a man from India
   Has got the pip, needs noodling and I,
   Not knowing how, was asking her advice.
   I'm a poor fool, alas, in matters such as these,
   And love my chickens like a mother.
WALTER: Come now, be seated. Hear the plaintiff's case.
   And you, Clerk of the Court, set down the record.
ADAM: Is it your worship's wish I try the case
   According to the regular rules or as
   We usually do things here in Huisum?
WALTER: According to the legal regulations
   As usual in Huisum, and not otherwise.
ADAM: Ah, very good. I can give satisfaction.
   Clerk, are you ready?
LICHT: Willing and able.
ADAM: — Then, justice, take your proper course.
   Plaintiff, step forward.
FRAU MARTHE: Here I am, Judge Adam.
ADAM: And who are you?
FRAU MARTHE: Who?
ADAM: You.
FRAU MARTHE: Who, me?
ADAM: Say who!
   Name, occupation, domicile, etc.

FRAU MARTHE: The judge will have his joke.

ADAM: His joke? Not so.
  I sit in the name of justice here, Frau Marthe,
  And justice must discover who you are.

LICHT: (*in an undertone*) Ask something that makes sense.

FRAU MARTHE: You poke
  Your head in at my window every Sunday
  When you walk out of town.

WALTER: You know the woman?

ADAM: She lives just round the corner, excellency,
  If you come up the footpath through the hedges,
  Widow of a janitor, midwife nowadays,
  An honest woman else, well spoken of.

WALTER: Being so perfectly informed, Judge Adam,
  Questions of that kind are superfluous.
  Set down her name and write beside it:
  Well known to the court.

ADAM: That too.
  You are not one for the formalities.
  Do as his worship asks that it be done.

WALTER: Now ask after the subject of the suit.

ADAM: Do what?

WALTER: (*impatiently*) Discover what the matter is.

ADAM: Likewise, a jug. Forgive me.

WALTER: How, likewise?

ADAM: A jug. Merely a jug. Set down a jug
  And write beside it: well known to the court.

LICHT: My casual supposition, Judge ... Will you
  On that ...

ADAM: God damn me, what I tell you write
  You write. Is it not a jug, Frau Marthe?

FRAU MARTHE: It is. This jug.

ADAM: What did I say?

FRAU MARTHE: Broken ...

ADAM: Pedantic detail.

LICHT: Pardon me!

ADAM: Who broke the jug? That lout, for certain.

FRAU MARTHE: Yes him, that lout.

ADAM: (*aside*)   Oh perfect, perfect.

RUPRECHT: It is not true, your worship.

ADAM: (*aside*)   Adam, old son, awake!

RUPRECHT: She's lying through her teeth.

ADAM: Less noise, dolt.
  You'll break your teeth on dry bread soon enough.
  — Clerk of the Court, set down a jug, as stated,
  And his name with it who demolished it.
  We'll have this matter settled speedily.

WALTER: Judge Adam! Heavens! Such a rough proceeding!

ADAM: How so?

LICHT: Should you not formally ...?

ADAM: Not so.
  His worship is no lover of formalities.

WALTER: If hearing the evidence in proper form, Judge Adam,
  Is something you are ignorant how to do
  This place is not the place to teach you.
  If otherwise than this you can't adjudicate
  Step down: perhaps your clerk here can.

ADAM: Forgive me. I did it as is usual in Huisum.
  Your worship's orders were to that effect.

WALTER: My orders ...?!

ADAM: Word of honour.

WALTER: I ordered you
  To judge the case here as our laws require
  And here in Huisum thought those laws to be
  As elsewhere in the United Provinces.*

ADAM: There I must humbly beg your pardon.
  We have here, with your worshipful permission,
  Statutes, peculiar ones, in Huisum,
  Not written-down ones, as I must confess,
  But come to us, tried and trusted, through tradition.
  From this way, I dare hope, of doing things
  Not one inch have I deviated.
  But also in your other way of doing things,
  The imperial way perhaps, I am at home.
  Do you want proof? Only command me to.
  I can judge cases now this way, now that.

WALTER: You give me bad opinions, Judge Adam.
  So be it though. Begin the case again. —

ADAM: Be assured, your worship will be satisfied.
  Observe. — Frau Marthe Rull, present your suit.

FRAU MARTHE: My suit, as I have said, concerns this jug.
  But let me first, before I tell the court

What happened to the jug, explain
What it has been to me.
ADAM: You are free to speak.
FRAU MARTHE: You see this jug, your honours,
　You see this jug?
ADAM: We do, indeed we do.
FRAU MARTHE: You don't, you'll pardon me, you see the bits.
　Of all jugs the most beautiful is smashed.
　Right on this hole, where there is nothing now,
　All of the provinces of the Netherlands
　Were handed over to Philip of Spain.
　Here in his robes stood Emperor Charles the Fifth.
　All you see standing now of him's his legs.
　Here Philip, on his knees, received the crown.
　He's in the inside now, except his backside,
　And even that received a walloping.
　There his two aunties, moved to tears,
　The Queen of France, the Queen of Hungary,
　Were wiping their eyes. If you see one of them
　Lifting her hand still with her hanky in it
　You'd say the tears she weeps were for herself.
　There in the entourage there's Philibert
　Who would have taken the clout the Emperor took
　Still leaning on his sword. But now he'll fall
　And so will Maximilian — oh, the lout! —
　Because their swords are swiped away below.
　Here in the middle, with his holy hat on,
　You saw the Archbishop of Arras standing
　But he's gone to the devil well and truly
　And left his lanky shadow on the cobbles.
　Here in the background stood the bodyguard
　With halberds, crowding round, and spears
　And here, see, houses in the marketplace in Brussels
　And at his window here a looker-on
　But what there is to look at now, who knows.
ADAM: Spare us the treaty that was knocked to bits
　Unless it matters here. The hole is our concern,
　Frau Marthe, not the Provinces
　That where that hole is now were handed over.
FRAU MARTHE: Yes, but how fine my jug was matters here.* —
　That jug was won by Childerich,

The tinker, when the Prince of Orange
Overran Briel with his Sea Beggars.
A Spaniard had it, filled with wine,
Already at his lips when Childerich
Flung down the Spaniard from behind and seized
The jug and emptied it and went his ways.

ADAM: A worthy Sea Beggar.

FRAU MARTHE: Thereafter
The jug came down to Fear-the-Lord, the gravedigger,
A sober man, he drank no more than thrice
And always mixed with water from the jug.
First as a man of sixty when
He married a young wife; then three years on
When she did more and made a happy father of him;
And when she'd brought forth fifteen further children
He drank a third time, when she died.

ADAM: And that's not bad either.

FRAU MARTHE: Next for the jug
Was Zaccheus of Tirlemont, a tailor,
Who told my husband, rest his soul, what I
Shall now tell you, this tale himself.
He flung, during the plundering by the French,
This jug and all his goods out of the window
And jumped himself and clumsily broke his neck.
The jug, however, the earthen jug, mere clay,
Fell on its feet, intact.

ADAM: To the point,
Frau Marthe Rull, if you don't mind, to the point.

FRAU MARTHE: Then in the terrible fire of '66
By then my husband had it, God rest his soul.

ADAM: The devil take mine, woman, have you still not done?

FRAU MARTHE: — If I am not to have my say, Judge Adam,
I might as well not be here and will go
And find a court where I'll be listened to.

WALTER: You are to have your say, but not on things
Foreign to your suit. If you tell us
That jug was valuable to you we know
All that we need to know to make a judgment

FRAU MARTHE: How much you need to know to make a judgment
I do not know and will not seek to know
But what I do know's this: to bring an action

I must be allowed to tell you what about.

WALTER: Well then. To a conclusion. What befell the jug?
What did? — What happened to the jug in '66
In the Great Fire? Shall we be told?
What happened to the jug?

FRAU MARTHE: What happened to it?
Nothing, I beg your pardon, gentlemen,
Nothing, in '66, happened to it.
Whole it remained, whole in the fire's midst,
And out of the ashes of the house I lifted it
Glazed, the next morning, shining
As though it came that moment from the kiln.

WALTER: Well now. Now we know the jug. We know what
Has happened to it, everything, and what has not.
What else is there?

FRAU MARTHE: Well then, this jug, see here, this jug
Smashed as it is still worth one whole, this jug
Not for a lady's mouth, not for the Stadholder's
Wife's lips herself unfit,
This jug here, honourable judges both,
This jug that lout there broke for me.

ADAM: Who did?

FRAU MARTHE: Him there, Ruprecht.

RUPRECHT: That's a lie,
Judge Adam.

ADAM: Speak when you're spoken to.
Your turn, yours too, will come later, for speaking.
— Is all this noted down?

LICHT: Indeed it is.

ADAM: Recount the event, my dear Frau Marthe.

FRAU MARTHE: Eleven yesterday ...

ADAM: I beg your pardon, when?

FRAU MARTHE: Eleven o'clock.

ADAM: A.M.?

FRAU MARTHE: Forgive me, no — at night.
And was in bed and blowing my candle out
When loud men's voices, a hullabaloo,
There in the far room where my daughter sleeps,
As if the Spaniards had come, alarmed me.
In no time down the stairs, I find
The bedroom door forced open, insults,

As I approach, assault my ears
And lifting up my light to see the scene
What do I see, Judge Adam, what do I see?
I see my jug in pieces on the floor,
A piece in every corner, and the girl
Wringing her hands and that great good-for-nothing
Full on, shouting his mouth off, like a madman.

ADAM: (*flabbergasted*) Well I'll be damned!

FRAU MARTHE: What?

ADAM: Damned, Frau Marthe!

FRAU MARTHE: Yes,
And then, as if, full of a righteous rage,
I grew ten arms and every one of them
I felt grow talons like the birds that kill,
I asked him, facing up to him, what he
Thought he was doing in the middle of the night
Smashing my jugs like someone raving mad
And he, he answered, guess what he answered me,
The cheek of it, him there, that limb of Satan,
I'll see him drawn and quartered or I'll never
Rest easy ever again, he says
Somebody other knocked the jug
From off the sill, I ask you, someone else
Who fled the bedroom just a moment since
And heaps, himself there, insults on the girl.

ADAM: A likely tale. And then?

FRAU MARTHE: When I hear this
I question her with looks. She stands there
Like someone dead and I say: Eve! —
And she sits down and was it someone else,
I ask. Joseph and Mary, you as well, mother,
She shouts, what are you getting at? — So tell me who.
Who else? she says. — And who else could it be?
And swears to me he was the one it was.

EVE: Swore what? What did I swear to you? I swore
You nothing. Never.

FRAU MARTHE: Eve!

EVE: You're telling lies.

RUPRECHT: D'you hear?

ADAM: Devil, will you, damned devil, hush!
Your gob will have my fist in for a stopper.

You wait your turn. Your turn's not now.

RUPRECHT: You say you never ...?

EVE: No, Mother. That's not the truth.
  Deep in my heart, believe me, I am sorry
  To say this thing here in a public place.
  But I swore nothing, nothing, I swore nothing.

ADAM: Be reasonable, my dears.

LICHT: Strange, is it not?

FRAU MARTHE: You tell me, Eve, you didn't promise me
  And call on Joseph and the Mother of God?

EVE: Not for an oath, not swearing. See I swear it now
  And call on Joseph and the Mother of God.

ADAM: Friends, come now. Come, Frau Marthe. See how
  You frighten the poor child. Why be like this?
  Once she has weighed the matter up and brought
  To mind, all in her own good time, what happened,
  Mark me, what did and what, should she
  Not say what she's supposed to say, still might,
  You mark my words she'll testify today
  Like yesterday, whether she can swear to it or not.
  Leave Joseph and the Virgin Mary out of it.

WALTER: Oh come, Judge Adam, come, come. This is
  Equivocal guidance that you give the parties.

FRAU MARTHE: If she, the shameless thing, can tell me to my face,
  The good-for-nothing trollop, if she tells me
  That it was somebody not Ruprecht there,
  Let her, for all I care — I won't say what.
  But me, Judge Adam, I can assure you, I can,
  Even if I can't exactly say she swore it,
  That yesterday she said it, I swear to that
  And call on Joseph and the Virgin Mary.

ADAM: That much the girl herself ...

WALTER: Judge Adam!

ADAM: Your worship? — What? — Didn't you, Eve, my chuck?

FRAU MARTHE: Open your mouth. Did you not say that to me?
  Did you not yesterday, did you not say it to me?

EVE: When did I say I didn't?

ADAM: There we are.

RUPRECHT: You slag, you.

ADAM: Write this down.

VEIT: How can she?

WALTER: I find myself quite at a loss, Judge Adam,
  To understand your conduct. Were you yourself
  The one who smashed the jug you could not be
  Keener to shift suspicion from yourself
  On to this youth than you are now. —
  Our clerk will set down nothing more, I hope,
  Than the young woman's admission
  Of yesterday's admission, not of the fact.
  — Is it her turn to testify?
ADAM: Damn me,
  Her turn? Perhaps it isn't. In these matters
  To err, your excellency, is only human.
  Whom should I question? Should I have? The accused?
  I'm always pleased to learn, I promise you.
WALTER: So unabashed! — Yes, question the accused.
  Question him, make an end of it, please do.
  This is the last case you conduct.
ADAM: The last? What? Yes indeed! Hear the accused.
  What was his old self thinking of, I wonder.
  God blast that guinea fowl, God blast its pip.
  I wish the plague had done for it in India.
  I've got that dollop of noodles on the brain.
WALTER: You've got ...? What sort of dollop ...?
ADAM: The dollop of noodles,
  Forgive me, I'm supposed to give the fowl.
  If I can't get the beast to take its pill
  God damn my soul if I know what will happen.
WALTER: God stap me, man. Do what you are here to do.
ADAM: Let the accused step forward.
RUPRECHT: Here, Judge Adam.
  Ruprecht, Veit's son, the cottager's, from Huisum.
ADAM: And did you hear, just now, before the court,
  The suit Frau Marthe brought against you?
RUPRECHT: I did, Judge Adam.
ADAM: You have the nerve, do you,
  To wish to say something in your defence?
  Do you confess? Or will you have the face
  To stand there like a heathen sinner and deny it?
RUPRECHT: To say something in my defence,
  Judge Adam? Well this, with your permission,
  That not one word of what she says is true.

ADAM: I see. And you can prove it, can you?

RUPRECHT: Oh yes.

ADAM: My dear Frau Marthe, my good lady,
  Set your mind at rest. All will be well.

WALTER: Why should Frau Marthe so concern you, Judge?

ADAM: Why me? By God! What Christian man would ...?

WALTER: You
  Say what you have to say in your defence. —
  Are you, Clerk, able to conduct the case?

ADAM: Oh come!

LICHT: Am I ...? Well, if your excellency ...

ADAM: What are you gawping at? What have you got to say?
  Don't stand there gawping like a half-wit, idiot.
  What have you got to say?

RUPRECHT: What have I got to say?

WALTER: Yes, you. You are to say what happened.

RUPRECHT: And so I will, as soon as I am let.

WALTER: It is indeed intolerable, Judge Adam.

RUPRECHT: Ten it would be about at night, —
  And warm, although a January night,
  As May, — when I said to my father: Father,
  I'll step over to Eve's a minute.
  For, let me say, I had a mind to marry her,
  A fine young woman, she is, I saw at haymaking
  How everything she did went quick and right,
  The hay, like magic, stacked in no time.
  I asked her: Will you? And she answered: Och,
  The twaddle you talk. — And afterwards said yes.

ADAM: Keep to the point. The twaddle! What?
  I asked her would she and she answered yes.

RUPRECHT: Yes, on my honour, Judge.

WALTER: Go on, go on.

RUPRECHT: Well, then
  Father, I said, d'you hear me? Let me.
  We'll have some talk together at the window.
  Well then, he says, be off. You'll stay outside?
  God's honour, I say. I promise. Well, he says,
  Be off, he says, and be back here by eleven.

ADAM: Well then, you say, and twaddle and no end of it.
  Well then, have you soon done?

RUPRECHT: Well then, I say,

Give you my word, and put my cap on
And reach the bridge and must go back
Through the village again because the stream is out.
Drat this, I think, Ruprecht, and damn and blast,
The garden gate at Marthe's will be shut,
Eve only leaves it open till ten o'clock,
If I'm not there by ten I'll not get in.

ADAM: No way to run a house.

WALTER: And then what?

RUPRECHT: Then — as I'm getting nearer Marthe's down
The avenue of limes and overhead they are
As close and dark as the cathedral in Utrecht
I hear the garden gate creak further on.
And hark, I say, Eve's still there after all
And where my ears had brought me news,
A happy man, I send my eyes after —
And tell them off, when they come back to me,
For being blind and send them out again
Forthwith, to take a better look,
And call them good-for-nothing tittle-tattlers,
Trouble-makers, worthless gossips,
And send them out a third time, thinking
They've always done as they were bid till now
And can't bear being bid to quit my head
And take up any other kind of service.
It's Eve, I recognize her by her dress,
And someone else is there as well.

ADAM: Oh someone else was there, was there? And who,
Clever dick?

RUPRECHT: Damn me if I know.

ADAM: Well then!
Can't hang a villain till you catch him, can you?

WALTER: Continue. Have your say. Let the man be.
Why must you interrupt him, Judge?

RUPRECHT: I wouldn't swear it on the book, the night
Was black as coal and things all looked alike,
But let me tell you this: The cobbler,
Lebrecht, the one they let off serving recently,
For some while now's been sniffing round her.
I said last autumn: Listen, Eve,
That man won't stay away, I don't like it,

Tell him to smack his lips at someone else
Or damn my soul if I don't throw him out.
She says you leave me be and says
Neither this nor that to him, neither do nor don't
So off I go and throw the beggar out.
ADAM: Ah, ha! Lebrecht's the fellow's name?
RUPRECHT: Yes, Lebrecht.
ADAM: Good.
We have a name. It all falls into place.
— Clerk of the Court, you've taken note of that?
LICHT: Indeed I have. That and the rest, Judge Adam.
ADAM: Go on, Ruprecht, go on, my son.
RUPRECHT: Well then,
Meeting this twosome at eleven like that —
I always left at ten — it riles me.
Hold on, I think, it's not too late yet, Ruprecht,
Your antlers haven't started growing yet
But feel here on your forehead carefully
Whether there's not something a bit like horn
Sprouting already — and crept in at the gate
And hid myself behind the taxus hedge
And hear a whispering and a tittering
And tussling, Judge, a tussling to and fro,
God damn, I think, I'll have ...
EVE: What wickedness
That is, oh shame on you!
FRAU MARTHE: Devil!
Wait till I get you on your own again,
I'll have your blood. You don't know what I'm like
And what things I might do. Time you found out.
RUPRECHT: Quarter of an hour or so it lasts. I'm thinking
Where will this end? Even before the wedding ...
And while the thought's still turning over in me
Suddenly they've gone inside, before the parson ...
EVE: Come Mother now, I don't care how this ends.
ADAM: You hush, you over there, take my advice.
Thunder and lightning blast you, gasbag.
You wait to speak until I tell you to.
WALTER: Very strange, by God.
RUPRECHT: Judge, it comes up in me
Like apoplexy. Let me breathe!

And buttons popping on my shirt-front. Breathe!
And tear my shirt open. Now let me breathe!
And go and shove and kick and batter in
Finding it, when I shove against it, locked
With one great kick the trollop's door.
ADAM: Bravo! Some spirit!
RUPRECHT: Just as it crashes open
   That jug there, off the sill, falls to the floor
   And through the window, whoosh! somebody jumps
   For it. I see his coat-tails flapping.
ADAM: And was that Lebrecht?
RUPRECHT: Who if it wasn't, Judge?
   The girl stands there, I shove her over,
   Run to the window quick and find the man
   Still hanging on the uprights in the trellis where
   The vine comes up, by tendrils, to the roof
   And since I've got the handle in my hand still
   From busting down the door I fetch
   Him with the metal end one on the nob, for there,
   Judge Adam, I could reach him, good and heavy.
ADAM: Was it a handle?
RUPRECHT: What?
ADAM: It was ...
RUPRECHT: The door handle.
ADAM: No wonder.
LICHT: You thought it was a sword handle.
ADAM: A sword? Me, why?
RUPRECHT: A sword?
LICHT: Easy enough
   To mishear, I should say. A door handle
   Is very like a sword handle.
ADAM: I think ...
LICHT: Sure as I live! The shaft of it, Judge Adam?
ADAM: The shaft!
RUPRECHT: The shaft! But that's not what it was.
   It was the end, the handle's turned round end.
ADAM: The turned round end of the handle's what it was.
LICHT: Well, well.
RUPRECHT: But where you hold it was a lump of lead,
   Much like, that's true, the pommel of a sword.
ADAM: Yes, like a pommel.

LICHT: Good, like the pommel of a sword.
  A solid sort of weapon, whatever it was,
  It must have been. That much I knew already.
WALTER: The point, gentlemen, please, keep to the point.
ADAM: Nothing but fiddle-faddle, Clerk. — Continue, you.
RUPRECHT: He topples off, and I'm about to turn
  But see him in the dark finding his feet
  And think: Not dead then, eh? And climb the sill
  And have a mind to halt him down below
  When, gentlemen, as I'm tensed up to jump
  Into my eyes, like hail, like flying hail —
  God blast me dead if man below and night
  And universe and window sill
  I'm standing on don't all go black —
  Comes sand, coarse grains of it, a fistful.
ADAM: Damn me! I never! Who did that?
RUPRECHT: Who? Lebrecht.
ADAM: Villain!
RUPRECHT: Villain's the word. If it was him.
ADAM: Who else?
RUPRECHT: As though a pelting hail had flung me
  Sixty feet off a mountainside
  Crash I go off the sill into the room
  And tell you: I thought I'd stove the floorboards in.
  But didn't break my neck, nor yet my back
  Nor hip, nor any other bones either
  But meanwhile lost my chance of having him
  And sit wiping my eyes. She comes
  And Oh dear heaven, she cries and Ruprecht, oh
  What have you done? I land out with my foot,
  By God I do, good job I couldn't see where.
ADAM: Was that the sand?
RUPRECHT: The sand flung at me, yes.
ADAM: Damn me! It hit.
RUPRECHT: Then when I'm up again
  I think why should I shame my fists on her?
  And lash her with my tongue: Common as dirt,
  You whore. And think that's good enough for her
  But tears, would you believe it, choke my voice.
  For then Frau Marthe coming in the room
  Lifting the lamp and I see that girl there

Before me, trembling fit to break your heart,
Whose look before was good and warm and sweet
It seems to me I'd rather have no eyesight
And would have given my eyes away
For marbles anyone can have a game with.

EVE: What wickedness. He isn't fit ...

ADAM: You hold your noise.

RUPRECHT: You know the rest.

ADAM: How so? What rest?

RUPRECHT: Didn't Frau Marthe come and start her yapping
And Ralf the neighbour come and neighbour Hinz
And Aunty Sus and Aunty Liese come
And maids and servant lads and cats and dogs
And make a scene and didn't Frau Marthe ask
The girl there who it was who broke the jug
And her, you know already, she said I did?
God damn my soul, she's not so very wrong.
I smashed the pitcher she was carrying to the well
And holed the cobbler's head —

ADAM: Frau Marthe
How do you answer what he says?
Speak up.

FRAU MARTHE: How do I answer what he says?
Judge, what he says has come in like a marten
And murders truth like a squawking hen.
Who loves what's right should reach for clubs
And do this beast of the night to death.

ADAM: We must have proof from you.

FRAU MARTHE: And so you shall
And gladly. — Here is my witness. — Speak.

ADAM: The daughter? No, Frau Marthe.

WALTER: No? Why not?

ADAM: As witness, excellency? In the Penal Code —
Rule Four, would it be? Or Five? — does it not read
If jugs or anything else for that matter
Are smashed by ruffianly young males
Then daughters cannot witness for their mothers.

WALTER: Learning and error are kneaded in your head
So thoroughly, like dough, in one,
With every slice you give me some of each.
The girl will make a statement now, not witness.

Whether and whom she wishes to witness for
And can, her statement will reveal.
ADAM: A statement, yes indeed. Rule Six.
But what she says no one believes.
WALTER: Step forward, child.
ADAM: Hey, Lies! — I beg your pardon,
My mouth is drying up. — Margrete!

Scene 8

Enter a MAID
ADAM: A glass, and water.
MAID: At once.
                                        [*She exits*]
ADAM: Yourself, may I ...?
WALTER: No, thank you.
ADAM: French? A Mosel? What you will.
    (WALTER *refuses, politely. The* MAID *brings water, and exits*)

Scene 9

ADAM: — If I may make so bold, your excellency,
It seems the parties could be brought to settle.
WALTER: Settle? I don't see how, Judge Adam.
Reasonable people, it is true, may settle,
But how you have in mind to get them to,
Much of the matter being still obscure,
I should be pleased to have you tell me.
How shall you manage it? Explain.
Have you come to your judgment?
ADAM: God damn me!
Left in the lurch by the Law itself, if I
Turn for assistance to philosophy
Then it was — Lebrecht —
WALTER: Who?
ADAM: Or Ruprecht —
WALTER: Who?
ADAM: Or Lebrecht broke the jug.
WALTER: Which then? Lebrecht, was it? Or Ruprecht?
You dive in with your judgment, we observe,
As with your fist into a sack of peas.
ADAM: Allow me.

WALTER: Silence. Be silent, please.
ADAM: Just as you like.
  God's truth, I should be perfectly content
  If it were both of them who did it.
WALTER: Enquire, and you'll be told.
ADAM: With pleasure.
  Call me a crook though if you get it out of them.
  — Clerk, are you ready there to take this down?
LICHT: Quite ready.
ADAM: Good.
LICHT: And start a fresh page for it,
  Eager to see what will be written there.
ADAM: A fresh page? Also good.
WALTER: Speak up now, child.
ADAM: Speak, Eve, d'you hear, little Miss Eve, speak up now.
  Give God, d'you hear, my pet, give, damn me,
  Him and the world, give Him some of the truth.
  Remember you stand before God's throne of judgement
  And by denials and by blabbing about
  What doesn't belong here mustn't aggravate
  Your judge. What am I saying? You'll be sensible.
  A judge, you know, never stops being a judge
  And when you'll need one you can never tell.
  If you say Lebrecht did it: fine. If you
  Say it was Ruprecht, that is also fine.
  Say one or the other and I'm a lying rogue
  If things don't fall out how you want them to.
  But give me twaddle about someone else,
  Some third party, and name me silly names —
  Look out, my chuck. I'll say no more.
  No one in Huisum will believe you, Eva,
  And no one in the Netherlands, God string me up.
  Walls may have ears but they can't testify.
  That other someone will protect himself
  And your boy Ruprecht goes his way to hell.
WALTER: Refrain from making further speeches, will you,
  Muddled as they are and neither rhyme nor reason.
ADAM: Your worship cannot follow them?
WALTER: Get on!
  You've sat too long there holding forth already.
ADAM: My word, I'm not a scholar, excellency.

If gentlemen from Utrecht find me difficult
It may be different with the common people here.
The girl, I'll bet, knows what I'm getting at.

FRAU MARTHE: What does this mean? Out with it now. Speak
plainly.

EVE: Oh dearest mother.

FRAU MARTHE: You ...! I'm warning you.

RUPRECHT: Truly it's hard, Frau Marthe, speaking plain
With a bad conscience at your throat.

ADAM: Less mouth! Less yapping, clever dick!

FRAU MARTHE: Who was it?

EVE: Jesu.

FRAU MARTHE: Him, was it, numbskull? Him, the villain!
Jesu! As good as call the girl a whore.
Lord Jesus, was it?

ADAM: Be reasonable, Frau Marthe!
I never heard ... Give the poor girl a chance.
Frightening the child ... A whore ... a nincompoop.
That way will get us nowhere. She'll remember.

RUPRECHT: Aye, that she will.

ADAM: You hush your noise there, dolt.

RUPRECHT: The cobbler — give her time — he'll come to mind.

ADAM: Limb of the devil! Usher! Call Hanfriede!

RUPRECHT: Easy, Judge. Let it be now. I'll keep quiet.
She'll bring my name up soon enough, you'll see.

FRAU MARTHE: You listen, you, don't show me up, d'you hear?
Forty-nine years, d'you hear, I've lived
Unstained, and wish to make it fifty.
My birthday is the third of February.
Today's the first. Be brief. Who was it?

ADAM: All right by me. All right, Frau Marthe Rull.

FRAU MARTHE: Your father said, passing away, Hear this, Martha:
Find me a decent husband for the girl
And if she goes to the bad, the trollop,
You give the gravedigger a threepenny bit
And have him put me on my back again.
God damn me, I'll be turning in my grave.

ADAM: And that's not bad either.

FRAU MARTHE: Eva, my love,
To honour thy father and thy mother as the fifth
Commandment says, if you must say it do: I let

The cobbler or some third person, d'you hear,
In my bedroom. Not him I'm promised to.
RUPRECHT: I'm sorry for her. Forget the jug, will you.
I'll take it to Utrecht. A jug like that ...
I wish I had smashed it to smithereens.
EVE: How mean you are. How shameful it is of you
That you don't say: Well then, I broke the jug.
Shame on you, Ruprecht, shame on you that you
Can't trust me in the thing that I am doing.
Did I not give you my word and answer yes
That day you asked me: Will you have me, Eva?
Do you not think yourself as good as him?
And even had you spied me through the keyhole
Drinking with him, the cobbler, from that jug
You should have thought still: Eve is honest
And all will be to her credit in the end
And if not here, in this life, then in the next.
We'll bide our time until the resurrection.
RUPRECHT: God's truth, I can't be patient that long, Eva.
I put my trust in things I can seize hold of.
EVE: Suppose it was Lebrecht, even suppose,
Why in the name of everything that's holy
Would I not there and then have told you so?
But why in front of lads and maids and neighbours?
Suppose I had a reason to conceal it
Why then, my only love, Ruprecht, tell me
Shouldn't I say it was you and you trust me?
Why not? Why shouldn't I? Why shouldn't I have?
RUPRECHT: The devil, say it then. What do I mind?
If you can spare yourself disgrace in church.
EVE: How vile you are! How thankless! Fit
I should spare myself for! Fit
That with one word of honest truth
I bring myself and you into perdition.
WALTER: Well then, and this one word? Do not detain us.
It wasn't Ruprecht?
EVE: No, your excellency,
Since he himself wants it to be like that.
Only for his sake did I not say so.
It wasn't Ruprecht broke the earthen jug
And if he says that too you can believe him.

FRAU MARTHE: Eva! Not Ruprecht?

EVE: No, Mother, no. And if
I said it yesterday, that was a lie.

FRAU MARTHE: Wait for it, you. I'll thrash the living daylights —
                    (She puts the jug down)

EVE: Do as you will.

WALTER: *(threateningly)* Frau Marthe!

ADAM: Ho there! Usher! —
Damned baggage! Fling her out! Who says
There's only Ruprecht that it might have been?
Were you there with a candle coupling, eh?
I'd say the one who knows is the girl herself.
Call me a villain if it wasn't Lebrecht.

FRAU MARTHE: Well was it? Was it Lebrecht? Was it?

ADAM: Speak up, Eva my chuck, was it not Lebrecht, sweetheart?

EVE: Have you no shame at all? Are you so base?
How can you say that it was Lebrecht?

WALTER: Come now,
Young woman, you forget yourself. Where's the
Respect you owe the Judge?

EVE: Respect!
For that judge there? Fit to be standing
Before the court himself, full of his sins,
Who knows better than anybody who it was.
                    (Turning to the village JUDGE)
Did you not yesterday send Lebrecht into town
To Utrecht, to the levying board,
With his certificate? How can you say
That it was Lebrecht when you know
Full well that Lebrecht is in Utrecht?

ADAM: Who else? If Lebrecht isn't it — God rack the lot —
And Ruprecht not, and not Lebrecht — Well, you?

RUPRECHT: True word, Judge Adam, let me tell you
What she says there at least might not be lies.
I met him yesterday, Lebrecht, myself,
Eight in the morning, heading for Utrecht,
Him with his bowly legs, unless
He had himself transported there, by ten
That night the man could not have got back here.
Might well be some third party did it.

ADAM: His bowly legs, my foot! Dimwit! The man,

Well as the next man will, can step along.
Call me an unforked radish if a dog,
A German sheepdog of a middling size,
Would not have trouble keeping up with him.

WALTER: Tell us what happened.

ADAM: Pardon me, excellency!
I doubt the girl can help you further.

WALTER: Not help? Not help me? And why ever not?

ADAM: Simple, you know. A good enough girl, but simple,
Still wet behind the ears, scarcely confirmed,
Mention a man, she blushes. You know the sort,
They'll let you in the dark but in the daylight
Before a judge they'll swear they never did.

WALTER: How kind you are and quick to make allowances,
Judge Adam, in all things that concern the girl.

ADAM: To tell the truth, your excellency,
Her father was a friend of mine. If you,
Your worship, were disposed to leniency
We could fulfil the letter of our duty
And let his daughter go.

WALTER: I feel
In me a strong desire, Judge Adam,
To get to the bottom of the matter, fully. —
Be bold, my child: Who was it broke the jug?
You stand here at this moment before no one
Who could not pardon you an error.

EVE: Please, in your goodness, sir, and in your mercy
Do not let me be forced to say what happened.
And do not think amiss of this refusal.
It is the strange determining of heaven
That in this matter lays a finger on my lips.
That Ruprecht never knocked against the jug
If you require me to I'll lay it down
On the holy altar with an oath.
But for the rest of yesterday's event
In every detail it belongs to me
And Mother can't demand to unknit it all
All for the sake of one sole thread
Belonging to her that runs through everything.
Who it was who broke the jug I mustn't say here
Or I'd be bound to touch on secrets

Not mine, and wholly not to do with the jug.
Sooner or later I will say it to her
But here, before the court, is not the place
Where she's a right to interrogate me for it.

ADAM: No right, indeed. God's honour, no she hasn't.
The girl knows what the rules are well enough.
If she will swear her oath before the court
The mother's charge is void, and there
The matter ends, beyond dispute.

WALTER: What do you say, Frau Marthe, to her statement?

FRAU MARTHE: If for a minute nothing sensible, your worship,
Occurs to me, I do beg you believe me
It is the shock of it has lamed my tongue.
There are examples that a desperate man
To do himself some good in the eyes of the world
Forswears himself in court, but that a girl
Should swear a false oath on the holy altar
Only to pillory herself
No one has heard of such a thing before today.
Suppose that somebody sneaking yesterday
Into her bedroom, somebody not Ruprecht,
Were fact, your excellency,
Or even possible it were a fact
Hear me aright: I wouldn't linger in this place.
I'd put a chair, to be her furniture,
Outside the door for her and say be off now, child,
The world's your oyster, you can live in it rent free,
And your inheritance includes long hair
By which, when you think fit, to hang yourself.

WALTER: Easy, Frau Marthe, easy.

FRAU MARTHE: But because
Here I can prove my case another way
Than only by her help who will not help me do it
And being through and through convinced that only he
Broke, no one else, my jug in pieces,
Seeing how keenly they deny it
Makes me suspect a thing to be ashamed of.
Last night conceals some other wrongdoing
Than merely the ruination of my jug.
Your worship must be told that Ruprecht
Has been conscripted, soon, in a day or two,

He has to take the oath, in Utrecht, on the flag.
The young men of our country take French leave.
Suppose last night he said: Eva, my pet,
What do you say? The world's a big place. Come.
You have the keys to safe and strongbox, don't you?
And she, Eva, she made him some objection:
The rest then, when I interrupted them —
Him out of spite, her still for love of him —
Much as it did happen might well have done.
RUPRECHT: Baggage! How dare she say such things!
  Safe and the strongbox ...
WALTER: Hush.
EVE: And him desert!
WALTER: Keep to the point. The jug's the matter here. —
  Proof, give us proof that Ruprecht broke it.
FRAU MARTHE: Very well, your honour. First I shall prove
  That Ruprecht broke my jug. And then
  Conduct enquiries in my house. — For see
  I'll fetch a tongue who will bear witness
  To every word he spoke and should at once
  Have brought it forward in due order
  Had I had any notion this one here
  Would not use hers for me. Now though
  Have Frau Brigitte summoned if you will,
  Who is his aunt, and she will serve me
  Since she'll affirm what is the central point.
  For she, she caught, ten thirty in the garden,
  And note this carefully, before the jug was smashed,
  Eva and him she caught them having words,
  And how the fairy tale put up by him
  Is split in two by this from top to toe
  By this one tongue, I leave it to you,
  Eminent judges both, to realize.
RUPRECHT: Who?
VEIT: Sister Briggy?
RUPRECHT: With Eve, me? In the garden?
FRAU MARTHE: Yes you, with Eve, in the garden, half past ten,
  Before you, as you told the tale, at eleven
  Bust down the door and fell upon the room:
  Exchanging words, now tenderly, now roughly,
  As if trying to turn her mind to something.

ADAM: (*aside*) Damn me, the devil looks after his own.

WALTER: Summon this woman.

RUPRECHT: Gentlemen, I beg you.
   This isn't true. It isn't possible.

ADAM: You wait, jailbird. — Hey, usher! Hey, Hanfriede! —
   Jugs break when people up and run, of course. —
   Clerk, will you go and send for Frau Brigitte.

VEIT: Listen here you, damned lout you, what's this then?
   I'll break your neck.

RUPRECHT: And why?

VEIT: You tell me why
   You kept it quiet that you were with this trollop
   Fooling with her, in the garden, by half past ten.
   Why keep that quiet?

RUPRECHT: Why did I keep that quiet?
   Because, God blast me dead, it's not true, Father.
   If Aunty Briggy swears it is then hang me
   And her too, from my feet, for all I care.

VEIT: But *if* she swears it, look out for your life,
   You and herself, your precious Eva Rull.
   Whatever you're acting like before this court
   You're hand in glove with her, there's something
   Secret to be ashamed of still that she
   Well knows and keeps it quiet to save you.

RUPRECHT: Secret? What secret?

VEIT: Why'd you pack your things?
   Last night, eh? Why'd you pack your things?

RUPRECHT: My things?

VEIT: Your jackets, trousers, linen,
   A bundle, just the sort a travelling man
   Slings on.

RUPRECHT: I've got to go to Utrecht, that's why.
   I've got to join the regiment. God blast it,
   You think I ...?

VEIT: To Utrecht? Oh ho, to Utrecht!
   Some hurry you were in to get to Utrecht!
   Day before yesterday you never knew
   Whether you'd have to leave the fifth or sixth.

WALTER: Are there things you might tell the court, Father?

VEIT: — Nothing, your worship, I can say for sure yet.

The hour the jug broke I was home and nor
Concerning any other enterprise
To tell the truth and when I weigh the facts
To cast suspicion on my boy have I seen anything.
Fully persuaded of his innocence
I came here bent, after this squabble's settled,
On breaking the engagement off
And asking back the little silver chain
And silver threepenny bit he gave her for a pendant
This girl, last autumn, when they were betrothed.
What my grey head is having heaped on it
This talk of dirty tricks and flitting
Is news to me, your honour, as to you.
The devil break his neck though if it's true.

WALTER: Fetch Frau Brigitte here, Judge Adam.

ADAM: — Surely
The matter will fatigue your worship
For it drags on and on. Your worship
Still has the registry
And my accounts ... What time is it?

LICHT: Half past just struck.

ADAM: Past ten?

LICHT: Past eleven, pardon me.

WALTER: No odds.

ADAM: The clock's not right, or you're not in the head.
                    (*He looks at the clock*)
Well I'm a liar. What are your orders then?

WALTER: I had a mind ...

ADAM: To call a halt? So be it.

WALTER: You'll pardon me. I had a mind to carry on.

ADAM: You have a mind. — So be that too. Else I,
God's honour, nine tomorrow, would end
The matter to your satisfaction.

WALTER: You know my wishes.

ADAM: As you command.
Clerk, send the ushers off. They are
To ask Frau Brigitte to the court at once.

WALTER: And kindly — to save me time that matters —
See to the thing yourself a little, please.

                                        [*Exit* LICHT]

Scene 10

ADAM: (*rising*) One could meanwhile, if that were agreeable,
  Arise and stretch one's legs?
WALTER: Pardon? Indeed.
  What I was going to say ...
ADAM: And will you likewise
  Allow the parties, till Frau Brigit appears ...?
WALTER: What's that? The parties?
ADAM: Yes, outside, if you ...
WALTER: (*aside*) Damnation!
  (*Aloud*)   Judge Adam, I'll tell you what.
  Give me a glass of wine, will you, meanwhile.
ADAM: Gladly, with all my heart. Hey, Margarete!
  Your worship makes a happy man of me. — Margarete!
                          Enter the MAID
MAID: You called?
ADAM: What shall it be? — Fall out, you people.
  French? — In the hall outside. — Or Rhenish?
WALTER: Or Rhenish.
ADAM: Good. — Until I call you. Off!
WALTER: Where to?
ADAM: Some under seal, Margarete. — What?
  Only in the hall outside. — Here, you. — The key.
WALTER: Hm. Stay!
ADAM: Quick march! — Be off now, Margarete.
  And butter, freshly churned, Limburger cheese,
  And goose, some of the fat smoked Pomeranian goose.
WALTER: Stay still. One moment. Please, Judge Adam,
  I beg you, this is too much fuss.
ADAM: You folk,
  Get to the devil, I say. And you do as you're told.
WALTER: Judge, are the people sent away?
ADAM: Your worship?
WALTER: I asked ...
ADAM: They will withdraw, with your permission.
  Only withdraw, till Frau Brigitte appears.
  Or not? Or should ...? Perhaps ...?
WALTER: Hm. As you like.
  One wonders is it worth the trouble.
  Do you suppose it will take such a time

Before they find her?

ADAM: Today is wood day,
   Excellency. Most of the women
   Are in the forest foraging for sticks.
   It might well be that ...
RUPRECHT: Aunty's home.
WALTER: Home is she? Let be then.
RUPRECHT: She won't be long.
WALTER: She won't be long appearing. Bring the wine.
ADAM: (aside) Oh damn!
WALTER: Continue. But nothing to eat, I beg you,
   Except dry bread, a slice of it, and salt.
ADAM: (aside) Two minutes with the trollop on my own ...
   (Aloud) Dry bread? Come, come. And salt? You jest.
WALTER: I do not.
ADAM: Mercy! A piece of Limburg cheese, at least. —
   The tongue needs cheese to make it taste the wine.
WALTER: Well then, a piece of cheese, but nothing more.
ADAM: Be off. And a cloth, a white one, damask.
   Plain but proper.

                                        [*Exit the* MAID]

                    The bachelor's state
   That no one thinks well of has this advantage:
   That we what others are obliged to share
   Tightly and bitterly with wife and child
   Can with a friend when the time is right
   Wholly enjoy.
WALTER: I had a mind to ask:
   How did you get your injury, Judge Adam?
   The devil of a hole your head has in it.
ADAM: — I fell.
WALTER: You fell. I see. And when? Last night?
ADAM: Today, five thirty, pardon me, A.M.
   Early, as I was rising.
WALTER: And what was it
   You fell over?
ADAM: Over — your excellency —
   To tell the truth, your honour, over me.
   I went down headfirst full against the stove
   And why, I couldn't tell you even now.
WALTER: Backwards?

ADAM: Forgive me? Backwards ...
WALTER: Or forwards?
  You have two injuries, one front, one back.
ADAM: Frontwards and backwards. — Margarete!
  (*Enter the two maids with wine etc. They lay the table and exit*)
  First so. Then so. Against the stove's edge first
  Frontwards and beat my forehead in, and then
  Rebounded off the stove and hit the floor
  And smashed my head, the back of it, to boot.
                    (*He pours some wine*)
  May I?
WALTER: (*reaching for the glass*) Were you a married man
  I should be thinking some strange things about you,
  Judge Adam.
ADAM: How so?
WALTER: My word of honour,
  Wherever I look, nothing but rips and scratches.
ADAM: (*laughing*) Ah, no, thank God. That's not a woman's nails.
WALTER: I'm sure. Another bonus for the bachelor.
ADAM: (*still laughing*) Twigs for silkworms that somebody fixed
  There on the corner of the stove to dry. —
  Your very good health.
                    (*They drink*)
WALTER: And then to lose your wig
  So strangely and on this day of all days.
  It would at least have hidden your injuries.
ADAM: Troubles, they say, never come singly.
  Here, some of the soft one now ... May I?
WALTER: A mouthful. Limburger?
ADAM: The real thing, excellency.
WALTER: — But how the devil, tell me, did it happen?
ADAM: Did what?
WALTER: Getting without your wig.
ADAM: Like this:
  Yesterday evening I was sitting reading
  A case, and having put my spectacles
  The wrong place somewhere I had bent so low
  Over the issue that the candle flame
  Set my wig on fire. I thought to myself
  God's fire was falling on my sinful head
  And seized the wig to fling it from me

But hadn't undone the drawstring at the back
Before the lot had burned like Sodom and Gomorrhah
And I could barely save my own three hairs.
WALTER: Be damned! And your other one's in town?
ADAM: At the wigmaker's. — But down to business.
WALTER: Steady now, steady, Judge, I beg you.
ADAM: Come, come. Time marches on. Another glass. Allow me.
                    (*He fills their glasses*)
WALTER: The man Lebrecht — if our friend told the truth —
    He must have had a nasty knock, him too.
ADAM: Indeed he must.
                        (*He drinks*)
WALTER: Suppose this matter here,
    As I'm afraid it may, remains unsettled,
    You'll easily, you in the village, know
    The malefactor by his injury.
                        (*He drinks*)
    Niersteiner?
ADAM: What's that?
WALTER: Or decent Oppenheimer?
ADAM: Nierstein. I say, my word, a connoisseur.
    Nierstein, as sure as if I'd fetched it here myself.
WALTER: Three years ago I drank it where it grows.
                    (ADAM *fills their glasses again*)
    — How high's your window? — Yours, Frau Marthe.
FRAU MARTHE: My window?
WALTER: Yes, the window of the room
    The girl sleeps in.
FRAU MARTHE: The room itself is only
    A first-floor room, and storage under it,
    The window nine foot from the ground, not more,
    But when you weigh it up, for jumping from
    Very unsuitable. You see, a vine
    Stands out two foot from the wall
    And branches in a knotty way the width
    Of the wall in all directions through a trelliswork.
    Even the window's in its clutches.
    A wild boar, armed with tusks,
    Would have a hard time breaking through.
ADAM: But did.
                (*He pours himself more wine*)

WALTER: I beg your pardon?
ADAM: Nothing, nothing.
                    (*He drinks*)
WALTER: (*to* RUPRECHT) Where did you smite the sinner? On the
                                                        head?

ADAM: Come now.
WALTER: Enough.
ADAM: Your glass.
WALTER: Is still half full.
ADAM: Half empty.
WALTER: I said enough.
ADAM: The rule of three.
WALTER: No more now.
ADAM: Come, come. Pythagoras' principle.
                    (*He pours* WALTER *more wine*)
WALTER: (*to* RUPRECHT *again*)
    How often did you smite the sinner on the head?
ADAM: One for Peter, two for Paul, three for
    The Lord's anointed. Three is something like.
    A man can taste the sun when he drinks his third
    And God's own heaven when he drinks the rest.
WALTER: How often did you hit the sinner's head?
    You, Ruprecht, you, I'm asking you there.
ADAM: Well?
    How often did you smite him? Speak, will you.
    God strike me if he knows himself whether ...
    Forgotten, have we?
RUPRECHT: With the handle?
ADAM: Whatever it was.
WALTER: Down from the window, when you swiped at him.
RUPRECHT: Twice, gentlemen.
ADAM: Damned rogue. He won't forget it.
                    (*He drinks*)
WALTER:
    Twice! You could have killed him hitting him twice
    Like that. Then what?
RUPRECHT: If I'd have killed him
    I'd have him here. And I'd be glad. If he
    Lay dead here I could say: Your honours,
    This is the one and what I said is true.
ADAM: Dead, yes. Indeed. But as things are ...

(*He pours more wine*)

WALTER: And in the dark you couldn't tell who it was?

RUPRECHT: Couldn't at all, your worship. How could I?

ADAM: Should've opened your eyes, I'd say. — Your health.

RUPRECHT: Opened my eyes? I did open my eyes.
The devil threw sand in them.

ADAM: (*into his beard*)   He did that. Sand!
Shouldn't have had them that wide open, should you?
— Here's looking at your worship. Raise a glass.

WALTER: — To all things right and honourable, Judge Adam.
(*They drink*)

ADAM: Now, if you're minded to, one last one, shall we?
(*He pours more wine*)

WALTER: Doubtless you're at Frau Marthe's now and then,
Judge Adam. Who comes and goes there,
Tell me, apart from Ruprecht?

ADAM: Not very often,
I beg your pardon, excellency.
Who comes and goes I couldn't tell you.

WALTER: Strange. Would you not now and then
Call on the widow of your departed friend?

ADAM: Indeed, no. Only very rarely.

WALTER: Have
You and Judge Adam fallen out, Frau Marthe?
He says he doesn't call on you any more.

FRAU MARTHE: Hm. Fallen out, your honour? I wouldn't say so.
I think he calls himself my good friend still.
But that I often see him in my house,
Kin though he be, I can't pretend I do.
Nine weeks it is since he last stepped inside
And only passing by it was even then.

WALTER: What are you saying?

FRAU MARTHE: What?

WALTER: Nine weeks since …?

FRAU MARTHE: Nine,
Yes, ten come Thursday. He came for seeds
From me, carnations and auriculas.

WALTER: And — Sundays — when he's going out of town …?

FRAU MARTHE: Yes then, maybe, he'll look in at the window
And give me and my daughter a good morning

But goes his ways again.

WALTER: (*aside*)   Well, well. What if
  I've done the man ... (*He drinks*) I was supposing
  Since now and then you have the girl to help
  At home, and her being kin, you might by way
  Of thanks visit the mother now and then.

ADAM: How so, your excellency?

WALTER: How so? You said the girl
  Will get your fowls back on their feet again
  That fell sick in your yard. Did she not
  Only this morning give you such advice?

FRAU MARTHE: She does, your excellency, indeed she does.
  He sent her round a guinea fowl sick,
  Day before yesterday, already nearly dead.
  Last year she saved one from the pip
  And this one too she'll cure with noodles.
  Still though, to thank her, he has not appeared.

WALTER: (*confused*) — Another glass, Judge Adam, if you please.
  Pour me another. We can drink one more.

ADAM: Your servant. I'm a happy man. Allow me.
                (*He fills* WALTER's *glass*)

WALTER: Good health to you! — Judge Adam, surely
  Sooner or later he'll call by.

FRAU MARTHE: You think so?
  I doubt it. If I'd a Niersteiner such as
  You're drinking and the janitor, my dear departed,
  Such as was in his cellar now and then
  To serve my kin, his worship, then he might.
  But as things are, being a poor widow,
  I've nothing in my house to tempt him in.

WALTER: So much the better.

Scene 11

Enter LICHT, FRAU BRIGITTE *with a wig in her hand,*
and the MAIDS

LICHT: Here, Frau Brigitte, this way.

WALTER: Clerk of the Court, is this the woman?

LICHT: This is our Frau Brigitte, your excellency.

WALTER: Ah good. Now let us settle matters.

Maids, clear away here.

[*Exit the* MAIDS *with glasses etc.*]

ADAM: (*meanwhile*)　　　Eva, my pet
Administer the pill the way you should,
D'you hear, and I'll be round, this evening
And eat a dish of carp with you. The swine
Must get it down, right down, if it's too big,
The pill, he'll choke and croak on it.

WALTER: (*notices the wig*) What's this that Frau Brigitte's bringing
us,
That wig?

LICHT:　　Your worship?

WALTER:　　　　　　That woman there, what is
That wig?

LICHT:　　Ahem.

WALTER:　　　What?

LICHT:　　　　　　Pardon me.

WALTER: Will no one answer?

LICHT:　　　　　　　　Be so kind, excellency,
And ask his worship to ask that woman there
And whose the wig is will and all the rest,
I don't doubt, be revealed.

WALTER: — I have no wish to know whose wig it is,
But how the woman got it, where she found it.

LICHT: The woman found it in Frau Marthe Rull's
Trellis, this wig, impaled,
Hanging like a nest in the vine's entanglement
Up close under the window where the girl sleeps.

FRAU MARTHE: What, my house? In the trellis?

WALTER: (*aside*)
If you have anything to say to me, Judge Adam,
I beg you, for the good name of our courts,
Be kind enough to say it.

ADAM:　　　　　　I, to you?

WALTER: Nothing? You haven't …?

ADAM:　　　　　　Upon my honour …
(*He seizes the wig*)

WALTER: The wig here, this wig, is not yours then?

ADAM: The wig here, gentlemen, this wig *is* mine!
It is, God's bolts and thunder, the selfsame wig
I gave that lad a week ago
To take to Utrecht, to Mehl's, the wigmaker's.

WALTER: You gave it who? What?
LICHT: Ruprecht?
RUPRECHT: Me?
ADAM: Scoundrel,
  Did I not last week when you went to Utrecht
  Entrust this wig to you, so that the barber
  Would spruce it up, and tell you give it him?
RUPRECHT: Did you ...? Well, yes. You gave me ...
ADAM: Why then,
  Jailbird, did you not leave the wig? Why did you,
  As you were told, not leave it there
  In the workshop at the wigmaker's?
RUPRECHT: Why I ...? God's blasts! God's smoke and flame!
  I did. I left it in the workshop. Mehl took it,
  The wigmaker.
ADAM: You left it there? And now
  It's hanging in the vine trellis at Marthe's.
  You wait, you trash. That won't save you. Sounds like
  Disguises here. Sounds like, I shouldn't wonder,
  Insurrection. — Will you permit me
  At once to interrogate the woman?
WALTER: Your wig, you say ...
ADAM: Excellency,
  When that young man there last Tuesday
  Went off to Utrecht with his father's oxen
  He called at court and said: Judge Adam,
  Anything I can do for you in town?
  My boy, I answered, if you'll be so kind
  You'll have this wig here freshened up for me —
  But what I never said was go and hide it
  Away at home and wear it in disguise
  And leave it hanging in the trelliswork at Marthe's.
FRAU BRIGITTE: Gentlemen, Ruprecht, begging your pardon, sirs,
  I don't think that could have been it. For last night
  Going to a cousin's out of town
  Whose time is nearly come I heard this maid
  Not loud but scolding in the garden at the back.
  She had no voice almost for rage and fear:
  Shame on you, you, you leave me be, you villain,
  What are you doing to me? I'll call my mother.
  As if the Spaniards had come. So then

Eve, through the hedge, Eva, I shout,
What's wrong? What is it? — Then there's silence.
Answer me, will you? Then: What is it, Aunty? —
What are you doing? I ask. — What do you think? —
Is that Ruprecht? Yes, yes, it's Ruprecht.
Nothing's wrong. She means: Mind your own business.
I think: they pet like others quarrel.

FRAU MARTHE: And then?

RUPRECHT: And then?

WALTER: Quiet! Let the woman finish.

FRAU BRIGITTE: On my way back from being out of town
Around midnight, and just when I'm
Under the limes by Marthe's garden
Comes some chap rushing past me bald-headed
And with a clubfoot and behind him
A stink like burning pitch and hair and sulphur.
I say a Hail Mary and swivel round
In dread and see, upon my soul,
His bald dome, gentlemen, as it vanishes
Like rotten wood, shining down the walk of limes.

RUPRECHT: You what! God's bolts!

FRAU MARTHE: Have you gone mad, Frau Briggy?

RUPRECHT: The devil, you think ...? You think ...

LICHT: Shush! Shush!

FRAU BRIGITTE: Upon my soul,
I do know what I saw and what I smelled.

WALTER: (impatiently) Whether you saw the devil, woman,
Is no concern of mine. He's not accused.
Say what you can say about someone else
But leave that sinner out of it.

LICHT: Your worship, be so kind and let her finish.

WALTER: Such dolts these people are.

FRAU BRIGITTE: As you command.
This gentleman, the Clerk, will be my witness though.

WALTER: How so? A witness? You?

LICHT: One might say so, indeed.

WALTER: Truly then, I don't know ...

LICHT: With all respect
I beg you let the woman have her say.
I will not claim it was the devil. However,
Clubfoot, bald head and fumes behind,

All that, unless I'm very much mistaken,
Is absolutely right. — Continue.
FRAU BRIGITTE: Hearing today then with astonishment
  What happened at Frau Marthe Rull's and wishing
  To find him out, the jug-smasher who met me
  There by the trellis in the night
  And when I search the place where he leaped down
  I find a trail, your honours, in the snow —
  What sort of trail, you ask me, in the snow?
  Clear on the right and always neatly cut
  A proper human foot, but on the left,
  Misshapen, grossly stamped.
  A monstrous lumpy hoof.
WALTER: (crossly)   Drivel,
  Insanity, offensive to the ears ...!
VEIT: Not possible, woman!
FRAU BRIGITTE: Honest to God!
  First by the trellis where he did his jump
  The snow churned up in a wide circle
  As if a sow had rolled around in it
  And human foot and hoof going from there
  And human foot and hoof and human foot and hoof
  Across the garden into the wide world.
ADAM: Damn me. — Suppose he had the nerve, the rogue,
  To dress up like the devil ...?
RUPRECHT: Who? Me?
LICHT: Hush! Hush!
FRAU MARTHE: After a badger if he finds the scent the hunter
  Couldn't be gladder than I was myself.
  Clerk, I said, seeing him, this gentleman
  Sent after me by you coming towards me,
  Clerk, I said, save yourselves a session
  You'll not have justice on the jug-smasher.
  Where can you send him worse than where he is?
  In hell. See here this trail's the way he went.
WALTER: You were persuaded, were you?
LICHT: That concerning
  The trail, your worship, all that is correct.
WALTER: A hoof?
LICHT: Foot of a human being, I beg your pardon,
  But *praeter propter** like a horse's hoof.

ADAM: Gentlemen, upon my soul, this thing is serious.
  We've had some very caustic writings
  Unwilling to concede that God exists.
  However, the devil, so far as I'm aware
  No atheist has yet quite proved away.
  The case before us seems to merit
  Particular airing. I therefore propose
  That we, before we reach a verdict,
  Should make enquiry of the Synod at The Hague
  Whether this court has the authority
  To assume it was Beelzebub who broke the jug.
WALTER: The sort of thing you would propose. And what
  Is your view, Clerk?
LICHT: Your excellency
  Will judge without the Synod's help. Allow
  Frau Brigit there to finish her account
  And with the falling into place of things
  I trust the matter will become transparent.
FRAU BRIGITTE: So then the Clerk and I, I said to him
  Suppose we follow the trail a while and see
  Where the devil got away to maybe,
  And good, he said, a good idea, Frau Brigit,
  We may not go much out of our way
  Going to the village judge's house, Judge Adam's.
WALTER: Well then? And then you found ...?
FRAU BRIGITTE: And then we find
  Beyond the garden, in the avenue of limes,
  The place where, giving off his sulphur fumes,
  The devil hit up against me, and an arc
  Such as a dog, say, makes around a cat
  There spitting in his face.
WALTER: And then what?
FRAU BRIGITTE: Soon after then he left a souvenir
  Against a tree. That gave me a bad turn.
WALTER: A souvenir? What sort of ...?
FRAU BRIGITTE: What? Well yes a ...
ADAM: (aside) My blasted bowels.
LICHT: Hurry on by,
  I beg you here, Frau Brigit, hurry by.
WALTER: I wish to know where you were led to by the trail.
FRAU BRIGITTE: Where to? God's honour, the quickest way to you,

Just as this gentleman, the Clerk here, said.
WALTER: To us? To here?
FRAU BRIGITTE: Yes, from the avenue of limes
　Over the mayor's field, by the carp pond,
　That path, diagonally across the graveyard,
　To here, I tell you, here to Judge Adam's.
WALTER: Here, to Judge Adam's?
ADAM: Here, to me?
FRAU BRIGITTE: To you, just so.
RUPRECHT: You'll not be telling us
　The devil lives in the courthouse?
FRAU BRIGITTE: My word,
　Whether he lives here I don't know, but here,
　Or I'm a liar, he paid a call. The trail
　Comes in the back way to the doorstep.
ADAM: Did he pass through here maybe ...?
FRAU BRIGITTE: Yes,
　Or passed through here. Could be. That too.
　The trail out at the front ...
WALTER: Front? Was there one?
LICHT: Out at the front, begging your worship's pardon, none.
FRAU BRIGITTE: Just so, out at the front the way was trampled.
ADAM: Trampled. Passed through here. Call me a crook.
　The rogue, you mark my words, has put a jinx on
　The laws in this place. Call me a liar if
　There's not a bad smell in the registry.
　If my accounts, and I don't doubt they will be,
　Are in a muddle when you come to look at them,
　You'll know, my word of honour, who to blame.
WALTER: We shall. (*Aside*) Hm. Can't remember. Was it the left
one?
　Was it the right? One or the other foot. —
　Judge Adam, your snuff box. — Be so kind.
ADAM: Snuff box?
WALTER: Your snuff box, pass it me.
ADAM: (*to* LICHT) Will you?
WALTER: Come, come. There's not a yard from you to me ...
ADAM: Already done. Give it his excellency.
WALTER: I should have liked a little word with you.
ADAM: After, shan't we?
WALTER: No matter, then or now.

(*Once* LICHT *has sat down again*)
Tell me, gentlemen, does no one locally
Have feet that are misshapen?
LICHT: Ahem. There is
Indeed a person here in Huisum.
WALTER: There is? And who?
LICHT: Your worship will do best to ask
The judge.
WALTER: Judge Adam?
ADAM: I know of no such thing.
Ten years I've occupied this seat in Huisum
And never heard of anything growing crooked.
WALTER: (*to* LICHT) Who was it you meant here then?
FRAU MARTHE: Leave your feet out!
Looking embarrassed and hiding them like that
Under the table so you'd think he left
The trail.
WALTER: Who did? Judge Adam?
ADAM: Me? The trail?
Am I the devil? Is that a horse's hoof?
                        (*He shows his left foot*)
WALTER: No word of a lie. The foot's a good foot.
(*Aside*) At once now bring this session to a close.
ADAM: A foot like that, why if the devil had one
That good he'd go out dancing.
FRAU MARTHE: Indeed
He would. Who says our village judge ...?
ADAM: Twaddle! What me?
WALTER: At once, I tell you, finish.
FRAU BRIGITTE: Only the one thing doesn't fit, your honours,
And that's, it seems to me, this splendid head-dress.
ADAM: What splendid ...?
FRAU BRIGITTE: Here, this wig. Whoever saw
The devil arrayed in anything like this?
A structure more piled up and lumped with tallow
Than any canon's in the pulpit.
ADAM: Out here we know very imperfectly,
Frau Brigit, what the fashion is in hell.
They say he wears his own hair usually.
On earth however, I feel very sure,
He slips into a wig, the better

To mingle with the quality.
WALTER: Villain,
  Fit to be hounded from the court disgraced
  Before the people! What protects you
  Is solely the honour due the Law.
  Finish your session.
ADAM: I hope I may ...
WALTER: Be done with hoping. Extricate yourself.
ADAM: Do you suppose that I, the judge, last night
  Was parted from my wig in the trelliswork?
WALTER: No, God forbid. Your wig went up in flames
  Like Sodom and Gomorrah.
LICHT: Or rather yesterday —
  Forgive me, excellency — the cat
  Had kittens in it.
ADAM: Gentlemen
  I may seem damned here by appearances
  But take your time. At stake is whether
  I swap my honourable name for ignominy.
  So long as the girl is silent I can't see
  What right you have to accuse me. I sit here
  On the judge's bench in Huisum
  And lay the wig down on the table. Whosoever
  Asserts the wig is mine I summons him
  Before the high court in Utrecht.
LICHT: Hm. The wig does fit you though. God's honour it does,
  As though your head were where it grew.
                    (*He puts it on him*)
ADAM: A slander!
LICHT: Does it not?
ADAM: Too wide if it were a cape
  Around my shoulders let alone my head.
            (*He looks at himself in the mirror*)
RUPRECHT: The face, the nerve of him!
WALTER: You hold your tongue.
FRAU MARTHE: Oh, what a damned and blasted judge!
WALTER: Again,
  Will you at once or shall I end the matter?
ADAM: Just as you wish.
RUPRECHT: (*to Eve*) Eve, tell us: Is it him?
WALTER: You keep your place. How dare you?

VEIT: Hold your noise,
  D'you hear?

ADAM: Savage, you wait, I'll have you.

RUPRECHT: Damned clubfoot, you!

WALTER: Usher! I say. Here, usher!

VEIT: Your trap, I said.

RUPRECHT: You wait, this time I'll have you.
  You won't blind me with sand like last time.

WALTER: Have you not sense enough, Judge ...?

ADAM: With your excellency's
  Permission I'll pass sentence now.

WALTER: Good. Do so.
  Pass your sentence.

ADAM: The case is settled then
  And Ruprecht, that rogue there, he did it.

WALTER: Very good so far. Continue.

ADAM: I put him in
  The stocks, and since he has behaved
  In an unseemly fashion towards his judge
  He goes behind bars as well. For how long
  I will determine at some future date.

EVE: Ruprecht ...?

RUPRECHT: Behind bars, me?

EVE: Him, in the stocks?

WALTER: Don't fret yourselves. — Will that be all?

ADAM: The jug
  He pays for or he doesn't, I don't care.

WALTER: Good. That concludes the case. And Ruprecht
  Appeals at the appeal court in Utrecht.

EVE: Him, he appeals? In Utrecht? Not till then ...?

RUPRECHT: I what?

WALTER: God hang me, yes. And till that time ...

EVE: And till that time ...?

RUPRECHT: I go to jail?

EVE: He sits
  In the stocks? Are you a judge as well?
  Him sitting there, that brazen face, it was
  Himself ...

WALTER: You hear me, damn it. Hush. Till then
  Let no one harm a hair of his head.

EVE: Oh Ruprecht

At him now. Judge Adam broke the jug.
RUPRECHT: You wait you.
FRAU MARTHE: Him?
FRAU BRIGITTE: Him there?
EVE: Yes, him. Oh at him,
Ruprecht. He was at Eve's last night.
Seize him and thump him how you like now.
WALTER: (rises) Stop this! Any disorderly ...
EVE: What does it matter?
Do something for the stocks. Here Ruprecht
Tumble him down now off the judge's bench.
ADAM: Excuse me, gentlemen.
             (He runs away)
EVE: Be sharp!
RUPRECHT: Grab hold!
EVE: Quick!
ADAM: What?
RUPRECHT: Damned cripple-devil!
EVE: Got him?
RUPRECHT: Strike and blast me!
Only his robe.
WALTER: Be off! Summon the usher
RUPRECHT: (beats the robe)
Damned swine, take that. And swine. Take that
And that and that. I wish it was his hump.
WALTER: Disgraceful lout! — Let me have order here.
— You quieten down at once or what was said
Concerning stocks will happen, and forthwith.
VEIT: Oaf! Madman! Quieten down.

Scene 12

They come to the front of the stage
RUPRECHT: Oh Eva
How shamefully I have insulted you
This day, oh God strike me, and yesterday
Sweet girl of mine, bride of my heart,
All your life long will you ever forgive me?
EVE: (throws herself at the Assessor's feet)
Oh sir, if you don't help us we are lost!
WALTER: Lost? Why so?

RUPRECHT: Dear God, what is it?

EVE: Save Ruprecht from the levy. For the men
  Being levied now — Judge Adam
  Disclosed this to me as a secret —
  Are for the East Indies, and from there
  You must know only one in three comes back.

WALTER: For where? The East Indies? Madness, child.

EVE: For Bantam, excellency. Admit it.
  Here is the letter, the instructions,
  Secret and undercover, that the government,
  Concerning our militia, issued lately.
  You see, I am informed of everything.

WALTER: (*takes the letter and reads it*)
  Was ever there a wickeder deception?
  The letter's forged.

EVE: Forged?

WALTER: Forged, true as I live.
  You tell us, Clerk, is this the instruction
  Issued you lately from Utrecht?

LICHT: The instruction! What! The villain. This is tripe
  Concocted by himself. — The troops
  Now being levied are intended
  For duties here at home. Nobody
  Has ever dreamed of sending them out east.

EVE: Never at all, sirs?

WALTER: On my honour, no.
  And for a proof of what I say: Your Ruprecht,
  Should it be as you said, I'll buy him out.

EVE: Oh heavens, how wickedly he lied to me.
  For with this terrible worry he
  Tortured my heart and came, at night-time,
  To force a thing written for Ruprecht on me
  Because to falsely certify him sick
  Would get him off all military service.
  So he explained and promised and came creeping
  To draw it up for me into my room,
  Gentlemen, asking such disgraceful things of me
  No girl would have the face to utter them.

FRAU MARTHE: Shameful, evil, deceiving her like that!

RUPRECHT: Forget him and his hoof, my darling girl.
  I'd be more jealous had it been a horse in there

Smashing the jug than I am now of him.
                    (They kiss)
VEIT: And so say I. Kiss and make up. Love one another
  And have a Whitsun wedding if you like.
LICHT: *(at the window)*
  See there, look there, I beg you, how Judge Adam
  Uphill and down, as though the hangman
  Were after him, stamps through the winter ploughlands.
WALTER: What's that? Is that Judge Adam?
LICHT: Indeed it is.
SEVERAL TOGETHER: He's at the road. Oh look, look there,
  See how the long wig whips his back.
WALTER: Hurry, Clerk, go at once and fetch him in
  Before he makes a bad thing worse.
  True, I relieve him of his office here
  And lend you, until further notice,
  The authority to hold it in these parts
  But if, as I hope, the accounts are right
  I will not force the man to quit.
  Hurry, be kind enough to fetch him back.

                                    [*Exit* LICHT]

Scene 13

FRAU MARTHE: Tell me, your excellency, where do I find
  The administration in Utrecht.
WALTER: What for, Frau Marthe?
FRAU MARTHE: *(with some feeling)* What for? I don't know ...
  Shall this jug here go without justice done it?
WALTER: Forgive me. No. You want the Big Market.
  Tuesdays the sessions are, and Fridays.
FRAU MARTHE: Good. I'll present myself this time next week.

AMPHITRYON
(A comedy after Molière) *

Dramatis Personae

JUPITER	in the form of Amphitryon
MERCURY	in the form of Sosias
AMPHITRYON	Theban general
SOSIAS	his servant
ALCMENE	Amphitryon's wife
CHARIS	Sosias's wife
OFFICERS/GENERALS	in the Theban army

Scene: Thebes, outside AMPHITRYON's *palace*

ACT I, Scene I

It is night
Enter SOSIAS *carrying a lantern*
SOSIAS: Who's there? Who's that there creeping? Hoy! — I'd be
Happier if daybreak broke. The night is ... What?
Friend, gentlemen. Your road is mine —
The man you've met is the most honest man,
You take my word for it, under the sun,
Or moon, more like, under the moon, I meant ...
Either it's villains and they're cowardly wretches
Not man enough to set upon me
Or it was the wind, making the leaves rustle.
The least sound echoes round the mountains here.
Steady now. Slowly. — But if I don't soon
Hit up against the walls of Thebes
I'll carry on to blackest hell instead.

God string me up, whether I'm brave or not
And have some stomach, there were other ways
My lord and master might have tried to find that out.
Fame crowns his head, the whole world says, and honour.
Sending me out in the middle of the night however
Is a poor sort of joke. Some thoughtfulness
And love thy neighbour as thyself would be as welcome
As that great fist of other virtues
He smashes enemies to pieces with.
Sosias, he said, be up and doing, servant.
You are to announce my victory in Thebes
And warn the gentle ruler of my heart
That my arrival home is imminent.
Wouldn't tomorrow have been time enough?
I'll be a horse and saddle up, if not.
See though. Looks like our house appearing.
You have arrived, Sosias. Victory!
Forgiveness now to all your enemies.
And now, friend, think of your commission:
You will be brought, with ceremony, to the lady
Alcmene, and the account, in every detail
And properly composed, you owe her of the battle
Won for the country by Amphitryon.
— How shall I, how the devil, not having been
Present myself? Oh damn. I wish I'd peeped
Out of the tent occasionally
When the two sides were at it hand to hand.
So what! I'll speak of blows and bolts
And shan't do any worse than others have
Who also never heard the arrows whizz. —
Still, best rehearse the part. Well thought of,
Sosias, excellent. See how you do.
Here's where I'll be received and this lantern's
Alcmene, on her throne, awaiting me.
                    (He places the lantern on the ground)
Worshipful lady, Amphitryon,
My lord and master and your noble husband,
Sends you, by me, the happy tidings of
His victory over the Athenians. —
A good beginning! — 'Ah, truly, dearest
Sosias, my joy at seeing you again

Is uncontainable.' — Your kindness,
Excellent lady, humbles me though certainly
Anyone else it would swell up with pride.
— And that's not bad either! — 'And the dear
Beloved of my soul, Amphitryon,
How is he?' — Great lady, I'll be brief: He is
As a man of courage on the field of honour is.
— Hear that? The language! — 'When is he coming then?'
Surely no later than his duty allows
Though doubtless not so soon as he would wish.
— Well, strike me dead! — 'And was there nothing more, Sosias,
He said to you for me?' — He says little,
Does much, and the earth quakes at his name.
— Pox carry me off! Where's it all coming from? —
'They yield then, so you say, the Athenians?'*
— They yield, and Labdacus is dead, their leader,
Pharissa's taken and where there are mountains
They echo with our shouts of victory. —
'Oh dearest Sosias, see here, all this
You must recount to me in every detail.'
— Lady, I'm at your service, for indeed
I can, I flatter myself, furnish you with
The whole news of this victory.
Picture, if you will be so kind,
On this side here —
                    (He indicates the places on his hand)
                              Pharissa
– Which is a city as you doubtless know
As large in compass, *praeter propter*,
Without exaggerating, if not larger
Than Thebes. Here is the river. Our men
In battle order on an eminence here,
And in the valley there, in droves, the foe.
First sending up to heaven such a vow
As made the encircling clouds tremble,
They teem, having their orders dealt them out,
Like rivers on us with a roar.
But we, no less brave, showed them
Their way back — and how we did, you'll see.
Here first of all they met our front men
Who gave. Then hit against the archers here

Who backed away. Then going on boldly
They pressed the slingsmen, who let them come, and now
Full of presumption, nearing our main corps
These fall — Stop! With the main corps something's wrong.
I hear a noise there, as it seems to me.

ACT I, Scene 2

MERCURY, *in the form of* SOSIAS, *comes out of* AMPHITRYON'S
house

MERCURY: (*aside*) If I don't speedily remove
That lout and nuisance from this door
By Styx* the happiness is put at risk
For whose enjoyment in Alcmene's arms
This day, in the appearance of Amphitryon,
Zeus, the Olympian, came down to earth.

SOSIAS: (*not noticing* MERCURY)
Though it was nothing and my fears have vanished
Still, to evade adventures,
I'll finish off my coming home
And discharge my commission.

MERCURY: (*aside*)   Either
You'll get the better of Mercury, my friend,
Or I'll have ways of stopping you.

SOSIAS: Oh but this night's interminably long.
If I've not been five hours on my way,
Five hours by the sundial here in Thebes,
I'll pot them one by one out of the sky.
Either my lord, being drunk on victory,
Mistook the evening for the morning, or
Dissolute Phoebus* is still asleep
After a few more than he should have had last night.

MERCURY: With what irreverence this louse
Speaks of the gods. Patience a while. Soon
My arm will teach him some respect.

SOSIAS: (*noticing* MERCURY)
Oh by the gods of darkness now I'm done for!
Some thug and thief is creeping round the house
Whom sooner or later I shall see strung up.
— Have to be bold now, show a cocky face.
(*He whistles a tune*)

MERCURY: (*aloud*) What kind of clown is it who has the nerve,
As though he lived here, to afflict my ears
With a row of whistling? Should he perhaps
Be beaten with my stick and dance to it?
SOSIAS: — Not one for music then.
MERCURY: A week since I
Found anyone to thrash the living daylights out of.
I'm stiff in the arm from inactivity.
A hump like yours, a good broad hump's
Exactly what I need to get back into practice.
SOSIAS: Where in the devil's name did he come from?
I feel the fear of death seize hold of me
And can't get breath. If hell itself
Had flung him up his apparition
Could not be deadlier to my spirit.
— Nevertheless, the dolt might be like me
And only acting like a fire-eater
To put the wind up me. Hold it, joker.
If you can, so can I. Besides
I'm one, so's he. I've got two fists,
He'll not have more. Also, if things go badly
My safe retreat is there — Onwards!
MERCURY: (*barring his way*) Halt! Who goes there?
SOSIAS: Me.
MERCURY: What sort of me?
SOSIAS: Mine, pardon me. And mine, I'd say, like anyone's,
Can come and go here. Courage, Sosias.
MERCURY: Hold it. You don't get off that lightly.
What standing do you have?
SOSIAS: Standing?
I stand on two feet, as you see.
MERCURY: Master or servant's what I want to know.
SOSIAS: Look at me this way, look at me that,
I'm boss or servingman accordingly.
MERCURY: Enough. I dislike you.
SOSIAS: I'm sorry for that.
MERCURY: In brief, impostor, I require to know,
Skulker, scoundrel, hanger around street corners,
Who you might be, where from and to you're going
And what you want here tarrying and dallying.
SOSIAS: There's nothing I can answer you

But this: I am a man, coming from there
And going there, and have a thing to do
Already growing to be tiresome to me.
MERCURY: A wit, I see, and going all out
    To fob me off with very little, but I
    Have a desire to lengthen our acquaintance
    And to initiate involvement
    Here with this hand of mine I'll clout your head.
SOSIAS: Mine?
MERCURY: Indeed. And here's your proof of it.
    Tell me your thinking now.
SOSIAS: God blight me!
    You thump as if you meant it, friend.
MERCURY: One of my middling clouts. At other times
    I land them better.
SOSIAS: If I were minded
    The way you are we'd have a pretty battle.
MERCURY: Would suit me nicely. Nothing like a battle.
SOSIAS: But, having some business, I must take my leave.
                    (He makes to leave)
MERCURY: *(barring his way)* Where to?
SOSIAS: You mind your own.
MERCURY: I wish to know,
    I tell you, where you are going to.
SOSIAS: To get
    That gate there opened for me. Let me pass.
MERCURY: Go any nearer to that palace gate,
    Have the audacity, and I promise you
    A storm of blows, a thunderstorm, will pelt you.
SOSIAS: I beg your pardon? May I not go home?
MERCURY: Go home? Say that again.
SOSIAS: All right. Go home.
MERCURY: Is what you're saying that you are of this house?
SOSIAS: Why not? Is this house not Amphitryon's?
MERCURY: This house Amphitryon's? Indeed it is,
    Jailbird, it is indeed Amphitryon's house,
    The palace of the Thebans' first commander.
    What follows from that? —
SOSIAS: What follows?
    That I go in. I am his servant.
MERCURY: His ser — ?

SOSIAS: His servant.
MERCURY   You?
SOSIAS: Yes, me.
MERCURY: Amphitryon's servant?
SOSIAS: Amphitryon's, the Theban general's, servant.
MERCURY: Your name's ...?
SOSIAS: Sosias.
MERCURY: So — ?
SOSIAS: *Sosias.*
MERCURY: Listen, I'll beat you to a jelly.
SOSIAS: Are
  You mad?
MERCURY: What right have you, the cheek of it,
  To take Sosias' name?
SOSIAS: Not take,
  I didn't take it, I was given it.
  Go and ask my father what for if you like.
MERCURY: Was ever there such impudence? You dare,
  You have the gall to tell me to my face
  That you're Sosias?
SOSIAS: Indeed I do.
  And for the right and proper reason that
  The great gods wish it so. Because
  I do not have it in my power to fight them
  And wish to be another than I am
  I must be me, Amphitryon's servant,
  Though I might ten times rather be Amphitryon
  Or else his cousin or his brother-in-law.
MERCURY: Wait now. Let's see if you can be transformed.
SOSIAS: Citizens! Thebans! Thieves! Assassins!
MERCURY: Stop yelling, wretch.
SOSIAS: I beg your pardon?
  You beat me and I'm not allowed to yell.
MERCURY: And don't you know it's night-time, sleeping-time,
  And in the palace here Alcmene,
  Wife of Amphitryon, is asleep?
SOSIAS: Oh rot you!
  I come off worse because, as you well see,
  I don't have, unlike you, a stick to hand.
  But doling blows out and not taking any,
  There's nothing brave in that. I tell you straight:

Showing your bravery's a poor thing when
Others are stopped by fate from showing theirs.
MERCURY: To the matter then. Who are you?
SOSIAS: (*aside*)   If I get clear
Of him I'll spill a bottle of wine, the half
Of it, on the earth, for an offering.
MERCURY: Are you Sosias still?
SOSIAS: Oh let me go.
Your stick can make me so I cease to be
But not that I'm not me, because I am.
The one thing changed is this: I feel I am
Sosias now that somebody has thrashed.
MERCURY: Enough, worm. Say your prayers.
                              (*He threatens him*)
SOSIAS: Leave off!
Stop coming on at me.
MERCURY: I will
When you stop ...
SOSIAS: Very good. I've stopped.
Not another word. What you say stands,
Whatever you propose my answer's yes.
MERCURY: Then are you still Sosias, swindler?
SOSIAS: Och
I'm what you like. What shall it be? Just tell me.
Your stick makes you the master of my life.
MERCURY: You said you used to call yourself Sosias?
SOSIAS: True. I was under the illusion
Until this minute that that might be right,
But by your reasons, by their weight,
I am persuaded that I was mistaken.
MERCURY: I'm the one calls himself Sosias.
SOSIAS: You?
Sosias?
MERCURY: Yes, Sosias. And whoever quibbles
Can look out for this stick.
SOSIAS: (*aside*)   Eternal gods
Above! am I to abdicate
From me myself and have my name
Stolen away from me by some impostor?
MERCURY: I hear you muttering.

SOSIAS: But nothing,
   I promise you, that might tread on your toes.
   But by the gods, all of the gods, of Greece,
   I do beseech you, rulers of you and me,
   By them, allow me for one little minute
   To address you candidly.
MERCURY: Speak then.
SOSIAS: Your stick, though, will not have a speaking part?
   Will not join in the conversation? Promise
   That we agree a truce.
MERCURY: So be it.
   I grant you that much.
SOSIAS: Tell me then
   How in the world did it occur to you
   To have the cheek to thieve my name off me?
   My coat, my supper, I could understand,
   But why my name? Can you dress up in it?
   Eat it? Drink it? Turn it into cash?
   What use then is this larceny to you?
MERCURY: What's this? You dare, do you ...?
SOSIAS: Leave off, leave off,
   We made a truce, remember.
MERCURY: Shameless
   And fit-for-nothing wretch.
SOSIAS: Indeed. By all means.
   I don't mind insults. Insults are a kind
   Of conversation.
MERCURY: You call yourself Sosias?
SOSIAS: Well, I admit, there was a story,
   Though unconfirmed, that I ...
MERCURY: Enough. I break
   The truce and take my promise back again.
SOSIAS: Oh go to hell! I can't annihilate nor
   Metamorphose myself, and quit my skin
   And hang my skin around your shoulders, can I?
   Was ever such a thing since time began?
   Is this a dream? Did I, to get me going,
   This morning take more than I usually do?
   Am I not fully mindful of my self?
   Was I not sent here by Amphitryon

To announce his coming to the lady?
Am I not to recount the victory
He won to her and how Pharissa fell?
Have I not just arrived here in this place?
Is this a lantern in my hand? Did I not find you
Hanging around this house's door and when
I made to approach the aforementioned door
Did you not take your stick and bruise
In the most inhuman way my back for me
Affirming to my very face it was not me
But you who is the servant of Amphitryon?
All that, alas, I feel is all too true
And would to God I were a man possessed.

MERCURY: Jailbird, beware. My anger, any minute,
Will pelt like hail on you again. What you
Have said, all of it, every bit
Is true of me, except the being thrashed.

SOSIAS: Of you? — This lantern here, by all the gods,
Be witness ...

MERCURY: Liar, I say, impostor.
I was the one Amphitryon sent here.
Me it was yesterday the Thebans' general
When he, still dusty from the murderous battle,
Leaving the temple, having sacrificed to Mars,
Gave proper orders to announce his victory
In Thebes and that by him, by his own hand,
The enemy's leader Labdacus was killed.
For I am, let me tell you, Sosias,
His servant, son of Davus, honest shepherd
In these parts, brother of Harpagon
Who died abroad, husband of Charis
Whose moods drive me insane, Sosias
Who did time in the tower and whose bum
Not long ago got fifty of the best
For being honester than he should have been.

SOSIAS: (aside) He's right. And without being Sosias
Yourself these things he seems to know about
It is impossible to know about.
Dear me, you have to credit him a bit.
What's more, now that I look at him close up

His shape's like mine and build and way of him
Also his scoundrelly manner's just like mine.
— I need to ask him a few questions which
Should settle this.
(*Aloud*)   Tell me, the booty
Found in the enemy camp, how did Amphitryon
Reward himself there and what fell to him?
MERCURY: He had the diadem of Labdacus
Which was discovered in that leader's tent.
SOSIAS: And what was done then with this diadem?
MERCURY: The initial of Amphitryon was graven
Brilliantly in the golden brow of it.
SOSIAS: Doubtless he wears it now himself ...?
MERCURY: Alcmene
Shall have it. To commemorate
The victory adorn her breast with it.
SOSIAS: And from the camp to her the present came
How?
MERCURY: In a golden casket on to which
Amphitryon impressed his coat of arms.
SOSIAS: (*aside*) Nothing he doesn't know. — Oh devils in hell
Now I begin to doubt myself in earnest.
First through his brazen cheek and through his stick
He was Sosias. Now all he needed, grounds
To be it, he has those as well.
True, when I feel myself I'd take an oath
This flesh is Sosias. — What way
Is there for me out of this labyrinth? —
What I did being wholly on my own,
What no one saw, no one can know
Who isn't really me as I am me.
— Good, with this question I shall clear things up.
What then? I'll catch him out. — Well, we shall see.
(*Aloud*) When the two armies were at it hand to hand
What were you doing, tell me, in the tents
Where, craftily, you found a place to skulk?
MERCURY: From off a ham ...
SOSIAS: (*aside*)   Have this man and the devil ...?
MERCURY: That I discovered in the corner of the tent
I cut myself a slice, juicy and meaty,

And smartly broached a field canteen
Thus for the battle being fought outside
To work a little courage up in me.

SOSIAS: *(aside)* That's that then. Now, for all I care,
The earth can swallow me here where I stand.
For no one drinks out of a field canteen
Unless, like me, by accident, in his pocket,
He happens to have found the key that fits it.
(Aloud) Old friend, I do see now that you
Are all the portion of Sosias
That can have any function here on earth.
More seems to me superfluous.
Far be it from me to importune you
And gladly I make way for you. Only
Do me the kindness, please, and tell me,
Since I am not Sosias, who I am.
For something, you'll concede, I have to be.

MERCURY: When I am not Sosias any more
You be him. That suits me. I give you leave.
But while I am, you risk your neck if you
Are impudent enough to think you are.

SOSIAS: Very well. My head is dizzy with it.
I see the way things are, indeed I do,
Without yet fully comprehending them.
However, it's time this business had an end
And, to conclude, the wisest course for me
Is go my ways. — Goodbye.

(He goes towards the house)

MERCURY: *(pushing him back)* What! Gallows fodder, must I thrash
you

Black and blue?

(He strikes him)

SOSIAS: Just gods above,
Where are you when I need you? I'll be sore
Across the back for weeks and whether or not
Amphitryon lifts *his* stick. So be it then.
I leave this devil in peace and back to camp
Black though it looks still in this hellish night. —
A famous embassy that was! How will
The master welcome you, I wonder, Sosias?

[Exit]

ACT I, Scene 3

MERCURY: At long last! Had you quitted sooner
  You would have spared yourself some wicked knocks.
  And what's a wretch like that care for the honour
  Of having a good hiding from a god?
  I gave it good and proper too.
  Well, well. He's sinned enough, deserves,
  If not precisely here and now, a thrashing.
  Let's say he had it on account. —
  I hope the hullabaloo the villain raised,
  As though I'd spitted him to roast alive,
  Didn't wake the lovers. — See here though:
  Zeus risen already. See where he comes, our father
  In heaven, and tenderly as though he were
  Her dear husband Amphitryon, Alcmene with him.

ACT I, Scene 4

Enter JUPITER *in the form of* AMPHITRYON, *and with him*
      ALCMENE *and* CHARIS. *Torches*

JUPITER: Keep back, my dearest Alcmene,
  The torches there. They light up, it is true,
  The greatest loveliness in flower on earth
  And none of the Olympians ever saw a greater.
  And yet — what shall I say? They betray him
  Whom this same loveliness lured here, beloved,
  And better it will be if it remains a secret
  That your Amphitryon was here in Thebes.
  They are stolen from war, these moments
  Which I have come and offered up to love.
  This theft, the world might misinterpret it,
  And I would rather have no other witnesses
  Of it than her on whom I have bestowed it.
ALCMENE: Amphitryon! And you are leaving me?
  How burdensome, beloved, such fame is!
  The diadem you won, how gladly
  I would exchange it for a bunch of violets
  Picked one by one around a simple dwelling.
  What have we any need of but ourselves?
  Why must so much that is remote to us,
  A crown, the soldier's staff, be forced on you?

True, when the people shout and call you
Name upon great name with lavish joy
The thought is sweet that you belong to me,
But this brief pleasure, can it compensate
For what I feel when in the savage wars
The arrow aims at this dear heart?
How barren, without you, this house is, how dull,
When you are gone, the cheerful round
Of the hours that ought to lift the days up for me.
Oh what our native country robs me of
Only today, my dear Amphitryon,
Do I feel fully, having you two brief hours.

JUPITER: Beloved, how you enchant me. But
One worry you arouse in me which I,
Frivolous though it may sound, must speak of.
You know there is a law in marriage and
A duty too and should a man not win love
Going before a judge he may demand it.
This law, do you see, it mars my highest happiness.
To you yourself, your heart, my dearest
I want all favours owed and do not want
You fitting yourself to some formality
Perhaps believing you are bound to it.
These trivial doubts you may dispel with ease.
Speak from your secret heart and say
Whether it was the husband you are bound to
Or whether the lover whom this night you took.

ALCMENE: Lover or husband!* What language is this?
Am I not solely through this sacred tie
Entitled to receive you? How can a law,
A worldly law, torment you which,
Far from in any way constraining us,
For all aroused desires, however bold,
Joyously rather tears down all constraints?

JUPITER: What I, dearest Alcmene, feel for you
Exceeds, do you see? by the distances of suns,
What any husband owes you. Wean yourself,
Beloved, off your legal spouse
And make a difference between me and him.
It pains me, this demeaning mixing up,
And it is more than I can bear to think

That all you took was the mere nincompoop
Who coldly thinks he has a right to you.
My wish, sweet radiance, is to have appeared
To you peculiarly in my own being,
Your conqueror because to conquer you
The art was taught me by the almighty gods.
Why let the Thebans' vain commander
Meddle in here who for a noble house
Latterly wooed a wealthy prince's daughter?
What do you say? My wish is, do you see?
To leave that public clown your virtue and
For me, for me myself, reserve your love.

ALCMENE: Amphitryon, you jest. If the people here
Heard you thus heaping insults on Amphitryon
They would be bound to think you someone else,
I don't know who. Not that I have not learned
In this past joyous night how it may be
Often the lover who outdoes the husband,
But since one and the other by the gods
Were joined in you for me with all my heart
If one did fail me I forgive the other.

JUPITER: Promise me then the joyous celebration
Enjoyed in honour of our blithe reunion
You never will let lapse from memory
And this day, like a day of heaven, dearest,
You will keep separate from all the poor
Day in day out continuance of your marriage.
Promise, I say, that you will think of me
Still in that future when Amphitryon returns.

ALCMENE: Why yes. What can I say to that?

JUPITER: I thank you.
It has more rhyme and reason than you think.
Farewell now. Duty calls.

ALCMENE: And must you go.
And not end this brief night, that on
Ten thousand wings has flown, with me, beloved?

JUPITER: Did this night seem to you more brief than other nights?

ALCMENE: Oh.

JUPITER: Sweet child, for our happiness
Aurora could not do more than she did.
Farewell. I'll see the others

Do not last longer than earth needs them to.
ALCMENE: He's tipsy with it, I think. And I am too.

[*Exit* JUPITER *and* ALCMENE]

ACT I, Scene 5

CHARIS: (*aside*) Now that's what I call tenderness and being true.
   That's how it should be — sweet — when man and wife
   After long absence see each other again.
   But that yokel, the one I'm yoked to, him,
   He's no more tender than a lump of wood.
MERCURY: (*aside*) Now I must hurry and give Night the word
   Or all the cosmos will be out of order.
   Our amiable goddess did a coupler's work
   And lingered seventeen hours over Thebes today.
   She can continue now and veil
   Other adventures too.
CHARIS: (*aloud*)   See
   Not a feeling in him. Leaving!
MERCURY: Well
   And am I not to follow Amphitryon?
   I'm surely not, while he returns to camp,
   To lay me down and do nothing?
CHARIS: You might say something.
MERCURY: Pah! there's time for that. —
   The thing you asked you know already. Basta!
   I'm one for saying little on that subject.
CHARIS: A clod, that's what you are. You might say: Sweetheart,
   Think of me. How I'll miss you. Things like that.
MERCURY: In hell's name, what a notion! You expect me
   To pass the time here mouthing stuff with you?
   Eleven years wed I've no talk left in me
   And all there was I said aeons ago.
CHARIS: Heartless. And see Amphitryon, he shows,
   As the humblest do, his tenderness
   And shame on you that in devotion to
   His wife and in his married love
   A great and public man outdoes you.
MERCURY: He's still on honeymoon, woman. There's
   A time of life when anything is proper.
   What suits these young people I wouldn't want

To be in the vicinity if we tried it.
Some spectacle if fools our age
Tried feeding one another titbits.
CHARIS: The foul mouth! Hear his language!
Am I not fit to then? —
MERCURY: I didn't say that.
Your obvious damage can be overlooked.
It's all one in the dark. But here,
In public, there would be a riot
If the devil made me fool about with you.
CHARIS: How can you? Didn't I go, the minute you came,
To the pump? Did I not comb my hair?
And put this clean dress on? And all
To have you hurl insults at me.
MERCURY: A clean dress! Pah! If you could take
The dress off nature gave you
I would not mind what dirty thing you wore.
CHARIS: When you were courting me you liked it.
Cooking, washing, haymaking, that was
The only dress you wanted me in. How
Could I stop time wearing it out?
MERCURY: You couldn't, wife. But I can't mend it either.
CHARIS: Devil, you don't deserve to have had
A woman of honour with a good name for a wife.
MERCURY: I wouldn't mind you less a woman of honour
If you would only not destroy my ears
By always scolding.
CHARIS: Pardon me? Unhappy,
Are you, that I've always kept myself
Honourable and won respect?
MERCURY: Heaven forfend! You cultivate your virtue.
Only don't drive it like a brewer's dray
Forever jingling through the streets and marketplace.
CHARIS: You want the sort of wife there is in Thebes,
A sly one, full of wicked ways,
A wife who'll stew you in sweet words
To make you swallow being cuckolded.
MERCURY: As far as that goes, honest to God, I tell you
Only a fool has an uneasy mind.
Indeed, I envy any man whose friend
Advances him the dues of marriage. He lives long

And lives the lives of all his children.
CHARIS: You'd have the cheek to tempt me? Have
  The actual face to encourage me to add
  That amiable Theban who's round here
  Most evenings after me, to you?
MERCURY: Oh devil take me, yes. So long as you
  Don't make me listen to an account of it.
  Comfortable sinning I think quite as good
  As bothersome virtue. And my motto is:
  Not so much honour in Thebes, more peace and quiet.
  Goodbye now, darling Charis. I have to leave.
  Amphitryon will be in camp already.

                                                    [*Exit*]

CHARIS: Why do I lack the necessary nerve
  To punish him, contemptible as he is,
  With an open act? Ah, you gods above
  How I regret now that the world thinks me
  Incapable of irregularity.

ACT II, Scene 1

It is daylight

AMPHITRYON: Here, wretch, I tell you, damned and blasted
  Villain. The tripe you talk, must you be told,
  You worse than useless dolt, will get you hanged.
  And if my anger had a stick with it
  You'd get the treatment you deserve to get.
SOSIAS: If that's the tone you take I'll say nothing.
  If you say so I'm dreaming or I'm drunk.
AMPHITRYON: Serving me tales like that. You have a nerve.
  Stories the nurses tell their children
  At bedtime, fairy stories. —
  Am I supposed to swallow stuff like that?
SOSIAS: Not likely. You give the orders here.
  Do what you want and don't do what you don't.
AMPHITRYON: Well then. I curb my rage, I force myself
  To have the necessary patience
  And hear the whole thing through again
  From the beginning — I shan't set foot in there
  Until I've sorted this damned muddle out.
  So now: collect your thoughts,

Answer me point by point, as I ask you.

SOSIAS: But sir, fearful, forgive me, of offending
I beg you first, before we make a start,
To indicate the tone of the proceedings.
Shall it be after my own understanding
As an honest fellow, if you follow me,
Or as they do at court, that I address you?
D'you want the truth straight out or should I
Conduct myself like someone well brought up?

AMPHITRYON: Enough damned tripe. Do what I tell you to
Which is: deliver me a frank account.

SOSIAS: I will. Very well. Your wish is my command.
Over to you now. Throw the questions at me.

AMPHITRYON: When I gave you my orders ...

SOSIAS: I proceeded
Through a night-time black as hell as if
The day had sunk ten thousand fathoms deep
Damning and blasting you, you and your orders,
Along the way to Thebes and your royal palace.

AMPHITRYON: Louse, *what* are you telling me?

SOSIAS: The truth, sir.

AMPHITRYON: Continue then. And as you made your way ...

SOSIAS: I put one foot in front of the other
And left my tracks behind.

AMPHITRYON: What! Whether
Anything happened to you, tell me, will you.

SOSIAS: Nothing, sir, except, you'll pardon me,
My soul was full of fear and trembling.

AMPHITRYON: Arriving here then ...

SOSIAS: I did a little
Rehearsing of the speech I had to make
And made believe, a pretty idea, this lantern
Was her royal ladyship, your wife.

AMPHITRYON: That done ...

SOSIAS: I was interrupted. Now we come to it.

AMPHITRYON: Interrupted? How? Who interrupted you?

SOSIAS: Sosias.

AMPHITRYON: And what does that mean?

SOSIAS: What that means?
God's truth, that's asking me too much.
Sosias interrupted my rehearsal.

AMPHITRYON: Sosias? What Sosias? What sort of
   Gallows fodder, wretch, of a Sosias
   Who has that name in Thebes as well as you
   Came interrupting your rehearsal?
SOSIAS: Sosias. The one who is your servant,
   The one you sent off yesterday from camp
   To tell them in the palace you were coming.
AMPHITRYON: You? What?
SOSIAS: Yes, me. A me that has
   Knowledge of all our confidentialities
   And knows about the casket and the diamonds
   Entirely like the me talking to you.
AMPHITRYON: What fairy stories!
SOSIAS: True ones.
   God strike me dead, sir, if I'm telling you lies.
   That me had got here earlier than me
   And I was here, in that case, heaven help me,
   Before I'd got here.
AMPHITRYON: Twaddle, demented
   Hogwash. What is the cause of this?
   Dreams? An inebriation? Brain
   Slippage? A joke?
SOSIAS: I'm being
   Utterly serious, sir, and you will give me
   Credence on my word of honour if
   You'll be so kind. I swear it to you
   That I, who left the camp a singleton
   Arrived in Thebes doubled; that I,
   With popping eyes, met myself here;
   That here this me standing in front of you,
   Fatigue and hunger having worn him out,
   Found the other one, when *he* appeared,
   Devilishly fresh and fit; and that
   These rogues, the both of them, being jealous,
   Each, to carry out your orders,
   Got into strife at once; and I
   Was forced to toddle back to camp again
   For being a brainless good-for-nothing.
AMPHITRYON: Only a man as even-tempered,
   As peaceable and self-controlled as I
   Would let a servant talk the way you talk.

SOSIAS: Sir, if you get het up I'll hold my tongue.
Let's speak of other things, shall we?
AMPHITRYON: Continue then. See how I calm myself.
I'll give you patient hearing till the end.
But tell me, on your conscience, now
Whether what you are offering me as true
Looks anything like a thing that might be true.
Who could see sense or rhyme or reason in it?
SOSIAS: Perish the thought! Who's asking that of you?
The madhouse, I'd say, is where anyone belongs
Who says he can make head or tail of this.
Nobody anywhere ever heard the like,
A mad and bad occurrence, like a fairy tale,
And yet it is so, as the sunshine is.
AMPHITRYON: Given the usual five senses, how
Is this believable?
SOSIAS: The same as you, believe you me,
I had trouble enough believing it.
I thought myself a man possessed when I
Found me stood here making a noise
And quite a while I called me an impostor
Until I realized I had to recognize
Me and the other me, the both of them.
As though the air were a mirror, it faced me here,
A being fully like my own, having
My bearing, do you follow, and my stature.
Two peas in a pod are not more similar.
Indeed, had it been a friendlier thing,
Not such a surly lout, I could have been,
I tell you straight, very content with it.
AMPHITRYON: What feats of self-control he damns me to!
In the end did you go in or did you not?
SOSIAS: The house? What? Thank you kindly! How?
Did I permit it? Listen to reason? Didn't I
Stubbornly, constantly, deny me entry?
AMPHITRYON: How so? The devil blight you!
SOSIAS: How? A stick,
My back still carrying the marks of which.
AMPHITRYON: So you were beaten?
SOSIAS: Well and truly.

AMPHITRYON: Who,
  Who did? Who dared beat you?
SOSIAS: Me.
AMPHITRYON: You? Beat you?
SOSIAS: Yes, me. I did. Truly. Not this me here,
  The damned and blasted me outside the house
  Who whacks like half a dozen blacksmiths.
AMPHITRYON: Misery dog you giving me this talk.
SOSIAS: Sir, I can show you if you want me to.
  My witness, a trustworthy one, is my
  Companion in misfortune, viz.: my back.
  — The me that chased me off from here had some
  Advantage over me: courage for one thing,
  Arms like a bruiser for another.
AMPHITRYON: Finish this now. Did you speak to my wife?
SOSIAS: No.
AMPHITRYON: Did not? Why not?
SOSIAS: Could not, could I?
AMPHITRYON: Who made you, feckless wretch, neglect
  Your duty, louse, worse than useless louse?
SOSIAS: Must I go on and on repeating it?
  Myself, I told you, me, the devil-me
  That got command over the door there,
  The me that claims to be the one and only me,
  Me of the house there, me of the stick,
  The me that thrashed me black and blue.
AMPHITRYON: The creature must have lost
  What bit of brain he ever had in drink.
SOSIAS: The devil carry me off if I have drunk
  More than my regulation tot today.
  Heavens, if I cross my heart, you must believe me.
AMPHITRYON: — Maybe you had more sleep than is good for you,
  — Saw in a bad dream maybe
  The semblance of these lunatic events
  That you have given me for reality?
SOSIAS: No, no. No, not at all. I last slept yesterday
  And had no wish to sleep in the woods either.
  I was awake, completely, on arrival
  And very awake and very alert was the other
  Sosias thrashing me the way he did.
AMPHITRYON: Be quiet. I must be mad myself, wearing

My brain out listening to such eyewash,
Drivel, feeble claptrap,
No human sense, no human meaning in it.
Follow me.

SOSIAS: (*aside*) That's how it is: from my mouth
It's idiot's stuff, not fit to listen to.
But if some toff had beaten himself up
They'd say God moves in a mysterious way.

AMPHITRYON: Let me go in. — But look, here comes
Alcmene herself. This will surprise her
For now, of course, she is not expecting me.

ACT II, Scene 2

Enter Alcmene and Charis

ALCMENE: Come, Charis, let us lay a sacrifice
Gratefully on the altar of the gods
And further their large holy watchfulness
Let me entreat upon the best of husbands.
                              (*Seeing Amphitryon*)
Oh God, Amphitryon!

AMPHITRYON: The heavens forbid
That seeing me my wife should feel alarm!
I am not fearful that Alcmene after
This brief absence will welcome me less lovingly
Than her Amphitryon returns to her.

ALCMENE: So soon returned ...?

AMPHITRYON: What! Your remark indeed
Seems an equivocal sign to me
Even though the gods did grant that wish.
This 'so soon returned' is not, by heaven,
At all the welcome of a passionate love.
Fool that I was I had supposed the war
Had kept me far too long from here already
And late, as I reckoned it, I was coming home.
But now I learn from you that I was wrong
And realize, unhappily, that I
Descend upon you inconveniently.

ALCMENE: I do not know ...

AMPHITRYON: Alcmene, no. Forgive me.
Saying what you did you came with water

And doused my burning love. In all the time
I have been absent from you not one glance,
One fleeting glance, have you given the clock.
Here time's wingbeat was never hearkened to
And in a rush of pleasures in this house
Five counted months have flown
As though they were so many minutes.

ALCMENE: Dear love, I find it difficult to grasp
What you may have as grounds for this reproach.
If you complain that I am cold to you
You find me at a loss to know how I
Might satisfy you. Yesterday, I think,
When in the twilight you appeared to me,
I paid the debt, that you remind me of,
Abundantly, from the warm heart of me.
If there is more you want, more you desire,
I must confess the poverty of my means.
Truly, I gave you everything I had.

AMPHITRYON: How so?

ALCMENE: How can you ask? Did I not yesterday —
I was at my work and you were in the room
Without my knowing, when you kissed my bowed neck —
Did I not fall on your heart as though plucked from the world?
How could joy in a lover be shown more?

AMPHITRYON: What are you telling me?

ALCMENE: What are you asking?
You were yourself brimful of the wildest joy
To see yourself so loved, and when I laughed
And wept betweentimes, swore to me
With an oath I felt a queer shudder to hear
That never had Juno* so pleased Jupiter.

AMPHITRYON: Eternal gods!

ALCMENE: Then at the blush of daybreak
However I pleaded would not keep you with me.
You would not stay even for the sun
But left, I lay down, but the morning
Was hot, I could not fall asleep,
Being too moved, and wished to make the gods
A sacrifice — and meet you as I leave!
An explanation, surely, you owe me
Whom your return surprises, even,

If you will, bewilders. Still there are
No grounds in this to scold me and be angry.

AMPHITRYON:
Could it have been a dream announced me to you,
Alcmene? Was it in your sleep perhaps
That you received me and so suppose you have
Settled the dues of love with me already?

ALCMENE: Has some bad spirit stolen your memory,
Amphitryon? Or has some god perhaps
Confused your lucid senses and that causes you,
In mockery, to strip your wife's chaste love
Of what is good and right in it?

AMPHITRYON: You dare to tell me, do you, that at twilight
Yesterday I entered here without your knowing
And teasingly, on your bowed neck ...? By hell!

ALCMENE: You dare deny it, do you, that at twilight
Yesterday you entered here without my knowing
And every freedom that a husband properly
May claim as his, you took it, over me?

AMPHITRYON: — You jest. Let us return to seriousness
For jesting of this kind is out of place.

ALCMENE: *You* jest. Let us return to seriousness
For jesting of this kind is coarse and hurts me.

AMPHITRYON: — And every freedom that a husband properly
May claim as his, I took it, over you?
Was that not what you said?

ALCMENE: How hateful you are.

AMPHITRYON: Oh heaven, what a blow has struck me,
Sosias, my friend.

SOSIAS: She needs a dose of something.
Something's the matter in her upper storey.

AMPHITRYON: Alcmene, by the gods, do you not see
The things that may ensue from this talk here?
Bethink yourself. Collect your spirits.
From now on what you say I shall believe.

ALCMENE: Whatever may ensue, Amphitryon
I want you to believe me, will not have you
Suppose me capable of improper jesting.
You see me very calm as to the outcome.
If you in earnest to my face can tell me
You never appeared in the palace yesterday

Unless the gods have punished you terribly
— Excuse it how you like, I do not care.
You cannot make me lose my inner peace
Nor in the world, I hope, my good opinion.
All I shall feel is the tearing in my heart
At this, my dearest's, cruel wish to hurt me.

AMPHITRYON: Unhappy woman! What are you saying? — And
have you
Already assembled evidence on your side?

ALCMENE: How dare he say these things? The servants,
All in the house, are witnesses. The flagstones
You walked on would, the trees, the dogs
That pressed against your legs, for me would all
Speak out in witness for me if they could.

AMPHITRYON: The servants, all our servants, would? Impossible.

ALCMENE: Then shall I give you, whom I cannot fathom,
The proof, the decisive proof? From where
Did I receive this necklace here?

AMPHITRYON: A necklace? What? Already? You? From me?

ALCMENE: The diadem, you said, of Labdacus,
In the final battle overthrown, by you.

AMPHITRYON: You liar there. What shall I make of this?

SOSIAS: Sir, let me speak. These are poor tricks.
I have the diadem in my own hands.

AMPHITRYON: Where?

SOSIAS: Here.
(He takes a casket from his satchel)

AMPHITRYON: The seal is still unbroken.
(He looks at the necklace on Alcmene's breast)
And yet, or all my senses are deceiving me ...
(To SOSIAS)
Quickly, undo the lock.

SOSIAS: Dear heaven, the place is empty.
The devil has conjured it away,
The diadem of Labdacus is not here.

AMPHITRYON: O you omnipotent divinities
That rule the world, what have you laid on me?

SOSIAS: What's laid on you? You have been doubled.
Amphitryon of the stick was here, you are
A happy man, by God, I'd say.

AMPHITRYON: Be quiet, villain.

ALCMENE: (*to* CHARIS) What in the world so agitates him?
   Why does it shake and take the soul from him
   To see this stone that he already knows?
AMPHITRYON: At other times I've heard of miracles,
   Of supernatural appearances that from
   Another world stray into ours; but here
   The thread from over there has fastened
   Around my honour and is throttling it.
ALCMENE: (*to* AMPHITRYON) After this evidence, my strange love,
   Will you deny still you appeared to me
   And what was due to you I paid you then?
AMPHITRYON: No; but relate the event to me, will you?
ALCMENE: Amphitryon!
AMPHITRYON: You hear, I do not doubt you.
   The diadem cannot be argued with.
   Merely that certain reasons make me wish you
   To tell the story of my hours here
   In the palace to me in every detail.
ALCMENE: Love, are you ill perhaps?
AMPHITRYON: Ill no, not ill.
ALCMENE: Maybe some worry of the war burdens
   Your head and spoils, being very pressing,
   The clear activity of your mind?
AMPHITRYON: I feel,
   It is true, bewildered in the head.
ALCMENE: Come then and rest a little.
AMPHITRYON: Leave me be.
   There's time for that. It is, as I said, my wish
   Before I set foot in the house to hear
   The account of this arrival yesterday.
ALCMENE: There's little to tell. Evening was coming on
   And I was in my room, spinning and dreaming
   Myself, with the noise of the wheel, into the field,
   Myself among warriors and weapons when I
   Heard shouts of joy at the outside gate.
AMPHITRYON: And whose?
ALCMENE: Our people's .
AMPHITRYON: Then?
ALCMENE: Then I
   Forgot it again, and even in my dreaming
   I had no thought yet of the joy

The kind gods had in store for me
And had just taken up the thread again
When all my body felt a shudder through it.

AMPHITRYON: I know.

ALCMENE: You know already.

AMPHITRYON: Then?

ALCMENE: Well then
There was talk and laughter, any amount,
And questions all pell-mell and crossing constantly
And then we sat — and you related to me,
In a warrior's voice, the events lately
At Pharissa, and Labdacus, you told me
How he was sunk into eternal night
— And every bloody encounter in the battle.
And then — the splendid diadem was given me
For a present, costing me a kiss,
And in the candlelight was much regarded
— And I attached it to a chain forthwith
And your hand hung it on my breast.

AMPHITRYON: (aside) Could one, I wonder, feel the knife
more keenly?

ALCMENE: Then supper was served, but neither you nor I
Gave any attention to the ortolan*
We had before us, nor much to the wine
Either. You said in jest
That you were living on the nectar of my love,
That you were a god, and what things else delight,
Given its liberty, brought to your tongue.

AMPHITRYON: — Given its liberty, brought to my tongue!

ALCMENE: — Just so, brought to your tongue. And after that ...
Why do you look so blackly, love?

AMPHITRYON: And after that ...?

ALCMENE: We rose from table, and then ...

AMPHITRYON: And then ...?

ALCMENE: When we had risen from table we ...

AMPHITRYON: When you had risen from table you ...?

ALCMENE: We went ...

AMPHITRYON: You went ...

ALCMENE: We went ... Well, but we ...
Why has such redness risen in your face?

AMPHITRYON: This knife has struck into the life of me.

No, no, betrayer of me, I wasn't the man.
Whoever it was who in the twilight yesterday
Crept in here as Amphitryon
He was the vilest of all womanizers.
ALCMENE: Oh, this is foul of you!
AMPHITRYON: Betrayal! Ingratitude! —
Now leave me, moderation, and you too,
Laming my honour's just demands, you, love,
And memories, leave, and hope and happiness,
Leave me to revel in rage and vengeance now.
ALCMENE: Leave me yourself. From you who are my husband
And mean in spirit, this heart tears itself free
Bleeding. Your trick revolts me, it is vile.
If you have turned your face towards someone else,
Because love's arrow made you, your wishes,
Confided to me decently, would as soon
As this weak trick have got you what you sought.
You see me now determined to undo
The bonds oppressive to your fickle heart
And before evening comes in
You are released from everything that binds you.
AMPHITRYON: Shameful as the insult is that has
Been done to me this is the very least
My honour, bleeding from its hurt, can ask.
That I am being deceived is obvious
Even though my senses cannot grasp
The accursed web of it. But witnesses
Now I will summon who will rip it up.
Your brother, I'll summon him, the generals
For me, and all the Theban army
Out of whose midst I did not move
Until today's first rays of morning light.
So I shall fathom out this riddle,
And woe on him, I say, who has deceived me.
SOSIAS: — Sir, shall I perhaps ...
AMPHITRYON: Be quiet. I've heard enough.
Stay here. I will be back. Stay till I am.

[*Exit*]

CHARIS: What shall I do, lady?
ALCMENE: Be quiet. I've heard enough.
I wish to be alone. Don't follow me.   [*Exit*]

ACT II, Scene 3

CHARIS: What sort of scene was that? I ask you:
  To claim he slept the night just past
  Out there in the camp, the man must be deranged. —
  Well, when her brother comes, then we shall see.
SOSIAS: This is a hard blow for my master.
  — Is something similar in store for me?
  Best if I sound her out a little.
CHARIS: (aside)
  What's this? He has the brazen cheek, him there,
  To keep his grumpy back turned.
SOSIAS: I feel,
  By heavens I do, a shudder down my back
  At the thought of fingering the ticklish point.
  I've half a mind to ask no questions.
  In the end a thing's as broad as it is long
  If you don't fetch a light and scrutinize it. —
  Courage! We'll take a chance. I have to know.
  — God bless you, Charis.
CHARIS: What! You approach me,
  Traitor, do you? You have the brazen cheek,
  The face, when I am angry, to address me?
SOSIAS: Just gods above, what is it now? Don't people
  Say something when they see each other again?
  The way you raise your hackles over nothing!
CHARIS: You call it nothing? What do you call nothing?
  What are you calling over nothing, villain?
SOSIAS: What I call nothing is, to tell you the truth,
  What's called nothing in prose or verse,
  And nothing, as you know, is about as much
  As nothing, you follow me, or very little. —
CHARIS: Can't understand what keeps my hands
  Off him. I'm itching, so it's nearly more
  Than I can bear, to scratch your eyes out
  And show you what a woman's rage is like.
SOSIAS: The gods be kind to me! What an attack!
CHARIS: You call it nothing, do you, nothing
  The way you saw fit to behave to me?
SOSIAS: I saw fit what? What has been happening?
CHARIS: To me? See here! All innocence!

Next thing, just like his master, he'll be telling me
He never was in Thebes till now.
SOSIAS: Believe me
  On that matter I'm telling you I'm not
  Making a mystery for fun. We've drunk
  Some of the devil's own brew
  And had our wits washed clean away by it.
CHARIS: You think a tale like that will get you off?
SOSIAS: No, Charis. Word of honour, call me a villain
  If I wasn't here once yesterday already.
  But what occurred, I've no idea. The world
  And I were speaking different tongues.
CHARIS:
  So you don't know now, do you, how you treated me
  Yesterday evening when you came in?
SOSIAS: The devil I do. I've less idea than none.
  But tell, I'm very biddable, as you know.
  I'll damn myself if I've done any wrong.
CHARIS: Wretch, it was midnight gone and long since
  The lord and lady newly-weds in bed
  And you still dawdling in Amphitryon's
  Apartments, not having shown yourself
  One minute at home. In the end, perforce,
  It is the wife herself who stirs her stumps
  And comes to find you and what does she find?
  Where do I find you, runaway from duty,
  I find you with your head down on a pillow
  As though that were your place, and not at home.
  To my complaint, in my tender distress,
  You answer Amphitryon, your master, wishes it,
  You musn't oversleep the time for leaving,
  He has a mind to start from Thebes early,
  And more old tripe of that sort. Not one word
  Comes from your lips at all friendly,
  And when I lean down lovingly for
  A kiss, you turn, how dare you, wretch,
  Your face to the wall and tell me let you sleep.
SOSIAS: Honest old Sosias, well done.
CHARIS: I beg your pardon?
  Did I hear you congratulate yourself?
  I believe I did.

SOSIAS: Come now, you must forgive me.
   I had been eating horseradish
   And did right, Charis, not to breathe on you.
CHARIS: So what? I shouldn't have noticed it.
   At midday we had horseradish ourselves.
SOSIAS: Well, well. I never knew. You can't tell then.
CHARIS: Don't try to wriggle out of it.
   Sooner or later the contempt with which
   I see myself treated will want revenge.
   It irks me, and I shan't get over it,
   What I was forced to listen to at dawn today.
   Sure as I'm honest I shall use against you
   The liberty you gave me.
SOSIAS: What was the liberty I gave you?
CHARIS:
   You said, and knew full well what you were saying,
   That wearing horns wouldn't bother you. Indeed,
   You said that you'd be very well content
   If that young Theban helped me pass my time
   Who's always at my heels here, as you know.
   So, friend, very well, thy will be done.
SOSIAS: Some donkey told you that, not me.
   Enough jokes now. I'm no party to that.
   In this matter you will behave yourself.
CHARIS: What if it gets the better of me though?
SOSIAS: Quiet now, Alcmene's here, the mistress.

ACT II, Scene 4

ALCMENE: Charis!
   What terrible thing has happened to me? Say
   What have I suffered? See this jewel.
CHARIS: What is the jewel, lady?
ALCMENE: It is
   The diadem of Labdacus, my dear
   And splendid present from Amphitryon
   In which the letter of his name is carved.
CHARIS: This? This is the diadem of Labdacus?
   Here there's no letter of Amphitryon's name.

ALCMENE:
  Ill luck on you, are you robbed of your reason?
  No letter here that can be read with fingers,
  No graven-in in gold big letter A?
CHARIS: Certainly not. What a delusion, lady.
  The initial here is of some other name.
  It is a J.
ALCMENE: A J?
CHARIS: A J. For certain.
ALCMENE: Alas for me then, oh alas. This dooms me.
CHARIS: What is it, tell me, that so troubles you?
ALCMENE: How shall I find the words, dear Charis,
  To explain to you what cannot be explained?
  Back in my room again bewildered and
  Not knowing was I awake or had I dreamed
  The insane and insolent assertion
  That someone other had appeared to me;
  But measuring all the same Amphitryon's
  Passionate pain and this, his final word,
  That he would go and fetch to vouch against me
  My brother, think of that, my own brother;
  And when I ask myself: Were you in error then?
  For one of the two of us is mocked by error,
  Not he nor I are capable of malice;
  And that equivocal jest came back
  Sharply to memory when Amphitryon
  The lover, I don't know if you heard it,
  Reviled, to me, Amphitryon the husband
  And then what shock, what dread seized hold of me
  And all my faithless senses fled from me —
  Then, dearest Charis, I seize upon this stone,
  Precious like nothing else as unique proof
  And for a witness wholly trustworthy
  I take it up to press the loved initial,
  Which is my darling liar's own contradictor,
  Much moved, to my delighted lips
  And see another, an unfamiliar mark
  And feel lightning has struck: a J.
CHARIS: But this is fearful. Were you perhaps deceived?
ALCMENE: Deceived?
CHARIS: Here, in the mark, I mean.

ALCMENE: Oh, in the mark, you mean — it almost seems so.
CHARIS: Well then?
ALCMENE: Well what then?
CHARIS: Calm yourself.
   All will be well still.
ALCMENE: Charis,
   I'd sooner be deluded in myself,
   Sooner suppose my innermost feeling
   Got as an infant at my mother's breast,
   The feeling that tells me I am Alcmene,
   Suppose myself a Persian or a Parthian.
   Is this hand mine? This breast here, is it mine?
   Does the image the mirror casts belong to me?
   Him stranger to me than I am myself?
   Blind me, I hear him. Deafen me, I feel him,
   And take my feeling from me: I still breathe him.
   Take eyes and ears, feeling and sense of smell,
   Take all my senses, leaving but the heart:
   So doing you leave me all the guide I need.
   From the whole world still I shall find him out.
CHARIS: For sure. How could I ever doubt it, lady?
   No woman makes mistakes in things like that.
   You take the wrong dress or some kitchen thing
   But seize the right man, be it ever so dark.
   Besides, was he not seen by all of us?
   Did not the whole household when he appeared
   Joyously make him welcome at the gate?
   It was still daylight. Not to see him
   Midnight must have covered a thousand eyes.
ALCMENE: Yet this strange letter here ... Why did
   A mark so unfamiliar
   That no one's unharmed senses could mistake it
   Not strike my eye and mind at once? Dear Charis,
   Answer me. If I can't tell apart
   Two such names might there, is it possible,
   Be two men bearing them who likewise
   Could not more easily be told apart?
CHARIS: I hope, however, you are certain, lady.
ALCMENE:
   As of my untouched soul. As of my innocence.
   You misinterpret else my sense that I

Never before found him so beautiful.
I might have taken him for his own image,
For an artist's portrait of him, let me say,
Done true to life but raised to the divine.
His standing there was like, I don't know, like
A dream and the feeling seized me beyond words
Of my own happiness, never so felt before
When yesterday in glory, radiant,
He came to me as conqueror of Pharissa.
It was Amphitryon, a son of heaven,
Only he seemed to me already one of them
In splendour, I might almost have asked him
Had he descended to me from the stars.

CHARIS: Imagination, lady, love's appearance.

ALCMENE: Oh, and the equivocal jesting, Charis,
Over and over again distinguishing
Between him and Amphitryon. If he
Was the one I gave myself to why
Did he forever call himself the lover,
The thief merely, stealing my sweets? A curse
On me for smiling blithely at this jest
If any other than my husband's mouth spoke it.

CHARIS: Don't be so quick to pain yourself with doubts.
Did not Amphitryon, being shown the diadem
By you today, himself acknowledge the letter?
Here is, for certain, some mistake, lady.
If this strange mark did not deflect him then
It must, it follows, be the stone's own mark.
Illusion yesterday deceived and blinded us.
Today, though, everything is as it should be.

ALCMENE: What if he only glanced at it
And now returns with all his generals
And furiously repeats the assertion that
He never crossed our house's threshold
Not only am I stripped of every witness
The stone here witnesses *against* me.
What can I, now confused, answer it with?
Where shall I run from pain to, from extinction,
When the suspicious men have tested it?
Must I not then admit that this initial
Is not the initial of Amphitryon?

Admit a gift cannot, that comes
With another's mark on, come to me from him?
Oh were I to swear at once upon the altar
That he, last night, gave me the stone himself,
Answer me: Am I certain that last night
I had the sign too, visible here, from him?

CHARIS:
Compose yourself. He is here. It will be solved now.

ACT II, Scene 5

Enter JUPITER

ALCMENE: My lord and husband, give me your permission
To kneel and place this jewel in your hands.
My life in faithfulness I lay down at your feet.
If you gave me this stone, consider it well,
Marked with the initial of another's name
For joy I'll kiss it and weep tears on it.
If you did not, and tell me you did not,
If you deny the stone, let death be dealt me
And in eternal night bury my shame.

JUPITER: Beautiful spouse, shall I accept the stone
When such worth lies before me in the dust?
Stand up. What do you want? Compose yourself.

ALCMENE: My confident utterance insulted you.
I felt myself then innocent and strong.
But since I saw this strange initial
I will mistrust my innermost feeling.
I will ... believe ... some other ... appeared to me
If your lips still can tell me it was so.

JUPITER: My noble spouse, how you put me to shame!
How can you let such untruths leave your lips?
How could another man appear to you?
Who comes near you, oh you before whose soul
Only the one and only's features ever rise?
Holy as you are, a diamond-hard refusal
Surrounds you against every access.
Even the happy man you do receive
He leaves you innocent still and pure and all
That ever nears you is Amphitryon.

ALCMENE: Will you, for pity, oh my husband, tell me
Was it you, was it not you? Speak. It was.

JUPITER: It was. Whoever it was. Be ... be at ease.
What you saw, touched and thought and felt
Was me: who else but me, beloved?
Whoever it was who crossed your threshold
Throughout, my dearest, I was the one received
And for whatever favours you bestowed on him
I am your debtor and I thank you.
ALCMENE: No, my Amphitryon, there you are wrong.
Goodbye for ever now. This was the state of things,
Beloved, I set myself to face.
JUPITER: Alcmene!
ALCMENE: Goodbye! Goodbye!
JUPITER: What do you mean?
ALCMENE: Away, away, away!
JUPITER: Light of my eyes!
ALCMENE: Leave me, I said.
JUPITER: Listen.
ALCMENE: I will not, not to anything, will not live
If the heart in me is not now free of wrong.
JUPITER: Adored spouse, what sense is in your speech?
What wrong, being holy, could you ever do?
Suppose it was a devil last night appeared to you
And from the depths of hell he voided over you,
Laced with his spittle, all the mire of sin,
With not one spot could he soil the lustre of
The bosom of my spouse. Madness to think he could.
ALCMENE: I am a woman shamefully deceived.
JUPITER: He was
The one deceived, my idol, him
Himself, not you, his wicked arts deluded,
Not your feeling that is infallible. When he
Supposed himself in your embrace you lay
On Amphitryon's beloved heart, when he
Was dreaming kisses you were pressing your lips
On Amphitryon's beloved mouth. A thorn,
Believe me, is working in him now
And from his heart, that love inflames, not all
The science of the gods can pluck it out.
ALCMENE: I wish Zeus flung him shattered at my feet.
Oh God, we must be parted for all time.
JUPITER: That kiss you gave him as a gift

Binds me to you faster than all the love
That ever flamed out from your heart for me.
And if from the flying dance of the days
I could as easily fling yesterday
As if it were a sparrow, dearest lady,
For the Olympians' blessedness, for Zeus'
Own everlasting life I would not do it.

ALCMENE: And death I'd give myself to, ten times over.
You will not see me in your home or show me
To any woman in Hellas ever again.

JUPITER: To the whole circle of the Olympians,
Alcmene. — What a language! I will lead you
Radiant into the host of all the gods
And were I Zeus, when you approached their company,
I'd make eternal Hera stand for you
And the strict Artemis bid you welcome.

ALCMENE: Your goodness crushes me. Hush, let me go.

JUPITER: Alcmene.

ALCMENE: Leave me.

JUPITER: Spouse of my soul.

ALCMENE: Amphitryon, you hear. I wish to leave.

JUPITER: Do you suppose you can escape these arms?

ALCMENE: Amphitryon, I wish it. You must let me.

JUPITER: And if you fled to distant lands, away
Towards the desert's abominable lives,
To the sea's shores I would follow you
And catch and kiss you there and weep
And lift you in my arms and carry
You home in triumph to my bed.

ALCMENE: Since you so wish it then I swear to you
And summon up the gods' whole company,
The terrible avengers of a broken oath:
This body of mine, while there is breath in it,
I'll lay in the grave sooner than in your bed.

JUPITER: Your oath, by birthright powers, *I* break
And fling its pieces in the air. It was
No mortal who appeared to you.
Zeus visited you, himself, the Thunderer.

ALCMENE: Who?

JUPITER: Jupiter.

ALCMENE: Who, are you mad, do you say?

JUPITER: Jupiter, I say, himself.
ALCMENE: Jupiter himself?
   You dare to, are you so depraved ...?
JUPITER: Jupiter, I say,
   And say again that he, and no one else,
   In this past night appeared to you.
ALCMENE: You accuse, you dare to, the Olympians
   Of the crime, blasphemer, that was perpetrated?
JUPITER: Accuse the Olympians of a crime? Give thought
   To what you say, and never let me
   Hear such things from your mouth again.
ALCMENE: Such things
   From my mouth, mine ...? Not call it a crime ...?
JUPITER: Silence, I say, obey me.
ALCMENE: You are lost.
JUPITER: Though you may not be sensible of the glory
   Of mounting the stairway to the immortal gods
   I am, and you will kindly let me be.
   And if you do not envy high Callisto,
   Nor Leda, nor Europa,* I do envy,
   For certain, let me tell you, Tyndarus
   And wish for sons like the Tyndarides.*
ALCMENE: Do *I* envy Callisto and Europa?
   Women of Hellas raised to splendour?
   The high elect of Jupiter who dwell now
   In the eternal and ethereal realms?
JUPITER: Why should they indeed seem enviable to you
   Who by the fame are wholly satisfied
   Of seeing at your feet one mortal man?
ALCMENE: This talk exceeds belief! Who am I
   To allow myself even the thought? Would I
   Not fade to nothing in such radiance?
   Would I, had it been him, still here
   In this warm breast enjoy the feel of life?
   Sinner that I am, unworthy of such grace?
JUPITER: Your worthiness or not of grace is not
   For you to judge. You will let come upon you
   Whatever his judgement of you is. So poor
   In vision, do you think to be his teacher
   Who knows the workings of all human hearts?
ALCMENE: Let be, Amphitryon, I understand you.

Your generosity touches me to tears.
I know you say this as a thing thrown out
To lure me from the thought that gives me torment.
But to that thought my soul comes back again.
Go now, my dearest darling, all and only,
And find your happiness with another wife
And let me live my life out weeping who
Am not allowed to be your happiness.

JUPITER: Dear spouse! You move me. See
The stone you are holding in your hands.

ALCMENE: You gods above, protect me from delusion.

JUPITER: Is it not his name, and yesterday was mine?
Is all here being revealed not wondrous?
Did I not have this diadem locked
Today still, sealed up in its casket?
And opening it, to offer you the jewel,
Find only the empty imprint bedded there?
And see it radiant on your breast already?

ALCMENE: Shall my soul think this? Jupiter?
The gods' eternal father and mankind's?

JUPITER: Who else could cheat the instant
Exquisite weighing by your feelings
And circumvent the fine
Outreaching touches of your woman's soul
And yet not cause to sound, although the softest
Breath will do it, your bosom's warning chimes?

ALCMENE: Himself! Him!

JUPITER: Only the almighty gods
Can visit as brashly as this stranger did
And I am proud to have such rivals.
It pleases me to see the omniscient gods
Discovering the pathway to your heart
And see them, who are omnipresent, near you.
And must they not, beloved, be themselves
Amphitryon and steal his features
To be received by you into your soul?

ALCMENE: Well yes.
                    (She kisses him)

JUPITER: Celestial woman!

ALCMENE: How happy I am!
And glad, how glad I am to be still happy!

And glad now to have felt the pain
Done me by Jupiter, so long as everything
Is kind to me as it was kind before.

JUPITER: Shall I say what my thought is?

ALCMENE: Say it.

JUPITER: And what, if revelation is not given us,
  I'm even inclined to feel is my belief?

ALCMENE: Say it. What is it? You frighten me.

JUPITER: What if
  You have — don't be alarmed — made him displeased?

ALCMENE: Him? Me? Displeased?

JUPITER: Is he a presence to you?
  Truly, do you apprehend his mighty work, the world?
  Do you see him when the evening
  Falls streaming red through silent trees?
  Do you hear him in the soodling of waters
  And in the raised song of the passionate nightingale?
  Does not the mountain, piled at heaven,
  Speak to you in vain of him, in vain to you
  The chute of cataracts vapoured by the rocks?
  And when the lifted sun shines in his temple
  And rung there by the pulse-beat of their joy
  All creatures of all kinds praise him
  Do you not then descend into your heart's shaft
  To adore your idol?

ALCMENE: You terrify me.
  What are you saying? Can anyone be more
  Pious in worship of him or more child-like?
  Does any day conclude without my bowing
  To thank him for my life and for yours too,
  With all my heart, beloved, at his altar?
  Did I not in the starry night just past
  Lie on my face before him, low and fervent,
  Sending to heaven, hot as the fumes of sacrifice,
  Out of the milling of my feelings, adoration?

JUPITER: Why on your face? — Was it not because
  In the drawings done by strokes of lightning
  You saw features that are well known to you?

ALCMENE: Inhuman, terrible! How can you know that?

JUPITER: Who is it you pray to at his altar? Him,
  Do you, truly, who is above the clouds?

Truly can you grasp him with your hampered senses?
Used to their nest, how can your feelings
Ever nerve themselves for such a flight?
Is it not Amphitryon, the beloved, always
Him before whom you lie there in the dust?
ALCMENE: I am an unhappy woman. How you trouble me!
Can one do wrong things never knowing it?
Am I to pray to a white marble wall?
I need the features of a face to think of him.
JUPITER:
There now. Did I not say so? Do you not suppose
It irks him, such idolatry? Will he be pleased
Foregoing your beautiful heart? Not feeling
Himself by you too idolized with passion?
ALCMENE: Ah no, he will not. Where is the sinner
Whose worship is not pleasant to the gods?
JUPITER: Indeed. He came to you, when he descended,
Only to make you bound to think of him
And be revenged on you, who had forgotten.
ALCMENE: Terrible.
JUPITER: Have no fear. He'll punish you no more
Than you deserve. But in the future, understand me,
You will think of him who appeared to you at night,
Him only, at his altar, and not me.
ALCMENE: I will. My holy word on it. I know
What he was like in every last expression
And never again will muddle him with you.
JUPITER: Do not. You risk else he will come again.
Whenever you see the initial of his name
Cut in the diadem you will be mindful
Passionately of his appearance;
Remember the event in every detail;
Remember how at him, the immortal,
Shock went through you at the spinning wheel;
What you gave for the jewel and who it was
Assisted you putting it on and what
Happened at table. And should your husband
Intrude you ask him in a friendly way
To leave you to yourself for an hour.
ALCMENE: Very well. I shall be as you wish me.
At every first hour of the morning

No further thought of mine shall think of you.
But after that I will not think of Jupiter.
JUPITER: If now therefore in all his radiance
  Touched by this large improvement
  The eternal cloud-shaker revealed himself
  To you, beloved, how would you bear yourself?
  Tell me.
ALCMENE: A terror for my eyes. If only
  I had, at his altar, always thought of him
  Since he is scarcely different from you.
JUPITER:
  You have not seen the form he has in heaven,
  Alcmene, yet. Your heart will lift at him —
  Oh, in a thousand kinds of bliss. And what
  You feel for him will seem like fire to you
  And ice your sentiments for Amphitryon.
  Why, if he touches your soul now
  And comes again as he returns to Olympus
  You will experience the unbelievable and weep
  That you are not allowed to follow him.
ALCMENE: No, no, never think that, Amphitryon.
  And in my life could I go back a day
  And in the innermost room of mine
  Against all gods and heroes lock and bolt myself
  I would ...
JUPITER: Truly, would you? Would you do that?
ALCMENE: With all my heart I would say yes to that.
JUPITER: (aside)
  Curse the deluded hopes that lured me here!
ALCMENE: What is it? Are you cross? Did I offend you,
  My love?
JUPITER: My pious child, are you unwilling
  To sweeten the immensity of his life for him?
  Would you deny him, when he seeks to rest
  His head from governing the world,
  The softness of your breast? Alcmene,
  Even Olympus is a desert without love.
  What can the adoration of the peoples of the earth,
  Face in the dust, give to a heart that thirsts?
  Not their illusion of him but himself
  Wants love. Forever veiled, his longing is

To mirror himself in a person's soul and have
Tears of rapture cast his image back.
See now, beloved, unending wealth of joy
He pours out between heaven and earth:
Were you decided on by fate to pay
The thanks of creatures in such millions,
The whole of his demand upon creation,
To pay him that in one sole smile
Would you still not for him ... I cannot think it,
I beg you let me not ... let me ...

ALCMENE: Far be it from me
To fight the vast decisions of the gods.
Were I elected for so holy an office
Let him who made me govern over me.
But ...

JUPITER: What?

ALCMENE: If I am left my choice ...

JUPITER: If you are left ...?

ALCMENE:
My choice, my reverence would still go to him,
And still to you my love, Amphitryon.

JUPITER: What if this god, it seemed to you, were me?

ALCMENE: Were you ...?
— What then? If I thought you the god?
— I don't know, should I kneel before you?
Or not? Are you, am I to think you him?

JUPITER: Decide yourself. I am Amphitryon.

ALCMENE: Amphitryon ...

JUPITER: Amphitryon, to you, yes. But
What if, I ask, it seemed to you that I
Were him, this god, descended lovingly to you
From heaven, how would you bear yourself?

ALCMENE:
If you, my love, were him, as it seemed, the god,
Not knowing then where was Amphitryon
I'd follow you, wherever you go, even if
You went to Orcus like Eurydice.*

JUPITER: Not knowing where Amphitryon was. But what
If now Amphitryon showed himself?

ALCMENE: If now Amphitryon ... You are tormenting me.
How can Amphitryon show himself to me

When in my arms I hold Amphitryon?
JUPITER: Yet you might easily be holding in your arms
    The god, believing him Amphitryon.
    Why should your feelings take you by surprise?
    If I, the god, held you here in my arms
    And now your own Amphitryon showed himself
    How would your heart explain itself?
ALCMENE: If you, the god, held me here in your arms
    And now Amphitryon showed himself to me
    Why ... I'd be sad, so sad, and wish
    He was the god for me and you remained
    Amphitryon for me, just as you are.
JUPITER: Sweet creature, see, I worship you!
    Rejoice in you! Am blessed, so blessed in you!
    True to the unspoilt truth of God's idea
    In form and measure, fashioning and tone,
    Such as in eons has not left my hand.
ALCMENE: Amphitryon!
JUPITER: Be easy, easy, easy.
    Everything will issue in your triumph.
    The god lusts after showing himself to you
    And even before the ranks of stars have trod
    Their measure through the silent fields of night
    Your heart will know who has enkindled it.
    — Sosias!
SOSIAS: Sir.
JUPITER: Now serve me faithfully
    To make this day splendid. Alcmene
    Lovingly has reconciled herself to me.
    And you, go now and summon where you meet them
    In camp my people for the celebration.

                              [*Exit* JUPITER *and* ALCMENE]

                     ACT II, Scene 6

CHARIS: (*aside*) What have you heard, unlucky woman?
    That it was gods, the Olympians, and the one
    Pretending to me he is Sosias
    Himself one of the immortals,
    Apollo, Hermes, say, or Ganymede?*
SOSIAS: (*aside*)
    God of the lightning! So it was Zeus, was it?

CHARIS: (aside)
  The shame of it! The way I acted with him.
SOSIAS: (aside)
  He had a good man looking after him,
  I must say that. A man who stood his ground
  And fought like a tiger for his gentleman.
CHARIS: (aside)
  Who knows, I might be wrong. I'd better test him.
  (Aloud) Come now, let's make it up too, Sosias.
SOSIAS: Some other time. There's no time for it now.
CHARIS: Where are you going?
SOSIAS: I have to summon the generals.
CHARIS: Allow me a word first, husband, will you, please.
SOSIAS: Husband ...? Oh very gladly.
CHARIS: Did you hear
  That yesterday at twilight to my lady
  And to her faithful servingwoman
  Two great Olympians came down,
  And Zeus, god of the thunderclouds, was here
  With lovely Phoebus for companion?
SOSIAS: Yes, if it's true, Charis. I did hear it, alas.
  I always found such marriages distasteful.
CHARIS: Distasteful? Why? I can't think ...
SOSIAS: Hm,
  It's like one, to be honest with you, of
  Horse with ass.
CHARIS: Horse with ass! A god
  And a great lady! (Aside) He's not from
  Olympus either, I shouldn't think. (Aloud) It pleases you
  To jest with your poor handmaiden.
  A triumph such as this come over us
  Never was heard the like in Thebes before.
SOSIAS: It was a bad deal I got out of it.
  A decent measure of disgrace
  Would do me just as well as these damned trophies
  So splendidly displayed on both my shoulders.
  But I must hurry.
CHARIS: What I meant was ...
  Who ever dreamed of visitors like these?
  Who'd have believed that in poor human flesh

Two of the immortal gods had veiled themselves?
It must be said that certain good sides
That stayed unnoticed very much within
We might have turned more outwards than we did.

SOSIAS: Indeed, I'd have been glad of that, Charis.
You were about as gentle with me
As a wild cat. You will mend your ways.

CHARIS: I'm not aware that I insulted you,
Said more to you than ...

SOSIAS: Not insulted me?
Call me a villain if this morning
You didn't deserve such handling with knocks
Bad as a woman anywhere was dealt.

CHARIS: But what ... what happened then?

SOSIAS: What happened then,
Fishface? Did you not say you'd have
That Theban in I not long since, the louse,
Already threw out once? And did you not
Promise me a pair of horns and shamelessly
Invest me with the name of cuckold?

CHARIS: Och,
A joke, for sure.

SOSIAS: Oh yes, a joke. You come
That joke with me again I'll fetch you such —
Be damned if I don't — a clout ...

CHARIS: Heavens,
What is this?

SOSIAS: Trollop.

CHARIS: Do not look so fierce.
I feel this heart of mine broken in pieces.

SOSIAS: Blaspheming woman, shame on you for joking
Like that about your sacred wifely duties.
Watch you don't sin that way again,
I'm warning you ... and when you see me next
You'll do me sausages and mash for dinner.

CHARIS: As you command. What am I waiting for?
Why am I dithering? It's him. Is it him?

SOSIAS: It's who?

CHARIS: I lie in the dust.

SOSIAS: Are you not well?

CHARIS: I lie before you humbled in the dust.

SOSIAS: Have you gone mad?
CHARIS: You are him. Oh, you are!
SOSIAS: Are who?
CHARIS: Oh why deny yourself to me?
SOSIAS: Has everyone gone raving mad?
CHARIS: Did I
   Not glimpse in the flaming anger of your eyes
   Apollo, the Archer's, deadly beams?
SOSIAS: Apollo, me? Are you possessed? —
   One of them makes a dog of me, the other
   A god. — I am the old and same as ever
   Clown Sosias.

                                              [*Exit*]

CHARIS: Sosias? What? My old
   And same as ever clown are you indeed?
   Sosias? I'm glad to know it. You're out of luck
   If you're expecting something hot when you get back.

                                              [*Exit*]

ACT III, Scene 1

AMPHITRYON: The faces of my generals, how repellent
   They are to me. All must deliver their
   Congratulations on the battle won
   And each and all of them I must embrace
   And every one of them I damn to hell.
   Not one among them has a heart such as
   My own, so full, could be disburdened to.
   To steal a jewel out of its locked
   Container and not break the seal
   That may be possible: conjurors can magic
   Things from a distance out of our very hands.
   But purloining the shape and manners of a man
   And doing the office of his marriage with
   His wife, is devilish, a trick from hell.
   In rooms lit up by candlelight
   Till now, being sound in all five senses,
   One never mistook one's friends. Eyes
   From their sockets laid down on a table,
   Limbs, ears and fingers taken off a body
   And packed in boxes would have been enough
   To know one's husband by. It will be necessary

Henceforth to brand the married men and bell
Their necks like wethers. She is
As capable of black deceit as is
Her turtle dove. I should rather believe
In the honesty of rogues escaped the rope
Than in any duplicity in this woman.
— She has gone mad, and at daybreak tomorrow
It is certain I shall have to send for doctors.
— If only I could reattach myself.

ACT III, Scene 2

Mercury appears on the balcony

MERCURY: (*aside*) Following you to earth on this lovesick
Adventure, Father Jupiter, no one
Less your good friend than Mercury would have done it.
By Styx, I am as bored as I can be.
For with the lady's maid in this affair,
With Charis, I have no great wish
To play the husband closer than I need.
— I'll try for some amusement now
And madden the man there in his jealousy.
AMPHITRYON: Why have they locked the house in daylight?
MERCURY: Hey!
Be patient, will you. Who's that knocking?
AMPHITRYON: Me.
MERCURY: Who? Me!
AMPHITRYON: Oh, open the door.
MERCURY: The door! And who are you
To make that racket, lout, and take that tone with me?
AMPHITRYON: It seems you don't know who I am.
MERCURY: I do.
There's no one lifts the latch that I don't know.
Don't know the man indeed!
AMPHITRYON: Has everyone in Thebes
Had something in their drink and lost their minds?
Sosias! Hey, Sosias!
MERCURY: Yes, Sosias,
That is my name. The rogue is bellowing it
As if he feared I might forget it else.
AMPHITRYON: Just gods above, man. Can't you see me?

MERCURY: Perfectly.
  What is it?
AMPHITRYON: What is it, you devil!
MERCURY: In hell's name then
  What isn't it? Say what, we'll answer you.
AMPHITRYON: You wait, you dreg. I'll be up there
  And teach you, with a stick, to talk to me like that.
MERCURY: Hallo! Someone down there wants teaching manners.
  You'll pardon me.
AMPHITRYON: Devil.
MERCURY: Compose yourself.
AMPHITRYON: Hallo! Is no one home?
MERCURY: Philippus!
  Where are you all? Charmion!
AMPHITRYON: The insolence!
MERCURY: We'll have to see to you.
  But bide your time in patience till they come
  And if you knock that knocker again
  Once more, from here above I'll send you down
  A pelting sort of answer on your head.
AMPHITRYON:
  Impudence! Brazen cheek! Him there, a thing
  I've often kicked, a thing if I'd a mind to
  I could have crucified.
MERCURY: Well then?
  Well, have you done? Have you done staring at me?
  With your big bulging eyes will you be long yet
  Measuring me up? See how he gawps.
  If looks were teeth and he could bite with them
  Long before now he would have ripped me up.
AMPHITRYON: I quake myself, Sosias, when I think
  What you are asking for with talk like this.
  Such blows, so many and terrible, await you.
  — Come down here now and open up.
MERCURY: At last.
AMPHITRYON: Don't make me wait. The affair is urgent.
MERCURY: So
  Now we discover what it is you want.
  You want me to open up the door down there.
AMPHITRYON: I do.
MERCURY: Very well. A man might ask politely.

Who is it you want?

AMPHITRYON: Who is it I want?

MERCURY: Who is it —
God damn you, are you deaf? — you want to speak to?

AMPHITRYON:
To speak to, who? Creature, I'll tread your bones
To powder once my house is opened to me.

MERCURY: Now listen, friend. I counsel you to leave.
Don't aggravate me. Go away, I say.

AMPHITRYON: Low form of life, you will discover
What sort of handling a servant can expect
Who mocks his master.

MERCURY: Master? Mock
His master, me? And you, are you my master?

AMPHITRYON: Next thing he'll say I'm not.

MERCURY: I only know
One master and that one's Amphitryon.

AMPHITRYON: And who except me is Amphitryon,
You squinnying wretch who'd mix up night and day?

MERCURY: Amphitryon?

AMPHITRYON: Amphitryon, I tell you.

MERCURY: Ho, ho. People of Thebes, come here. Hear this.

AMPHITRYON: The shame of it. Oh let the earth swallow me.

MERCURY: Listen, my friend. Say where it was you drank
Yourself into this happy state.

AMPHITRYON: Oh heaven.

MERCURY: A young wine or an old?

AMPHITRYON: You gods above.

MERCURY: Why stop it where you did? You could
Have drunk yourself into the King of Egypt.

AMPHITRYON: I'm done for now.

MERCURY: Run along, old lad.
You break my heart. Go home and go to bed.
Amphitryon lives here, the Theban general.
Be off. Leave him in peace.

AMPHITRYON: What's that you say?
You say Amphitryon is there inside?

MERCURY: Inside here, yes, him and Alcmene.
Be off, I tell you once again, beware
You don't disturb the lovers' happiness
Unless you wish him to appear himself

And punish your insolence.

[*Exit* MERCURY]

ACT III, Scene 3

AMPHITRYON: I am unhappy, I am smitten down,
The blow destroys me, there is nothing of me left.
I am already buried and my widow
Already mated with another husband.
What resolution can I come to now?
Shall I broadcast it to the world
Or hide it that disgrace has struck my house?
Spare nothing here. Nothing in all
My deliberations has a voice except
The sentiment that burns: revenge.
And my one tender care shall be
Not to let him, the impostor, off alive.

ACT III, Scene 4

Enter SOSIAS *and the* GENERALS

SOSIAS: Here you see all the company, sir,
That I could gather in so short a time.
You may not want me feasting at your table.
God's honour though, I've earned a meal.

AMPHITRYON: See here then, you!

SOSIAS: Well?

AMPHITRYON: Dreg! And now you die.

SOSIAS: Me? Die?

AMPHITRYON: Now you discover who I am.

SOSIAS: God stap me, don't I know?

AMPHITRYON: You knew, did you?

                    (He lays his hand on his sword)

SOSIAS: Gentlemen, save me, please.

FIRST GENERAL: Forgive me.

                    (He intervenes)

AMPHITRYON: Stand aside.

SOSIAS: Say what I've done.

AMPHITRYON:
You ask me that? — Stand aside, I say, and let
My just vengeance have satisfaction.

SOSIAS: Before you hang a man you tell him why.

FIRST GENERAL: Be good enough.

SECOND GENERAL: Say what his fault is.

SOSIAS: Stand firm, sirs, if you'll be so kind.

AMPHITRYON: What? This sorry serf, only a minute since,
    Would not open the door though I stood there
    But gave me such abundant shameless lip
    All of it fit to have him nailed up high.
    Die, wretch!

SOSIAS: I'm dead already.

                    (He falls to his knees)

FIRST GENERAL: Calm yourself.

SOSIAS: Gentlemen! Ah!

SECOND GENERAL: What is it?

SOSIAS: Has he stabbed?

AMPHITRYON: Stand aside, I say again. Him there
    I must reward him, fully, for the insult
    He did me only a moment since.

SOSIAS: What can I have done wrong now when
    These last nine hours of the clock
    I was, as you commanded, in the camp?

FIRST GENERAL: It is the truth. He invited us to dine
    With you. He left the camp two hours ago
    And never our sight.

AMPHITRYON: Who gave you this command?

SOSIAS: Who? You did. You yourself.

AMPHITRYON: When? Me!

SOSIAS: When you
    Were reconciled, you and Alcmene,
    And you were full of joy and called at once
    Throughout the palace for a celebration.

AMPHITRYON: O heaven, every hour and every step
    Into the labyrinth leads me deeper and deeper.
    Dear friends, what must I think of it?
    Are you informed of what has happened here?

SECOND GENERAL: What this man told us is so little
    Suited to being grasped that your concern
    For now must be, boldly and quickly
    To rip the riddle's whole deceiving mesh.

AMPHITRYON:
    We'll do it then. And I need your assistance.
    My lucky star has led you here to me.

I stake my happiness, my whole life's, now.
Here in my heart I burn to be enlightened
And oh I fear it as a man fears death.
                    (*He knocks*)

ACT III, Scene 5

(Enter JUPITER)

JUPITER: What is this noise I have to come down for?
  Who's knocking at my door? Is it you, comrades?
AMPHITRYON: Who are you? Oh, you almighty gods!
SECOND GENERAL: O heaven,
  What am I seeing? Two Amphitryons!
AMPHITRYON:
  My soul is stiff with terror through and through.
  This solves the riddle. Oh, my unhappy soul.
FIRST GENERAL: Which of the two of you is Amphitryon?
SECOND GENERAL:
  Two beings so made in one another's image,
  Truly, no human eye can tell between them.
SOSIAS: Gentlemen, this one is Amphitryon.
  The other's a rogue, deserving punishment.
                    (*He goes and stands by* JUPITER)
FIRST GENERAL: (*pointing at Amphitryon*)
  Not credible! And this one here a cheat?
AMPHITRYON: Enough enchantment. It demeans me.
  The time has come to end the mystery.
                    (*He lays his hand on his sword*)
FIRST GENERAL: Stop!
AMPHITRYON: Stand aside!
SECOND GENERAL: What do you mean?
AMPHITRYON: I mean
  To punish a foul deception. Stand aside!
JUPITER: Control yourself. You insist too much.
  A man so worried about his name
  Will have poor grounds for bearing it.
SOSIAS: I say so too. He has filled his belly out
  And put some colour on his face, the impostor,
  To impersonate the master of the house.
AMPHITRYON: Traitor! For your outrageous mouthings
  Three hundred lashes will be the punishment

Dealt you by three men taking turns.
SOSIAS: Ho, ho. My master is a man of spirit.
He'll teach you not to beat his people.
AMPHITRYON: Stand back, I say, and let me rinse
The insult away in that impostor's heartblood.
FIRST GENERAL: Forgive us, sir. We can't allow
This combat of Amphitryon with Amphitryon.
AMPHITRYON: What? You ... you can't allow ...?
FIRST GENERAL: You must compose yourself.
AMPHITRYON: Generals, is that your friendship for me?
That the support you promised? You who should
Get me revenge yourselves for my dishonour
You take the impostor's wicked part
And halt the just fall of the sword of vengeance?
FIRST GENERAL: If your judgement were free, as it is not,
You would allow the rightness of our conduct.
Which of the two of you is Amphitryon?
You are. Very well. But he is likewise.
We need a god to indicate with a finger
In which identical two bodies lurks
In hiding an impostor's heart.
When that is done we shall, don't doubt it,
Know also where our vengeance must be aimed.
However, so long as here the sword's edge
Could only flail and choose its object blindly
Better, without a doubt, we keep it sheathed.
Let us investigate the matter calmly
And if indeed you feel you are Amphitryon
As we in this queer case do hope
But on the other hand must also doubt
You will not find it harder than he would
To prove the fact and give us evidence.
AMPHITRYON: Me, prove the fact ...?
FIRST GENERAL: With telling evidence.
Nothing will be resolved until you do.
JUPITER: You are right, Photidas. And the like appearance
We see established here between us
Excuses you your faltering choice of me.
It will not anger me if I am weighed
Myself against him. I do renounce

The cowardly decision of the sword
And have in mind to summon all of Thebes
And in the packed assembly of the people
To demonstrate whose blood I am. Himself,
Him there, he shall acknowledge my royal line
And that in Thebes I am the lord. He shall
Bow down his features in the dust before me
And call the abundant fields of Thebes
And all the herds and flocks covering the pastures
All mine, and mine this house, and mine also
The mistress ruling quietly in its rooms.
The whole orb of the earth shall learn
That no disgrace has come upon Amphitryon.
And the suspicion of it that fool raised
Someone stands here who will annihilate it.
Soon all of Thebes will gather here, but come
Meanwhile, and favour with your presence
The feast Sosias called you to.

SOSIAS:

My heavens, I knew it. — With these words, gentlemen,
All the remaining doubts are blown away.
He is the real Amphitryon and in
His house at noon now you will feast yourselves.

AMPHITRYON: You just and everlasting gods!

Can any man be abased as low as this?
To have stolen from me by the wickedest impostor
Wife, honour, governance and name!
And friends tying my hands?

FIRST GENERAL: You must,

Whoever you are, be patient for a while.
In a few hours we shall know. And then
Speedily vengeance will be executed
And woe, I say, woe on the one it strikes.

AMPHITRYON:

Go, with your faint hearts! Honour the impostor!
Friends still remain to me other than you.
I shall still meet with men in Thebes
Whose hearts will feel with me the pain I have
And who will not deny me their avenging arms.

JUPITER: Very well. You call them. I shall wait for them.

AMPHITRYON:

You loudmouthed rogue, you will meanwhile
Make for the open country by the back door.
Still you will not run clear of my revenge.

JUPITER: You go and summon me your friends here.
Then I shall say a word or two, not now.

AMPHITRYON:

By Zeus, you are right, by the cloud god Zeus.
For it is certain I shall find you out.
A word or two is all you will say, fiend.
My sword will fill your throat up to the handle.

JUPITER: Summon your friends. I might say nothing.
I'll speak with looks if that is what you wish.

AMPHITRYON: Quickly away now or he will escape me.
Grant me, you gods, you must, the pleasure
Of sending him down to your hell today.
I shall come back here with a host of friends
All armed, and net the exits of this house
And like a wasp will press my sting
Into his heart, and suck, and then the winds
Will play with his dry bones to my contentment.

[*Exit* AMPHITRYON]

ACT III, Scene 6

JUPITER: Now gentlemen, if you will. Honour this house
By entering.

FIRST GENERAL: I swear to God, my wits
Are all at sea with this adventure

SOSIAS: Now call a truce with your astonishment
And feast and tipple till the morning comes.

[*Exit* JUPITER *and the* GENERALS]

ACT III, Scene 7

SOSIAS: What joy to sit myself down
And bravely when the talk
Turns to the war how I will tell my tale!
I long to speak about the fighting at
Pharissa and never in all my days
Did I have such a wolfish hunger.

ACT III, Scene 8

Enter MERCURY

MERCURY: Where to? You poke your shameless nose in here
As well, I see, crawling the kitchens.
SOSIAS: Beg pardon, no.
MERCURY: Be off, I tell you, you there, off.
Or do you want your headgear straightening out?
SOSIAS: Why? What? O generous and noble self,
Be calm. Go easy on Sosias,
Sosias. Why be so grimly set
On always coming at yourself with blows?
MERCURY: Are these your tricks again, you fit and good
For nothing, stealing the name from me,
Stealing the name Sosias from me?
SOSIAS: What's that? Heaven forbid, excellent self.
Would I be such a churl, so mean to you?
Have it, go halves in it, this name,
Have it, this piece of junk, all, if you like.
Even if Castor or Pollux was my name,
Brother of mine, would I not share it with you?
I let you be here in my master's house,
You let me likewise be in brotherly love,
And while the two Amphitryons
Jealously break each other's necks
Let the Sosiases sit down in harmony
Together and raise a glass and drink
Long life and happiness to the both of them.
MERCURY: Oh no. — The idea of it. Insanity.
And me chew nothing but my fingernails?
The table's set for one.
SOSIAS: Nevertheless
One mother's womb gave birth to us,
One little house was shelter for us both,
We slept together in one bed, were clothed
As one, as brothers, and dealt one fate
So let us eat our victuals off one plate.
MERCURY: This bond is news to me. I've been
All on my own since boyhood
And never shared a bed nor any clothing
Nor any bite of bread.

SOSIAS: Think back on it.
  We are two twin brothers.
  You are the elder, I make do with less.
  In all things you have precedence over me.
  You take the first and all the odd numbers,
  The second spoon and all the even, I take.
MERCURY: Oh no. I need my whole ration
  And anything left over I shall save.
  I'd show him what was what, by God I would,
  Who pushed his fingers anywhere near my plate.
SOSIAS: Well let me be there as your shadow at least
  That falls behind you where you sit and eat.
MERCURY: Not even as my footstep in the sand.
  Be off.
SOSIAS: Heartless savage, steely thing
  Shaped on an anvil by a splitting thunderbolt!
MERCURY: Do you expect me like some journeyman
  To lie down in the grass outside the gates
  And live off nothing but fresh air?
  Great gods, no horse ever deserved
  An ample helping the way I do today.
  Didn't I come from camp here overnight?
  Wasn't I sent away again at daybreak
  To drum up company for the banquet?
  And on these hellish trips have I not worn
  My dutiful old legs down
  Almost to the hips with stepping out?
  There's sausage today and red cabbage warmed up.
  Exactly what I need to set me right.
SOSIAS: How right you are. And over the blasted
  Roots of pines criss-crossing the path
  You break your legs, as good as, and your neck.
MERCURY: Well then.
SOSIAS: — I am abandoned by the gods.
  So Charis has got sausages?
MERCURY: She has.
  Fresh ones. But not for you. They killed a pig.
  And I got Charis on my side again.
SOSIAS: Fine, fine. I lay me down and die. And cabbage?
MERCURY: Red cabbage, yes, warmed up. And anyone
  Whose mouth is watering over it he'll have

Charis and me to reckon with.
SOSIAS: Don't mind me.
Eat your cabbage. I hope you choke on it.
And keep your sausage. He who nourishes
The fowls of the air will nourish too, I'd say,
Honest old Sosias.
MERCURY: You still, impostor,
Give the name yourself, do you, you louse,
You dreg of everything, you dare ...?
SOSIAS: Not so.
Not me. I meant an elderly related
Sosias once a servant here
Who used to thrash the other servants. Then
One day some fellow fell from heaven, it seemed,
And threw him out, just on dinnertime.
MERCURY: I say one thing to you: be careful.
Be careful's my advice, unless you're happy
Not being among the living any longer.
SOSIAS: (*aside*) Wouldn't I knock you silly if I dared,
You born a bastard swindler you,
Puffed up with your own conceit!
MERCURY: What's that?
SOSIAS: What?
MERCURY: Seemed you were saying something.
SOSIAS: Me?
MERCURY: You.
SOSIAS: Not a peep.
MERCURY: Knocking a person silly, didn't I hear,
Unless I'm wrong, and born a bastard swindlers?
SOSIAS: A parrot. It will have been a parrot.
They chatter when the weather's fine.
MERCURY: Very well.
You are not dead yet. But if your back itches
I'll be indoors and you can ask for me.

                              [*Exit* MERCURY]

ACT III, Scene 9

SOSIAS: Damned cocky devil from hell, I hope
You die on it, the pig they slaughtered. Someone
Come near your plate, you'll show him will you?

I'd rather go shares with a bulldog
Than share a dish with him, he'd see his father
Starve to death in front of him
Sooner than let him have even as much
As lodges in your cavities when you chew.
— See though, it serves you right for being a traitor.
If I'd a sausage now in each hand here
I wouldn't take a bite at either one.
Leaving an honest man, my poor master,
When brute force drove him out of house and home!
— But there he comes with fighting friends already
— And here come droves of citizens. What is this?

ACT III, Scene 10

Enter AMPHITRYON *with* OFFICERS *from one side,*
CITIZENS *from the other*

AMPHITRYON: Welcome. Who summoned you, my friends?
CITIZEN: Heralds were crying throughout the city
  We were to congregate outside your palace.
AMPHITRYON: Heralds! And for what purpose?
CITIZEN: So we should witness, we were told,
  How one decisive utterance of your mouth
  Would solve the riddle that has thrown the town
  Wholly into consternation.
AMPHITRYON: (*to the* OFFICERS) What nerve he has!
  Could any brazenness be worse than this?
SECOND CITIZEN: He'll even show himself.
AMPHITRYON: So what? Let him.
FIRST OFFICER: Be easy. Argatiphontidas is here.
  Once I have got him in my sights
  He'll dance his dance of death over my sword.
AMPHITRYON: (*to the* CITIZENS)
  Listen to me, citizens of Thebes.
  You were not summoned here by me, although
  In droves assembling thus you are
  With all my heart welcome. He did it,
  The lying devil from hell who wants
  Me out of Thebes, out of my wife's heart,
  Out of the remembrance of the world and even,
  If he could do it, he would drive me out

Of the very stronghold of my consciousness.
Therefore collect your senses now and were you
Each an Argus* with a thousand eyes
Able at the midnight hour to recognize
A cricket by his traces in the sand
Still open wide — exert yourselves —
Your eyes as moles do now when they
At the hour of midday search after the sun.
Fling all these eye-glances into one lens
And bring to bear the whole full beam on me
Playing it up and down from head to toe
And tell me, utter it, and answer me:
Who am I?
CITIZENS: Who you are? Amphitryon.
AMPHITRYON:
Very well. Amphitryon. So be it. But when
That son of the dark appears there,
That monstrous human being on whose head
The curl of every hair is as on mine,
When your tricked senses in confusion cannot find
Even so small a mark as mothers need
To know their newest infants by
And when between us two as though between
Two drops of water you are required to choose
And one is sweet and pure and genuine and silver
And poison, trickery, murder, death the other,
Remember then, you citizens of Thebes,
That I am Amphitryon, the one who now
Snaps, so it droops, this helmet's plume.
CITIZENS: No, no. What are you doing? Spare the plume,
So long as we have you, thriving, in our sight.
SECOND OFFICER: Do you suppose we too ...?
AMPHITRYON: Friends, let me do it.
I feel in my right mind, know what I am at.
FIRST OFFICER:
Do as you wish. But meanwhile I shall hope
This foolery was not for my sake. Just because
Your generals showed hesitation here
When the ape appeared, Argatiphontidas
Is not the sort to follow suit. If we
Are needed in a matter of honour by a friend

What's wanted is to pull the helmet down
And close with the enemy. Leaving your man
Hours to shout his mouth off at you
Old women might. For my part I
Was always for the quickest way of doing things.
In cases of this kind best to begin
Directly and no ifs and buts, and stick
Your blade through him and out the other side.
Argatiphontidas will, in a word,
Show himself slaughterous today
And by no other hand, in the name of Ares,*
This rogue will bite the dust, you'll see, than mine.

AMPHITRYON: Forward then.

SOSIAS: I throw myself down at your feet,
O my real, noble, persecuted master.
Wholly I've come to realize it
And now await the punishment of my sins.
Beat, clout, thrash, poke and trample on me,
Put me to death, I will not murmur, promise.

AMPHITRYON: Get up. What has occurred?

SOSIAS: Of what was served
To eat not even a whiff of it they gave me.
The other me, servant of the other you,
The devil utterly possessed him once again.
In brief, I have been desosiatized
As you've been deamphitryonized.

AMPHITRYON: You hear this, citizens.

SOSIAS: Yes, Theban citizens!
Here is the real Amphitryon.
The one in there, sitting at table,
Is fit to be a meal himself, for crows.
Up now and storm the house, if you'll be so kind.
The cabbage won't be cold yet.

AMPHITRYON: Follow me.

SOSIAS: But look. He's coming out. Himself and her.

ACT III, Scene 11

Enter JUPITER, ALCMENE, MERCURY, CHARIS *and*
the GENERALS

ALCMENE: So cruel to me! A mortal man, you say,

And wish to shame me, showing me to his eyes?
CITIZENS: Eternal gods, what is it we see now?
JUPITER: The whole world, my beloved, must be shown
  That *nobody* came near your soul
  Except your husband, except Amphitryon.
AMPHITRYON:
  Lord of my life! Oh the unhappy woman!
ALCMENE:
  No one. Can you change things already happened?
OFFICERS: Olympian gods! There is Amphitryon.
JUPITER: Dearest, you owe it yourself, you owe it me.
  You *must*, you will, my life, force yourself to it.
  Come now, collect yourself, a triumph awaits you.
AMPHITRYON:
  God's bolts and devils of hell, must I see this?
JUPITER: Citizens of this town, I welcome you.
AMPHITRYON:
  Murderous fiend, they have come to butcher you.
  At him now!
                   (*He draws his sword*)
SECOND GENERAL: (*barring his way*) Halt.
AMPHITRYON: At him, Thebans, I say.
FIRST GENERAL: (*pointing at Amphitryon*)
  And I say seize him, Thebans, the impostor.
AMPHITRYON: Argatiphontidas!
FIRST OFFICER: Am I bewitched?
CITIZENS: Can any human eye distinguish here?
AMPHITRYON: Death! Devils! Rage without revenge!
  Annihilation!
                   (*He falls into* SOSIAS's *arms*)
JUPITER: Fool, hear a word or two.
SOSIAS: He hardly will, I promise you. He's dead.
FIRST OFFICER: What good's the drooping plume he broke?
  'Open your eyes like moles.' The one
  Is the one his own wife recognizes.
FIRST GENERAL: Officers, Amphitryon is standing here.
AMPHITRYON: (*waking*) Which does his own wife know?
FIRST OFFICER: She knows the one,
  She acknowledges the one she left the house with.
  Whom would she fasten round like vine tendrils
  Except her stock and stem, Amphitryon?

AMPHITRYON:
  Would there were strength enough left in me still
  To tread the tongue that said that in the dust.
  She doesn't acknowledge him.
                    (*He raises himself*)
FIRST GENERAL: You are a liar.
  Do you suppose you can confuse the people's judgement
  When they can see these things with their own eyes?
AMPHITRYON:
  She doesn't acknowledge him. I say it again!
  If she can recognize him for her husband
  Then I will not ask further who I *am*
  And I will greet him as Amphitryon.
FIRST GENERAL: So be it. Speak now.
SECOND GENERAL: Lady, declare yourself.
AMPHITRYON: Alcmene, wife of mine, declare yourself.
  Bestow on me the light of your eyes again.
  Say you acknowledge him as husband
  And swiftly, swiftly, as the flash of the thought itself
  This sword will free you from the sight of me.
FIRST GENERAL: So. Judgment is coming now.
SECOND GENERAL: Do you know him?
FIRST GENERAL: Do you know the stranger there?
AMPHITRYON: Can I suppose this breast unknown to you?
  Who have so often listened at the heart of it
  Counting the beats that beat with love for you?
  And this my speech, will you not recognize it
  That has so often been stolen by your eyes
  From off my lips before its utterance?
ALCMENE: Would I could sink into eternal night.
AMPHITRYON: I knew it. Citizens of Thebes, observe:
  Sooner will swift Peneus* flow upstream,
  Sooner the Bosporus* bed itself on Ida,*
  Sooner a dromedary travel over oceans
  Than she will recognize that stranger there.
CITIZENS: Can it be? She havers. Him Amphitryon?
FIRST GENERAL: Speak.
SECOND GENERAL: Say then.
THIRD GENERAL: Tell us.
SECOND GENERAL: Lady, say one word.
FIRST GENERAL: If she keeps silent longer we are lost.

JUPITER: Give truth, child, give the truth your voice.
ALCMENE: The one here, friends, he is Amphitryon.
AMPHITRYON: Him there Amphitryon! Almighty Gods!
FIRST GENERAL:
    Very well. Your lot is cast. Remove yourself.
AMPHITRYON: Alcmene!
SECOND GENERAL: Away, impostor! Unless you wish
    That we should execute the judgment on you.
AMPHITRYON: Beloved!
ALCMENE: Miscreant! Foul thing!
    You dare to call me by that name?
    Even in my husband's gaze that should compel
    Your fear have I no safety from your rage?
    You monstrous thing, filthier to me
    Than any swollen being that beds in swamps,
    What did I do to you that you approached me
    Under the covering of hell's own night
    And slavered your poison on my wings?
    What more than that I shone into your eyes,
    Still, like a glow-worm, evildoer?
    I see now what deceit deluded me.
    I needed the illumination of clear sunlight
    To tell the cheap build of a common serf
    From these royal limbs marshalled so splendidly
    And tell apart the dray horse and the stag.
    Oh curse the senses that surrendered
    To such coarse duping! Curse the heart
    That gives forth such false tones!
    Oh curse the soul not even good enough
    To mark her own beloved for herself!
    To the peaks of mountains I will run away
    Into a dead wasteland and have the visit
    Not even of the owl if there's no guardian
    To shield the heart of me from doing wrong. —
    Be off. Your mean deceit has worked
    And my soul's peace is bowed and broken-necked.
AMPHITRYON: Unlucky woman! Am I the one then
    Who in the night just past appeared to you?
ALCMENE: Enough, enough. Husband, release me now.
    Be merciful and shorten this
    Bitterest of my life's hours a little.

Let me escape these thousand eyes whose looks,
Converging on me, beat me down like clubs.
JUPITER: Goddess-like woman! More radiant than the sun!
A triumph awaits you such as never came
Before on any daughter of a noble house in Thebes.
You must remain a moment longer.

(To AMPHITRYON)

Now do you believe I am Amphitryon?
AMPHITRYON: Now do I believe you are Amphitryon?
You human creature — more terrible
Than breath of mine will reach to utter it! —
FIRST GENERAL: Impostor! What? Do you refuse?
SECOND GENERAL: Do you deny?
FIRST GENERAL:
Have you perhaps in mind to seek to prove
That we are lied to by this lady?
AMPHITRYON:
Oh all her words, each every one, is truthful.
Gold purified ten times is not so true.
If I read what the lightning inscribed
Into the night and thunder spoke to me
I would not trust that oracle so much
As what her never falsifying mouth has said.
Even I'll swear an oath now on the altar
And die the death forthwith seven times over
And nothing move me from my fixed belief
That he is Amphitryon to her.
JUPITER: Very well. You are Amphitryon.
AMPHITRYON: I am! —
Who then, ghost terrifying us, are you?
JUPITER: Amphitryon. I thought you knew it.
AMPHITRYON:
Amphitryon. No mortal man can grasp that.
Be so we understand.
ALCMENE: What has he said?
JUPITER: Amphitryon! You fool! Do you still doubt?
Argatiphontidas and Photidas,
The hill of Cadmus* and the land of Greece,
The light, the pure blue air, the watery element,
That which was there and is and always will be.
ALCMENE: Terror.

GENERALS: What sense has this event?
JUPITER: (*to Alcmene*)
  You think Amphitryon appeared to you?
ALCMENE: Leave me for ever thinking it. My soul
  Goes dark for ever if you enlighten me.
JUPITER:
  Cursed be the bliss you gave me as your gift
  If I must not be here for you for ever.
AMPHITRYON:
  Tell us in open language now. Who are you?
    (*Thunder and lightning. The scene is veiled in cloud. Out of
      the clouds an eagle descends, bearing a thunderbolt*)
JUPITER: Do you wish to know?
              (*He seizes the thunderbolt. The eagle flies away*)
CITIZENS: The gods!
JUPITER: Who am I?
GENERALS AND OFFICERS: Him in his terrible power! Jupiter!
ALCMENE: O gods of heaven, protect me!
              (*She falls into* AMPHITRYON'*s arms*)
AMPHITRYON: In the dust
  We worship you. You are the Thunderer,
  The Almighty. All I have is yours.
CITIZENS: Him! In the dust! Our faces in the dust!
    (*All throw themselves to the ground, except* AMPHITRYON)
JUPITER: It pleased Zeus being in your house,
  Amphitryon, and you shall have a sign
  Of his divine contentment.
  Now let your black griefs fly away from you
  And open your heart up to a triumph.
  What you, in me, did for yourself, will do you
  No harm with me in what I am eternally.
  If you will think my debt to you your recompense
  Then I will leave you with the farewell of a friend.
  Your fame henceforth will, like my world,
  Have limits only in the stars.
  If you are not contented by this thanks
  Very well: Your dearest wish shall be fulfilled
  And I give it a tongue to speak before me.
AMPHITRYON: No, I am not contented, Father Zeus!
  And for my heart's wish I will find my tongue.
  What you did once for Tyndarus, do

Also for Amphitryon: bestow a son,
Great as the children of Tyndarus, on him.
JUPITER: So be it. To you there will be born a son,*
And name him Hercules. In fame
No hero of the earlier world will touch him,
Not even my undying Dioscuri.
Twelve monstrous labours he will pile
Into a towering everlasting monument.
And when this pyramid, completed,
Raises its crown to the clouds' hem
Then he will mount the steps of it heavenwards
And on Olympus there I'll welcome in a god.
AMPHITRYON:
Thanks be. — And you won't steal her from me, here
Not breathing? Look.
JUPITER: She will remain for you
But if she is to you must leave her be. —
Hermes!
(*He is lost among the clouds which meanwhile have opened in
the heights to show the summit of Olympus on which the
Olympians are reclining*)
ALCMENE: Amphitryon!
MERCURY: Lord God, at once!
As soon as I have told that clown there
That I am weary of wearing
His ugly face and with ambrosia
Will wash it now off my Olympian cheeks;
That he was dealt blows fit for poets to sing;
And that I'm neither more nor less than Hermes,
The god whose feet have wings.

                                    [*Exit* MERCURY]

SOSIAS: I'd rather you had left me eternally
Unsung. In all my days I never saw
Such a bruiser, such a punisher.
FIRST GENERAL: Truly, such a triumph ...
SECOND GENERAL: So much fame ...
FIRST OFFICER: You see us touched to the heart ...
AMPHITRYON: Alcmene!
ALCMENE: Oh.

THE PRINCE OF HOMBURG
A Drama

ACT I

*Scene: Fehrbellin. A garden in the classical French style. In the
background a palace to which a slope ascends. — It is night*

Scene 1

The PRINCE OF HOMBURG, *bareheaded, his shirt open at the
neck, is sitting half awake, half asleep under an oak tree,
plaiting himself a wreath. — The* ELECTOR, *his wife,*
PRINCESS NATALIE, COUNT HOHENZOLLERN, CAVALRY
OFFICER GOLZ *and others emerge stealthily from the palace
and look down on him from the parapet above the slope. —*
PAGES *with torches*

COUNT HOHENZOLLERN:
   The Prince of Homburg, our brave cousin, who
   For three days at the cavalry's head
   Busily has harried the retreating Swedes
   And here at Fehrbellin,* at headquarters,
   Appeared only today, breathless:
   His orders are, from you, to linger here
   Three hours, no more, to feed and water,
   And then again, at once, against Wrangel*
   Dug in already, where he could, along the Rhyn,
   To push forward, into the Hackel Hills?
ELECTOR: Just so.
HOHENZOLLERN: The company commanders all
   Instructed then, after the plan, for leaving town
   At ten in the night, this duly done
   He flings himself down like a hunting dog,
   Panting, to let, in preparation for
   The battle awaiting us at crack of dawn,
   A little at least, his fagged limbs rest.
ELECTOR: I heard
   As much. — What then?
HOHENZOLLERN: Then when the hour strikes
   And all the cavalry are mounted
   And treading the field to mud outside the gates
   They are missing — whom? The Prince of Homburg, their
   Commander. He, our hero, being searched for with
   Torches, lights, lanterns, we find him — where?

(He takes a torch from a PAGE's *hand)*
See, as a sleepwalker, on that seat there
Where, in his sleep, though you would not believe me,
The moonlight lured him, occupied, dreaming,
As though he were his own posterity,
Plaiting himself the glorious wreath of fame.
ELECTOR: What!
HOHENZOLLERN: Truly. Look down here. See where he sits.
(He shines the light down from the balustrade on to the
PRINCE)
ELECTOR: Sunk in his sleep? Impossible.
HOHENZOLLERN: Fast asleep.
Call him by name and he will fall to the ground.
(Pause)
ELECTRESS: The young man's ill. So much is obvious.
NATALIE: He needs a doctor ...
ELECTRESS: One ought to help, I'd say,
Not use the moment to make fun of him.
HOHENZOLLERN: *(giving back the torch)*
You ladies pity him but he is as fit,
By God, and well as I am myself. Tomorrow
The Swedes when we meet them will find that out.
It is nothing more, I give you my word on it,
Than a mere bad habit of his mind.
ELECTOR: Well, well. This seemed far-fetched. — Follow me,
                                           friends,
And let us look at him more closely.
(They come down the slope)
A COURTIER: *(to the* PAGES) Keep the torches back.
HOHENZOLLERN: Let be, let be.
The whole place might go up in flames
And still his mind feel no more of it
Than would the diamond he wears on his finger.
(They surround him, the PAGES *illuminate him with their*
torches)
ELECTOR: *(bending over him)*
What leaves are they he's plaiting? — Willow leaves?
HOHENZOLLERN: Willow, sir? — These are laurel leaves
As he has seen them in the portraits of the heroes
Hung in the armoury in Berlin.
ELECTOR: — Where did he find a laurel in my sandy land?

HOHENZOLLERN:
  There you must ask the just gods for an answer.
COURTIER: In the garden perhaps, behind. The gardener
  Cultivates other foreign plants there too.
ELECTOR: Strange, by heaven. But all the same I know
  What's working in the heart of this young fool.
HOHENZOLLERN: Tomorrow's battle, sir, that's what.
  I'll wager in his mind he sees astronomers
  Already plaiting him a victory wreath of stars.
                    (The PRINCE contemplates the wreath)
COURTIER: Now he has done.
HOHENZOLLERN: A pity, such a pity
  There is no mirror here to hand. As vain
  As any girl he would approach it
  And try the wreath on now this way, now that
  As she would try a flowery bonnet.
ELECTOR: By God, I must find out how far he'll go.
    (The ELECTOR takes the wreath from his hand; the PRINCE
    blushes and looks at him. The ELECTOR winds his chain
    of office around the wreath and gives it to the PRINCESS;
    excitedly the PRINCE gets to his feet. The ELECTOR backs
    away with the PRINCESS, who has lifted up the wreath;
      the PRINCE follows her with outstretched arms)
HOMBURG: (in a whisper) Natalie! Beloved girl! My bride!
ELECTOR: Quick, come away!
HOHENZOLLERN: The fool! What is he saying?
COURTIER: What did he say?
                  (All go back up the slope)
HOMBURG: Friedrich! My prince! Oh, Father!
HOHENZOLLERN: Hell and devils!
ELECTOR: (backing away)   Open the gate!
HOMBURG: Oh, Mother!
HOHENZOLLERN: Madman. He is ...
ELECTRESS: Who does he mean by this?
HOMBURG: (reaching out for the wreath)
  Natalie, dearest, why do you run away?
          (He tears a glove from the PRINCESS's hand)
HOHENZOLLERN: Merciful heaven, what was that he seized?
COURTIER: The wreath?
NATALIE: No, no.
HOHENZOLLERN: (opening the gate)

Quickly, in here, your majesty,
So all the image will vanish for him again.
ELECTOR: Back into nothingness, Sir Prince of Homburg!
Nothingness! Nothingness! On the field of battle,
If you will be so kind, we'll meet again.
Such things are not attainable by dreaming.
(*They exit, the gate clangs shut in front of the* PRINCE. *Pause*)

Scene 2

(*The* PRINCE OF HOMBURG, *with a look of wonderment on
his face, stands for a moment outside the gate; then, deep in
thought and pressing the hand holding the glove against his
forehead, he comes down the slope; but turns as soon as he is
down, and looks back up at the gate*)

Scene 3

(COUNT HOHENZOLLERN *enters from below, through a trellis
gate.* A PAGE *comes after him*)
PAGE: (*softly*)
Count, listen to me, will your lordship, please.
HOHENZOLLERN: (*impatiently*)
Hush with your chatter. — What then?
PAGE: I am sent ...
HOHENZOLLERN:
You mind he doesn't wake up with your noise.
— Well then. What is it?
PAGE: Sent by the Elector here.
He orders you you must not say a word
To the Prince when he awakes about the joke
He allowed himself with him a moment since.
HOHENZOLLERN: (*softly*)
Well, well. You go and curl up in a cornfield
And sleep your sleep. I knew not to. Be off.

[*Exit the* PAGE]

Scene 4

HOHENZOLLERN: (*positioning himself at a little distance
behind the* PRINCE *who is still staring fixedly up the slope*)
Arthur!

(The PRINCE *falls down)*

Down he goes; a bullet would do no better.

(He approaches him)

Now I am curious to hear the tale
He will invent to explain to me why he
Lay down and slept in this place.

(He bends over him)

Hey!

Arthur! Are you insane? What are you doing here
And how and why in the middle of the night?

HOMBURG: Oh, my dear friend.

HOHENZOLLERN: I say now, really!
The cavalry you are commander of
Are gone ahead an hour already
And you, you lie here in the garden, sleeping!

HOMBURG: What cavalry?

HOHENZOLLERN: The Mamelukes!* — As true
As I am standing here he has forgotten
He is commander of the cavalry of Brandenburg.

HOMBURG: *(getting to his feet)*
Quickly! My helmet! The armour!

HOHENZOLLERN: Yes, where are they?

HOMBURG:
There, on the right, Heinz — right — there on the stool.

HOHENZOLLERN: Where? On the stool?

HOMBURG: Yes there. I thought I laid ...

HOHENZOLLERN: *(looking at him)*
Then take them up again from off the stool.

HOMBURG: — What is this glove?*

(He stares at the glove in his hand)

HOHENZOLLERN: And how should I know that?
(Aside) Be damned! He took it unbeknown up there
From off the niece's, the Princess's, arm.
(Abruptly) Hurry now, come. Why are you dallying?

HOMBURG: *(throwing the glove aside)*   Coming.
Hey Franz! The scoundrel! He was told to wake me.

HOHENZOLLERN: *(looking at him)* Mad, he is raving mad.

HOMBURG: I swear to God,
Heinrich I cannot, friend, tell where I am.

HOHENZOLLERN:
In Fehrbellin, you muddle-minded dreamer,

In one of the byways of the garden
That lies extensively behind the palace.
HOMBURG: (*aside*)
I wish the night would swallow me. Again
I have been wandering in the moonlight unawares.
                    (*He pulls himself together*)
Forgive me. Now I know. The heat last night,
You know, was hardly to be borne in bed.
I crept into the garden here exhausted
And when the night enfolded me so sweetly
Blonde-haired, running with scents, oh as
A Persian bride receives her groom,
I lay down in her lap. — But now
What time is it?
HOHENZOLLERN: Half past eleven.
HOMBURG: And
The squadrons, did you say, have ridden off?
HOHENZOLLERN:
Of course. At ten. As it was planned they should.
Princess Natalie's own regiment,
I do not doubt it, at their head
Already will have reached the heights of Hackelwitz
Where in the morning, facing Wrangel, they must cover,
The stealthy moving forward of our forces.
HOMBURG: No matter. Old Kottwitz has command of them
And he knows all the intentions of this move.
Besides, I should have had to come back here
To headquarters, at two in the morning,
Because we must be given our orders still.
Thus it was better staying where I was.
Come, let's be gone. The Elector knows nothing?
HOHENZOLLERN:
How could he? In bed long since and sleeping.
    (*They are about to leave when the* PRINCE *stops short, turns
            round and picks up the glove*)
HOMBURG: Such a strange dream I dreamed! — It was as if
Radiant with gold and silver
Suddenly a sovereign's palace opened
And from on high down a slope of marble
A company descended to me
Of all the people my heart loves, the Elector,

Her royal wife Elisa and — the third,
—   What was her name?
HOHENZOLLERN: Whose?
HOMBURG:
(*He seems to be searching*) Hers, the one I mean.
A man born mute would still be able to name her.
HOHENZOLLERN: The Platen girl?
HOMBURG: No, no.
HOHENZOLLERN: Or Ramin's girl?
HOMBURG: My dear friend, no, not so.
HOHENZOLLERN: '   Or Bork or Winterfeld?
HOMBURG: No, no. I beg you. You can't see the pearl
For the ring in which the pearl is set.
HOHENZOLLERN:
Be damned then. Tell me. Can we guess her face?
— What lady do you mean?
HOMBURG: No matter. No matter.
The name, since I awoke, has gone from me
And for an understanding does not matter.
HOHENZOLLERN: Good. Then continue.
HOMBURG: But do not interrupt. —
And he, the Elector, with the brow of Zeus,
He held a crown of laurel in his hand
And stood himself close up before my face
And wound, so fully to inflame my soul,
The chain around, that hangs about his neck,
And proffered it, to set it on my head ...
Oh, my dear friend!
HOLLENZOLLERN: To whom?
HOMBURG: Ah, friend!
HOLLENZOLLERN: Say, then.
HOMBURG: — Probably it was the Platen girl.
HOLLENZOLLERN: Platen? Her? The one gone into Prussia?
HOMBURG: The Platen girl. No doubt. Or Ramin's girl.
HOHENZOLLERN: Ah, her! Ramin's, the redhead. — Platen,
The one with eyes like violets and rascally
We know you like her.
HOMBURG: Yes I do like her. —
HOHENZOLLERN:
And she, you say, she offered you the wreath?
HOMBURG: Lifting it up, up high, she seemed to be

The spirit of fame, and with the wreath, from which
The chain dangled, to wish to crown a hero.
I reached, more moved than I can say,
I reached my hands out to seize hold of it
And would have fallen at her feet
But as a sweet haze floating over valleys
Will be dispersed by a fresh wind's breath
So all the group, climbing the slope, eluded me.
The slope, when I begin it, endlessly
Continues, to the very gates of heaven,
And I grasp left and right around me
Anxious to seize on one of them so dear to me.
In vain! Suddenly the palace opens,
A blinding light, flashed from within, engulfs them,
The gates fit back together with a rattle,
Only a glove, in my pursuit and roughly
I peeled from the arm of that same dream shape
And here a glove, O you almighty gods,
When I awoke I was holding in my hand.

HOHENZOLLERN:
Be damned you were. — And now the glove, you think,
It must be hers.

HOMBURG: Whose?

HOHENZOLLERN: Platen's girl, of course.

HOMBURG: Platen's, of course. Indeed. Or Ramin's girl. —

HOHENZOLLERN: (*laughing*)
You and your visions. What a rogue you are.
Who knows what idle interlude indeed
Spent wideawake here, flesh and blood,
Has left this glove still clinging to your hand.

HOMBURG: What, mine? By the one I love ...!

HOHENZOLLERN: Be damned
What do I care? Say it was Platen's girl
Or else Ramin's. Sunday the post goes out to Prussia
And you can find out soonest that way
Whether your ladylove's missing this glove. —
Come now. It's twelve. Why are we chattering here?

HOMBURG: (*sunk in his own dreams*)
— You are right. Let us go to bed.
But what I meant to ask you, my dear friend,
Was whether the Elector's wife is here and her

Pretty niece still, the Princess of Orange,
Who joined us in the camp not long ago?
HOHENZOLLERN: And why? I do believe the fool ...
HOMBURG: Why?
I was to send them thirty troopers
To escort them out from where the fighting is.
I had to give Ramin orders about it.
HOHENZOLLERN:
Oh, them! They've gone long since. Gone or about to.
At least, Ramin, all ready for departure,
Stood at the gates the whole night through.
But come. It's twelve. Before the battle starts
I'd like to rest myself a little yet.

[*Both exit*]

Scene 5

*Scene: Fehrbellin, a room in the palace. Firing is heard in the
distance. The* ELECTOR'S WIFE *and* PRINCESS NATALIE,
dressed for travelling, led by a COURTIER, *enter and seat
themselves to one side.* LADIES-IN-WAITING. *Then enter the*
ELECTOR, FIELD MARSHAL DÖRFLING, *the* PRINCE OF
HOMBURG *wearing the glove in his collar,* COUNT
HOHENZOLLERN, COUNT TRUCHSS, COLONEL HENNINGS,
CAVALRY OFFICER GOLZ *and several other* GENERALS,
COLONELS *and* OFFICERS

ELECTOR: What is that firing? — Is it Götz?
DÖRFLING: Colonel Götz, your majesty?
Who took the advance guard forward yesterday.
He has already sent an officer
To set your mind at rest on this at once.
A Swedish company, of a thousand men,
Has made a move into the Hackel Hills
But Götz stands surety to you for these hills
And says, through me, you may of course proceed
As though his vanguard had already taken them.
ELECTOR: (*to the* OFFICERS)
Gentlemen, the Marshal knows the plan of battle.
Be ready will you, please, to take it down.
        (*The* OFFICERS *gather on the other side around the* FIELD
        MARSHAL *and take out their writing tablets*)

ELECTOR: (*turning to the* COURTIER)
Ramin is waiting with the carriage?
COURTIER: This moment, sir. — They are hitching up.
ELECTOR: (*seating himself behind his wife and the* PRINCESS)
Ramin will be my dear Elisa's escort
And thirty brave riders with him.
You are going to Kalkhuhn's house, my chancellor's,
Near Havelberg, across the Havel river,
Where not a Swedish soldier now remains.
ELECTRESS: And is the ferry there restored?
ELECTOR: At Havelberg? — The matter is in hand.
Also, it will be light before you get there.
(Pause)
Natalie is so quiet, my darling girl?
— What ails you, child?
NATALIE: I feel afraid, Uncle.
ELECTOR: And yet my little girl is very safe.
She was not safer in her mother's womb.
(Pause)
ELECTRESS: When, do you think, shall we be reunited?
ELECTOR: If God grants me my victory as I do not doubt
He will, perhaps in a day or two.
(PAGES enter and serve the ladies a breakfast. — FIELD
MARSHAL DÖRFLING is dictating. — The PRINCE OF
HOMBURG, pencil and writing tablet in hand, is staring
at the LADIES)
DÖRFLING: The aim of the plan of battle, gentlemen,
Devised by his majesty the Elector, is
Wholly to fragment the fleeing Swedish army
By severing them from the bridgehead
They cover their backs with now on the Rhyn river.*
Colonel Hennings ...
HENNINGS: Here!
(He begins to write)
DÖRFLING: Who has command today,
By the Elector's wish, of the right wing of our army,
Stealthily through the wooded Hackel valley
Will seek to round the enemy's left wing
Get boldly between him and the three bridges
And in conjunction with Count Truchss —
Count Truchss!

TRUCHSS: Here!
                        (He begins to write)
DÖRFLING: In conjunction with Count Truchss —
                        (He pauses)
Who on the heights meanwhile, facing Wrangel,
Has taken up position with the cannon ...
TRUCHSS: *(writing)* Position with the cannon ...
DÖRFLING: Have you written that?
                        (He continues)
Will seek to drive the Swedes into the marshes
Lying behind their right wing.
                        Enter a FOOTMAN
FOOTMAN: Madam, the carriage is at the door.
                        (The LADIES *rise)*
DÖRFLING: The Prince of Homburg ...
ELECTOR: *(also rising)*   — Is Ramin ready?
FOOTMAN: Already mounted and waiting at the gate.
        (The LADIES *and* GENTLEMEN *take leave of one another)*
TRUCHSS: *(writing)* Lying behind their right wing.
DÖRFLING: The Prince of Homburg ...
Where is the Prince of Homburg?
HOHENZOLLERN: *(in a whisper)* Arthur!
HOMBURG: *(with a start)*   Here!
HOHENZOLLERN: Have you lost your wits?
HOMBURG: Your orders, Field Marshal?
        *(He blushes, presents himself with pencil and paper and begins
                        to write)*
DÖRFLING:
To whom his majesty the Elector as at Rathenow*
Once again entrusts the glorious
Command of all the cavalry of Brandenburg ...
                        (He pauses)
But without prejudice to Colonel Kottwitz
Who will be at his side and counsel him ...
                (Aside to CAVALRY OFFICER GOLZ*)*
Is Kottwitz here?
GOLZ: Field Marshal, no, he is not.
He sent me in his stead, do you see,
To hear the battle orders from your mouth.
                (The PRINCE *is again staring across at the ladies)*

DÖRFLING: (*continuing*)
Takes up position near the village of Hackelwitz
On the flat, facing the enemy's right wing,
And out of range of cannon shot.
GOLZ: (*writing*) And out of range of cannon shot.
(*The* ELECTOR'S WIFE *is fastening a scarf around the*
PRINCESS'S *neck. The* PRINCESS, *about to put on her gloves,*
looks about her as if she were missing something)
ELECTOR: (*going up to her*) What is it, child?
ELECTRESS: Have you lost something?
NATALIE: I don't know, Aunt, my glove ...
(*They all look about them*)
ELECTOR: (*to the* LADIES-IN-WAITING)   Ladies,
Be good enough to help her, will you?
ELECTRESS: (*to the* PRINCESS) It's in your hand, child.
NATALIE: The right. Where is the left?
ELECTOR: Would it be in the bedroom still perhaps?
NATALIE: Dear Bork, will you ...?
ELECTOR: (*to the girl*)   Be quick.
NATALIE: On the mantelpiece.
(*Exit* LADY-IN-WAITING)
HOMBURG: (*to himself*) My living soul! Did I hear aright?
(*He takes the glove out of his collar*)
DÖRFLING: (*consulting a paper in his hand*)
And out of range of cannon shot ...
(*He continues*)
His Highness will ...
HOMBURG: She is looking for the glove ...
(*He looks from the glove to the* PRINCESS *and back again*)
DÖRFLING: By the Elector's express command ...
GOLZ: (*writing*) By the Elector's express command ...
DÖRFLING: Whatever be the course the battle takes
Not quit the spot he has been ordered to ...
HOMBURG: — Quickly, to find out is it hers.
(*He drops his handkerchief and with it the glove; picks up*
his handkerchief but leaves the glove lying where anyone may
see it)
DÖRFLING: (*in some surprise*) What is his Highness doing?
HOHENZOLLERN: (*in a whisper*)   Arthur!
HOMBURG: Here!
HOHENZOLLERN: Are you possessed?

HOMBURG: Your orders, Field Marshal?
(He takes up his writing things again. DÖRFLING *looks at him*
curiously for a moment. — Pause)
GOLZ: *(as he finishes writing)*
Not quit the spot he has been ordered to ...
DÖRFLING: *(continues)*
Until, being pressed by Hennings and by Truchss ...
HOMBURG: *(aside to* GOLZ *and looking at what he has written)*
Who? My dear Golz! What? Me?
GOLZ: Yes, you. Who else?
HOMBURG: I must not quit ...?
GOLZ: Indeed not.
DÖRFLING: Well? All clear?
HOMBURG: *(aloud)*
Not quit the spot I have been ordered to ...
                                   (He writes)
DÖRFLING: Until, being pressed by Hennings and by Truchss ...
                                   (He pauses)
The enemy's left wing, coming undone,
Collapses on his right and all his ranks,
Then faltering, crowd into the pastures
And in the marshes there threaded with ditches
The plan, precisely, is to annihilate them.
ELECTOR: Pages, some light! — My darlings, let me lead you.
         (He makes to leave with his WIFE *and the* PRINCESS*)*
DÖRFLING: Then he will sound the trumpet for the charge.
ELECTRESS: *(since some of the officers are bowing to her)*
Gentlemen, goodbye. Don't let us interrupt.
         *(*FIELD MARSHAL DÖRFLING *likewise bows to her)*
ELECTOR: *(suddenly halting)*
Look there! The lady's glove. Quick! Lying there.
COURTIER: Where?
ELECTOR: At the Prince's, at our cousin's, feet.
HOMBURG: *(courteously)*
At mine? I beg your pardon. Is this yours?
         (He picks up the glove and brings it to the PRINCESS*)*
NATALIE: I am grateful to you, Prince.
HOMBURG: *(confused)*   Is this glove yours?
NATALIE: Mine, yes. The one that I was missing.
                 (She takes it from him and puts it on)
ELECTRESS: *(to the* PRINCE *as they leave)*

Farewell. Farewell. Good luck and blessings on you.
See that we soon and happily meet again.
          [Exit the ELECTOR *with the* WOMEN. LADIES-IN-WAITING,
                              COURTIERS *and* PAGES *follow]*
HOMBURG: *(stands for a moment as though thunderstruck; then,*
   with a triumphant step, re-enters the circle of the OFFICERS)
Then he will sound the trumpet for the charge!
                    (He pretends to write)
DÖRFLING: *(consulting his papers)*
Then he will sound the trumpet for the charge. —
However, the Elector, so there shall not be
Misunderstanding and the assault be premature ...
                    (He pauses)
GOLZ: *(writing)*
Misunderstanding and the assault be premature ...
HOMBURG: *(to* HOHENZOLLERN, *aside and in great agitation)*
Oh, Heinrich!
HOHENZOLLERN: *(impatiently)*
          Well? What is it? What is it you want?
HOMBURG: Did you not see?
HOHENZOLLERN: See what? For God's sake hush.
DÖRFLING: *(continues)*
Will send an officer to him from his suite
And he — note this — will bring him
The express command to attack the enemy.
Sooner than that he will not sound the charge.
                    (The PRINCE *stands in a dream)*
Noted?
GOLZ: *(writing)*
          Sooner than that he will not sound the charge.
DÖRFLING: *(raising his voice)*
Your Highness, have you ...?
HOMBURG: Field Marshal?
DÖRFLING: I ask have you noted that?
HOMBURG: Sounding the charge?
HOHENZOLLERN: *(aside, impatiently, vehemently)*
The charge! Be damned! You do not, not till he ...
GOLZ: *(likewise)* Till he himself ...
HOMBURG: *(interrupting them)*   Of course not. Not until ...
But then he'll sound the trumpet for the charge.
                    (He writes. — Pause)

DÖRFLING: If Colonel Kottwitz, Baron Golz, note this,
  Can make it possible I wish to speak to him
  Before our forces are engaged, in person.
GOLZ: (*pointedly*) I will inform him. Be assured of that.
                        (*Pause*)
ELECTOR: (*returning*) Well, generals and colonels, first light
  Is in the sky. — Are the orders taken down?
DÖRFLING: It is accomplished, sir. Your plan of battle
  Exactly allocated to your generals.
ELECTOR: (*taking up his hat and gloves*)
  Prince Friedrich, my advice to you is: steady.
  Not long since, you remember, on the Rhine
  You threw away two victories. Curb yourself
  And don't deprive me of a third today.
  For nothing less than throne and empire rest on it.
  (*To the* OFFICERS) Come then. — Hey, Franz!
GROOM: (*entering*)   Here!
ELECTOR: Quickly, my white horse!
  — Let me be in the field before the sun is.
              [*Exit.* GENERALS, COLONELS and OFFICERS *follow him*]

<hr>

Scene 6

HOMBURG: (*to front stage*)
  Fortune, oh vast good fortune, now a breath
  Has raised your veil, and lifts
  It like a sail, roll on your wheel my way.
  You have touched the hair of my head lightly already
  And from your horn of plenty, smiling,
  Already in passing thrown me down a pledge.
  Today I'll seek you on the battlefield,
  Child of the gods, fleeting, and seize and tip
  Your blessing at my feet, the whole of it,
  No matter were you fastened sevenfold
  With iron chains to the Swedes' triumphant chariots.

                                              [*Exit*]

ACT II

Scene 1

Battlefield near Fehrbellin. Enter, leading the cavalry, COLONEL
KOTTWITZ, COUNT HOHENZOLLERN, CAVALRY OFFICER
GOLZ *and other* OFFICERS

KOTTWITZ: *(still offstage)* Cavalry, halt here! Dismount!

HOHENZOLLERN AND GOLZ: *(entering)*   Halt! — Halt!

KOTTWITZ:
Which of you gentlemen will help me from my horse?

HOHENZOLLERN AND GOLZ: Coming, old friend!

                            [They exit again]

KOTTWITZ: *(still offstage)*   Thank you. — The devil! Ouf!
A noble son to each of you who will
Do you a like service when you decay.
  (He enters, HOHENZOLLERN, GOLZ *and others following him)*
Yes, on a horse I feel I am full of youth
When I get off though such a quarrel begins
As if body and soul were parting company.
           (He looks about him)
Where is the Prince, our leader?

HOHENZOLLERN: His Highness
Will join you soon.

KOTTWITZ: Where is he?

HOHENZOLLERN:
He rode into the village that you came past.
The trees hide it. He will be back at once.

OFFICER: I hear in the night he tumbled with his horse.

HOHENZOLLERN: I believe he did.

KOTTWITZ: He fell?

HOHENZOLLERN: *(turning)*   It was nothing.
His black horse reared up at the mill. However
He slid off lightly sideways
And did himself no injury at all.
There's not a shadow of a cause for worry.

KOTTWITZ: *(climbing a rise)*
A beautiful day, true as I live and breathe,
A day the Lord God of our world has made
For sweeter things than fighting. Through the clouds
There is a faint red shimmer of sunshine
And feelings flutter upwards with the lark

Carolling to the scented limpid sky. —
GOLZ: Did you find Marshal Dörfling?
KOTTWITZ: (*coming forward*)   Damn me, no.
  What was his excellency thinking of?
  Am I an arrow or a bird or thought
  That can be hurtled over all the battlefield?
  I tried the vanguard on the Hackel Heights
  And in the Hackel Valley tried the rearguard
  And found, whoever else I found, no marshal.
  That done, I found my regiment again.
GOLZ: He will be very sorry. It seems he had
  Something to impart to you that mattered.
OFFICER: Here comes the Prince, our leader.

Scene 2

Enter the PRINCE OF HOMBURG *with a black kerchief around
his left hand*

KOTTWITZ:
  Greetings, my young and noble Prince. See here
  How I, whilst you were in the village,
  Have ranged our horsemen where the road dips down.
  You will, I think, not be displeased with me.
HOMBURG: Good morning, Kottwitz. — Friends, good morning.
  Whatever you do, you know that I commend it.
HOHENZOLLERN:
  What were you doing, Arthur, in the village?
  You seem so serious.
HOMBURG: I ... was in the church.
  It caught the light among the village's quiet trees,
  The bells were ringing as we passed
  For early service. I was moved
  To kneel among them praying at the altar.
KOTTWITZ: A godfearing young man, I must say.
  The work, believe me, that begins with prayer
  Salvation, fame and victory will crown it.
HOMBURG: Something I had to say to you, Heinrich ...
            (*He leads Hohenzollern forward a little*)
  What was the thing concerning me that Dörfling
  Gave out last night when we were being briefed?
HOHENZOLLERN: — You were distracted. That was obvious.

HOMBURG:

Distracted ... split. I don't know what was wrong.

Being dictated to confuses me. —

HOHENZOLLERN:

— Happily this time nothing much for you.

Hennings and Truchss, commanding the infantry,

The assault on the enemy is their business,

And what is asked of you is to bide here

In the dip, with the cavalry, all ready

Until you are sent the order to attack.

HOMBURG: (*after a pause in which, head bowed, he has been dreaming*)

A strange event!

HOHENZOLLERN: Which, my dear friend?

(*He looks at him. — A cannon fires*)

KOTTWITZ: Hark at that, gentlemen! Mount! Mount!

That will be Hennings. The battle has begun.

(*They all climb a slope*)

HOMBURG: What is it? Who?

HOHENZOLLERN: Colonel Hennings, Arthur,

Who has got by stealth behind the back of Wrangel.

Come up, from here you oversee it all.

GOLZ: (*on the hillock*)

Look how he menaces along the Rhyn.

HOMBURG: (*shielding his eyes*)

— And that is Hennings there on our right flank?

FIRST OFFICER: It is, your Highness.

HOMBURG: In hell's name, why?

Yesterday, surely, he was on our left.

(*Distant cannon fire*)

KOTTWITZ: God's thunder! Look: from a dozen mouths

How Wrangel works his fire on Hennings!

FIRST OFFICER: The Swedes are well dug in.

SECOND OFFICER: My God they are.

They've thrown up walls almost as high

As the church tower in the village at their backs.

(*Firing close by*)

GOLZ: That's Truchss!

HOMBURG: Who? Truchss?

KOTTWITZ: Indeed yes, Truchss

From forward now going to Hennings's aid.

HOMBURG:

How comes it Truchss today is in the centre?

(Violent cannonade)

GOLZ: Heavens, look there! Is that the village burning?

THIRD OFFICER: God's truth, it is.

FIRST OFFICER: On fire! On fire!

The flames are up around the tower already.

GOLZ: Look at their runners scurrying everywhere!

SECOND OFFICER: They are moving out!

KOTTWITZ: Where?

FIRST OFFICER: Their right flank. —

THIRD OFFICER: Indeed. In columns. With three regiments.

It seems they want to reinforce their left.

SECOND OFFICER: I swear to God! And cavalry moving up

To give the advance of their right wing some cover.

HOHENZOLLERN: *(laughing)*

Ha! They'll vacate the place again

When they see us here hidden in the hollow.

(Musket fire)

KOTTWITZ: Look, comrades, look!

SECOND OFFICER: And hearken!

FIRST OFFICER: Musket fire!

THIRD OFFICER: Now they're at one another at the trenches! —

GOLZ: By God, I never heard a din of fire

Like that before in all my days.

HOHENZOLLERN:

Fire! Fire! And burst the womb of the earth!

The rift you make will be your corpses' grave.

(Pause. — Distant shouts of victory)

FIRST OFFICER: Dear God above, giver of victories!

Wrangel has turned.

HOHENZOLLERN: Not possible!

GOLZ: By heaven, friends. On their left flank from the

Redoubt he and his guns are pulling back.

ALL: Victory! Victory! Hurrah! Hurrah!

HOMBURG: *(coming down from the hill)*

Now, Kottwitz, follow me.

KOTTWITZ: Steady now, steady.

HOMBURG: Away, follow me now, sound the charge.

KOTTWITZ: Steady, I tell you.

HOMBURG: (*beside himself*) All the devils of hell!

KOTTWITZ: His Majesty at the briefing yesterday
Instructed us to wait for orders.
Golz, read this gentleman the instruction.

HOMBURG: For orders? Are you so sluggish, Kottwitz?
Have you not had your orders from your heart?

KOTTWITZ: Orders?

HOHENZOLLERN: I beg you, Arthur!

KOTTWITZ: From my heart?

HOHENZOLLERN: Hear reason, Arthur.

GOLZ: Heed us, sir.

KOTTWITZ: (*insulted*)
Oho, young man, is that what you are meaning? —
The nag you ride on, if it comes to it,
I'll fasten to mine's tail and drag along.
Move, gentlemen. Trumpeter, sound the charge.
Forward, to battle! Kottwitz will be there.

GOLZ: (*to Kottwitz*) No, colonel, no. This cannot be.

SECOND OFFICER:
Hennings has not yet reached the Rhyn.

FIRST OFFICER: Take away his sword.

HOMBURG: My sword?
(*He pushes him back*)
You insolent young fool! Did you never learn
The Prussian Ten Commandments?*
I'll have yours and its scabbard.
(*He tears the sword and swordbelt from him*)

FIRST OFFICER: (*staggering*)
This treatment, Prince ... By God ...

HOMBURG: (*coming at him*) Still answering back?

HOHENZOLLERN: (*to the officer*) Hush! Are you raving?

HOMBURG: (*handing over the sword*) Guards,
Conduct him as a prisoner to headquarters.
(*To* KOTTWITZ *and the other* OFFICERS)
The word now, gentlemen, is this: he is a rogue
Who will not follow his commander into battle.
— Which of you won't?

KOTTWITZ: You heard. Why make these speeches?

HOHENZOLLERN: (*to placate him*)

All we intended was to counsel you.
KOTTWITZ: On your head be it. I will follow you.
HOMBURG: (*placated*)
 On my head be it. Follow me, friends.

[*All exit*]

Scene 3

A room in a village. Enter a COURTIER *in boots and spurs. —*
A PEASANT *and his* WIFE *are sitting at a table working*

COURTIER: Greetings, good people. Have you room
 Here in your house to welcome guests?
PEASANT: Indeed. Gladly.
WIFE: May we know who?
COURTIER: Our country's mother. No one less than her.
 Leaving the village the carriage axle broke
 And since we hear the victory is won
 Our further journey is unnecessary.
PEASANT AND HIS WIFE: (*rising*)
 The victory won? — O heaven!
COURTIER: You did not know?
 The Swedish army has been smitten,
 If not for ever for a year at least
 The Mark* is safe against their fire and sword.
 — But here our sovereign lady comes already.

Scene 4

The ELECTRESS, *pale and distressed,* PRINCESS NATALIE *and*
several LADIES-IN-WAITING *following her*
ELECTRESS: (*still in the doorway*)
 Bork! Winterfeld! Support me!
NATALIE: (*hurrying to her*) Dear Aunt!
LADIES-IN-WAITING: She is white. She is fainting. Oh!
                              (*They support her*)
ELECTRESS: Lead me to a chair. I must sit down.
 — Dead, he says, dead?
NATALIE: Oh, my dear Aunt.
ELECTRESS: I'll speak to
 This bringer of evil news myself.

Scene 5

Enter CAVALRY OFFICER MÖRNER, *wounded and supported
by two* COMRADES

ELECTRESS: Herald of horrors, what have you brought me?
MÖRNER: A thing, dear lady, that, alas, these eyes
 To their eternal grief witnessed themselves.
ELECTRESS: Well then. Tell it.
MÖRNER: The Elector is dead.
NATALIE: Dear God
 Must we be smitten by so hideous a blow?
      (She covers her face)
ELECTRESS: Give me the account of how he fell.
 — And as the lightning when it strikes a traveller
 One last time lights his world in crimson
 So let your words be. Night, when you have spoken,
 May clap together then around my head.
MÖRNER: *(comes forward supported by his comrades)*
 The Prince of Homburg had, soon as the enemy,
 Pressed by Truchss, were wavering where they stood,
 Advanced on to the plain against Wrangel.
 Two lines already, with his cavalry,
 He had broken through and smashed them in their flight.
 And then he hit on earthworks in the field.
 Here such a murderous pelting iron
 Came at him that his host of riders
 Buckled and lay down like a reaping.
 Among the trees and hillocks he had to halt
 And gather in again his scattered corps.
NATALIE: *(to the* ELECTRESS*)* Dearest, be brave.
ELECTRESS: Let be, let be, my dear.
MÖRNER: At that moment, clear of the dust,
 We saw the Sovereign: he was with the standards
 Of Truchss's corps, riding at the enemy.
 He sat there on a white horse, splendid,
 Sunlit, lighting the way of victory.
 All of us gathered at this sight
 On a hillside, gravely anxious,
 To see him full in the middle of the fire
 When he, the Elector, horse and rider,
 Sank down in the dust before our eyes.

Two standard bearers fell on top of him
And covered him over with their colours.

NATALIE: Dear Aunt.

FIRST LADY-IN-WAITING: O heaven.

ELECTRESS: Go on. Go on.

MÖRNER:

Then pain gripped, at the sight of this horror,
Immeasurable pain the Prince's heart
And like a bear, goaded by rage and vengeance,
With us he broke headlong at their redoubt.
The ditch, the earthwork covering it,
We took flying and the men there, flung them
Strewed them over the field, rubbing them out.
Cannon and colours, drums and standards
And all the wargoods of the Swedes were seized
And had the bridgehead on the Rhyn
Not hampered us in slaughtering not one
Would ever have reached the hearth of home to say
At Fehrbellin I saw their hero fall.

ELECTRESS:

The victory cost too much. I do not like it.
Give me the sum it cost me back again.
                              (She faints)

FIRST LADY-IN-WAITING:

Oh help her, God in heaven, she is fainting.
                    (NATALIE *weeps*)

Scene 6

Enter the PRINCE OF HOMBURG

HOMBURG: Dearest Natalie, oh my dear girl!
          (Moved, he lays her hand against his heart)

NATALIE: Then it is true?

HOMBURG: Could I but say it is not,
Could I with blood from this true heart of mine
But call his own heart back to life. —

NATALIE: (*drying her tears*)
Have they already found his body?

HOMBURG: Oh till this moment all my business was
Vengeance on Wrangel. How could I
Till now devote myself to that concern?

But I dispatched a company of men
To search the field of death for him. By nightfall,
I do not doubt it, they will bring him in.
NATALIE: Who in this terrifying struggle now
   Will hold the Swedes in check? Who will
   Protect us in the world of enemies
   His fortune and his fame have brought on us?
HOMBURG: (*taking her hand*)
   Myself, lady. I will take on your cause.
   I'll be an angel with a flaming sword
   There at the orphaned steps that climb your throne.
   The Elector wished, before the turn of the year,
   To see the marches free. So be it. I
   Will be the accomplisher of that last wish.
NATALIE: My dear and precious cousin.
                    (*She withdraws her hand*)
HOMBURG: Oh Natalie!
                    (*He pauses for a moment*)
   What are your thoughts now on your future?
NATALIE: Indeed, what can I, after this thunderbolt
   Opening the ground beneath me, contemplate?
   My father rests and my dear mother rests
   Entombed in Amsterdam. Dortrecht lies
   In rubble, under ash, that was my family's home.
   Harassed by tyrannous Spanish armies
   Moritz, my cousin of Orange, hardly knows
   Where he should bring his own children to safety
   And now my final stock and staff has fallen
   That held upright my vine of happiness.
   Today I have my second orphaning.*
HOMBURG: (*putting his arm around her*)
   Oh my dear friend, if now were not
   Sacred to grieving I should say to you:
   Entwine your further growing round this body
   That longs, having for years flourished alone,
   To breathe the sweet scent of your flowering.
NATALIE: My dear kind cousin!
HOMBURG: — Will you? Will you?
NATALIE: — If I can grow into the heart of it.
                    (*She leans herself against him*)
HOMBURG: What was it you said?

NATALIE: Stand away.
HOMBURG: (*holding her*)   Into its core,
  Into the core of the heart of it, Natalie!
          (*He kisses her, she tears herself away*)
  Ah God, were he here whom we grieve for now
  To see this union. If only we
  Could look to him and beg a father's blessing.
   (*He covers his face with his hands.* NATALIE *turns back to the*
                ELECTRESS)

Scene 7

Enter a SERGEANT *in haste*

SERGEANT:
  I hardly dare, your Highness, by the living God
  Report the rumour that has gone about.
  — The Elector is alive.
HOMBURG: Alive!
SERGEANT: By heaven
  Count Sparren has brought the news.
NATALIE: Dear God of life! Aunt, do you hear this?
 (*She throws herself down before the* ELECTRESS *and embraces her*)
HOMBURG: No, tell ... Who brings me ...?
SERGEANT: Georg, Count Sparren
  Who saw him safe and sound, with his own eyes,
  In Hackelwitz, with Truchss's forces.
HOMBURG:
  Hurry, friend, run and bring him here to me.

                          [*Exit* SERGEANT]

Scene 8

Enter COUNT SPARREN *and the* SERGEANT

ELECTRESS: Oh do not cast me twice into the abyss.
NATALIE: Dear Aunt, no.
ELECTRESS: Friedrich is alive?
NATALIE: (*with both hands holding her steady on her feet*)
  The summit of life welcomes you back again.
SERGEANT: (*entering*) Here is the officer.
HOMBURG: Count Sparren,
  You saw our sovereign fit and well
  In Hackelwitz, with Truchss's forces?

COUNT SPARREN:
  Indeed, your Highness, in the pastor's yard
  Where he, among his staff, was ordering
  The burial of the dead of both armies.
LADIES-IN-WAITING: Oh God, what happiness!
                    (They embrace one another)
ELECTRESS: Oh my dear child!
NATALIE: Joy such as this can almost not be borne.
                (She buries her face in her aunt's lap)
HOMBURG: Did I not, from a distance, where I led,
  See him beaten to death by cannon fire
  And foundering in the dust with his white horse?
COUNT SPARREN:
  The horse indeed fell and the rider with it.
  However, that rider, Prince, was not the Elector.
HOMBURG: Was not? Was not the Elector?
NATALIE: Oh what joy!
        (She rises and stands by the ELECTRESS's side)
HOMBURG: Tell us.
  Your words fall heavy as gold into my heart.
COUNT SPARREN:
  Hear then the account of an event more touching
  Than ever anybody heard before.
  The Elector who, ignoring every warning,
  Again rode that same shiningly white horse
  That Froben* bid and got for him in England lately,
  Became again, as all along he has been,
  The target of the enemy's cannon fire.
  Scarcely a man could, of his entourage,
  Get nearer to him than a hundred paces.
  Grenades and cannon balls and grape-shot
  In one wide river of death rolled in
  And everything alive there sought the banks.
  Only he, the intrepid swimmer, never faltered
  And always signalling to his friends he beat
  Blithely towards the heights, where the source was.
HOMBURG:
  By heaven, yes. The blood was chilled to see it.
COUNT SPARREN: Equerry Froben, in the entourage
  Following the closest, called to me:
  'I curse the shining whiteness of that horse today

Got recently in London for a deal of gold.
I'd give another fifty guineas now
To have a cover on it like a mouse's grey.'
He approached him then, in warm concern, and said:
'Your horse is shying, sir, you must
Allow me again to try correcting him.'
So saying, he got down from his sorrel
And seized the Elector's animal by the bridle.
The Elector smiled. 'Old friend,' he said, dismounting,
'The tricks you have in mind to teach him
I doubt he'll learn while this day lasts.
Walk him behind those rises, will you, at a distance
Where the enemy cannot observe his faults.'
Mounted the sorrel then Froben was riding
And turned again back where his office called him.
Hardly was Froben on the white horse though
Than murderous lead, shot from their walls and trenches,
Flailed horse and rider to the ground.
He sank in dust, a sacrifice to loyalty,
And no sound more did anyone hear from him.

(Short pause)

HOMBURG: His debt is paid. — If I had ten lives
I could not use them better than he did his.
NATALIE: Froben was brave.
ELECTRESS: Noble and good.
NATALIE: A lesser man would still be worth our tears.

(They weep)

HOMBURG:
Enough. To business now. Where is the Elector?
Has he moved his command to Hackelwitz?
SPARREN: Forgive me, no. The Elector is in Berlin
And all the officers of his command
Are ordered to proceed there after him.
HOMBURG: Berlin? How so? — Is the campaign over?
SPARREN: Is all this strange to you? I am amazed. —
Count Horn, the Swedish General, came to us.
And through our lines, as soon as he was there,
A truce was called. If I
Correctly understood Field Marshal Dörfling
Negotiations were initiated
And peace itself may well ensue.

ELECTRESS: Heavens, how happily everything is ending.
                    (*She rises*)
HOMBURG: Come, let us follow him to Berlin at once.
    Might you, for greater speed, make room
    For me to travel with you in your carriage?
    I have a note to write to Kottwitz first
    And will be with you in one instant.
                    (*He sits down to write*)
ELECTRESS: Gladly, very gladly.
HOMBURG: (*folds the letter and hands it to the* SERGEANT. *Then,
    turning to the* ELECTRESS *again and laying his arm gently around*
    NATALIE'*s waist*)
                                Something is on my mind
    It makes me shy to ask you but I will
    Unburden myself of it on the way.
NATALIE: (*freeing herself*) My scarf, Bork, please. Be quick.
ELECTRESS: To ask me? You?
FIRST LADY-IN-WAITING:
    Princess, your scarf is round your neck.
HOMBURG: (*to the* ELECTRESS) Can you not guess?
ELECTRESS: I cannot.
HOMBURG: Not an inkling? —
ELECTRESS: (*breaking off*)
    And all the same. — No supplicant on earth
    Hears no from me today, whatever it is,
    And you, victorious in battle, least of all.
    — Now let us go.
HOMBURG: Oh lady! Mother! Can I lend
    Your words the meaning I wish them to have?
ELECTRESS: I said let us go. More in the carriage.
HOMBURG:
    Come then, give me your arm. — Immortal Caesar,
    I set my ladder now against your star.
                (*He escorts the* LADIES *out. Everyone follows*)

Scene 9

*Berlin. A pleasure garden in front of the old palace. In the
background the palace chapel, with steps up to it. Bells are
tolling, the chapel is brilliantly lit,* FROBEN'*s corpse is carried
by and laid down on a splendid bier*

Enter the ELECTOR, FIELD MARSHAL DÖRFLING, COLONEL
HENNINGS, COUNT TRUCHSS *and several other* OFFICERS.
Opposite the bier one or two OFFICERS *are to be seen with
dispatches.* — *In the church and on the square before it are
people of all ages*

ELECTOR: Whoever it was who led the cavalry
In battle and before, by Colonel Hennings,
The enemy's bridges could be destroyed,
Advanced, himself deciding to,
Before I gave the order, forcing them to flee,
His offence is capital, I state that now,
And summon him before a courtmartial.
— The Prince of Homburg did not lead them?
COUNT TRUCHSS: No, your Majesty.
ELECTOR: Who tells me that?
COUNT TRUCHSS: Men of the cavalry can confirm it
Who swore to me, before the battle began,
The Prince fell with his horse and he was seen
Severely injured in the head and legs
In a church being bandaged.
ELECTOR: None the less
The victory today is radiant. Tomorrow
At the altar I shall give my thanks to God.
But were it ten times greater that would not excuse
The man through whom mere chance bestows it on me.
I have more battles than this last to fight
And I will have the law obeyed.
Whoever it was who led them into battle,
I say it again, he has forfeited his head
And herewith I courtmartial him.
— Now, friends, accompany me into the church.

Scene 10

Enter the PRINCE OF HOMBURG *with three Swedish standards
in his hands,* COLONEL KOTTWITZ *with two,* COUNT
HOHENZOLLERN, CAVALRY CAPTAIN GOLZ, COUNT REUSS
each with one, several other OFFICERS, CORPORALS *and*
CAVALRYMEN *with standards, drums and colours*

FIELD MARSHAL DÖRFLING: (*seeing the* PRINCE)
The Prince of Homburg! — What has happened? — Truchss!

ELECTOR: (*stopping short*) Where have you come from, Prince?
HOMBURG: (*stepping forward a few paces*) From Fehrbellin, sir
And bring you these trophies.
(*He lays the three standards down before him, the* OFFICERS,
CORPORALS *and* CAVALRYMEN *follow with theirs*)
ELECTOR: (*astonished*) You are hurt,
I hear, and seriously. — Count Truchss!
HOMBURG: (*cheerfully*) Forgive me.
COUNT TRUCHSS: This is astonishing.
HOMBURG: My horse stumbled before the battle began.
This hand here, bandaged for me by the field surgeon,
Does not deserve that you should call it hurt.
ELECTOR: It was you, therefore, who led the cavalry?
HOMBURG: (*looking at him in surprise*)
Me? Of course. Do you need me to tell you?
— I laid the proof of it here at your feet.
ELECTOR: — Arrest him. Take away his sword.
DÖRFLING: (*shocked*) Take whose?
ELECTOR: (*stepping among the standards*) You are welcome,
Kottwitz.
TRUCHSS: (*aside*) Oh, be damned.
KOTTWITZ: By God, I am exceedingly ...
ELECTOR: (*looking at him*) What is that you say?
See what a crop was reaped here for our fame.
— Surely this standard is the Swedish bodyguard's?
(*He takes up a standard, unrolls it and examines it*)
KOTTWITZ: Elector?
DÖRFLING: My sovereign?
ELECTOR: Indeed it is.
From Gustavus Adolphus' time moreover.
— What is the inscription?
KOTTWITZ: I think ...
DÖRFLING: *Per aspera ad astra.**
ELECTOR: That did not hold at Fehrbellin. —
(*Pause*)
KOTTWITZ: (*timidly*) May I
Be allowed one word, my sovereign?
ELECTOR: What is it?
Take all the colours, drums and standards
And hang them from the columns of the church.
I mean to use them when we celebrate tomorrow.

(The ELECTOR *turns to the* COURIERS, *takes their dispatches,
opens and reads them)*

KOTTWITZ: *(aside)* That, by the living God, is going too far.
  *(*KOTTWITZ, *after some hesitation, takes up his two standards,
  the other* OFFICERS *and* CAVALRYMEN *follow suit. Finally,
  since the* PRINCE's *three standards are left lying there,*
  KOTTWITZ *takes up those as well so that now he is carrying
  five)*

AN OFFICER: *(approaching the Prince)*
  Your sword, your Highness, please.

HOHENZOLLERN: *(coming with his standard to the Prince's side)*
                                Be calm now, friend.

HOMBURG: Is this a dream? Am I awake? Alive? Not mad?

GOLZ: Be advised. Say nothing, Prince. Give up your sword.

HOMBURG: Under arrest?

HOHENZOLLERN: That is the case.

GOLZ: You heard.

HOMBURG: And may one know what for?

HOHENZOLLERN: *(with some vehemence)* Not now.
  — You thrust yourself too early, as we said
  At the time, into the battle. Your orders were
  To not move from the spot until told to.

HOMBURG: Help me, friends, help. I am going mad.

GOLZ: *(interrupting him)*   Hush now.

HOMBURG: Was Brandenburg's army defeated then?

HOHENZOLLERN: *(stamping his foot)*
  That is not the point. — Orders must be obeyed.

HOMBURG: *(bitterly)* I see. I see.

HOHENZOLLERN: *(moving away from him)*
                        It won't be the end of you.

GOLZ: *(likewise)* Perhaps by tomorrow you will be free again.
  (The ELECTOR *folds the letters and re-enters the circle of his
                        OFFICERS)*

HOMBURG: *(having unfastened his swordbelt)*
  My cousin Friedrich wants to play the part of Brutus*
  And sees himself already done in chalk
  On canvas seated on the consul's chair
  The Swedish standards in the foreground
  And on a table our articles of war.
  By God, in me he will not find the son
  Who under the axe will still admire him.

My heart is German in the old way,
Accustomed to generosity and love
And if he comes at me in this time now
In all the stiffness of antiquity
So much the worse for him. I pity him.
          (He gives his sword to the OFFICER *and exits)*
ELECTOR: Take him to Fehrbellin, to headquarters,
And order the courtmartial that will judge him.
          [*Exit the* ELECTOR *into the church. The standards are carried
               in after him and as he and his entourage kneel and pray at*
          FROBEN's *coffin they are hung from the pillars. Solemn music.*]

ACT III

Scene 1

Scene: Fehrbellin. A prison. The PRINCE OF HOMBURG. — *In the background two* CAVALRYMEN *as guards.* — *Enter* COUNT HOHENZOLLERN

HOMBURG:
Now see who is here! Heinrich, my friend! Welcome.
The arrest is lifted and I'm free again?
HOHENZOLLERN: (*amazed*) Praise God in the heights!
HOMBURG: What's that you are saying?
HOHENZOLLERN: Free?
Has he returned your sword to you?
HOMBURG: To me? No.
HOHENZOLLERN: No?
HOMBURG: No.
HOHENZOLLERN: — On what grounds free then?
HOMBURG: (*after a pause*)
I thought you came for that, that *you* did. Still.
HOHENZOLLERN: — I have heard nothing.
HOMBURG: Still, I say. But still.
He'll send me word by someone else.
                    (*He turns and brings two chairs*)
Sit down. — What news then? Tell me.
— The Elector is returned now from Berlin?
HOHENZOLLERN: (*distracted*) Last night.
HOMBURG: And was, as it was planned to be,
The victory celebrated there? — Indeed!
His Majesty was present in the church?
HOHENZOLLERN: He and the Electress and Natalie. —
The church was fittingly illuminated,
During the Te Deum guns were heard
Before the palace firing with solemn pomp,
The colours and the standards of the Swedes
Hung down as trophies from the pillars
And by his Majesty's express command
Your name, as being the victor,
Was given mention from the pulpit.
HOMBURG:
So I heard. — What else is new? What can you tell me?
— Your look, it seems to me, is less than cheerful, friend.

HOHENZOLLERN: Have you seen anybody?
HOMBURG: Golz, just now,
  In the palace where, as you know, my hearing was.
(Pause)
HOHENZOLLERN: (looking at him meaningfully)
  Arthur, what do you think of your position
  Now it has changed so strangely?
HOMBURG: Me? Why, what you and Golz do — and the judges.
  The Elector has done what duty said he must,
  Now he'll obey his heart also.
  You have done wrong, he will tell me earnestly
  And mention, maybe, death and prison.
  However, I give you back your freedom —
  And around the sword, that won him victory,
  Some pretty mark of favour might be wound.
  — If not, very well. For I have not deserved it.
HOHENZOLLERN: Oh, Arthur.
(He pauses)
HOMBURG: Well?
HOHENZOLLERN: — Are you so sure of this?
HOMBURG: So it looks to me. I know I matter to him,
  Matter like a son. Since earliest childhood
  His heart has proved it to me with a thousand proofs.
  What kind of doubt is it that troubles you?
  Did he not seem to take almost more delight
  In the growth of my young fame than I did?
  Am I not everything I am through him?
  And now this plant that he has raised himself
  Would he unlovingly merely because
  It flowered a little soon and brashly
  Trample it down in pique now in the dust?
  I wouldn't believe that from his vilest enemy
  Much less from you who know him and love him.
HOHENZOLLERN: (pointedly)
  Arthur, you stood before a courtmartial
  And still think that?
HOMBURG: Precisely because I did! —
  By the living God no man would go that far
  Who did not have in mind to pardon.
  It was precisely there, before that court,
  Confidence came back to me.

Was it a crime that merits death
To have laid the power of Sweden in the dust
Two minutes earlier than ordered to?
And what wrong otherwise weighs in my heart?
How could he have me fetched before that bench
Of judges, heartlessly, like owls who sang me
Their dirge of the firing squad, over and over,
Were he not with a lord's serene announcement
About to step into their circle like a god?
No, friend, he is gathering these clouds
Around my head only to rise and beam
Through their black vapours like the sun on me.
And truly such a treat I don't begrudge him.

HOHENZOLLERN:
And yet the court, I am told, has given its judgment.

HOMBURG: Yes, so I hear. Death.

HOHENZOLLERN: (*astonished*)   You know already?

HOMBURG: Golz, who was present at their verdict,
Informed me what it was.

HOHENZOLLERN:
Dear God then, does the fact not touch you?

HOMBURG: Me? Not in the least.

HOHENZOLLERN: You are quite mad.
What does your certainty rest on?

HOMBURG: The feeling
I have of him.

                        (*He gets to his feet*)
              Stop this now, please.
Why should I be tormented by false doubts?
    (*He considers the matter for a while, then sits down again. —*
                        Pause)
The verdict of the court had to be death.
The law says so, by which it makes its judgments.
But sooner than have that verdict carried out,
Sooner than give this heart that loves him loyally
Over to bullets at the given signal
He'd bare, believe me, his own breast and wet
The dust with his own blood, drop by drop.

HOHENZOLLERN: Arthur, I do assure you ...

HOMBURG: (*impatiently*)   My dear friend!

HOHENZOLLERN: The Marshal ...

HOMBURG: (*impatiently*)   Enough of this.
HOHENZOLLERN: One final thing.
  If it does not weigh with you I'll be silent.
HOMBURG: (*turning back to him*)
  I know it all, I tell you. — Well, what is it?
HOHENZOLLERN:
  The Marshal, this is very strange, just now
  Was at the palace with the death sentence for him
  And he, instead of pardoning you, which by
  The verdict he is free to do, he ordered
  That it come back to him for signing.
HOMBURG: All the same, I tell you.
HOHENZOLLERN: All the same?
HOMBURG: For signing?
HOHENZOLLERN: My word of honour. I do assure you.
HOMBURG: The sentence? — No. The minutes? —
HOHENZOLLERN: The death sentence.
HOMBURG: — Who told you this?
HOHENZOLLERN: He did, the Field Marshal.
HOMBURG: When?
HOHENZOLLERN: Just now.
HOMBURG: Returning from the Elector?
HOHENZOLLERN:
  Coming downstairs from seeing the Elector. —
  He added, since he saw my consternation,
  All was not lost, not yet, there still remained
  Tomorrow to pardon you.
  His lips were pale however and contradicted
  His own words and said: I do not think so.
HOMBURG: (*rising*) Could he — no! — turn so monstrous
  A resolution in his heart? For a flaw,
  Under the glass scarcely discernible,
  In the diamond he has just accepted
  To tread the giver in the dust? Do what
  Would burn the Dey of Algiers* white, with wings
  Fit Sardanapalus* so that he shone
  Silvery like the cherubim and sort
  The line of ancient Roman tyrants,* all of them,
  Like children dying on their mother's breast,
  Not guilty on to God's right hand?
HOHENZOLLERN: (*having likewise got to his feet*)

You must, my friend, persuade yourself it is so.

HOMBURG: And the Marshal, he was silent and said nothing?

HOHENZOLLERN: What should he say?

HOMBURG: Dear heaven! Oh, my hope!

HOHENZOLLERN: Have you perhaps by taking any step
  Whether knowingly or unbeknown
  Come closer than you should to his proud spirit?

HOMBURG: Never.

HOHENZOLLERN: Think.

HOMBURG: Never, in heaven's name.
  The very shadow of his head was holy to me.

HOHENZOLLERN: Arthur, forgive me if I doubt that.
  Count Horn arrived, the Swedish emissary,
  His business, so the certain story is,
  Concerns Princess Natalie.
  Something her aunt, the Electress, said
  Struck at the Elector in the deepest way.
  They say the lady has already made her choice.
  Are you in any way a party here?

HOMBURG: Dear God, what are you telling me?

HOHENZOLLERN: Are you? Are you?

HOMBURG: I am, dear friend, now everything is clear.
  Their seeking this flings me into perdition.
  Listen: I am the cause of her refusal.
  The Princess has engaged herself to me.

HOHENZOLLERN:
  Fool! Thoughtless fool! What have you done?
  How often, loyally, did I warn you?

HOMBURG: Oh friend, help, save me! I am lost.

HOHENZOLLERN:
  Indeed, out of this pass what way is there?
  Will you speak to her aunt perhaps, the Electress?

HOMBURG: (turning) Guard!

CAVALRYMAN: (rear stage) Sir!

HOMBURG: Call your officer! —
    (Quickly he takes a cloak from the wall, wraps himself in it
        and puts on a plumed hat that was lying on the table)

HOHENZOLLERN: (assisting him)
  The move may, properly managed, bring salvation.
  — For if the Elector at the price
  We know of can make peace with Carl of Sweden

You'll see: he will be reconciled with you
And soon, in a few hours, you will be free.

Scene 2

Enter the OFFICER

HOMBURG: *(to him)* Stranz, I am in your custody.
　Allow me to absent myself
　A while on a matter that is urgent.
OFFICER: Prince, I do not have custody of you.
　The instructions I was given state
　I am to let you go wherever you will.
HOMBURG: Strange. — I am not a prisoner then?
OFFICER:
Forgive me. — You are, of course, bound by your word.
HOHENZOLLERN: *(leaving)* Just so. All the same. —
HOMBURG:　　　　　　　　　　Very well. Goodbye then.
HOHENZOLLERN:
　What binds the Prince goes with him every step.
HOMBURG: Only to the palace to see the Electress.
　In two minutes I shall be back.

　　　　　　　　　　　　　　　　　　　[All exit]

Scene 3

The ELECTRESS's *room. Enter the* ELECTRESS *and* NATALIE

ELECTRESS: Now, my child, now. This is your chance.
　Count Gustav Horn, the Swedish emissary,
　And all the company have left the palace.
　I see the light still in your uncle's rooms.
　Come, take your cloak and go in secret to him
　And see if you can save your friend.

　　　　　　　　　(They are about to leave)

Scene 4

Enter a LADY-IN-WAITING

LADY-IN-WAITING:
　The Prince of Homburg, madam, is at the door.
　Truly, I hardly know if I have seen aright.
ELECTRESS: *(astonished)* Dear God!
NATALIE:　　　　　　　　　The Prince?

ELECTRESS: Is he not under arrest?

LADY-IN-WAITING:

He is outside, in a plumed hat and a cloak,
And begs, with desperate passion, for a hearing.

ELECTRESS: (*with some annoyance*) Folly! To break his word!

NATALIE: Who knows

What is compelling him?

ELECTRESS: (*after some thought*) Let him come in.
                    (*She sits down*)

Scene 5

Enter the PRINCE OF HOMBURG

HOMBURG: Oh Mother!
           (*He goes down on his knees before her*)

ELECTRESS: Prince, what do you want here?

HOMBURG: Oh Mother, let me clasp your knees.

ELECTRESS: (*controlling her emotion*) You are
In custody and yet you have come here.
Why add new wrong, Prince, to the old?

HOMBURG: (*urgently*) Do you know what has happened to me?

ELECTRESS: I know it all.
But what can I, the weakest, do for you?

HOMBURG:

Oh Mother, you would not speak like this if death
Were closing cold on you as it is on me.
You seem endowed, you and the lady Princess,
You and your women and everything around
With heaven's powers, to save. Your household's
Lowest menial, your horseminder, I'd fall
About his neck and beg him: save me!
Alone, on God's wide earth, only I
Am helpless, am abandoned, can do nothing.

ELECTRESS:

You are distraught — entirely. What has happened?

HOMBURG: Oh, on the way that brought me here to you
I saw my grave, by torchlight, opening
To take my body into it tomorrow.
Oh look, lady, these eyes that see you now
They want to overcast with night, this breast
Of mine drill through with murderous bullets.

The windows on the marketplace are booked
That give on that bleak spectacle
And a man today on the summit of his life
Still viewing the future like a fairyland
Will scent the little space between two planks tomorrow
And a slab will say of him: He was.*
   (The PRINCESS *who until now has been leaning at a distance*
   on the shoulder of a LADY-IN-WAITING *at these words sits*
   down at a table, overcome, and weeps)
ELECTRESS: My son, if heaven wills it so
   You'll arm yourself with courage and composure.
HOMBURG: Oh God's world, Mother, is so beautiful.
   Let me not, I entreat you, go below
   To those black shades before it is my time to.
   Can he not, if I erred, punish me otherwise?
   Why must it be the bullet and only that?
   Let him deprive me of my offices,
   Discharge me, if that is the law,
   Dishonourably from the army. God in heaven
   Since seeing my grave I want nothing but life
   In honour or not I do not mind now.
ELECTRESS:
   Stand up, my son, stand up. What are you saying?
   You are too shaken by it. Compose yourself.
HOMBURG: Mother, if you will swear, and only then,
   To go before his countenance on your knees
   And save my life, entreating him.
   She gave to you at Homburg when she died,
   Hedwig, your childhood friend, gave me and said:
   'Be a mother to him when I no longer am.'
   You bowed, much moved, kneeling at her bed,
   Over her hand, and answered: 'He shall be
   To me as though I had given birth to him.'
   Now I remind you of that thing you said.
   As though you had borne me go to him and say:
   I beg for mercy, mercy, set him free.
   Oh then come back to me and say: You are.
ELECTRESS: *(weeping)*
   My precious child, that has already happened.
   But all my pleading did no good.
HOMBURG: I give up every claim on happiness.

Natalie — be sure to tell him this —
I have no more desire for, in my heart
All tender feelings for her are extinguished.
She is as free as forest deer again,
Her hand and lips, as though I had never been,
And can bestow herself and if the Swedish king,
Carl Gustav, is the one she has my blessing.
I shall go to my property on the Rhine
And there I'll work at building and unbuilding
And there I'll sweat and there I'll sow and harvest
As though for wife and child, enjoy alone
And when I've harvested I'll sow again
And keep life moving through a ceaseless round
Until, come evening, it lies down and dies.

ELECTRESS: Very well. But go home to your prison now.
That is the first condition of my favour.

HOMBURG: (*rising and turning to the* PRINCESS)
Poor girl there weeping, the sun today
Lights all your hopes into the grave.
The choice of your first feelings fell on me
And now your look tells me, as true as gold,
You never will cherish another man.
So poor, what can I offer you for comfort?
Go to the Main, I'd say, to the nunnery,*
To your cousin Thurn and in the hills
Find for yourself a boychild blond as I am,
Buy him for gold or silver, press him
Against your breast and teach him to say 'mother'
And when he is older let him know
The dead need somebody to close their eyes.
The happiness ahead of you is only that.

NATALIE: (*courageously and upliftingly as she rises and puts her
hand in his*)
Go, my young hero, back into your jail
And on the way there look again
Calmly at the grave being opened for you.
It is no darker and not one whit larger
Than you have seen it, a thousand times, in battle.
True to you meanwhile unto death I'll try
A word of rescue for you to my uncle.
Perhaps I will succeed and move his heart

And liberate you from all trouble.
                    (Pause)
HOMBURG: *(sunk in contemplation of her clasps his hands)*
    Had you two wings, girl, on your shoulders
    Truly I'd take you for an angel. —
    Dear God, did I hear aright? You'll speak for me?
    Where until now was the quiver of your speech
    Kept hidden, child, that you will dare
    Approach his Majesty for such a thing? —
    Oh light of hope, suddenly refreshing me!
NATALIE: God will hand me the arrows that hit home. —
    But if the Elector cannot, cannot
    Alter the law's decree, well then, a brave man
    Bravely you will submit to it. A man
    A thousand times victorious in life
    In death too he will see his way to victory.
ELECTRESS:
    Go now. — The time is wasting that is favourable.
HOMBURG: Now all the saints go with you as protectors.
    Farewell. Farewell. Whatever you achieve
    Send me some sign of your success.
                                        [All exit]

ACT IV

Scene 1

The ELECTOR's *room. The* ELECTOR *is standing with papers in his hands at a table illuminated by candles. — Enter* NATALIE *through the middle door. She goes down on her knees at some distance from him*

(*Pause*)

NATALIE: (*kneeling*) My noble uncle, Friedrich of Brandenburg!
ELECTOR: (*laying aside his papers*) Natalie!
                    (*He seeks to raise her to her feet*)
NATALIE: No! No!
ELECTOR: What do you want, child?
NATALIE: In the dust before your feet, as it behoves me,
    To beg for mercy for my cousin Homburg.
    I do not wish that he be saved for me —
    My heart desires him and admits it to you —
    I do not wish that he be saved for me.
    Let him be married to what woman he will.
    Dear uncle, all I ask is that he live
    For himself, freely apart and independent,
    Like a flower I can take pleasure in.
    I plead for this, my highest lord and friend
    And know that you will listen to such a plea.
ELECTOR: (*raising her*)
    My darling girl, what do you mean by this?
    — You know what wrong our cousin Homburg did.
NATALIE: Oh my dear Uncle.
ELECTOR: Did he do none then?
NATALIE: This misdemeanour, blond, blue-eyed,
    Even before it stammered: I am sorry
    Forgiveness ought to raise it from the ground.
    You would not spurn it from you with your foot,
    You'd press it to your heart for the mother's sake
    Who gave it birth and say: 'Come, dry your tears,
    You are as dear to me as loyalty itself.'
    Was it not hunger, when the armies met,
    For the honour of your name that led him on
    To break through the barrier of the law
    And oh, that barrier youthfully broken through,

Did he not, like a man, then tread the dragon down?
First, for his victory, crown him then behead him —
History does not ask you to do this.
It would be so high-minded, my dear uncle,
It might be called inhuman
And God made no one gentler than you.

ELECTOR: My sweet child, see, were I a tyrant
    Your words, I feel it keenly, would have thawed
    The heart already in my iron breast.
    But I ask you yourself: Am I allowed
    To quash the verdict that the court has given?
    What then, do you think, would be the consequences?

NATALIE: For whom? For you?

ELECTOR: For me? No! — What? For me?
    Do you know nothing higher, girl, than me?
    Are you quite ignorant of the sacred thing
    A soldier calls his fatherland?

NATALIE: But sir, what is your worry? This fatherland
    Under an impulse of your mercy
    Will not, forthwith, disintegrate and founder.
    Truly what you, raised among soldiers,
    Call a disorder — that in this case you,
    To suit your whim, tear up the judges' verdict —
    Seems to me the loveliest order there might be:
    The laws of war, I do know that, must govern
    But so too must the feelings of the heart.
    The fatherland that you have founded for us
    Stands, a firm fortress, noble uncle:
    And it will weather worse and other storms,
    Indeed, than this unlicensed victory.
    It will grow splendidly in future years
    Under the hands of grandchildren, extend
    More beautifully with turrets, a fabulous
    Rich joy to friends and terror to every foe.
    It does not need this cold unfruitful
    Binding with friendly blood to live beyond
    My uncle's peaceful and abundant autumn.

ELECTOR: Does cousin Homburg think this?

NATALIE: Cousin Homburg?

ELECTOR: Does he think it no matter to our country
    Whether what governs there is whim or law?

NATALIE: Oh that young man!

ELECTOR: Well?

NATALIE: Oh my dear uncle,
For answer all I have is tears.

ELECTOR: (*surprised*)
Why so, my darling? What has happened?

NATALIE: (*hesitantly*)
His one thought now is this: How to be saved?
Down the levelled barrels of the firing squad
He looks into such horror that every wish
Is shocked and sick and mute, except to live.
He might see all the territory of Brandenburg
Sink under lightning and thunderbolts
And yet not ask you: What is happening?
— He was a brave man. You have broken him.
              (*She turns away and weeps*)

ELECTOR: (*in extreme astonishment*)
Never, my dear Natalie, impossible!
Can that be true? — He begs for mercy?

NATALIE: Oh
If you had not condemned him, oh if only!

ELECTOR: No, speak. He begs for mercy? — God in heaven,
My dear child, what has happened, why do you weep?
You spoke to him? Tell all. You spoke to him?

NATALIE: (*leaning against him*)
Just now, in my aunt's room, where he,
Himself, in a cloak and a plumed hat,
The twilight hiding him, came creeping:
Distressed, abashed, in secret, wholly unworthy,
Abject, a pitiable sight.
To such sad depths, I should have thought, no one
Would sink who had the name of hero.
See here, I am a woman and start away
In terror from an insect near my heel
But so ground down, so without grip, so wholly
Unheroic, death in the form
Of any hideous beast would not find me.
— Oh what is human greatness, human fame!

ELECTOR: (*confused*) Well, by the God of heaven and earth,
Then take heart, child; then he is free.

NATALIE: What does my sovereign mean?

ELECTOR: That he is pardoned. —
I will at once do what is necessary.
NATALIE: My dearest friend! Oh is this true?
ELECTOR: You hear me.
NATALIE: He'll be forgiven? Now he will not die?
ELECTOR: My word of honour. I swear it. How should I
Oppose the opinion of such a soldier?
I have in my heart, as you must surely know,
Respect in the highest degree for what he feels.
If he can hold the judgment to be unjust
I will annul it: he is free. —
                    (He brings her a chair)
Will you sit down a moment?
          (He goes to the table, seats himself and writes. Pause)
NATALIE: *(aside)*   Heart,
Why do you beat thus at your dwelling place?
ELECTOR: *(writing)* The Prince is over in the palace still?
NATALIE: Forgive me, no. He is back in custody. —
ELECTOR: *(finishes and seals the letter and returns with it
to the* PRINCESS)
My little girl, my little niece, was weeping,
And I, entrusted with her happiness, have been
The one to cloud the heaven of her eyes.
               (He puts his arm around her)
Shall you give him the letter yourself? —
NATALIE: In prison? How?
ELECTOR: *(pressing the letter into her hand)*
                    Why not? — Hey! Footmen!
               (Enter FOOTMEN)
Bring the carriage round. The Princess
Has business with the Prince of Homburg.
                              [*Exit* FOOTMEN]

Then he can thank you for his life at once.
               (He embraces her)
My dear child. Now are we friends again?
NATALIE: *(after a pause)*
Sir, what so rapidly has aroused your favour
I do not know and will not seek to know.
But this much, be assured, I do feel in my heart
You never would ignobly make a mock of me.
The contents of the letter be what they may

I shall believe they save him — and I thank you.
                    (She kisses his hand)
ELECTOR: Indeed, my child, indeed. As surely
As it accords with cousin Homburg's wishes.

                                        [*Both exit*]

Scene 2

PRINCESS NATALIE's *room. Enter the* PRINCESS, *two* LADIES-
IN-WAITING *and* CAVALRY OFFICER COUNT REUSS *following
her*

NATALIE: (*in haste*)
What have you there, Count? — From my regiment?
Is it important? Will tomorrow do?
COUNT REUSS: (*handing her a letter*)
Lady, a letter from Colonel Kottwitz.
NATALIE: Quickly then. Give it me. What is it?
                    (She opens it)
COUNT REUSS: It is,
A petition, forthrightly, as you will see,
But humbly addressed to the Elector
In our commander's cause, the Prince of Homburg.
NATALIE: (*reading*) 'Petition, in all humility, presented by
The Regiment Princess of Orange ...'
                    (Pause)
In whose hand is it?
COUNT REUSS: As you might guess
From the uncertain forming of the letters
Colonel Kottwitz is himself the writer. —
His noble name, moreover, heads it.
NATALIE: The thirty signatures that follow his?
COUNT REUSS: Madam, the names of all the officers
Ordered by rank and company by company.
NATALIE: And me, the petition comes to me?
COUNT REUSS: Lady, respectfully to ask will you
Set likewise, as our colonel-in-chief,
Your name there at the head, in the vacant space.
                    (Pause)
NATALIE: The Prince, it is true, my noble cousin, is,
So I hear, on the Elector's own impulse
To be pardoned, and such a move not needed.

COUNT REUSS: (*delighted*) Is this so? Truly?
NATALIE: Yet, under a script
  That in his Majesty's decision, cleverly used,
  May weight the scales and, doing so, perhaps,
  To bring things to their issue, will even be
  Welcome to him, I will not refuse ...
  And so, as you desire, I place myself
  Foremost among you with my name.
                    (*She goes to write*)
COUNT REUSS: Truly, you put us deep into your debt.
                    (*Pause*)
NATALIE: (*turning back to him*)
  I only see my regiment, Count Reuss.
  Why are the Bomsdorf cuirassiers not there
  Nor Götz's nor the Anhalt Pless dragoons?
COUNT REUSS:
  Not, as perhaps you fear, because their hearts
  Are less fervent for him than our hearts are. —
  It is unfortunate for our petition
  That Kottwitz's station is far off, in Arnstein,
  Which separates him from the other regiments
  In barracks here, in this town. So our letter wants
  Freedom of movement to dispense its power
  Safely and easily in all directions.
NATALIE:
  As the letter is, it does, I think, lack weight. —
  Count, are you sure if you were in the town
  And spoke with the gentlemen congregated here
  They would likewise support the plea?
COUNT REUSS:
  Here in the town, your Highness? — To a man!
  All of the cavalry would pledge themselves
  By name. God is my witness, I believe
  The army of Brandenburg entire
  Would add, if they were asked, their signatures.
NATALIE: (*after a pause*) Why then not send out officers
  Who could promote the matter here in the barracks?
COUNT REUSS: Forgive me. — Our commander has refused to.
  — He would not, as he said, do anything
  Capable of sinister interpretation.
NATALIE: How strange he is. Now bold, now timorous. —

Happily the Elector, it occurs to me,
Being pressed by other matters, requested me
To order Kottwitz, since the stabling there is tight,
To remove hither. — I shall at once
Sit down and do it.

(She sits down and writes)

COUNT REUSS: By heaven, your Highness,
This falls very well. For our petition
No event could be more opportune.

NATALIE: *(writing)*
Use it, Count Reuss, in the best way you can.

(She finishes the letter, seals it, rises)

For the time, of course, this letter must remain
Safely in your care. You are not to leave
For Arnstein and deliver it to Kottwitz
Until I give you more particular orders.

(She hands him the letter)

Enter a FOOTMAN

FOOTMAN: The carriage, madam, as the Elector ordered
Is ready in the courtyard, waiting for you.

NATALIE: Then bring it round. I will be down at once.

*(Pause in which, deep in thought, she crosses to the table and
pulls on her gloves)*

Will you come with me to the Prince of Homburg,
Count? I have a mind to speak with him.
There is room for you in my carriage if you wish.

COUNT REUSS: Your Highness, such an honour, truly ...

(He offers her his arm)

NATALIE: *(to the* LADIES-IN-WAITING*)*
Follow me, friends. — In that place
I may decide at once about the letter.

[*All exit*]

Scene 3

The PRINCE OF HOMBURG's *prison. He hangs his hat on the
wall and seats himself apathetically on a cushion spread out on
the ground*

HOMBURG: Life, so the dervish* tells us, is a journey,
A brief one. Indeed. A span above
The earth, and then a span below

And I will make my resting place halfway.
Today you hold your head up high,
Tomorrow you tremble and your head hangs down
And lies the next day at your feet.
True, we are told the sun shines over there
As well and over brighter fields than here
And I believe it. Pity the eyes are rotting
That should be the observers of that splendour.

Scene 4

Enter PRINCESS NATALIE *escorted by* CAVALRY OFFICER
COUNT REUSS, LADIES-IN-WAITING *following. Ahead of them*
a FOOTMAN *with a torch*

FOOTMAN: Your Highness, the Princess.
HOMBURG: (*rising*)   Natalie!
FOOTMAN: Already come.
NATALIE: (*bowing to the* COUNT) Leave us a moment, will you?
                    [*Exit* COUNT REUSS *and the* FOOTMAN]
HOMBURG: My dear lady!
NATALIE: Dear cousin, my good friend!
HOMBURG: (*leading her forward*)
What news then? Say. How do things stand with me?
NATALIE: Well. All is well. As I told you earlier
You have your pardon, freedom. Here is a letter
Written by him, that will confirm it.
HOMBURG: It is not possible. No. It is a dream.
NATALIE: Read. Read the letter. See how it is yourself.
HOMBURG: (*reads*) 'Prince Friedrich, when I had you arrested
Because of the charge you led, too early,
I thought all I was doing was my duty
And counted on you to approve it.
If you believe yourself unjustly done by
I beg you, say so in a word or two —
And I will send you back your sword at once.'
        (NATALIE *turns pale. Pause. The* PRINCE *looks at her*
                    questioningly)
NATALIE: (*with an expression of sudden delight*)
See, there it is. Only a word or two!
Oh my sweet precious friend!
                (*She presses his hand*)

HOMBURG: My dear lady!
NATALIE: Now is the moment of my happiness! —
  Here now, take this. Here take this pen and write.
HOMBURG: And here, his signature?
NATALIE: The F. His way of signing. —
  Oh Bork! Be glad then. — Oh his mercy
  Is limitless, I knew it, as the ocean. —
  Bring us a chair here. He must write at once.
HOMBURG: He says: 'If it is my opinion ...'
NATALIE: (*interrupting him*)   Just so.
  Quickly. Sit down. I shall dictate it to you.
                    (*She places a chair for him*)
HOMBURG: — The letter, let me look it through again.
NATALIE: (*snatching the letter from his hand*)
  What for? — Did you not see the vault in church
  With open jaws already gaping at you?
  The moment presses. Sit and write.
HOMBURG: (*smiling*) Truly, you act as though that grave
  Were, like a panther, at my back and pouncing.
                    (*He sits down and takes a pen*)
NATALIE: (*turns aside and weeps*) Write, or I will be cross.
          (*The* PRINCE *rings for a* SERVANT. *Enter a* SERVANT)
HOMBURG: Fetch me
  A pen and paper, sealing wax and seal.
  (*The* SERVANT, *having found these things, goes out again. The*
                    PRINCE *writes. — Pause*)
HOMBURG: (*tearing up the letter he has begun and throwing it
  under the table*)
  A stupid start!
                    (*He takes another sheet*)
NATALIE: (*picking up the letter*) Why so? What did you say? —
  It is good, in heaven's name, it will do perfectly.
HOMBURG: (*to himself*)
  Pah! — As a rogue would write it, not a prince.
  I'll find some other turn of phrase.
          (*Pause. — He reaches for the* ELECTOR's *letter which the*
                    Princess is holding in her hand)
  What was it he said in the letter actually?
NATALIE: (*withholding it*) Nothing.
HOMBURG: Show me.
NATALIE: You read it.

HOMBURG: (*seizing it*)   All the same.
Only to see how I should frame myself.
                    (*He opens it and reads it over*)
NATALIE: (*aside*)
Dear God of heaven and earth, now he is done for.
HOMBURG: (*surprised*)
See here, most odd, true as I live and breathe.
Doubtless you overlooked the place?
NATALIE: No! Which?
HOMBURG: He calls me to decide the thing myself.
NATALIE: Well, yes.
HOMBURG: Truly courageous, truly fit,
Truly how a noble heart should frame itself.
NATALIE: Dear friend, his generosity is boundless.
But you play your part now and write
As he requests. Do you see, it is the pretext,
Only the outward form that has to be.
Soon as a word from you is in his hand
At once the quarrel is all over.
HOMBURG: (*laying aside the letter*)   No, my love.
I will reflect upon the matter till tomorrow.
NATALIE: Then I don't understand you. Such a turn! —
And why? For what?
HOMBURG: (*rising in great emotion from his chair*)
                    I beg you, do not ask me.
You have not weighed the content of the letter.
That he has done me wrong, as I am asked to,
I cannot write that to him. If you force me
To give him, in the mood I am in, my answer
By God I'll say: You have served me aright.
    (*Folding his arms he sits down at the table again and looks at
                        the letter*)
NATALIE: (*pale in the face*) Madman! What are you saying?
                    (*She bends over him, moved*)
HOMBURG: (*pressing her hand*)
Still for a minute. It seems to me ...
                    (*He ponders*)
NATALIE: What did you say?
HOMBURG: In a moment I shall know what I must write.
NATALIE: (*distressed*) Homburg!
HOMBURG: (*taking up the pen*) I hear you. Well?

NATALIE: Oh my sweet friend,
  I praise what suddenly has moved your heart.
  But I swear this to you: The riflemen
  Are chosen already who will perform tomorrow
  When you are lowered in, above your tomb
  The rites of death and reconciliation.
  If you, being nobleminded, cannot oppose
  The verdict, cannot, to annul it, do
  What in this letter he asks you to do,
  Then, I assure you, he will comport himself
  Nobly, as the thing demands, towards you and will
  Tomorrow, with compassion, carry it out on you.
HOMBURG: (*writing*) So be it.
NATALIE: So be it?
HOMBURG: Let him do as he may.
  Me it behoves to act here as I ought.
NATALIE: (*horrified, comes nearer*)
  Maddest of madmen, have you written that?
HOMBURG: (*finishing*) 'Homburg, at Fehrbellin, the twelfth ...'
  I have finished. — Franz!
                    (He folds and seals the letter)
NATALIE: Dear God in heaven!
HOMBURG: (*rising*)
  Take this to the palace, to the man I serve.
                                    [*Exit the* SERVANT]
  I will not, since he faces me so fitly,
  Confront him in an unfit way.
  Guilt, more than a little, weighs on me
  As I acknowledge. If he can
  Forgive me only if I dispute it with him
  Then I will do without his mercy.
NATALIE: (*kissing him*)
  Take this kiss. — And if twelve bullets forthwith
  Drilled you to dust I could not stop myself
  But would rejoice and weep and say: I like you so!
  — Meanwhile, if you follow your heart
  It is permitted me to follow mine.
  — Count Reuss!
          (The FOOTMAN *opens the door. Enter the* COUNT)
COUNT REUSS: Here!
NATALIE: Go with your letter now

To Arnstein, go, to Colonel Kottwitz.
The regiment moves, his Majesty orders it,
By midnight I expect them here.

[*All exit*]

ACT V

Scene 1

Scene: A room in the palace. The ELECTOR *comes, half undressed, out of an adjoining room. After him come* COUNT TRUCHSS, COUNT HOHENZOLLERN *and* CAVALRY OFFICER GOLZ. — PAGES *with lights*

ELECTOR: Kottwitz? With the Princess's dragoons?
   Here in the town?
COUNT TRUCHSS: (*opening the window*) Yes, your Majesty.
   He is drawn up here, under the palace window.
ELECTOR: Well, gentlemen, will you explain this riddle?
   — Who called him here?
HOHENZOLLERN: That I don't know, your Majesty.
ELECTOR: The place I stationed him is Arnstein.
   One of you, quickly, go and fetch him.
GOLZ: Sir, he will be before you in a moment.
ELECTOR: Where is he?
GOLZ: In the council, so I hear,
   Where all the commanding officers
   Who serve your house have gathered.
ELECTOR: And why? To what end?
HOHENZOLLERN: — That I do not know.
TRUCHSS: May we, my sovereign, be permitted
   Briefly to join them there?
ELECTOR: Them where? In the council?
HOHENZOLLERN: At the gathering.
   We gave our word that we would be there too.
ELECTOR: (*after a short pause*) — You are dismissed.
GOLZ: Come, gentlemen.
                              [*Exit the* OFFICERS]

Scene 2

ELECTOR: How strange. — Were I the Dey of Tunis
   At such suspicious goings-on I'd sound the alarm.
   I'd lay the silk cord* ready on my desk
   And bring up cannons and howitzers
   Before my barricaded gates. But since
   It is Hans Kottwitz, born in Priegnitz,

Come in on me unordered, as he pleases,
I'll do things as they are done in Brandenburg
And take him by a curl, one of the three
Still shining silver on his skull,
And lead him gently, with his dozen squadrons,
Back to his headquarters in Arnstein.
Why wake the town out of its sleep?
*(Having again stood at the window for a moment he crosses to
the table and rings. Enter two* SERVANTS)

ELECTOR:
Run down, will you, and ask, as though for you,
What's happening in the council room.

SERVANT: At once, sir.

                                                       [*Exit* SERVANT]

ELECTOR: (*to the other* SERVANT)
And you, bring me my clothes, will you.
(The SERVANT *goes and fetches the* ELECTOR'*s clothes. The*
ELECTOR *dresses, putting on all his regalia)*

Scene 3

Enter FIELD MARSHAL DÖRFLING

DÖRFLING: Rebellion, your Majesty!

ELECTOR: (*still getting dressed*)   Calm down.
I do detest it, as you know full well,
When people enter unannounced.
— What do you want?

DÖRFLING: Sir, an event, forgive me,
Brings me here, of very great importance.
Colonel Kottwitz has, without orders,
Moved into town, about a hundred officers
Are gathered round him in the council chamber.
Among them, circulating, is a paper
Whose aim is interference in your powers.

ELECTOR: I know. — What will it be
More than a movement in the Prince's favour
The law having condemned him to the bullet?

DÖRFLING: Exactly so. By God, exactly right!

ELECTOR: Well then. — My heart is with them.

DÖRFLING: It is said
They have in mind, the madmen,

To hand you their petition in the palace,
And should you, still unmoved, still harsh,
Uphold the verdict then — I scarcely dare tell you —
To free him from imprisonment by force.
ELECTOR: (*grimly*) Who told you that?
DÖRFLING: Who told me that?
Madame Retzow, a lady you can trust,
My wife's cousin. This afternoon
She was at her uncle's, Governor Retzow's, house
Where officers, arriving from the camp,
Proposed this shameless action openly.
ELECTOR:
I will believe that when I have it from a man.
I'll stand my boot outside his door —
That will protect him from these heroes.
DÖRFLING: Sir, I beseech you, if you are minded,
In the end, to grant the Prince his pardon
Do it before a loathsome move is made.
An army loves its heroes, as you know.
Do not allow this spark alight in it
As fire to spread and rage beyond all succour.
Kottwitz does not yet know nor does the host
Assembled by him that I have loyally warned you.
Send then, before he comes, the Prince his sword,
Send it him back, as he deserves you should.
So doing you give the news one great deed more
And one less wrong to pass from mouth to mouth.
ELECTOR: First I should have to ask the Prince
Whom, as you doubtless know, not arbitrariness
Arrested and so cannot release. —
I'll speak to the gentlemen when they arrive.
DÖRFLING: (*aside*)
Be damned! There's nothing he's not proof against.

Scene 4

Enter two FOOTMEN. *One is holding a letter*
FIRST FOOTMAN:
The colonels Kottwitz, Hennings, Truchss and others
Ask to be admitted.

ELECTOR: (*to the* SECOND FOOTMAN, *taking the letter from his hand*)

                    From the Prince of Homburg?

SECOND FOOTMAN: Yes, my sovereign.

ELECTOR: Who gave it you?

SECOND FOOTMAN: The Swiss* at the gate on guard duty.

  The Prince's messenger handed it to him.

ELECTOR: (*stands at his desk and reads the letter. Having done so he turns and calls to a* PAGE)

  Prittwitz! — Bring me the death sentence.

  — Also the passport for Gustav Count of Horn,

  The Swedish emissary, I'll have that too.

                          [*Exit the* PAGE]

            (*To the* FIRST FOOTMAN)

  Tell Kottwitz and those with him to come in.

Scene 5

Enter KOTTWITZ, HENNINGS, TRUCHSS, HOHENZOLLERN, SPARREN, REUSS, GOLZ, STRANZ *and other* COLONELS *and* OFFICERS

KOTTWITZ: (*with the petition*) Elector, sovereign, permit

  That I in the name of all the army

  Humbly present this paper to you.

ELECTOR: Kottwitz, before I take it, tell me, will you

  Who summoned you here into this town?

KOTTWITZ: (*with a look of surprise*) With the dragoons?

ELECTOR: With the regiment.

  Arnstein was the place I stationed you.

KOTTWITZ: Sir, it was your orders summoned me.

ELECTOR: What? — Show me the orders.

KOTTWITZ: Here, my sovereign.

ELECTOR: (*reads*) 'Natalie, signed at Fehrbellin, on my

  Uncle's behalf, the Elector Friedrich.' —

KOTTWITZ: Dear God, your Majesty, I hope

  The order was known to you.

ELECTOR: Of course. I meant ...

  Who was it who brought the orders to you?

KOTTWITZ: Count Reuss.

ELECTOR: (*after a moment's pause*)

                No indeed. You are welcome here. —

  It falls to you, with your twelve squadrons,

To show our last respects tomorrow
To Colonel Homburg whom the law has judged.
KOTTWITZ: (*shocked*) What did my sovereign say?
ELECTOR: (*giving him back the orders*)   The regiment
Is out in the pitch black still before the palace?
KOTTWITZ: Pitch black, forgive ...
ELECTOR: Why have they not moved in?
KOTTWITZ: They have moved in, sir. They have taken up,
As you commanded, quarters in this town.
ELECTOR: (*turning to the window*)
What? Two minutes since ... Good heavens, yes.
You have been speedy finding stabling. —
So much the better. Again, welcome.
What brings you here now? What's the news?
KOTTWITZ: Sir, this petition from your loyal army.
ELECTOR: Give it to me.
KOTTWITZ: But the word your lips have uttered
Dashes all my hopes to earth.
ELECTOR: Why then
A word may raise them up again.
                              (*He reads*)
'Petition, begging our sovereign's clemency
For our leader condemned to die,
Colonel Prince Friedrich Hesse-Homburg.'
                    (*To the* OFFICERS)
Gentlemen, a noble name, not at all unworthy
That you, in such number, should move to help him.
                    (*He looks again at the petition*)
Who is the author of this plea?
KOTTWITZ: I am.
ELECTOR: The Prince is apprised of it?
KOTTWITZ: He has
Not the least inkling. In our own midst
It was conceived and done.
ELECTOR: Be patient
One moment with me, will you.
   (*He goes to his desk and reads their composition through.* —
                    Long pause)
Hm. Very strange. — You, you old soldier,
Defend the Prince's action, justify his
Falling on Wrangel before ordered to.

KOTTWITZ: Sir, yes indeed. That is what Kottwitz does.
ELECTOR: Your view was different on the battlefield.
KOTTWITZ:
  Sir, when I weighed things up then I was wrong.
  I should have let myself without demur
  Be ruled by the Prince, who understands war well.
  The Swedes were faltering on their left flank
  And offering assistance from their right.
  If he had waited for your order they
  In the ditches would have stood their ground again
  And you would never have got the victory.
ELECTOR: So you like to suppose. I had,
  As you well know, sent Colonel Hennings
  To take possession of the Swedish bridgehead
  Covering Wrangel's back. Had you
  Not disobeyed your orders Hennings
  Would have succeeded in this action.
  Given two hours he would have fired the bridges
  And taken up positions on the Rhyn
  And Wrangel wholly, root and branch, would have,
  In dykes and marshes, been annihilated.
KOTTWITZ: Only an amateur, not you,
  Goes after Fate's very highest wreath.
  You always took, till now, what Fate offered.
  The dragon ravaging your marches as it liked
  Was hit about the head and chased away:
  What more could happen in a single day?
  Why should you mind if he lies in the sand
  Gasping and licks his wounds another week or so?
  Now we have learned the art of beating him
  And feel an eagerness to practise it some more.
  Let us meet Wrangel boldly face to face
  Another time, and that will finish it
  And he will tumble back into the Baltic.
  Rome was not built in a day.
ELECTOR: What grounds,
  You fool, do you have for hoping that,
  If, while I drive the chariot of war,
  Anyone, as he likes, may seize the reins?
  Do you suppose that Fortune always will
  Crown disobedience with laurels, as lately?

I do not want a victory that is
The bastard child of chance. I want
The law upheld which is the mother of my crown
To bear me a whole family of victories.
KOTTWITZ: Sir, the law, the highest, chiefest law
    That should be the mover in your generals' hearts,
    That law is not the letter of your will,
    It is the fatherland, it is the crown
    And you yourself upon whose head it rests.
    What do you care, I ask you, by what rule
    The foe is beaten, just so long as he
    With all his colours sinks before you?
    The rule that beats him is the highest rule.
    Would you turn the army, passionately yours,
    Into a tool like the sword that lies
    Dead in your golden scabbard? Miserable
    The mind and not a reacher for the stars
    Who ever taught such a thing. And poor
    And short-sighted the polity that for
    One case where feeling did some harm
    Forgets ten others in the course of things
    Where feeling is the one and only hope!
    Do I, in battle, spill my blood in the dust
    For you for pay, be it gold or honour?
    May God forbid! My blood's too good for that.
    I tell you I take pleasure, I delight
    Freely, for myself, quietly, because I chose to,
    In your surpassing excellence and splendour,
    In the renown and growth of your great name.
    Those are the wages that have bought my heart.
    Suppose, on account of this unbidden victory
    You judge the Prince to death and I, suppose
    Tomorrow, I, likewise unbidden to it,
    Encountered victory in the woods and rocks somewhere,
    Say like a shepherd, with my squadrons,
    By God, I'd be a worthless rogue did I
    Not cheerfully repeat the Prince's deed,
    And if you, law-book in your hand, then said:
    'Kottwitz, you've forfeited your head', I'd say
    'I knew that, sir, here have it, here it is,
    When my oath bound me to your crown, body

And soul, my head was not left out and I'd
Be giving you nothing not already yours.'
ELECTOR: You and your queer ideas, old friend,
Are more than I can manage. You seduce
Me with your tricky rhetoric
Who am fond, as you know, of you, and now
I shall call an advocate to end this dispute,
One who will put my case.
                    (He rings. Enter a SERVANT)
                    The Prince of Homburg,
Let him be brought from prison to me here.

                                        [*Exit* SERVANT]

He will instruct you, I can promise you,
What discipline and obedience are. At least
I have a text from him that reads unlike
The casuistical ideas of freedom you,
Like a boy, have been developing for me.
            (He returns to his desk and reads)
KOTTWITZ: (astonished) Fetch who? Call who?
HENNINGS: Himself?
TRUCHSS: Impossible!
    (The OFFICERS congregate in some agitation and converse with
                    one another)
ELECTOR: Who is the author of this second paper?
HOHENZOLLERN: Sir, I am.
ELECTOR: (reading)   'Proof, that Elector Friedrich
Himself, for the Prince's deed ...' By heaven now
I call that impudence!
What! The cause, the wrong he let himself commit
In battle, you lay the cause of it on me?
HOHENZOLLERN: On you, my sovereign, yes. I, Hohenzollern.
ELECTOR: By God, this goes beyond belief.
One of them tells me that he is not guilty,
The other, worse, that I am! —
How will you prove a claim like that to me?
HOHENZOLLERN:
You will remember, sir, that night when we
Came on the Prince, sunk deep in sleep,
Under the plane trees in the garden:
Dreaming perhaps of next day's victory
He held a wreath of laurel in his hand.

You, as it were to try his innermost heart,
Took the wreath from him, wound the chain you wear
Around your neck, smilingly round his laurel
And handed chain and laurel, thus entwined,
Over to the lady, your noble niece.
The Prince, at such a wondrous sight, stood up
Blushing; and having such sweet things and by
So dear a hand offered, he sought to seize them:
But you, leading the Princess so she backed away,
Hurriedly eluded him, the doors closed on you,
Lady and chain and wreath of laurels vanished
And all alone — holding a glove which he
Had torn, he did not know himself from whom —
In the lap of midnight he remained behind.
ELECTOR: What was that glove?
HOHENZOLLERN: Sir, let me finish.
The business was a joke, but of what sense
For him I was soon to recognize.
For when I, through the back gate of the garden,
Crept in to him, as if by accident,
And woke him and he gathered his wits again
The memory flooded him with joy. Truly
Nothing more touching is imaginable.
The whole event, as though it were a dream,
In the minutest detail he presented to me.
Never was any dream, he said, more vivid —
And the sure belief grew up in him
That heaven had given him a sign
That everything his spirit had seen,
Lady and laurel wreath and chain of honour,
God next time on the battlefield would grant him.
ELECTOR: Hm. Very strange. — And the glove?
HOHENZOLLERN: Indeed
That part of the dream become substantial to him
At once destroyed and strengthened his belief.
At first, wide-eyed, he stared at it —
White was its colour, it seemed, by sort and shape,
From a lady's hand — but that night in the garden
There being no one he had spoken to
Or could have had it from — and when I crossed his musing
By calling him to hear his orders in the palace

He let go what he could not grasp
And tucked the glove, not thinking, in his collar.
ELECTOR: And then?
HOHENZOLLERN: With pen and paper then he entered
The palace, to hear, from the Field Marshal's mouth,
With proper attention, his orders for the battle.
The Electress and the Princess, ready to leave,
Happened to be also present among the men.
But who can measure the vast astonishment
That seized him when the Princess missed
The glove that he had fastened in his collar?
The Marshal called, not once but often: 'Sir,
Prince Friedrich!' 'What are the Marshal's orders?' he
Replied, and sought to gather his wits. But he,
With wonders ringing him around, the thunder
Of heaven might have fallen on the palace ...
                    (He pauses)
ELECTOR: The glove was the Princess's?
HOHENZOLLERN: Indeed it was.
          (The ELECTOR *becomes thoughtful)*
(HOHENZOLLERN *continues)*
He was turned to stone. Pen in hand
True he still stood there like a living person
But all sensation, as though by strokes of magic,
Had been put out in him; not till next day,
The guns already thundering from our ranks,
Did he return to life and ask me: Friend,
What was it, tell me, Dörfling yesterday
Was saying, when we were briefed, concerning me?
DÖRFLING: Sir, what is said here, truly I endorse it.
The Prince, as I remember, of all my speech
Took in not a word. I often saw him vague.
However, in that degree wholly not present in
His body never so before that night.
ELECTOR:
And now you pile, if I have understood you,
Cause and effect on me as follows:
Had I not played equivocal games with this
Young dreamer's state he would have done no wrong:
Would not have been distracted at the briefing,

Would not in battle then have been unruly.
Not so? Not so? Is that your thinking?
HOHENZOLLERN: Sir,
The conclusions I may leave to you.
ELECTOR: Fool that you are and muddlehead, had you
Not called me down into the garden I,
Following the impulse of my curiosity, should not
Have had my harmless joke with him, that dreamer.
Thus I assert, quite with an equal right,
The one who caused his wrongdoing was you. —
The delphic wisdom of my officers!
HOHENZOLLERN:
It is enough, your Majesty. I am sure
My words, like weights, have settled in your heart.

Scene 6

Enter an OFFICER

OFFICER: The Prince, sir, will be here forthwith.
ELECTOR: Good. Let him in.
OFFICER: In two minutes. —
In passing, quickly, he had the graveyard
Opened by the gatekeeper for him.
ELECTOR: The graveyard?
OFFICER: Yes, your Majesty.
ELECTOR: What for?
OFFICER: To tell the truth, I do not know. It seemed
He wished to see the vault that has
Been opened for him there at your command.
     (*The* SENIOR OFFICERS *congregate and speak with one
                                   another*)
ELECTOR: No matter. When he arrives let him come in.
          (*He goes back to his desk and looks at the papers*)
TRUCHSS: The guard are bringing in the Prince.

Scene 7

Enter the PRINCE OF HOMBURG *and an* OFFICER *with the*
GUARD

ELECTOR: My dear young Prince, I call you to assist me.
Colonel Kottwitz brings me, in your favour,

This letter here, one after the other, look,
Signed by a hundred men of rank.
The army, so it says, desires your freedom
And disapproves of what the court decided. —
Read it yourself, will you, and see.
(He hands him the letter)
HOMBURG: (having glanced at it turns and looks around among
the officers)
Kottwitz, give me your hand, old friend.
You have done more for me than I, in battle,
Deserved of you. But now quickly go back
To Arnstein where you came from
And do not move. I have thought about it.
I wish to suffer the death imposed upon me.
(He gives him back the letter)
KOTTWITZ: (in surprise)
No, never, Prince. What are you saying?
HOHENZOLLERN: He wishes to suffer ...?
TRUCHSS: He shall not, must not die.
SEVERAL OFFICERS: (pressing forward)
Elector! Sir! My sovereign! Hear us!
HOMBURG: Be still. It is my wish, unalterably.
I wish, having transgressed it in the view
Of all the army, now to glorify
By a willing death the holy law of war.
What does the victory, comrades, matter to you,
One poor one more, that I perhaps
Might wrest from Wrangel, set beside
The triumph over the worst of enemies
In us, self-will and hubris,
Gloriously won tomorrow? Let the foreigners
Seeking to subjugate us perish
And freely in their mothers' land the Brandenburg
People assert themselves. That land is theirs
And only tilled for them their fruitful fields.
KOTTWITZ: (moved)
My son! My friend! Every dear thing to me!
TRUCHSS: God be my witness ...
KOTTWITZ: Come, let me embrace you.
(They press around him)

HOMBURG: (*turning to the* ELECTOR)
  My sovereign who bore once alas now
  Forfeited a sweeter name for me
  I lay myself with all my feeling at your feet.
  If I, when things were fought for, served you eagerly
  Too soon, forgive me now. Death now
  Washes me clean of every guilt. Allow
  My heart, serenely now and not at odds with you
  Bowing to your verdict, this to comfort it:
  That your heart too renounces every quarrel
  And in this hour of parting as a sign of that
  Graciously grant me one request.

ELECTOR:
  Ask, as a brave man may. What is it you wish?
  You have my word of honour as a soldier
  Whatever it is, it is already granted.

HOMBURG: Sir, do not barter with your niece's hand
  For peace from Gustav Carl. Send away
  The go-between out of your camp
  Who made you that proposal without honour.
  Write him an answer with a run of shot.

ELECTOR: (*kissing him on the forehead*)
  Be it as you say. With this kiss, my son,
  I grant your last request.
  Why should it need that sacrifice as well,
  Got from me only through bad luck in war,
  When out of every word that you have spoken
  A victory flowers that will grind him into dust.
  She is, I'll tell him, Prince Homburg's betrothed
  Who fell to the law because of Fehrbellin.
  He must dispute her with the Prince's ghost
  In battle, striding before our colours, dead.
          (*He kisses him again and raises him up*)

HOMBURG: See now you have given me my life again.
  Now I beg down upon you every blessing
  That, from their throne of clouds, the seraphim
  Joyfully pour upon the heads of heroes.
  Sir, go and combat and defeat
  The world if it defies you. You are fit to.

ELECTOR: Guard! Conduct him back to prison.

Scene 8

NATALIE *and the* ELECTRESS *appear in the door*, LADIES-IN-
WAITING *following them*

NATALIE:
Please, Aunt, don't speak to me of right behaviour.
The thing most right at this time is to love him.
My dear unhappy friend.

HOMBURG: (*seeking to leave*) Away!

TRUCHSS: (*holding him*)   No, Prince, never!
                (*Several* OFFICERS *bar his way*)

HOMBURG: Lead me away.

HOHENZOLLERN: Elector, can your heart ...?

HOMBURG: (*tearing himself free*)   Tyrants, would you
Prefer me dragged to the firing squad in chains?
Away! — I have paid the world my debt.
                                [*Exit with the* GUARD]

NATALIE: (*leaning against her aunt*)
Oh earth receive me now into your lap.
Why should I see the sunlight any more?

Scene 9

DÖRFLING:
Oh God in heaven. Did it have to come to this?
(*The* ELECTOR *speaks secretly and urgently with an* OFFICER)

KOTTWITZ: (*coldly*) Sovereign and lord, this having happened
Are we dismissed?

ELECTOR: No you are not. Not yet.
I'll tell you when you are dismissed.
(*He looks fixedly at him for a moment. Then he takes up from
the table the papers the page has brought and turns with them
                to* FIELD MARSHAL DÖRFLING)
This passport to the Swede, Count Horn. Tell him
The Prince, my cousin, made me a request
That I am honour bound to grant:
The war resumes in three days' time.
                (*Pause. — He glances at the death sentence*)
Well, gentlemen, judge for yourselves. The Prince of Homburg
Has in the last year wilfully, frivolously,
Cost me two splendid victories. A third
Likewise he gravely marred for me.

Having gone through the school of these last days
Will you risk it a fourth time with him?
KOTTWITZ AND TRUCHSS: (*speaking at once*)
  Sir! What? Dear sovereign lord! Revered ...!
ELECTOR: Will you? Will you?
KOTTWITZ: By the living God
  You might stand on the very brink of ruin
  And he, to help you, would not even,
  To save you, draw his sword, unless you ordered it.
ELECTOR: (*tearing up the death sentence*)
  Follow me, friends, into the garden then.

                                                    [*All exit*]

                              Scene 10

  Scene: Palace with the stairway leading down into the garden
  as in Act I. — It is night again. The PRINCE OF HOMBURG,
  blindfolded, is led on by CAVALRY OFFICER STRANZ *through*
  the lower garden gate. OFFICERS *with the* GUARD. *— In the*
            distance drums are heard, beating a death march
HOMBURG: Now immortality you are wholly mine.
  You beam through the blindfold covering my eyes
  At me with the radiance of a thousand suns.
  Wings have put forth on both my shoulders,
  My spirit lifts through the ether's silent spaces
  And as a ship, the wind's breath carrying her,
  Sees sinking away the cheerful harbour town
  So all life sets for me in twilight now.
  Now I distinguish colours still and shapes
  And now below me everything has misted.
  (*The* PRINCE *seats himself on the bench which, in the centre of*
  the square, is fitted around the trunk of the oak tree. CAVALRY
    OFFICER STRANZ *moves away from him and looks up at the*
                              stairway)
HOMBURG: Oh such a sweet scent from the violets!
  Can you not smell them?
                        (STRANZ *comes back to him*)
STRANZ: They are nightscented stocks
  And carnations.
HOMBURG: Nightscented stocks, how so? —
  How do they come to be here?

STRANZ: I don't know. —
It seems that they were planted by a girl. — Can I
Hand you a carnation?
HOMBURG: Dear friend,
At home I'll put it in some water.

Scene 11

The ELECTOR, *carrying the laurel wreath around which the*
golden chain is wound, ELECTRESS, PRINCESS NATALIE,
FIELD MARSHAL DÖRFLING, COLONELS KOTTWITZ,
HOHENZOLLERN, GOLZ, *etc.,* LADIES-IN-WAITING,
OFFICERS *and torches appear on the stairway leading down*
from the palace. — HOHENZOLLERN *comes to the balustrade*
holding a handkerchief and waves to CAVALRY OFFICER
STRANZ *with it.* STRANZ *then moves away from the* PRINCE
OF HOMBURG *and speaks, at the rear of the stage, with the*
GUARD

HOMBURG: Dear friend, what light is that, spreading?
STRANZ: *(coming back to him)*
Prince, be kind enough to stand, will you?
HOMBURG: What is it?
STRANZ: Nothing that need alarm you. —
I wanted merely to open your eyes again.
HOMBURG: Has the last hour of my ordeals come?
STRANZ: It has. –
Hail to you now and blessing, as you deserve.
(*The* ELECTOR *gives the wreath, from which the chain is*
hanging, to the PRINCESS, *takes her by the hand and leads her*
down the stairway. The LADIES *and* GENTLEMEN *follow. The*
PRINCESS, *surrounded by torches, approaches the* PRINCE *who*
rises to his feet in astonishment. She places the wreath on his
head, hangs the chain around his neck and presses his hand
against her heart. The PRINCE *faints*)
NATALIE: Oh heaven! The joy of it has killed him.
HOHENZOLLERN: *(supporting him)* Help him.
ELECTOR: Let thundering cannon wake him.
(*Cannon-fire. A march. The palace is illuminated*)
KOTTWITZ: Hail,
Hail to the Prince of Homburg.
OFFICERS: Hail, hail!

ALL: The victor in the Battle of Fehrbellin!

                (*Momentary pause*)

HOMBURG: No, say. Is it a dream?

KOTTWITZ: A dream, what else?

SEVERAL OFFICERS: To war! To war!

TRUCHSS: To battle!

DÖRFLING: And victory!

ALL: In the dust with every enemy of Brandenburg!

PROSE

MICHAEL KOHLHAAS
(From an old chronicle)

On the banks of the Havel,* around the middle of the sixteenth century, there lived a horsedealer by the name of *Michael Kohlhaas*, the son of a schoolmaster and one of the most honest and most terrible human beings of his time. — This extraordinary man could have stood, until his thirtieth year, as the very model of a good citizen. He owned, in a village that still bears his name, a farm on which, by his trade, he earned a quiet livelihood; the children his wife had borne him he brought up in the fear of God to be loyal and hardworking; there was not one among his neighbours who had not enjoyed some benefit from his charity and fairness; in brief, posterity would surely have blessed his memory had he not, in one virtue, gone to extremes. His sense of justice turned him into a robber and a murderer.

He was leaving his homeland one day with a string of young horses, all well groomed and glossy, and was considering how he would use the profit he hoped to make on them at the markets: some, as any good businessman would, to make more profit, but also some for present enjoyment: when he reached the Elbe and, at a magnificent castle, on Saxon territory, met a barrier he had never encountered on that road before.* He halted with his horses, just as the rain came on very violently, and shouted for the tollbooth keeper, who did then soon show his bad-tempered face at the window. The horsedealer asked to be let through. 'What's this then?' he said when the keeper, after a good while, emerged from the house. 'Royal privilege,' said the keeper, opening the way, 'granted to the Junker Wenzel von Tronka.' — 'Oh?' said Kohlhaas. 'So the Junker is called Wenzel?' And he contemplated the castle that with shining turrets looked out across the fields. — 'Is the old one dead?' 'Died of a stroke,' the tollbooth keeper replied, raising the barrier. — 'A pity,' said Kohlhaas. 'A fine old gentleman who liked to see people in dealings with one another, helped trade along whenever he could, and once had a stone causeway built because a stallion of mine, back there where the road goes into the village, broke its leg. Ah well. What do I owe you?' he asked and began, with difficulty, to fetch out from under his coat, that was flapping in the wind, the amount demanded of him by the tollbooth keeper. 'Yes, friend,' he added as the keeper, cursing the weather, muttered at him to hurry up, 'if that pole had never left the forest it would have been better for both of us'; and so saying he gave him the money and was setting off again. But he had scarcely got under the barrier when a new voice shouted behind him from the tower: 'Stay where you are, horsedealer!' And he saw the castle steward slamming a window shut and hurrying down. 'Now what?' Kohlhaas wondered, and halted with his horses. The steward, buttoning an extra jacket around his ample form, approached and, leaning into the weather, asked to see his pass. — Kohlhaas asked: 'My pass?' He said, somewhat taken aback, that so far as he knew he had no pass; but if someone would tell him what manner of thing it was then it could be that he had one with him after all. The steward, looking at him askance, replied that without written permission from the court no horsedealer was allowed over the border with horses. The horsedealer assured him that without any such pass he had crossed the border seventeen times in his life already; that he was fully cognizant with all the court's regulations pertaining to his trade; that this was doubtless a mistake, as they would realize if they thought about it; and that, since he had a long day's journey ahead of him, would they please not hold him up for no good reason any longer. But the steward replied that he would not slip through the eighteenth time; that the order in question had only recently been issued, and that he must either acquire a pass forthwith or go back where he came from. The horsedealer, whom these illegal demands were beginning to anger, having thought for a moment got down from his horse, gave it to a servant to mind, and said he would speak to the Junker von Tronka himself about the matter. And he went into the castle; the steward followed him, muttering about skinflints and money-grubbers and how it was necessary to bleed them now and then; and together, exchanging hostile looks, they entered the hall. As it happened, the Junker and some of his cheerfully noisy friends were in there drinking and, at some joke or other, a colossal laughter broke out among them just as Kohlhaas approached with his complaint. The Junker asked what he wanted; the knights, seeing the stranger, fell silent; but scarcely had Kohlhaas broached the matter of his horses than the whole company called out: 'Horses? Where?' — and hurried to the windows, to look. Seeing how glossy the beasts were they raced then, at the Junker's suggestion, down into the courtyard. The rain had ceased; steward, bailiff and servants all gathered around the horses, inspecting them. One man praised the sorrel with the blaze, another liked the chestnut best, a third was stroking the dapple grey; and all were of the opinion that the horses were like stags and that in the whole country none better were being raised. Kohlhaas answered cheerfully that the horses were no better than the knights who would be their riders; and invited them to buy. The Junker, very tempted by the powerful sorrel stallion, did then ask the price; the bailiff urged him to buy the black pair since, being short of horses, he thought he could use them on the estate; but when the horsedealer named his prices the knights found them too high, and the Junker said he would have to ride to the Round Table and find King Arthur if he was going to ask that much. Kohlhaas, who saw the steward and the bailiff whispering together and casting looks, whose import was obvious, at the black horses, felt some faint foreboding of ill, and did all he could to let his horses go to them. He said to the Junker: 'Sir, I bought the black pair six months ago for twenty-five gulden. Give me thirty and they are yours.' Two knights who were standing near the Junker expressed the view, with some definiteness, that the horses were surely worth so much; but the Junker declared that he might be willing to spend money on the sorrel stallion but not on the black pair, and made to leave; whereupon Kohlhaas said that perhaps they might do business the next time he passed through with his nags; bowed to the Junker; and seized the reins of his horse, to ride on his way. At that moment the steward stepped forward out of the group and said to Kohlhaas that without a pass, as he had been told, he would not be allowed to travel. Kohlhaas turned and asked the Junker whether it was true that such a requirement, which would destroy his whole business, was indeed in force? The Junker answered with an embarrassed face, as he left: 'Yes, Kohlhaas, you must have a pass. Speak with the steward and be on your way.' Kohlhaas assured him that it was not at all his intention to circumvent any regulations there might be with regard to the exportation of horses; promised that as he went through Dresden* he would get himself issued with a pass in the Chancellery offices and asked, this once, since he had known nothing whatsoever about the requirement, to be allowed to proceed. 'Well then,' said the Junker as the weather at that moment again became severe and howled through his thin limbs, 'let the fool go. Come', he said to the knights, turned away and was making for the castle. The steward said, turning to the Junker, that he must at least leave something behind as security that he would indeed take out a pass. The

Junker halted in the castle gate. Kohlhaas asked what should be the value then, in money or goods, of the security which, on account of the black horses, he should leave behind. The bailiff, muttering into his beard, was of the opinion that he might as well leave the black horses themselves behind. 'Indeed yes,' said the steward, 'that would be the most appropriate. Once he has his pass he can pick them up again at any time.' Kohlhaas, taken aback by the shamelessness of this demand, said to the Junker who, shivering, was wrapping himself in the tails of his coat, that he was of course wanting to sell the horses; but the Junker, since at that moment a gust of wind drove rain and hail through the gate in vast amounts, cried out, to make an end of the matter: 'If he won't leave them here you send him packing', and left the scene. The horsedealer, seeing very well that he must give way to force, decided, since there was nothing for it, to fulfil the demand; and unharnessing the black horses he led them into a stable as the steward directed. He left a stableman with them, provided him with money, charged him, until his return, to take good care of the horses, and with those remaining, uncertain whether perhaps after all, on account of the burgeoning of their own studfarms, some such regulation might not have been introduced in the Saxon lands, he continued on his way towards Leipzig, where it was his intention to attend the fair.

In Dresden where, in one of the suburbs, he owned a house with a few stables, since from here he took his business out to the country's smaller markets, he went immediately after his arrival to the Chancellery and learned from its officials, some of whom he was acquainted with, what he had been inclined to believe all along, namely that the story about his needing a pass was a fiction. Kohlhaas, to whom the displeased officials, at his request, issued a written attestation of this invalidity, smiled at the skinny Junker's joke, without quite understanding what he meant by it; and some weeks later then, having, to his satisfaction, sold the horses he had with him, he returned with no more bitterness than what was due to the general plight of the world, to the castle at Tronka. The steward, to whom he showed the attestation, had nothing further to say on the subject and replied, when the horsedealer asked him could he now have his horses back, that he could go down and fetch them if he wished. But even as he was crossing the courtyard Kohlhaas was unpleasantly surprised to learn that his stableman, having behaved badly it was said, had, only a few days after being left behind at Tronkenburg, been given a thrashing and chased away. He asked the boy who told him this what the stableman had done and who had looked after the horses meanwhile, to which the boy replied that he did not know and thereupon opened for the horsedealer, whose heart was already full of foreboding, the stable in which they were kept. His astonishment then was very great when he saw, instead of his two glossy well-fed black horses, a pair of skinny and ill-used nags; bones one might have hung things from; mane and hair, for lack of being looked after, now all matted together: surely the most wretched spectacle in all of the animal kingdom! Kohlhaas's anger was extreme. The horses made a feeble movement and whinnied in his direction. He asked what had happened to them and the boy, standing by him, replied that no misfortune had befallen them, that they had also had proper feeding, but that, since it was harvest time and there was a shortage of animals for the wagons, they had been used in the fields a little. Kohlhaas swore over this disgraceful and calculated injury but, feeling his own powerlessness, he swallowed his rage and was already making preparations, since there was nothing for it, to take himself and his horses out of that den of thieves when the steward, drawn there by the raised voices, appeared and asked what was the matter. 'The matter?' Kohlhaas replied. 'Who gave the Junker von Tronka and his people permission to use my horses, left here with him, for work in the fields?' He added: was it a humane thing to have done? tried to raise the exhausted creatures with a stroke of his riding crop, and showed the steward that they did not stir. The steward, after staring at him defiantly for a while, replied: 'Hark at the lout!' The oaf, he continued, should thank God that his nags were alive at all. Who, he asked, since the stableman had run away, was supposed to look after them? Wasn't it right and proper that the horses should earn in the fields the food they had been given? To conclude, Kohlhaas should hush or he would call the dogs and soon restore order in the place with them. — The horsedealer felt the thumping of his heart. He felt powerfully inclined to fling the fat-bellied good-for-nothing in the dirt and tread on his brassy face. But his sense of justice, delicate as a goldsmith's scales, still wavered; he was, before the bar of his own heart, still uncertain what weight of wrong his opponent was carrying; and swallowing the insults he crossed to the horses and laying their manes straight, silently thinking things over, he asked, in a lowered voice, for what misdemeanour then the stableman had been ejected from the castle. The steward answered: 'Because the villain was troublesome around the place. Because he would not accept a change of stabling when it was necessary and wanted us, when two young gentlemen visited Tronkenburg, to let their horses stand out in the street all night, for his pair's sake.' — Kohlhaas would have given what the horses were worth to have the stableman there and had he been able to compare his account with that of the loud-mouthed steward. He was still standing there and, with his fingers, combing out the plugs in the horses' manes and wondering what in his situation it would be best to do, when suddenly the scene changed and Junker Wenzel von Tronka with a host of knights, servants and dogs burst into the courtyard, from hare-hunting. The steward, when the Junker asked him what was happening, spoke up first, and whilst the dogs on the one side at the sight of the stranger set up a devilish baying at him, and the knights, on the other, ordered them to be silent, he reported, grievously distorting the facts, that the horsedealer, because his horses had been put to use a little, was creating a great disturbance. He said, with a sneer, that the man was refusing to acknowledge the horses as his. Kohlhaas cried: 'Those are not my horses, sir! Those are not the horses that were worth thirty gulden. I want my well-fed glossy horses back.' — The Junker, a brief pallor coming into his face, dismounted and said: 'If the clown doesn't want his horses back, so be it. Come along, Günter!' he called — 'Hans, come along!' and shook the dust from his trousers; and 'Bring some wine!' he called, already passing through the door with his companions; and went into the house. Kohlhaas said that he would sooner send for the knacker and dump the horses in his yard than lead them back in that condition into his stables at Kohlhaasenbrück. Then he paid them no further attention and left them standing where they were; and swearing that he would not fail to get justice for himself he mounted his chestnut stallion and rode away.

He was already at full tilt on the road to Dresden when, at the thought of the stableman and the complaint made in the castle against him, he slowed to walking and before he had done another thousand paces turned his horse and, first to hear the stableman's account of events, as seemed to him politic and just, took the road to Kohlhaasen-brück. For a proper sense of the world, born of familiarity with its fragile ordering, inclined him, despite the insults he had suffered, should in fact, as the steward asserted, any guilt be ascribable to the stableman, to put up with the loss of the horses as its fair consequence. But an equally admirable feeling, a feeling that rooted deeper and deeper the further he rode and at every stopping place heard of the injustices daily perpetrated against travellers at Tronkenburg, this feeling said to him that if the whole incident, as seemed very likely, was merely trumped up, then he with all his strength now had a duty to the world to get satisfaction for the offence done him and security for his fellow citizens against any further such.

Arriving at Kohlhaasenbrück, as soon as he had embraced his faithful wife Lisbeth and kissed the children pressing joyfully around his knees, he asked after Lerse, the chief stableman, and whether anything had been heard of him. Lisbeth said: 'Oh Michael, our poor Herse! Would you believe it, he arrived two weeks ago, poor man, he had been terribly beaten about; indeed, so beaten about he could not breathe properly. We put him to bed, he was spitting blood, and we heard from him, in answer to our repeated questions, a story that nobody could understand. How you had left him behind at Tronkenburg with some horses not allowed to go through; how he had been forced, by the worst possible ill-treatment, to quit the castle; and how he was not able to take the horses with him.' 'I see,' said Kohlhaas, taking off his coat. 'Is he better now?' — 'More or less,' she replied, 'except for spitting blood. I wanted to send a man to Tronkenburg at once to look after the horses until you got there. For since Herse has always been truthful and more loyal to us than any other I had no grounds for doubting his story, with so much to support it, and for supposing, say, that he had lost the horses in some other fashion. But he begged me not to ask anyone to venture into that den of thieves and to give up the animals rather than sacrifice a person's life on their account.' — 'Is he still in bed?' Kohlhaas asked, ridding himself of his neck-cloth. — 'He has been out and about,' she replied, 'for some days now. To conclude,' she went on, 'you will see that everything he says is true and that this occurrence is one among the wrongs that lately the people at Tronkenburg have been doing to strangers.' — 'I must enquire into it first,' Kohlhaas replied. 'Call him in here to me, will you, Lisbeth; if he is up.' So saying, he seated himself in his armchair; and his wife, very gladdened by his composure, went and fetched the stableman.

'What did you do at Tronkenburg?' Kohlhaas asked as Lisbeth came into the room with him. 'I am not very pleased with you.' — The stableman, whose pale face at these words showed a patchy red, was silent for a while; then 'You are right, sir,' he answered, 'for, as God willed it, I had a fuse of sulphur on me and could have sent the den they drove me out of up in flames but I heard the crying of a child in there and threw my sulphur in the Elbe instead, and thought: Let God's bolts burn it, I won't.' — Kohlhaas was astonished and said: 'But how did you get yourself driven out of Tronkenburg?' Herse's answer: 'By a bad move, sir,' and he wiped the sweat off his brow. 'But what's done cannot be undone. I did not want the horses worked to death in the fields and said they were still young and had never been in harness.' — Kohlhaas replied, whilst seeking to conceal the confusion of his feelings, that he had not been entirely truthful in saying this since at the beginning of the year they had been in harness once or twice. 'In the castle,' he went on, 'where you were after all a sort of guest, you might now and then, when the need arose, to get the harvest in quickly, have shown willing.' — 'So I did, sir,' said Herse. 'I thought, since they were looking at me askance, it won't be the death of the beasts, and on the third morning I harnessed them and brought in three waggon-loads of grain.' Kohlhaas, his heart swelling up, looked down at the ground and answered: 'Nobody told me that, Herse.' — Herse assured him that it was so. 'Where I didn't show willing,' he said, 'was in this: that at midday, when they had hardly finished feeding, I wouldn't let them be put back in their halters; and when the steward and the bailiff suggested I should take feed for them gratis and pocket the money you left me to feed them with, I said what I might like to do to *them*; and turned and walked away.' — 'But that,' said Kohlhaas, 'is not what you were driven out of Tronkenburg for?' 'God forbid!' cried the stableman. 'It was a downright wickedness. For that evening the horses of two gentlemen who arrived at Tronkenburg were led into the stable and mine were tethered to the stable door. And when I asked the steward, who brought them in himself and handed mine over, where they were supposed to go, he showed me a pigsty put together out of laths and planks against the castle wall.' — 'You mean,' said Kohlhaas interrupting him, 'it was such a poor place for horses that it was more like a pigsty than a stable.' — 'Sir, it was a pigsty,' Herse replied, 'really and truly one with the pigs running in and out and I couldn't stand up in it.' — 'Perhaps no other accommodation could be found for the horses,' said Kohlhaas. 'In a sense the knights' horses came first.' — 'Space,' the stableman replied, dropping his voice, 'was tight. By now there were seven knights housing in the castle altogether. If it had been you, you would have squeezed the horses up a little. I said I would try and rent a stable in the village, but the steward replied that he must have the horses always in his sight and I mustn't dare take them out of the castle.' — 'Hm,' said Kohlhaas. 'What was your response to that?' — 'Because the bailiff said the two guests would only stay the night and ride on the next day I put the horses in the pigsty. But the next day passed and they had not ridden on and on the third day the word was they would stay another few weeks in the castle.' — 'In the end, Herse,' said Kohlhaas, 'it wasn't as bad in the pigsty as you thought when you first looked in.' — 'True,' Herse replied. 'When I'd swept the place out a bit, we could manage. I gave the girl a penny to put the pigs somewhere else. And during the day I saw to it as well that the horses could stand upright. At first light, I took the roof planks off the laths and laid them back on again in the evening. So they poked out through the roof like geese and turned their heads towards Kohlhaasen-brück or wherever else it would have been better to be.' — 'Well then,' Kohlhaas asked, 'why on earth did they chase you away?' — 'Sir, I tell you,' said the stableman, 'because they wanted rid of me. Because so long as I was there they couldn't work the horses to death. Everywhere I went, in the yard or in the servants' quarters, they gave me sour looks, and because I said to myself pull all the faces you like and see if I care they invented an occasion and threw me out.' — 'But the reason!' Kohlhaas cried. 'They must have had some reason.' — 'Oh indeed,' Herse replied, 'and a very fair one at that! On the evening of my second day in the pigsty I took the horses which, naturally, had got filthy in there and wanted to ride them down to the watering place. And just as I had reached the castle gates and was about to move away I heard the steward and the bailiff with men and dogs and sticks come in a rush out of the servants' quarters after me and crying "Stop, thief! Stop, you villain!" like men possessed. The gatekeeper barred my way and when I asked him and the demented mob running at me what the matter was, the steward answered: "What the matter is?" and seized my black pair by their bridles. "Where do you think you are going with the horses?" he asked, and held me by the front of my coat. "Where am I going?" I said. "God in heaven I'm going where I can give them a wash. Did you think I ...?" "For a wash?" the steward shouted. "I'll give you a wash, here on the road to Kohlhaasenbrück, I will, you lying rogue", and flung me, with a devilish tug, him and the bailiff, who had me by the foot, down from off my horse so I measured my length in the muck. "God blast you," I cried, "harness and covers are back there and a bundle of washing, in the stable there"; but he and the men while the bailiff led the horses away were at me with their feet and whips and sticks and I went down half dead at the castle gate. And when I said: "You thieving devils, where are you taking my horses?" and got to my feet, "Out!" yelled the steward, "Get out!" and "Seek him, Prince! Seek him, Fang!" they shouted and "Seek him, Towser!" and a pack of a dozen or more dogs was on me. Then I broke a pole or something from off the fence and laid out three dogs dead in front of me but when, terribly ripped, I had to give some ground, there comes a loud whistle, the dogs back in the yard, the gates shut, bolted, and I fell down on the highway in a faint.' — Kohlhaas said, white-faced, with a forced roguishness: 'Did you really not want to abscond, Herse?' And when Herse, flushing darkly, looked down at the floor, 'Admit it,' he said, 'you were not happy in the pigsty, you thought to yourself I'd be better off in the stables at Kohlhaasen-brück.' — 'God blast it!' Herse cried. 'I left the harness and the covers and a bundle of my linen in the pigsty. Wouldn't I have put the three gulden in my pocket that I had hidden in my red silk handkerchief behind the trough? Hellfire and devils! When you talk like that I wish I could light the sulphur fuse again that I threw away.' 'There, there,' said the horsedealer, 'I didn't mean any ill. What you have told me, look, I believe it every word and if it comes to being said I'll swear to it myself, on the body of God. I am sorry that in my service you have not fared better than this. Off you go now, Herse, go back to bed, have them give you a bottle of wine, and be comforted, you shall have justice.' And with that he rose, drew up an inventory of the things his stableman had left behind in the pigsty; specified the value of them, also asked what he estimated the costs of his treatment were; and having once again shaken hands, let him go.

Next then he related to Lisbeth, his wife, the whole sequence and sense of the events, explained to her that he was determined to seek justice from the law and had the pleasure of seeing that in this intention she supported him wholeheartedly. For she said that many another traveller, perhaps less patient than he was, would pass by that castle; that it was doing God's work to put a stop to such irregularities; and that, never fear, she would manage to get together the costs he would incur by going to law. Kohlhaas called her his trusty wife, took pleasure that day and the next in her and his children's company and set off then, as soon as his business at all permitted it, for Dresden, to bring his case to court.

There, with the help of a lawyer of his acquaintance, he drew up a document of complaint in which, after a detailed description of the crime committed against him and his stableman Herse by Junker Wenzel von Tronka, he sought the punishment of the law on the man, restoration of the horses into their former state and compensation for the damage both he and the servant had suffered. The case was indeed clear-cut. The fact that the horses had been illegally detained cast a decisive light over all the rest; and even had one been prepared to accept it as mere bad luck that the horses had fallen sick still the horsedealer's demand that they be returned to him fit and well was just. Nor, as he looked about him in the capital, did Kohlhaas at all lack friends promising him their active support in his affair; his widespread business with horses and his honesty in prosecuting it had got him the acquaintance and the goodwill of the most important men in the land. Several times he dined very cheerfully with his lawyer, who was himself a man of standing; and a few weeks later, leaving with him a sum of money to meet the legal costs and having been completely reassured by him as to the outcome of the case, he returned to his wife Lisbeth in Kohlhaasenbrück. But months passed, the year was almost up before from Saxony even any response to the complaint he had lodged there let alone any resolution of it reached him. In a private letter, after several times addressing himself to the lawcourts, he asked his advocate what was causing such excessive delay; and learned that his suit, through some intervention from on high, had, in the Dresden courts, been wholly rejected. — When the horsedealer wrote again, asking in astonishment after the reason, the advocate reported: that Junker Wenzel von Tronka was related to two young noblemen, Hinz and Kunz von Tronka, one of whom was the Elector's cupbearer and the other actually his chamberlain. — He advised him besides to make no more efforts at law but to seek to have back the horses still at Tronkenburg; gave him to understand that the Junker, presently sojourning in the capital, seemed to have directed his people to release them to him; and concluded with the request that, if he were not willing to be content with this, he would at least not bother him any further in the matter.

Kohlhaas happened at this time to be in Brandenburg where the governor, Heinrich von Geusau, in whose administrative region Kohlhaasenbrück lay, was just then occupied in setting up, out of a considerable sum of money which had fallen to the town, a number of charities for the sick and the needy. One chief project was to make it possible for invalids to make use of a certain mineral water that rose up in a village in that region and of whose healing powers more was expected than the future in fact delivered; and because Kohlhaas, through business dealings during his time at court, was known to him he allowed Herse, the chief stableman, who since that evil day at Tronkenburg still had pains in his chest when he drew breath, to try the powers of the little spring now roofed and walled around. It happened that the governor, making certain arrangements, was present on the edge of the pool in which Kohlhaas had laid Herse, at the very moment when, by a messenger sent after him by his wife, he, Kohlhaas, received the letter of rejection from the advocate in Dresden. The mayor, noting whilst in conversation with the doctor that Kohlhaas let fall a tear on to the letter he had received and opened, approached him in a warm and friendly way and asked what misfortune he had suffered; and when the horsedealer, without replying, handed him the letter, this estimable man, knowing of the abominable injustice done him at Tronkenburg, as a result of which Herse, perhaps for the rest of his life, lay sick, clapped him on the shoulder and said not to lose heart, he would help him get satisfaction. That evening when the horsedealer, obeying his summons, called on him in the palace, his advice was simple: that he draw up a petition, with a brief presentation of the occurrence, to the Elector of Brandenburg, attach the advocate's letter, and beg his sovereign's protection in the face of the violence that had been perpetrated against him on Saxon territory. He promised to include the petition in another packet, already made up, and bring it thus into the hands of the Elector who then infallibly, if circumstances permitted, would intercede for him with the Elector of Saxony; and more than such a step would not be necessary to get him justice, despite the machinations of the Junker and his clique, in the lawcourts of Dresden. Kohlhaas, keenly delighted, gave the governor warmest thanks for this new proof of his goodwill; said he regretted not having at once, without making any move in Dresden, presented his case in Berlin; and having then drawn up his complaint in the city's law office exactly as required and handed it to the governor he returned to Kohlhaasenbrück, easier in his mind than ever as to the outcome of his affair. But only a few weeks later he was distressed to learn, through a magistrate travelling to Potsdam on business of the governor's, that the Elector had passed on the petition to his chancellor Count Kallheim and that he, instead of going straight, as seemed most practical, to the Dresden court for investigation into and punishment of the wrongdoing, had gone instead, for preliminary further details, to the Junker von Tronka. The magistrate who, halting in his carriage outside Kohlhaas's house, seemed to have been given the job of divulging this to him, could not, to the astonished question why they had proceeded thus, give him any satisfactory answer. All he added was that the governor bade him be patient; seemed in a hurry to go on with his journey; and only as their brief conversation ended did Kohlhaas deduce, from some casual remarks, that Count Kallheim was related by marriage to the house of Tronka. — Kohlhaas, who had no joy now in the raising of horses, nor in his house and land, and scarcely even in his wife and children, endured the next month in a gloomy apprehension of what would come; and, wholly according to his expectation, when that time had elapsed Herse, to whom the baths had brought some relief, came back from Brandenburg with a letter, accompanying a more ample document, from the governor, saying: he was sorry, he could do nothing in his case; he was sending him the State Chancellery's resolution, addressed to him; and advised him to collect the horses he had left at Tronkenburg and thereafter to let the matter drop. — The resolution read: He was, according to a statement of the lawcourts in Dresden, a litigious nuisance; the Junker, with whom he had left the horses, was in no sense withholding them from him; he should send to the castle and fetch them, or at least let the Junker know where he should return them to him; but whatever else, would he please refrain from bothering the Chancellery with any further stink and fuss. Kohlhaas, for whom the horses were not the issue — he would have felt the same grief had it been a matter of a couple of dogs — Kohlhaas foamed with rage when he received this letter. He looked, whenever there was a noise in the yard, in the unhappiest anticipation ever to trouble his heart, towards the way through his gates, to see whether it might not be the Junker's servants come, perhaps even with an apology, to deliver him his horses, starved and broken down; and this was the first time ever that his soul, well educated by the world, had prepared itself to bear something not in accordance with its feelings. But he soon heard from an acquaintance who had travelled the road that his nags, as before, like the rest of the Junker's horses, were being used in the fields at Tronkenburg; and in the midst of the pain it gave him to see the world in such monstrous disorder he felt a sudden access of inner satisfaction that at least his own heart was in order now. He invited in his neighbour, a councillor, who had long entertained the idea of increasing his own estate by the purchase of the plots of land adjoining it, and asked him, when they were seated together, what he would give him for his properties in Brandenburg and Saxony, houses and land, the whole lot, fixtures and movables. Lisbeth, his wife, went pale at these words. She turned, lifted up her youngest child who was playing on the floor behind her, and past the red cheeks of the boy, whom now the fastenings on her collar were amusing, she stared with death in her eyes at the horsedealer and at a paper in his hand. The councillor, looking at him in astonishment, asked what was the cause of such sudden strange ideas; to which Kohlhaas, with as much cheerfulness as he could manage, replied: the idea of selling his dairy farm on the banks of the Havel was not so very new; they had already, the two of them, often discussed it; his house in the suburbs of Dresden was, in comparison, a mere appendage, of no importance; and in brief if he would do as he wished and take on both the properties he was ready to sign a contract with him to that effect. He added, with rather forced jocularity, that Kohlhaasenbrück was not the whole world; there might be things to do in comparison with which heading a household as a decent father was less important and indeed unworthy; and, in brief, his heart, he must tell him, was set on great things which he would hear of soon enough perhaps. The councillor, reassured by these words, said, jokingly, to the woman, who did not leave off kissing her child: he wouldn't want payment there and then, would he?; laid his hat and stick, which he had been holding between his

knees, down on the table and took the paper, which the horsedealer had
in his hand, to read it through. Kohlhaas, moving closer, explained that
it was a contract of sale drawn up by him to come into effect, if they
wished, in four weeks' time; indicated to him that it lacked nothing but
the signatures and to have the sums inserted, both the sale price and the
forfeit which he bound himself to pay should he, within four weeks,
withdraw; and again cheerfully urged him to make an offer, assuring
him that he would be reasonable and settle without fuss. The woman
went to and fro in the living room; the agitation of her bosom was such
that the shawl, at which the boy had been tugging, threatened to fall
completely from her shoulders. The councillor said that of course he had
no way of judging the value of the property in Dresden; whereupon
Kohlhaas, pushing towards him letters exchanged at the time of
purchase, answered that he estimated it at a hundred gold gulden;
although from the letters it was clear that he had paid nearly half as
much again. The councillor, re-reading the contract and finding that,
particularly, on his side too the freedom to withdraw was a stipulation,
said, already half decided: that he would not, of course, have any use for
the stud-horses in the stables; but when Kohlhaas replied that he did not
in fact wish to part with the horses and that some weapons, which hung
in the armoury, he intended keeping also, then the councillor hesitated
and still hesitated and at last repeated an offer that he had made him
once already, not long since, half in jest, half in earnest, whilst they were
out walking together, one derisively below the value of the property.
Kohlhaas pushed pen and ink towards him, to write; and when the
councillor, doubting his own senses, had asked him again was he serious
and the horsedealer with a touch of annoyance had answered: did he
suppose he was making game of him? the councillor, with some
uneasiness in his look, did then take up the pen, and wrote; but crossed
out the clause which dealt with the forfeit to pay should the seller regret
the deal; engaged himself to a loan of one hundred gulden against the
mortgage of the property in Dresden whilst not at all wishing to acquire
it as a purchase; and left Kohlhaas complete freedom to withdraw from
the deal within two months. The horsedealer, touched by this conduct,
shook him with great warmth by the hand; and when they had then
agreed, as a chief condition, that a quarter of the purchase price should
be paid without fail in cash immediately and the rest within three
months into the Bank of Hamburg, he called for wine to celebrate a
piece of business so happily concluded. He said to a maid, entering with
the bottles, that Sternbald, the stableman, should saddle him his
chestnut stallion; he was obliged, he let it be known, to ride to the

capital where he had things to arrange; and gave them to understand that soon, when he returned, he would expound more candidly what for the present he had to keep to himself. Thereupon, filling the glasses, he enquired after the Poles and the Turks, just then at odds with one another; involved the councillor in various political conjectures on the subject; drank finally once more to the success of their business, and bade him good day. — When the councillor had left the room Lisbeth fell on her knees before her husband. 'If you at all,' she said, 'hold me in your heart, me and the children I have borne you; if we are not already, for what reason I do not know, cast out: then tell me what these terrible measures mean.' Kohlhaas said: 'Dearest wife, nothing by which, things being as they are, you need be disquieted. I have received a ruling in which I am told that my complaint against Junker Wenzel von Tronka is a stink about nothing. And since there must be a misunderstanding here I have decided to bring my complaint once more, in person, to the Elector.' — 'Why do you want to sell your house?' she cried, rising to her feet in evident distress. The horsedealer, pressing her gently against him, answered: 'Because, dearest Lisbeth, I do not wish to remain in a land where I will not be protected in my rights. I'd rather be a dog, if I am to be kicked, than a human being. I am certain my wife thinks in this as I do.' — 'How do you know?' she asked him in furious tones, 'that you will not be protected in your rights? If you approach your sovereign humbly, as it behoves you to, with your petition, how do you know it will be cast aside or answered with a refusal to listen to you?' — 'Naturally,' Kohlhaas answered, 'if my fears are groundless I shall not sell my house. The sovereign himself is, I know, just; and if I can only succeed in getting through those who surround him to his own person I do not doubt that I will get justice for myself and return in good spirits before the week is out to you and to my old occupations. Then all I ask,' he added, kissing her, 'is to abide with you till the end of my days. — But it is advisable,' he continued, 'to prepare myself for every eventuality; and so I should like you to absent yourself for a while, if that is possible, and go with the children to your aunt in Schwerin,* whom you have in any case for a long time now intended visiting.' — 'What?' his wife cried. 'I am to go to Schwerin? Over the border with the children to my aunt in Schwerin?' And horror choked her voice. — 'Indeed, yes,' Kohlhaas replied, 'and at once, if that is possible, so that in the steps I wish to take in my affair I will not be hindered by any considerations.' — 'Oh I understand you,' she cried. 'All you need now is weapons and horses; the rest whoever wants it he can have it.' And with that she turned, threw herself down in a chair and wept. —

Kohlhaas, concerned, said: 'Dearest Lisbeth, what are you doing? God
has blessed me with a wife and children and with worldly goods. Shall I
today for the first time wish it were otherwise?' — Lovingly, as she at
these words blushed and flung her arms around his neck, he sat down by
her. — 'Tell me,' he said, brushing the curls off her forehead, 'what shall
I do? Shall I give up my case? Shall I go to Tronkenburg and ask the
Junker to give me my horses back, and mount and ride them home here
to you?' — Lisbeth did not dare say: 'Yes! Yes! Yes!' — Weeping, she
shook her head, hugged him close and covered his breast with
passionate kisses. 'Well then!' Kohlhaas cried. 'If you feel that I must
have justice or I cannot continue with my trade, grant me then also the
freedom I need to get it.' And with that he stood up and said to the
stableman, who had come in to tell him that the chestnut was saddled
and ready, that tomorrow the brown horses would have to be harnessed
also, to convey his wife to Schwerin. Lisbeth said she had an idea. She
rose, wiped the tears from her eyes and asked him, now seated at a desk,
would he give her the petition and let her, instead of him, go to Berlin
and hand it to the Elector. Kohlhaas, for more than one reason touched
by this move, drew her down on to his lap and said: 'Dearest wife, that
would hardly be possible. The Elector is densely surrounded and anyone
approaching him will face all kinds of unpleasantness.' Lisbeth
answered that there were a thousand occasions on which it would be
easier for a woman to approach him than a man. 'Give me the petition,'
she repeated, 'and if all you want is to know that it is in his hands, I
promise you: he shall have it.' Kohlhaas, having already had many
proofs both of her courage and of her ingenuity, asked how she thought
to manage it; to which, looking bashfully down, she replied: that the
constable of the Elector's palace in earlier days when his employment
was in Schwerin, had courted her; that he was now, admittedly, married
and had several children, but that she had still not quite been forgotten;
— and in a word, that he should leave it to her to derive from this, and
from various other circumstances too complicated to go into, some
advantage. Kohlhaas, greatly delighted, kissed her and said he accepted
her proposal; informed her that if she lodged with the constable's wife
she would then be able to approach the Elector in the palace itself, gave
her the petition, had the brown horses harnessed, saw her snugly
ensconced and, with Sternbald, his faithful servant, sent her on her way.
    But of all the unsuccessful steps that he had taken in his case this
journey was the most unhappy. For after only a few days Sternbald drew
into the yard again, leading one pace at a time the carriage in which the
woman lay stretched out, dangerously hurt in the chest. Kohlhaas,

white, crossed to the carriage, but could learn nothing coherent on what
had caused this misfortune. The constable, as the servant said, had not
been at home; they had been obliged to put up at an inn near the palace;
which inn Lisbeth had left the next morning, ordering the servant to stay
behind with the horses; and not until evening had she returned, in that
condition. It seemed she had pushed forward too boldly towards the
person of the Elector and, without his being to blame, through the mere
rude zealousness of one of the guards around him, had been jabbed in
the chest with the shaft of a spear. That at least was the account given
by the people who brought her unconscious towards evening to the inn;
for she herself, hampered by blood welling from her mouth, could say
little. Later a knight had taken the petition off her. Sternbald said that it
had been his wish to get on a horse at once and bring him news of this
unhappy occurrence; but she had insisted, despite representations made
by the surgeon they had called, on being transported without any prior
notice to her husband in Kohlhaasenbrück. Kohlhaas brought her,
entirely broken by the journey, to bed and there, painfully striving to get
breath, she lived a few days longer. It was in vain that attempts were
made to bring her back to consciousness in the hope of learning more
about what had happened; she lay with fixed and already glazing eyes
and did not answer. Only shortly before her death did her senses return
to her. For as a priest of the Lutheran religion (which creed, then
burgeoning, she had followed her husband and espoused) was standing
by her bed and in a loud and feelingly ceremonious voice reading out to
her a chapter of the bible, suddenly she frowned at him and, as though
there were nothing in it to read out to her, took the bible from his hands
and turned and turned its pages and seemed to be seeking something;
and with her index finger showed Kohlhaas, seated by her bed, the verse:
'Forgive thine enemies; do good to them that hate thee.'* — Then, with
a look in which all her soul was contained, she pressed his hand and
died. — Kohlhaas thought: 'May God never forgive me as I forgive the
Junker' — kissed her and, weeping copiously, closed her eyes and left
the room. He took the hundred gold gulden that the councillor, for the
stables in Dresden, had already made over to him and ordered a funeral
that seemed less one for her than for a princess: an oak coffin heavily
studded with metal, cushions of silk with gold and silver tassels, a grave
eight foot deep and lined with stones and whitened. He stood there
himself, his youngest child on his arm, watching the work. On the day
of the funeral the corpse, white as snow, was displayed in a hall which
he had caused to be hung with black drapes. The priest had just
concluded a moving oration at the bier when the Elector's response to

the petition, which the dead woman had delivered, was brought to Kohlhaas. It read: that he should collect his horses from Tronkenburg and, on pain of being thrown into prison, now let the matter rest. Kohlhaas pocketed the letter and had the coffin laid on the carriage. As soon as the earth was mounded on the grave, the cross set on it and the mourners who had assisted at the burial had left, he threw himself down once more by her now desolate bed, and then at once took up the business of revenge. He sat down and composed a judgment in which, by virtue of the authority inborn in him, he commanded that the Junker Wenzel von Tronka should, within three days of receiving it, fetch the two black horses, which he had taken from him and worked to exhaustion in the fields, back to Kohlhaasenbrück and in person in the stables there feed them up to their former weight and health. He sent this judgment to him by a special messenger whom he instructed to return to Kohlhaasenbrück immediately after delivering it. When the three days passed and the horses had not been handed over he sent for Herse; revealed to him what, concerning their restitution to weight and health, he had required of the Junker; asked him two things: whether he would ride with him to Tronkenburg and fetch the Junker; and also whether, having fetched him and should he in the stables at Kohlhaasenbrück be dilatory in fulfilling the terms of the judgment, he would be willing to use the whip; and when Herse, as soon as he understood, cried out in jubilation: 'Sir, this very day!' and, flinging his cap in the air, promised him to have a lash made with ten knots in it, to give the man lessons in the art of currycombing — Kohlhaas sold the house; sent away his children, packed into a carriage, across the border; summoned, as night fell, his remaining men, seven of them, all true as gold; armed them and gave them horses, and set off for Tronkenburg.

With this small band then, promptly at nightfall on the third day, trampling down the tollbooth keeper and the gatekeeper who were standing in conversation under the gatehouse, he entered the castle and whilst Herse, amid the sudden roaring, as they set fire to them, of all the sheds and shacks within the castle walls, rushed up the winding staircase into the steward's tower and, slashing and stabbing, fell upon the steward and the bailiff who were sitting, half undressed, at cards, Kohlhaas broke into the heart of the place, for Junker Wenzel. The Avenging Angel comes down from heaven thus; and the Junker, just then amid much raucous laughter reading aloud to his entourage of young friends the judgment the horsedealer had sent him, when he heard his voice in the yard below he went corpse-white, called out to the gentlemen: 'Save yourselves, brothers!', and disappeared. Kohlhaas, entering the hall and, approached by a certain Junker Hans von Tronka, seizing him by the shirtfront and flinging him into a corner so that his brains spurted out against the stones, asked, whilst his followers overwhelmed and dispersed the other knights, who had reached for their weapons, where the Junker Wenzel von Tronka was. And when he, faced with the ignorance of the dumbfounded men, kicked open the doors of two rooms leading into the wings of the castle and, traversing the extensive building in all directions, had found nobody, he went down, cursing, into the courtyard, to have the exits guarded. Meanwhile, reached by the fire among the sheds, the castle itself, in all its extent, had caught and thick smoke billowed from it into the sky; and whilst Sternbald, with three busy companions, was dragging out everything not nailed down and tipping it by the horses as fair booty, down came to Herse's cheers from the open windows of their quarters in the tower the bodies of the steward and the bailiff and their wives and children too. Kohlhaas, when, as he came down the stairs, the Junker's old gout-ridden housekeeper had flung herself at his feet, he halted on the step and asked her where the Junker Wenzel von Tronka was; and when she answered in a faint and trembling voice: she believed he had taken refuge in the chapel, he summoned two of his men with torches, broke in, since he lacked the key, with crowbars and axes, overturned pews and altars and still, to his savage grief, did not find the Junker. It happened that a young stableboy, employed at Tronkenburg, hurried by, just as Kohlhaas was leaving the chapel, to bring out the Junker's warhorses from a spacious stone stable threatened by the fire. Kohlhaas, at that moment noticing in a small straw-covered shed his own black pair, asked the boy: why did he not rescue them? and when the boy, putting the key into the stabledoor, answered: because the shed, as they could see, was already alight, Kohlhaas, wrenching the key violently out of the door, flung it over the wall and drove the boy under a hail of blows with the flat of his sword into the burning shed and forced him, amid the terrible laughter of the bystanders, to rescue the black horses. But when the boy, pale with terror, a few moments before the shed collapsed behind him, stepped out of it, leading the horses, Kohlhaas had gone; and when he went to the men assembled in the space before the castle and asked the horsedealer, who repeatedly turned his back on him, what he should do with the creatures — Kohlhaas suddenly, with a terrifying gesture, raised his foot and the kick, had he delivered it, would have been the boy's death — then, giving no answer, mounted his chestnut stallion, positioned himself under the castle gateway and, whilst his men continued their activities, he waited in silence for daybreak.

When dawn came the whole castle, but for the walls, had burned down and no one was left in it but Kohlhaas and his seven men. He dismounted and in the clear daylight again searched through the place in every corner now lit by the sun, and being then, hard though it was for him, obliged to realize that his action against the fortress had failed, with pain and grief in his heart he sent forth Herse and one or two others to find out in what direction the Junker had fled. He was particularly disquieted by a large convent, called Erlabrunn, that lay on the banks of the Mulde* and whose abbess, Antonia von Tronka, was known in the region as a pious, charitable and holy woman; for it seemed only too likely to the unhappy Kohlhaas that the Junker, stripped as he was of every necessity, had taken refuge in this establishment, the abbess being his aunt by blood and the educator of his early childhood. Kohlhaas, informed of this circumstance, climbed the steward's tower, where one room was still habitable, and composed what he called a 'Kohlhaas Mandate' in which he urged the country to give no assistance to Junker Wenzel von Tronka, against whom he was waging a just war; indeed, he ordered every inhabitant, not excepting relatives and friends, to deliver him up or suffer death and the certain destruction by fire of all they might call their own. By travellers and others not local he distributed this declaration throughout the region; and giving Waldmann, one of his men, a copy of it, he instructed him particularly to hand it to the Lady Antonia at Erlabrunn. Next he had discussions with some of the Tronkenburg retainers who were discontented with the Junker and, excited by the prospect of booty, wished to enter his service; armed them, in the manner of foot soldiers, with crossbows and daggers and showed them how to sit up behind his own men on their mounts; and having turned to money everything his men had raked together and distributed it among them he rested for a few hours under the gatehouse from his wretched work.

Towards noon Herse came and confirmed what his own heart, always inclined to the worst presentiments, had told him already: that the Junker was in the nunnery at Erlabrunn with the old abbess Antonia von Tronka, his aunt. He had, it seemed, escaped through a door in the back wall of the castle into the open air, and down a narrow stone staircase which, under a little roof, descended to the Elbe and a few boats there. At least, Herse reported that, to the astonishment of the people congregating because of the fire at Tronkenburg, he had appeared about midnight, in a boat without oars or rudder, at a village on the Elbe, and in a village wagon had travelled on to Erlabrunn. — At this news Kohlhaas gave a deep sigh; he asked had the horses been fed and, being told they had, he ordered his company to mount and three hours later stood before Erlabrunn. With distant thunder muttering along the horizon, he and his men, carrying torches they had lit outside the place, were entering the courtyard of the nunnery and as Waldmann, his servant, came up and reported that the mandate had indeed been delivered, he saw the abbess and the steward of the place approaching through the gateway, arguing and distressed; and whilst the latter, the steward, a small, old, snow-white man, with fierce glances at Kohlhaas was having his armour put on him and in a determined voice was calling to the servants around him to ring the alarm bell, she, the abbess, the silver image of Christ Crucified in her hand, white as linen came down the slope and with all her nuns threw herself on the ground before Kohlhaas's horse. Whilst Herse and Sternbald overwhelmed the steward, who had no sword in his hand, and led him as a prisoner among the horses, Kohlhaas asked her where the Junker von Tronka was; and when she, detaching a great ring of keys from her belt, answered: 'My respects to you, Kohlhaas. He is in Wittenberg', and in a trembling voice added: 'Fear God and do no evil' — Kohlhaas, flung back into the hell of unfulfilled vengeance, turned his horse and was about to cry out: 'Burn it down!' when a vast thunderbolt fell to earth very close to him. Kohlhaas, again turning his horse, asked had she received his mandate, and when the abbess in a weak, scarcely audible voice answered: 'Just now' — 'When?' — 'Two hours, so help me God, after the Junker, my nephew, had already departed' — and Waldmann, the servant, to whom Kohlhaas, frowning grimly, now turned, stammered that it was so because, as he said, the waters of the Mulde, swollen by rain, had prevented him from arriving sooner than a moment ago: then Kohlhaas composed himself; a sudden deluge of rain, extinguishing the torches and falling with a din on the cobbles of the courtyard, released the grief in his unhappy heart; he turned his horse, first briefly touching his hat to the abbess, and, with the words: 'Follow me, brothers. The Junker is in Wittenberg', drove in the spurs and left the convent.

As night fell he halted at an inn on the highway and there, the horses being greatly fatigued, was obliged to rest a day; and since he knew very well that with a company of ten men (for that was his strength now) he could not take on a place like Wittenberg, he composed a second mandate in which, after a brief account of his experiences in the country, he urged 'all good Christians', as he put it, 'on the promise of bounty and other benefits of war', to take up his cause against the

Junker von Tronka as against the enemy of all of Christendom. In another mandate, appearing soon after, he termed himself 'a man subject to no law of the Empire or the world, but only to God's'; a fanatical nonsense, sick and misbegotten, which none the less, at the sound of his gold and at the prospect of booty, brought him in abundant reinforcements from among the rabble put out of work by the peace with Poland: so that he numbered thirty and more when, to burn Wittenberg, he returned to the right bank of the Elbe. He camped with horses and men under the roof of an old dilapidated brick-built barn in the remoteness of a dark wood which in those days surrounded the place, and had no sooner heard from Sternbald, whom he had sent in disguise into the town with the mandate, that it was known there, than he advanced with his forces and on the evening before Whit Sunday, as the citizens lay fast asleep, set fire to the town in several places simultaneously. And whilst his men were plundering in the suburbs he affixed a proclamation to the doorpost of a church, saying: he, Kohlhaas, had set fire to the town and would, if they did not deliver up the Junker to him, burn it so thoroughly that there would not, as he put it, 'be a wall left standing for him to hide behind'. — The inhabitants' horror at this unprecedented crime was indescribable; and no sooner had the flames, which, it is true, in a — fortunately — almost windless summer night had destroyed no more than nineteen houses but with them a church also, no sooner had they been brought, towards daybreak, to some degree at least under control, than the elderly governor, Otto von Gorgas, sent forth a troop of fifty men to take the fearful savage into custody. But the captain leading it, whose name was Gerstenberg, managed so badly that the whole expedition, far from undoing Kohlhaas, helped him instead to an extremely dangerous fame as a warrior; for when the captain divided his company into several small units in order, as he thought, to encircle and to crush him, he was attacked by Kohlhaas, who kept his men together, in separate places, and beaten; with the result that by the evening of the following day not one man of the whole troop, in whom the country's hopes were invested, still stood in the field to oppose him. Kohlhaas, who had lost a few people in this fighting, once more on the morning of the following day set fire to the town, and his murderous procedures were so effective that again a good number of houses and almost all the barns in the suburbs were reduced to ash. Again he affixed his notorious mandate, and indeed to the very walls of the town hall itself, and added a note on the fate of Captain von Gerstenberg, whom the governor had sent against him and whom he had destroyed. The governor, exceedingly enraged by this defiance, set himself with several knights at the head of a company of a hundred and fifty men. He gave the Junker von Tronka, at his written request, an armed guard to protect him against the violence of the common people who wanted him ejected from the town without more ado; and having set guards in all the neighbouring villages and also sentries around the city walls to cover the place against an attack he went forth himself, on St Jervis's Day,* to capture the dragon that was laying waste the land. The horsedealer was astute enough to avoid this troop; and having by canny marches lured the governor twenty miles or so away from the town and by various strategies induced him to believe that, being pressed by a superior force, he would retreat into Brandenburg, he turned suddenly, at nightfall on the third day, came back, forcing the pace, to Wittenberg and set fire to the town for the third time. Herse, creeping in in disguise, carried out this frightful coup; and the inferno, thanks to a sharp north wind, was so deadly and extensive that in less than three hours forty-two houses, two churches, several monasteries and schools and the governor's own ministry were in ash and rubble. The governor who, as day broke, believed his enemy to be in Brandenburg, when, informed of what had happened, he marched hastily back again, he found the city in a general uproar; the people had established themselves in thousands before the Junker's house — now barricaded with planks and stakes — and were calling in frenzied voices for his expulsion from the town. Two mayors, Jenkens and Otto by name, appearing in full official dress at the head of the whole city council, declared in vain that it was absolutely necessary to await the return of a messenger sent to the president of the State Chancellery for permission to convey the Junker to Dresden where he himself, for a variety of reasons, wished to go; the unreasoning mob, armed with pikes and staves, paid no heed to these words and, with some manhandling of certain councillors who were demanding strong measures, they were about to storm the house the Junker was in and raze it to the ground, when the governor, Otto von Gorgas, appeared in the town leading his mounted company. This estimable gentleman, accustomed to inspiring respect and obedience in the people by his very presence, had succeeded, as a sort of compensation for the failed expedition he was returning from, in capturing, close by the gates of the town, three men who had got detached from the murdering and fire-raising band; and when he, whilst before all the people the captives were being laden with chains, assured the council, in a skilful address, that he was confident of shackling and bringing in Kohlhaas himself before long, being already on his trail: he managed, by dint of all these soothing factors, to disarm the fear of the assembled multitude and to calm them somewhat concerning the Junker's residence among them until the return of the messenger from Dresden. He dismounted, together with some of his knights, and, after the clearing away of the barricades and stakes, entered the house where he found the Junker, passing from one faint into the next, in the hands of two doctors who with essences and stimulants were striving to restore him to life; and since Otto von Gorgas could see very well that this was not the moment to have words with him about the conduct he was guilty of he merely requested him, with a look of silent contempt, to dress and, for his own safety, to follow him to an apartment in the prison reserved for gentlemen. When the Junker had had a jerkin put on him and a helmet and when, with his shirt still half open, since he could not get breath, and leaning on the governor and his own brother-in-law Count Gerschau, he appeared on the street, blasphemous and terrible maledictions rose to heaven against him. The people, held back only with great difficulty by the soldiery, called him a blood-sucker, a miserable blight on the land and a tormentor of its people, the curse of the city of Wittenberg and the ruination of Saxony; and after processing lamentably through the rubbled town and several times, without noticing, losing his helmet and a rider behind him setting it on again, they at last reached the prison into one of whose towers under the protection of a strong guard he vanished. Meanwhile the return of the messenger with the Elector's decision threw the city into new anxiety. For the state assembly, immediately petitioned with great urgency by the citizens of Dresden, would hear nothing, until the murderous fire-raiser had been defeated, of the Junker's residing in the capital; on the contrary, they enjoined the governor to use the forces at his disposal to give him protection where he was, since he had to be somewhere; but informed the good people of Wittenberg, for their comfort, that an army of five hundred men, under the command of Prince Friedrich of Meissen, was marching their way to shield them against any further depredations. The governor, seeing perfectly well that a resolution of this kind would do nothing to calm the people: not only because several small successes won by the horsedealer at different points outside the town had spread extremely disagreeable rumours about the strength he had grown to; also the war his rabble were waging in the darkness of night, in disguise, with pitch, straw and sulphur, would, unheard of and without example as it was, have rendered ineffectual even a greater force than that with which Prince Friedrich was advancing: the governor, having briefly reflected on the matter, decided to suppress entirely the resolution he had received. All he did was affix a letter, in which Prince Friedrich announced his arrival, on street corners in the town; a curtained carriage, departing from the prison at daybreak, left town on the Leipzig road, escorted by four heavily armed knights who, without being explicit, let it be known that their destination was Pleissenburg;* and the people being thus calmed on the wretched Junker's account, who brought with him fire and sword wherever he went, the governor himself set out with a troop of three hundred to join forces with Prince Friedrich of Meissen. Kohlhaas meanwhile, thanks to the strange position he was assuming in the world, had indeed grown to number one hundred and nine men; and since in Jessen* he had got possession of a stock of weapons and equipped his company very thoroughly with them, he resolved, being warned of the double thunderstorm advancing against him, to meet it with the speed of a tempest himself, before it broke over him. Accordingly, only one day later, he fell upon Prince Friedrich near Mühlberg,* at night; in this skirmish, to his great grief, lost Herse, who went down at his side under the very first shots; but enraged by this loss, in a battle lasting three hours, so battered the Prince, who never managed to collect himself in the place, that with many grievously wounded and his whole troop in disarray, he was obliged to take the road back to Dresden. Emboldened even to recklessness by this advantage Kohlhaas turned back for the governor before he should hear what had happened, fell upon him near the village of Damerow* in the clear light of midday, in the open fields, and fought with him, sustaining terrible losses it is true, but with equal successes, until night came on. Indeed, next morning with his remaining company he would certainly have attacked the governor again, who had withdrawn into the churchyard at Damerow, but the latter, through his scouts, had learned of the defeat suffered by the Prince at Mühlberg and, like him, deeming it wiser to retreat, had done so, to Wittenberg, to await a better moment. Five days after routing these two forces Kohlhaas appeared before Leipzig and fired the city on three sides. — He called himself, in the mandate he distributed on this occasion, 'a viceroy of Michael, the Archangel, come with fire and sword to punish in the persons of all who might take the Junker's part in the quarrel the wickedness into which the whole world had sunk'. At the same time, from the castle at Lützen* which he had taken and in which he had established himself, he called on the people to join him in setting up a better order of things; and the mandate, approaching insanity, concluded: 'Signed here at the fortress of Lützen, the seat of our provisional world government.' The citizens of Leipzig were fortunate in that the fire, because of steady rain falling from the heavens, did not spread, so

that thanks to the speed with which the available resources were
employed only a few small shops around the Pleissenburg went up in
flames. Nevertheless the town's dismay at the presence of this raving and
murderous fire-raiser and at his mistaken conviction that the Junker was
in Leipzig, was indescribable; and when a troop of one hundred and
eighty horsemen sent out against him returned to the town undone, the
council, not wishing to risk the city's riches, had no alternative but to
stop all coming and going through the gates and have the citizens on
guard day and night outside the walls. In vain did the city council affix,
in the surrounding villages, categorical declarations that the Junker was
not in the Pleissenburg; the horsedealer, in similar announcements,
insisted that he was and declared that if he wasn't he, Kohlhaas, would
none the less act as though he were until his real whereabouts, the name
of the place, had been revealed to him. The Elector, informed by urgent
messenger of the plight the city of Leipzig was in, announced that he
was already gathering together an army of two thousand men and
would place himself at the head of it, to capture Kohlhaas. To Otto von
Gorgas he issued a severe reprimand for the equivocal and incautious
trick he had employed to get rid of the murderous fire-raiser from the
vicinity of Wittenberg; and words cannot describe the confusion seizing
the whole of Saxony, and the capital especially, when they learned that
in the villages around Leipzig a declaration had been posted, by whom it
was not known, addressed to Kohlhaas, to this effect: that Junker
Wenzel was with his cousins Hinz and Kunz in Dresden.

In these circumstances Dr Martin Luther undertook to try with the
power of soothing words and on the basis of the authority given him by
his standing in the world to press Kohlhaas back under the curb of
human order; and laying upon that which was good in the heart of the
murderer and arsonist he addressed the following open letter to him and
had it posted up in all the Elector's towns and villages:

'Kohlhaas, you say you are sent, do you, to wield the sword of justice?
What overweening lunacy is this, how can you dare to, mad and blind
with passion and injustice itself filling you up entirely from top to toe?
Because your sovereign, to whom you are subject, has denied you your
rights, your rights in a dispute over a nothing, for that then, reprobate,
you have risen in revolt with fire and sword and fallen like the wolf of the
wilderness into the peaceable commonwealth that he protects. By this
claim, full of untruth and wickedness, leading men astray, do you suppose,
sinner that you are, that on that future day, standing before God in the
light that will shine into every corner of all our hearts, your claim will save

you then? How can you say your rights were denied you when, in the bitterness of your heart and goaded by the itch for a miserable private vengeance, you would not, after the first slight efforts had failed, exert yourself any further for those rights? Is a bench of beadles and servants of the court who suppress a letter that is brought to them or withhold some ruling they are duty bound to give, are they the authority over you? And must I say to you, damnable as you are, that the authority over you knows nothing of your case? — indeed, the sovereign you are in revolt against does not even know your name, so that should you one day appear before God's throne supposing to accuse him, he, with untroubled looks, will be able to say: 'I did this man no wrong, Lord, for my soul is ignorant of his very existence.' Know this: the sword you wield is the sword of pillage and murderousness, a rebel is what you are and not a warrior of the God of justice and your end on earth will be the gallows and the wheel and after that the damnation which is decreed for evildoing and godlessness.

Wittenberg, etc.   Martin Luther.'*

At Lützen castle meanwhile, much tormented, Kohlhaas was turning over a new plan to reduce Leipzig to ashes — for he gave no credence to the announcements in the villages that Junker Wenzel was in Dresden since nobody, let alone the city council as he had demanded, had signed them — when Sternbald and Waldmann, to their great consternation, noticed the proclamation which had been nailed in the night to the castle gate. For days they hoped in vain that Kohlhaas, whom they were unwilling to approach on the matter, would notice it himself; grim and oblivious he did appear at evening but only to issue his curt orders, and saw nothing; so that one morning when he was to hang two of his men for plundering in the region against his will, they resolved to draw the proclamation to his attention. Through a crowd that parted timidly for him on either side he was returning from the place of execution with the show that had become habitual since his last mandate: a great sword like that of the Cherubim, on a red leather cushion, decorated with tassels of gold, was carried before him and twelve men followed after with burning torches: when Sternbald and Waldmann, their swords under their arms in a way that must strike him as odd, stepped forward around the pillar on which the letter was posted. Kohlhaas, sunk in thought, his hands behind his back, as he came under the gate he raised his eyes, and stopped short; and when the two men now before him respectfully made way, he gave them distracted glances and approached the pillar in a few quick strides. No words can describe what went on then in his soul when he saw the letter affixed there accusing him of injustice and signed with the name of all the names he knew best loved and fittest to be revered: Martin Luther. A dark red rose into his face; twice, taking off his helmet, he perused the writing from beginning to end; turned then, with an uncertain look, there among his men, as though to say something, and said nothing; took down the sheet, read through it again, and called out: 'Waldmann, get my horse saddled!' and then: 'Sternbald, follow me!' and disappeared into the castle. In the utter reprehensibility of his situation Luther's few words were enough to disarm him on the spot. Hastily he disguised himself as a Thuringian farmer; told Sternbald that a matter of particular importance obliged him to go to Wittenberg; made over to him, in the presence of some of his very best men, the command of the troop who would remain at Lützen; and assuring him that before three days were up, during which time there was no fear of an attack, he would be back again, he departed for Wittenberg.

Under an assumed name he put up at an inn and there, as soon as night had fallen, in a cloak and armed with a brace of pistols he had taken as booty from Tronkenburg, he entered Luther's room. Luther, sitting at his desk amidst books and papers, seeing the strange man open the door and lock it behind him, asked who he was and what he wanted; and the man, who held his hat respectfully in his hand, had no sooner replied, in a shrinking apprehension of the horror he would cause, that he was Michael Kohlhaas, the horsedealer, than Luther exclaimed: 'Stand back!' and, rising from his desk and hurrying for a bell, added: 'Your breath is a pestilence, your presence perdition!' Kohlhaas, not moving from where he stood and drawing his pistol, said: 'Honoured sir, this pistol, if you touch the bell, will stretch me out dead at your feet. Be seated and listen to me; among the angels whose psalms you transcribe you could not be safer than you are with me.' Luther, sitting down, asked: 'What do you want?' Kohlhaas replied: 'To refute the view you have of me, that I am an unjust man. You said in your proclamation that my sovereign knows nothing of my case: well then, get me safe conduct and I will go to Dresden and present it.' — 'Damnable, terrible man!' cried Luther, at once confused and reassured by his words. 'Who gave you the right — other than you yourself — to fall upon the Junker von Tronka and then, not finding him in his castle, to visit with fire and sword the whole community that is protecting him?' Kohlhaas replied: 'Sir, as I now see: no one. I was deceived, led astray, by news I received from Dresden. The war I am waging on the community of humankind is an evil deed if I was not, as you assure me I was not, expelled from it.' 'Expelled!' Luther cried, and stared at him. 'What madness seized your thinking? Who could have expelled you from the community of the state in which you lived? Indeed, has it ever been the case, since states existed, that any man, whoever he might be, has been expelled from one?' — 'Expelled,' said Kohlhaas, clenching his hand, 'is what I call a man denied the protection of the law. For I need that protection or my peaceable trade cannot prosper; indeed for that same protection I take refuge, with the sum of all I have earned, in the community; and whoever denies it me casts me out among the savages in the wilderness; he hands me, how can you deny it, the weapon to protect myself.' — 'Who has denied you the protection of the law?' Luther cried. 'Did I not write to you that the complaint you brought remained unknown to the sovereign to whom you brought it? If behind his back the servants of the state suppress a case or otherwise, unbeknown to him, make a mock of his sacred name: who else but God can call him to a reckoning for his choice of such servants, and do you, a damned and terrible human being, have the authority to judge him?' — 'Very well,' Kohlhaas replied, 'if the sovereign has not cast me out, I shall return into the community which he protects. Get me, I ask you again, safe conduct to Dresden and I will disperse the company I have gathered at Lützen castle and will present the complaint which I have had rejected at the lawcourts of the country once again.' — Luther, showing his annoyance, rummaged at the papers lying on his desk, and said nothing. The defiant posture which this strange individual had adopted in the state exasperated him; he thought of the declaration the man had issued from Kohlhaasenbrück to the Junker, and asked: what he was asking of the courts in Dresden. Kohlhaas answered: 'Punishment of the Junker in accordance with the law; restoration of the horses to their previous condition and compensation for the damage I and my stableman Herse, who died in the fighting at Mühlberg, have suffered because of the violent wrong that was done to us.' — Luther exclaimed: 'Compensation for the damage! You have raised huge sums of money, from Jews and Christians, on bank drafts and securities, to finance your savage private vengeance. Will all that too be on the bill if we ask to see it?' — 'God forbid,' Kohlhaas replied. 'I am not asking for the restitution of my house and land and of the prosperity I once possessed; nor for the costs of burying my wife. Herse's old mother will supply a statement of what his cure cost and an inventory of the things he lost at Tronkenburg; and what I lost by not selling the two black horses, the authorities can have some qualified person calculate that.' — Luther said: 'Madman, incomprehensible, frightful madman!' and gazed at him. 'After your sword has taken revenge, the worst imaginable, on the Junker, what now impels you to insist on a ruling against him whose effect, should it finally be given, will touch him with so slight a force and severity?' — Kohlhaas replied, and a tear rolled down his cheek: 'Sir, it has cost me my wife. Kohlhaas wishes to show the world that she did not die in an unjust cause. Do my will in this matter and have the court give me a verdict, and I will do yours in whatever else may be at issue.' — Luther said: 'See here, what you ask, if things are other than they are officially deemed to be, is just; and had you managed, before taking it upon yourself to seek a private vengeance, to bring your quarrel to the sovereign's consideration, your demands, I do not doubt, would have been met, in every item. But would you not, all things considered, have done better to have forgiven the Junker for your Saviour's sake and to have taken your two black horses, skinny and worn to nothing as they were, and mounted and ridden home to Kohlhaasenbrück and fed them up again in your stables there?' — Kohlhaas answered: 'Maybe', and crossed to the window. 'Maybe. Maybe not. Had I known I should have to get them back on their feet again with blood from the heart of my dear wife: Sir, maybe I should have done as you have said and not begrudged a peck or two of oats. But since now, as it is, they have cost me so dear, my view is: let things take their course. Let me have the judgment I am entitled to and make the Junker feed my horses up.' — Luther, thinking various thoughts and again reaching for his papers, said that he would approach the Elector on his account. Meanwhile he should bide peacefully at Lützen castle; if the sovereign granted him safe conduct this would be made known to him by means of a notice posted in a public place. — 'But,' he continued, as Kohlhaas bent to kiss his hand, 'whether the Elector will temper justice with mercy, I do not know; for, as I hear, he has gathered an army and is about to seize you in the castle at Lützen; meanwhile however, as I have already said, I shall do what I can.' And with that he stood up and made to dismiss him. Kohlhaas said that by this intercession in the matter his mind was entirely set at rest concerning it; whereupon Luther raised a hand in farewell, but he then suddenly went down on one knee before him and said he had another thing to ask him that was weighing on his heart. At Whitsun, he said, when it was his habit to present himself at the table of the Lord he had, because of the warfare he was engaged in, missed going to church; would he, Luther, be so indulgent as to receive his confession unprepared and grant him, in exchange for it, the blessing of holy communion. Luther, having thought for a while and looking at him closely, said: 'Yes, Kohlhaas, I will. But the Lord, whose body you desire, forgave his enemies. — Will you,' he added, as Kohlhaas looked at him, abashed, 'likewise forgive the Junker who has done you wrong and go to Tronkenburg and ride home your two black horses to Kohlhaasenbrück and feed them up yourself?' — 'Sir,' said Kohlhaas, blushing and seizing his hand, — 'Well?' — 'The Lord himself did not forgive all his enemies. Let me forgive the Electors, my two sovereigns,* the steward and the bailiff and those two gentlemen Hinz and Kunz and whoever else may have offended against me in this matter: but the Junker, if it is possible, let me force him to feed my two black horses up again.' — At these words Luther, with a displeased look, turned his back on him and rang the bell. When a manservant, thus summoned, announced his arrival with a light in the adjoining room, Kohlhaas rose to his feet, wiping his eyes, abashed; and since the servant was trying the door in vain, for the bolt was drawn across, and since Luther had sat down to his papers again, it was Kohlhaas who opened for the man. Luther, glancing aside at the stranger, said to the manservant: 'Light the way out'; whereupon the man, somewhat unhappy to see a visitor there, took the house key from the wall and, waiting for him to leave, withdrew through the half-open door of the room. — Kohlhaas, agitatedly taking up his hat in both his hands, said: 'So I may not, sir, partake of the blessing I begged you for, that of being reconciled?' Luther answered him briefly: 'With your Saviour, no.* With your sovereign — that depends on an approach I shall make, as I promised you.' And with that he indicated to the manservant that he should do what he had asked him to do without further delay. Kohlhaas, his painful feelings very evident, raised his two hands to his breast, followed the man who was lighting his way downstairs, and disappeared.

Next morning Luther issued a letter to the Elector of Saxony in which, after a caustic aside on the subject of those gentlemen around his person, Hinz and Kunz, Chamberlain and Cupbearer von Tronka who, as was generally known, had suppressed the complaint, he expounded to the sovereign, with characteristic candour, his view that, things being as bad as they were, there was nothing for it but to accept the horsedealer's proposal and in the light of what had happened and so that the case might be reopened, to grant him an amnesty. Public opinion was, he observed, in a most dangerous way on the man's side, to such an extent that even in Wittenberg, three times burned by him, there were voices in his favour; and since, if his offer were turned down, he would infallibly and with spiteful observations broadcast it among the people, they could easily be so led astray that it would be impossible further to employ the forces of the state against him. He concluded by saying that in this extraordinary case it was necessary to override the scruples one might have about entering into dealings with a citizen who had taken up arms; that the man had been indeed, by the procedures adopted against him, in a certain sense put outside the bond of the state; and that, in brief, he should be thought of more as an invading foreign power (which as a citizen of Brandenburg he might to some extent claim to be) than as a rebel in revolt against the throne. — When the Elector received this letter Prince Christiern von Meissen, Imperial Commander-in-Chief and uncle of Prince Friedrich von Meissen, defeated at Mühlberg and still sick from his wounds; the Lord Chancellor, Count Wrede; Count Kallheim, President of the State Chancelleries; and the two gentlemen Hinz and Kunz von Tronka, the latter chamberlain, the former cupbearer, and both longstanding friends and intimates of the sovereign, all happened to be present in the palace. Kunz, the chamberlain, who, in his capacity as a privy councillor, saw to the sovereign's private correspondence and was authorized to use his signature and his seal, spoke first, and having once again and at great length explained that he would never have presumed on his own sole authority to suppress the complaint brought to the courts against the Junker, his nephew, by the horsedealer had he not, misled by false submissions, deemed it to be an entirely groundless and merely irritating triviality, he came to the present state of things. He observed that neither by the law of God nor by the law of man was the horsedealer entitled, on account of that mistake, to permit himself such monstrous acts of private vengeance; he spoke of the glory that would descend, if he were negotiated with as a legal force of war, upon his accursed head; and the disgrace that would thereby rebound on the sacred person of the Elector seemed to him so intolerable that he, in the fervour of his oratory, would rather, he said, suffer the worst and see the rebellious madman's resolution carried out and the Junker, his nephew, conveyed away to Kohlhaasenbrück, to feed up the pair of black horses there, than that the proposal made by Doctor Martin Luther should be accepted. The Lord Chancellor, Count Wrede, half turning to him, expressed his regret that the delicate concern he was now, in attempting to resolve this admittedly awkward matter, showing for the sovereign's good name had not inspired him at the outset and cause of it. He was, he explained to the Elector, unhappy to see the power of the state enlisted to execute a manifestly unjust measure; he observed, with a warning glance at the constant support the horsedealer was getting in the country, that in this way the chain of ill-doing threatened to extend itself into infinity and declared that only by a plain doing of what was right, by immediately and unreservedly making good the transgression they had made themselves guilty of, could the chain be broken off and the government safely extricate itself from the whole ugly business. Prince Christiern von Meissen, asked by his sovereign what he thought of this, replied, turning with every mark of esteem towards the Lord Chancellor: that the attitude of mind thus enunciated filled him with the greatest respect, but that, in assisting Kohlhaas to get his rights, he was forgetting that he thereby disregarded Wittenberg, Leipzig and all the country that had been maltreated by him, in their just demands for compensation or, at least, for his punishment. The order of the state was, in respect of this man, so out of joint that it would hardly be possible to set it right again by the application of any principle of jurisprudence. For that reason he would, following the view of the chamberlain, vote to employ the means at their disposal in such cases: gather together an army of sufficient size and with it capture or crush the horsedealer in his base at Lützen. The chamberlain, fetching chairs for him and the Elector from against the wall and in a very obliging manner bringing them forward, said: he was delighted that a man of such probity and insight should concur with him on the means of settling this equivocal affair. The Prince, holding the chair in his hand and not sitting down, looked at him and said: that he had no reason at all to be delighted since the concomitant and first measure would be to issue an order of arrest against him and try him for an abuse of the sovereign's name. For if necessity required that a veil be lowered before the throne of justice over a series of criminal acts which, proliferating beyond all compass, exceeded what could ever be summoned to account before that throne, that did not apply to the first, which had caused them; and only a capital proceeding against the first offence could justify the state in crushing the horsedealer whose cause was, as everybody knew, a just one and who had had the very sword he wielded put into his hands. The Elector, when at these words Junker Kunz looked at him in alarm, turned away, his whole face blushing red, and went to the window. Count Kallheim, after an embarrassed silence on all sides, said that this was no way out of the sorcerer's circle in which they were all confined. With as much justice his own nephew Friedrich could be put on trial; for he too, in the strange campaign he had waged against Kohlhaas, had in many ways overstepped his instructions, so that if one enquired into the extensive host of those who had caused the embarrassment in which they now found themselves, he too must be named among that number and called to account by his sovereign for what had happened at Mühlberg. The cupbearer, Hinz von Tronka, whilst the Elector, with uncertain looks, crossed to his desk, took his turn and said: he did not understand how what it was necessary for the state to do could have escaped the collective wisdom of such a gathering of men. The horsedealer had, so far as he knew, promised that in exchange for no more than safe conduct to Dresden and the reopening of his case he would disperse the company with which he had invaded the land. It did not follow from that that he should be given an amnesty for his criminal acts of private vengeance: two points in law which both Doctor Luther and the State Council seemed to be confusing. 'When,' he continued, laying a finger against his nose, 'the courts in Dresden have given their verdict, whatever that may be, in the matter of the black horses, there is nothing to stop us arresting Kohlhaas for all his burning and pillaging: an astute move politically which would unite the advantages of both these councillors' points of view and be certain to win the approval of our age and of ages to come.' — The Elector, since both the Prince and the Lord Chancellor answered this speech by Hinz the cupbearer merely with a look and the discussion seemed to be at an end, said that he would himself now, until the next sitting of the council, weigh the different opinions they had presented to him. — It seemed that the measure the Prince had said must be taken first had robbed him, susceptible as he was to the claims of friendship, of any desire to proceed with the campaign against Kohlhaas for which everything was prepared. At least, he kept back the Lord Chancellor, Count Wrede, whose view seemed to him the most practical; and when the Count then showed him letters to the effect that the horsedealer's strength had indeed by now grown to four hundred men; and that before long, because of the general discontent aroused by the chamberlain's improprieties, he would be able to count on double or treble so many, the Elector decided to accept without more ado the advice that Doctor Luther had given him. Accordingly, he made over to Count Wrede the whole handling of the Kohlhaas business; and only a few days later a proclamation appeared whose chief contents we set down here as follows:

We etc. etc. Elector of Saxony, in especial and gracious consideration of the intercession made to us by Doctor Martin Luther, extend to Michael Kohlhaas, horsedealer, citizen of Brandenburg, on condition that within three days of receiving this notice he lays down the arms he has taken up, safe conduct to Dresden, for the reopening of his case; but in this sense that if he, which we do not expect, should have his plea concerning his horses turned down by the courts in Dresden, we shall proceed against him, for having on his own authority sought his rights, with all the severity of the law; but in the other event justice will be tempered with mercy and he and all his company will be granted total amnesty for the acts of violence he has committed in Saxony.

No sooner had Kohlhaas, through Doctor Luther, received a copy of this proclamation, which had been displayed in all the public places of the land, than he, conditional though its language was, dismissed his entire company with gifts, thanks and good advice. He deposited with the courts in Lützen, as property of the Elector, all the money, weapons and implements he had acquired as booty; and having despatched Waldmann with letters to the councillor in Kohlhaasenbrück, to buy back his farm, if that should be possible, and Sternbald to Schwerin, to fetch his children whom he wished to have with him again, he left Lützen castle and went, incognito, carrying the rest of his small fortune in papers, to Dresden.

Day was just breaking and the whole city was still asleep when he knocked at the door of the small property in the suburb of Pirna which the honesty of the councillor in Kohlhaasenbrück had allowed him to keep, and said to Thomas, the elderly man who kept house there and who opened the door to him now in astonishment and consternation, that he should go and inform the Prince of Meissen at the Chancellory that he, Kohlhaas the horsedealer, had come. The Prince of Meissen, thinking it expedient, on receiving this message, to discover for himself at once how they stood with this man, found in the streets leading to Kohlhaas's dwelling, where he arrived soon after with a company of horsemen and his guard, an immeasurable multitude of people already gathered. News that the Avenging Angel, who pursued the oppressors of the people with fire and sword, was there had roused all Dresden, the city and its suburbs; it was necessary to bolt the house door against the press and curiosity of the mob, and boys climbed up at the windows to have a sight of the murderer and arsonist breakfasting within. As soon as the Prince, the guard making a way through for him, had got into the house and entered Kohlhaas's room, he asked him, who was standing half dressed at a table, was he Kohlhaas the horsedealer, whereupon Kohlhaas, taking a portfolio of papers pertaining to his situation out of his belt and handing them to him with every mark of respect, answered yes, and added that having dispersed his army and in enjoyment of the freedom granted him by the Elector he was in Dresden to bring charges against the Junker von Tronka on account of the two black horses. The Prince, looking him over swiftly from head to foot, went through the papers in the portfolio; had him explain what an attestation among them meant that the court in Lützen had issued with reference to a

deposition made there in favour of the Elector's treasury; and having
further ascertained the nature of the man, with questions of various
kinds concerning his children, his fortune, and the life he intended
leading henceforth, and found him in all respects such that one could be
easy on his account, he returned the papers to him and said: that now
nothing stood in the way of his case and that to initiate it he had only to
apply directly to the Lord Chancellor, Count Wrede. 'Meanwhile,' said
the Prince, after a pause in which he crossed to the window and
surveyed with a look of astonishment the people congregated before the
house, 'you will, for the first days, have to have a guard who will protect
you both in your house and when you go out.' — Kohlhaas, taken
aback, looked down and said nothing. The Prince said: 'Very well then,'
and left the window. 'But what comes of it is your own doing'; and with
that he turned to the door, intending to leave the house. Kohlhaas,
having thought about the matter, said: 'Your Highness, do as you wish.
Give me your word that you will withdraw the guard as soon as I ask
and I have no objection to the measure.' The Prince replied that it went
without saying; and having made it clear to the three soldiers who were
brought in for the purpose that the man in whose house they would
remain was free and that they were only to follow him for his protection
when he went out, the Prince took leave of the horsedealer with a
condescending wave of the hand, and departed.

Towards noon Kohlhaas, accompanied by his three soldiers and
followed by immense crowds of people who however, having been
warned by the police, did nothing at all to harm him, went to the Lord
Chancellor, Count Wrede. The Count, according him in an antechamber
a kindly welcome, spoke with him for a full two hours, and having had
him relate the whole course of the matter from beginning to end he
directed him, for the immediate formulation and submission of his suit,
to one of the city's best advocates, one employed by the courts
themselves. Kohlhaas, without further delay, proceeded to this man's
dwelling place; and having drawn up the suit exactly as the first that had
been dismissed, for punishment of the Junker in accordance with the
laws, restoration of the horses to their former condition and compensation for his own losses as well as those suffered by his stableman Herse,
dead at Mühlberg, these now in favour of Herse's old mother, he
returned, accompanied by a crowd still gazing open-mouthed at him, to
his house, fully determined not to leave it again unless called forth by
any necessary business.

The Junker himself meanwhile had been released from his incarceration in Wittenberg and having just recovered from a dangerous

inflammation of the foot, he was summoned by the High Court in peremptory form to present himself in Dresden and answer the charges brought against him by the horsedealer Kohlhaas that he had illegally taken two of that man's horses and worked them into the ground. The two brothers von Tronka, the chamberlain and the cupbearer, fief-cousins of Junker Wenzel, received him, arriving in their house, with the greatest annoyance and contempt; they called him a wretch and a good-for-nothing who had brought shame and disgrace on the whole family, and warned him that he would now inevitably lose his case and ordered him to take steps at once to recover the two black horses since he would be condemned by the court to feed them up again and become in so doing the laughing stock of the world. The Junker, in a feeble and trembling voice, replied that he was the most pitiable man on earth. He swore that he had known little about the whole cursed affair that was now his undoing, and that the steward and the bailiff were to blame for everything in that they had used the horses for the harvest without his in the least knowing it or wishing it, and by excessive labours, also in their own fields, had worked them into the ground. He sat down as he said this and begged them not to thrust him back by idle insults and hurtful remarks into the illness from which he had only just recovered. The next day the two gentlemen Hinz and Kunz, who owned properties in the vicinity of the burned-out castle at Tronkenburg, wrote, at the request of the Junker, their cousin, having no alternative, to their stewards and tenants there, to get news of the black horses gone missing on that unhappy day and nothing having been heard of them since. But all they could learn, the whole place having been laid to waste and most of the inhabitants butchered, was that a stableboy, driven by blows with the flat of the arsonist's sword, had rescued them out of the burning shed in which they stood but afterwards asking where he should take them to and what he should do with them he had received from the incensed fiend only a kick for an answer. The Junker's old gout-ridden housekeeper, who had fled to Meissen, assured him, when he wrote and asked, that his boy on the morning following that terrible night had moved away towards the Brandenburg frontier with the horses; but all the enquiries undertaken in that area were fruitless and it seemed the information might be based on an error since the Junker did not have a stableboy living in Brandenburg or even along the road there. Men from Dresden, who a few days after the fire at Tronkenburg had been in Wilsdruf, said in their statements that at the time in question a boy leading two horses by a halter had arrived there and had left the animals, because they were very wretched and could go no further, in the cowshed of a herdsman who was willing to bring them back to health. It seemed for various reasons very probable that these were the two black horses at the centre of the case; but the herdsman from Wilsdruf* had already, as people coming from there said for certain, sold them on, but to whom it was not known; according to a third rumour, the author of it remaining undiscovered, the horses had already gone to their Maker and were buried in the bone pit in Wilsdruf. The gentlemen Hinz and Kunz, to whom this turn of events was, understandably, the most welcome, since it would relieve them of the necessity of feeding up the horses in their own stables, the Junker, their cousin, having none, nevertheless wished, for the sake of being quite sure, to confirm this circumstance. Accordingly, Wenzel von Tronka, hereditary, feudal and judicial lord of the place, issued a letter to the courts in Wilsdruf asking them, after an extensive description of the black horses which, as he said, had been entrusted to his care and by an accident had gone missing, to be so kind as to search out their present whereabouts and to urge and require their owner, whoever he might be, to deliver them, all his expenses being amply reimbursed, to the stables of Chamberlain Kunz in Dresden. Consequently, only a few days later, the man to whom the herdsman of Wilsdruf had sold them did indeed appear and led them, skinny and tottering, tied to the pole of his cart, into the city marketplace; but unfortunately for Junker Wenzel, and even more so for the honest Kohlhaas, the man was the knacker of Döbbeln.*

As soon as Wenzel, in the presence of the chamberlain, his cousin, had heard the uncertain rumour that a man with two black horses saved from the fire at Tronkenburg had arrived in town, both betook themselves, accompanied by a few servants of the house hastily gathered together, to the square before the palace where he was standing, and intended, if these really were Kohlhaas's, to take them from him, repay him his costs, and lead them home. But the gentlemen were greatly disconcerted when they saw around the two-wheeled cart to which the horses were tied a mob drawn thither by the spectacle, already large and getting larger by the minute, and calling out to one another, amid endless jeering, that the horses causing the state to totter had already been at the knacker's yard. The Junker, who had circled the cart and contemplated the wretched animals that seemed they might drop dead at any moment, said, in embarrassment, that those were not the horses he had taken from Kohlhaas; but Kunz, the chamberlain, casting at him a look of wordless rage which, had it been of iron, would have broken him into pieces, stepped across to the knacker, opening his coat as he did

so to reveal his insignia and his chain, and asked him were those the
black horses acquired by the herdsman at Wilsdruf and which the
Junker Wenzel von Tronka, to whom they belonged, had asked the
court there to search for. The knacker, who with a bucket of water in his
hand was busy giving a drink to the fat and very solid nag that pulled his
cart, said: 'The black pair?' — Setting down the bucket he removed the
bit from the horse's mouth and said that the black horses tied to the pole
had been sold him by the swineherd in Hainichen.* Where he had got
them from and whether they came from the herdsman in Wilsdruf, he
did not know. Himself, he said, taking up the bucket again and resting it
on the shaft and his knee, himself, the messenger from the courts in
Wilsdruf had told him he was to take them to Dresden, to the von
Tronka house; but the Junker he was told to find was called Kunz. So
saying he turned with the rest of the water left in the bucket by his own
horse and tipped it over the cobbles. The chamberlain, stared at on all
sides by the jeering crowd and unable to get the man, who was going
about his business with an oblivious zest, to look at him, said that he
was the chamberlain, Kunz von Tronka; but the black horses he was
seeking had to be ones belonging to Junker Wenzel, his cousin; come to
the herdsman in Wilsdruf via a stableboy who had escaped the fire at
Tronkenburg and originally belonging to the horsedealer Kohlhaas. He
asked the fellow who was standing there with his legs apart and hoisting
his trousers up whether he knew anything about that. And whether the
swineherd of Hainichen had not perhaps, and on this detail everything
hinged, acquired them from the Wilsdruf herdsman or from some third
person who had himself bought them from him, the herdsman. — The
knacker, who had faced the cart and relieved himself against it, said he
had been told to bring the black horses to Dresden and would have his
money for them in the von Tronka house. He did not understand what
the chamberlain was meaning; and it was all the same to him, since they
weren't stolen, whether the herdsman from Wilsdruf had them before
the swineherd from Hainichen, or anyone else for that matter. And so
saying, and with the whip held diagonally across his broad back, he
went over to an inn on the square intending, since he was hungry, to
take some breakfast. The chamberlain, who had not the remotest idea
what he should do with horses sold by the swineherd of Hainichen to
the knacker of Döbbeln and belonging, for all he knew, to the devil
himself, urged the Junker to say something; but when he, with pale and
quivering lips, replied the wisest thing would be to buy the horses
whether they belonged to Kohlhaas or not, the chamberlain, cursing the
mother and father who had given him life and again throwing open his

coat, withdrew from among the crowd still wholly uncertain what he should do or not do. He hailed the Baron von Wenk, an acquaintance, who was just then riding across the street, and defiantly refusing to move from the scene, for the very reason that the mob was staring at him derisively and seemed, with handkerchiefs pressed against their mouths, only to be waiting for his departure to burst out laughing, he begged him to call at the Lord Chancellor's, Count Wrede's, house and through him fetch out Kohlhaas to inspect the horses. It happened that Kohlhaas, having been summoned by a messenger from the courts to give certain explanations regarding the deposition made at Lützen, was present in the Chancellor's room when the baron, with the aforementioned purpose, entered; and as the Lord Chancellor, with a look of irritation, rose from his seat and asked Kohlhaas, not known to the baron, to stand aside with the papers he was holding, the baron represented to him the embarrassment in which the von Tronka gentlemen found themselves. The knacker von Döbbeln, in response to a less than perfect instruction of the courts of Wilsdruf, had appeared with horses whose condition was so lamentable that Junker Wenzel was rightly reluctant to acknowledge them to be Kohlhaas's; and thus, if they were nevertheless to be accepted from the knacker so that, in the gentleman's stables, an attempt might be made to restore them, it was first necessary that Kohlhaas should inspect them with his own eyes and put their identity beyond any doubt. 'Therefore be so good,' he said in conclusion, 'to send a guard to fetch Kohlhaas from his house and conduct him to the marketplace, where the horses are.' The Lord Chancellor, taking his spectacles off his nose, said that he was doubly mistaken; first, if he believed that the circumstance under discussion could only be decided by Kohlhaas's carrying out an inspection with his own eyes; and secondly, if he imagined that he, the Lord Chancellor, had the authority to have Kohlhaas conducted by a guard to wherever the Junker pleased. So saying, he introduced the horsedealer, who was standing behind him, and, taking his seat again and resuming his spectacles, he begged the baron to address himself in the matter to the man in person. — Kohlhaas, who gave no sign at all of what was going on in his soul, said that he would be willing to follow him to the marketplace and inspect the black horses which the knacker had brought into town. Whilst the baron turned round to him in astonishment he approached the Lord Chancellor's desk again, and having given him from among the papers in his portfolio further information concerning the deposition made in Lützen, he took his leave; the baron who, blushing red all over his face, had crossed to the window, likewise said his goodbyes; and both then, escorted by the three soldiers whom the Prince of Meissen had assigned to the job and with a crowd of people following after, proceeded to the square before the palace. The chamberlain, von Kunz, who in the meantime, despite the urgings of several friends who had gathered around him, had stood his ground among the populace, facing the knacker, as soon as the baron approached with the horsedealer he approached the knacker and asked him, whilst holding his sword with pride and dignity under his arm, whether the horses standing behind the cart were his. The horsedealer, turning respectfully to face the gentleman asking him this question, whom he did not know, tipped his hat, made no answer, and, together with all the knights, approached the knacker's cart. Ten yards away from the creatures, who stood there on unsteady legs, bowing their heads and not eating the hay the knacker had laid down for them, he halted and appraised them briefly. 'Sir,' he said, turning back to the chamberlain, 'the knacker is quite right: the horses tied to his cart belong to me.' And with that, looking round at the whole circle of gentlemen, he tipped his hat again and, accompanied by his guard, went out of the square. At these words the chamberlain stepped, with a stride so rapid it shook the plume on his helmet, across to the knacker and threw him a purse of money; and whilst he, the purse in one hand, combed back the hair off his forehead with a leaden comb and contemplated the money, the chamberlain ordered a servant to untie the horses and lead them home. The boy, who at the gentleman's summons had left a group of his friends and relations among the crowd, approached the horses, stepping over the large puddle of filth that had collected at their feet and blushing a little as he did so, but no sooner had he taken hold of the halter to untie them than his uncle, Master Himboldt, seized him by the arm and with the words: 'You leave that trash alone!' flung him away from the cart. Turning then to the chamberlain, who stood there speechless at this occurrence, and stepping gingerly over the pool of filth, he added that he must get himself a knacker's boy if he wanted such work done. The chamberlain, foaming with rage, contemplated Master Himboldt for a moment; turned then and over the heads of the gentlemen surrounding him called for the guard; and when, summoned by the Baron von Wenk, an officer with a number of the Elector's bodyguard appeared from the palace, he ordered him, first describing the disgracefully rebellious conduct of the citizens, to arrest the ringleader, Master Himboldt. He accused the latter, seizing him by the coat, of flinging his servant, who had been obeying his orders and untying the horses, away from the cart and manhandling him. Master Himboldt, with one deft movement freeing himself from the chamberlain and forcing him back, said: 'Your Grace, telling a lad of twenty what he should do is not rebellious conduct. Ask him will he go against tradition and decency and deal with the horses tied to that cart. If he will, after what I have said, so be it. He can gut them and flay them for all I care.' At these words the chamberlain turned round to the boy and asked him would he object at all to obeying his order and untying the horses that belonged to Kohlhaas and leading them home; and when the boy, timidly and withdrawing into the crowd, replied that first the horses would have to be made decent again before anyone could ask that of him, the chamberlain came after him from behind, tore off his hat, which bore the arms of the von Tronka house, and having trampled on it drew his sword and drove the boy with savage swipes at once out of the square and out of his service. Master Himboldt cried: 'Madman! Murderer! Fling him down!' and whilst the citizens, outraged by this scene, closed up and forced the guard away, he seized the chamberlain from behind and flung him down, tore off his cloak, collar, helmet, twisted the sword out of his hand and hurled it, with a furious throw, far away across the square. In vain did Junker Wenzel, escaping from the tumult, call out to the knights to go to the aid of his cousin; before they had taken one step to do so they were dispersed by the press of the people, with the result that the chamberlain, who had hurt his head in falling, was given up to the entire fury of the crowd. Only the appearance of a troop of mounted soldiers, who happened to be passing through the square and whom the officer of the Elector's bodyguard summoned to assist him, could save the chamberlain. The officer, having chased away the mob, seized the raging Master Himboldt and whilst he was being carried away to prison by horsemen, two friends raised the unfortunate chamberlain all bloody from the ground, and conveyed him home. This was the unhappy outcome of the well-meant and honest effort to get the horsedealer satisfaction for the wrong that had been done to him. The knacker of Döbbeln, whose business was finished and who had no wish to tarry, when the crowd began to disperse he fastened the horses to a lamp post and there they remained all day, nobody doing anything about them, a laughing stock for the street urchins and the idlers; until in the end, since they were given no care or attention, they became the responsibility of the police who towards nightfall summoned the Dresden knacker to look after them, until further notice, in the knacker's yard outside the city.

This occurrence, however little the horsedealer was to blame for it, did nevertheless arouse even among better and more moderate people in the country a mood that was exceedingly dangerous for the outcome of his case. His relationship with the state was thought to be quite intolerable, and in private houses and in public places opinion grew that it would be better to do him an obvious wrong and again reject his whole complaint than to allow him, in such a trivial matter and merely for the satisfaction of his mania, justice won by violence. Poor Kohlhaas was then quite undone by the Lord Chancellor himself who, out of excessive probity and, deriving from that, out of a hatred for the von Tronka family, involuntarily contributed to the hardening and spreading of this mood. It was very unlikely that the horses now being looked after by the Dresden knacker would ever again be restored to the condition in which they had left the stables at Kohlhaasenbrück; but even supposing that with skill and sustained care this might have been possible the disgrace that, things being as they were, would fall from it on the Junker's family was so great that, because of their social importance as one of the first and noblest families in the land, the most suitable and practicable thing seemed to be to offer a monetary compensation for the horses. All the same, when the President, Count Kallheim, in the name of the chamberlain, himself prevented by his sickness, some days later wrote to the Lord Chancellor suggesting this the Chancellor did, it is true, address a letter to Kohlhaas advising him not to dismiss such an offer out of hand, should it be made to him; but in a brief and not especially friendly reply to the President himself he begged him not to bother him in future with private commissions within the case, and urged the chamberlain to deal directly with the horsedealer, whom he characterized as a very fair and modest man. The horsedealer, whose will had indeed been broken by the occurrences in the marketplace, was himself then only waiting, in accordance with the Lord Chancellor's advice, for an overture on the part of the Junker or his relatives to meet them with complete amenability and forgiveness of all that had happened; but their family pride was such that making this overture was painful to them; and deeply embittered by the answer they had received from the Lord Chancellor they showed it to the Elector who, the next morning, had visited the chamberlain in his room as he lay there sick of his wounds. The chamberlain, in a voice made weak and plaintive by his condition, asked him whether, having risked his life in the effort to settle the matter according to his wishes, he must now expose his honour to the scorn of the world and appear with a plea for settlement and indulgence before a man who had brought every conceivable shame and disgrace upon him and his family. The Elector, when he had read the letter, asked Count Kallheim in some embarrassment whether the court was not entitled, without further reference to Kohlhaas, to make the assumption that the horses were not able to be restored and to rule therefore, just as if they were dead, that a simple monetary compensation would suffice. The Count answered: 'Sir, they *are* dead, in a legal sense they are dead because they have no value, and will be so physically before they are fetched from the knacker's yard to the von Tronka stables'; whereupon the Elector, pocketing the letter, said he would speak to the Lord Chancellor himself about it, reassured the chamberlain, who had half sat up and had seized his hand in gratitude, and having again urged him to be chary of his health he rose, all kindness, and left the room.

So things stood in Dresden when a second and more significant storm gathered over poor Kohlhaas from the direction of Lützen; and its lightning the clan were clever enough to direct upon his unhappy head. For Johann Nagelschmidt, one of the men recruited by Kohlhaas and then, after the publication of the Elector's amnesty, dismissed, had seen fit a few weeks later on the Bohemian frontier to gather some of that rabble together again and with them, ready as they were for any atrocity, to continue the trade Kohlhaas had led him into, but now as his own master. This good-for-nothing, partly to inspire fear in the soldiery pursuing him, partly, in the accustomed fashion, to seduce the populace into joining him in his criminal deeds, called himself Kohlhaas's viceroy; with an astuteness learned from his master he put it about that in the cases of several men returning peaceably to their homes the amnesty had not been honoured, indeed that Kohlhaas himself had on his arrival in Dresden been arrested and put under guard, faith with him broken thus in a way that cried to heaven; and in proclamations very similar to Kohlhaas's own he presented his gang of murderers and arsonists as an army risen up for the glory of God and for the purpose of seeing that the amnesty promised them by the Elector was observed; all this, as already stated, not at all for the glory of God nor out of loyalty to Kohlhaas, whose fate they cared nothing whatsoever about, but so that under the protection of such pretences they might burn and pillage with all the more impunity and ease. The von Tronka clan, as soon as the first news of this reached Dresden, could not repress their delight, for the event gave the whole affair a new complexion. With wise and disapproving sideways glances they alluded to the error made, despite their urgent and repeated warnings against it, in granting Kohlhaas an amnesty; for must it not have seemed that the intention in so doing was to signal to all manner of wicked men that they might follow him along his way? And not content with giving credence to Nagelschmidt's claim that he had taken up arms only in support and for the protection of his oppressed master they even uttered the decided opinion that his appearance on the scene was nothing but a strategy devised by Kohlhaas himself to intimidate the government and to hasten and achieve a verdict which would suit his frenzied self-interest in every point. Indeed the cupbearer, Hinz, to various hunting cronies and courtiers gathered around him after dinner in the Elector's antechamber, even described the dissolution of the robber band at Lützen as a devilish blind; and ridiculing the Lord Chancellor's love of justice he demonstrated, on the basis of some wittily assembled circumstances, that the band, now as before, were present in the country's forests and only waiting for a sign from the horsedealer to break forth again with fire and sword. Prince Christiern von Meissen, very unhappy at this development which threatened to sully the good name of his patron in a most palpable way, went to him in the palace immediately; and fully understanding that the von Tronkas' objective was to undo Kohlhaas, if they possibly could, with new transgressions, he asked the Lord Chancellor's permission to interrogate the horsedealer forthwith. The horsedealer, rather taken aback at being fetched to the Chancellery by an armed sergeant, appeared with Heinrich and Leopold, his two youngest boys, in his arms; for Sternbald, his servant, had arrived with all five the day before from Mecklenburg where they had been staying; and a variety of thoughts too extensive to be detailed here moved him to pick up the two boys, who as he was leaving begged him to with floods of childish tears, and take them with him to the hearing. The Prince, with kindly looks for the two children, whom Kohlhaas had seated by himself, and having in a friendly fashion asked them their names and ages, revealed to him what liberties his former underling Nagelschmidt was taking in the valleys of the Erzgebirge;* and handing him the so-called mandates issued by the man he requested him to say what he could to justify himself against them. The horsedealer, greatly alarmed though he was by these disgraceful and treacherous writings, had all the same little difficulty in satisfactorily demonstrating, to a man as fair-minded as the Prince, that the accusations thus aroused against him were without foundation. For not only had he, so it seemed to him, for the settlement of his case, now proceeding admirably, no need of help from any third party: it emerged from papers which he had on him and which he showed to the Prince that for quite particular reasons it was unlikely that Nagelschmidt should feel inclined to lend him assistance of that kind, since just before dispersing the band in Lützen he had been intending to have the man hanged, for rape and other misdeeds committed in the country; so that only the announcement of the Elector's amnesty, which annulled the relationship between them, had saved him and they had parted next day sworn enemies. Kohlhaas at his own proposal, which the Prince accepted, sat down and composed an open letter to Nagelschmidt, in which he declared that his claim to have risen to uphold a dishonoured amnesty was a disgraceful and pernicious fiction; informed him that on arrival in Dresden he had been neither imprisoned nor put under guard, that his case was proceeding as he wished, and that for the acts of murder and arson committed in the Erzgebirge after the proclamation of the amnesty he delivered him up to the full vengeance of the law, as a warning to the rabble gathered around him. And the horsedealer appended some portions of the criminal proceedings which he had begun against him at Lützen castle for the above-mentioned atrocities, so that people should know the truth about this good-for-nothing who had been intended for the gallows and had only escaped, as already mentioned, when the Elector issued his edict. Thereupon the Prince reassured Kohlhaas concerning the suspicions which, necessarily in the circumstances, had been voiced in the course of the hearing; promised him that so long as *he* remained in Dresden the amnesty granted him would in no wise be broken; shook hands again with the boys, giving them presents of fruit from his table, and with courteous words dismissed Kohlhaas. The Lord Chancellor, nevertheless recognizing the danger hanging over the horsedealer, did his utmost to conclude the man's affair before new events should complicate and confuse it; but that precisely was what the astute von Tronkas wished and intended, and instead of, as before, tacitly admitting guilt and fighting only for a more lenient judgment, they now began by devious and quibbling means to deny guilt altogether. First they pretended that Kohlhaas's black horses had been detained at Tronkenburg by the steward and the bailiff acting on their own authority, and that the Junker had not known about it, or only imperfectly; next they asserted that the beasts on arrival there had been sick of a violent and dangerous cough, and claimed they had witnesses, whom they could produce; and when, after extensive enquiries and dispute, they were defeated in these arguments they even produced an electoral decree in which, twelve years previously because of an epidemic among livestock, the import of horses from Brandenburg into Saxony was indeed forbidden: this as conclusive proof not only that the Junker was right to but that he was actually obliged to halt the horses Kohlhaas had brought over the border. — Kohlhaas, having in the meantime bought back his farm from the honest councillor at

Kohlhaasenbrück, paying him in addition only a small sum to make good his losses, now wished, in order, so it seems, to settle the matter legally, to leave Dresden for a few days and return home; a decision all the same, we do not doubt, in which the aforementioned business, pressing though it was since the winter sowing must be put in hand, played a lesser part than an intention to review his position in circumstances so strange and worrying; and reasons of another kind were working in him too which we leave all who know their own hearts free to guess at. Accordingly, leaving behind the guard that had been assigned to him, he betook himself to the Lord Chancellor and with the councillor's letters in his hand explained to him that it was his wish if, as seemed to be the case, he was not needed in court, to leave the city and for a period of between eight and twelve days, within which time he promised to be back again, to journey into Brandenburg. The Lord Chancellor, with a look at once unhappy and disquieting, cast down his eyes and answered: he was bound to say that Kohlhaas's presence at that moment was more necessary than ever since the court, because of the malicious and hairsplitting objections being raised by the defendants, would need his statements and explanations in a thousand instances that could not be foreseen; but when Kohlhaas referred him to his advocate, who was well briefed in the case, and with a respectful urgency, promising to restrict himself to eight days, persisted in his plea, the Lord Chancellor, after a silence, said, as he dismissed him, only this: he hoped that if he applied to Prince Christiern von Meissen he would be given the necessary passes. — Kohlhaas, who understood the look on the Lord Chancellor's face very well indeed, sat down at once, all the more determined, and, giving no reason, applied to the Prince of Meissen, head of the Chancellery, for eight-day passes to Kohlhaasenbrück and back. In reply to this letter he received a Chancellery note, signed by the palace governor, Baron Siegfried von Wenk, to the effect that his application for passes to Kohlhaasenbrück would be laid before his Majesty the Elector and the passes would be issued just as soon as the sovereign had approved them and the approval had been received. When Kohlhaas enquired of his advocate how it could be that the note from the Chancellery was signed by a Baron Siegfried von Wenk and not by Prince Christiern von Meissen, to whom he had addressed himself, he was told that the Prince had left for his estates three days ago and that for the period of his absence Chancellery matters had been handed over to Baron Siegfried von Wenk, a cousin of the gentleman of that name mentioned above. — Kohlhaas, whose heart amid all this was beginning to beat uneasily, waited several days for his application, laid in a worryingly laborious fashion before the sovereign himself, to be decided upon; but a week passed, and more time still, and neither did the decision arrive nor, despite its being definitely promised him, did the court give its verdict, so that on the twelfth day, firmly determined now to have the government's feelings towards him, whatever they might be, put into words he sat himself down and again, in an urgent representation, applied to the Chancellery for the passes he had requested. But he was then very taken aback when on the evening of the following day, which had likewise passed without the expected reply, still mulling over his predicament and especially the amnesty arranged for him by Doctor Luther, he crossed to the window of his back parlour and in the small annexe in the yard which he had given them as their living quarters he did not see the guard assigned to him on his arrival by the Prince of Meissen. Thomas, the old caretaker, when he summoned him and asked what this meant, answered with a sigh: 'Sir, things are not as they should be. The soldiers, of whom there are more today than usual, at nightfall distributed themselves all around the house; two, well armed, are standing on the street at the front door; two at the back door in the garden; and two more are lying in the hall on bales of straw and saying that they will sleep there.' Kohlhaas, the colour vanishing from his face, turned and replied: no matter, so long as they were there, and to give them a light, when next went out into the hall, so that they could see. And having, under the pretext of emptying a bowl, opened the front shutters and convinced himself of the truth of what the old man had revealed to him, for just then, without a sound, the guard was being changed, which until that moment throughout the period of the arrangement nobody had thought of doing: he went to bed, though little inclined to sleep, and had very soon resolved what to do next day. For the thing he disliked most about the government he had to deal with was their pretence of justice, when in fact they were breaking the amnesty they had promised him; and if he was indeed now a prisoner, as seemed beyond doubt, he wished to force them into a definite and unequivocal statement that this was the case. Accordingly, at dawn the next day, he had his servant Sternbald harness the horses and bring the carriage round in order, as he announced, to drive to Lockewitz,* to the steward there, who, as an old acquaintance, had spoken to him in Dresden a few days previously and invited him and the children to visit him when they liked. The guards, conferring together over the visible activity this caused in the house, sent one of their number secretly into town, whereupon a few minutes later an official from the Chancellery appeared with several armed officers and went into the house opposite as though they had business there. Kohlhaas who, busy dressing his boys, himself now noticed this activity and deliberately kept the carriage waiting outside the door longer than was quite necessary, as soon as he saw that the police had completed their measures he stepped out with his children, ignoring them; and saying, in passing, to the soldiers at the door that he did not need them to accompany him he lifted the boys into the carriage and kissed and comforted the tearful little girls who, as he had arranged it, were to stay behind with the old caretaker's daughter. Scarcely had he got into the carriage himself than the Chancellery official, followed by his men, approached him out of the house opposite and asked where he was going. When Kohlhaas replied that he wished to drive into the country, to Lockewitz, to his friend there, the steward, who a few days previously had invited him with the two boys, the Chancellery official answered that in that case he must wait for a few moments since, in accordance with the orders of the Prince of Meissen, a few mounted soldiers would accompany him. Kohlhaas, smiling down from the carriage, asked him did he suppose there would be any danger to his person at the house of a friend who had offered to entertain him at his table for the day. The official replied in a cheerful and agreeable manner that indeed the risk was not great; and added that the soldiers would not be in his way at all. Kohlhaas answered very seriously that the Prince of Meissen, on his arrival in Dresden, had left him free to make use of the guard or not, as he chose; and when the official expressed surprise at this and in cautious phrases referred to their use throughout his time there: the horsedealer recounted to him the event which had first occasioned the placing of the guard in his house. The official assured him that by the orders of the palace governor, Baron Wenk, who was at the moment chief of police, it was his duty to protect him, Kohlhaas, continuously; and begged him, should he not wish to be escorted, to go to the Chancellery himself and rectify the error there must be there. Kohlhaas, giving the official a meaningful look, determined now to force the issue, said he would do that; with a beating heart got down from his carriage, had the caretaker carry the children into the hall, and whilst his servant stayed with the horses at the house, he proceeded with the official and his guards into the Chancellery. It happened that the governor, Baron Wenk, was at that moment busy interrogating a band of Nagelschmidt's men, brought in the evening before, having been captured in the vicinity of Leipzig, and they were being questioned by the knights with him about many things it was desirable to know, when the horsedealer and his escort entered the room. The baron, as soon as he caught sight of the horsedealer, while the knights at once fell silent and broke off the interrogation, crossed over to him, and asked him what he wanted; and when the horsedealer, in a respectful manner, had expressed to him his intention of taking his midday meal at the house of the steward in Lockewitz and his wish to be allowed to leave behind the soldiers, having no need of them, the baron, changing colour and seeming to swallow back a different reply, answered that he would do well to bide quietly at home and put off for the time being his meal at the steward's in Lockewitz. — And with that, breaking off the whole conversation, he turned to the Chancellery official and said to him that the order he had given concerning the man stood and that he was not to leave the city except in the company of six mounted soldiers. — Kohlhaas asked: was he a prisoner and was he to believe that the amnesty, solemnly promised him before the eyes of the world, had been broken, whereupon the baron, his face burning red, suddenly turned to him and coming up close and looking him in the eyes replied: 'Yes, yes, yes!' — turned away, left him standing there and went back to Nagelschmidt's men. Thereupon Kohlhaas left the room and although he saw that by the steps he had taken he had greatly increased the difficulty of the one means of saving himself, flight, still he approved his move since now for his part too he considered himself released from honouring the stipulations of the amnesty. Arriving home, he had the horses unharnessed, and accompanied by the official from the Chancellery went to his room, very downcast and troubled; and while the man assured the horsedealer, in a way which disgusted him, that it must all be because of a misunderstanding that would soon be cleared up, the guards, directed by him, locked every exit into the yard, the official asssuring him meanwhile that as before the front main entrance would remain open for him to use as he liked.

Meanwhile Nagelschmidt in the forests of the Erzgebirge was so pressed on all sides by police and soldiery that, wholly lacking the means to act out the role he had taken on, he hit upon the idea of really engaging Kohlhaas; and being, through a traveller along the road, pretty exactly informed about the state of the legal battle in Dresden he believed that despite the open enmity existing between them he might induce the horsedealer into a fresh association with him. Accordingly, he dispatched a man with a letter for him, written in scarcely readable German, to this effect: If he would come to Altenburg and take over the leadership of the company which had formed itself there out of the remnants of the old one, he, Nagelschmidt, offered with horses, men and money to help him escape from his captivity in Dresden; and promised in the future to be more obedient and altogether more orderly and better than before and as proof of his loyalty and devotion swore to come into the neighbourhood of Dresden itself and effect his release from prison. Now the fellow charged with delivering this letter had the misfortune, in a village close to Dresden, to fall into a hideous fit of a kind he had been subject to since childhood; whereupon the letter, which he was carrying in his breast pocket, was found by the people coming to his assistance and he himself, as soon as he recovered, was arrested and, accompanied by a large crowd, conveyed to the Chancellery by the guard. As soon as the governor, von Wenk, had read this letter he proceeded at once to the Elector in the palace, where he found the two gentlemen Kunz and Hinz, the former now recovered from his injuries, and the President of the Chancellery Count Kallheim also present. The Junkers were of the opinion that Kohlhaas must without more ado be arrested and, on the grounds of secret dealings with Nagelschmidt, brought to trial; for they would have it that such a letter could not have been written unless others, from the horsedealer too, had preceded it and unless altogether a criminal and wicked connection, for the devising of new atrocities, existed between them. The Elector steadfastly refused, on the basis merely of this letter, to break the promise of safe conduct he had given to Kohlhaas; he was on the contrary of the opinion that out of Nagelschmidt's letter might be deduced a sort of probability that no previous intercourse had taken place between them; and all he would undertake to do, to clear the matter up, and then only after much hesitation, was, at the President's suggestion, to deliver the letter to Kohlhaas by the man Nagelschmidt had sent with it, just as if he had not been arrested, and see whether he would reply. Accordingly the man, who had been put into a prison, next morning was conveyed to the Chancellery where the governor gave him back the letter and promising him that he was free and would be let off the punishment he had incurred, ordered him to deliver it to the horsedealer as though nothing had happened; and for this miserable stratagem the fellow without more ado allowed himself to be used and with a pretence of secrecy, under the pretext of selling crayfish which the Chancellery official had supplied him with from the market, he came to Kohlhaas in his room. Kohlhaas, reading the letter while the children played with the crayfish, would certainly, had things been otherwise, have taken the rogue by the collar and handed him over to the soldiers outside the door; but since, opinion by then being what it was, even that act would not have been interpreted favourably for him, and since he was fully persuaded that nothing in the world now could extricate him from the business he was caught up in: he looked sadly into the man's

familiar face, asked him where he was staying, and said he should come
back a few hours later when he would inform him of his decision
regarding his master. He told Sternbald, who happened to come through
the door, to buy some crayfish off the man in the room; and when this
transaction was completed and both, without recognizing one another,
had left, he sat down and wrote as follows to Nagelschmidt: First, that
he accepted his proposition that he take over the command of his men in
Altenburg;* that accordingly, to free him and his five children from their
present captivity, he should send a carriage and two horses to Neustadt,
near Dresden; that he would also, for a speedier getaway, need another
pair of horses on the road to Wittenberg, that detour, for reasons he had
not space to give, being the only way he could come to him; that
although he hoped to win over the soldiers guarding him by bribery, he
wished there to be, in case force should be necessary, a few courageous,
canny and well-armed men ready in Neustadt; that to cover the costs of
these arrangements he was sending him, with the messenger, a rouleau
of twenty gold crowns and would ask him for an account of them when
the business was concluded; that finally, because it was unnecessary, he
would ask him not to be present himself at the rescue in Dresden; indeed
he gave him explicit orders to remain behind in Altenburg to command
the company a while longer, since they could not be without a leader. —
When the messenger returned towards evening Kohlhaas handed him
this letter; rewarded him richly and urged him to take good care of it. —
His intention was to go to Hamburg with his five children and from
there to take a ship to the Levant or the East Indies or to wherever else
out of a blue sky the sun shone down on human beings other than those
he knew. For in his heart sorely troubled and also disinclined to have
Nagelschmidt as an ally in his cause he no longer wanted his two black
horses feeding up again. — Scarcely had the man taken this reply to the
governor than the Lord Chancellor was removed from office, the
President, Count Kallheim, appointed Chief Justice in his stead, and
Kohlhaas, by an order in council issuing from the Elector himself,
arrested and conveyed in heavy irons to jail in the city tower. On the
grounds of his letter, which was displayed throughout the town, he was
brought to trial; and when, at the bar, asked did he acknowledge the
handwriting to be his, he answered to the clerk holding it before him:
'Yes', and when, asked did he have anything to say in his defence, he
cast down his eyes and answered: 'No', he was sentenced to be pinced
with red-hot tongs and quartered and his body burned between the
wheel and the gallows by the knacker's men.

So things stood for poor Kohlhaas when the Elector of Brandenburg appeared on the scene to rescue him out of the hands of arbitrary power and claimed him, in a note delivered to the electoral Chancellery in Dresden, as a subject of Brandenburg. For the honest city governor, Heinrich von Geusau, had related to him, on a walk along the banks of the Spree, the story of this strange and not wholly reprehensible man, and on that occasion, pressed by the questions of his astonished sovereign, he had had no option but to mention the blame which, as a result of the improprieties of his Lord Chancellor, Count Siegfried von Kallheim, attached to his own person; whereupon the Elector, vastly indignant, having confronted the Lord Chancellor and established that his being related to the von Tronka family was at the root of everything, removed him from office immediately with many marks of displeasure, and appointed Heinrich von Geusau in his stead.

Now it happened that precisely at this time the crown of Poland, having, for what reason we do not know, a quarrel with the house of Saxony, was repeatedly urging the Elector of Brandenburg to make common cause against them; so that Lord Chancellor Geusau, who had some skill in such matters, saw the possibility of fulfilling his sovereign's wish to get justice for Kohlhaas, cost what it might, without putting the stability of the whole any more at risk than was justified by consideration for an individual. Consequently, the Lord Chancellor not only demanded that Kohlhaas, having been the victim of procedures whose arbitrariness was offensive to God and men, should at once and unconditionally be returned so that, if guilty of anything, he could be judged according to the laws of Brandenburg on charges which the court of Dresden could make via an advocate in Berlin; but he went further and requested passes for an advocate whom the Elector wished to send to Dresden to get justice for Kohlhaas against Junker Wenzel von Tronka, for the black horses taken from him on Saxon territory and for other outrageous and violent ill-treatment. The Chamberlain, Kunz von Tronka, who in the changes among the government posts in Saxony had been made President of the State Chancellery and who, for various reasons, in the predicament in which he found himself, did not wish to offend the court of Brandenburg, replied in the name of his sovereign, who was very cast down by the note he had received: that they were surprised by the unfriendliness and unfairness with which the court of Dresden's right to judge Kohlhaas for crimes committed in their country was disputed, since it was well known that he owned a sizeable property in the capital and himself did not deny his Saxon citizenship. But since the crown of Poland, for the prosecution of its claims, was already assembling an army of five thousand men along the border with Saxony,

and the Lord Chancellor, Heinrich von Geusau, declared that Kohlhaasenbrück, the place from which the horsedealer took his name, lay in
Brandenburg and that if the sentence of death which had been passed on
him were carried out they would regard this as a breach of international
law: the Elector, on the advice of Kunz, his chamberlain, himself, who
wished to withdraw from the affair, recalled Prince Christiern von
Meissen from his estates and decided, after briefly consulting this
sensible gentleman, to deliver Kohlhaas to the court of Berlin in
accordance with their demand. The Prince who, though unhappy at the
improprieties that had occurred, was obliged at the bidding of his
beleaguered sovereign to take over the direction of the Kohlhaas case,
asked him what charges he now wished to see brought against the
horsedealer at the high court in Berlin; and since they could not base
anything on the unfortunate letter to Nagelschmidt, because of the
equivocal and unclear circumstances under which it had been written,
and could not refer to the earlier acts of pillage and arson because of the
proclamation pardoning him for them: the Elector then decided to
present to the Emperor in Vienna an account of Kohlhaas's armed
incursion into Saxony, to complain about this breach of a peace
established by imperial law itself, and to ask that the Emperor, who was
of course not bound by any amnesty, should, through his own
prosecutor, bring Kohlhaas to account for these things at the lawcourts
in Berlin. A week later the horsedealer was fetched by the knight
Friedrich von Malzahn, whom the Elector of Brandenburg had sent with
six riders to Dresden, and, still in chains, was placed in a carriage and
along with his five children who, at his request, had been assembled
again from orphanages and homes for foundlings, was transported to
Berlin. It happened that the Elector of Saxony, at the invitation of his
provincial governor, Count Aloysius von Kallheim, who in those days
owned a good deal of land on the Saxon border, in the company of
Chamberlain Kunz and his wife, Lady Heloise, daughter of the governor
and sister of the President, not to mention other brilliant ladies and
gentlemen, squires and courtiers, had travelled to Dahme* for a great
stag-hunt which, to lift his spirits, had been arranged for him; with the
result that, under awnings that were bright with flags and rose up a
slope right across the road, the whole company, still covered with the
dust of the chase, waited on by page boys and young courtiers and a
cheerful music sounding over towards them from under an oak, were
sitting at table when the horsedealer and the riders accompanying him
came slowly down the road from Dresden. For one of the young and
delicate Kohlhaas children had fallen sick, obliging von Malzahn, the

knight escorting them, to remain for three days in Herzberg;* and being only responsible to the sovereign he served he had not thought it necessary to inform the government in Dresden of this measure. The Elector, his shirt open at the neck and his plumed hat decorated with evergreen in huntsman's style, was seated next to Lady Heloise, who in his early youth had been his first love; and his spirits being cheered by the enchanting festivity all around him, he said: 'Let us go down and offer this goblet of wine to that unhappy man, whoever he may be.' Lady Heloise, all her beauty in the look she gave him, stood up at once and, ransacking the whole table, filled a silver bowl, handed to her by a page, with fruit, cakes and bread; and the whole company, with refreshments of every kind, had swarmed from the tent when the Marshal came towards them with embarrassment on his face and begged them to keep away. When the Elector, taken aback, asked what had happened to cause him such consternation, the governor, turning to the chamberlain, stammered that Kohlhaas was in the carriage; upon which information, incomprehensible to all of them since it was general knowledge that he had departed six days ago, Chamberlain Kunz took his goblet of wine and, turning back towards the tent, poured it into the sand. The Elector, redder and redder in the face, set his down on a tray held out to him for that purpose by a page at a nod from the chamberlain; and while the knight Friedrich von Malzahn, respectfully saluting the company, whom he did not know, slowly proceeded on the road towards Dahme among the tent-ropes crossing it, the party, paying him no further attention, withdrew under the awning as the governor invited them to. The governor, as soon as the Elector had resumed his seat, sent secretly to Dahme to get the magistrates there to move the horsedealer on immediately; but since von Malzahn, the day being already far advanced, expressed a decided wish to stay the night in that place, the best that could be done was accommodate him quietly in a farm belonging to the magistrates which lay off the road and was hidden among trees. Now it happened that towards evening when wine and the enjoyment of a rich dessert had driven the whole incident from the party's minds the governor proposed that, another herd of stags having been sighted, they should again try for a kill; which suggestion the company took up with delight, and in pairs, having armed themselves with guns, hurried off over ditches and hedges into the nearby forest; with the result that the Elector and Lady Heloise who, to be present at the spectacle, had linked arms with him, were led by a servant who had been assigned to them, directly, to their astonishment, through the courtyard of the house in which Kohlhaas and the Brandenburg escort were staying. The lady, when she heard this, said: 'Oh, come, sir, do come', and reaching for the chain that hung about his neck teasingly she hid it inside his silk shirt: 'Let us creep into the farm before the rest arrive and see the wondrous person accommodated there.' The Elector, blushing and seizing her hand, said: 'Heloise, what can you be thinking of?' But when, looking at him in surprise, she replied: that disguised as he was in hunting clothes of course nobody would recognize him, and tugged him along and when, just at that moment, two country noblemen who had already satisfied their curiosity emerged from the house and assured them that in fact, thanks to precautions the governor had taken, neither the riders nor Kohlhaas knew what company it was that had gathered in the vicinity of Dahme, the Elector, smiling, pulled his hat down over his eyes and said: 'Folly, you govern the world, and the lips of a beautiful woman are your dwelling place.' — As it happened, Kohlhaas, seated on a bale of straw and leaning back against the wall, was feeding white bread and milk to the child who had fallen sick in Herzberg, when the Elector and his party entered the farmstead to visit him; and when the lady, to initiate a conversation, asked him who he was and what was the matter with the child, what he had done wrong and where he was being taken to under such an escort, he touched his leather cap and to all these questions, whilst continuing to feed the child, he gave her sparse but satisfactory answers. The Elector, standing behind the two country gentlemen and noticing a small leaden locket that hung on a silk string around his neck, asked him, for want of any better topic of conversation, what its significance was and what it contained. Kohlhaas replied: 'Ah yes, sir, my locket' — and with that drew it over his head, opened it up and took out a small folded paper sealed with a wafer of glue — 'it is a strange thing, this locket. Perhaps seven months ago, precisely on the day after my wife's funeral, and I had left Kohlhaasenbrück, as perhaps you know, to lay my hands on the Junker von Tronka, who had done me great wrong, when for some business that I know nothing about the Elector of Saxony and the Elector of Brandenburg met in Jüterbock,* a market town through which I had to pass to carry out my raid; and when towards evening they had reached the desired agreement, they strolled, in amicable conversation, through the streets of the town to view the fair then cheerfully in progress. There they came upon a gypsy woman who, sitting on a stool, was telling fortunes to the crowd around her and, jokingly, they asked her whether she had anything agreeable to reveal to them also. Myself, having just dismounted at an inn with my men and being there on the spot where this took place, from where I stood, at the back of the crowd, by a church door, I could not hear what the strange woman said to the gentlemen; and when the people laughed and whispered to one another that she would not tell her secrets to all and sundry and because of the spectacle thus in the making pushed and shoved, I, not so much curious as making room for those who were, stepped up on to a stone seat that was cut into the church porch behind me. From this vantage point, nothing blocking my view, I had no sooner taken in the two Electors and the woman who, sitting on the stool before them, seemed to be scribbling something, than she stood up suddenly, leaning on her crutches, and looking around in the crowd, fixed her gaze on me, who had never before exchanged a word with her nor ever sought her knowledge; but she pushed through the whole dense press of people to me and said: "There! If the gentleman wants to know he can ask you." And with that, sir, from her thin and bony hands I received this scrap of paper. And when, taken aback, as all the crowd turned round to me, I asked: "What is it you are giving me, old lady?" she replied, after much that was unintelligible but in which to my great astonishment I heard my name: "An amulet, Kohlhaas the horsedealer. Take care of it. One day it will save your life!", and vanished. — Well,' Kohlhaas continued amiably, 'to tell the truth, though things turned very bad in Dresden it did not cost me my life; and how I shall fare in Berlin and whether I shall survive with it there also, time will tell.' — At these words the Elector sat down on a bench and although when the lady asked him what the matter was he answered: 'Nothing. Nothing at all', he fell to the floor in a faint before she had time to hurry across and take him in her arms. Von Malzahn, on some business at that very moment entering the room, said: 'In heaven's name, what is the matter with the gentleman?' The lady cried out: 'Bring some water!' The two country gentlemen lifted him up and carried him through to a bed in the adjoining room; and consternation reached its height when the chamberlain, fetched by a page boy, after several vain attempts to summon him back to consciousness declared that to all appearances he had suffered a stroke. The governor, whilst the cupbearer sent a messenger on horseback to Luckau,* to fetch a doctor, when the Elector opened his eyes, he had him transferred to a carriage and conveyed then at walking pace to a hunting lodge of his in the vicinity; but this journey, after he arrived there, brought on two further faints, with the result that not until late the following morning, when the doctor arrived from Luckau, did he recover somewhat, and even then with the decided symptoms of an approaching nervous fever. As soon as he was master of his senses again he raised himself up in bed a little and his first question was:

'Where is Kohlhaas?' The chamberlain, misinterpreting the question, said, taking him by the hand, that he should be easy now on that frightful person's account who, as agreed, after that strange and incomprehensible occurrence, had remained at the farm in Dahme, in the custody of Brandenburg. He asked him, with protestations of the liveliest sympathy and with the assurance that he had reproached his wife in the bitterest terms for her irresponsible frivolity in causing him to meet that man, what was it in their conversation that had troubled him so strangely and inordinately. The Elector answered that he must confess it was the sight of a scrap of paper the man carried on him in a leaden locket which was to blame for the whole unpleasant accident that had befallen him. He added various details in explanation of this circumstance which the chamberlain did not understand; confessed to him suddenly, pressing his hand between his own, that to possess this paper was of the utmost importance to him; and begged him to mount forthwith, ride to Dahme and procure the paper for him from Kohlhaas at whatever cost. The chamberlain, finding it hard to conceal his embarrassment, assured him that if the paper was of value to him nothing in the world was more necessary than to conceal that fact from Kohlhaas; for should he by any incautious utterance learn of it, not all the royal riches would suffice to get it by purchase out of the hands of that heartless and in his lust for vengeance insatiable man. He added, to calm him, that they must think of some other means and that perhaps by cunning, through some third party, someone wholly uninvolved, since the miscreant doubtless was not, for itself, especially attached to it, they might manage to get possession of the paper that was, to him, of such importance. The Elector, wiping the sweat off his face, asked whether to that end word could be sent to Dahme at once and the transportation of the horsedealer be halted for a while until, by whatever means, the paper had been obtained. The chamberlain, who could not believe his ears, assured him that unfortunately, by all probable reckoning, the horse-dealer must have left Dahme by now and be already over the border on Brandenburg soil where any attempt to hinder his removal or, worse, fetch him back would cause difficulties of the most disagreeable and far-reaching kind, indeed such difficulties as would perhaps not be able to be overcome. Then he asked the Elector, who with the gesture of a man bereft of all hope had laid himself back in silence on the pillow, what was in the paper and by what strange and inexplicable accident did he know that the contents concerned him. But to this the Elector made no reply, only glancing equivocally at the chamberlain whose eagerness to please in this matter he mistrusted. He lay there rigid, his heart beating unsteadily, and stared down at the corner of a handkerchief that, lost in thought, he was holding in his hands; abruptly then asked him to call in von Stein, a young, vigorous and resourceful gentleman whom he had several times employed on secret business, under the pretext that he had other things to settle with him. Having explained the matter to him and told him of the importance of the paper in Kohlhaas's possession, he asked this gentleman did he wish to be assured of his eternal friendship by getting him that paper before Kohlhaas reached Berlin; and when, so soon as he had to some extent grasped the situation, strange as it was, the man promised him that he was entirely at his service, the Elector's orders were that he should ride after Kohlhaas and, since he was probably not to be moved by money, to come at him in a skilful parley and offer him freedom and his life; indeed, should he insist on it, to lend him immediate though cautious assistance, with horses, men and money, to escape from the Brandenburg riders transporting him. Von Stein, having asked for a note in the Elector's hand, as authority, set off at once with a small company and, since he did not spare the horses, was fortunate enough to come upon Kohlhaas at a village on the border where, with von Malzahn and his five children, he was taking a midday meal that had been laid in the open air outside the door of a house. Von Malzahn, to whom the gentleman introduced himself as a foreigner who, travelling through, wished to have a sight of the strange man in his charge, at once courteously sat him down and presented him to Kohlhaas; and since von Malzahn had to come and go in the preparations for departure, and the riders were taking their meal at a table on the other side of the house, the Elector's man soon had an opportunity to reveal to the horsedealer who he was and with what particular commission he had come to him. The horsedealer, already aware of the rank and name of the person who at the sight of the locket in question had fainted in the farmhouse at Dahme, and only needing, to crown the excitement into which this discovery had thrown him, some insight into the secrets of the paper which, for various reasons, he was resolved not to open out of mere curiosity: the horsedealer, remembering how ungenerously and ignobly, despite his own utter readiness to make every possible sacrifice, he had been treated in Dresden, answered: that he wished to keep the paper. Asked by the gentleman what moved him to this strange refusal, since he was being offered in exchange nothing less than life and liberty, Kohlhaas replied: 'Sir, if your sovereign came and said: I will annihilate myself with all the band of those who help me rule — annihilate himself, do you understand me, which is of course my soul's dearest wish — I would still refuse to give him the paper which matters more to him than his existence, and should say: "You can bring me to the scaffold, but I can do you injury, and I will." Thereupon, with death in his face, he called over one of the riders and urged him to help himself to the food still remaining, in good amount, in the dish. Then for the rest of his stay in the village ignoring von Stein, who sat on at the table, only when he was climbing into the carriage did he turn back to him and, with a look, give him a goodbye. — The condition of the Elector when he received this news worsened to such a degree that the doctor, during three fateful days, feared greatly for his life assailed simultaneously from so many sides. However, having resources in his native health, after several anxious weeks of sickness he did recover; to the extent at least that he could be carried to his carriage and, well provided with cushions and blankets, be conveyed back to Dresden and to his responsibilities as a ruler. So soon as he had arrived in that city he summoned Prince Christiern von Meissen and asked him how things stood with regard to the departure of Justice Eibenmayer, whom it had been intended to send to Vienna as advocate in the Kohlhaas case, to charge him before his Imperial Majesty with breach of the imperial peace. The Prince replied that in accordance with orders left behind when the Elector departed for Dahme he, Eibenmayer, had gone to Vienna immediately after the arrival of advocate Zäuner, whom the Elector of Brandenburg had sent to Dresden to bring his charges relating to the pair of black horses against Junker Wenzel von Tronka. The Elector, blushing and crossing to his desk, said he was surprised at this haste since he had, he believed, stated that the definitive departure of Eibenmayer should wait on more precise and particular orders, it being necessary beforehand to refer back to Doctor Martin Luther, who had negotiated the amnesty for Kohlhaas. So saying, with a look of repressed displeasure, he rummaged among the letters and papers on his desk. The Prince, gazing at him in amazement for a time, replied that he was sorry if he had failed to satisfy him in the matter; but he could show him the resolution of Council requiring him to dispatch the advocate on that date. He added that there had been no mention whatsoever in Council of any reference back to Doctor Luther; that it might have been proper earlier to have considered that churchman's views because of his intercession on Kohlhaas's behalf, but no longer, now that they had broken the amnesty before the eyes of all the world, arrested him and delivered him to the courts of Brandenburg for sentencing and execution. The Elector said: dispatching Eibenmayer was indeed not a very serious mistake; but now it was his wish that for the time being until further notice he should not exercise his function as prosecutor in

Vienna, and asked the Prince to instruct him to this effect at once by an express messenger. The Prince replied that, alas, the order came just too late since Eibenmayer, according to a report which had arrived that very day, had already proceeded in that capacity and filed the action at the lawcourts in Vienna. To the Elector's astonished question how all this was possible in so short a time, he replied that three weeks had already elapsed since the man's departure and by instructions given him he had been required to seek to press ahead with the business immediately on arrival in Vienna. Any delay, the Prince observed, would in this case have been all the more inappropriate since Zäuner, the lawyer from Brandenburg, was proceeding against the Junker Wenzel von Tronka with aggressive vigour and had already applied to the court for a provisional removal of the horses out of the hands of the knacker, for their future restoration, and despite all objections on the part of the defendants had got his way. The Elector, tugging at the bell, said: no matter, it was of no importance, and having turned back to the Prince with idle questions on how things stood otherwise in Dresden and what had happened in his absence, he made a gesture of farewell and, unable to conceal his innermost state, dismissed him. That same day he sent to him in writing for all the Kohlhaas papers, under the pretext that because of its political importance he wished to conduct the case himself; and since the thought of destroying the only man he could learn the secrets of the locket from was intolerable to him, he wrote in his own hand to the Emperor begging him, in heartfelt and urgent tones, to be permitted, for important reasons which he would perhaps soon set before him more explicitly, temporarily, pending a further decision, to withdraw the charge that Eibenmayer had submitted against Kohlhaas. The Emperor, in a note dispatched through the Chancellery, replied that this, as it seemed, so sudden change of heart perturbed him very greatly; that the report submitted by Saxony had made the case of Kohlhaas a matter for the entire Holy Roman Empire; that, as a consequence, he, the Emperor, as its head, had felt duty-bound to address the house of Brandenburg and bring charges there; with the result that since the imperial assessor, Franz Müller, acting as advocate, had gone to Berlin to call Kohlhaas to account for breach of the peace of the Empire, it would be quite impossible now to withdraw the charge and the case must take its course according to the law. By this letter the Elector was utterly cast down; and when, before long, to his extreme dismay, private letters came in from Berlin reporting the presentation of the case at the High Court and commenting that, despite all the efforts of the advocate assigned to him, Kohlhaas would probably end on the scaffold, the

unhappy man decided to make one more attempt and in an address in
his own hand begged the Elector of Brandenburg for the horsedealer's
life. It would, he pretended, be improper to carry out a death sentence
on a person to whom an amnesty had been granted; he swore that,
despite the apparent severity with which they had proceeded against
him, it had never been his intention to let him die; and would it not, he
wrote, be very wretched for the horsedealer if the protection they
claimed they wished to see extended to him from Berlin were finally, in
an unexpected twist, to turn to something more to his disadvantage than
if he had remained in Dresden and his case had been decided according
to Saxon law? The Elector of Brandenburg, to whom much in this
representation seemed equivocal and unclear, replied that because of the
zeal with which his Imperial Majesty's advocate was proceeding it
would be wholly impossible to deviate, in the way that he had requested,
from the strict requirements of the law. He observed that the anxiety
expressed by the Elector surely went rather too far, since the charge
concerning the crimes forgiven Kohlhaas in the amnesty was not
brought to the High Court in Berlin by the person who had granted him
the amnesty, but by the head of the Empire, who was not in the least
bound by that amnesty. He also put it to him that since Nagelschmidt
was continuing his depredations, extending them indeed, with unprecedented impudence, even into Brandenburg territory, it was very
necessary to make an example of Kohlhaas, as a deterrent, and begged
him, should all this not weigh with him, to appeal directly to the
Emperor, since if any intervention were to be made on Kohlhaas's behalf
it could only be on the basis of a declaration from that quarter. The
Elector, grieved and angered by these repeated failures, fell sick again;
and when the chamberlain visited him one morning he showed him the
letters he had sent to Vienna and Berlin to keep Kohlhaas alive and so at
least win time in which to acquire the paper in his possession. The
chamberlain went down on his knees before him and begged him by
everything he held dear and holy to tell him what was in that note. The
Elector said he should lock the door and sit down on the bed; and
having taken his hand and, with a sigh, pressed it against his heart, he
began as follows: 'Your wife, as I hear, has already told you that on the
third day of our meeting in Jüterbock the Elector of Brandenburg and I
came upon a gypsy woman; and when the Elector, with the quickness
typical of him, decided that by making fun of her in the view of all the
people he would destroy the reputation of this colourful person whose
powers had been spoken about, in a way that was not proper, at the
meal we had just left, he stood before her at her table and, folding his

arms, demanded that, if she were to tell his fortune, she first give him some sign whose truth could be proved that very day, saying that he could not otherwise give any credence to her words, not even if she were the Roman sibyl herself. The woman, appraising us fleetingly from head to foot, said the sign would be that the great antlered stag being reared in the park by the gardener's son would come to meet us in the market where we were standing before we left the place. Let me tell you that this stag which was destined for the kitchens in Dresden was kept under lock and key in a close surrounded by a high fence and overshadowed by the oak trees of the park so that, considering also that on account of other smaller game and birds the park altogether as well as the garden leading to it were very carefully secured, it was inconceivable that the beast, as the strange claim required it to, should come to meet us in the square where we were all standing; nevertheless the Elector, fearing some trickery at the back of it, after a brief word with me and being determined, in order to ridicule her, that whatever she might utter should be conclusively demolished, sent word to the palace that the stag should be slaughtered at once and prepared for table on a following day. Thereupon he turned back to the woman in front of whom this business had been openly conducted and said: "Well now. What can you tell me about my future?" The woman, looking at his hand, said: "Hail to you, my sovereign and lord! Your Majesty's reign will be long, and of long duration will be the house you come from, and your descendants will grow strong and splendid and be more powerful than all the lords and princes of the world." The Elector, after a silence in which he looked at the woman thoughtfully, said, under his breath, taking a step towards me, that he was almost sorry now to have sent a messenger who would annul the prophecy; and whilst money from the hands of the gentlemen in his entourage rained down in quantities amid a general rejoicing into the woman's lap, the Elector himself, reaching into his pocket and contributing a gold piece, asked her whether the salutation she had for me would sound as silvery as his. The woman, having opened a box which stood at her side and sorted the money into it according to kind and amount, taking her time and all very deliberately, when she had closed the box again she raised her hand against the sun as if it were troubling her and looked at me; and when I repeated the question and jokingly, while she examined my hand, said to the Elector: "She seems not to have anything very pleasant to tell *me*", she seized her crutches, raised herself slowly from off her stool on them and coming up close against me, holding her hands out in a mysterious manner, she whispered, loud enough to hear, into my ear: "No!" — "I see," I said, in confusion, and stepped back a pace from the figure who with a cold and lifeless look, as if out of eyes of marble, sat down again on the stool behind her: "And from what side is my house threatened by danger?" The woman, taking up paper and charcoal and crossing her legs, asked should she write it down for me; and when, in embarrassment and only because in the circumstances I could do nothing else, I answered: "Yes, do so", she answered: "Very well. I shall write out three things for you: the name of the last ruler of your house, the year he will lose his kingdom, the name of the man who by force of arms will seize it from him." This done, and the whole crowd watching, she rose, stuck down the paper with a glue which she wetted in her lifeless mouth and pressed a lead signet ring on it that she wore on her middle finger. And when, more curious, as you will easily imagine, than words can tell, I made to grasp the note she said: "Ah no, my lord", and turned and lifted up one of her crutches: "From that man there, the man with the feather in his hat, standing on the seat in the church porch behind the crowd, from him, if you wish, you can claim the message." And with that, before I had rightly understood what she was saying, she left me standing in the square, speechless with astonishment; and clapping together the box behind her and flinging it over her shoulder, she went in among the crowd of people surrounding us so that I could not see what else she did. Then, greatly to my comfort indeed, the knight appeared whom the Elector had sent to the palace, and reported, with a smile, that the stag had been slaughtered and before his eyes had been dragged into the kitchens by two of his huntsmen. The Elector, cheerfully linking arms with me, to lead me away from the square, said: "There now. The prophecy was the usual cheat and not worth the time and money it has cost us." But how great was our astonishment when, even while these words were being spoken, a cry went up throughout the square and all eyes turned upon a colossal butcher's dog bounding our way from the direction of the palace and it had seized the stag in the kitchens by the neck and carried it off and pursued by servant boys and servant girls dropped it on the ground three paces away from us: so that in truth the woman's prophecy, as the guarantee of everything she uttered, was fulfilled and the stag, though dead, had come to meet us in the marketplace. Lightning falling from heaven on a winter's day cannot strike more annihilatingly than did this sight at me, and my immediate endeavour, as soon as I could escape the company around me, was to find the man with the feather in his hat whom the woman had pointed out to me; but none of my people, sent out for a full three days to enquire unceasingly, could give me even the remotest news of him: and

then, my friend, a few weeks ago, in the farmhouse at Dahme, I saw the
man with my own eyes.' — And so saying he let go of the chamberlain's
hand; and wiping the sweat from his face sank back again upon his bed.
The chamberlain, thinking it a waste of effort to oppose and seek to
correct the Elector's view of events with his own, begged him to try
some means of obtaining the paper, and then to leave the fellow to his
fate; but the Elector replied that he saw absolutely no means of doing
this even though the thought of not having it, or worse of seeing its
message vanish with that man, was driving him into misery and despair.
Asked by his friend whether he had made efforts to find the gypsy
woman herself, the Elector replied that the Chancellery, following an
order he issued to them under a pretext, had been and still were
searching for her throughout the country, in vain; himself however, for
reasons he refused to elaborate, he doubted whether she was to be found
in Saxony at all. Now the chamberlain, as it happened, on account of
several sizeable properties in the Neumark bequeathed to his wife by
Count Kallheim, the former Lord Chancellor, who had died shortly after
being removed from office, wished to go to Berlin; and, being truly fond
of the Elector, he asked him, after a moment's thought, would he give
him complete freedom in the matter, and when the Elector, warmly
pressing the chamberlain's hand against his heart, replied: 'Act as
though you were me, and get me that paper!', the chamberlain, having
delegated his duties, brought forward his departure by a few days and
leaving his wife behind and accompanied only by a few servants set off
for Berlin.

Kohlhaas, having in the meantime, as already stated, arrived in Berlin
and by special order of the Elector been housed with his five children as
comfortably as possible in a prison for men of noble birth, was brought
to the bar of the High Court as soon as the Emperor's advocate arrived
from Vienna and charged with breach of the imperial peace; and
although he answered in his defence that his armed incursion into
Saxony and the acts of violence he had perpetrated there were not
actionable because of the accommodation reached at Lützen with the
Elector of Saxony, his misapprehension was corrected and he learned
that his Imperial Majesty whose advocate was pressing the charges
could take no account of it and very soon, when the thing was explained
to him and he was told that on the other hand from Dresden, in his case
against Junker Wenzel von Tronka, he would receive complete satisfaction, he accepted his situation. Accordingly then it happened that on the
very day of the chamberlain's arrival in Berlin judgment was given and
he was sentenced to death by the sword; a sentence which, though

merciful, nobody, seeing how complicated things were, believed would be carried out but which the whole city, knowing how well-disposed towards Kohlhaas the Elector was, confidently expected to see commuted to mere, though perhaps harsh and lengthy, imprisonment. The chamberlain, who none the less saw that there was no time to lose if the commission given him by his sovereign was to be accomplished, began his efforts by one morning allowing Kohlhaas, at his prison window idly watching the passers-by, a full and certain sight of him in his customary court dress; and judging, from a sudden movement of the head, that the horsedealer had seen him, and with great satisfaction also noticing an involuntary reaching of his hand towards his breast where the locket lay, he thought what had occurred at that moment in the horsedealer's soul a sufficient preparation for a next step in the attempt to get hold of the paper. He summoned an old pedlar woman, one on crutches whom he had seen about the streets of Berlin among a band of wretches like her dealing in rags and who in age and dress seemed similar enough to the one the Elector had described to him; and assuming that Kohlhaas would have no very exact memory of the features of the woman who had appeared briefly before him and handed him the paper, he decided to substitute his own for her and, if it could be done, have her act for him with Kohlhaas as though she were the gypsy. Accordingly, to enable her to do this, he informed her thoroughly of what had occurred between the Elector and the gypsy in Jüterbock, and since he did not know how far that woman had gone in her disclosures to Kohlhaas he was careful to instil in her particularly the three secret facts which the paper contained; and when he had explained to her how she must in a disconnected and unintelligible fashion drop hints that certain measures were being taken, either by cunning or by force, to get hold of this paper so important to the Saxon court, he instructed her to ask Kohlhaas, under the pretext that it was no longer safe with him, to give it her to look after till the ominous days had passed. The pedlar woman, on the promise of a substantial payment, a part of which, at her demand, the chamberlain was obliged to make her in advance, at once undertook to do the job; and since the mother of Kohlhaas's man Herse, killed at Mühlberg, had the authorities' permission to visit him occasionally and had moreover for some months been acquainted with the pedlar woman, this latter managed, on one of the following days, by means of a small gift to the jailer, to get access to the horsedealer. — But Kohlhaas, when this woman entered the room, thought, from a signet ring she was wearing on her hand and a coral necklace around her neck, that he recognized in her the old gypsy herself who had given him the paper in Jüterbock; and as probability and truth are not always on the same side it was the case that something had happened here which we relate but leave anyone inclined to doubt it free to do so: the chamberlain had made the most monstrous mistake and in the pedlar woman picked up from the streets of Berlin to impersonate the gypsy he had hit upon the mysterious gypsy herself whom he wanted impersonating. At least, the woman's story as she, leaning on her crutches, stroked the cheeks of the children who, alarmed by her strange appearance, pressed against their father, was this: that she had returned some while ago out of Saxony into Brandenburg and hearing on the streets of Berlin the chamberlain's incautious enquiry after the gypsy who early in the previous year had been in Jüterbock, she had at once pushed herself forward and under a false name had offered to do the job he wanted done. The horsedealer, who noticed a strange resemblance between her and his dead wife Lisbeth, so much so that he might have asked her was she her grandmother: for not only did the features of her face, her hands, still beautiful in their bony shape and especially the use she made of them when speaking, remind him of her in the liveliest possible way but also a mole which had marked his wife's neck he noticed on hers too — the horsedealer, in a strange welter of thinking, urged her to be seated and asked why in the world she should come to him on business of the chamberlain's. The woman, whilst Kohlhaas's old dog snuffled around her knees and wagged its tail under the caresses of her hand, replied that the commission she had from the chamberlain was to disclose to him what three questions important to the Saxon court the mysterious paper contained the answers to; to warn him against an agent, now in Berlin, sent to get possession of it; and to ask him, on the pretext that it was no longer safe where he wore it on his breast, to give her the paper. But her real purpose in coming was to tell him that the threat of depriving him of the paper by trickery or force was a feeble and empty lie; that under the protection of the Elector of Brandenburg, in whose custody he was, he need have not the least fear for his locket; indeed it was far safer with him than with her and he must beware of losing it by handing it over to whomsoever on whatever pretext. — None the less she concluded that he would be wise to use the paper as she had intended he should when she gave it to him at the fair in Jüterbock: close with the offer made him at the frontier by the Junker von Stein and hand over the paper, which could be of no further use to him, to the Elector of Saxony in exchange for life and liberty. Kohlhaas, rejoicing in the power thus granted him to wound his enemy mortally in the heel just as it was grinding him into the dust, replied: 'Not for worlds, old lady, not for worlds', and pressed her hand and wished to know how the fateful questions were answered in the note. The woman, lifting up the youngest child, who had been crouching at her feet, and taking him on her lap, replied: 'Not for worlds, Kohlhaas the horsedealer, but for this pretty little boy with his blond hair', and so saying she laughed and cuddled and kissed the child, who was staring at her wide-eyed, and in her thin hand gave him an apple out of her apron. Kohlhaas, troubled, said that the children themselves when they were grown up would commend him for what he had done and that for them and their grandchildren he could do nothing more salutary than keep the paper. And he asked her who, after what he had experienced, could guarantee him against further treachery and whether he might not deliver up the note to the Elector, as he had recently delivered up his army assembled at Lützen, and gain nothing by it? 'A man who once goes back on his word to me,' he said, 'I never let him give me his word again, and only if you ask me for it, definitely and unequivocally, lady, will I part with this scrap of paper which, in so strange a fashion, gets me satisfaction for all I have suffered.' The woman, setting down the child, said that in some ways he was right and he could do as he pleased. And with that she took up her crutches again and was about to leave. Kohlhaas repeated his question concerning the contents of the strange note; and when she answered him cursorily that he could always open it, though it would only be out of curiosity if he did, there were a thousand other things he wanted to be told before she left him: who she really was, how she had come into the knowledge she possessed, why she had refused to give the note to the Elector — for whom after all it was written — and handed the wondrous document to him out of so many thousands of people when he had never sought her knowledge? — Now, as it happened, at just this moment they heard the noise of certain officers of the prison climbing the stairs; so that the woman, seized by a sudden fear that they might discover her in his rooms, replied: 'Goodbye, Kohlhaas, goodbye. When we meet again you will not want for understanding of all these things.' And with that, turning to the door, she cried: 'Farewell, children, farewell', kissed the little tribe one after the other, and was gone.

Meanwhile the Elector of Saxony, at the mercy of his miserable thoughts, had summoned two astrologers, Oldenholm and Olearius, who at that time were highly respected in Saxony, and consulted them concerning the mysterious paper whose contents were of such importance to him and all the tribe of his descendants; and when the two men, after profound investigations over several days in the palace tower, still could not agree whether the prophecy had to do with future centuries or with the present time, and the crown of Poland was meant by it, since dealings there were still very belligerent, the distress, not to say despair, in which the unfortunate man found himself, far from being relieved by these learned disputes was only aggravated and increased, in the end, to something more than his soul could bear. It happened in addition that around this time the chamberlain wrote to his wife, who was about to follow him to Berlin, that before she left she must tactfully make known to the Elector how little hope there was, after an abortive attempt he had made through a woman who had since vanished, of getting hold of the paper in Kohlhaas's possession, because the sentence of death passed on him had now, after a thorough examination of the papers, been signed by the Elector of Brandenburg and the day of execution set for the Monday before Easter; hearing which news the Elector of Saxony, his heart torn by grief and regret, like a lost man locked himself in his room, for two days sick of life, taking nothing to eat, and on the third then suddenly, with a brief note to the Chancellery that he had gone to visit the Prince of Dessau to hunt, he disappeared from Dresden. Where he went in fact and whether he did go to Dessau, we leave open to question since the chronicles,* collating which we offer this account, curiously contradict one another here and cancel one another out. We can say for certain that at that time the Prince of Dessau was unfit to go hunting and lay sick in Braunschweig at the house of his uncle Duke Heinrich; also that on the evening of the following day Lady Heloise, accompanied by a Count von Königstein whom she presented as her cousin, rejoined Chamberlain Kunz, her husband, in Berlin. — Meanwhile, on the orders of the Elector, Kohlhaas had had the sentence of death read out to him, his shackles removed, and the papers concerning his estate, denied him in Dresden, returned to him; and when the jurists assigned to him by the court asked him how he wished his possessions to be disposed of after his death, he drew up a will, with the help of a notary, in favour of his children and appointed the councillor in Kohlhaasenbrück, his trusty friend, to be their guardian. That done, nothing could equal the peace and contentment of his final days; for in accordance with a quite particular decree of the Elector's, the prison itself in which he was housed soon afterwards was opened and all his friends, of whom he had a great number in the city, were granted free access to him day and night. Indeed, he had the satisfaction of being visited in his cell by the theologian Jakob Freising, who came as an emissary of Doctor Luther with a letter in his own hand, which must doubtless have been a very remarkable document but which has been lost, and from that priest, in the presence of two Brandenburg deacons who assisted him, he had the solace of Holy Communion. Then, amid general agitation among the citizens, who still could not give up the hope that an intervention from above would spare his life, the fateful Monday before Easter arrived, on which day he was to make amends to the world for having tried too hastily to get himself justice in it. Heavily guarded, and carrying his two sons (a favour he had expressly sued for from the dock) he was just issuing forth through the gateway of the prison, led out by the theologian Jakob Freising, when amid a doleful press of acquaintances all shaking his hand and bidding him farewell the constable of the Elector's palace approached him with a troubled look and gave him a note which, he said, an old woman had left for him. Kohlhaas, looking at the man, whom he scarcely knew, in some surprise, opened the note whose seal, imprinted on the gum, at once reminded him of his friend the gypsy woman. But how shall we describe the astonishment seizing him when he read the communication that follows here: 'Kohlhaas, the Elector of Saxony is in Berlin; he has gone ahead to the place of execution and you will recognize him, if it matters to you, by a hat with blue and white plumes. I do not need to tell you what his purpose in coming is. He will have the capsule dug up as soon as you are buried and the paper in it opened. — Your Elizabeth.' — Kohlhaas, turning to the constable in the greatest possible turmoil of feelings, asked him whether he knew the strange woman who had given him the note. But the constable answered: 'Kohlhaas, the woman' — and in the midst of his speech halted oddly, and being carried away then by the procession at that moment resuming, Kohlhaas never heard what the man, seeming to tremble in all his limbs, uttered. — Arriving at the place of execution he found the Elector of Brandenburg and his entourage, among them the Lord Chancellor, Heinrich von Geusau, all there on horseback among an immeasurable crowd of people: on his right, holding a copy of the death sentence, the imperial advocate Franz Müller; on his left, with the verdict of the High Court in Dresden, Kohlhaas's own advocate, the jurist Anton Zäuner; a herald in the middle of this semi-circle, which the populace completed, held a whole bundle of items and by him the two black horses glossy with health stamping the earth with their hooves. For the Lord Chancellor had pressed the claim against the Junker von Tronka, lodged in Dresden in the Elector's name, through to the end, without concession, in every item; and the horses, first restored to a condition of honour by having a flag waved over their heads, had been removed from the knacker's care, fed back to health by the Junker's people and, in the presence of a commission set up for that purpose, handed over to the advocate in the market square in Dresden. The Elector therefore, as Kohlhaas, escorted by the guard, climbed the little mound towards him, said: 'Well now, Kohlhaas, today is the day on which you will have justice. See, here I give back to you everything taken from you by force at Tronkenburg, everything that I, as your sovereign, was duty bound to recover for you: horses, kerchief, coins of the realm, linen, even the cost of treatment for your stableman Herse who fell at Mühlberg. Are you content with me?' — Kohlhaas, when the verdict, at a nod from the Lord Chancellor, was handed to him, set down the two children he was carrying and read it through with wide and shining eyes; and finding in it also a paragraph in which Junker Wenzel was sentenced to two years' imprisonment, then, quite overwhelmed by his feelings, he crossed his arms on his breast and knelt, at a distance, before the Elector. Rising then and laying his hand on his heart, joyfully he assured the Lord Chancellor that now his dearest wish on earth was fulfilled; went up to the horses, appraised them, patted their plump necks; and returning to the Chancellor, declared to him cheerfully that he made a present of them to his two sons Heinrich and Leopold. The Chancellor, Heinrich von Geusau, inclining to him kindly from horseback, promised, in the Elector's name, that his last wishes would be respected, and urged him also to dispose of the articles in the bundle as he saw fit. Thereupon Kohlhaas called forth Herse's aged mother, whom he had noticed in the square, from among the crowd and handing her the things he said: 'Here, my old friend, these are for you', and added the amount that had come to him as compensation, which was there in the bundle with the other money, as a further gift, for her care and extra comfort in her declining years. — The Elector cried: 'Now Kohlaas the horsedealer, satisfaction having thus been given to you, prepare yourself now, for your part, to give satisfaction to his Imperial Majesty, whose advocate is standing here, for the breach of his peace.' Kohlhaas, taking off his hat and flinging it on the ground, said he was ready, and having lifted up his children once more and hugged them to his breast he handed them to the councillor from Kohlhaasenbrück and stepped, whilst they were led from the square with silent tears, to the block. He was removing the kerchief from around his neck and opening his shirt when, glancing around quickly in the circle made by the crowd, he noticed at only a little distance from himself, between two noblemen whose bodies almost hid him, the man he knew very well wearing plumes of blue and white. With a sudden step, surprising his guard, Kohlhaas came close up to him, and removed the capsule lying under his shirt; he took out the paper, unsealed it, read it: and staring fixedly at the man with the blue and white plumes, who was already beginning to entertain sweet hopes, he put it into his mouth and swallowed it. The man with the blue and white plumes, seeing this, fell down unconscious, twitching violently. Kohlhaas however, whilst that man's astonished companions bent down to him and lifted him from the ground, turned to the scaffold where his head fell under the executioner's axe. Here the story of Kohlhaas ends. Amid the general lament of the people his body was laid in a coffin; and whilst the bearers raised it, to carry it to a decent burial in a churchyard* in the suburbs, the Elector called the dead man's sons to him and, with a word to the Lord Chancellor that they were to be brought up among his pages, he knighted them. The Elector of Saxony, riven in body and soul, returned shortly afterwards to Dresden, and what followed can be read about in history. But in Mecklenburg, even in the last century, Kohlhaas still had robust and cheerful descendants living.

THE MARQUISE OF O.

(Based on a real event but the place has
been shifted from the north to the south.)*

In M., an important town in northern Italy, the widowed Marquise of
O., a lady of excellent reputation and the mother of two well-brought-
up children, announced in the newspaper: that she had, without
knowing it, become pregnant, and would the father of the child she was
to bear kindly declare himself since she was resolved, out of consideration for her family, to marry him. The lady who under the pressure of
unalterable circumstances was with such self-assurance taking this
extraordinary step and exciting society's ridicule in doing so, was the
daughter of Lord G., the Commandant of the fortress near M. About
three years previously, whilst he was travelling to Paris on family
business, she had lost her husband, the Marquis of O., having been most
tenderly and deeply devoted to him. After his death, at Lady G.'s, her
mother's, request, she had left the country seat near V., her home till
then, and had returned with her two children to her father's house, in
the fortress. Here, occupying herself with art and literature, with the
education of her children and the càre of her parents she had spent the
following years quite out of the world: until the ——— War* suddenly
filled the surrounding country with troops of nearly all the powers,
Russians among them. Colonel G., who had been ordered to defend the
place, urged his wife and daughter to withdraw either to the latter's
estate or to his son's, which lay near V. But before any assessment of
what risks they might be exposed to in the fortress or what brutalities in
the open country had weighed in the ladies' deliberations the citadel was
already beset by Russian forces and called on to surrender. The
Commandant informed his family that he would now act as though they
were not there, and answered with grenades and bullets. The enemy, for
their part, bombarded the citadel. They set fire to the magazine,
captured an outwork, and when the Commandant, again called on to

surrender, hesitated to do so, they ordered a night attack and took the fort by storm.

Just as the Russian troops, powerfully supported by howitzers, were forcing their way in, the west wing of the Commandant's house caught fire and the women were obliged to quit it. The Commandant's wife, hurrying after her daughter who was fleeing downstairs with the children, shouted that they should stay together and seek shelter in the vaults below; but a grenade at that moment exploding in the house completed an utter confusion there. The Marquise came with her two children into the front courtyard where, the battle being very fierce, firing lit up the night and drove her, desperate to know where to turn, back into the burning building. Here, unhappily, just as she was seeking to escape by the back door, she was met by a troop of enemy sharpshooters who, seeing her, suddenly fell silent, shouldered their weapons and gesturing abominably led her away. In vain did the Marquise, tugged hither and thither by the fearful pack fighting among themselves, call out for help to her women fleeing back in terror through the gate. She was dragged into the rear courtyard and there, vilely maltreated, was falling to the ground when, drawn by the lady's screams, a Russian officer appeared and with furious blows dispersed the beasts who were lusting for that prey. He seemed one of heaven's angels to the Marquise. Ramming his sword handle into the last man's face, so that the murderous savage took his hands off her slim waist and staggered back with blood spewing from his mouth, he addressed the lady courteously in French, offered her his arm and led her, stricken dumb by all these scenes, into the wing of the house not yet caught alight, and, losing consciousness entirely, she fell to the floor. Thereupon — when, soon after, her terrified women appeared, he arranged for a doctor to be called; assured them, putting on his hat, that she would soon recover; and returned to the battle.

In a brief while all the space before the house had been taken, and the Commandant, still fighting only because no one would as yet give him quarter, was retreating with failing strength towards the entrance when the Russian officer, very heated in the face, emerged from there and called on him to surrender. The Commandant replied: that was what he had been waiting to be asked to do, handed him his sword and asked permission to go into the house and look for his family. The Russian officer who, to judge by the part he was playing, seemed to be one of the leaders of the assault, let him do so, under guard; with some speediness then set himself at the head of a detachment of men, settled the struggle wherever it was still in doubt and very rapidly occupied all the strong points of the fort. This done, he was soon back where the troops were mustering, gave orders that the fire, which was beginning to advance with great fury, should be brought under control and in this business was himself wonderfully active when his orders were not obeyed with sufficient zeal. At one moment he was aloft among blazing gables with a hosepipe in his hands, directing the jet of water; at another, a terror to the Asiatics under his command, he was deep in the arsenals, rolling out powder kegs and mines already loaded. The Commandant, who in the meantime had gone indoors, when he heard what had befallen the Marquise his consternation was extreme. The Marquise who, without the doctor's help, was already, as the Russian officer had foretold, fully recovered from her faint and in her delight at seeing her family safe and sound was staying in bed only to calm their excessive anxiety, assured him that all she wanted was to be allowed to get up and express her gratitude to her rescuer. She knew already that he was Count F., a lieutenant-colonel in the —th Hussars and the bearer of various military honours and decorations. She begged her father to implore him not to leave the fortress without first appearing in the house for a moment. The Commandant, honouring his daughter's feelings, went back at once into the fort and finding no better occasion, since the Count was perpetually dashing to and fro on military business, it was on the earthworks, where he was reviewing his battered troops, that the grateful lady's wishes were made known to him. He assured the Commandant that just as soon as he could wrest one moment free from his duties he would come and pay her his respects. And he enquired how the lady Marquise was feeling; but by several officers and their reports was pitched back then into the mêlée of the war. At daybreak the Commander-in-Chief of the Russian forces appeared and looked over the fort. He was respectful to the Commandant, condoled with him that his courage had not been better supported by good fortune, and gave him, on parole, the freedom to come and go as he liked. The Commandant thanked him and said how much that day he was indebted to the Russian forces altogether and to the young Count F., lieutenant-colonel of the —th Hussars in particular. The General asked what had happened; and when he learned of the criminal assault upon the Commandant's daughter his indignation was extreme. He called the Count's name, and made him step forward. Having first, in a short speech, commended him for his own noble conduct, the Count blushing crimson as he did so, he finished by saying that as for the miscreants who had sullied the Czar's good name, he would have them shot; and ordered the Count to say who they were. Count F., in a confused speech, replied that he was not in a position to give their names since he had been unable to recognize their faces in the dim light from the lamps in the courtyard. The General, who had heard that at that time the house was in flames, expressed some surprise at this; but observed that if it was dark one might surely recognize familiar people by their voices; and he ordered the Count, who shrugged his shoulders and looked embarrassed, to enquire into the matter with all possible diligence and rigour. At that moment a man pushing forward from the rear of the assembly reported that one of the malefactors wounded by Count F., having collapsed in the corridor, had been dragged into a place of custody by the Commandant's people, and was still there. The General had him fetched out by the guard and summarily tried; and the whole gang, five of them, when the first had given their names, he then had shot. This done, the General ordered that a small party be left behind to occupy the fort and that the rest should depart; the officers returned in haste to their units; the Count, in all the confusion of this hurried dispersal, approached the Commandant and said that things being as they were he must regretfully send to the Lady Marquise his humble respects and bid her farewell; and in less than an hour the whole fort was empty of Russian troops.

The family were left wondering how they might ever, in the future, find an opportunity of giving the Count some indication of their gratitude; and it was a great shock to them when they learned that on the very day of his departure from the fort, in a skirmish with the enemy's troops, he had met his death. The courier who brought this news to M. had with his own eyes seen him, mortally wounded in the chest, being borne away to P.,* in which place, as was reliably reported, he had died just as the stretcher bearers were setting him down. The Commandant, who went to the posting house himself and asked for more details of what had happened, learned that on the battlefield, at the moment when he was hit, he had cried out: 'Julietta! This bullet avenges you!', and had closed his lips then for ever. The Marquise was inconsolable that she had let slip the opportunity of throwing herself at his feet. Bitterly she reproached herself that when, perhaps out of modesty, as she supposed, he had refused to come to the house she had not gone and sought him out; she grieved for the unhappy woman, her namesake, who had been his last thought as he died; made efforts, but in vain, to discover where she lived and tell her of this unhappy and touching event; and some months went by before she could forget him herself.

The family were obliged to give up the Commandant's house to the Commander-in-Chief of the Russian forces. They wondered at first whether they should not retire to the Commandant's estates, and that would have been the Marquise's decided preference; but since the Commandant disliked country life they moved into a house in town and made it suitable to be their permanent dwelling place. Now the old order of things was restored. The Marquise resumed the education of her children, after its long interruption; and for her leisure hours she took out her easel and books; but then, having always been the picture of good health, she began to be plagued by repeated indispositions which for weeks at a time made her unfit for society. She felt nauseous, dizzy, faint, and this strange condition was a puzzle to her. One morning when the family were drinking tea and her father had left the room for a moment the Marquise, waking out of a long vacancy, said to her mother: 'If a woman told me that she had had such a feeling as I had just now when I took up my cup my thought would be that she was with child.' Lady G. said she did not understand her. The Marquise explained herself, saying again that she had just felt as she did when she was pregnant with her second daughter. Lady G. said perhaps she would give birth to Phantasus, and laughed. 'Then Morpheus would be the father,' the Marquise replied, 'or one of his entourage of dreams'; and she laughed as her mother had done. But then the Commandant returned, the conversation was broken off and the whole subject, since within a few days the Marquise felt better again, was forgotten.

Soon afterwards, at a time when the Chief Forester G., the Commandant's son, also happened to be present in the house, the family were peculiarly shocked to hear a valet, entering the room, announce Count F. 'Count F.!' said father and daughter together, and everyone was dumbfounded. The valet assured them that he had heard and seen aright and that the Count stood waiting in the next room. At once the Commandant himself sprang to his feet, to open the door for the Count who did indeed then enter, handsome as a young god and a little pale in the face. After scenes of wonder and incomprehension and when the Count, answering the parents' remonstrance that he was supposed to be dead, had assured them that he was alive, he turned to the daughter, with much emotion in his face, and his first question was: how did she feel? Very well, the Marquise assured him, and was herself only interested in knowing how *he* had come back to life. But he, insisting on his subject, replied that she was not telling him the truth; there was a strange fatigue in her face; unless he was much mistaken she was unwell and suffering. The Marquise, gladdened by the warmth with which he said this, answered: well then, the fatigue might, if he liked, count as the trace of an indisposition she had suffered from some weeks previously;

but she had in the meantime ceased to fear that it would have any lasting bad effect. Whereupon he, with a sudden flaring up of joy, replied that he had no such fears either, and added: would she marry him? The Marquise was at a loss to know what to make of this behaviour. Blushing red, she looked at her mother, who, in embarrassment, looked at the father and son; whilst the Count approached the Marquise and taking her hand, as though to kiss it, asked had she understood him. The Commandant said would he not sit down; and politely, but with a serious look, placed a chair for him. The Commandant's wife said: 'Really, we shall think you a ghost until you divulge to us how you rose from the grave you were laid in at P.' The Count sat down, letting go of the lady's hand, and said that circumstances obliged him to be very brief; that mortally wounded in the chest he had been brought to P.; that there for months he had despaired of his life; that during that time the Lady Marquise had been his only thought; that the joy and pain embracing in that one conception were indescribable; that finally, having recovered, he had gone back to the army; that there he had suffered the most acute unease; that he had several times taken up his pen to give his heart some relief in letters to the Commandant and the Lady Marquise; that he had suddenly been sent to Naples with dispatches; that he could not be sure that from there he might not be ordered on further, to Constantinople; that he might even have to go as far as St Petersburg; that it had in the meantime become impossible for him to live without some clear answer to a necessary demand of his soul; that, passing through M., he had not been able to resist the urge to take certain steps towards this end; in brief, it was his wish that he might be blessed with the Marquise's hand in marriage, and that in the most respectful, pressing and urgent way possible he begged for the kindness of an answer. — The Commandant, after a long pause, answered: that this proposal, if, as he did not doubt, seriously meant, seemed to him indeed a very flattering one. But that after the death of her husband, the Marquis of O., his daughter had decided not to enter into any second marriage. However, having recently been put by him, the Count, under so great an obligation it was not impossible that this might cause her decision to be altered, in accordance with his wishes; but he asked meanwhile on her behalf to be allowed to think the matter over quietly for a time. The Count assured him that this kind declaration did indeed satisfy all his hopes; that it would, in other circumstances, have rendered him entirely happy; that he was sensible of the utter impropriety of not contenting himself with it; but that very pressing factors, upon which he was not in a position to elaborate, made him exceedingly desirous of obtaining a yet more definite response; that the carriage which was to bring him to Naples stood ready and waiting; and he begged them from the bottom of his heart that if anything in their house spoke in his favour — here he looked at the Marquise — they would not let him depart without a favourable reply. The Commandant, rather taken aback by this behaviour, replied that the gratitude the Marquise felt for him did indeed justify him in making large presumptions, but not so large; in a matter in which her whole life's happiness was at stake she would not act without a proper prudence. It was imperative that his daughter, before she declared herself, should have the pleasure of his closer acquaintance. He invited him to return to M. when his journey on business was concluded and then for a time to be a guest in his house. Then if the Lady Marquise could hope to be made happy by him, but not before, he would himself be delighted to hear that she had given him a definite answer. The Count, blushing, replied that all the way there he had warned his impatient wishes that this would be the outcome; that it flung him now into the greatest possible distress; that in the unfortunate role he was now obliged to play a closer acquaintance would indeed be advantageous; that as to his reputation, if that most equivocal of qualities must be taken into account, he believed he could vouch for it; that the one unworthy deed he had ever committed in his life was unknown to the world and he was himself moreover about to make up for it; that he was, in a word, an honourable man, and begged them to accept his assurances that what he was assuring them of was true. — The Commandant replied, and smiled a little, though without any irony, as he did so, that he subscribed to all these declarations. He had never before made the acquaintance of any young man who in so short a time had revealed so many excellent traits of character. He was inclined to believe that a brief period of reflection would resolve the present indecisiveness; but until he had had some consultation with his own as well as with the Count's family no other response was possible except the one already made. Thereupon the Count stated that he had no parents and that he was free. His uncle was General K.,* and he could vouch for his consent. He added that he was in possession of a substantial fortune and that he would not be averse to settling in Italy. — The Commandant bowed to him courteously, said again what his own wishes were and begged him now to let the matter rest until after his journey. The Count, after a short pause during which he displayed the marks of a very great unease, said, turning to the Marquise's mother, that he had done his utmost to avoid being sent on this journey; that the representations he had, not without risk, made to the Commander-in-

Chief and to General K., his uncle, could not have been more determined; but that it had been thought that the journey would shake him out of the melancholy still lingering in him after his illness; and now, by that selfsame journey, he found himself plunged into utter misery. — The family did not know what to say to this. Rubbing his forehead the Count went on to say that if there were any hope it might bring him closer to the attainment of his wishes he would postpone his journey by a day and even by rather more than a day, to make the attempt. — So saying, he looked in turn at the Commandant, the Marquise and her mother. The Commandant looked down at the floor in some annoyance, and made no reply. His wife said: 'My dear Count, be on your way now, go to Naples; when you return give us the pleasure of your company for a while; and the rest will surely follow.' — The Count sat still for a moment and seemed to be wondering what he should do. Rising then and removing his chair he said that since he must acknowledge the hopes he had entered the house with to be premature and since the family, as he thought right and proper, were insisting on a closer acquaintance, he would send his dispatches back to headquarters at Z.,* to be carried forward from there by somebody else, and accept the kind invitation to be their guest for a week or two. And thereupon, holding the chair in his hand and standing by the wall, he paused for a moment and looked at the Commandant. The Commandant replied that he would be exceedingly sorry if the passion he seemed to have conceived for his daughter were to bring him into what would surely be very serious trouble; but that he, the Count, doubtless knew best what it was up to him to do or not do, and should then, if he so wished, send back the dispatches and move into the rooms that would be his. At these words he was seen to lose colour; humbly he kissed the mother's hand, bowed to the others and withdrew.

Left in the room the family did not know what to make of what they had witnessed. The mother said it was scarcely possible that he intended sending back to Z. dispatches with which he was travelling to Naples merely because, passing through M., he had not managed, in a five-minute interview, to persuade a lady he was wholly unacquainted with to marry him. The Chief Forester remarked that for such irresponsible behaviour he would most certainly be arrested. And cashiered as well, the Commandant added. But there was no risk of that, he continued. It was only a shot in the air in the assault; doubtless he would come to his senses before he sent the dispatches back. The mother, when she knew of the danger, expressed the keenest concern that he would indeed send them back. That passionate will of his, set as it was on one objective, seemed to her capable of just such a thing. She begged the Forester most urgently to go after him at once and dissuade him from an action threatening his ruin. The Forester replied that to do so would achieve a contrary result and only strengthen him in the hope that his strategy would be successful. The Marquise was of the same opinion, but felt certain, she said, that not to do so would result without any doubt in the dispatches being sent back, since he would sooner be ruined than lose face. All were agreed that his behaviour was very strange and that it seemed to be his way to take a lady's heart by storm, like a fortress. At that moment the Commandant noticed the Count's carriage and the horses in harness before it outside his door. He called the family to the window and in astonishment asked a servant, entering at that moment, whether the Count was still in the house. The servant replied that he was down below, in the servants' quarters, with an adjutant, writing letters and sealing packages. The Commandant, suppressing his consternation, hurried down with the Forester and asked the Count, whom he saw busy at tables unsuitable for his purposes, would he not like to move to his rooms. And whether he had any other requirements. The Count, still writing rapidly, replied that he was grateful, but no, the job was almost done; asked, as he sealed the letter, what time it was, and wished the adjutant, handing him the whole portfolio, a safe journey. The Commandant, who could not believe his eyes, said, as the adjutant left the house, 'My dear Count, unless you have very important reasons —' 'Overriding ones,' said the Count, interrupting him; accompanied the adjutant to the carriage, and opened the door for him. 'In that case,' the Commandant continued, 'I should at least send the dispatches ...' 'Impossible,' the Count replied, helping the adjutant into his seat. 'The dispatches are no good in Naples without me. I thought of that too. Off you go!' — 'And the letters from his excellency, your uncle?' the adjutant cried, leaning out through the carriage window. 'Will reach me,' the Count replied, 'in M.' 'Drive on,' said the adjutant, and the carriage took him away.

Thereupon Count F., turning to the Commandant, asked would he be so kind as to have the servants show him to his rooms. 'At once,' said the Commandant, in confusion, he would do so himself, it would be an honour; called to his own and to the Count's people to take up the baggage and conducted him to the rooms set aside for visitors and there, stiffly, took his leave of him. The Count changed his clothes; went out then to announce his presence to the town's military governor, and for the rest of the day making no appearance in the house he returned there only a short while before supper.

The family meanwhile were in a very agitated state. The Forester
recounted how decidedly the Count had answered certain points of view
put to him by the Commandant; he was acting, as it seemed to the
Forester, in a quite premeditated way; what in heaven's name were the
reasons for this courtship at a gallop? The Commandant said he could
not make head or tail of the business, and begged the family to say
nothing more about it in his presence. The mother kept looking out of
the window to see if he had regretted his irresponsible behaviour and
were coming back to make amends. At last, when it got dark, she joined
the Marquise who was seated at a table very busy over some work and
apparently not wishing to talk. She asked her in a whisper, while the
father paced up and down, whether she had any idea where things were
leading. With a timid glance towards the Commandant the Marquise
replied that if her father had managed to get him to go on to Naples all
would have been well. 'To Naples!' the Commandant replied, having
overheard this. 'Should I have fetched a priest? Or had him arrested and
sent to Naples under guard?' — 'No,' the Marquise answered, 'but
sharp and forceful arguments do have an effect'; and with some
impatience she looked down at her work again. — At last, as night came
on, the Count appeared. They were only waiting, after the first
politenesses, for the subject to come up again, in order to join forces and
urge him, if it were still possible, to undo what in his foolhardiness he
had done. But in vain, throughout the meal, did they wait for such a
moment. Scrupulously avoiding anything that might lead to it he
discussed war with the Commandant and hunting with the Forester.
When he mentioned the fighting at P., in which he had been wounded,
the mother drew him into the story of his illness, asked him how he had
fared in such a small place, whether he had had all the proper comforts.
Thereupon he recounted several little things made interesting by his
passion for the Marquise: how throughout his sickness she had sat at his
bedside; how in the fever brought on by his wound he had constantly
confused his image of her with the image of a swan that he had seen, as
a boy, on his uncle's estates; that one memory had moved him
especially, of how once he had thrown dirt at this swan, which had then
gone silently under water and had risen again pure white; that she had
swum to and fro without end on a fiery flood and he had called out
Thinka, which was the name of the swan, but that he had never been
able to lure her towards him for all her delight had been in paddling and
in breasting the waves; declared suddenly, crimson in the face, that he
loved her exceedingly: looked down at his plate and was silent. In the
end they had to leave the table; and since the Count, after a brief

conversation with the mother, then at once bowed to the company and withdrew to his room, they stood there again, not knowing what to think. The Commandant was of the opinion that the thing should be allowed to run its course. Probably, in doing what he had done, he was relying on his relations. Otherwise a dishonourable discharge from the army would be the cost. Lady G. asked her daughter what she thought of him. And whether it was likely that she would be able to say the sort of thing by which disaster might be averted. The Marquise replied: 'My dear mother! That is not possible. I am sorry that my gratitude is being tested so severely. But it was my decision not to marry again; I do not wish to risk my happiness on any second venture, especially with so little forethought.' The Forester observed that if she was quite decided in this such a declaration itself might help the Count and that it really seemed they must tell him something definite. Lady G. answered that since this young man, who had so many extraordinary qualities to recommend him, had declared his willingness to settle in Italy, it was her view that his proposal deserved some consideration and the Marquise's decision some thinking about. The Forester, sitting down beside her, asked her how, in a personal sense, she liked the Count. The Marquise replied, in some embarrassment: 'I like him and don't like him'; and asked what the others felt. Lady G. said: 'If he came back from Naples and if the enquiries which we would in the meantime have been able to make about him did not contradict the general impression you have of him already, what would your answer be should he then repeat his proposal?' 'In that case,' the Marquise replied, 'I would — since his wishes do indeed seem very heartfelt — I would ...' — she paused and her eyes shone as she said this — 'because of the debt I owe him grant him their fulfilment.' The mother, who had always hoped that her daughter would remarry, had difficulty concealing her delight at these words, and pondered what use might be made of them. The Forester, in some agitation rising to his feet again, said that if the Marquise thought it at all possible that she might one day make the man happy by her acceptance it was necessary at once to take a step in that direction and so prevent the ill effects of his lunatic behaviour. The mother was of the same opinion and declared that it was not such a risky thing after all in that, given the numerous excellent qualities he had displayed in the night when the Russians stormed the fort, it was scarcely to be feared that his conduct elsewhere in his life would be any different. With every appearance of being greatly agitated the Marquise looked down at the floor. 'One might at least,' the mother continued, seizing hold of her hand, 'let him have an assurance that you will not, before his return from Naples, enter into any other union.' The Marquise said: 'My dear mother, such an assurance I can give him; my only fear is that it would not content him, and might engage us too far.' 'Let me take care of that,' her mother replied, overjoyed and turning to look at the Commandant. 'Lorenzo,' she asked, 'what do you think?', and made to rise from her seat. The Commandant, who had heard everything, looked out on to the street and said not a word. The Forester assured him that armed with this harmless declaration he would undertake to get the Count out of the house. 'Do it then, do it, do it!' the father cried, turning. 'Seems I must surrender to this Russian a second time.' — Thereupon the mother sprang to her feet, kissed him and her daughter and asked, while the father smiled at her busyness, how this declaration might at once be conveyed to the Count. It was decided, at the Forester's suggestion, to send word asking, if he had not already retired to bed, would he be so kind as to join them again for a moment. The Count's reply was that he would have the honour of appearing before them forthwith, and scarcely had the servant returned to say this than he himself, propelled by joy, entered the room and went down on his knees before the Marquise, with a passionate tenderness. The Commandant was about to speak: but he, getting to his feet, replied that he understood, kissed his and the mother's hand, embraced the brother, and asked only that they be so kind as to help him obtain some means of transport. The Marquise, although moved by this scene, none the less said: 'I trust, my dear Count, that in your eagerness you will not hope for more than ...' 'Not at all! Not at all!' the Count replied. 'We are as we were if the results of any enquiries you choose to make about me contradict the feeling which called me back into this room.' Thereupon the Commandant embraced him most warmly, the Forester at once offered him his own carriage, a servant hastened to the posting station to secure some horses, and there was more joy at this departure than ever at an arrival. He hoped, said the Count, to catch up with his dispatches at B., and from there he would take a shorter route to Naples than via M.; in Naples he would do everything possible to avoid being sent on with further business to Constantinople; and since he was determined, if things came to the worst, to declare himself sick he could assure them that unless insuperable obstacles intervened he would be back in M. without fail within four to six weeks. At that moment his servant announced that his carriage was waiting and that everything was ready for departure. The Count took his hat, approached the Marquise and seized her hand. 'Well, Julietta,' he said, enclosing her hand in his, 'I am in some measure contented, though it had been my dearest wish to marry you before I left.' 'Marry!' all the members of the family exclaimed. 'Marry,' said the Count again, kissed the Marquise's hand and assured her, when she asked him was he out of his mind, that there would come a day when she would understand him. The family were about to be displeased with him, but he at once, in the warmest fashion, said his goodbyes to them all, and begging them to give no further thought to what he had said, he left.

Several weeks passed, during which time the family, with their very different feelings, waited in some suspense for the outcome of this strange affair. From General K., the Count's uncle, the Commandant received a polite communication; the Count wrote himself from Naples; what they learned through their enquiries spoke pretty well in his favour; in brief, the engagement seemed as good as settled when the Marquise's indisposition came on again, more acutely than before. She noticed an incomprehensible alteration in her person. She was entirely candid with her mother and said that she did not know what to make of her condition. The mother, made very fearful for her daughter's health by these strange occurrences, insisted that she seek the advice of a doctor. The Marquise, hoping her own nature would give her victory, demurred; she spent several days, ignoring her mother's advice, in the most acute discomfort: until certain feelings, constantly recurring and of the oddest kind, plunged her into an extreme unease. She sent for a doctor whom her father trusted and, her mother happening not to be present, made him sit down on the sofa and after a brief preamble, in a jocular tone, revealed to him what state she believed herself to be in. The doctor gave her a quizzical look and after examining her thoroughly still said nothing for a while: then with a very grave face answered that her Ladyship's opinion was quite correct. When he then, upon her asking him what he meant by this, expressed himself in unequivocal terms and said, with a smile he was unable to suppress, that she was in good health and had no need of a doctor, the Marquise rang the bell, looked at him askance and very severely, and asked him to leave. She added in an undertone, as though to herself and as though he were a negligible person, that she had no taste for any levity with him on subjects of that sort. The doctor replied rather touchily that it was to be wished she had always been so little inclined to levity as now; took up his hat and his stick and was about to leave. The Marquise promised him that her father would hear of these insults. The doctor replied that he would stand by his statements in a court of law: opened the door, bowed, and made to leave the room. The Marquise, as he stooped for a glove he had dropped on the floor, asked: 'And how could that possibly be, doctor?'

The doctor replied that she surely did not need him to explain the first cause of things; bowed once again, and left.

The Marquise was thunderstruck. She pulled herself together and was about to run to her father; but the strange gravity of the man by whom she thought herself insulted paralysed her limbs. In great agitation she threw herself down on the couch. Now becoming mistrustful of herself she went over every moment of the past year and reaching the last thought she must be out of her mind. Finally her mother appeared, and being asked, in some anxiety, why she was so distraught, the daughter related what the doctor had just told her. Lady G. called him shameless and a good-for-nothing and supported her daughter's determination to report this insult to her father. The Marquise assured her that he had been entirely serious and that he seemed resolved to repeat his insane assertion to her father's face. Lady G., more than a little shocked by this, asked did she then believe in the possibility of such a condition. 'Sooner believe,' said the Marquise, 'that the grave itself were fruitful and the wombs of the dead gave birth.' 'Well then, my poor dear child,' said Lady G., hugging her close: 'Why be uneasy? If your conscience absolves you why should you be troubled by one opinion and even if it were that of a whole board of doctors? Whether his was due to error or malice: is it not all the same to you? But it would be proper to tell your father.' — 'Dear heaven!' said the Marquise with a convulsive movement: 'How can I feel easy? Do I not have my own inner feeling against me, a feeling I know only too well? Would I not, if I knew of such feelings in another woman, myself be of the opinion that what was said of her was right?' 'This is frightful,' Lady G. replied. 'Malice! Error!' the Marquise continued. 'Why should this man, whom until today we have always thought worthy of our esteem, now insult me in so idle and despicable a fashion? Me, who never offended him? Who received him trustingly and in the anticipation of owing him my gratitude? To whom he came, as his first words proved, in the pure and honest intention of giving help and not of actually causing me pain worse than the pains I had already? And if, because it must be one or the other,' she continued, whilst her mother looked at her in some surprise, 'I am inclined to believe in its being an error: is it really possible that a doctor, and were he even only moderately skilled, could be wrong in such a case?' — Lady G. said, rather tartly: 'Error or malice, it must necessarily have been one or the other.' 'My dear mother,' the Marquise replied, crimson in the face and with a look of injured dignity kissing her hand: 'it must. Though the circumstances are so extraordinary that I may be permitted to have my doubts. I swear to you, since such an assurance is required, that my conscience is as clear as my children's. Even you, my dearest mother whom I respect exceedingly, your own could not be clearer. Nevertheless I beg you to send for a midwife so that I can convince myself of the truth of what is and be at ease then whatever it is.' 'A midwife!' cried Lady G., affronted. 'A clear conscience and a midwife!' And words failed her. 'My dear mother, a midwife,' the Marquise replied, and went down on her knees before her, 'and at once, or I shall go mad.' 'Gladly,' Lady G. replied, 'but please find somewhere else for your confinement.' And with that she stood up and made to leave the room. The Marquise, following with outstretched arms, prostrated herself utterly and embraced her knees. 'If a blameless life,' she cried with all the eloquence of suffering, 'if a life lived after your example gives me any right to your respect, if in your bosom still, at least until my guilt is proven beyond doubt, some motherly feeling speaks on my behalf: do not abandon me at this terrible hour.' — 'What is it that troubles you?' her mother asked. 'Is it only the doctor's words? Only your own inner feeling?' 'Only that, Mother,' the Marquise replied, and laid her hand on her breast. 'Nothing else, Julietta?' her mother continued. 'Think. A transgression, unspeakably painful though it would be to me, would in the end be forgivable and I should have to forgive it; but if to escape a mother's reprimand you invent some tale by which the order of things is overturned and blasphemously protest your innocence to force your story on my all too credulous heart: that would be disgraceful and you and I would never be reconciled.' — 'May heaven one day be as open to me as my soul is to you,' the Marquise cried. 'My dear mother, there is nothing I have not told you.' — These words, pathetic in their utterance, shook the mother. 'Dear heavens!' she cried, 'my darling child, how you move me!' And raised her up and kissed her and pressed her close against her heart. 'What in the world are you afraid of? Come, you are very ill.' And she sought to lead her away to bed. But the Marquise, whose tears would not be kept back, assured her that she was very well and that there was nothing the matter with her except that strange and incomprehensible condition. — 'Condition!' the mother cried again. 'What condition? If your memory of the past is so certain what fearful madness has seized hold of you? Might not an inner feeling, only dimly stirring after all, might it not be deceiving you?' 'No, no,' said the Marquise, 'I am not deceived. And if you send for the midwife you will learn that this frightful thing, this thing that annihilates me, is true.' — 'My dearest child, come now,' said Lady G., beginning to fear for her sanity. 'Come now, come with me, come to bed. What was it you thought the doctor said to you? How flushed you are. And shaking like a leaf. What was it then that the doctor said to you?' And with that she was leading the Marquise away, no longer believing her account of what had happened. — The Marquise said: 'You are good and kind. I am not out of my mind.' And she smiled through her tears. 'The doctor told me I am carrying a child. Send for the midwife and as soon as I hear from her that it is not true I shall be calm again.' 'Very well,' Lady G. replied, suppressing her fears. 'She shall come at once; if you want her to laugh at you let her come at once and tell you you are a dreamer and not quite right in the head.' And so saying she rang the bell and dispatched one of the servants to fetch the midwife.

The Marquise, still agitated, her bosom still heaving, was lying in her mother's arms when the woman appeared and Lady G. told her the bizarre idea her daughter lay sick with. The lady Marquise, she said, swore that her conduct had been blameless and yet, misled by an incomprehensible feeling, she had thought it necessary to have her condition examined by a woman expert in such matters. The midwife, being told more about this condition, spoke of the passions of youth and the wicked ways of the world; said, having completed her business, that she had met such cases before; young widows finding themselves in her situation would always have you believe they had been living on desert islands; told the Marquise there was nothing to worry about and said she felt sure that whoever the happy mariner was who had come ashore one night, he would appear again. At these words the Marquise fainted. Lady G., giving in to her motherly feelings, did, with the help of the midwife, revive her. But indignation was victorious as soon as she opened her eyes. 'Julietta,' her mother cried in acute distress, 'will you be honest with me, will you tell me who the father is?' And still seemed inclined to be forgiving. But when the Marquise said she felt she would go mad her mother, rising from the sofa, said: 'Out of my sight! You are unworthy of us. I curse the hour I bore you.' And left the room.

The Marquise, again near to losing consciousness, drew the midwife down to her and, trembling violently, laid her head on her breast. She asked in an unsteady voice what the ways of nature were really like. And whether an unwitting conception were a possibility. — The midwife smiled, loosened the Marquise's bodice, and said that would scarcely be her Ladyship's own case. No, no, the Marquise replied, hers was not unwitting, she was only curious to know in a general way whether in the natural world such a thing ever happened. The midwife answered that it had to the Virgin Mary but not to any other woman on earth. The Marquise was trembling ever more violently. She believed she might give birth at any moment and clinging to the midwife in spasms of terror she

begged her not to go. The midwife soothed her. She assured her that her
confinement was still far off, suggested the means by which, in such a
case, the world's bad opinion might be avoided, and was of the view
that everything would turn out well in the end. But since these
consolations went through the poor lady's heart like so many knives she
pulled herself together, said she felt better and asked her companion to
withdraw.

Scarcely had the midwife left the room than the Marquise was
brought a communication from her mother in which the lady expressed
herself thus: Lord G. wished her, in the circumstances, to leave his
house. He enclosed the papers having to do with her finances and hoped
God would spare him the torment of ever seeing her again. — Here and
there the letter was wetted with tears; and a smudged word in one
corner read: 'Dictated.' — The Marquise's grief welled from her eyes.
Bitterly weeping over her parents' error and over the injustice into which
such excellent people had been misled, she went to her mother's rooms.
Her mother was with her father, she was told; she staggered to her
father's rooms. There, finding the door locked, she fell down, calling on
all the saints as witnesses of her innocence. Lay for some minutes; then
the Forester came out, with burning cheeks, and asked: had she not been
told that the Commandant did not wish to see her? The Marquise cried:
'Oh, my dear brother!' sobbing uncontrollably; forced her way into the
room and cried: 'Oh, my dear father!' and stretched out her arms
towards him. The Commandant, at the sight of her, turned his back and
hurried into his bedchamber. He cried out, as she followed him: 'Keep
away!' and tried to fling the door shut; but when she, beseeching him, in
her anguish prevented it from closing, he suddenly gave way and fled, as
the Marquise entered, towards the far wall. She had just flung herself
down at his feet and though he had turned his back on her she was
clinging to his knees when a pistol he had seized went off at the very
moment of his tearing it from the wall and shattered into the ceiling.
'Dear God,' the Marquise cried; rose, deathly pale, from her knees and
fled from his rooms. 'The carriage at once,' she said, entering her own;
sat down, almost lifeless, on a chair, quickly dressed her children and
had her things packed. She had the youngest between her knees and was
wrapping a scarf around her and everything being ready for departure
was about to get into the carriage when the Forester arrived and
demanded that, on the Commandant's orders, she leave the children
behind and hand them over. 'These children?' she asked; and stood up.
'Tell your inhuman father that he may come and shoot me down but
may not tear my children from me.' And armed with all the pride of her

innocence she lifted up the children, carried them, her brother not daring to halt her, to the carriage and drove away.

Thus through this beautiful exertion coming to self-knowledge she lifted herself suddenly, as though by her own hand, clear out of the depths into which fate had flung her. The commotion tearing her apart subsided once she was outside the house; again and again she kissed the beloved children she had carried off, and thought with great self-satisfaction of the victory which, by force of her guiltless conscience, she had won over her brother. Her reason, strong enough to withstand the strangeness of her situation, gave itself up entirely to the large and holy and inexplicable ordering of the world. She saw the impossibility of convincing her family of her innocence, understood that she must cease grieving over it or perish, and only a few days after her arrival in V. her grief had been replaced completely by the heroic resolve to arm herself with pride against the world's assaults. She resolved to withdraw entirely into her innermost self, dedicate herself with an exclusive zeal to the education of her two children and to caring for the third, as a gift that God had bestowed on her, with all of a mother's love. She took steps so as to begin in a few weeks' time, as soon as she was over her confinement, the restoration of her beautiful but, after long absence, somewhat run-down estate; sat in an arbour and pondered, as she knitted little bonnets and leggings for the child, what best use she should make of the rooms and which she should fill with books and in which her easel and painting things could best be accommodated. And in this way before Count F. was due to return from Naples she had already fully reconciled herself to the idea of living for evermore as secludedly as a nun. The porter had orders to admit nobody. But one thought was unbearable to her: that the young creature whom she had conceived in utter innocence and purity and whose origins precisely because they were more mysterious also seemed more heavenly than those of other mortals, would be marked in civil society by a mark of shame. A strange means had occurred to her by which the father might be discovered, a means which, when she first thought of it, she let her knitting fall from her hands in fright. Whole nights long, in a restless sleeplessness, she turned it this way and that to grow used to its nature which was offensive to her innermost feelings. She still recoiled from entering into any dealings with the person who had abused her so, rightly assuming that whoever it was must belong, beyond any redemption, among the ordures of his kind and wherever one might suppose his abode on earth to be his origins must lie in the mire where it was foulest and most trampled. But the sense of independence becoming ever stronger in her and when she considered that the stone keeps its value whatever the setting, she one morning, as the new life stirred in her again, screwed up her courage and placed in the newspapers of M. the strange request we read at the start of this story.

Count F., detained in Naples by business he could not avoid, had in the meanwhile written a second time to the Marquise urging her, whatever strange circumstances might arise, to remain true to the unspoken promise she had made him. Having managed to refuse the further errand to Constantinople and as soon as his other affairs allowed it he at once quitted Naples and only a few days after the time he had himself appointed he duly arrived in M. The Commandant received him with an embarrassed look, said that essential business obliged him to leave the house, and asked the Forester to speak to him meanwhile. The Forester led him to his room and asked, after briefly welcoming him, whether he already knew what had happened in the Commandant's house during his absence. The Count, turning pale for an instant, answered: 'No.' Thereupon the Forester told him of the disgrace which the Marquise had brought upon the family and related the things that our readers have just learned. The Count smote his brow. 'Why were so many obstacles put in my way?' he cried, forgetting himself. 'If the marriage had taken place all the shame and unhappiness would have been spared us.' The Forester, staring at him, asked was he insane enough to wish to be married to so worthless a woman. The Count replied that she was worth more than all the world despising her; that he found her assertion of innocence entirely believable and that he would go at once to V. and make his proposal of marriage to her again. And he did indeed then seize his hat forthwith, took his leave of the Forester, who thought him out of his mind, and left the room.

He mounted his horse and galloped out to V. Dismounting at the gateway, when he wished to go through into the first courtyard he was told by the porter that the Marquise would not see anyone. The Count asked whether this rule devised against strangers would also apply to a friend of the house; to which the porter answered that he knew of no exceptions and a moment later, in an equivocal manner, added: was he perhaps Count F.? The Count, searching him with a look, answered: 'No', and said, turning to his servant but so that the porter could hear him, that in the circumstances he would put up at an inn and announce his presence to the Marquise in a letter. But as soon as he was out of sight of the porter he turned a corner and crept around the wall of a large garden that extended behind the house. Through a gate, that he found open, he entered the garden, wandered its paths and was about to

climb the slope towards the back of the house when to one side, in a
bower, busily working at a small table, he saw the Marquise in a sweet
secrecy. He approached her in such a way that she could not catch sight
of him until he stood at the entrance of the bower, scarcely three paces
from her feet. 'Count F.,' said the Marquise as she raised her eyes, and a
blush of surprise spread over her face. The Count smiled, stood a while
longer at the opening, not moving; seated himself by her then, with such
modesty in his presumptuousness as was necessary if she were not to be
alarmed, and before she, in the strangeness of her situation, had made
any decision gently he put his arm around her. 'Where have you come
from? How is it possible?' the Marquise asked — and looked shyly
down at the ground. The Count said: 'From M.', and pressed her very
gently against him; 'through a back gate that I found open. I believed I
might count on your forgiveness, and I entered.' 'Did they not tell you in
M. —?' she asked, and moved not a muscle in his embrace. 'Everything,
my dear lady,' the Count replied; 'but wholly convinced of your
innocence ...' 'What!' the Marquise cried, standing up and disengaging
herself; 'and you have come despite that?' — 'In despite of the world,' he
continued, holding her fast, 'and in despite of your family, and even in
spite of this sweet appearance here.' And so saying he bowed his head
against her breast in a passionate kiss. — 'Keep away!' the Marquise
cried. — 'As convinced,' he said, 'Julietta, as if I were all-knowing, as if
my soul were dwelling in your breast ...' The Marquise cried: 'Let me
go.' 'I have come,' he concluded — and did not let her go — 'to repeat
my proposal of marriage to you and to receive, if you will grant me what
I ask, a life of bliss henceforth from your hand.' 'This minute let me go!'
the Marquise cried, 'I order you to', and she tore herself forcibly out of
his arms and fled. 'Beloved, my revered lady,' he whispered, getting to
his feet and following her. — 'You hear me,' the Marquise cried and
turned and eluded him. 'One moment's whispered, private ...' said the
Count and made to seize hold of her smooth-skinned arm, but she
escaped. — 'I wish *to know nothing*,' the Marquise replied, repulsed
him with a violent push against his chest, hurried to the path that rose
towards the house, and disappeared.

He was climbing after her to get himself a hearing cost what it might
when the door slammed shut ahead of him and the bolt, in haste and
distress, was slid across. For a moment undecided what was to be done
in the circumstances he stood and debated whether to climb through an
open window at the side and pursue his purpose until he achieved it; but
hard though it was in every sense for him to turn back, necessity this
time seemed to demand it, and bitterly angry with himself for letting her

out of his arms he crept down the slope and left the garden, to look for his horses. He felt that he had forfeited the one opportunity he would have of explaining himself in her embrace, and he rode at walking pace back to M., meditating the letter he was now obliged to write. That evening, in the worst of all possible moods dining at an inn, he met the Forester who at once enquired whether in V. he had been successful in his suit. The Count answered curtly: 'No', and was very inclined to dismiss the man with an angry turn of phrase; but for the sake of politeness he added after a while: that he had decided to address himself to her in writing and would soon, by that means, conclude things satisfactorily. The Forester said: he was sorry to see that his passion for the Marquise had robbed him of his wits. He must however inform him that she was already in the process of making another choice; rang for the latest newspapers and handed him the one containing the Marquise's request to the father of her child. The Count, with the blood rushing to his face, scanned the text. A variety of feelings went to and fro in him. The Forester asked did he not think that the person the Marquise was looking for would be found? — 'Without a doubt,' the Count replied, in a trance over the newspaper, greedily devouring what it said. Thereupon, after he had for a moment, folding the newspaper, stepped across to the window, he said: 'Now all is well. Now I know what to do'; turned then and asked the Forester, in very courteous tones, whether he would be seeing him again before very long; said goodbye and, wholly reconciled to his fate, left the room. —

Meanwhile in the Commandant's house there had been some very animated scenes. By her husband's destructive violence and by her own weakness in allowing him to command her in the tyrannical banishing of their daughter Lady G. was incensed. When the shot was fired in the Commandant's bedroom and their daughter rushed forth she had fallen in a faint from which, it is true, she quickly recovered; but the Commandant, as she came round, had said nothing more than that he was sorry she had been alarmed for nothing, and had thrown the empty pistol on to a table. Later, when he said he would demand the children, she plucked up the courage to declare, in timid tones, that they had no right to take such a step; she begged him, in a voice made weak and touching by what she had suffered, to avoid any violent scenes in the house; but all the Commandant said in reply was, turning to the Forester and foaming at the mouth with rage: 'Go and get me them!' When the Count's second letter arrived the Commandant had ordered that it be sent on to the Marquise in V. and she, as they learned from the messenger afterwards, had laid it aside and said: 'Very good.' Lady G., puzzled by so many things in the whole affair and especially by the Marquise's readiness to enter, quite without passion, into a second marriage, sought in vain to have this circumstance discussed. The Commandant repeatedly begged her, in the manner of a man giving an order, to be silent; asserted, on one such occasion taking down a portrait of her that still hung on the wall, that he wished to eradicate her entirely from his memory; and declared that he no longer had a daughter. Soon afterwards the Marquise's strange proclamation appeared in the newspapers. Lady G., astounded by it, took the paper, which she had received from the Commandant, through into his room, where she found him working at a desk, and asked him what in the world he made of it. The Commandant went on with his writing and said: 'Oh she is innocent.' 'What!' Lady G. exclaimed in the most extreme astonishment. 'Innocent?' 'She did it in her sleep,' said the Commandant without looking up. 'In her sleep!' Lady G. replied. 'And such a monstrous event might be ...?' 'The fool!' the Commandant cried, threw all his papers into disorder, and left the room.

When next there were newspapers Lady G., as both were sitting at breakfast, read out the following reply in print still wet from the press:

If the Lady Marquise of O. will present herself on the 3rd at
11 in the morning in the house of Lord G., her father, the
man she is seeking will be there, to prostrate himself at her feet.

Lady G.'s voice failed her before she was halfway through this outrageous announcement; she hurried over the rest and handed the paper to the Commandant. He read it three times, as if he could not believe his eyes. 'Now tell me, in heaven's name, Lorenzo,' Lady G. exclaimed, 'what do you make of it?' 'Oh how vile she is!' the Commandant replied, and stood up. 'Such cunning, such hypocrisy! Ten times the shamelessness of a bitch and couple it with ten times the slyness of a fox and still you fall short of hers! And what a look she has! What a pair of eyes! The eyes of a cherub could not look more truthful.' — And he fell to lamenting and was unable to calm himself. 'But what in the world,' Lady G. asked, 'if this is a subterfuge does she hope to achieve by it?' — 'Achieve by it? To get her vile deception through by force, that's what,' the Commandant replied. 'They have learned their fairy story off by heart, the pair of them, and we are to swallow it here on the third at eleven in the morning. "My darling little girl," I am supposed to say, "these are things I did not know, who would have thought, forgive me, have my blessing and be friends with me again." But there's a bullet for the man who crosses my threshold on the morning of the third. Except that it would be more decent to have him thrown out by the servants.' — Lady G. said, after another reading of the newspaper, that if of two incomprehensible things she was obliged to give credence to one she would sooner believe in some unprecedented quirk of fate than in such baseness in their daughter who had always been exemplary. But even before she had finished the Commandant shouted: 'Do me the kindness of being silent!' and left the room. 'Even to hear of it is detestable to me.'

A few days later the Commandant received from the Marquise in connection with the announcement in the newspaper a letter in which, respectfully and touchingly, she asked him whether, since she was denied the favour of appearing in his house, he would be so kind as to send whoever presented himself on the morning of the third out to her at V. Lady G. happened to be present when the Commandant received this letter; and seeing from the expression on his face that he was confused now in his feelings: for now what motive, if this really were a deception, could he ascribe to her since she seemed not to be making any bid for his forgiveness? — emboldened by this, Lady G. came forward with a plan that she had for a long time harboured in her doubt-ridden heart. She said, as the Commandant continued blankly gazing at the paper, that she had an idea. Would he permit her to go out to V. for a couple of days? She believed she could place the Marquise, should she really already be acquainted with the man who had answered her through the newspapers as one unknown to her, in such a situation that she must inevitably betray her innermost heart no matter how superlatively well practised in deception she might be. The Commandant replied, and with a sudden violent movement he tore up the letter: that she knew that he wanted nothing to do with her and that he forbade her to enter into any dealings whatsoever. He put the torn-up pieces of the letter in an envelope, wrote the Marquise's address on it and gave it to the messenger as his reply. Lady G., bitterly angered in her heart by this obstinacy and wilfulness that destroyed any possibility of an explanation, decided to carry out her plan now against his will. She took one of the Commandant's coachmen and drove out with him next morning, while her husband was still in bed, to V. When she arrived at the gate of the country house the porter told her that nobody was admitted to the Marquise. She replied that she knew of this rule but that he should go nevertheless and announce that Lady G. was there. To this he replied that it would be of no use doing so since there was nobody in the world the lady Marquise was willing to see. Lady G. replied that she would be seen by her since she was her mother and that he should not delay any longer but go and do his duty. But scarcely had the porter gone into the house on this, as he maintained, none the less vain endeavour, than the Marquise was seen to emerge from there, hurry to the gate and throw herself down on her knees beside Lady G.'s carriage. Lady G., assisted by the coachman, got out and in some agitation raised up the Marquise from the ground. The Marquise bowed, overwhelmed by emotion, deep over her hand and frequently giving in to tears led her, with every mark of respect, into the rooms of the house. 'Dearest mother!' she cried, having seated her on the sofa and herself remained standing, drying her eyes. 'To what happy chance do I owe this visit whose value to me is higher than I can say?' Lady G., affectionately taking hold of her daughter, replied that what she had to say was this: that she had come to ask forgiveness for her harsh expulsion from her father's house. 'Forgiveness!' cried the Marquise, interrupting her, and made to kiss her hands. But her mother, not allowing it, continued: 'For not only has the response published in the latest newspapers to your advertisement convinced both your father and myself of your innocence, but I must also tell you that yesterday, to our great and joyful astonishment, he appeared in person in our house.' 'Who did?' the Marquise asked and sat down by her mother; 'what person appeared?', her expression through and through one of suspense. 'He did,' Lady G. answered, 'the author of that reply, himself, in person, the one your appeal was addressed to.' — 'Well then,' said the Marquise, breathless in her agitation, 'who is it?' And again: 'Who is it?' — 'That,' Lady G. replied, 'I think I will let you guess. Imagine, yesterday, at tea-time, just as we were reading that extraordinary newspaper a person we know very well indeed burst into the room, in despair by the look of him, and flung himself first at your father's and a minute later at my feet. We, not knowing what to make of it, urged him to speak. Thereupon he said: that his conscience would not let him rest; he was the vile scoundrel who had abused the Marquise, he had to know what the judgment on his crime would be and if vengeance were to be visited upon him then he had come in person to give himself up to it.' 'But who? who? who?' the Marquise interposed. 'As I said,' Lady G. continued, 'a young and otherwise honourable person, whom we should never have thought capable of such a wicked act. But you will be relieved, child, when I tell you that he is from the lower classes and wholly without any qualification to be your husband.' 'All the same, my dear mother, he cannot be wholly unworthy since it was at your feet he threw himself first, not mine. But who? who? Do tell me: who?' 'Well,' said the mother, 'it is Leopardo, the coachman whom your father sent away far from the Tyrol not long ago and whom I, if you even noticed him, have brought with me to introduce him to you as your bridegroom.' 'Leopardo the coachman!' the Marquise cried and with a look of desperation pressed her hand against her forehead. 'Why are you so shocked?' Lady G. asked. 'Do you have grounds for doubting it?' — 'How? Where? When?' the Marquise asked, in confusion. 'Those,' her mother replied, 'are things he will only divulge to you. Shame and love, he claimed, made it impossible for him to explain matters to anyone but you. But if you wish we can open the door, he is in the next room waiting with bated breath for the outcome; and you can see whether, if I step outside, you can induce him into telling you his secret.' 'Dear God in heaven!' the Marquise cried. 'I fell asleep once in the middle of the day when it was hot and saw him going away from my couch when I woke.' — And with that she hid her face, crimson with shame, in her little hands. Hearing what she said her mother went down on her knees before her. 'Oh my child,' she cried, 'my paragon of virtue', and put her arms around her, 'and oh I am contemptible!' and hid her face in her daughter's lap. The Marquise asked in consternation: 'What is it, Mother?' 'Listen,' Lady G. continued, 'you are purer than angels are and of all I said to you nothing is true. My corrupted soul could not believe in innocence such as you wear around you like a holy light and only through this despicable subterfuge could I be convinced of it.' 'Dear Mother,' the Marquise cried and with a joyous tenderness bowed over her and sought to raise her up. But she replied: 'I will stay here at your feet until you tell me whether you, in your more than earthly virtue, can forgive me the baseness of my behaviour.' 'Forgive you? My dearest mother, stand up,' the Marquise cried, 'I beseech you.' — 'You heard,' said Lady G., 'I want to know whether you can still love me and honour me truly as you used to.' 'But I worship you!' the Marquise cried and herself went down on her knees before her. 'Reverence and love for you never left my heart. Who could, the circumstances being so extraordinary, have faith in me? How happy I am that you are persuaded of my guiltlessness.' 'Well then,' Lady G. replied and supported by her daughter she got to her feet, 'my beloved child, I will have you in my tender care. You shall have your baby in my house and I will cherish you and honour you as though it were a little prince you were giving me. All the days of my life now I shall never leave your side. I defy all the world. Henceforth I want no other honour than your disgrace so long as you forgive me and will forget the harshness with which I cast you out.' The Marquise sought with endless caresses and beseechings to comfort her; but evening came and midnight struck before she had succeeded. Next morning, when the old lady's emotions, which in the night had brought on a fever, had subsided a little, mother, daughter and grandchildren drove as if in triumph back to M. They were in excellent spirits along the way, joked about Leopardo the coachman sitting forward on the box, and the mother said to the Marquise that she noticed her blushing whenever she looked at his broad back. The Marquise answered, with a start that was half a sigh and half a smile: 'Who knows who it will be after all who appears in our house on the third at eleven in the morning.' — Then the closer they got to M. the more serious their mood became in the apprehension of the decisive scenes still awaiting them. Lady G., revealing nothing of her plans, conducted her daughter, when they got out of the carriage outside the house, back into her old rooms; said to make herself comfortable, she would be with her again in no time, and crept away. She came back an hour later, very flushed in the face. 'What a Thomas!' she said with some secret inner satisfaction, 'what a doubting Thomas! Has it not just taken me one full hour of the clock to convince him? But now he is sitting there weeping.' 'Who?' the Marquise asked. 'Him,' the mother replied. 'Who else but the one who has most cause to?' 'Not my father?' the Marquise cried. 'Like a child,' the mother answered, 'so that I should have laughed at him as soon as I got outside the door, had I not had tears of my own to dry.' 'And because of me?' the Marquise asked, and stood up; 'and here I am ...' 'Do not move,' said Lady G. 'Why did he dictate that letter to me? He can come and look for you here if he ever wants to be with me again so long as I live.' 'My dearest mother,' the Marquise cried, begging her. — 'Implacable!' said Lady G., interrupting. 'Why did he reach for his pistol?' — 'But I beseech you.' — 'You *shall* not,' Lady G. replied, pressing her daughter back into her seat. 'And if he is not here before evening, tomorrow I will leave this place with you.' The Marquise called this a harsh and unjust measure. But her mother replied: 'Calm yourself', for she had just heard somebody drawing nearer, sobbing. 'Here he is.' 'Where?' asked the Marquise, and listened. 'Is there somebody outside the door? The loud ...' 'Indeed yes,' Lady G. replied. 'He wants us to open the door for him.' 'Let me then,' the Marquise cried, and stood up in haste. But: 'If you really have forgiven me, Julietta,' Lady G. answered, 'stay where you are'; and at that moment the Commandant came in, holding a handkerchief over his face. The mother stood in front of her daughter, turning her back on him. 'Dearest father!' the Marquise cried, and stretched out her arms towards him. 'Stay where you are,' said Lady G. 'Do you hear?' The Commandant stood there in the parlour, weeping. 'Let him beg your pardon,' Lady G. continued. 'Why is he so violent? And why is he so stubborn? I love him, but I love you too; I honour him, but I honour you too. And if I have to make a choice you are a better person than he is and I stand by you.' The Commandant bent double and howled. The walls rang with it. 'Dear God in heaven!' the Marquise cried, suddenly ceased struggling against her mother and took out a handkerchief, to let her own tears flow. Lady G. said: 'It is just that he cannot speak', and moved a little to one side. Thereupon the Marquise got to her feet, embraced the Commandant and begged him to calm himself. She was herself weeping violently. She asked would he not like to sit down; she tried to manoeuvre him into a chair; pushed one towards him so that he should sit in it: but he made no reply; he could not be budged; nor would he be seated but merely stood there bowing down his face almost to the floor and weeping. The Marquise said, holding him upright and half turning towards her mother: that he was going to be ill; the mother herself, since he was behaving as if in a fit, seemed about to lose her steadfastness. But when finally the Commandant, repeatedly urged to by his daughter, had seated himself and she, ceaselessly caressing him, had sunk down at his feet, she spoke again and said it served him right, now perhaps he would see reason, withdrew from the room and left them alone.

Once outside she dried her own tears, wondered whether the violent agitation she had thrown him into might not after all be dangerous and whether it might not be advisable to send for a doctor. In the kitchen she cooked him, for the evening, a meal of all the fortifying and calming things she could lay hands on, made up and warmed his bed to lay him in it just as soon as he should appear hand in hand with his daughter, and crept, when he still had not come and the evening meal was ready to serve, to the Marquise's room to find out, by listening, what was happening there. She could hear, when she laid her ear softly against the door, a gentle murmuring, just dying away, that seemed to be coming from the Marquise; and, as she saw through the keyhole that lady was sitting on the Commandant's lap, a thing he had never permitted in his life before. Then at last she opened the door and saw — and her heart swelled up in her for joy: the daughter, lying still in her father's arms, her head thrown back and her eyes tight shut; whilst he, sitting in the armchair, his wide eyes full of shining tears, was kissing her lips, at length, with passion, greedily: exactly like a lover. The daughter said nothing, he said nothing, he sat there with his face bowed over her as over the first girl he had ever loved, and arranged her mouth and kissed her. The mother felt like one of the blessed; unnoticed, standing behind his chair, she was loath to intrude upon such pleasures and interrupt the heavenly joyous reconciliation that had visited her house. She approached the father at last and bending around the side of the armchair watched him as he busied himself once more in unspeakable pleasure over his daughter's mouth. The Commandant, catching sight of her, bowed down his face already crumpling again and was about to say something; but she cried out: 'What sort of a face is that?' and herself now kissed it into better shape and with pleasantries brought all the emotion to an end. She invited and led in the two of them, walking like a bridal pair, to table and over the meal, although the Commandant was very cheerful, he did not eat or speak much but sobbed from time to time and looked down at his plate and played with his daughter's hand.*

Then the question was: who in all the world would present himself at eleven o'clock on the following day; for that day was the third of the month, the day they dreaded. Father and mother and also the brother, who had made his appearance, to be reconciled, were, if the person should be in the least degree tolerable, decidedly in favour of marriage; everything at all possible was to be done to make the Marquise's situation a happy one. However, if the person's circumstances were such that they would, even after favours and assistance, be still too far below the Marquise's, then in that case the parents were opposed to a marriage; they were resolved to keep the Marquise with them as before, and to adopt the child. The Marquise on the other hand seemed willing whatever the case, unless the person were wholly wicked, to keep her word and get the child a father cost what it might. That evening the mother asked how the reception of the person should be managed. The Commandant thought it would be most proper if the Marquise were left alone at eleven o'clock. But the Marquise insisted that both parents and her brother should be present, for she wished to share no secrets with that person. It was also her view that a similar wish seemed contained in the reply, since the person had suggested the Commandant's house for the meeting; one circumstance which, as she candidly admitted, had made her very pleased with that reply. The mother observed that there was something improper in the roles the father and the brother would have to play; begged the daughter to allow the men to absent themselves and would then agree to her request and be present herself to receive the person. The daughter thought for a moment, and finally this last proposal was adopted. Then, after a night spent in very great suspense, the morning of the third, of the day they dreaded, broke. As the clock struck eleven the two women, ceremoniously dressed as though for a betrothal, were seated in the reception room; their hearts were beating so that they would have been audible had the noises of the day ceased. The eleventh hour was still reverberating when Leopardo, the servant hired by the father from Tyrol, came in. Seeing him the women went white. 'Count F.,' he said, 'has arrived and asks to be announced.' 'Count F.!' they exclaimed at once, flung from one kind of shock into another. The Marquise cried: 'Close the doors! We are not at home to him!' — rose to lock the room herself immediately and was pushing the servant, who stood in her way, outside when the Count himself, in battledress with medals and weapons just as he had been when the fort was taken, came in to her. The Marquise felt she would sink into the ground in her confusion; she reached for a handkerchief that she had left lying on the chair, and made to escape into an adjoining room; but Lady G., seizing her hand, cried out: 'Julietta!' and her voice, as though choked by thoughts, failed her. She kept her eyes fixed on the Count and repeated: 'Julietta, I beg you', pulling her after her: 'Whom were we expecting then?' The Marquise, turning suddenly, exclaimed: 'Not him for sure', and struck home in him with a look that seared like lightning while the pallor of death went over her face. The Count had gone down on one knee before her; his right hand was pressed against his heart, his head bowed meekly on his breast; he kneeled there with a burning face and gazed at the floor and said nothing. 'Who else,' Lady G. exclaimed in a hampered voice, 'who else — were we out of our minds? — but him?' The Marquise stood rigid over him and said: 'Mother, I shall go mad.' 'Fool,' her mother replied, drew her close and whispered in her ear. The Marquise turned and, covering her face with her hands, flung herself down on the sofa. The Mother cried: 'What is it, child? What is the matter? What has happened that you were not prepared for?' — The Count did not move from Lady G.'s side. Still on his knees, he took up the outermost hem of her dress and kissed it. 'Dear lady, gracious lady, worthier of respect than words can say,' he whispered, and a tear rolled down his cheek. Lady G. said: 'Stand up, Count, stand up. Comfort her; then we are all friends again and everything is forgiven and forgotten.' The Count stood up, weeping. Before the Marquise he went down on his knees again, gently he took her hand as though it were made of gold and the aura of his own might tarnish it. But she: 'Go away! Go away! Go away!' she cried, rising to her feet. 'I was prepared for a vicious man but not for a ... devil!' — opened, avoiding him like a leper, the room door and said: 'Call the Commandant!' 'Julietta!' Lady G. cried in astonishment. The Marquise stared with a lethal wildness now at the Count, now at her mother, her breath came fast, her face was flaming: the gaze of a fury is not more terrible. The Commandant and the Forester came in. 'To this man, Father,' she said before they were through the door, 'I cannot be married', dipped her hand into a stoup of holy water affixed to the back of the door and in one large throw sprinkled father, mother and brother with it, and vanished.

The Commandant, surprised by this apparition, asked what had happened; and went white at that decisive moment seeing Count F. there in the room. The mother took the Count by the hand and said: 'Ask no questions. With all his heart this young man regrets what has occurred. Give him your blessing; do it, do it; then everything will still end happily.' The Count stood like a man annihilated. The Commandant laid his hand on him; his eyelashes twitched, his lips were as white as chalk. 'May heaven's curse be lifted from off this head!' he cried. 'When is it your intention to marry?' — 'Tomorrow,' said the mother, answering for him since he could not speak, 'tomorrow or today, as you like. The Count, who has shown such admirable eagerness to make good his wrongdoing, the soonest opportunity will suit him best.' — 'Then I shall have the pleasure of meeting you tomorrow at the Augustinians' church at eleven,' said the Commandant, bowed to him, summoned wife and son to follow him into the Marquise's room, and left him standing where he was.

They tried in vain to get the Marquise to tell them why she had behaved so strangely; she lay in a high fever, would not hear a word about a marriage and begged to be left alone. Being asked: why had she suddenly changed her mind and what made the Count more hateful to her than anyone else she looked distractedly at her father with wide eyes, and gave no answer. Lady G. said: had she forgotten that she was going to have a child? To which she replied that in her situation she must think of herself more than her child; and again, calling on all the saints and angels to be her witnesses, she swore that she would not marry. The father, seeing the obvious over-excitement of her emotions, declared that she must keep her word; left her and, after the proper consultation in writing with the Count, made the arrangements for the wedding. He presented the Count with a marriage contract in which he was to renounce all the husband's rights and agree to all the duties that would be imposed on him. The Count returned the paper signed and soaked with his tears. When next morning the Commandant handed this paper to the Marquise her spirits were a little calmer. She read it through several times, sitting up in bed; folded it thoughtfully, opened it and read it through again; and then announced that she would be there in the Augustinians' church at eleven o'clock. She rose, dressed, without saying a word, got into the carriage with her family as the clock was striking, and drove off.

Only in the church porch was the Count permitted to join the family. Throughout the ceremony the Marquise stared fixedly at the painting on the altar; not one fleeting glance did she grant the man with whom she exchanged rings. When the priest had joined them the Count offered her his arm; but as soon as they were outside the church the Countess bowed and withdrew from him; the Commandant asked would he have the honour of seeing him in his daughter's apartments from time to time, to which the Count stammered something that nobody understood, took off his hat to the company, and disappeared. He took an apartment in M., and spent some months there without once setting foot in the Commandant's house, where the Countess remained. It was entirely owing to his delicate, dignified and exemplary behaviour on all occasions when he came at all into contact with the family that, after the Countess had given birth to a son, he was invited to the christening. The Countess who, wrapped in shawls, was sitting on her bed, saw him only for a moment when he appeared in the door and greeted her from a distance with great reverence. Into the cradle, among the gifts with which the guests had welcomed the new arrival, he threw two documents: the one, as was discovered after his departure, being a gift of twenty thousand roubles to the boy, and the other a testament in which, in the event of his death, he made the mother the heir of all his fortune. From that day forth, at the instigation of Lady G., he was often invited, the house was open to him, soon no evening passed without his putting in an appearance. He began, since his feelings told him that on all sides now, in a world as fallible and fragile as ours is, he was forgiven, his courtship of the Countess, his wife, over again; and a year later, for the second time, she said yes to him, and a second marriage was celebrated too, more joyous than the first, at the conclusion of which the family removed to V. Quite a series of little Russians now followed the first; and when the Count, in a happy moment, asked his wife why on that terrible third of the month when she seemed prepared to face a vicious man she had fled from him as though he were the devil, she replied, putting her arms around him: he would not on that occasion have appeared to her like a devil had he not on his first appearance seemed to her an angel.

THE CHILEAN EARTHQUAKE

In Santiago, the capital of the kingdom of Chile, at the very instant of
the great earthquake of 1647 in which many thousands of people lost
their lives, a young man accused of a crime, a Spaniard by the name of
Jeronimo Rugera, stood by a pillar of the prison in which he had been
confined, and was about to hang himself. *Don Henrico Asteron*, one of
the richest noblemen of the city, had, about a year before, banished him
from his house, in which he was employed as a tutor, because of the
tender understanding that existed between him and Don Asteron's only
daughter, *Donna Josephe*. When a secret assignation was betrayed to
the elderly Don by his proud and mischievously watchful son he was so
incensed, having given her already very emphatic warnings, that he put
her with the Carmelites in the convent of our Dear Lady of the
Mountain.

There, by a lucky chance, Jeronimo had managed to resume the
liaison and the garden of the convent one stolen night was the scene of
his attaining the summit of his happiness. It was at the feast of Corpus
Christi* then and the solemn procession of the nuns with the novices
following them had just got under way when the unfortunate Josephe,
as the bells rang out, sank down on the steps of the cathedral in labour
pains.

This occurrence caused an extraordinary stir; the young sinner,
notwithstanding her condition, was fetched away to jail forthwith and
no sooner was her confinement over than, on the orders of the
Archbishop, she was subjected to the harshest rigour of the law. Among
the citizens the discussion of this scandal was so outraged and such
opprobrium was heaped upon the whole convent in which it had taken
place, that neither the pleading of the Asteron family nor even the
wishes of the Abbess herself, who had grown fond of the young girl on
account of her otherwise blameless conduct, could lessen the severity of

the monastic law under whose power she lay. All that could happen was that death at the stake, to which she had been sentenced, was commuted by the intercession of the Viceroy to death by beheading, which greatly incensed the matrons and the maidens of Santiago.

Windows were rented out along the streets through which the procession would pass to the execution, house roofs were removed, and the pious daughters of the city invited in their friends to view this spectacle offered to the vengeance of God in their sisterly company.

Jeronimo, who in the meantime had also been imprisoned, came near to losing his wits when he heard of the monstrous turn events had taken. Vainly he pondered how he might escape; wherever the wings even of the boldest thinking took him he hit against walls and padlocks, and an attempt to saw through the bars of his cell, when it was discovered, only brought him even closer confinement. He threw himself down before the image of the Holy Mother of God and prayed with limitless fervour to her as the only one by whom he might yet be rescued.

But the day he had dreaded duly came and with it in his heart the conviction of the utter hopelessness of his situation. The bells accompanying Josephe to the place of execution were ringing out, and despair took possession of his soul. Life seemed detestable to him and he resolved to kill himself by means of a rope left there fortuitously. He was standing, as we have said, by a pillar in the wall and fastening the rope, that would pluck him from this world of suffering, to an iron bracket embedded in the pillar's capital, when suddenly the greater part of the town, with a crash as though the firmament were falling in, sank and buried under its rubble everything that lived and breathed. Jeronimo Rugera went stiff with terror; and just as though all his consciousness had been broken into pieces he sought to keep his footing now by clinging to the pillar from which he had desired to hang himself. The ground rocked under his feet, all the walls of the prison were torn asunder, the whole structure tilted towards collapsing into the street and was only prevented from doing so utterly because, in its slow fall, it was met by the fall of the building opposite and made an accidental arch with that. Trembling, his hair on end, his legs giving under him, Jeronimo slid over the tilted floor towards the opening torn in the front wall of the prison by the collision of the two buildings.

He was scarcely out when the whole street, already shaken, fell in completely as the earth moved for a second time. At a loss as to how he might save himself from the general perdition he hurried, while death rose up at him everywhere, over rubble and fallen timbers towards one of the nearest of the city's gates. Another house collapsed; and by the wide volleys of its masonry he was driven into a side street; then into another, in terror, by fire flashing forth through clouds of steam from every gable end; and into a third he was carried with a roaring noise by the Mapocha river lifted from its bed and rolling at him. There were heaps of dead, there was groaning under the rubble; there were people on burning rooftops, screaming down; men and animals battling with the flood; there was a brave man struggling to help and save; and another, a man as white as death, stood speechlessly lifting his trembling hands to heaven. Reaching the gate and when he had climbed an eminence beyond it Jeronimo sank down there in a faint.

He lay for perhaps a quarter of an hour in the deepest unconsciousness, but woke at last and with his back to the city half raised himself from the earth. He felt his forehead and his breast and did not know what to make of his condition, and a feeling of unspeakable bliss took hold of him when a westerly wind, from the sea, blew upon the life returning in him and his eyes looked this way and that over the loveliness of the land around Santiago. Only the droves of people in distress, everywhere to be seen, depressed his spirits; he did not understand what could have brought them and himself to where they were, and only when he turned and saw the city behind him, sunk, only then did he remember the terrible moments he had gone through. He bowed down so low that his brow touched the ground, to thank God for his miraculous rescue; and as though the one fearful impression had driven all previous impressions from his mind he wept for joy that life in its sweetness so full of bright phenomena was still his to delight in.

Then, catching sight of a ring on his finger, suddenly he remembered Josephe too, and with her the prison, the bells he had heard from it and the moment that had preceded the prison's collapse. Again now his heart filled up with a deep grief; he began to regret his prayer of thanks; and whatever thing it is that rules above the clouds, fearful it seemed to him now. He joined the people who, busy saving their possessions, were tumbling through the gates, and timidly asked after Asteron's daughter and whether the execution had been carried out; but there was nobody who could answer him in any detail. A woman, bowed almost to the ground by the weight of utensils hung around her neck and with two children hanging at her breast, said in passing, as though she had seen it herself, that the girl had been beheaded. Jeronimo turned; and since he himself, when he calculated the time, could not doubt that it was indeed accomplished he sat down among some trees apart and gave himself up wholly to his grief. He wished that Nature's forces of destruction would break over him once more. He could not comprehend why, when death, which his tribulated soul desired, had freely offered him salvation on all sides, why in those moments he had fled from it. He resolved now not to waver even if the oak trees should be uprooted and fall on him headfirst. Then, having wept all he could and when hope had appeared to him again through the worst of his tears, he stood up and in one direction after another searched the fields. He visited every hilltop where people had collected; approached them on all the roads wherever they were still in flight; trembling, he went wherever a woman's dress flapped in the wind; but never was it Asteron's beloved daughter wearing it. The sun and with it all his hope was setting again when he came where the steep ground fell away and a broad valley, with few people in it, was opened to his view. He passed from group to group, unsure what he should do, and was about to turn back when suddenly he caught sight of a young woman bathing a child in the waters of the valley's irrigating stream. And the heart in him leapt at the sight, he sprang down over the stones in a happy surmise, called out: 'Holy Mother, Holy Mother of God!', and recognized Josephe as timidly she turned to face him at the noise. What bliss they had in embracing one another thus rescued from their misfortune by a heavenly miracle.

Josephe, on her way to death, had already come very close to the place of execution when suddenly the whole procession was flung asunder by the thunderous collapsing of the city's buildings. In terror her first steps were towards the nearest gate; but she soon bethought herself and turned to hurry to the convent where her helpless little child had been left. She found the convent already all in flames and the Abbess, who in the moments that were to have been Josephe's last had promised to care for the infant, there at the gates at that very instant was crying out for help, that he might be saved. Josephe, unafraid, plunged through the heaving steam into the building itself already collapsing on all sides, and as though all the angels of heaven were protecting her she came forth with him, unhurt, out at the gate again. She was about to embrace the Abbess, who was clapping her lifted hands, when that lady together with almost all her nuns was killed in a hideous fashion by a falling beam. At the sight of this horror Josephe started back; hastily she closed the Abbess's eyes and fled, thoroughly terrified, to rescue from destruction the beloved boy restored to her by heaven.

She had not gone many paces before she came upon the corpse of the Archbishop that precisely then was being dragged all broken out of the ruins of the cathedral. The Viceroy's palace had fallen down, the court in which sentence had been passed on her was in flames and in the place of her father's house there was now a lake boiling with a red vapour.

Josephe summoned up all her strength, not to lose hold on herself. Keeping grief away from her heart bravely she strode with her prize from street to street and was close to the gate when she saw that the prison in which Jeronimo had sorrowed was also in ruins. Seeing this she faltered and was near to sinking down unconscious in a corner; but at that very moment a building already entirely undone by the quakes collapsed behind her and fortified by terror she was driven to her feet; she kissed the child, wiped the tears from her eyes and paying no more attention to the horrors around her she reached the gate. Once out in the open she soon came to the conclusion that not everybody who had inhabited a building now destroyed must necessarily have been crushed by it.

At the next parting of the ways she stood still and waited for one whom she loved best in all the world after little Philip to appear to her. But when nobody came and the press of people grew she went on and turned again and again waited; and crept in tears into a dark valley shaded by pine trees to say prayers for his soul which she believed had fled away; and found him there, her beloved, in the valley, and such happiness as though it were the vale of Eden.

She recounted all this now with emotion to Jeronimo and handed him, as she finished, the child for him to kiss. — Jeronimo took him and cuddled him with a father's love and tenderly with kisses more than can be counted hushed his mouth, when the strange face made him cry. Night had come down meanwhile, lovelier than any night before, softly perfumed, a wonder, still and silvery, as only a poet might have imagined it. Everywhere along the valley's stream in the shimmering moonlight people had settled down and were making themselves soft beds of moss and leaves to recover in sleep from a day so full of torments. And because many in their misfortune were still lamenting, for the loss of a home, or wife and child, or everything, Jeronimo and Josephe crept away where the trees were denser so as to give no one any further grief by the secret jubilation of their souls. They found a splendid pomegranate tree that spread its boughs, full of scented fruit, out wide; and from its leafy crown came the passionate fluting of a nightingale. Here Jeronimo sat down against the trunk and with Josephe in his lap and Philip in hers they rested, covered by his cloak. The tree's shadow, with its scattered lights, passed away over them and the moon had paled into the reddening dawn before they fell asleep. For there was no end of things to talk about — the convent garden, their prisons and what each had suffered on the other's account; and were deeply moved when they considered how much misery had to come upon the world to make their happiness possible.

They decided that as soon as the tremors had ceased they would go to La Concepcion where Josephe had a close friend and with a small advance of funds which they hoped to obtain from her would take a ship to Spain where Jeronimo had relatives on his mother's side; and there they would live out their days in happiness. Then, with much kissing, they slept.

When they awoke the sun was already high in the sky and near them they saw several families busy over fires in the preparation of a frugal morning meal. Jeronimo himself was wondering how he would feed his family when a well-dressed young man with a baby on his arm came up to Josephe and, with all humility, asked whether she would nurse the poor thing for a while whose own mother lay there injured under the trees. Josephe felt some embarrassment, for she recognized the man; but when, misconstruing her embarrassment, he continued: 'Only for a little while, Donna Josephe. This child since the moment which brought unhappiness to us all has had no nourishment', she said: 'If I did not answer — it was for another reason, Don Fernando. In these terrible times no one would refuse to share whatever he might have', and took the little stranger, giving her own child to his father, and laid him at her breast. Don Fernando was very grateful for this kindness and asked would they not come with him and join the company there preparing a little breakfast over the fire. Josephe replied that she would accept the offer gladly and followed him, since Jeronimo also made no objection, to his family where she was received with the utmost warmth and gentleness by Don Fernando's two sisters-in-law whom she knew already as two very estimable young women.

Donna Elvire, Don Fernando's wife, who was severely injured in both feet and lay on the ground, when she saw her weakened child at Donna Josephe's breast she drew her down where she lay and showed her great affection. Don Pedro too, his father-in-law who was injured in the shoulder, bowed his head to her in a kindly way. —

Strange thoughts were stirring in Jeronimo and Josephe now. Seeing themselves treated with so much warmth and kindness they were at a loss to know what to make of the past events, of the scaffold, the prison, the bell; had they only dreamed them? It was as though all hearts and minds, after the fearful shock that had passed through them, were reconciled now. They could remember back no further than that shock. Only Donna Elisabeth, who had been invited to watch the previous morning's spectacle at the house of a friend but had declined, now and then rested her eyes on Donna Josephe musingly; but whenever another terrible misfortune was related this wrenched her soul, scarcely wandering from the present, back into it.

There were stories of how throughout the city, immediately after the first big shock, numerous women had given birth in full view of the men; and of how the monks in the city, with crucifixes in their hands, had run around screaming that the end of the world had come; how soldiers seeking to evacuate a church and invoking the authority of the Viceroy were told there was no viceroy in Chile any more; how at the worst of it all the Viceroy had to set up gallows to put a stop to thieving, and how an innocent man, who had made his escape through a burning house, was caught by the over-hasty owner at the back, and at once strung up.

Donna Elvire, whilst Josephe was busy seeing to her injuries, had found an opportunity, just when the swapping of stories was at its height, to ask her how she had fared on that terrible day. And when Josephe, uneasy in her heart, told her some of the chief things, she had the gratification of seeing tears in that lady's eyes; Donna Elvire seized her hand and pressed it, and signalled her to say no more. It seemed to Josephe she was now among the blessed. She was moved irresistibly to call the day that had passed, for all the misery it had brought upon the world, a blessing such as heaven had never bestowed on her before. And indeed, in that hideous time, when all the people's earthly goods were lost and the whole of Nature was threatened with destruction, the human spirit itself, like a beautiful flower, seemed to be putting forth. In the fields, as far as the eye could see, people of all the classes were lying without distinction, princes and beggars, patrician wives and peasant women, the state's officials and day labourers, monks and nuns, they were seen extending pity and help to one another and gladly sharing whatever they might have saved for their own sustenance, as if the general misfortune had made one family of all who had survived.

Instead of the meaningless tea-table conversations, whose stuff had been as the world provided it, now there were stories of colossal deeds: people previously little noticed by society had shown a Roman virtue; innumerable instances of fearlessness, of a cheerful contempt for danger, of selflessness and more than human self-sacrifice, of people laying down their lives without any hesitation as though, like a material possession of no value, it might be taken up again at the next step. Indeed, since there was nobody to whom that day some affecting thing had not occurred or who themselves had not done something brave, the pain in every human heart was mixed with so much joy and sweetness that, as she thought, it might be wondered whether the total of human happiness had not increased on the one hand by as much as it had decreased on the other.

Jeronimo, when both had fallen silent among these reflections, took Josephe by the arm and led her, in more blitheness of spirit than words can tell, up and down under the shady pomegranate trees. He told her that, hearts and minds being now as they were and all former circumstances so overthrown, he had abandoned his decision to take a ship to Europe; that if the Viceroy, who had always been sympathetic to him in his plight, were still alive he was resolved to petition him, and that he was hopeful (here he kissed her) of being able to remain with her in Chile. Josephe replied that similar thoughts had risen in her too; that she herself no longer doubted that, if her father were still alive, he could be conciliated; but that rather than throwing themselves at the Viceroy's feet they should go to La Concepcion and conduct the business of reconciliation with him by letter; for there, whatever the outcome, they would be near the port and, if things went well and as they hoped, they could easily come back to Santiago. Having reflected a little Jeronimo acknowledged the wisdom of this strategy, and a while longer, surveying the happiness ahead of them, they continued their promenade, before returning to the company.

The day had advanced meanwhile into the afternoon and the swarms of refugees, as the shocks grew less and less, were just beginning to be easier in their minds when word spread that in the church of the Dominicans, the only one the earthquake had spared, a solemn mass would be celebrated by the prelate himself, to beseech heaven that there would be no further tribulation.

On all sides the people were departing in haste and crowding into the city. It was asked in Don Fernando's little company whether they should not also be present at this solemn occasion and join the general throng. Donna Elisabeth, in some dismay, reminded them of the evil that had happened in the church the day before; such thanksgiving would be bound to be repeated and then, when the danger was more definitely past, they might entrust themselves to the mood with greater serenity and peace of mind. Josephe, rising in some enthusiasm, said that she had never felt the urge to bow down her countenance before her creator more keenly than now, at this time when his awful and incomprehensible power had been made so manifest. Donna Elvire, in passionate tones, declared herself to be of the same mind as Josephe. She insisted that they should attend the mass and called on Don Fernando to conduct them; whereupon everyone, Donna Elisabeth included, rose. But when they saw this lady prolonging the little preparations for departure and hardly able to get breath and when she replied to their question: 'What is the matter?' by saying that she had bad forebodings, she could not tell what, Donna Elvire reassured her and urged her to stay behind with her and her sick father. Josephe said: 'Donna Elisabeth, you must have this little darling back from me. As you see, he has found his way here to me again.' 'Very gladly,' Donna Elisabeth replied, and made to take hold of him; but when he began to wail at the wrong being done him and would absolutely not agree to it Josephe smiled and said she would keep him after all and kissed him until he was quiet. Thereupon Don Fernando, charmed by the dignity and grace of her behaviour, offered her his arm; Jeronimo, carrying little Philip, escorted Donna Constanze; the others who had joined their company followed; and in that order they set off towards the town.

They had scarcely gone fifty paces when they heard Donna Elisabeth, who had in the meantime been whispering agitatedly with Donna Elvire, call out: 'Don Fernando!' and saw her hurrying after them in some distress. Don Fernando halted and turned; waited for her without letting go of Josephe and asked, when as if waiting for him to advance she paused at a little distance, what she wanted. Then Donna Elisabeth approached, albeit, as it seemed, reluctantly, and murmured, but so that Josephe could not hear them, a few words in his ear. 'Well?' Don Fernando asked: 'And what ill can come of it?' Donna Elisabeth, with a troubled face, continued her whispering into his ear. Don Fernando's face began to colour with impatience; he replied: 'That will do, Donna Elvire must calm herself'; and led the lady on his arm away. —

When they reached the church of the Dominicans the splendid music of the organ could already be heard and inside a measureless multitude was heaving to and fro. The throng extended far beyond the doors out on to the square before the church, and high up on the walls, in the frames of paintings, boys were perched, looking forth expectantly, their caps in their hands. Light poured down from all the chandeliers, the pillars, as dusk came on, cast eerie shadows, the great rose window shone from the back of the church like the evening sun by which its coloured glass was illuminated, and silence reigned, as the organ ceased, in the whole assembly, as if no one had a sound in his own heart. Never from any Christian minster did such a flame of fervour beat against heaven as on that day from the Dominican minster in Santiago; and no hearts contributed more warmly than Jeronimo's and Josephe's.

The service commenced with a sermon from the pulpit by one of the oldest of the canons in all his ceremonial finery. He began at once with praise and thanksgiving, his hands in the vast sleeves of his surplice lifted tremblingly to heaven, that in that part of the world collapsing into rubble there were still human beings capable of addressing themselves in all humility to God. He reminded them of what, at a sign from the Almighty, had occurred; Judgement Day itself cannot be more terrible; and when, pointing to a crack in the fabric of the minster, he called the earthquake of the day before none the less only a foretaste of the day of reckoning a shudder ran through the congregation. He came then, on the flood of his priestly rhetoric, to the people's turpitude; indicted them for horrors such as Sodom and Gomorrah had not seen; and only, he said, because God's forbearance was infinite had their city not been wiped off the face of the earth.

But like daggers instantly it entered the hearts of our two unfortunates, already lacerated by this preaching, when the canon now alluded in detail to the wickedness committed in the garden of the Carmelite convent; called the leniency of the world towards it godless and in a short excursus, laced with maledictions, commended the souls of the perpetrators, naming their names, to all the lords of hell. Donna Constanze, tugging at Jeronimo's arm, cried out: 'Don Fernando!' But he with as much emphasis as could be compressed into a whisper replied: 'You will be silent, madam. Do not move so much as an eyelid, but pretend to faint, and we shall leave the church.' But before Donna Constanze could employ this stratagem to save them a voice, loudly interrupting the canon's sermon, cried out: 'Citizens, stand back! The sinners are among you. There they are!' And when another voice, full of dread, while a wide circle of horror formed around them, called out: 'Where?' 'Here!' a third person answered, and full of a holy savagery dragged down Josephe by the hair so that with Don Fernando's child she would have fallen to the floor had he not held her. 'Are you mad?' the young man cried and put his arm around Josephe. 'I am Don Fernando Ormez, son of the Commandant of Santiago, whom you all know.' 'Don Fernando Ormez?' It was a cobbler, close up against him, who had done work for Josephe and knew her at least as well as he did her small and shapely feet. 'And who is the father of this child?' turning, as he said this, with an ugly insolence, to Asteron's daughter. Don Fernando went pale at the question. He glanced nervously at Jeronimo, he searched the congregation for somebody who knew him. Josephe, pressed by horrific circumstances, cried out: 'Master Pedrillo, this is not my child as you believe', glancing as she said this with a boundless fear in her soul at Don Fernando. 'This young gentleman is Don Fernando Ormez, son of the Commandant of the city, whom you all know.' The cobbler asked: 'Citizens, who among you knows this young man?' And of the others around him several said again: 'Who knows Jeronimo Rugera? Let him step forward.' Now it happened that at that very moment little Juan, frightened by the tumult, struggled to leave Josephe's breast and reach Don Fernando's arms. 'He *is* the father!' a voice screamed; and 'He *is* Jeronimo Rugera!' screamed another; and 'They *are* the blasphemers!' a third; and: 'Stone them! Stone them!' all Christianity gathered there in the house of Jesus. Then at once Jeronimo: 'Stay still, you monsters. If you are looking for Jeronimo Rugera, here he is. Let that man go, he is innocent.' —

The enraged rabble, confused by Jeronimo's declaration, faltered; several holding Don Fernando let go; and when at that moment a high-ranking naval officer hurried forward and pushing through the tumult asked: 'Don Fernando Ormez, what is the matter here?' the latter, now entirely released, replied with truly heroic composure: 'My word, Don Alonzo, only look at these assassins! I was done for had not this excellent gentleman, to calm the mob in their insanity, given himself out to be Jeronimo Rugera. Arrest him, if you will be so kind, along with this young lady, for their own protection, and this rogue' — seizing Master Pedrillo — 'who stirred up the riot, arrest him too.' The cobbler cried: 'Don Alonzo Onoreja, I ask you on your conscience, is not this girl Josephe Asteron?' When Don Alonzo, who knew Josephe very well, hesitated with his answer and a number of voices, inflamed by this to rage again, cried out: 'She is! She is!' and: 'Kill her!' then Josephe placed little Philip, whom Jeronimo had been holding, along with Juan into Don Fernando's arms and said: 'Go now, Don Fernando, save your two children and leave us to our fate.'

Don Fernando took the children and said he would rather die than allow anyone in his company to suffer harm. He offered Josephe, having borrowed the naval officer's sword, his arm and instructed the pair behind to follow him. And they came indeed, as, after such measures, people, sufficiently respectful, made way for them, out of the church, and thought themselves safe. But no sooner had they stepped on to the equally crowded square than a voice from the incensed mob following them called out: 'Citizens, that is Jeronimo Rugera. I am his own father' and with one blow of a colossal club laid him out on the ground at Donna Constanze's side. 'Jesus and Mary!' Donna Constanze cried, and fled to her brother-in-law, but: 'Whore!' came a cry, 'Whore of a nun!' and a second blow, from another quarter, felled her, lifeless, next to Jeronimo. 'Monster!' cried a man unknown to them, 'that was Donna Constanze Xares.' 'Why did they tell us lies?' the cobbler answered. 'Find us the right one and kill her.' Don Fernando, seeing Constanze's corpse, reddened with rage; he drew and swung his sword and struck at the murderous fanatic who had caused these atrocious deeds and would have cleft him had he not dodged aside and escaped the furious stroke. But since he could not overpower the crowd pressing in on him: 'Farewell to you, Don Fernando and the children!' Josephe cried — and: 'Murder me then, inhuman butchers that you are!' and threw herself of her own volition among them, to end the struggle. Master Pedrillo felled her with his club. Then, all bloody from her, 'Send the bastard after her to hell!' he roared, and pressed, his lust for murder still unsatisfied, forward again.

Don Fernando, a god-like hero, stood now with his back against the church; on his left arm he held the children, in his right hand the sword. With every stroke, like a lightning bolt, he struck another to the ground; a lion fighting for its life could not do better. Seven of the killer dogs lay dead before him, the prince of the satanic pack himself was wounded. But Master Pedrillo did not rest until, by the legs, he had torn one of the children from Don Fernando's breast and swinging him high around had smashed him against a pillar of the church. Thereupon it was quiet and everyone withdrew. Don Fernando, seeing his little Juan before him with his brains spilling out, lifted his eyes, full of a nameless pain, to heaven.

The naval officer now returned to his side, sought to comfort him and assured him that, though many circumstances excused him, he felt his inactivity while the catastrophe was taking place to be regrettable; but Don Fernando said he had nothing to reproach himself with and asked only that he help remove the corpses. They were borne, as the darkness of night came down, all of them into Don Alonzo's house and there Don Fernando, weeping and weeping over the countenance of baby Philip, followed them. He spent the night at Don Alonzo's too and for a long while, with false excuses, delayed informing his wife of the whole compass of the calamity; in the first place because she was ill and then because he did not know how she would judge his conduct in the events; but soon afterwards, learning by chance from a visitor all that had happened, that excellent lady wept her motherly grief out in privacy and with tears still shining in her eyes one morning fell upon his neck and kissed him. Don Fernando and Donna Elvire then took the little stranger to be their foster son; and when Don Fernando thought of Philip and Juan together and how he had come by both he felt, almost, as though he must rejoice.

BETROTHAL IN SAN DOMINGO

In Port au Prince, in that part of the island belonging to the French, at the beginning of this century when the blacks were murdering the whites, there lived an old negro, a terrifying man, Congo Hoango by name, on M. Guillaume de Villeneuve's plantation. This person, who came from the Gold Coast and seemed in his youth to be of a loyal and honest disposition, had been infinitely well treated by his master for having saved his life once on a crossing to Cuba. Not only did M. Guillaume grant him his freedom there and then and on returning to San Domingo put him in possession of a house and home, but a few years later, contrary to what was usual in that country, he appointed him overseer over his considerable property and, since he did not wish to remarry, assigned to him, in lieu of a wife, a mulatto* from the plantations, Babekan by name, with whom, through his first wife, he was distantly related. Moreover, when the negro reached his sixtieth year he gave him his leisure and a handsome pension and crowned all his benefactions with this: that he left him a legacy in his will; but all these proofs of M. Villeneuve's gratitude did not save him from the fury of this fearsome man. Congo Hoango, in the general orgy of vengeance flaring up on those plantations as a result of the reckless measures of the National Convention, was one of the first to seize a gun and, mindful of the tyranny which had torn him away from his native land, he put a bullet through his master's head. He set fire to the house in which Mme Villeneuve and her three children and the other whites from the plantation had taken refuge, laid waste the whole plantation on which the heirs living in Port au Prince might have made a claim and then, when all the buildings belonging to the property had been razed to the ground, he took the blacks he had assembled and armed and roamed the countryside with them, to be of assistance to his fellows in their struggle against the whites. He ambushed any travelling the island in armed bands; or in broad daylight fell on the planters themselves in their fortified homes and put all he found there to the sword. Indeed, in his inhuman lust for vengeance he demanded that old Babekan herself, together with her daughter, a young mestiza* by the name of Toni, only fifteen years of age, should participate in the cruel war in which he himself was quite rejuvenated; and since the largest house on the plantation, now his dwelling place, lay in an isolated position on the highway and, during his absences, fleeing whites or creoles* often called there seeking food or shelter, he instructed the women to detain the white vermin, as he called them, until his return, by giving them assistance and showing them kindness. Babekan, consumptive as a result of a cruel punishment meted out to her when she was young, would, when such occasions arose, dress up the youthful Toni in her best clothes, for the girl's complexion, tending to the yellowish, made her particularly serviceable in this hideous ruse; she encouraged her to allow their visitors every intimacy, except the last, which was forbidden her on pain of death: and when Congo Hoango returned with his company of blacks from marauding in the country round about, an immediate death was the fate of the unfortunates who had let themselves be duped by these wiles.

Now it is generally known that in 1803 when General Dessalines advanced with his thirty thousand blacks against Port au Prince all whose colour was white hastened thither, to defend the place. For this was the last stronghold of French power on the island and if it fell the whites, one and all, were doomed. Thus it happened that precisely during one of the absences of old Hoango, who had set off with his blacks to transport a supply of powder and lead right through the French lines to General Dessalines, in all the darkness of a night of wind and rain somebody knocked at the back door of his house. Old Babekan, already in bed, rose and, only flinging a skirt around her waist, opened the window and asked who was there. 'In the name of Mary and all the saints,' said the stranger in a whisper, positioning himself under the window, 'answer me one question before I tell you.' And so saying he stretched out his hand through the darkness of the night to seize the old woman's hand, and asked: 'Are you a negress?' Babekan said: 'You must certainly be a white man if you would rather look this pitchblack night in the face than a negress. Come in,' she added, 'and have no fear. It is a mulatto who lives here and nobody else is in the house except my daughter, a mestiza.' And with that she closed the window as though to come down and open the door for him; but crept, under the pretext that she could not find the key, upstairs to the bedroom with some clothes

hurriedly collected from the cupboard, and woke her daughter. 'Toni!'
she said: 'Toni!' — 'What is it, mother?' — 'Hurry,' she said. 'Get up
and dress. Here are some clothes, white underwear and stockings. There
is a white man at the door, being hunted, and he wants us to let him in.'
— Toni asked: 'A white man?' and sat up in bed. She took the clothes
the old woman had in her hand and said: 'But is he alone, Mother? And
have we nothing to fear if we let him in?' — 'Nothing at all,' the old
woman replied as she lit a candle. 'He is unarmed and alone and shaking
with fear that we might fall on him.' And so saying, whilst Toni rose and
put on her skirt and stockings, she lit the big lantern in the corner of the
room, quickly put up the girl's hair, in the local way, and having
fastened her bodice set a hat on her head, put the lantern in her hand
and ordered her to go down into the yard and fetch the stranger in.

Dogs in the yard meanwhile by their barking had woken a boy,
Nanky by name, whom Hoango had fathered on a negress outside
marriage and who slept with his brother Seppy in the outbuildings; and
seeing in the moonlight a solitary man standing on the back steps of the
house he did as he had been told to do on such occasions and hurried to
the yard gate, through which the man had entered, to lock it. The
stranger, not knowing what this meant, asked the boy whom, to his
horror, when he came near, he saw to be a negro child, who lived in the
settlement; and on his reply that since the death of M. Villeneuve the
property had fallen to the negro Hoango was about to fling the boy to
the ground, tear the gate key from his hand and escape, when Toni, the
lantern in her hand, came out of the house. 'Quickly,' she said, seizing
his hand and pulling him towards the door, 'in here.' She was careful,
saying this, to hold the light so that the full beam of it fell on her face. —
'Who are you?' the stranger cried, resisting her and staring in an
astonishment that had more than one cause at her youthful and lovable
appearance. 'Who lives in this house in which, as you pretend, I will be
safe?' — 'Nobody, by the light of the sun,' said the girl, 'except my
mother and myself,' and sought with might and main to drag him after
her. 'How so, nobody?' the stranger cried, stepping backwards a pace
and freeing his hand. 'Has not this boy just told me that a negro,
Hoango by name, is in there?' — 'I tell you, no,' said the girl, and with
an impatient expression stamped her foot; 'and even if the house does
indeed belong to a monster of that name he is not in it at present but is
fifty miles away.' And so saying, with both hands she dragged the
stranger into the house, ordered the boy to tell nobody who had come
and having reached the door she seized the stranger's hand and led him
upstairs to her mother's room.

'Now,' said the old woman who, from the window above, had eavesdropped on the whole conversation and had noticed, in the lamplight, that he was an officer, 'what is the meaning of the sword there under your arm? It looks ready to be used. We,' she added, pressing a pair of spectacles on to her nose, 'have risked our lives to offer you shelter in our house. Have you entered after the custom of your compatriots to repay this kindness with treachery?' — 'Heaven forbid!' the stranger replied, coming close up to her chair. He seized the old woman's hand, pressed it against his heart and having cast a few fearful glances around the room and unbuckled the sword from his hip, he said: 'You see before you the unhappiest of men, but nobody bad or ungrateful.' — 'Who are you?' the old woman asked; and with her foot shoved a chair towards him and ordered the girl to go to the kitchen and prepare him a meal, the best she could, but quickly. The stranger replied: 'I am an officer in the French army though not, as perhaps you can tell, a Frenchman. Switzerland is my country and my name is Gustav von der Ried. Would I had never left there and exchanged my home for this unhappy island! I have come from Fort Dauphin where, as you know, all the whites have been murdered and my intention is to reach Port au Prince before General Dessalines manages, with the troops under his command, to cut the place off and besiege it.' — 'From Fort Dauphin!' the old woman cried. 'And you managed, with your white face, to travel that vast distance through a land of blackamoors in revolt?' 'God and all his saints,' the stranger replied, 'were my protectors. — And I am not alone. With me, though I have left them behind now, are a venerable old gentleman, my uncle, with his wife and five children; not to mention maids and servants belonging to the family; in all a company of twelve whom I, with the help of two wretched mules in unspeakably arduous marches through the night, for we dare not show ourselves on the highway in daylight, must carry with me.' 'Dear heaven!' the old woman cried and shaking her head in pity took a pinch of snuff. 'And where are your companions at this minute?' — 'To you,' the stranger replied after a moment's thought, 'to you I can entrust myself. There is in the colour of your face a glimmer of my own colour, and it shines forth at me. The family, let me tell you, are about four miles from here, near the Gull Pond, in the forest bordering on it from the mountains: hunger and thirst obliged us to seek shelter there the day before yesterday. Last night we sent our servants out to procure a little bread and wine among the inhabitants of those parts, but in vain; fear of being captured and killed prevented them from taking the decisive measures that were necessary, so that I have myself now, putting my life at risk, been obliged to set off and try my luck. Heaven, unless I am much mistaken,' he continued, pressing the old woman's hand, 'has led me among kindhearted people who do not share in the hatred and savagery beyond belief that have seized all the inhabitants of the island. Show your kindness now and for a rich reward fill me some baskets with things to eat and drink; we are only five days from Port au Prince and if you provision us to reach that town we shall always remember that you were our saviours.' — 'Ah, the rage and hatred,' said the old woman piously. 'Is it not as if the hands of a body or the teeth of a mouth were to set upon one another merely because they are not all made the same? How can I — whose father was from Cuba, from Santiago — help it that a shimmer of lightness dawns on my face when daybreak comes? And how can my daughter, conceived and born in Europe, help it that the full daylight of those parts is reflected in hers?' — 'What!' cried the stranger. 'To judge by the form of your face you are a mulatto and, what is more, of African origin, and are you and the pretty young mestiza who opened up the house for me, are you accursed as we are, we the Europeans?' — 'By heaven,' the old woman replied, taking the spectacles off her nose, 'what we have laboured years in misery and hardship to acquire, little as it is, that pack of thieves and murderers from hell lust after it, you may be sure. If we were not able, by cunning and by all the ways and means the weak invent in their own self-defence, to secure ourselves against our persecutors: believe me, the shadow of kinship visible in our faces would not itself do it.' — 'Impossible!' the stranger cried. 'And who on this island persecutes you?' 'The owner of this house,' the old woman replied, 'the negro Congo Hoango. Since the death of M. Guillaume, the former owner of the plantation, who fell by his cruel hand when the revolt broke out, we his relatives, who manage his household, are at the mercy of his violent whim. He pays us in abuse and beatings for every bit of bread, every sip of refreshment that we, out of our humanity, might grant one white man or another as they pass in flight from time to time along the road; and his chief desire is to bring down the vengeance of the blacks upon us white and creole mongrels, as he calls us, partly in order to be rid of us, since we speak against his savage treatment of the whites, and partly so that he might appropriate what little fortune we should leave behind.' — 'You are indeed unfortunate,' said the stranger. 'I pity you. — And where is this monster at present?' 'With General Dessalines's army,' the old woman replied. 'He and the other blacks belonging to this plantation have taken him the supplies of lead and gunpowder he needed. We expect him back, unless he undertakes other things, in ten or twelve days' time; and should he then find out, which God forbid, that we have given shelter and hospitality to a white man making for Port au Prince whilst he with might and main is engaged in the effort to cleanse this island of the whole race of them, we are doomed, you may be sure.' 'Heaven that loves compassion and human kindness,' the stranger replied, 'will protect you in what you do for an unhappy man. — And since,' he added, moving closer to the old woman, 'you would in that case have incurred the negro's wrath, and obedience thereafter, even if you were to obey him again, would avail you nothing, could you not, for any reward you cared to name, bring yourself to give my uncle and his family, who have been terribly weakened by the journey, shelter in your house for a day or two, until they have recovered a little?' — 'Young man,' said the old woman, taken aback, 'do you know what you are asking? How in a house on the highway would it be possible to accommodate a company as large as yours without the local people finding out?' — 'Why should it not be?' the stranger answered in urgent tones. 'If I myself now went at once to the Gull Pond and led my people into the plantation before daybreak; if they were all, masters and servants together, given shelter in one and the same room and perhaps, to prevent the worst occurring, if one took the further precaution of carefully closing the doors and windows?' — The old woman replied, having considered the proposition for a while, that if he were to try that night to lead his company from the ravine into the plantation they would infallibly as they returned from there meet a troop of armed blacks whose arrival along the highway had already been announced by scouts sent on ahead. — 'Very well,' the stranger replied. 'We shall content ourselves for the moment with sending those poor unfortunates a basket of provisions and put off the business of conducting them into the plantation until the following night. Will you be our dear friend and do this for us?' — 'Well,' said the old woman as kisses from the stranger's lips rained down in any number on her bony hand, 'for the sake of the European, my daughter's father, I will do you, his compatriots in distress, this favour. When day breaks sit yourself down and write a letter to your people inviting them to make their way to me here in the plantation; then the boy you saw in the yard can take them the message along with the provisions, stay with them, for safety's sake, in the mountains overnight and be their guide here, if they accept the invitation, at dawn on the following day.'

Meanwhile Toni had returned with a meal she had prepared in the kitchen and glancing at the stranger asked the old woman in teasing tones while she laid the table: 'Well, Mother, what do you say? Has the gentleman recovered from the shock he had outside? Does he believe now that neither poison nor the knife are in store for him and that the negro Hoango is not at home?' Her mother sighed and said: 'Once bitten, as the saying goes, twice shy. The gentleman would have been foolish to enter the house before ascertaining what race its inhabitants belonged to.' The girl approached her mother and explained how she had held the lantern in such a way that its beam fell full upon her face. 'But in his imagination,' she said, 'there was nothing but blackamoors and negroes and if a lady from Paris or Marseilles had opened the door for him still he would have taken her for a black.' The stranger, gently putting his arm around her waist, said, in some embarrassment, that the hat she was wearing had prevented him from seeing her face. 'Had I been able,' he continued, pressing her hard against him, 'to look into your eyes as I can now, willingly, even were everything else about you black, I would have drunk from a poisoned chalice with you.' The mother made him, blushing as he said these words, sit down and Toni sat by him at the table, her chin in her hands, and gazed, as he ate, into his face. The stranger asked her how old she was and the name of her place of birth, whereupon her mother intervened and told him that she had conceived and given birth to Toni fifteen years ago in Paris on a journey to Europe she had taken with the wife of her former master M. Villeneuve. She added that although the negro Komar, whom she had married later, had accepted the child as his own her real father was a rich merchant from Marseilles, called Bertrand, and after him her full name was Toni Bertrand. — Toni asked the stranger whether he knew any such gentleman in France. He answered: no, the country was large and during his brief stay there when embarking for the West Indies he had not come across anyone of that name. The old woman replied that indeed M. Bertrand, according to the pretty certain information she had gathered, was no longer in France. 'His spirit,' she said, 'was too ambitious and energetic for him to be content in the private citizen's usual round; when the Revolution broke out he involved himself in public affairs and in 1795 went with a French legation to the court of Turkey and still, so far as I know, has not returned from there.' The stranger smiled and, taking Toni's hand, observed that if that were the case she was a rich and respectable young woman. Why, he said, she should press her claims to these advantages and might hope one day at her father's hand to be introduced into more brilliant circumstances than those in which she was living now. 'Scarcely,' said the old woman, with more feeling than she showed. 'M. Bertrand, when I was pregnant in Paris, because he was ashamed on account of the rich young lady he wished to marry, denied in court that he was the father of my child. I shall never forget the oath he had the nerve to look me in the face and swear; a gall-fever followed it, and soon after that sixty lashes given me on the orders of M. Villeneuve which have left me consumptive to this day.' — Toni, resting her head thoughtfully on her hand, asked the stranger who he was, where he came from and where he was going to, whereupon he, after a moment's embarrassment brought on by the old woman's bitter account, replied that with Herr Strömli's, his uncle's, family, whom he had left behind in the mountain forests by the Gull Pond under the protection of two young cousins, he had come from Fort Dauphin. He recounted, in response to the girl's questions, numerous details of the revolt which had broken out in that town; how at midnight, when all were sleeping, a signal was given and the blacks' treacherous slaughter of the whites began; how the leader of the negroes, a sergeant in the French pioneers, perfidiously had set fire at once to all the ships in the harbour to cut off the whites' escape to Europe; how the family had scarcely had time to get through the city gates with a few belongings and how, since the revolt had flared up simultaneously in all the coastal towns, their only option had been to set off to traverse the island, with two mules they had managed to get hold of, towards Port au Prince which, being protected by a strong French force, was still, so far, holding out against the ever more triumphant power of the blacks. — Toni asked how the whites there had made themselves so detested. — The stranger, taken aback, replied: 'Generally through the relationship in which, as masters of the island, they stood to the blacks which I would not myself, if I am honest, presume to defend but which has existed in that form for many centuries already. The madness of liberation which has seized all the plantations drove the blacks and the creoles to break the chains by which they were oppressed and to be revenged upon the whites for many wrongs done them by a few reprehensible members of that race. — The act of one young girl,' he continued after a moment's silence, 'seemed to me especially terrible and remarkable. She, a negress, when the revolt flared up, lay sick of yellow fever which, making things yet worse, had broken out in the town. Three years earlier she had been the slave of a planter, a white, who, piqued when she would not comply with his wishes, had been hard on her and afterwards sold her to a creole planter. When the girl learned on the day of the general uprising that her former master was sheltering from the rage of the blacks, who were pursuing him, in a nearby shed she, mindful of how he had abused her, sent her brother to him at dusk to invite him to spend the night with her. The unfortunate man, not even aware that the girl was ill let alone what sickness she had, came and in the grateful belief that he was saved enfolded her in his arms; but after little more than half an hour of kisses and caresses in her bed she sat up suddenly with a look of savage and icy rage and said: "The girl you have been kissing has the plague and death is in her lungs. Go now and give the yellow fever to all of your kind."' — The officer, while the old woman loudly expressed her abhorrence at this, asked Toni would *she* be capable of such a deed. 'No,' said Toni, looking down in confusion. The stranger, placing his napkin on the table, replied that, heart and soul, he felt there could be no justification, however tyrannous the whites had been, for an act of such base and abominable deceit. The vengeance of heaven, he said, and rose in passion to his feet, was disarmed by it, the angels themselves, outraged, sided with those who were in the wrong, and for the upholding of order, human and divine, took up their cause. So saying, he crossed to the window for a moment and looked out into the night where black clouds were hurrying by across the moon and stars; and because he had the impression that mother and daughter were looking at one another, though not, so far as he saw, making any signs, suddenly he felt unhappy and ill at ease; he turned and asked to be shown the room where he might sleep.

The mother, glancing at the clock on the wall, remarked that it was indeed nearly midnight, took a lamp in her hand and instructed the stranger to follow her. She led him down a long corridor to the room that was to be his; Toni carried the stranger's coat and a number of other things that he had set down; the mother showed him the comfortably pillowed bed he was to sleep in and having ordered Toni to prepare a footbath for the gentleman she wished him goodnight, and withdrew. The stranger stood his sword in the corner, took a brace of pistols from his belt and laid them on the table. Whilst Toni was pushing the bed forward and laying a white sheet over it he looked about the room; and soon deducing from the splendour and good taste everywhere manifest that it must have belonged to the former owner of the plantation, uneasiness settled like a vulture on his heart and he wished himself back, hungry and thirsty as he had come, among his people in the forest. Meanwhile the girl had brought in a bowl of warm water, steaming with fragrant herbs, from the kitchen near by, and urged the officer, who was leaning at the window, to enjoy the balm it would give. The officer, without a word relieving himself of his cravat and waistcoat, sat down on the chair; and beginning to remove his footwear and whilst the girl, crouching on her knees in front of him, was busy with the little preparations for washing his feet, he dwelled on the attractiveness of her appearance. Her dark hair, copious and wavy, had tumbled down over her young breasts when she knelt; there was a play of quite extraordinary grace about her lips and about the long lashes showing over her downcast eyes; but for her colour, which he found repellent, he would have sworn that he had never seen anything more beautiful. Also he was struck by a faint resemblance, he could not have said with whom, which he had noticed on first entering the house and by which his soul was won over entirely. He seized her when, at her tasks, she stood up, by the hand and judging quite correctly that there was only one way to test whether the girl had a heart or not he drew her down on to his lap and asked if she were already engaged to any man. 'No,' the girl whispered, in a sweet bashfulness, casting down her large black eyes. She added, without moving from his lap, that Konelly, the young negro in the neighbourhood, had admittedly, two or three months before, asked her; but she had refused him because she was too young. The stranger, clasping his hands behind her slim waist, said that in his country, according to a saying there, a girl of fourteen years and seven weeks was old enough to marry.* He asked, while she was contemplating a small golden cross that he wore on his breast, how old she was. — 'Fifteen,' Toni replied. 'Well then,' the stranger said. — 'Does he not have the wealth to set up house with you as you would wish?' Toni, without raising her eyes to him, answered: 'That isn't it. — On the contrary,' she said, letting go the cross she was holding in her hand, 'Konelly is, after recent events, a rich man; his father has acquired the whole plantation which used to belong to the planter, his master.' — 'Then why did you turn his offer down?' the stranger asked. Smiling, he brushed the hair off her forehead and asked: 'Did you not like him?' The girl, quickly shaking her head, laughed; and when the stranger whispered into her ear the teasing question whether perhaps only a white man would ever win her favour, abruptly, after a moment's dreamy reflection and her dark face blushing in an altogether charming way, she pressed herself against him. The stranger, moved by her grace and sweetness, called her his darling girl and, as though released by the hand of heaven from every anxiety, enfolded her in his arms. It was not possible for him to believe that all the shifts of feeling he had seen in her might be merely the sorry outward form of some cold and hideous deceit. The thoughts that had made him anxious departed from him like a host of frightful birds; he rebuked himself for having even for a moment misjudged her heart; and while he rocked her on his knee and breathed in the sweet breath of her lifted mouth he pressed, as though to

signal reconciliation and forgiveness, a kiss upon her forehead. Meanwhile the girl, suddenly and strangely alert, as though someone were
approaching the door along the corridor, had raised herself up;
pensively, dreamily, she put right the scarf over her breast where it had
been displaced; and only when she saw that she had been mistaken did
she turn back with a cheerful face to the stranger and remind him that
the water, if he did not make use of it soon, would grow cold. — 'Well?'
she said, taken aback when he said nothing and only dwelled on her in
thoughtful scrutiny. 'Why are you looking at me with such close
attention?' She did her best, seeing to her bodice, to conceal the
embarrassment that had come upon her, and laughed, saying: 'How odd
you are! What is it you can see in me?' The stranger, passing his hand
over his forehead, said, suppressing a sigh and lifting her down off his
lap: 'A wondrous resemblance between you and a dear friend.' — Toni,
seeing that his cheerfulness had been dispelled, took him in friendly
sympathy by the hand and said: 'With whom?' To which he, after a
moment's thought, began again and said: 'Her name was Mariane
Congreve and she was from Strasburg. I had got to know her in that
town, where her father was a merchant, shortly before the outbreak of
the Revolution and was so fortunate as to be accepted by her and then
to receive her mother's blessing too. Oh, she was the truest soul under
the sun; and the terrible and affecting circumstances in which I lost her
come back to me so forcibly when I look at you that for sadness I cannot
keep from weeping.' 'What?' said Toni, pressing herself close and
warmly against him. 'Is she no longer alive?' — 'She died,' the stranger
answered, 'and I knew the epitome of all goodness and excellence only
at the moment of her death. God knows,' he continued, in his
tribulation laying his head upon her shoulder, 'the fool I was. I made
remarks one evening in a public place about the fearful Revolutionary
Tribunal just then set up. I was denounced, they came looking for me;
and then, not finding me, since I had been lucky enough to escape out of
town, my pursuers, a savage mob, needing a victim, ran to the house of
my betrothed and, only enraged by her truthful assertions that she did
not know where I was, they dragged her, under the pretext that she and
I were in league together, with unbelievable heedlessness, to the place of
execution in my stead. No sooner had this terrible news been brought to
me than I emerged from my hiding place and pushing through the
crowds hurried to the square, crying: "Murderers! Here I am! Here!"
But she, already on the scaffold by the guillotine, when the judges, to
whom, as unlucky chance would have it, I was a stranger, questioned
her she turned away with a look that went into my soul for ever and

answered: "I do not know this man" — whereupon amid shouts and the rolling of drums the blade, as those impatient men of blood had wished, soon fell and severed her head from her body. — How I escaped I cannot tell; I found myself some fifteen minutes later in the house of a friend and from there, continually losing consciousness and half out of my wits, I was got into a carriage and across the Rhine.' — With these words the stranger, letting go of the girl, crossed to the window; and when she saw him deeply moved bowing his face into a handkerchief a human feeling, various in its origin, took hold of her; in a sudden movement she went after him, fell on his neck and mingled her tears with his.

What then ensued it is not necessary to report since any reader, reaching this point, will know. The stranger, when he had composed himself, could not tell where the thing he had done would lead; but for the time he understood this much: that he was saved and that in the house in which he found himself he had nothing to fear from the girl. He tried, when he saw her hugging herself and weeping on the bed, all in his power to calm her. He took off the little golden cross, a gift from the faithful Mariane, his dead betrothed, and bending over her and endlessly caressing her he hung it for a betrothal gift, as he said, around her neck. But when she only wept and would not listen to his words he sat down on the edge of the bed and told her, now stroking her hand, now kissing it, that in the morning he would ask her mother to permit them to marry. He described to her the little property he owned, in freedom and independence, on the banks of the Aare; a house that was comfortable and spacious enough to accommodate her and, if her age would allow her to make the journey, her mother also; fields, gardens, meadows and vineyards; and an elderly father whom she would revere and who would welcome her there with love and gratitude for having saved his son. She wept and wept, her tears were drenching the pillow. He took her in his arms and asked her, deeply moved himself, what harm he had done her and could she not forgive him? He swore that the love he felt for her would never go from his heart and that only in a delirious strange confusion of his senses, by the mixture of desire and fear she aroused in him, had he been led to do such a thing. He warned her at last that the morning stars were in the sky and that if she stayed any longer in his bed her mother would come and discover her there; he urged her, or she would be ill, to get up and take some rest for an hour or so in her own bed; he asked her, being thrown by her state into the most terrible anxiety, whether he should carry her to her bedroom in his arms; but when she gave no answer to anything he said but only lay there among the disordered pillows, her head in her arms in a wordless grief, he had no choice finally, for daybreak was brightening at both windows, but, without more ado, to lift her up and carry her, hung over his shoulder as though she were lifeless, downstairs to her room and there, having laid her on the bed and said again, ceaselessly caressing her, all he had said already, he called her once more his darling bride-to-be, kissed her on the cheeks and hurried back.

So soon as it was quite daylight old Babekan went upstairs to her daughter and, sitting on the bed, divulged to her what her plan was with regard not only to the stranger but also to his travelling companions. Since, she said, it would be two days before the negro Congo Hoango returned, they must at all costs keep the stranger in the house for that time without letting in the family accompanying him, whose presence, because of their numbers, might become dangerous. To this end, she said, her idea was to pretend to the stranger, that, having just had word that General Dessalines and his army were heading into the neighbourhood, they must wait two days until he had gone by, and only then would it be possible to have the family in the house as he, the stranger, wished, the risk otherwise being too great. Those people themselves, she concluded, must in the meantime, so that they would not continue their journey, be given provisions and also, so as to capture them later, must be deluded into believing that they would find a refuge in the house. It was an important matter, she added, for probably the family would have many belongings with them; and she urged her daughter to give her all possible assistance in the plan she had expounded. Toni, half sitting up in bed and a flush of disinclination colouring her face, replied that it was shameful and despicable thus to violate the laws of hospitality on a person inveigled into the house. In her view a man should be doubly safe with them if he were being pursued and he entrusted himself to their protection; and she assured her that, if she did not abandon the wicked plot she had just proposed she, Toni, would go at once and let the stranger know what a murderous den the house was in which he had thought himself safe and sound. 'Toni!' the mother said, hands on hips and staring at her wide-eyed. — 'Truly,' Toni replied, lowering her voice. 'What harm has the young man, not even a Frenchman by birth but, as we have heard, a Swiss, what has he done to us that we should fall on him like robbers and kill him and steal what is his? Do the grievances we have here against the planters count in the part of the island he comes from? Does not rather everything indicate that he is the best and noblest of men and surely not a party to whatever wrongs the blacks may accuse his race of?' — The old woman, while she studied the girl's strange expression, said, with trembling lips, only that she was amazed. Then she asked what harm had the young Portuguese done whom they had clubbed to the ground not long since at the gate. She asked what crime the two Dutchmen had committed who three weeks ago had gone down under the negroes' bullets in the yard. She asked to be told what had been laid at the doors of the three Frenchmen and so many other solitary white men fleeing for their lives who with guns, spears and knives had since the revolt began been put to death in their house. 'By the light of the sun,' the daughter said, rising in passion to her feet, 'you do very wrong to remind me of those bestial deeds. The inhuman things you force me to take part in have for a long time outraged my innermost feelings; and to turn aside from myself God's vengeance for all that has happened I swear to you that I would rather die ten times over than allow a single hair of that young man's head to be harmed so long as he is in our house.' — 'Very well,' said the old woman, suddenly appearing to give in, 'let the stranger go his ways. But when Congo Hoango comes back,' she added, rising to leave the room, 'and learns that a white man has spent the night in our house then you must answer for the pity that moved you to let him leave again despite the explicit commandment we are under.'

After these words in which for all their superficial mildness the old woman's obdurate anger betrayed itself none the less, the girl was left in considerable consternation alone in the room. She was too well aware of the old woman's hatred towards the whites to suppose she would let slip such an opportunity for gratifying it. Fearing that she might at once send to the neighbouring plantations and summon the blacks to overpower the stranger Toni dressed and followed her down without delay into the lower living room. Whilst her mother, looking troubled, moved from the food cupboard where, as it seemed, she had been busy and sat down at a spinning wheel Toni stood by the door to which was affixed a proclamation warning all blacks, on pain of death, not to give protection or shelter to the whites; and just as though with a shock of fear she had realized what a wrong thing she was doing she turned suddenly and, well aware that her mother had been watching her from behind, fell at her feet. She begged, hugging her knees, to be forgiven for the insanities she had uttered in the stranger's favour; blamed it on the state, half dreaming, half awake, she was in when her mother had surprised her, still in bed, with the plans for tricking him, and said that without any reservation she abandoned him to the vengeance of the law of the land which had after all decreed that he be destroyed. The old woman, after a pause during which she looked the girl full in the face,

said: 'By heaven, what you tell me now has saved his life for today at
least. His meal, since you were threatening to protect him, was already
poisoned and would have delivered him into Congo Hoango's power, as
we were ordered to, if not alive then dead.' And so saying she stood up
and tipped a pot of milk, that was standing on the table, out of the
window. Toni stared at her mother in disbelief and horror. The old
woman, sitting down again and raising up the girl still kneeling there,
asked what in the course of a single night had so altered her thinking.
Whether after preparing his bath she had stayed much longer with him?
And whether she and the stranger had had much conversation with one
another? But Toni, greatly agitated, said nothing in reply, or nothing
definite; her eyes cast down she stood holding her head and said she
must have been dreaming; but a glance at her unhappy mother's breast,
she added, quickly stooping and kissing her hand, brought all the cruelty
of this stranger's race to mind; and she assured her, turning away and
burying her face in her apron, that as soon as the negro Hoango arrived
she would see what sort of a daughter she had in her.

Babekan was still sitting deep in thought and wondering what might
be the cause of the girl's peculiar intensity when the stranger, with a note
written in his bedroom inviting the family to spend a few days on the
negro Hoango's plantation, came into the room. He greeted mother and
daughter in a very cheerful and friendly fashion and asked, as he gave
the old woman the note, that somebody be sent into the forest forthwith
and look after his people there according to the promise that had been
made him. Babekan stood up and said, looking uneasy and putting the
note away in the cupboard: 'Sir, we must ask you to return at once into
your bedroom. Many parties of blacks are passing along the highway
and they tell us that General Dessalines is heading this way with his
army. In this house, open to everybody, you will not have any safety
unless you hide yourself in your bedroom which looks out over the yard
and be sure to close your doors and your shutters.' — 'What?' said the
stranger in surprise. 'General Dessalines ...' The old woman interrupted
him: 'Ask no questions,' she said, and beat with a stick three times upon
the floor. 'In your bedroom, where I shall follow you, I will explain
everything.' The stranger, ushered from the room with anxious gestures
by the old woman, turned once more in the doorway and cried: 'But
should we not at least send the family waiting for me a messenger to ...?'
'All will be taken care of,' said the old woman, interrupting him, as the
bastard child, whom we have met already, came in, summoned by the
knocking; and she ordered Toni who, with her back to the stranger was
standing before the mirror, to take up a basket of provisions from the

corner; and mother, daughter, the stranger and the boy went up to the bedroom.

There the old woman, seating herself comfortably in the chair, told how the whole night through on the mountains along the horizon they had seen the flickering of General Dessalines's fires: which was in fact the case, though not a single negro of his army, advancing in a southwesterly direction against Port au Prince, had so far shown himself in their neighbourhood. In this way she managed to plunge the stranger into a turmoil of anxiety which however, by assuring him that even if the worst should happen and they had troops quartered on them, still she would do everything in her power to save him, subsequently she was able to assuage. On his repeatedly urging her at least, if things were so, to succour his family with some provisions she took the basket from her daughter's hand and gave it to the boy, saying: he should go to the Gull Pond among the trees in the hills close by and give it to the family, the stranger's people, he would find there. The officer himself, he should add, was well; friends of the whites who had themselves, on account of the cause they had espoused, suffered a good deal from the blacks were, out of pity, sheltering him in their house. She concluded by saying that just as soon as the highway was free of the blacks expected along it in armed gangs steps would at once be taken to accommodate them also, the family, in the house. — 'Is that clear?' she asked, having finished. The boy, settling the basket on his head, answered that he knew the Gull Pond she had described to him well since he would sometimes go fishing there with his friends and that he would pass on to the foreign gentleman's family camping by it everything just as he had been told to. The stranger, when asked by the old woman whether he had anything to add, took a ring off his finger and gave it to the boy, with the instruction that he should hand it, as a sign that the message he, the boy, was bringing was trustworthy, to the head of the family, Herr Strömli. Thereupon the mother did various things designed, as she said, to ensure the stranger's safety; ordered Toni to close the shutters and herself then, to dispel the darkness ensuing in the room, lit, with a flint and tinder on the mantelpiece, a lamp, but not without difficulty since the tinder would not catch. The stranger took advantage of that moment to put his arm gently around Toni's waist and to whisper into her ear: how had she slept and should he not inform her mother of what had happened? But to the first question Toni made no answer and to the second, escaping from his arm, said: 'No, not if you love me, not a word.' She concealed the dread all these deceitful measures aroused in her; and under the pretext of preparing breakfast for the stranger rushed downstairs into the lower living room.

She took from her mother's cupboard the letter in which the stranger, in his innocence, had invited the family to follow the boy into the settlement, and at the risk that her mother would miss it, resolved if the worst came to the worst to suffer death with him, she raced out after the boy already making his way along the road. For now, before God and her own heart, she saw the young man no longer as merely a guest to whom they had given protection and hospitality but as her betrothed and as her husband and was ready, just as soon as his party were in the house in sufficient strength, recklessly to tell her mother so, knowing very well into what consternation this would fling her. 'Nanky,' she said, after a breathless run catching up with the boy on the road, 'mother has changed her plan for Herr Strömli's family. Take this letter. It is addressed to Herr Strömli, the elderly head of the family, and invites him and all his party to spend a few days in our settlement. — Use your wits, do all you can to bring this about. Congo Hoango the negro will, when he returns, reward you for it.' 'Very good, cousin Toni,' the boy replied. And he asked as he carefully wrapped the letter and put it in his pocket: 'Shall I be the guide for the party on their way here?' 'Indeed so,' Toni replied. 'That goes without saying, since they do not know the country. But you must not, because there might be some movement of soldiers along the highway, begin your journey before midnight; but then move as quickly as you can, so that you arrive here before daylight. — Can we rely on you?' she asked. 'You can rely on Nanky,' the boy answered. 'I know why you want the white refugees in the plantation and Black Hoango will be content with me.'

Then Toni took up breakfast to the stranger and when it was cleared away mother and daughter returned to the front living room, to their household tasks. Some time later, as was bound to happen, the mother went to the cupboard and, naturally, missed the letter. For a moment she laid a hand, doubting her own memory, against her head and asked Toni where she might have put the letter the stranger gave her. Toni answered after a short silence during which she looked down at the floor: that she was sure the stranger had put the letter back in his pocket and upstairs in his room, while they were both there, had torn it up. The mother stared at the girl; she said she was sure she could remember taking the letter from his hand and placing it in the cupboard; but when after much fruitless searching she could not find it there and because, after several such occasions in the past, she did not trust her memory, in the end she had no option but to believe her daughter's version of events. Still she could not conceal how very put out she was by the circumstance; the letter, she said, would have been of the greatest importance to Black Hoango, to bring the family into the plantation. At noon and in the evening, when Toni served the stranger his meals, she several times, as she sat there at the table for some conversation with him, found an opportunity to ask about the letter; but Toni was clever enough to turn the talk or muddle it whenever it came near that dangerous subject; with the result that the mother was not enabled by anything the stranger said to learn for certain what had happened to the letter. So the day passed; after supper, as a precaution, she said, the mother locked the stranger's room; and having then deliberated with Toni by what stratagem they might again next day get possession of such a letter, she withdrew and ordered the girl likewise to go to bed.

As soon as Toni, who had longed for this moment, reached her bedroom and was sure that her mother was asleep she took the image of the Virgin Mary that hung by her bed, placed it on a chair and, clasping her hands, fell on her knees before it. She implored the Redeemer, the Virgin's divine son, in a prayer of infinite fervour, for courage and steadfastness to make to the man to whom she had given herself a full confession of the crimes that burdened her young conscience. She swore that no matter what it cost her heart she would keep nothing back from him, not even the intention, merciless and terrible though it was, in which the day before she had lured him into the house; but because of the steps she had already taken to save him she hoped that he would forgive her and take her with him as his loyal wife to Europe. Wonderfully strengthened by this prayer she rose and took the master key that opened all the rooms of the house and with it, but without a light, down the narrow corridor that divided the building, slowly she made her way to the stranger's bedroom. Softly she let herself in and approached the bed where he lay sleeping in a deep sleep. The moon shone on his youthful face and the night's breezes, entering through the open windows, played with the curls on his forehead. All gentleness, she bowed down over him and called him, breathing his sweet breath in, by his name; but a deep dream, of which she seemed to be the subject, was preoccupying him: at least she heard, again and again, from his passionate and trembling lips the whispered word: 'Toni!' Sadness beyond telling seized hold of her; she could not bring herself to wrench him out of the lovely heaven of his imagination down into the depths of a mean and wretched reality; and in the certainty that he must sooner or later wake of his own accord she knelt by the bed and covered his beloved hand with kisses.

Indescribable then was the horror a few moments later that clutched at her heart when suddenly inside the yard she heard the noises of men, horses and weapons and unmistakably among them the voice of Black Congo Hoango who with all his band had returned unexpectedly from General Dessalines's army. She leapt behind the curtains of the window, taking care to keep out of the moonlight that might have given her away, and heard her mother already informing the negro of all that had happened in the meantime and of the presence of the fugitive European in the house. The negro, in a hushed voice, quietened his men in the yard. He asked the old woman where the stranger was at that moment; she showed him the room and took her chance also at once to tell him of the strange and shocking conversation she had had, concerning the fugitive, with her daughter. She assured the negro that the girl was a traitor and that the whole attempt to capture him was in danger of failing. At least, the girl, in her wickedness, as she, her mother, had observed, had crept secretly when night fell to his bed and was still there in all tranquillity; and it was probable that the stranger, if he had not already fled, was even now being warned and ways and means being discussed to get him away. The negro, who had tried and tested the girl's loyalty on similar occasions in the past, replied: surely that was not possible? And: 'Kelly!' he cried in a rage, and: 'Omra! Bring your guns!' And thereupon, without another word, he and all his blacks following him climbed the stairs and entered the stranger's room.

Toni before whose eyes in the course of a very few minutes this whole episode had occurred, stood there as though lightning had struck her, in a complete paralysis. For a moment she thought of waking the stranger; but in the first place, since the yard was occupied, he had no chance of flight; and in the second she foresaw that he would reach for his weapons and, the blacks so outnumbering him, to be done to death would be his certain fate. Then of all the things she was bound to consider the most terrible was this: the unhappy man, if he found her by his bedside at that juncture, would believe she had betrayed him and instead of listening to her advice would in the madness of so desperate a delusion dash without the least pause for thought into the very arms of Black Hoango. In this unspeakable dread she caught sight of a length of rope which, heaven knows by what chance, was hanging from a beam in the wall. God Himself, she thought, tearing it down, had placed it there to be the salvation of herself and her friend. She entwined the young man with it at hands and feet with many loops and knots; and when, though he woke and struggled, she had drawn the ends tight and fastened them around the bedstead then, in her happiness at having got command of the situation, she pressed a kiss upon his lips and hurried to confront the negro Hoango already rattling on the stairs.

The negro, still not believing what the old woman had said on the subject of Toni, came, when he saw her emerging from the room in question, there on the corridor with his followers and their weapons and torches, astonished and in confusion to a halt. 'Traitor!' he cried. 'Renegade!' And turning to Babekan, who had advanced a few paces towards the stranger's door, he asked: 'Has the stranger gone?' Babekan, who had found the door open but had not looked in and was, as she returned, beside herself with rage, cried out: 'Deceitful devil! She has let him escape. Quick, stop the exits or he'll be clean away.' 'What is the matter?' Toni asked, looking in apparent astonishment at the old negro and the blacks surrounding him. 'The matter?' Hoango replied, and with that seized her by the bodice and dragged her to the room. 'Have you gone mad?' Toni cried, pushing the old man, stopped dead by the sight that met him, away from her. 'There is the stranger, tied up by me while he slept, and by heaven it is not the worst thing I ever did.' And so saying she turned her back on him and sat down, as though she were weeping, at a table. The old man turned to the mother standing in confusion a little aside, and said: 'Oh Babekan, what tales are these you have been telling me?' 'Thanks be to heaven,' the mother answered, examining, in some embarrassment, the cords fastening the stranger, 'he is still there. Though what the meaning of all this is I do not know.' The negro, putting his sword back into its scabbard, stepped to the bed and asked the stranger who he was, where he had come from and where he was going. But when he, struggling desperately to free himself, made no reply except, in tones of terrible sorrow: 'Oh Toni, oh Toni!' the mother intervened and said he was a Swiss, Gustav von der Ried by name, and that with a whole family of filthy Europeans, presently in hiding near the Gull Pond in the ravines, he had come from Fort Dauphin on the coast. Hoango, who saw the girl resting her head in sadness on her hands, approached her, called her his darling, pinched her cheeks and asked her to forgive him the overhasty suspicions he had voiced. The old woman, who likewise had approached the girl, stood with hands on hips, shaking her head, and asked: Why, since the stranger was wholly ignorant of the danger he was in, had she tied him to the bed with cords? Toni, in truth weeping for grief and rage, replied, suddenly facing her mother: 'Because you are blind and deaf. Because he knew very well what danger he was in. Because he was going to escape, because he had asked me to help him escape, because he had a scheme against your very life and at daybreak, without a doubt, if I had not tied him up while he

was asleep, would have executed it.' The old man caressed and soothed
the girl and ordered Babekan to say nothing more on the subject. He
called forward a few men with guns to visit at once upon the stranger
the penalty he had fallen liable to; but Babekan whispered secretly in his
ear: 'For heaven's sake, no, Hoango!' — She took him aside and put it
to him that the stranger, before they executed him, must compose an
invitation by means of which the family, whom it would be in many
respects dangerous to engage with in the forest, could be lured into the
plantation. — Hoango, considering that the family would almost
certainly be armed, thought this proposal a good one; he set, since it was
too late to get the letter written as agreed, two sentries over the fugitive
white man; and having, to make sure, examined the cords and also,
finding them too loose, summoned a couple of men to pull them tighter,
he left the room, he and all his fellows, and gradually the household
settled down to sleep.

But Toni who, as the old man squeezed her hand again, had said
goodnight but only made a pretence of going to bed, got up again as
soon as she saw that the house was quiet, crept out through a back gate
into the open country and ran, nearly mad with desperation, on a path
crossing the highway towards the region from which Herr Strömli's
family would be bound to come. For the contempt in the looks the
stranger had given her from his bed had cut into her heart as painfully as
knives; into her love for him there entered also now something bitter
and burning, and she rejoiced in the thought of dying in this attempt to
save him. She took up a position, anxious not to miss the family, against
the trunk of a pine tree past which, if the invitation had been accepted,
the family must come, and scarcely had dawn, the time agreed, begun to
show its first light along the horizon than the voice of Nanky, the boy
who was serving the people as their guide, could be heard in the distance
among the forest trees.

The company consisted of Herr Strömli and his wife, the latter riding
on a mule; their five children, two of whom, Adelbert and Gottfried,
young men of eighteen and seventeen, were walking by the mule; three
servants and two maids, one of whom, with an infant at her breast, was
riding the other mule; twelve persons in all. They were proceeding
slowly down the track bumpy with roots, to the pine: when Toni, as
quietly as she could, to startle nobody, stepped forward out of the
shadow of the tree and called: 'Halt!' The boy recognized her at once
and upon her asking him who Herr Strömli was, whilst men, women
and children surrounded her, he cheerfully introduced her to the elderly
head of the family, Herr Strömli. 'Sir,' said Toni, in a firm voice

interrupting his courtesies, 'Black Hoango and all his band have, to our surprise, returned to the settlement. You cannot now without great peril to your lives go in there; moreover your cousin who, unhappily for him, was given refuge there, is lost unless you take up your weapons and to free him from the captivity in which Black Hoango is holding him, follow me.' 'God in heaven!' all the family, seized with terror, cried; and the mother, who was sick and whom the journey had exhausted, fell from the mule to the ground in a faint. Whilst the maids, summoned by Herr Strömli, hurried forward to help their mistress, Toni, the youths assailing her with questions, for fear of the boy Nanky, took Herr Strömli and the other men aside. She told them, unable as she did so to hold back her tears of shame and remorse, all that had happened; what the circumstances were in the house when the young man entered it; how her conversation alone with him had changed them beyond all understanding; what almost mad with fear she had done when the negro arrived and how she would now lay down her life if need be to deliver him out of the captivity into which she herself had thrown him. 'My weapons!' cried Herr Strömli, hurrying to his wife's mule and taking out his musket. He said, as Adelbert and Gottfried, his strapping sons, and the three trusty servants likewise armed themselves: 'More than one of us owes his life to cousin Gustav; now is our chance to repay him'; and so saying he lifted his wife, who had recovered, back on to the mule; ordered that the boy Nanky, as a sort of hostage, should, as a precaution, have his hands tied; sent the whole party of women and children under the sole protection of his thirteen-year-old son Ferdinand, also armed, back to the Gull Pond; and having questioned Toni, who had herself put on a helmet and taken up a spear, about the strength of the blacks and their disposition in and around the yard and promised her to spare in the coming action if at all possible both Hoango and her mother, bravely, trusting in God, he placed himself at the head of his little army and, led by Toni, set off for the plantation.

Toni, as soon as the band had crept in at the back gate, showed Herr Strömli the room in which Hoango and Babekan were sleeping; and whilst Herr Strömli silently entered the open house with his people and possessed himself of all the blacks' muskets there stacked together, she slipped away to the sheds where Seppy, the five-year-old half-brother of Nanky, slept. For Nanky and Seppy, old Hoango's bastard children, were very dear to him, and especially the latter whose mother had died not long since; and because even if they were able to free the young man from his captivity the return to the Gull Pond and their flight thence to Port au Prince, which she intended joining, would still expose them to many difficulties: she judged, not incorrectly, that holding the two boys as a sort of surety would be of great advantage to the company, should the blacks pursue them. She managed, without being seen, to lift the boy from his bed and carry him still half asleep into the main house. Herr Strömli meanwhile had, as stealthily as possible, got into the doorway of Hoango's room with his men; but instead of finding him and Babekan in bed as he had thought, both, woken by the noise, were up, though helpless and half naked, and standing there in the middle of the room. Herr Strömli, raising his musket, cried to them to surrender or be killed; but Hoango, by way of an answer, snatched a pistol from the wall and fired it off, grazing Herr Strömli's head, into the group. Herr Strömli's men, at this signal, fell upon him furiously; Hoango, after firing a second time and drilling one of the servants through the shoulder, was wounded in the hand by a sabre blow and both then, he and Babekan, were flung to the floor and bound with cords to the legs and struts of a heavy table. Meanwhile, woken by the firing, Hoango's blacks, more than a score of them, had rushed from their lodgings in the yard, and hearing old Babekan's screaming within the house they pressed forward furiously against it, to get possession of their weapons again. In vain did Herr Strömli, whose wound was of no significance, place his men at the windows and have them fire into the mob, to hold them in check; two were killed, and lay in the yard, but the rest made nothing of this and were fetching axes and crowbars to stave in the house door which Herr Strömli had bolted when Toni, shaking with fear and carrying the boy Seppy in her arms, entered Hoango's room. Herr Strömli, very glad of her arrival, snatched the boy from her arms; and turning to Hoango and drawing his hunting knife, he swore he would kill the child on the spot unless he shouted to the blacks that they must desist. Hoango, whose strength was broken by the slash across three fingers of his hand and who, had he refused, would have put his own life at risk, replied after a moment's thought and getting them to raise him from the floor: that he would do it. Led by Herr Strömli he stood at the window and waving, in his left hand, a handkerchief over the yard he called to the blacks that since no help was needed to save his life they should leave the door alone and return to their sleeping quarters. There was a lull in the battle; Hoango, at Herr Strömli's bidding, sent a black captured in the house down into the yard with a reiteration of the order; and though the blacks lingering and deliberating there could not comprehend what was happening still they were bound to heed the words of this formal ambassador and they abandoned their intended assault, for which all the preparations had been made, and one by one, though muttering and cursing, they withdrew to the sheds. Herr Strömli, having the boy Seppy's hands tied in full view of Hoango, told this latter: that his intention was, quite simply, to release the officer, his cousin, from the custody imposed upon him in the plantation and that so long as no obstacles were placed in the way of their flight to Port au Prince neither Hoango's life nor the lives of his children, who would be restored to him, were in any danger. Babekan, whom Toni approached and whose hand, with an emotion she could not suppress, she sought to clasp, thrust her violently away. She called her contemptible and treacherous and said, averting her face where she lay against the table-leg: God's vengeance, even before she had any pleasure from her shameful act, would overtake her. Toni replied: 'I did not betray you; I am a white and betrothed to the young man you are holding captive; I belong to the race you are in open warfare with and will answer to God for having aligned myself with them.' Then Herr Strömli set a guard over Hoango whom, as a precaution, he had had bound again and fastened to the door posts; he had the servant, who was lying unconscious on the floor with a shattered collar bone, lifted up and carried away; and having said again to Hoango that he could collect both children, Nanky as well as Seppy, in a few days' time, in Sainte Lucie where the first French outposts were, he took Toni, a prey to various feelings and unable to keep from weeping, by the hand and led her, cursed by Babekan and old Hoango, out of the bedroom.

Adelbert and Gottfried meanwhile, Herr Strömli's two sons, had hurried as soon as the first and chief battle at the windows was over, on the orders of their father, into their cousin Gustav's room and had been lucky enough, after a fierce resistance, to overcome the two blacks guarding him. One lay dead in the room; the other, with a severe bullet wound, had dragged himself as far as the corridor. The brothers, one of whom, the elder, was wounded, though only slightly, in the thigh, released their much loved cousin; they embraced and kissed him and in jubilation, giving him weapons, urged him to follow them into the front room where, since victory was won, Herr Strömli was doubtless making all preparations for their withdrawal. Cousin Gustav however, sitting up in bed, pressed them warmly by the hand; but beyond that he was quiet and seemed distracted and instead of seizing hold of the pistols they offered him he raised his right hand and rubbed his brow, more sorrowful in his appearance than can be said. The young men, who had sat down by him, asked what was the matter; and when he put his arms around them and in silence laid his head on the younger one's shoulder, Adelbert was getting to his feet to fetch him some water, wrongly supposing him to be feeling faint: at which moment Toni, the boy Seppy on one arm and Herr Strömli leading her by the hand, entered the room. Seeing her Gustav went pale; he stood up, holding tight, as though he might collapse, to both his friends; and before these two young men knew what he wanted with the pistol which he now took from them, he had fired it, his mouth twisting with rage, at Toni. She was hit full in the chest; and when she with a broken noise of pain still took some steps towards him and, before him then, handing the child to Herr Strömli, sank down: he flung the pistol over her away, pushed her from him with his foot and, calling her a whore, flung himself down on the bed again. 'Monster!' cried Herr Strömli and his sons. The youths fell on their knees by the girl and shouted, as they lifted her up, for one of the old servants who had on several similar desperate occasions done the work of a doctor for their party; but the girl, clutching at her wound, pressed her friends away and 'Tell him ...', she gasped, the rattle in her throat, pointing at the man who had shot her and said again: 'Tell him ...' 'What must we tell him?' Herr Strömli asked, for death was robbing her of her voice. Adelbert and Gottfried stood up and shouted to the man who had done this inconceivably terrible killing: did he know that the girl was his rescuer? That she loved him and that it had been her intention to flee with him, for whose sake she had sacrificed everything, parents and possessions, to Port au Prince? — They thundered 'Gustav!' in his ears, asked was he deaf, shook him and pulled him by the hair since he lay there insensible and not heeding them on the bed. Gustav sat up. He glanced at the girl there writhing in her blood and the rage that had caused this deed gave way naturally to a feeling of common pity. Herr Strömli, weeping for grief into his handkerchief, asked: 'Wretch, why did you do it?' Cousin Gustav, who had risen from the bed and, wiping the sweat from his brow, was contemplating the girl, replied: that in her wickedness she had bound him in the night and handed him over to Black Hoango. 'Oh!' Toni cried and with an indescribable look reached out her hand towards him: 'My dearest friend, I bound you because ...' But she could not speak nor could she reach him with her hand; she fell with a sudden lapsing of her strength back into Herr Strömli's lap. 'Why?' Gustav asked, white in the face and kneeling down to her. Herr Strömli, after a long silence broken only by Toni's agony, having hoped in vain for an answer from her, spoke up himself and said: 'Because, you unhappy man, once Hoango had arrived there was no other means of saving you; because she wanted to prevent the fight you would for certain have had to fight, because she wanted to win time until we, already hurrying here by her arrangement, could force your freedom with weapons in our hands.' Gustav hid his face. 'Oh,' he cried, without looking up, and felt the ground was opening under his feet, 'is what you tell me true?' He put his arms around her and stared, torn all to pieces by his grief, into her face. 'Oh,' Toni cried, and they were her last words, 'you should not have mistrusted me.' And so saying she breathed the beautiful spirit from her body. Gustav tore his hair. 'Oh that is true,' he said, as his cousins dragged him from the corpse: 'I shouldn't have mistrusted you, for you were betrothed to me by a vow even though we never said so.' Herr Strömli, sobbing, put back the clothing off the girl's breast. He urged the servant who, with a few inadequate instruments, was standing by him, to extract the bullet which, as he thought, must have lodged in the breastbone; but all their efforts were, as we have said, in vain; the lead had drilled her through and her soul had already departed to some better star. — Gustav meanwhile had gone to the window; and whilst Herr Strömli and his sons, weeping silently, were discussing what to do with the body and whether they ought not to summon the mother: Gustav blew his brains out with the other pistol's bullet. This new atrocity deprived his relatives of all power of comprehension. They turned now with their efforts to help him; but the poor man's skull was entirely shattered and parts of it, since he had put the pistol in his mouth, were hung around the walls. Herr Strömli was the first to pull himself together. For since daylight was already shining with full brightness through the windows and also word came that the blacks had appeared again in the yard there was nothing for it but to turn at once to the business of withdrawal. They laid the two bodies, which they were unwilling to abandon to the casual violence of the blacks, on a board and having reloaded the muskets the sorrowful procession set off for the Gull Pond. Herr Strömli, the boy Seppy on his arm, led the way; after him came the two strongest servants carrying the bodies on their shoulders; the wounded man, with a stick, tottered behind; and Adelbert and Gottfried, with muskets cocked, accompanied the slowly proceeding cortège on either side. The blacks, seeing how weak the company was, emerged from their quarters with spears and pitchforks, and seemed disposed to attack; but Hoango, whom they had taken the precaution of releasing, came out on the house steps and signalled the blacks to be still. 'In Sainte Lucie!' he called to Herr Strömli who, with the bodies, was already passing through the gate. 'In Sainte Lucie!' he replied; whereupon the procession, without pursuit, emerged into the fields and reached the trees. At the Gull Pond, when they rejoined the family, with much weeping they dug the bodies a grave; and having then exchanged the rings both wore on their hands they lowered them, with silent prayers, into the abode of eternal peace. Herr Strömli was fortunate enough, with his wife and children, to reach Sainte Lucie five days later and there, keeping his promise, he left the two black boys. Shortly before the start of the siege he entered Port au Prince and fought there on the walls in the whites' cause; and when the city after a stubborn defence fell to General Dessalines he escaped with the French army on to the English fleet. The family crossed then to Europe and without further misadventure reached their native country, Switzerland. Herr Strömli, with the remains of his small fortune, bought himself a property near the Rigi; and in 1807 among the bushes of his garden the monument was still to be seen that he had set up in memory of Gustav his nephew and Gustav's betrothed, the faithful Toni.

THE BEGGARWOMAN OF LOCARNO

At the foot of the Alps, near Locarno in Northern Italy, there stood a country house, belonging to a marquis, which nowadays, if you come from the Saint Gotthard, you see lying in ruins: a house with high and spacious rooms in one of which once, on straw thrown down for her, an old woman, in ill health, who had come to the door begging, was given a bed by the lady of the house, out of pity. The Marquis who, returning from the hunt, happened to go into that room, it being where he kept his gun, impatiently ordered the old woman to get up from the corner in which she was lying and remove herself to behind the stove. As the woman rose her crutch slid from under her on the polished floor and she fell, hurting her back in a dangerous way; with the result that she did, though with unspeakable difficulty, get to her feet and go diagonally across the room as she had been told to, but behind the stove, with groans and sighs of pain, she sank down and died.

Some years later when the Marquis, through war and poor harvests, had got into financial difficulties, a Florentine nobleman called on him, wishing, on account of its fine situation, to buy his house. The Marquis, to whom the sale was a matter of great importance, instructed his wife to accommodate their guest in the above-mentioned room which was unoccupied and very beautifully and splendidly furnished. But to the couple's great consternation the nobleman, in the middle of the night, came down to them, distressed and white in the face and swearing that by heaven the room was haunted, for something, invisible to the eye, with a noise as if it had been lying on straw, had risen in the corner of the room and with audible steps, slowly and feebly, had gone in a diagonal across the floor and behind the stove, with groans and sighs of pain, sunk down.

The Marquis, fearful, he did not himself know why, with an affected cheerfulness laughed at the Florentine and said he would rise at once and to set his mind at rest spend the night in the room with him. But the Florentine asked would he be so kind as to let him spend the night there, in an armchair, in the Marquis's own bedroom, and when morning came he called for his carriage, said his goodbyes, and departed.

This occurrence, which made a very great stir, frightened off, much to the Marquis's chagrin, several buyers; and so, since among his own servants, in a disquieting and incomprehensible way, it was being said that in that room at the hour of midnight something *walked*, he, wishing by a decisive move to put a stop to this talk, decided to investigate the matter himself the following night. How shaken he was then, at the first stroke of the witching hour, actually to hear the incomprehensible sounds; it was as if somebody rose from straw with a rustling, went in a diagonal across the room, and behind the stove with a sighing and a rattle in the throat sank down. The Marquise, the next morning, when he came down, asked him how the investigation had passed off; and when, looking about him with frightened and uncertain eyes and having locked the door, he assured her that it was true about the ghost: then never in her life had she been so afraid, and begged him, before he let it be widely known, to put the matter in her presence cold-bloodedly once more to the test. But, with a faithful servant whom they had fetched in with them, they did indeed, the following night, hear the same incomprehensible and ghostly sounds; and only the urgent desire to be rid of the house at all costs enabled them to suppress in the presence of their servant the terror by which they were seized and offer for the occurrence some insignificant and accidental cause which it was surely possible to discover. On the evening of the third day when the two of them, to get to the bottom of the mystery, again, with beating hearts, climbed the stairs to the guest room it happened that the household dog, let off his chain, was at that door; and without saying as much but perhaps in the involuntary wish that some living creature should be there besides themselves, they took the dog with them into the room. Man and wife, two lights on the table, the Marquise still fully dressed, the Marquis with sword and pistols, taken from the cupboard, to hand, seated themselves, towards eleven, each on a separate bed; and whilst they made conversation the best they could the dog curled up in the middle of the room and went to sleep. But then, exactly at midnight, the terrible sounds were heard again; someone, not able to be seen with human eyes, rose up on crutches in the corner of the room; the straw rustled; and at the first step, tap, tap, the dog woke, leapt to its feet, pointed its ears, growled, barked, just as if someone were advancing at it, and backed away, towards the stove. Seeing this the Marquise, her hair on end, rushed from the room; and whilst the Marquis, seizing his sword, called out 'Who's there?' and, nobody answering, slashed at the air in all directions like a madman, she called for her carriage, resolved to leave for the town at once. But flinging together a few belongings, she had scarcely rattled out of the gates when she saw the house going up in flames from every quarter. The Marquis, unhinged by his terror, weary of his life, had taken a candle and set the place, panelled throughout with wood, alight at all four corners. In vain she sent people in to save the unhappy man; he had lost his life already in the most lamentable way; and his white bones, gathered together by the country people, still lie in the corner of the room from which he had told the beggarwoman of Locarno to get up.

THE FOUNDLING

Antonio Piachi, a wealthy Roman broker, was sometimes obliged to travel great distances on business. Then he would usually leave his young wife *Elvire* behind in Rome, in the care of her relatives. One of these journeys brought him, with the eleven-year-old *Paolo*, his son by his first wife, to Ragusa. As it happened, a plague-like sickness had broken out there, greatly alarming the town and the environs. Piachi, only getting word of it when he was on his way, halted in the suburbs, to make enquiries as to its nature. But when he heard that the evil seemed to be worsening day by day and that there was talk of shutting the gates of the town, concern for his son outweighed all commercial interest: he took horses and drove away again.

He noticed, once he was clear of the town, a boy near his carriage whose hands were outstretched like a petitioner's and who seemed to be greatly agitated. Piachi halted the carriage; and to the question: what did he want? the boy, in his innocence, replied: he was infected, the police were after him to fetch him into the hospital where his father and mother had already died; he begged Piachi, by everything holy, to take him with him and not let him perish in the town. And he seized the old man's hand, pressed and kissed it and let his tears fall there. Piachi's first horrified instinct was to fling the boy far away from him; but when he at that moment lost his colour and fell to the ground in a faint the old man, in his goodness, was moved to pity: together with his son he got down, laid the boy in the carriage, and drove away, having not the least idea, however, what he should do with him.

At the first staging post he was in discussion with the innkeeper as to how he might be rid of the boy again when on the orders of the police, who had got wind of the matter, he was arrested and, under escort, he, his son, and Nicolo, as the sick boy was called, were brought back to Ragusa. All Piachi's protests at the cruelty of this measure were in vain;

arriving in Ragusa all three, under guard, were removed to the hospital where Piachi did not sicken and Nicolo, the boy, recovered from the sickness: but the son, the eleven-year-old Paolo, was infected by the latter and three days later died.

Now the gates were reopened and Piachi, having buried his son, was given permission to travel by the police. In the throes of his grief he had just got into his carriage and at the sight of the empty seat beside him had taken out his handkerchief, to weep: when Nicolo, cap in hand, approached the carriage and wished him a safe journey. Piachi leaned out through the door and asked him, in a voice broken by violent sobs, would he like to come with him. The boy, just as soon as he had understood the old man, nodded and said: yes, indeed he would; and when the guardians at the hospital, being asked by the merchant whether the boy was allowed to get in, smiled and assured him that he was a child of God whom nobody would miss, Piachi, much moved, lifted him into the carriage and took him, in place of his own child, with him to Rome.

On the road, outside the gates of the city, the land broker for the first time looked closely at the boy. He had a peculiar, rather frozen beauty, his black hair hung down over his forehead in plain ringlets, darkening a face which, serious and intelligent, never changed in its expression. The old man asked him several questions which however he answered only briefly: taciturn and introverted he sat there in the corner, his hands in his pockets, and gazed with shy and thoughtful eyes at things as the carriage hurried by. Now and again, with quiet little movements, he fetched a handful of nuts out of the bag he had on him, and, whilst Piachi wiped the tears from his eyes, took them between his teeth and cracked them open.

In Rome Piachi, briefly explaining what had happened, introduced him to Elvire, his excellent young wife who, it is true, thinking of Paolo, her little stepson whom she had greatly loved, could not hold back a heartfelt rush of tears; but strange and stiff though Nicolo was as he stood there before her, still she pressed him to her bosom, made over to him the bed in which Paolo had slept and gave him, as a present, all that child's clothes. Piachi sent him to school where he learned to read and write and do arithmetic and since, as may be easily imagined, the boy was dear to him for having cost him dear after only a few weeks, with the kind consent of Elvire, who could not hope for children now from the old man, he adopted him as his own son. Later, after dismissing a clerk whom he had found for a variety of reasons unsatisfactory, he was delighted, having replaced him in the comptoir with Nicolo, to see the latter managing his many and complex affairs with very great energy and success. Only one fault could his father, a sworn enemy of bigotry, find with him: that he had dealings with the monks of the Carmelite monastery who, on account of the considerable fortune that would fall to him one day in the old man's will, were very devoted to the youth; and only one fault his mother: that there stirred in him, rather early, as it seemed to her, a liking for the female sex. For he was only fifteen when, whilst consorting with the aforementioned monks, he was seduced by a certain *Xaviera Tartini*, the concubine of her bishop, and although he was at once, by the strict orders of Piachi, obliged to break off the liaison Elvire had many grounds for believing that his self-denial in that dangerous area was by no means great. But when Nicolo in his twentieth year married *Constanza Parquet*, a young and lovable Genoese, Elvire's niece, brought up in Rome under her supervision, the latter fault at least seemed blocked at its source; both parents were united in their satisfaction with him and, by way of showing it, they set him up splendidly, vacating a large part of their fine and extensive dwelling house in his favour. In brief, when Piachi was sixty, he did the last and greatest thing he could do for him: retaining only a small capital for himself, he made over to him, in proper legal form, the whole fortune on which his property business rested and with the good and faithful Elvire, who had few wishes in the world, he went into retirement.

There was a strain of quiet sadness in Elvire's character, the legacy of an affecting incident in her childhood history. Philippo Parquet, her father, a well-to-do dyer in Genoa, had a house which, as his trade required, backed on to the sea with an edge of square-cut stone; great beams fitted into the gable, on which the dyed cloths were hung, stuck out several yards above the water. Once, in an unhappy night, when the house caught fire and immediately, as though the place were made of pitch and sulphur, the blaze went up with a crackling in all the rooms together composing it, Elvire, then thirteen, chased everywhere by the flames, fled from floor to floor, and found herself, not knowing how, on one of these beams. The poor child, hanging between heaven and earth, had not the least idea how she might save herself; behind her the burning gable, the fire there, whipped along by the wind, already eating into the beam, and below her the wide and desolate and frightful sea. She was about to commend herself to all the saints and, choosing the lesser of two evils, leap into the waves; when suddenly a young Genoese, of a patrician family, appeared in the gable door, flung his cloak over the beam, seized hold of her and, with as much courage as dexterity, by means of one of the wet sheets hanging from the beam, let himself down with her into the sea. There they were taken up by gondolas afloat in the harbour and brought ashore amid the loud rejoicing of the people; but it transpired that this heroic young man, even as he was making his way through the house, had been severely injured in the head by a stone falling from an upper ledge, and soon, losing consciousness, he collapsed. The Marquis, his father, into whose mansion he was brought, seeing how long he was recovering, called doctors in from all over Italy who trepanned him on more than one occasion and took out several bones from the inside of his skull; but all their arts, by some incomprehensible dictate of heaven, were in vain: only rarely, supported by Elvire, whom his mother had summoned to nurse him, could he leave his bed; and after three years of lying sick and in much pain, during which time the girl never quitted him, once more he gave her his hand affectionately, and died.

Piachi, who did business with that gentleman's house and indeed had got to know Elvire there while she was nursing him and had married her two years later, was very careful never to mention his name in her presence or otherwise remind her of him; for he knew how violently it shook her frail and beautiful spirit if he did. The least thing reminding her however remotely of the time when the youth suffered for her and died would always move her to tears, and then she could not be comforted or calmed; wherever she might be she would leave and nobody went after her for they had learned that there was no cure but to let her exhaust her grief herself by solitary weeping. Only Piachi knew the reason for these strange and frequent crises, since never in her life had she uttered a single word concerning the event. It was usual to blame them on her nervous system left over-excitable after a high fever into which she had fallen immediately after her marriage; and that put an end to any further enquiries into their cause.

Now it happened that Nicolo, unbeknown to his wife, pretending to visit a friend, had gone in secret to the carnival in the company of Xaviera Tartini with whom, despite his father's prohibition, he had never quite ended his liaison, and in the costume he had chosen, which was, by chance, that of a Genoese nobleman, he came home late in the night when all were sleeping. As luck would have it the old man had suddenly felt unwell and to see to him in the absence of the maids Elvire had risen and gone into the dining room to fetch him a bottle of vinegar. She had just opened a cupboard in the corner and, standing on the edge of a chair, was searching among the glasses and the carafes: when softly Nicolo opened the door and with a candle he had lit in the hall and with plumed hat, cloak and sword passed through the room. Safely, not seeing Elvire, he reached the door that led to his bedroom and had just, to his consternation, found it locked: when Elvire behind him with bottles and glasses in her hands, catching sight of him, fell as though struck by invisible lightning from the chair she was standing on to the tiled floor. Nicolo, white with shock, turned and was about to hurry to the aid of the unfortunate lady; but since the noise she had made must necessarily alert Piachi his fear of a rebuke overcame all other considerations: in desperate haste he tore a bunch of keys from her that she had on her hip and finding one that fitted threw them back into the room and vanished. Soon afterwards, when Piachi, sick though he was, had sprung from his bed and lifted her up and when maids and servants also, at his ringing of the bell, had appeared with lights, Nicolo too came in, in his dressing gown, and asked what had happened; but since Elvire, her tongue stiff with terror, could not speak and beside her only he himself could give any answer to that question, the circumstances remained in eternal mystery; Elvire, trembling in all her limbs, was carried to bed and lay there several days in a violent fever, but did then by her own resources of health get over the accident and but for a strange melancholy, which remained, made a fair recovery.

A year went by and Constanze, Nicolo's wife, gave birth, and died with the child. This event, sad enough in the loss of a virtuous and dutiful creature, was doubly so in that it opened the way again to Nicolo's two passions, his bigotry and his love of women. Again now, pretending to console himself, he passed whole days in the monastery with the Carmelites and yet it was well known that in her lifetime the love and loyalty he had shown his wife were scant. Indeed, Constanze was not even buried when Elvire, entering his room one evening to discuss the funeral arrangements, found a girl with him who, painted and kilted up, was known to her only too well as Xaviera Tartini's maid. Elvire cast down her eyes at the sight, turned without saying a word and left the room; to neither Piachi nor to anyone else did she mention this occurrence but sick at heart only knelt and wept by the corpse of Constanze, who had loved Nicolo dearly. But as it happened Piachi, who had been in town, met the girl as he returned and fully understanding what her business had been he accosted her angrily and part by subterfuge, part by force, he got from her the letter she was carrying. He went to his room to read it. In it, as he had expected, Nicolo begged Xaviera, in very urgent terms, to tell him when and where he might meet her as he longed to. Piachi sat himself down and replied, disguising his handwriting, in Xaviera's name: 'At once, before nightfall, in the church of Mary Magdalene' — sealed the note with a seal that was not his own and had it delivered, as though it came from the lady herself, to Nicolo's room. The stratagem was entirely successful; there and then Nicolo took his cloak and forgetting Constanze, who lay in her open coffin, left the house. At that Piachi, deeply offended, cancelled the next day's splendid funeral, had the corpse, the coffin still open, lifted by bearers, and accompanied only by Elvire, himself and one or two relatives, had it laid down all in silence in the vault of Mary Magdalene, which had been made ready. When Nicolo, wrapped in his cloak and standing in an aisle of the church, to his astonishment saw a funeral procession approaching, of people all well known to him, he asked old Piachi, who was following the coffin: what this meant and whom were they carrying. But Piachi, his prayerbook in his hand, did not raise his head, and answered merely: 'Xaviera Tartini': whereupon the coffin, just as though Nicolo were not present, was unlidded again, the corpse blessed by those in attendance, and sunk then and sealed in the vault.

This event, deeply shaming to him, quickened a burning hatred against Elvire in his unhappy heart; for he thought that the humiliation visited upon him by Piachi in front of everyone was her doing. For several days Piachi said not a word to him; but because, on account of what he stood to inherit from Constanze, he needed Piachi's favour and goodwill, he felt obliged to seize hold of the old man's hand one evening and to promise him, with every appearance of remorse, that he would cast off Xaviera at once and for ever. But he was little disposed to keep this promise; on the contrary, the efforts to thwart him only fuelled his defiance and schooled him in the art of eluding the honest Piachi's surveillance. It was also the case that Elvire had never seemed to him more beautiful than at that moment when, for his undoing, she had opened the door of the room in which the girl was present, and closed it again. By the distaste then softly inflaming her cheeks, her face, that was gentle and only rarely moved by any passion, was made infinitely attractive to him; it seemed to him incredible that she, among so many enticements, should not sometimes herself follow the path for the plucking of whose flowers she had just and in so shameful a fashion punished him. And should that be the case, he burned to serve her in the old man's eyes as she had him, and wanted and sought nothing but the opportunity to put this purpose into practice.

One day then, at a time when Piachi was not at home, he was passing Elvire's room and to his surprise heard speech within. Malevolent hopes flashed through him on the spot and he bent with ears and eyes to the keyhole, and saw — in heaven's name! She lay there rapturously at somebody's feet, and though he could not make out who the person was he did hear very clearly and uttered in the accents of love the whispered word: 'Colino.' With beating heart he pressed himself back into the window on the corridor from where, without betraying his purpose, he could observe the entrance to the room; and supposed, at a noise made very softly by the bolt, that the inestimably precious moment had arrived when he would be able to unmask the hypocrite: but instead of the stranger he was expecting, Elvire herself, without any companion and casting his way from a distance an indifferent glance, emerged from the room. She had a length of linen under her arm that she had woven herself; and having locked the room with a key which she took from her hip she reached for the banister and went calmly downstairs. This dissimulation, this feigned nonchalance, seemed to him the height of impudence and cunning and scarcely was she out of his sight than he ran to fetch a master key and, first casting anxious looks all around, furtively he opened the door. To his astonishment he found the room quite empty and could discover nothing even resembling a human being in any of the four corners into which he spied: except, set up in a recess behind a red silk curtain and lit by a particular light, the life-sized picture of a young nobleman. Nicolo was shocked, he could not himself have said why: and face to face with the portrait, whose large eyes stared at him fixedly, he was visited by a whole host of thoughts and feelings: but before he could collect and order them the fear seized him that he might be discovered and punished by Elvire; and more than a little confused he locked the door again and went his ways.

The more he thought about this strange encounter the more important seemed to him the picture he had discovered and a curiosity as to whose portrait it was tormented him ever more keenly. For by her whole posture, when he had spied on her, she looked to be on her knees and he was certain that the person she had knelt before was the young nobleman on the canvas. Restless in his thoughts and unable to rid himself of them he went to Xaviera Tartini and told her of his wondrous experience. She, sharing his interest in the undoing of Elvire, since it was from her that all the difficulties in their dealings with one another stemmed, said she would like to see the portrait set up in Elvire's room. For she could boast a very large acquaintance among the noblemen of Italy and if the one in question had ever been in Rome and was of any consequence she might hope to recognize him. And before long, as luck would have it, Piachi and Elvire went into the country one Sunday, to visit a relative. Nicolo, as soon as the coast was clear, hurried to Xaviera and showed her, as a stranger, under the pretext of looking at paintings and embroidery, together with a little daughter she had from the Cardinal, into Elvire's room. But there, to Nicolo's amazement, the moment he lifted the curtain little Klara (that was the child's name) cried out: 'Heavens above, Signor Nicolo, it is a picture of you!' — Xaviera said nothing. The picture did indeed, the longer she looked at it, strikingly resemble him; especially if she imagined him, as in her memory she easily could, in the noble costume he had worn only a few months before to go in secret to the carnival with her. Nicolo tried, by joking, to counter the sudden blush suffusing his face. Kissing the little girl, he said: 'True enough, my darling Klara, the picture is as much like me as you are like the man who thinks himself your father.' — But Xaviera, bitter feelings of jealousy starting in her heart, gave him a glance and said, stepping to the mirror, that in the end it did not matter who the person was; bade him a rather cool goodbye and left the room.

This scene, as soon as Xaviera had gone, threw Nicolo into a great excitement. Joyfully he remembered the strange and violent shock he had given Elvire by his fantastical appearance in that night. The thought that he had aroused a passion in a woman parading as a model of virtue worked in him almost as much as did his desire to be revenged on her; and since a prospect now opened up to him of being able to combine the two interests in one act of satisfaction it was with very great impatience that he awaited Elvire's return and the moment when, by looking her in the eye, his wavering conviction would be crowned. Nothing gave him pause in all the rampage of his feelings except the definite memory that Elvire had addressed the picture she was kneeling before, when he spied on her through the keyhole, as Colino; but even this name, not very usual in those parts, had in its sound more than one element which, he did not know why, encouraged him to dream sweet dreams; and faced with the choice: which sense to disbelieve, his eyes or his ears? — naturally he inclined the way most gratifying to his desires.

But several days elapsed before Elvire came back from the country and since she brought with her from the house of the cousin she had visited a young female relative who wished to see the sights of Rome, when Nicolo, in very amiable fashion, helped her from the carriage she, busy being kind to her companion, merely glanced at him and the look said nothing. Several weeks were given over to the guest in the house and passed in more bustle than was usual there; within and without the city they visited everything likely to interest a young girl enjoying life as she did; and Nicolo, who because of his business in the comptoir was not invited on these trips, fell again, with respect to Elvire, into the worst possible mood. He began again, with very bitter and tormenting feelings, to think of the man unknown to him whom she in her secret devotions idolized; and these feelings tore at his dissolute heart especially when at last, as he had long desired, the young relative departed and that evening Elvire instead of now conversing with him sat for a whole hour at the dinner table in silence and busying herself with some small piece of womanly work. By chance a few days previously Piachi had enquired after a box of little ivory letters with which Nicolo had been taught as a boy and which now, since no one had any further use for them, Piachi had thought of giving away to a child in the neighbourhood. The maid asked to search them out from among many other old things had been unable to find more than the six making up the name: *Nicolo*; doubtless because the others, not being so connected with the boy, had been neglected and, on one occasion or another, thrown away. Now when Nicolo took up the letters, which had been lying on the table for some days, and whilst he, resting his arm on the surface and sunk in troubled thoughts, was idling with them he discovered — quite by chance indeed, for he was more astonished than ever in his life before — the combination which spelled the name: *Colino*. Nicolo, unaware until then of the anagrammatic properties of his name, was assailed again by furious hopes and cast a shy and uncertain glance at Elvire sitting beside him. The kinship thus revealed between the two words seemed to him more than mere chance; containing his joy he considered what scope this strange discovery might have, and taking his hands off the table he awaited with a beating heart the moment when Elvire would look up and see the name lying there openly. Nor was he at all deluded in his expectations; for no sooner had Elvire, resting a moment from her work, noticed that the letters were set out and innocently and unthinkingly, since she was a little shortsighted, bent over them, to read them: than she glanced in a strangely embarrassed way at Nicolo gazing down at them in apparent indifference; and with a sadness beyond all words took up her work again and blushing faintly let fall, unnoticed as she believed, tear upon tear into her lap. Nicolo, aware, without looking at her, of this inner trouble, felt certain now that in rearranging the letters so that they spelled Colino her only purpose was to hide his own name. He saw her with a gentle movement suddenly shuffle them and his mad hopes reached the summit of certainty when she stood up, put her work aside and disappeared into her bedroom. He was about to rise himself and follow her when Piachi entered and heard from a maid, when he asked where Elvire was, that she felt unwell and was lying down. Piachi, not showing much alarm, went to see what she was doing; and when a quarter of an hour later he returned with the news that she would not be coming to table and said not another word on the subject: then Nicolo believed he had found the key to all the mysterious scenes of that kind he had witnessed in the past.

Next morning, when he in his shameless joy was busy considering what advantage he might hope to draw from this discovery, he received a note from Xaviera asking him to come and see her since she had things to tell him concerning Elvire which would interest him. Xaviera had, through the bishop who kept her, very close dealings with the Carmelite monks; and since his mother went to confession in their church Nicolo felt certain that it would be possible for Xaviera to gather information about the secret history of her feelings which could corroborate his unnatural hopes. But after a strange and teasing welcome from Xaviera he was unpleasantly disabused when she with a smile drew him down beside her on the sofa and said: she felt bound to tell him that the object of Elvire's love was a man already twelve years in his grave. — Aloysius the Marquis of Montferrat, to whom an uncle in Paris, in whose house he had been brought up, had given the name *Collin*, later, in Italy, changed for fun to *Colino*, was the original of the portrait he had discovered in Elvire's room in the niche behind the red silk curtain: the young Genoese nobleman who in so chivalrous a fashion had rescued her from the fire when she was a child and had died of the injuries received in doing so. — She finished by begging him not to make any use of this information since it had been confided to her in the monastery under the seal of the most extreme secrecy by a person who himself had no real right to it. Nicolo, flushed in the face and white again by turns, assured her that she had nothing to fear; and being quite unable under Xaviera's teasing looks to conceal the embarrassment into which this revelation had thrown him, he pretended that he had business that called him away, and, his upper lip twitching in a hideous manner, he took his hat, said his goodbyes, and left.

Humiliation, lust and vengefulness combined now to breed the foulest act that ever was committed. He knew full well that he could have no access to the pure heart of Elvire but by deception; and no sooner had Piachi, departing to spend some days in the country, left the coast clear than he made preparations to execute the satanic plan he had devised. He procured for himself precisely the same costume in which a few months earlier returning home from the carnival at night he had appeared to Elvire; and wearing cloak, cape and plumed hat in Genoese style just as they were in the portrait, he crept, shortly before she would

retire to bed, into her room, hung a black cloth over the picture standing
in the recess and waited there, a staff in his hand precisely in the pose of
the young patrician, Elvire's idol, as the artist had painted him. Made
perspicacious by his shameful passion, as he had calculated so exactly
did it come to pass: for no sooner had Elvire, entering soon afterwards
and quietly and calmly undressing, no sooner had she, as was her wont,
drawn back the curtain covering the recess and seen him there, than she
cried out: 'Colino! Beloved!' and fell down in a faint on the tiled floor.
Nicolo stepped out; he stood for a moment sunk in the contemplation of
her delicate beauties paling even as he looked under the kiss of death;
but soon, since there was no time to lose, took her in his arms and
tearing down the black cloth from the picture carried her to the bed that
stood in the corner of the room. That done, he went to lock the door,
but found it locked already; and certain that even after the return of her
troubled consciousness she would offer no resistance to his fantastic
and, as it must seem, unearthly appearance, he went back to the bed and
sought to wake her with passionate kisses on her breasts and mouth. But
Nemesis, who follows hard on the heels of evildoers, had willed it that
Piachi, whom the wretch thought absent for several more days, should
return home unexpectedly at that very moment; softly, thinking Elvire
already asleep, he approached along the corridor and because he always
had the key with him he was able suddenly, without a noise giving any
warning, to enter the room. Nicolo stood thunderstruck; he threw
himself, since his wickedness could not possibly be covered up, at the
old man's feet and, promising he would never raise his eyes to look upon
his wife again, begged for forgiveness. And indeed Piachi was disposed
to settle the matter quietly; bereft of all words by what Elvire told him as
she, in his arms, with a terrible glance at the miscreant, recovered, all he
did was draw the curtains around the bed she lay on, take a whip from
the wall, open the door for Nicolo and show him the way he should
depart forthwith. But Nicolo, through and through a tartuffe, seeing the
failure of his first procedure, stood up abruptly and declared: he, the old
man, was the one who must vacate the house, for he, Nicolo, given
possession of it by valid documents, was the owner and would uphold
his rights against the world if necessary. — Piachi could not believe his
ears; as though disarmed by this unprecedented impudence he laid the
whip aside, took up his hat and stick and ran at once to his old friend in
the law Doctor Valerio, rang till a maid emerged and opened for him
and reaching his room fell down senseless by his bed, before he could
utter a word. Doctor Valerio, taking him and later also Elvire into his
house, hurried the very next morning to secure the arrest of the satanic

malefactor, who had many advantages; but while Piachi made what feeble moves he could to dislodge him from the properties once transferred to him, he, armed with an assignment to him of everything in them, fled to the Carmelites, his friends, and called on them to protect him against the old fool wishing to evict him. In brief, when he agreed to marry Xaviera, whom the bishop wanted rid of, wickedness triumphed and the government, petitioned by that man of the cloth, issued a decree confirming Nicolo in the property and commanding Piachi not to importune him.

Piachi had the day before buried the unhappy Elvire who, as a consequence of a high fever brought on by that event, had died. Maddened by this double grief he went, with the decree in his pocket, into the house and, given strength by his rage, flung Nicolo, a weaker man, down and crushed his skull against the wall. By the people in the house he was not observed until he had done the deed; they found him kneeling over Nicolo and stuffing the decree into his mouth. That done he stood up and surrendered all his weapons; was imprisoned, tried and condemned to death by hanging.

In the Papal States there is a law by which no criminal can be put to death until he has received absolution. Piachi, when the staff was broken over him, stubbornly refused absolution. In vain having tried all the means religion disposes of to bring home to him the culpability of his behaviour it was hoped that by the sight of the death awaiting him he might be shocked into a feeling of remorse, and he was led out to the gallows. There stood a priest who, in a voice like the last trump, conjured up for him all the horrors of hell into which his soul was about to descend; and there stood another with the body of Christ, the sacred means of forgiveness, in his hand and said how desirable were the mansions of everlasting peace. — 'Will you partake of the blessing of redemption?' both asked him. 'Will you not take communion?' — 'No,' Piachi answered. — 'Why not?' — 'I do not wish to be among the blessed. I wish to go down into the deepest pit of hell. I wish to find Nicolo again, and he will not be in heaven, and resume my revenge that I could not completely accomplish here.' — And so saying he climbed the ladder and called on the hangman to do his office. In brief, they were obliged to halt the execution and conduct the unhappy man, whom the law protected, back to jail. For three days following the same attempts were made, and always with the same success. When on the third day, not having been hanged, he was obliged to come down the ladder: in a savage gesture he raised his hands and cursed the inhuman law that would not let him go to the hell. He called on all the host of devils to come and fetch him; swore that his only wish was to be executed and damned and threatened to seize the first priest he could by the throat if he must, to get his hands on Nicolo in hell. When this was reported to the Pope he ordered that he be executed without absolution; he went without a priest and in silence, in the Piazza del Populo, he was strung up.

SAINT CECILIA *or* THE POWER OF MUSIC
(A Legend)

Around the end of the sixteenth century, when the image-breakers were raging in the Netherlands, three brothers, young men studying in Wittenberg, and a fourth, a predicant in Antwerp, met in Aachen. They were there to claim an inheritance left them by an old uncle, whom none of them had known; and having nobody in the place who might have accommodated them they put up at an inn. Some days later, days which they spent listening to the predicant's account of the remarkable scenes occurring in the Netherlands, it happened that the convent of Saint Cecilia,* situated at that time outside the walls, was to celebrate the Feast of Corpus Christi in a grand way; and the four brothers, fired up by youth and fervour and the Dutch example, resolved that the city of Aachen too should be given the spectacle of a bout of image-breaking. The predicant,* who had led such enterprises more than once already, gathered together, on the evening before, a number of young students and sons of tradespeople, all adherents of the new doctrine, and they passed the night at the inn, eating and drinking and cursing the papists; and when daylight had risen over the towers of the city they armed themselves with axes and with all manner of implements of destruction, to begin their violent work. Gleefully they agreed on a signal at which the smashing of the windows bright with stories from the bible would commence; and sure that among the townsfolk there would be much support they proceeded, in the determination to leave not one stone standing on another, into the church as the bells began to ring. The Abbess, warned at daybreak by a friend of the danger the convent was in, sent in vain on several occasions to the imperial officer commanding in the town for soldiers to protect the building. The officer, himself an enemy of the papists and as such, covertly at least, well disposed towards the new doctrine, suited his own position by assuring her that she was imagining things, that not the faintest semblance of any danger threatened her convent; and refused her the guard. Meanwhile the hour had come at which the ceremonies were to begin, and the nuns, with prayers, in fear and in a pitiable anticipation of the things that were said to be going to occur, prepared themselves for mass. Their only protector was the advocate of the place, a man of seventy, who took up his stance at the church door with a few armed stablemen. In the convents it is, as is well known, the nuns themselves who, skilled in the playing of every sort of instrument, perform their own music; and often with a precision, an understanding and a sensibility which, perhaps because of the femaleness of this mysterious art, one misses in orchestras of men. Now it so happened, to make their predicament doubly distressing, that the director of music, Sister Antonia, who was the usual conductor of the orchestra, had a few days earlier fallen gravely ill of a nervous fever;* with the result that the convent, besides the four blasphemous brothers, already noticed in their cloaks against the pillars of the church, had also over the performance of a fitting music a very keen anxiety. The Abbess, who on the evening of the previous day had ordered that they perform an ancient mass, by an unknown Italian master, with which the choir and orchestra had often, because of an especial holiness and splendour in its composition, already been notably successful, sent down again, insisting on her wishes more than ever, to Sister Antonia, to ask after her health; but the nun who did this errand returned with the news that the sister was lying there quite unconscious and that it was wholly unthinkable that she should direct the intended music. Meanwhile in the church, into which more than a hundred miscreants of all ages and classes, armed with axes and crowbars, had found their way, alarming scenes had already taken place. Some of the stablemen, standing at the doors, had been subjected to very indecent teasing and against the nuns, who were to be seen from time to time, singly, at their religious duties, in the nave or the aisles, things of a most insolent and shameless nature had been uttered; so that the advocate came to the sacristy and begged the Abbess on his knees to halt the ceremony and seek the protection of the commandant in town. But the Abbess was not to be moved, and insisted that the Feast in the deity's honour must be celebrated. She reminded the advocate that it was his duty to protect, with his life if necessary, the mass and the solemn proceedings that were to be held in the church; and, the hour striking precisely then, she ordered the nuns who were around her in fear and trembling to take an oratorio, no matter which nor of what worth it might be, and by performing it to make a start at once.

The nuns, in the organ gallery, were preparing to do so; the score of a work they had often performed was being distributed; violins, oboes and contrabasses were being checked and tuned; when suddenly Sister Antonia, fit and well, a little pale in the face, appeared at the top of the steps. She was carrying the score of that ancient Italian mass, on whose performance the Abbess had been so insistent, under her arm. To the nuns' astonished question where had she come from and how was it she had recovered so suddenly, she replied: 'No matter, friends, no matter'; distributed the score she was carrying and sat down herself, with a burning enthusiasm, at the organ to take over the direction of the wonderful work. Thereupon it was as if the comfort of heaven miraculously entered the hearts of those pious women; at once they stood in their places with their instruments; the anxiety they felt itself contributed to a conducting of their souls, as though on wings, through every heaven of harmony; the oratorio was performed with all possible musical splendour; not a breath stirred during the whole rendition in any of the pews or aisles; especially during the *salve regina* and even more so during the *gloria in excelsis* it was as if all those congregated in the church were dead; with the result that despite the four godforsaken brothers and their supporters not even the dust on the paving stones was wafted away, and the convent survived until the end of the Thirty Years War when, by an article in the Treaty of Westphalia,* it suffered dissolution after all.

Six years later, long after this event had been forgotten, the mother of the four young men arrived from The Hague and instituted, on the unhappy grounds that her sons had completely disappeared, judicial enquiries with the authorities in Aachen as to what road they might have taken from there. The last anyone in the Netherlands, where in fact they belonged, had heard of them was, she reported, a letter written before that period of six years, on the evening before a feast of Corpus Cnristi, by the predicant to his friend, a schoolteacher in Antwerp, in which, with great good humour, or rather unbridledness, he gave, on four closely written sides, prior notice of a planned action against the convent of Saint Cecilia, which the mother, however, was not prepared to be more particular about. After various unsuccessful efforts to discover the whereabouts of the persons whom the distressed woman was seeking it finally came to mind that for a period of years roughly matching that in the statement four young people, whose country and origins were unknown, had been inmates of the city's madhouse, founded, at the solicitous instigation of the Emperor, only recently. But since they were suffering from the abnormal development of a religious idea, and their behaviour, as the court dimly remembered having heard, was of an exceedingly morbid and melancholic kind, this was so unlike the brothers' character, which unhappily their mother knew all too well, that she could not give much credence to the suggestion, especially since it almost seemed to be the case that the persons concerned were Catholics. None the less, being strangely affected by various items in the description of them, she did one day, accompanied by a servant of the court, make her way to the madhouse and asked the overseers to be so kind as to give her access to and a chance to observe the four unhappy and deranged individuals in their custody. But beyond all words was the poor woman's horror when at the first glance as she came through the door she recognized her sons. They were sitting in long black gowns around a table on which stood a crucifix and they seemed, leaning forward in silence with folded hands, to be adoring it. When the woman, bereft of all her strength and sinking into a chair, asked what the men were doing the overseers answered: quite simply, they were engaged in the glorification of the Saviour, believing themselves, so they said, better able than others to perceive in him the true Son of the one and only God. The overseers added that the youths had lived this ghostly life for six years now; that they slept very little and took very little food; that not a sound passed their lips; except that at the hour of midnight they would rise from their seats and then, with voices that threatened to shatter the windows of the house, intone the *gloria in excelsis*. The overseers concluded by assuring her that with all this the young men were physically in perfect health; that there was undeniably a certain albeit very solemn and ceremonious cheerfulness in their bearing; that they, if anyone called them mad, would shrug their shoulders pityingly; and that they had more than once declared: that if the good citizens of Aachen knew what they knew they would lay aside their affairs and would, as the brothers did, gather around the crucifix of the Lord and sing the *gloria*.

The woman, not able to bear the grisly spectacle of these unfortunates and soon, unsteady in her limbs, asking to be taken home, went on the morning of the following day, for some enlightenment as to the cause of this monstrous occurrence, to one Veit Gotthelf, a cloth merchant well known in the town; for this man was mentioned in the predicant's letter and had been, as that letter revealed, a more than willing party to the projected destruction of the convent of Saint Cecilia on the day of the Feast of Corpus Christi. Veit Gotthelf, the cloth merchant, who had in the intervening time married, fathered several children and taken over his own father's considerable trade, received the woman with great kindness; and when he learned what her business with him was he locked the door and, having obliged her to sit down, he spoke as follows: 'My dear lady, I was six years ago a close associate of your sons. So long as it is not your intention to involve me in any proceedings on that count, then I do candidly and without reserve admit to you that we did indeed have the intention referred to in the letter. What caused our action, planned with great exactness, with a truly fiendish cleverness, to fail, is beyond my comprehension. Heaven itself seems to have taken the godly women's house into its own holy protection. For I must tell you that your sons, by way of leading into their more drastic interventions, had in their wantonness done things to disrupt the service once or twice already; more than a hundred miscreants from within our, in those days, errant city were there with axes and wreaths of pitch and only waiting for the signal, which the predicant was to give, to raze the church to the ground. However, at the onset of the music your sons suddenly in one simultaneous movement and in a manner very striking to us removed their hats; then, seeming deeply and inexpressibly moved, they bowed their faces into their hands and the predicant, after a momentous pause, suddenly turned and in a loud and terrible voice called to us all that we should likewise bare our heads. In vain did some companions with whispers and by boldly nudging at him with their elbows urge him to give the signal for the image-breaking to begin; the predicant, instead of answering, fell with his arms crossed on his breast to his knees and in a murmur, together with his brothers, pressing his forehead fervently into the dust, repeated one after another all the prayers which shortly before he had been ridiculing. Confused in their deepest hearts by this spectacle, the mob of pitiable fanatics, robbed of their ring-leaders, stood there undecided and inactive until the oratorio, coming down upon them with wonderful fullness from the gallery, was concluded; and since on the orders of the commandant at precisely that moment several arrests were made and certain malefactors who had indulged in disorderly acts were taken up by the watch and led away, all the wretched gang could do was remove themselves from the house of God with all possible speed under the protection of the congregation then dispersing. That evening, having several times enquired in vain at the inn after your sons, who had not returned, I went out terribly disquieted with a few friends to the convent again and asked the doorkeepers, who had given assistance to the imperial watch, if they knew where they were. My dear lady, how shall I describe to you my horror when I saw those four men still, as they had been, lying with clasped hands, kissing the floor with breast and brow, as though they were turned to stone, in passionate fervour stretched out flat before the altar! In vain did the advocate, arriving at that very moment, tug at their sleeves, shake them, and urge them to leave the church in which by now it was quite dark and no other human being present; like dreamers, half getting to their feet, they never heeded him, until he had his men lift them by the arms and lead them out through the great door and there, finally, although with sighs and frequently, in a heartrending way, turning to look back at the great church which shone behind us splendidly in the sunlight, they followed us into town. Gently, kindly, we asked again and again, the friends and I, as we returned, what in the world, what terrible thing capable of thus reversing their innermost being, had happened to them; they pressed our hands, gazing at us with affection; cast down their eyes in a deep thought and from time to time, oh with an expression that still breaks my heart, wiped away tears. Coming back to their rooms then, they plaited themselves a cross, rich in significance and pleasing to look upon, out of birch twigs and set it down, pressed into a small mound of wax, between two lamps with which the maid appeared, on the big table in the middle of the room, and whilst their friends, whose number was growing by the minute, stood aside wringing their hands and in scattered groups, speechless with grief, were spectators of their silent ghostly doings, they, as if their senses were closed to any other phenomena, went down on their knees around the table and, clasping their hands, prepared to worship. They wanted neither the food brought them by the maid as they had ordered it that morning for the feasting of their friends, nor later, at nightfall, the beds which, as they seemed tired, she put up for them in an adjoining room; and the friends, so as not to excite the indignation of the landlord, whom this performance disconcerted, were obliged to seat themselves at a copiously laden table on one side and to consume the dishes prepared for a numerous company, salting them as they did so with their bitter tears. Then suddenly midnight struck; your four sons, attending for a moment to the muffled sound of the bell, suddenly, all with one movement, rose from their seats; and as we, laying down our napkins, looked across at them in an anxious apprehension of what after this strange and disconcerting start might now ensue, they began, in terrifying and hideous voices, to intone the *gloria in excelsis*. Leopards and wolves sound much the same, I should say, when in the icy wintertime they bellow at the firmament; the pillars of the house, believe me, shuddered and the windows, smitten by the invisible breath of their lungs, rattled and, as though being pelted with handfuls of gravel, threatened to shatter. At this grisly occurrence we lost all composure, our hair stood on end, we fled; we dispersed, leaving hats and coats behind, into the surrounding streets which very soon, instead of with us, were filled with more than a hundred people frightened out of their sleep. The crowd, bursting open the outside door, pressed forward up the stairs into the dining room to seek out the source of that vile and horrendous bellowing which, as from the lips of sinners everlastingly damned, drove up from the deepest depths of the flames of hell to reach God's ears, piteously begging mercy. Finally, at the stroke of one, having heeded neither the anger of the innkeeper nor the deeply troubled cries of the people surrounding them, they closed their mouths; they wiped their foreheads with a cloth, for the sweat was falling in great drops on chin and breast; spread out their cloaks and lay down, to rest for a while from such a work of torment, on the tiled floor. The innkeeper, letting them have their way, as soon as he saw them sleeping made the sign of the cross over them; and glad to be free of the misery for the moment, with the promise that the morning would bring a change for the better he persuaded the throng still present and muttering among themselves, to leave the room. But alas, at the first crowing of the cock those unhappy men rose up and began again, in the presence of the cross on the table, the same barren and ghostly monastic life that only exhaustion had momentarily obliged them to break off. From the innkeeper, whose heart was melted by the pitiable sight of them, they would accept neither exhortation nor any help; they begged him to give a polite refusal to all their friends whose habit it had been to gather regularly in their company on the morning of every day; they wanted nothing of him except bread and water and, if possible, some straw for the night; with the result that the innkeeper, who in the past had made a good deal of money out of their cheerful spirits, now saw himself obliged to report the whole business to the authorities and to beg them to rid his house of these four people, in whom the devil himself must surely be at work. Whereupon, on the orders of the magistrates, they were examined by doctors and, being found mad, were, as you know, given rooms in the madhouse which, through the mercy of the late emperor, for the benefit of unfortunates of this kind, had been established within the walls of our city.' All this was said by the cloth merchant, Veit Gotthelf, and other things too which, believing that for an insight into the inner workings of the matter we have already said enough, we here suppress; and he again requested that, should there be any legal enquiries into this event, the woman would in no way implicate him in them.

Three days later when the mother, shaken in her innermost heart by this account, had, on the arm of a friend, gone out to the convent in the melancholy intention of, on a walk, the weather being fine, seeing with her own eyes the terrible place itself where God as though with invisible lightnings had destroyed her sons, the women found the great church, because building work was going on just then, blocked at the entrance with planks and through openings in the boards when, with difficulty, they lifted themselves up, all they could see of the inside was the wonderfully luminous rose window at the far end. On a light and intricate scaffolding many hundreds of workmen, singing cheerfully, were busy raising the towers a good third higher and covering their roofs and spires, until then only slated, with a strong bright copper that shone in the rays of the sun. Stormclouds meanwhile, deep black with gilded edges, stood in the sky behind the work of building; the thunderstorm had already spent itself over the region of Aachen and having once or twice more flung its by now feeble lightning in the direction of the church it sank, dissolving into vapour, muttering discontentedly, down in the east. It happened that as the women, from the steps of the convent's extensive living quarters and sunk in a variety of reflections, were contemplating this double spectacle, a nun, passing by, happened to learn who the woman standing there in the doorway was; with the result that the Abbess, who had heard of a letter she was carrying on the subject of the Feast of Corpus Christi, sent the sister down at once and asked the woman from the Netherlands to come up. She then, although for a moment shocked, nevertheless prepared herself, with all proper reverence, to obey the order which had been transmitted to her; and whilst her friend, following the nun's invitation, stepped aside into an antechamber hard by the main entrance, for the Dutch woman, who had to climb a flight of stairs, the double doors of the ornate upper room itself were opened. There she found the Abbess, a noble woman, still and queenly in her appearance, sitting in a chair and resting her feet on a stool that stood on dragon's claws; and at her side, on a lectern, lay a musical score. The Abbess, having ordered that the visitor be given a chair, explained to her that she had already heard of her arrival in the city, through the mayor; and having then, in a kindly way, asked after the condition of her unhappy sons and having urged her, regarding the fate that had befallen them, since nothing could alter it, to be as composed as possible, she expressed a wish to see the letter which the predicant had written to his friend, the schoolteacher in Antwerp. The woman, who had enough experience of the world to realize what might ensue from doing this, was for a moment thrown into uncertainty; but since it was impossible, seeing the Abbess's venerable face, not to trust her unconditionally and quite improper to suppose that her intention might be to make any public use of the contents, she did not deliberate much longer, but took the letter out of her bosom and gave it to her, fervently kissing that majestic lady's hand. The mother then, whilst the Abbess was reading the letter, glanced at the score which lay carelessly opened on the music stand; and since through Veit Gotthelf's account it had occurred to her that surely the power of the music itself had, on that terrifying day, destroyed and confused the minds of her poor sons, she turned to the sister standing behind her chair and asked timidly: whether this was the musical work which six years ago on the morning of that remarkable Feast of Corpus Christi had been performed in the church. When the young sister answered: yes, she remembered hearing of it and that since then, when not needed, its usual place was in the room of the most reverend Abbess herself, the mother, deeply troubled, rose and, agitated by a variety of thoughts, stood in front of the lectern. She gazed at the strange and magical signs with which, as it seemed, some terrible spirit was mysteriously marking out its own domain, and seemed to feel the earth gape under her when she saw that the score was open, precisely, at the *gloria in excelsis*. It was as if the whole horror of the mysteries of composition which had undone her sons was gathering with a rushing noise about her head; she felt as if by the mere sight of the score she was losing her wits and having then quickly, with a movement of infinite humility and obedience to divine omnipotence, pressed the page to her lips, she resumed her seat. Meanwhile the Abbess had read the letter to the end and, folding it, she said: 'God Himself, on that wondrous day, protected the convent against the sinful pride of your grievously errant sons. What means He employed in doing so may be of no interest to you, as a Protestant; also, you would scarcely comprehend what I could say to you on that subject. For the fact of the matter is this: nobody knows who it was who, in all the urgency of that terrible hour, when the image-breakers were about to fall on us, calmly sitting at the organ directed the work that you see opened there. By a document drawn up the following morning in the presence of our advocate and several other men and deposited in the archives it is attested that Sister Antonia, the only person capable of conducting the work, throughout the whole time of its performance lay in the corner of her cell sick, unconscious, absolutely incapable of moving her limbs; a sister who, being a blood relative, had been charged with her bodily care, did not, throughout the whole morning whilst the Feast of Corpus Christi was being celebrated in the church, move from her bedside. Indeed, Sister Antonia would without any doubt herself have testified to the fact that it was not she who, in so strange and disconcerting a way, appeared in the organ gallery, had the utter loss of her senses not prevented her from being asked and had she not that very evening, as a result of the nervous fever she lay ill of and which earlier had not seemed to threaten her life, died. Moreover, the Archbishop of Trier, to whom the event was reported, has uttered the only explanation of it; namely, that it was Saint Cecilia herself who performed that at once terrible and glorious miracle; and I have now had from the Pope a missive which confirms this.' And with that she gave back to the woman, promising to make no use of it, the letter which she had only asked to see in order to have more detailed information on what she knew already; and having then enquired whether there was any hope that her sons might recover and whether she could perhaps, with money or some other support, contribute anything towards that end, to which the woman, kissing her skirt and weeping, answered no, she raised a hand in a gesture of kindly farewell and dismissed her.

Here this legend ends. The woman, whose presence in Aachen was entirely useless, went back, leaving a small sum of money with the authorities for the benefit of her poor sons, to The Hague and there, a year later, much affected by what had happened, she returned to the bosom of the Catholic Church; her sons, however, died, at a great age, a cheerful and contented death, having once more, after their habit, sung the *gloria in excelsis*.

THE DUEL

Duke Wilhelm von Breysach who, since his secret union with a countess, Katharina von Heersbruck by name, of the house of Alt-Hüningen, who seemed below him, had lived in enmity with his half-brother Count Jakob Rotbart, was returning home towards the end of the fourteenth century, on the evening before the feast of St Remigius,* from a meeting in Worms with the German Emperor who had, at his request, agreed to legitimize, since none of the children of his marriage had survived, his natural son, Count Philip von Hüningen, born to his wife before their marriage. Looking to the future more cheerfully than at any time throughout his reign he had already reached the park which lay behind his castle: when suddenly, by an arrow loosed from out of the darkness of the trees, his body, hard under the breastbone, was transfixed. Friedrich von Trota, his chamberlain, deeply shocked by this occurrence, conveyed him with the help of some other knights into the castle where in the arms of his distressed wife he barely had the strength to read out the imperial act of legitimation to a meeting of vassals hastily convened by that lady; and when, not without strong opposition, since by law the throne went to his half-brother Jakob Rotbart, the vassals had done his last bidding and, on condition the Emperor would allow it, had recognized Count Philip as heir to the throne, his mother however, since he was a minor, as guardian and regent: Duke Wilhelm laid himself down and died.

The Duchess now without more ado, merely sending a deputation to her brother-in-law Count Jakob Rotbart, to inform him, ascended the throne; and what by several knights of the court, who reckoned to have seen through the latter's secretive nature, had been foretold did indeed, at least to all appearances, come about: shrewdly weighing up the situation Jakob Rotbart swallowed the wrong his brother had done him; at least, he refrained from taking any steps to thwart the Duke's last wishes, and heartily congratulated his young nephew on achieving the throne. He told the members of the deputation, receiving them very cheerfully and amiably at his table, that since the death of his wife, who had bequeathed him a royal amount, he lived a free and independent life in his own castle; that what he loved were the wives of the neighbouring nobility, his own wine and, in the company of some hearty friends, the hunt; and that a crusade to the Holy Land, on which he hoped to atone for the sins of his hasty youth still amassing, alas, as he grew older, was now the only enterprise to which, at the end of his life, he was looking forward. Bitterly but in vain did his two sons, raised in the definite hope of succeeding to the throne, reproach him for his nonchalant, unfeeling and very unexpected acquiescence in this unforgivable slighting of their claims; in a few contemptuous words he ordered them, still only youngsters, to be silent; obliged them, on the day of the great funeral ceremonies, to accompany him into town and there, at his side, as was proper, to see the old Duke, their uncle, lowered into the tomb; and having then in the throne room of the ducal palace, like all the other grandees of the court, in the presence of the Regent sworn his allegiance to the young prince, he returned to his castle, refusing all offices and honours offered him by that lady and taking with him the blessings of the people by whom for his generosity and moderation he was now doubly revered.

The Duchess, after this unexpectedly satisfactory settling of the first important matters, turned now to her second duty as regent, which was to begin the hunt for her husband's murderers, a whole pack of whom, it was claimed, had been seen in the park; and to that end she herself, together with Godwin von Herrthal, her chancellor, examined the arrow by which the Duke's life had been ended. But they found nothing about it that might have betrayed its owner, except perhaps that it was surprisingly elegant and splendid in its manufacture. Strong, crisped and brilliant feathers were mounted in a shaft of dark walnut full of grace and power; the end was clad in shining bronze and only the extreme tip, sharp as a fishbone, was of steel. The arrow seemed to have been made for the armoury of a man of wealth and standing, either one involved in feuds or a great lover of hunting; and recently, as a date inscribed in the grip revealed. The Duchess therefore, on the advice of the Chancellor, circulated the arrow, bearing the royal seal, among all the workshops in Germany and Switzerland to discover the master craftsman who had fashioned it and, if that were achieved, to find out from him the name of the man for whom it had been fashioned.

Five months later Lord Godwin, the Chancellor, to whom the

Duchess had handed over the entire investigation of the matter, received word from an arrowsmith in Strasburg that he, three years previously, had made three score such arrows and the quiver to go with them for Count Jakob Rotbart. The Chancellor, greatly astonished by this communication, held it back in his secret cabinet for several weeks; in part because he was, despite the Count's rather profligate life, too convinced of the nobility of his nature to suppose him capable of so abominable a crime as the murder of a brother; and in part not convinced enough of the Regent's sense of justice, despite her many other excellent qualities, to proceed in a matter concerning her worst enemy otherwise than extremely cautiously. Meanwhile in secret he followed the line of enquiry suggested by that strange pointer and when by chance through officials in the city Chancellery he discovered that the Count, who never or only very rarely left his castle, had done so during the night of the Duke's murder: then he thought it his duty to drop the secrecy and at one of the next sessions of the council to inform the Duchess in detail of the disturbing and strange suspicion that these two accusing facts cast on her brother-in-law Count Jakob Rotbart.

The Duchess, who thought herself fortunate to be on such friendly terms with the Count, her brother-in-law, and was above all else fearful of upsetting and angering him by any hasty steps, gave now, to the Chancellor's surprise, no sign at all of being pleased by this equivocal revelation; on the contrary, having read the papers twice with close attention, she expressed, with some vehemence, her displeasure that so uncertain and fraught a matter had been raised in open council. She was of the opinion that it must be a mistake or a slander and refused absolutely to allow the charge to be brought before the courts. Indeed, given the extraordinary, almost fanatical respect in which the people, naturally enough perhaps, had held the Count since his being cut off from the throne, the mere airing of the case in council seemed to her extremely dangerous; and since she foresaw that gossip on the subject would soon reach his ears she communicated to him, in a truly generous letter, the two points telling against him, together with the evidence on which they might be said to rest, calling them the accident of a strange misunderstanding and assuring him in very definite terms that she, persuaded in advance of his innocence, had no wish to hear him answer them.

The Count, at table in the company of friends, when the knight arrived with the Duchess's letter, he rose and welcomed him; and while the friends contemplated the messenger, who would not be seated and whose presence was solemn and ceremonious, he, in the embrasure of the window reading the letter, went pale and said, handing the sheets to his friends: 'See, comrades, what a disgraceful charge, the murder of my brother, has been concocted against me.' Eyes flashing, he took the arrow out of the knight's hand and, concealing the mortal harm done to his soul and while his companions gathered around him uneasily, he added: that the bolt was indeed his and that he had indeed, as was asserted, been absent from his castle in the night before the Feast of St Remigius. The friends, outraged by such base and malevolent scheming, cast suspicion of the murder back on the wicked accusers themselves and were on the point of becoming insulting towards the messenger, who had begun to defend the Duchess, his sovereign, when the Count, having read through the papers again, suddenly stepped among them and crying: 'Hush now, friends', took his sword that stood in the corner, handed it to the knight and said: he was his prisoner. To the knight's astonished question: had he heard aright and did he indeed acknowledge the two points in the charge drawn up by the Chancellor, the Count answered: 'Yes, yes, yes.' — But he hoped he could be spared the necessity of proving his innocence anywhere except at the bar of a court formally constituted by the Duchess. In vain did his followers, extremely unhappy with this statement, put it to him that at least if such were the case he owed an explanation of the facts of the matter to no one but the Emperor; the Count, in a strangely sudden change of attitude entrusting himself to the Regent's sense of justice, insisted that he would stand trial in her land and, tearing himself free of them, he had called through the window for his horses, ready, as he said, to follow the messenger at once into custody: when his comrades forcibly, with a suggestion that in the end he was obliged to accept, prevented him. The whole company composed a letter to the Duchess, demanding, as a right available to any gentleman in such a case, free passage for him and as surety that he would present himself before a court set up by her and comply with whatever that court might lay upon him, they offered a sum of twenty thousand silver marks.

The Duchess, receiving this unexpected and, to her, incomprehensible declaration, thought it advisable, given the atrocious rumours already circulating among the people as to the motivation for the charge, to withdraw, in her own person, entirely, and lay the whole case before the Emperor. She sent him, on the advice of the Chancellor, all the papers having to do with the matter and begged him, in his capacity as imperial sovereign, to relieve her of the investigations into a case in which she was herself an interested party. The Emperor, residing at that moment in Basel on account of negotiations with the Swiss, acceded to this request;

he set up a court there of three counts, twelve knights and two legal assessors; and having granted Count Jakob Rotbart, as his friends had requested and on a surety of twenty thousand silver marks, safe conduct, he summoned him to appear before the said court and give an answer to the two questions: how did the arrow, which by his own admission belonged to him, get into the hands of the murderer, and where was he on the night before the Feast of St Remigius?

It was on the Monday after Trinity that Count Jakob Rotbart with a splendid escort of knights answered the summons sent out to him and appeared before the court in Basel. There passing over the first question, which he was, he said, quite unable to answer, he expressed himself with regard to the second, which must be decisive in the matter, thus: 'My noble lords,' and he rested his hands on the rail and from under reddish brows his little eyes looked out with a fierce brightness at the gathering, 'you accuse me, despite the many proofs I have given of my indifference towards crown and sceptre, of the foulest deed that might be done, the murder of a brother who, though not, it is true, well disposed to me, was none the less dear; and as one of the grounds of your accusation you assert that I was in the night before the Feast of St Remigius, when the crime was committed, contrary to a habit of many years standing absent from my castle. Now I know very well that a knight secretly granted the favours of a lady is honour-bound to safeguard her good name; and truly, had heaven not so unexpectedly gathered this strange fate about my head, the secret slumbering in my heart would have died with me, gone into dust, and only when the graves spring open at the angel's trump would it have risen before God with me. But the question put to my conscience by his Imperial Majesty through you obliterates, as I am sure you will agree, all other considerations and concerns; and since you wish to know why it is neither probable nor even possible that I in person or indirectly had any part in the murder of my brother let me say now: that in the night before the Feast of St Remigius, thus at the time when it was done, in secret I was with the daughter of Governor Winfried von Breda, the beautiful widow Lady Littegarde von Auerstein, who is in love with me.'

Now it is necessary to know that the widowed Lady Littegarde von Auerstein was not only the most beautiful lady in the land but also, until the moment of this disgraceful accusation, one like no other quite without spot or blame. She had lived since the death of the Castellan von Auerstein, her husband, whom an infectious fever had taken from her only a few months after their marriage, quietly and privately in her father's castle; and it was only at the request of this old gentleman, who wished to see her married again, that she agreed to appear now and then at the hunts and banquets organized by the knights in her locality and by Jakob Rotbart most of all. Many noblemen from the best and wealthiest families in the country were there to court her on these occasions, and among them the dearest to her and best loved was Friedrich von Trota, the Chamberlain, who had once on a hunt braved the charge of a wounded boar, to save her life; but being anxious not to displease her two brothers, who were counting on her inheritance, she had not yet, for all her father's admonitions, made up her mind to give him her hand. Indeed, when Rudolf, the elder of the two, married a wealthy lady of the neighbourhood and after three years of childless marriage to the great joy of the family a son and heir was born to him: she then, moved by certain more or less explicit remarks, took formal leave, in a letter it cost her many tears to write, of her friend Friedrich, and to preserve the unity of the family she agreed to her brother's proposal that she become abbess of a convent on the banks of the Rhine not far from her father's castle.

At that very moment, as approval was being sought from the Archbishop of Strasburg and the plan was near to being carried out, the court set up by the Emperor sent Governor Winfried Breda notification of his daughter's disgrace and ordered him to send her to Basel to answer the charge brought against her by Count Jakob Rotbart. They gave him in their missive the exact time and place of the secret assignation the Count, in his evidence, claimed to have had with Littegarde and enclosed a ring, the gift of her late husband, which, he asserted, he had received from her hand when they parted, in memory of that night. Now on the day when this communication arrived Lord Winfried was suffering from a grievous and painful illness of old age; in an extremely nervous state he was taking unsteady steps around the room on his daughter's arm and the end that is set for all living things was already before his eyes; so that when he read that terrible notification instantly he suffered a stroke, let the paper fall, and collapsed with stricken limbs. The brothers, also present, in consternation raised him up, calling for a doctor who, to attend him, lived in rooms hard by; but all efforts to restore him to life were in vain; as Lady Littegarde lay unconscious in the arms of her women he gave up the ghost and she, when she recovered, was left without even the bitter-sweet consolation of having said a word at least, to go with him into eternity, in defence of her honour. The brothers' shock at this frightful event and their rage over the unhappily all too plausible accusation of misconduct made against their sister that had caused it, were indescribable. For they knew only too well that Count Jakob Rotbart had indeed throughout the previous summer courted her very pressingly; had staged several tournaments and banquets solely in her honour and in a manner very offensive even then had distinguished her among all the other women he drew into his company. Moreover, they remembered that Littegarde, precisely around the Feast of St Remigius, the day in question, had claimed to have lost, whilst out walking, that very ring she had had from her husband which now, in so strange a fashion, had come to light again in Count Jakob's hands; so that not for a moment did they doubt the truth of the statement made in court against her by the Count. In vain — while her father's body, amid the lamentations of the servants, was being borne away — did she clasp her brothers' knees and beg to be heard; Rudolf, red with indignation, turned to her and asked: could she call on any witness who would vouch for the groundlessness of the accusation? and when, trembling and quaking, she replied: alas no, only on the blamelessness of the life she had led, because her maid that night had not been with her in her bedroom but absent, visiting her parents: then Rudolf thrust her from him with his foot, drew a sword, hanging on the wall, out of its scabbard and commanded her, in his misbegotten rage summoning the servants and the dogs, instantly to leave her dwelling and the castle altogether. White as chalk, Littegarde stood up; silently evading his violence she begged him to allow her at least enough time to arrange her enforced departure; but Rudolf made her no other answer than, foaming with rage: 'Out, out of the house!' And when he would not heed his own wife standing in his way with a plea for clemency and humanity and in his madness with his sword hilt knocked her, bleeding, aside: the unhappy Littegarde, more dead than alive, left the room. She tottered, surrounded and stared at by the common crowd, through the courtyard to the gates where Rudolf allowed a bundle of clothes, to which he added a little money, to be handed out to her and behind her then, cursing and ill-wishing her, himself he shut the gates.

Being thus suddenly flung down from the heights of a serene and almost untroubled happiness into the depths of an unfathomable and utterly helpless misery was more than the poor woman could bear. Not knowing where to turn she staggered, clutching at the rail, down the stony path to find some shelter for the approaching night at least; but before she had reached the little village, whose houses were scattered through the valley, all her strength deserted her and she fell to the ground. She must have lain a good hour there, released from earthly suffering, and total darkness lay over the land, when she awoke with several inhabitants of the place in a commiserating ring around her. For a boy playing on the hillside had seen her there and had reported this strange and striking phenomenon to his parents in their house; whereupon they, recipients of Littegarde's charity in the past, had gone at once, appalled to hear of her in such a wretched state, to assist in any way they could. Through their ministrations she recovered soon enough and at the sight of the castle locked and barred behind her remembered everything; but when two women offered to conduct her back there, she declined, asking only that they would be so good as to find someone with a conveyance, to continue her journey. In vain did the people seek to persuade her that in her condition she was unfit to travel; claiming her life was threatened Littegarde insisted on leaving the precincts of the castle instantly; indeed when the crowd around her increased but did not help she made to free herself from them by force and in night and deepening darkness go on her way alone; whereupon they perforce, afraid the lords would hold them accountable should she meet with an accident, did what she wished and fetched a wagon which, when she had been asked repeatedly where did she want to go, set off with her towards Basel.

But before they had reached the village, having given her circumstances more careful consideration, she altered her decision and ordered her driver to turn about and take her to Trotenburg not many miles away. For it was clear to her that against such an opponent as Count Jakob Rotbart she would achieve nothing before the court in Basel unless she had assistance; and nobody seemed to her fitter to be entrusted with the defence of her honour than her admirable friend the excellent Chamberlain Friedrich von Trota who, as she knew, was still devotedly in love with her. It was about midnight and the lights of the castle were still faintly showing when she, greatly fatigued by her journey, arrived there in her cart. When a servant of the house came out to her she sent him up to announce her arrival to the family; but before he could do so Bertha and Kunigunde, Friedrich's two unmarried sisters, happening to be in the entrance hall for a household matter, appeared at the door. These two ladies, to whom Littegarde was well known, welcomed her joyfully and affectionately, helped her from the cart and, somewhat perturbed, led her upstairs to their brother who, immersed in the innumerable papers of some litigation, was sitting at a table. Friedrich's astonishment when, hearing sounds behind him he turned and the Lady Littegarde, pale and discomposed, the very image of despair, went down on her knees before him, was indescribable. Standing, he raised her from the floor and cried: 'My dearest Littegarde, what has happened to you?' Littegarde, sinking into a chair, told him what had occurred; what an evil accusation Count Jakob Rotbart, to clear himself of suspicion of the Duke's murder, had brought against her at the court in Basel; how the news of it had instantly caused her aged and already ailing father to suffer a stroke from which then a few moments later he had died in the arms of his sons; and how they, maddened by their anger at all this and without listening to what she might say in her defence, had visited abundant and frightful abuse and violence upon her and finally driven her like a common criminal from the house. She begged Friedrich to provide her with a suitable escort for the journey to Basel and to appoint a lawyer for her there who when she appeared before the court set up by the Emperor could be at her side and with shrewd and mature counsel combat the scandalous accusation. She assured him that had it come from the mouth of a Parthian or a Persian on whom she had never set eyes before, such a claim would not have been more unexpected than it was from the mouth of Count Jakob Rotbart whom in her deepest soul for his bad reputation as well as for his outward appearance she had always detested and whom at last summer's banquets when in his impudence he had sought to please her she had with the greatest coldness and contempt on every occasion spurned. 'Enough, my dearest Littegarde,' Friedrich cried, with a noble fervour taking her hand and pressing it to his lips: 'Waste no more words defending and establishing your innocence. In my heart a voice speaks for you more passionately and persuasively than all the assurances or indeed than all the proofs and legal grounds you might by fitting together events and circumstances be able to assemble and put to the court in Basel. Take me, since your unjust and ungenerous brothers have abandoned you, as friend and brother and allow me the glory of being your advocate in this affair; I will restore the radiance of your honour before the court in Basel and in the verdict of the whole wide world.' And with that he led Littegarde, moved to copious tears of gratitude by such noble words, upstairs to his mother, Lady Helena, who had already retired to her bedchamber; and presented her to this estimable old lady, who held her in particular affection, as a dear guest who because of a quarrel in her family had decided to reside in his castle for a little while; that very night a whole wing of the spacious dwelling was made over to her, the cupboards in it were filled with abundant clothing and linen from the sisters' store and servants assigned to her to attend her well, indeed royally, as befitted her rank: and only three days later Friedrich von Trota, giving no hint of how he intended to conduct his case before the court, was on the road to Basel with a numerous following of knights and squires.

Meanwhile the court in Basel had received a letter from Littegarde's two brothers, the von Bredas, in which they related what had happened at the castle and, either because they really did think her guilty or because they had other reasons for undoing her, they abandoned the poor woman utterly to the due processes of the law as a wrongdoer now exposed. At least, in an ignoble and untruthful fashion, they called her expulsion from the castle a voluntary departure from it; they claimed she had, being unable to offer anything at all in her own defence, at once, when a few indignant words escaped them, quitted the house; and it was their opinion after making, so they said, vain efforts to discover her whereabouts, that she was now wandering the country in the company of some other paramour, thus setting the seal on her disgrace. And they requested that, for the restitution of the family honour she had besmirched, her name be expunged from the rolls of the House of Breda and, advancing an array of points in law, they desired that as punishment for such unprecedented misdeeds she be declared to have forfeited all claims on the inheritance of her noble father whom she had hurried to the grave by her disgrace. Now there was no likelihood that the judges in Basel would allow this petition, nor were they even qualified to do so; but when Count Jakob, hearing this news, gave unequivocal and definite proofs of his sympathetic interest in Littegarde's fate and secretly, as it emerged, sent out riders to look for her and offer her hospitality in his castle: then the court no longer doubted the veracity of his testimony and resolved at once to set aside the charge still hanging over him that he was the murderer of the Duke. Indeed, his extending such sympathy to the unhappy woman in her hour of need worked in a manner greatly to his advantage on the minds of the common people wavering latterly in their goodwill towards him; they now excused what earlier they had severely condemned: that he had delivered up to the world's contempt a woman in love with him; and found that in such extraordinary and uncanny circumstances, when nothing less than his life and honour were at stake, the ruthless revelation of the adventure he had had in the night before the Feast of St Remigius was his only recourse. Accordingly, on the orders of the Emperor himself, Count Jakob Rotbart was summoned before the court again to be publicly cleared of the suspicion of involvement in the Duke's murder. In the spacious vaulted courtroom the herald had just read out the von Bredas' letter and the judges were preparing themselves, in accordance with the Emperor's resolution, to proceed to a

formal rehabilitation of the accused standing at their side: when
Friedrich von Trota approached the bar and asked, as any impartial
observer was entitled to, to see the letter for a moment. All eyes upon
him he was granted his request; but scarcely had Friedrich had the
missive from the herald's hands than, after glancing at it, he tore it
through from top to bottom and threw the pieces, wrapped together
with his glove, into Count Jakob Rotbart's face, declaring: that he was a
vile and disgraceful calumniator and that he, Friedrich, was resolved in
mortal combat before all the world with God as judge to prove Lady
Littegarde's innocence of the wrongdoing he, the Count, had accused
her of. — Count Jakob Rotbart having, white in the face, taken up the
glove, said: 'So surely as God's verdict in a trial by force of arms is just
so surely will I prove to you in combat as an honourable knight the truth
of what I was obliged to make public with regard to Lady Littegarde.
Noble lords,' he said, turning to the judges, 'report this gentleman's
intervention to his Imperial Majesty and request him to determine a time
and a place for us with sword in hand to meet and decide our quarrel.'
Accordingly the judges, suspending the session, sent a deputation to the
Emperor with an account of this occurrence; and since his belief in the
Count's innocence was more than a little shaken by the entry of
Friedrich as Littegarde's defender: he summoned, as the laws of chivalry
required, Lady Littegarde to Basel to be present at the duel, and for the
solving of the strange mystery in which the affair was shrouded he
named St Margaret's Day* as the time and the square before the palace
in Basel as the place, and then and there Friedrich von Trota and Count
Jakob Rotbart must meet in the presence of Lady Littegarde.

So it was decided and the midday sun was rising on St Margaret's Day
over the towers of Basel and an immeasurable crowd, for whom seating
and stands had been erected, were gathered in the square when at the
third shout of a herald standing before the judges' gallery Friedrich and
Count Jakob, clad both from head to foot in shining steel, entered the
lists to decide the case by combat. Almost all the chivalry of Swabia and
Switzerland was present on the rising ground below the palace; and on a
balcony there among his courtiers sat the Emperor himself, his wife and
the princes and princesses, his sons and daughters. Shortly before the
start of the combat, while the judges were dividing light and shadow
between the combatants, the Lady Helena and her two daughters Bertha
and Kunigunde who had accompanied Littegarde to Basel came again to
the gates of the square and asked the guards standing there for
permission to enter and speak with Lady Littegarde who, as custom
since time immemorial had required it, was seated on a platform within

the lists themselves. For although this lady's life seemed to command complete respect and a boundless trust in the truthfulness of her assertions, still the ring that Count Jakob could produce and even more the fact that in the night before the Feast of St Remigius Littegarde had allowed her maid, the only person who could have vouched for her, to be absent, did cause them to feel a very keen anxiety; they resolved to test once again how certain, now that the decisive moment pressed upon her, was the conscience of the woman who stood accused, and to make clear to her how vain and indeed blasphemous it would be, if in fact any guilt were weighing on her soul, to seek to cleanse herself of it by letting weapons speak a verdict; for in that holy combat infallibly the truth must come to light. And Littegarde did indeed have good reason to give careful thought to what Friedrich was even now undertaking on her behalf; death at the stake awaited both her and her friend, the knight Friedrich von Trota, if God in the judgment of iron decided not for him but for Count Jakob Rotbart and for the truth of the testimony he had given in court against her. Lady Littegarde, when she saw Friedrich's mother and sisters entering at the side, rose in the dignified manner that was natural to her and that the suffering by which all her being was now marked had rendered yet more poignant, and asked as she stepped towards them why they had come to her at such a fateful moment. 'My dear child,' said Lady Helena, taking her aside, 'will you spare a mother, whose only consolation in her desolate old age is that she has a son, the grief of having to weep over his grave; will you, before the duel begins, agree to be conveyed from here with abundant gifts and everything you might need and take one of our estates across the Rhine, where you will be fittingly and affectionately received, as a further gift from us?' Pallor passed over Littegarde's face; she stared at her for a moment; then, having grasped these words in all their import, went down on one knee. 'Madam,' she said, 'my revered lady, does the fear that God at this decisive moment will declare Himself against my soul's innocence have its origin in the heart of your noble son?' — 'Why?' Lady Helena asked. — 'Because if it does, if his hand wielding the sword does not have complete faith, I beseech him not to draw that sword but, making what decent excuse he can, to leave the lists to his opponent and, not heeding pity, which is not in place here and which I cannot at all accept, to abandon me to a fate that I place in God's hands.' — 'No,' said Lady Helena, confused; 'my son knows nothing of this. It would hardly be proper for him who gave his word in court to fight in your cause now when the hour strikes that will decide the matter to make you any such offer. Firmly believing in your innocence he stands, as you see, ready for combat, face to face with the Count, your enemy. It was a proposition that we, my daughters and I, beset by the moment, thought up in consideration of what might be best and to avoid unhappiness.' — 'Well,' said Lady Littegarde, fervently kissing the old lady's hand and wetting it with her tears, 'let him keep his word. My conscience is not spotted by any guilt and even if he went without armour into the fight God and all the angels will protect him.' So saying she rose and led Lady Helena and her daughters to chairs placed on the platform behind her own and on this then, which was covered with a red cloth, she herself sat down.

Thereupon the herald, at a sign from the Emperor, blew for the combat to begin and the two knights, sword and shield in hand, came at one another. With the first stroke Friedrich struck he wounded the Count; with the tip of his sword, which was not notably long, he hurt him between hand and arm through a joint in the armour; but the Count, startled by the sensation, sprang back and examining the wound found that although there was a good deal of blood only the surface of the skin had been scratched: and, when the knights on the slope behind began to murmur at the unseemliness of his conduct, he advanced again and continued the fight with renewed strength like a man not hurt at all. Now the struggle heaved to and fro between them like the meeting of two storm winds, like the confrontation of two thunder clouds that send their lightnings at one another and without mingling rear up and circle with a din of frequent thunder. Friedrich, presenting his sword and shield, stood on the ground as though he were rooting in it; into the earth, that had been cleared of its cobbles and deliberately loosened, he dug himself as far as his spurs, as far as his ankles and calves, warding off the blows that the Count, small and quick and attacking, as it seemed, from all sides simultaneously, dealt at his head and chest. Already, counting the pauses both parties were obliged to make to get their breath, the combat had lasted almost an hour and again there was a murmuring among the spectators in the stands. It seemed this time to be directed not against Count Jakob, whose keenness to push the fight to a finish was obvious, but against Friedrich's staking of himself to the spot and his odd and, as it seemed, almost cowed or at least perverse refusal to attack. Friedrich, though doubtless having good reasons for his tactics, abandoned them at once in all too ready deference towards those who at that moment were sitting in judgment on his honour. Emerging bravely from the position he had adopted at the outset, where, by the movement of his feet, he had fashioned a sort of natural rampart around himself, he reared up over his adversary, whose strength was beginning to ebb, and, not weakened himself, beat at his head, blow upon shattering blow, which he however, swaying very adeptly, was able to ward off with his shield. But in the very first minutes of the now altered combat Friedrich met with a misfortune that did not exactly seem to indicate the presence and governance over the struggle of any higher power: tripping in his spurs he stumbled and as, under the weight of his helmet and the armour encumbering his upper body, he fell to his knees and rested, to support himself, a hand in the dust, Jakob Rotbart, in no very generous or chivalrous fashion, thrust the sword into his side where he, in falling, had exposed it. Friedrich, crying in instant pain, leapt up. He pressed down his helmet and again turning rapidly to face his enemy sought to continue the fight: but as he bowed almost double under the pain and rested on his sword and darkness overwhelmed his eyes the Count twice more thrust in his flamberg* close under Friedrich's heart; so that he, in the din of his armour, crashed to the ground and let fall by him sword and shield. The Count, flinging aside these weapons, set a foot on his chest, the trumpets sounding thrice; and while all the spectators, first among them the Emperor, rose from their seats with choked exclamations of horror and pity, Lady Helena, followed by her two daughters, rushed to her beloved son writhing in the dust in his blood. 'Oh my Friedrich!' she exclaimed, kneeling by his head and lamenting; whilst Lady Littegarde, fainting, senseless, was lifted by two guards from the floor of the platform where she had sunk down and carried to a prison. 'And oh how wicked of her,' Lady Helena added, 'how damnable, how dare she come here, conscious in her heart of guilt, and arm the truest and the noblest of friends to win God's verdict for her in an unjust duel!' And with that, lamenting, she raised up her dear son, freed meanwhile of his armour by her daughters, and sought to still the blood that was gushing from his noble breast. But guards on the orders of the Emperor arrived and took him, fallen to the law, into custody also; doctors assisting, he was laid on a bier and, accompanied by a large host of people he, like Littegarde, was carried to a prison, Lady Helena however and the daughters being allowed to follow him there and be with him until he died as no one doubted he would.

But it very soon transpired that Friedrich's wounds, though they affected delicate and vital parts, were not, by a peculiar ordinance of heaven, mortal; on the contrary, only a few days later the doctors assigned to him could offer his family firm assurances that he would remain alive; indeed, that, since his constitution was a strong one, he would within a few weeks recover and his body be unblemished. As

soon as his reasoning powers, which for a long time pain had deprived
him of, returned, his persistent question to his mother was: what was
Lady Littegarde doing? He could not keep from weeping when he
thought of her in the desolation of a prison a prey to the most terrible
despair and he urged his sisters, touching their cheeks caressingly as he
did so, to visit her and comfort her. Lady Helena, surprised to hear him
speak like this, begged him to forget a woman so shameful and
despicable; it was her opinion that the crime referred to in court by the
Count and now by the outcome of the duel brought into the daylight,
could be forgiven, but not the shamelessness and effrontery of seeking
God's judgement as though she were innocent and knowing her guilt all
along and heedlessly sending to his doom her generous friend. 'Oh my
dear mother,' said the Chamberlain, 'what mortal person, and even if
the wisdom of the ages were his, will dare interpret the mysterious
verdict delivered by God in this duel?' 'What!' Lady Helena exclaimed.
'Is the meaning of that holy verdict obscure to you? Did you not in a
manner all too plain and unequivocal, alas, succumb to your adversary's
sword in the combat?' — 'Granted,' said Friedrich in reply, 'for a
moment I did succumb. But was I defeated by the Count? Am I not
alive? Am I not, as though breathed on by heaven, wonderfully risen up
again as if in a few days, doubly and triply armed with strength, to
resume the fight in which by a trivial accident I was interrupted?' —
'Fool!' his mother cried. 'Do you not know there is a law by which a
combat once, in the opinion of the judges, finished, may not, to dispute
the same affair, be taken up again in the holy court of law?' — 'What of
it?' the Chamberlain replied impatiently. 'What are these arbitrary
human laws to me? Can a combat not fought to the death of one of the
combatants be on any rational appraisal of the matter considered
finished? And might I, if I were permitted to resume it, not hope to undo
the accident which befell me and achieve with my sword a divine verdict
wholly other than what at present narrow-minded and shortsighted
people take for it?' 'All the same,' his mother insisted, 'these laws you
say you do not care about are what governs and rules; reasonably or
not, they enforce God's ordinances and will deliver up you and her, as a
criminal pair, an abomination, to the full severity of judicial process.' —
'Oh,' Friedrich cried, 'that is what casts me into sorrow and despair. The
staff has been broken over her as though her guilt were proven; and I
who desired to demonstrate her virtue and innocence before all the
world, I brought this misery upon her: one false step, the unhappy
tangling of my spurs, by which perhaps, quite separately from her case,
God wished to punish me for the sins of my own heart, and her youthful

body is given to the flames and her memory given over to eternal shame.'
— At these words a passionate and manly sorrow filled his eyes with
tears; he reached for a handkerchief and turned his face to the wall; and
Lady Helena and her daughters knelt by his bed in wordless pity, kissing
his hand and mingling their tears with his. Meanwhile the jailer had
entered with food for him and them and when Friedrich asked what
state Lady Littegarde was in the man in slovenly scraps of speech
informed him that she was lying on a bed of straw and since the day of
her incarceration had not spoken a word. By this news Friedrich was
flung into the most extreme anxiety; he requested him to tell the lady,
for her comfort, that he by a strange intervention of heaven was in the
process of a full recovery, and begged her permission, when he should be
quite restored and if the Governor allowed it, to visit her in her cell. But
the reply that the jailer, having shaken her many times by the arm as she
lay there like a madwoman on her straw neither hearing nor seeing, the
reply he claimed to have had from her was: no, she wished, so long as
she remained on earth, to see no one; — indeed, they learned that on the
same day she had sent a letter in her own hand to the Governor,
commanding him to allow nobody, whoever it might be, but least of all
von Trota, the Chamberlain, access to her; with the result that Friedrich,
driven by violent worry over her condition, on a day when he felt his
strength returning with particular vigour, rose up, got the Governor's
permission and, sure of her forgiveness, proceeded in the company of his
mother and sisters unannounced to her room.

But beyond all utterance was the unhappy Littegarde's horror when, a
noise being made at the door, she rose with undone hair and half
uncovered at the breast from the straw flung down for her and saw
instead of the expected jailer the Chamberlain, her noble and excellent
friend, entering on the arms of Bertha and Kunigunde, a melancholy and
pitiable appearance, much marked by the sufferings he had gone
through. 'Keep away!' she cried, and with an expression of despair flung
herself back on the covers of the bed and pressed her hands against her
face. 'If there is any glimmer of pity in your heart, keep away!' — 'But
my dearest Littegarde ...' Friedrich replied. Leaning on his mother he
came to her side and bowed, inexpressibly moved, over her to take her
hand. 'Keep away!' she cried, shuddering and on her knees retreating
before him some distance on the straw. 'Do not touch me, unless you
wish me mad. I fill with horror at the sight of you, fire is less terrible to
me, that burns, than you.' — 'Horror?' Friedrich answered in astonishment. 'My noble lady, how have I deserved this welcome?' — At these
words Kunigunde, motioned to by her mother, placed a chair for him

and said that, being weak still, he should sit. 'Oh Jesu,' Littegarde cried, throwing herself down before him and in the most terrible fear laying her face hard against the ground, 'oh my beloved, leave the room, leave me. Fervently, lovingly, I clasp your knees, I bathe your feet with my tears, I entreat you, as a worm writhing in the dust before you, do me this one act of mercy: oh my lord and master, leave the room, leave it at once, and me!' — Friedrich stood before her, shaken through and through. 'Is the sight of me so disagreeable, Littegarde?' he asked, looking down at her with great earnestness. 'Terrible, unbearable, annihilating,' Littegarde replied, and in a gesture of complete despair laid down her face in hiding between his feet. 'Hell with its horrors and terrors is sweeter to me and to look at lovelier than the springtime of your countenance turned thus towards me in devotion and love.' — 'Dear God,' the Chamberlain cried, 'what am I to make of this torment and abasement in your soul? Was God's verdict, unhappy woman, the true one and the crime the Count accused you of before the court, are you guilty of it?' — 'Guilty, proved guilty, cast out, now and in all eternity damned and condemned,' cried Littegarde, beating her breast as though she were raving. 'God is truthful and does not deceive. Go away, my senses will not hold and I am losing strength. Leave me alone with my grief and my despair.' — At these words Friedrich fainted; and whilst Littegarde covered her head with a veil and as though wholly departing from the world lay back upon her bed, Bertha and Kunigunde fell with shrieks upon their unconscious brother and sought to recall him to life. 'Curse you,' Lady Helena cried, as the Chamberlain opened his eyes again, 'be cursed with everlasting remorse this side of the grave and beyond it be damned everlastingly: not for the guilt you now confess but for your mercilessness and inhumanity in not confessing it until you had dragged my innocent son along with you into perdition. What a fool I was,' she continued, turning from her contemptuously, 'that I gave no credence, just before the holy ordeal began, to what I was told by the prior of our Augustinian monastery to whom, in pious preparation for the decisive hour ahead of him, the Count had made his confession. On the body of Christ he swore to him that the deposition he had made in court respecting this wretch was true; he told him the garden gate at which, as arranged, she had waited for him and welcomed him when night fell; described the room, a side room in the unoccupied tower of the castle, into which, unseen by the guards, she had led him; the bed with its baldaquin and plentiful soft pillows on which in secret and shameless luxury she lay with him. An oath sworn at a time like that will not contain a lie, and had I, blinded as I was, only given my son even at the very moment when combat commenced some word of this I should have opened his eyes and he would have staggered back from the abyss he stood over. — But come now,' Lady Helena cried, gently embracing Friedrich and kissing his brow: 'we do her an honour if we think her fit to hear our indignation. Let her see our backs and, annihilated by the reproaches we do not deign to make, let her despair.' — 'Oh that wicked man!' Littegarde replied and, stung by Lady Helena's words, sat up. In sorrow she rested her head on her knees and wept hot tears into her handkerchief. 'I remember,' she said, 'that my brothers and I were in his castle three days before the Feast of St Remigius; he had, as he often did, held a banquet in my honour and my father, who liked to see my youthful beauty celebrated, had urged me to accept the invitation in the company of my brothers. Late, when the dancing had ended, I climbed to my bedroom and found a note on my table: in an unknown hand, unsigned, it was a formal declaration of love for me. As it happened, my two brothers were present in the room to arrange our departure, set for the following day; and since I never did have any secrets from them I showed them, in my speechless astonishment, the strange find I had at that moment made. They, immediately recognizing the Count's script, foamed with rage and the elder was ready there and then to go to his room with the note; but the younger warned him this might be a risky step, since the Count had been shrewd enough not to sign the note; whereupon both, outraged by this deeply offensive conduct, that same night drove away with me, resolved never again to honour his castle with their presence and brought me to their father's house. — That is the only association,' she added, 'I have ever had with that despicable and good-for-nothing man.' — 'What!' cried the Chamberlain, turning his tearful face towards her: 'Those words were music in my ears. — Repeat them,' he said, after a pause during which he went down on his knees before her and clasped his hands: 'You never did betray me for that wretch and are you innocent of the wrong he accused you of in court?' 'Dear love,' Littegarde whispered and pressed his hand to her lips. — 'Are you?' the Chamberlain cried. 'Are you?' — 'As a newborn child, as a man come from confession, as a novice dying at the moment of her veiling in the sacristy!' — 'Oh Almighty God,' Friedrich cried, embracing her knees: 'have thanks from me. Your words have given me life again; death no longer frightens me and eternity, which only a moment since had stretched before me like an ocean of endless grief, now rises again like a realm of countless shining suns.' — 'Unhappy man,' said Littegarde, backing away, 'how can you give credence to the words of my mouth?' — 'Why should I not?' said Friedrich fervently. —

'You are mad,' Littegarde cried. 'You are raving. Was not God's holy judgement given against me? Were you not in that fateful duel defeated by the Count? Did he not prove by force of arms the truth of what he advanced in court against me?' — 'Oh my dearest Littegarde,' the Chamberlain cried, 'do not allow your senses to despair, raise up the feeling living in your heart like a rock: hold on to it and do not waver, not even if heaven and earth above you and below you founder utterly. Of two thoughts that confuse our senses let us think the one that is the more intelligible and able to be grasped, and before you believe yourself guilty believe that in the duel I fought for you I was the victor. — Dear God,' he added, 'Lord of my life,' suddenly covering his face with his hands: 'keep *my* soul from confusion! True as I look to heaven, I do believe I was not defeated by my enemy's sword, for though I was thrown down in the dust under his feet here I have risen into life again. Why should God Almighty in His wisdom indicate and declare the truth the moment we, the believers, ask Him to? Oh Littegarde,' he concluded, pressing her hand between his, 'in life let us look ahead to death and in death to eternity and be of the firm unshakeable belief: your innocence will be, and by the duel I fought for you, brought into the clear and happy light of day.' — At these words the Governor entered; and when he reminded Lady Helena, who was sitting at a table weeping, that so much agitation of the feelings might be harmful to her son: Friedrich, persuaded by his family and not without a sense of having given and received some comfort, returned to his prison.

Meanwhile, at the tribunal set up by the Emperor in Basel, charges had been brought against Friedrich von Trota and his friend Lady Littegarde von Auerstein for having sinfully invoked God's verdict in their case, and both had, in accordance with the law as it stood then, been sentenced to suffer a shameful death by burning on the very site of the duel. A deputation of councillors was sent to announce this to the prisoners and the sentence would have been carried out immediately after the Chamberlain's recovery had it not been the Emperor's secret intention to see Count Jakob, who still aroused a sort of mistrust in him, present there too. But he, in a way which was indeed very odd and remarkable, still lay sick of the small and, as it had seemed, insignificant wound given him at the start of the duel by Friedrich; an extreme corruption of his body's juices prevented it, day by day and week by week, from healing, and all the arts of the doctors called in one after another from Swabia and Switzerland were not able to close it. Indeed, a devouring putrescence, entirely unknown to medical science in that day and age, ate and spread like a cancer into the whole system of his hand, down to the bone, so that, to the horror of all his friends, it became necessary to amputate first the whole damaged hand and then, since even by this the rot devouring him could not be halted, the arm itself. But even by this means, vaunted as a radical cure, the evil, as nowadays one would easily have foreseen, instead of any improvement, was only aggravated; and the doctors, when gradually all his body dissolved in putrescence and decay, declared that he could not be saved and must die before the week was out. In vain did the prior of the Augustinian monastery, seeing, as he thought, the terrible hand of God in this strange turn of events, urge him in his quarrel with the Regent to confess the truth; the Count, shaken through and through, again on the holy sacraments asserted the veracity of his statements and offered up, with every sign of utter dread, his soul to eternal damnation if what he accused Lady Littegarde of was untrue and a slander. Thus, despite the immorality of his life, there were doubly grounds for believing in the inner honesty of this assurance: first because the sick man did indeed have a certain piety which seemed to rule out a false oath at such a moment, and then because from an interrogation of the guard in that tower of the von Breda castle, whom Jakob, to get secret access, claimed to have bribed, it did definitely emerge that this claim was well founded and that the Count in the night before the Feast of St Remigius really had been inside the von Breda home. Accordingly, the prior was left with almost no alternative but to believe that the Count himself had been, by some third person unknown, deceived; and the unhappy man, to whom, hearing of the Chamberlain's miraculous recovery, the same thought had occurred, did not attain the end of his life before that supposition was, to his despair, fully corroborated. It is necessary to know that the Count, long before he turned his desires on Lady Littegarde, had been in dealings of an infamous kind with Rosalie, her maid; almost every time her lady visited his castle he would have this girl, who was a frivolous and immoral creature, to his room at nights. When Littegarde then, during her last stay, with her brothers, in his castle, received from him that tender letter in which he declared his passion, this irked the girl and aroused her jealousy, since he had for several months neglected her; so that when Littegarde soon afterwards departed and she was obliged to accompany her, she left behind, in Littegarde's name, a note for the Count saying that her brothers' indignation at the step he had taken made an immediate meeting with him impossible but, to bring one about, she invited him to visit her in the apartments of her father's castle during the night before the Feast of St Remigius. He, full of joy at the success of his enterprise, dispatched a

second letter to Littegarde at once, informing her that he would for
certain be there in the said night and only asking, to avoid all going
astray, that she send a faithful guide to meet him, who would lead him
to her rooms; and since the maid, well practised in every kind of
intrigue, expected some such response she was able to intercept the letter
and to tell him in a second false reply that she would wait for him
herself at the door into the garden. Next, on the evening before the night
of this arrangement, she asked Littegarde, under the pretext that her
sister was sick and that she wished to visit her, for leave to go into the
country, and was given it; did indeed then leave the castle late in the
afternoon with a bundle of linen under her arm and set off in full view
of everybody towards where that woman lived. But instead of
completing the journey she returned at nightfall, with the excuse that a
storm was brewing, to the castle and because, as she said, she did not
want to disturb her Ladyship, it being her intention to go on with her
journey the following morning, she procured herself a bed for the night
in one of the empty rooms of the dilapidated and scarcely ever visited
castle tower. The Count who, with money, got past the gatekeeper into
the castle and at midnight, as arranged, was met at the door into the
garden by a veiled figure, had no suspicion, as may well be imagined, of
the trick being played on him; the girl kissed him quickly on the mouth
and led him by many stairs and corridors of that remote and neglected
wing into one of the most splendid rooms of the castle itself, the
windows of which she had taken the precaution of shuttering earlier.
Here, holding him by the hand, she first listened stealthily at all the
doors and in a whisper, pretending that her brothers slept close by,
urged silence, then, going to one side, lay down with him on the bed
there. The Count, deceived by that shape and form, luxuriated in the
satisfaction of, at his age, making such a conquest; and when at first
light she left him and, to remember the night spent, put on his finger a
ring that Littegarde had had from her husband and that she, Rosalie,
had purloined for that purpose the evening before, he promised her that
he would, as soon as he reached home, give her in exchange one his late
wife had bestowed on him on their wedding day. He kept his word and
three days later sent the ring, that Rosalie, again, was clever enough to
intercept, secretly to the castle; but then, doubtless because he feared the
adventure might lead him further than he wished to go, nothing more
was heard from him, and making various excuses he avoided any second
assignation. Later the girl, on pretty certain suspicion of a theft, was
dismissed and sent back to her parents on the Rhine; and when after the
lapse of nine months the consequences of her dissolute life became

apparent and her mother cross-examined her severely, she named Count Jakob Rotbart as the father of the child and revealed the whole deceit she had played out with him. Fortunately, afraid she would be thought to have stolen it, she had made only very timid attempts to sell the ring sent to her by the Count and in fact, because of its very great value, had not found anyone seeming keen to buy it: with the result that the truthfulness of her statement could not be doubted and the parents, on the grounds of this hard and fast evidence, sued Count Jakob in the courts for the child's maintenance. The courts, having already heard of the strange case brought in Basel, made haste to bring their discovery, of great importance for the outcome of that case, to the tribunal's notice; and since a councillor was just leaving for that city on public business they gave him, so that the terrible riddle preoccupying the whole of Swabia and Switzerland might be solved, a letter containing the girl's testimony in court and enclosing the ring, for Count Jakob.

It was on the day set for the execution of Friedrich and Littegarde which the Emperor, ignorant of the doubts now awakening in the bosom of the Count himself, had felt he could not postpone any longer, that the councillor, bearing the communication, entered the sick man's room and found him writhing on his bed in a lamentable despair. 'Enough,' he cried, having read the letter and received the ring, 'I no longer wish to behold the light of the sun. Carry me,' he turned to the prior, 'wretch that I am and my strength going all to dust, out to the place of execution. I will not die without first doing one just thing.' The prior, deeply shaken by this event, at once, as he wished, had him raised up on a bier by four servants; and together with an immeasurable crowd, gathering as the bells rang out around the stake to which Friedrich and Littegarde were already fastened, he arrived there with his miserable charge, who was holding a crucifix in his hand. 'Wait!' cried the prior, and had the bier laid down below the Emperor's balcony. 'Before you light the pyre hear what this sinner's mouth has to divulge to you.' — 'What!' cried the Emperor, rising pale as death from his seat. 'Did not God's holy verdict uphold the justice of his case and are we, after what has happened, even permitted to suppose that Littegarde might be innocent of the crime he charged her with?' — So saying he came in consternation down from his balcony and more than a thousand knights, followed down over benches and barriers by all the people too, crowded together around the sick man where he lay. 'Innocent,' he replied, clutching the prior and half rising up, 'as God Almighty on that fateful day before the eyes of all the gathered citizens of Basel decided it. For he, given three wounds, each mortal, blossoms, as you see, in strength and fullness of life; whereas a blow from him that seemed scarcely to touch the outermost husk of my life has reached in a slow and terrible continuation the kernel itself and felled my strength as the storm wind does the oak. But here, if any disbeliever still harbours doubts, are the proofs. It was Rosalie, her maid, who received me during the night before the Feast of St Remigius whilst I, a wretch, in the deception of my senses, thought that she, who had always spurned my advances with contempt, was the one I was holding in my arms.' The Emperor at these words stiffened as though where he stood he had turned to stone. He dispatched, turning to the stake, a knight with orders to climb the ladder himself and untie the Chamberlain and the lady, already lying unconscious in her mother's arms, and fetch them down to him. 'The angels have watched over you!' he cried, as Littegarde, her dress half open at the breast and her hair undone, led by Friedrich, her friend, whose own steps, in the emotion of this miraculous rescue, were unsteady, approached him through the circle of people making way for them in reverence and amazement. He kissed them both, as they knelt before him, on the forehead; and having begged from his wife the ermine she was wearing and wrapping it around Littegarde's shoulders under the eyes of all that assembled chivalry he took her arm, intending to lead her himself into the rooms of his imperial palace. He turned, whilst the Chamberlain too instead of the suit of penance he had on was adorned with the plumed hat and the cloak of a noble knight, back to the Count writhing pitiably on his bed, and moved by a feeling of compassion, since the Count had not after all entered into the combat which had destroyed him in any criminal or blasphemous fashion, he asked the doctor at his side: was there no hope for the unhappy man? — 'None,' Jakob Rotbart answered, resting, with terrible spasms, in his doctor's arms, 'and I have deserved the death I am dying here. For let it be known, since the temporal arm of the law will no longer reach me, I am the murderer of my brother, the noble Duke Wilhelm von Breysach. The miscreant who laid him low with that arrow from my armoury I had hired for the deed, which was to get me the crown, six weeks before.' — Making this statement he fell back on the bier and breathed the black soul out of him. 'Ha! the thing my husband, the Duke, himself suspected,' exclaimed, at the Emperor's side, the Regent, who likewise, in the Empress's entourage, had come down from the palace balcony into the square, 'and that he imparted to me at the moment of his death in broken words that then, it is true, I understood only imperfectly.' — The Emperor, indignant, replied: 'The arm of the law will reach your body after all. Take him,' he called, turning, to the guards, 'and deliver

him, judged as he is, at once to the executioners. Let him perish, so that
his memory may be marked with shame for evermore, at the very stake
where we, because of him, were about to sacrifice two innocents.' And
with that, whilst the wretch's corpse went up with a roar in reddish
flames and the breath of the north wind scattered it and it was lost, he
led Lady Littegarde, followed by all his knights, into the palace. He
reinstated her, by an imperial decree, in the wealth bequeathed to her by
her father and of which her brothers in their ignoble greed had already
possessed themselves; and only three weeks later the excellent pair were
married at the castle in Breysach, the Duchess Regent, delighted by the
whole turn of events, giving Littegarde a large portion of the Count's
estate, fallen in forfeit to the law, as a wedding gift. But the Emperor
immediately after the priest had joined them hung a chain of honour
around Friedrich's neck; and as soon as he, having concluded his
business with Switzerland, had returned to Worms he inserted into the
holy statutes governing trial by combat, everywhere where it is
presumed that by that means guilt will immediately be brought to light,
the words 'if it is God's will'.

ANECDOTES

HOSPITAL INCIDENT

The man run over by a coach not long ago, his name is Beyer, has suffered the same fate three times in his life already; so that when he was examined at the Charité Hospital by the consultant Mr K. the most laughable misunderstandings occurred. The consultant, first noticing his legs, which were crooked and out of line and covered with blood, asked him was it in these limbs he had been injured? To which the man however answered: no, his legs got in that state five years ago when another doctor ran over him. Then a surgeon assisting the consultant observed that his left eye was burst; but when asked was it there the wheel had hit him he answered: no, a doctor had knocked his eye out fourteen years ago running over him. Finally, to the astonishment of all present, it was discovered that his ribs on the left side had been turned, in a pitiable contorsion, quite into his back; but when the consultant asked him was it there the doctor's carriage had injured him he answered: no, his ribs had been squashed like that seven years ago by another doctor's carriage running over him. — Until finally it was revealed that in his last accident the cartilage in his left ear had been driven into the eardrum. — Our reporter interviewed the man himself about the incident and even those mortally sick lying on their beds around him in the ward could not help laughing at his comical and nonchalant way of telling it. — Moreover, he is recovering; and so long as he keeps clear of doctors when he goes out on the streets he may live a good while yet.

ANECDOTE

In very wet weather a Capuchin monk was accompanying a Swabian to
the gallows. The condemned man, as they went along, several times
complained aloud to God at being obliged to walk such a bitter way in
such unkind weather. The Capuchin, wishing to give him some
Christian comfort, said: 'Louse, count yourself lucky. You only have to
go but I, in this foul weather, have to come back again, the same way.'
— Anyone who has ever felt how desolating, even in fine weather, the
way back from the place of execution is, will admit the monk had a
point.

ANECDOTE

Two famous English boxers, one a Portsmouth man, the other from
Plymouth, who had for many years heard of one another but had never
met, decided, when they did then meet in London, to settle which of
them should be known as champion by having a public match.
Accordingly, before a crowd, they faced up with clenched fists in the
garden of a public house; and when very soon the Plymouth man hit the
Portsmouth man so hard in the chest that he spat blood the latter wiped
his mouth and cried: 'Bravo!' — But when soon after that, facing up
again, the Plymouth man took such a blow from the Portsmouth man's
right fist that he rolled his eyes and dropped, he, dropping, cried: 'And
that's not bad either!' — Whereupon the people, in a ring around them,
cheered and whilst the Plymouth man, hurt in the guts, was carried off
dead they named the Portsmouth man the champion. — The Portsmouth man however is said to have died next day of a haemorrhage.

A LATTER-DAY
(AND MORE FORTUNATE) WERTHER

Charles C., a young clerk living at L——e in France, was secretly in love
with the wife of his employer, D., a merchant, who was rich but old.
Knowing the woman to be virtuous and upright, and being moreover
bound to his employer by many ties of gratitude and respect, he made
not the least attempt to have her return his love. She, sympathizing with
him in his condition, which threatened to become harmful to his health,
urged her husband, on one pretext after another, to remove him from
the house; but her husband postponed a journey, on which he had
decided that his clerk should go, from one day to the next and in the end

said flatly that he could not do without him in his comptoir. One day then Monsieur D. went into the country with his wife, to visit a friend, and left young C. behind in the house, to look after his business. That night, when all were sleeping, the young man, driven by I don't know what feelings, got up to take another walk through the garden. He came by the beloved woman's bedroom, halted, laid his hand on the door handle, opened the room: at the sight of the bed she slept in his heart swelled up and, in brief, he committed the folly, after an inner struggle, since nobody was looking, of taking off his clothes and getting in. Later in the night, when he had already had several hours of sweet and peaceful sleep, the man and wife, for some good reason that does not matter here, came home unexpectedly; and when the old gentleman and his wife entered the bedroom they found young C., alarmed by the noise they made, sitting up in bed. Shame and confusion seized hold of him at the sight of them; and whilst husband and wife, in some surprise, disappeared into the adjoining room whence they had come, he rose, and dressed. Sick of his life he crept to his own room, wrote a brief letter, explaining the incident, to the lady, and with a pistol hanging on the wall shot himself through the chest. Here the story of his life seemed to have ended; and yet (strangely enough) only here and now did it begin. For instead of killing the one intended, the young man namely, the shot caused the old gentleman in the adjoining room to have a stroke: Monsieur D. died a few hours later, all the arts of all the doctors summoned being inadequate to save him. Five days later, Monsieur D. being long since under the ground, young C., the bullet, without endangering his life, having passed through his lung, woke up: and who can well describe — what shall I say: his grief, his joy? — when he learned what had happened and found himself in the arms of the beloved woman, the cause of his wishing to kill himself! A year later the lady married him and in 1801 both were still alive, their family then, as an acquaintance informs me, already numbering thirteen children.

STRANGE COURT CASE IN ENGLAND

As is well known, in England any man accused has for his judges a jury of twelve of his peers whose verdict must be unanimous and who, so that they will not be too long coming to it, are locked in without food or water until they are of one mind. Two gentlemen, living a few miles from London, had a violent quarrel in the presence of witnesses; one threatened the other and added that before twenty-four hours had passed he would regret his behaviour. Towards evening the man was found shot dead; suspicion fell naturally on the one who had uttered the threats against him. He was arrested, brought to trial, further proofs were assembled and eleven of those sitting in judgment condemned him to death; but the twelfth obstinately refused to join them, saying he thought him innocent.

His colleagues begged him to give them the reasons why he thought this; but he would not, and stuck to his opinion. It was already late at night and the judges were sorely plagued by hunger. At last one rose and declared that it was better to acquit one guilty man than to allow eleven innocents to starve to death. Accordingly, they moved to pardon him but presented at the same time the circumstances which had forced the court to do so. The public were wholly against the obstinate odd man out; the matter even came before the King, who asked to speak to him. The gentleman appeared and having got the King to promise that he would not suffer any ill consequences by being honest he told the monarch that, coming home in the dark from hunting and firing off his gun, it had unfortunately killed the nobleman in question who was standing behind a bush. 'Since there were,' he continued, 'no witnesses of my deed nor of my innocence I decided to keep silent; but when I heard that an innocent man had been accused I did everything I could to become one of the jury; for I was firmly resolved to starve to death rather than let the defendant die.' The King kept his word and the gentleman received his royal pardon.

ESSAYS

ON THE GRADUAL PRODUCTION
OF THOUGHTS WHILST SPEAKING
For Rühle von Lilienstern*

If there is something you wish to know and by meditation you cannot
find it, my advice to you, my ingenious old friend, is: speak about it with
the first acquaintance you encounter. He does not need to be especially
perspicacious, nor do I mean that you should ask his opinion, not at all.
On the contrary, you should yourself tell him at once what it is you wish
to know. I see astonishment in your face. I hear you reply that when you
were young you were advised only to speak of things you already
understood. But in those days, doubtless, you spoke in the presumption
of instructing others but my wish is that you speak in the sensible
intention of instructing yourself, and so, different rules applying in
different circumstances, both may perhaps be allowed to stand. The
French say 'l'appétit vient en mangeant'* and this maxim is just as true
if we parody it and say 'l'idée vient en parlant'. Often I have sat at my
desk over the papers of a difficult case and sought the point of view
from which it might be grasped. My habit then, in this striving of my
innermost being after enlightenment, is to gaze into the lamplight, as
into the brightest point. Or a problem in algebra occurs to me and I need
a starting point, I need the equation which expresses the given
relationships and from which by simple calculation the solution may be
found. And lo and behold! If I speak about it to my sister sitting behind
me at her work, I learn more than I should have arrived at by perhaps
hours of brooding. Not that she in any real sense *tells* me, for she is not
familiar with the penal code nor has she studied Euler* or Kästner*.
Nor is it that by skilful questioning she brings me to the crux of the
matter, though that might often be the way to do it, I daresay. But

because I do have some dim conception at the outset, one distantly related to what I am looking for, if I boldly make a start with that, my mind, even as my speech proceeds, under the necessity of finding an end for that beginning, will shape my first confused idea into complete clarity so that, to my amazement, understanding is arrived at as the sentence ends. I put in a few unarticulated sounds, dwell lengthily on the conjunctions, perhaps make use of apposition where it is not necessary, and have recourse to other tricks which will spin out my speech, all to gain time for the fabrication of my idea in the workshop of the mind. And in this process nothing helps me more than if my sister makes a move suggesting she wishes to interrupt; for such an attempt from outside to wrest speech from its grasp still further excites my already hard-worked mind and, like a general when circumstances press, its powers are raised a further degree. This, in my view, was how Molière* used his maid; for to allow her judgement to correct his, as he said he did, would show more modesty than I can believe he had. It is a strangely inspiring thing to have a human face before us as we speak; and often a look announcing that a half-expressed thought is already grasped gives us its other half's expression. I believe many a great speaker to have been ignorant when he opened his mouth of what he was going to say. But the conviction that he would be able to draw all the ideas he needed from the circumstances themselves and from the mental excitement they generated made him bold enough to trust to luck and make a start. I think of the 'thunderbolt' with which Mirabeau* dismissed the Master of Ceremonies who, after the meeting of 23 June, the last under the *ancien régime*, when the King had ordered the estates to disperse, returned to the hall in which they were still assembled and asked them had they heard the King's command. 'Yes,' Mirabeau replied, 'we have heard the King's command.' — I am certain that beginning thus humanely he had not yet thought of the bayonets with which he would finish. 'Yes, my dear sir,' he repeated, 'we have heard it.' — As we see, he is not yet exactly sure what he intends. 'But by what right ...' he continues, and suddenly a source of colossal ideas is opened up to him, 'do you give us orders here? We are the representatives of the nation.' — That was what he needed! — 'The nation does not take orders. It gives them.' — Which launches him there and then to the highest pitch of boldness. — 'And to make myself perfectly plain to you ...' — And only now does he find words to express how fully his soul has armed itself and stands ready to resist — 'Tell your king we shall not move from here unless forced to by bayonets.' — Whereupon, well content with himself, he sat down. — As to the Master of

Ceremonies, we must imagine him bankrupted by this encounter of all ideas. For a law applies rather similar to the law which says that if a body having no electricity of its own enters the zone of a body which has been electrified at once the latter's electricity will be produced in it. And just as in the electrified body, by a reciprocal effect, a strengthening of the innate electricity then occurs, so our speaker's confidence, as he annihilated his opponent, was converted into an inspired and extraordinary boldness. In this way it was perhaps the twitching of an upper lip or an equivocal tugging at the cuffs that brought about the overthrow of the order of things in France. We read that Mirabeau as soon as the Master of Ceremonies had withdrawn stood up and proposed (i) that they constitute themselves a national assembly at once, and (ii) declare themselves inviolable. For having, like a Kleistian jar,* discharged himself now he was neutral again. Returning from boldness, speedily he made way for caution and fear of the Châtelet.* — We have here a remarkable congruence between the phenomena of the physical world and those of the moral world which, if we were to pursue it, would hold good in the subsidiary circumstances too. But I shall leave my comparison and return to the matter in hand. La Fontaine also, in his fable 'Les animaux malades de la peste',* where the fox is obliged to justify himself to the lion and does not know what material to draw on, gives us a remarkable example of the gradual completion of thought out of a beginning made under pressure. The fable is well known. Plague is raging among the animals, the lion summons the grandees of the kingdom and informs them that heaven, if it is to be propitiated, must have a sacrifice. There are many sinners among the people, the death of the greatest must save the rest from destruction. Accordingly, he bids them make him a candid confession of all their crimes. He, for his part, admits that, driven by hunger, he has cut short the lives of many a sheep; dogs likewise, when they came too near; indeed, in delicious moments he has even been known to eat the shepherd. If no one is guilty of worse weaknesses than these then he, the lion, will gladly be the one to die. 'Sire,' says the fox, wishing to ward the lightning off himself, 'in your zeal and generosity you have gone too far. What if you have done a sheep or two to death? Or a dog, a vile creature? And: quant au berger,' he continues, for this is the chief point, 'on peut dire,' though he still does not know what, 'qu'il méritoit tout mal,' trusting to luck, and with that he has embroiled himself, 'étant,' a poor word but which buys him time, 'de ces gens là,' and only now does he hit upon the thought that gets him out of his difficulty, 'qui sur les animaux se font un chimérique empire.' — And he goes on to prove that the donkey, the bloodthirsty donkey (devourer of grass and plants) is the most fitting sacrifice. And with that they fall on him and tear him to pieces. — Speech of that kind is truly a thinking aloud. The ideas in succession and the signs for them proceed side by side and the mental acts entailed by both converge. Speech then is not at all an impediment; it is not, as one might say, a brake on the mind but rather a second wheel running along parallel on the same axle. It is a quite different matter when the mind, before any utterance of speech, has completed its thought. For then it is left with the mere expression of that thought, and this business, far from exciting the mind, has, on the contrary, only a relaxing effect. Thus if an idea is expressed confusedly we should by no means assume that it was thought confusedly too; on the contrary, it might well be the case that the most confusedly expressed ideas are the clearest thought. In any gathering where by a lively conversation a continuous insemination of minds with ideas is under way you will often see people who, not feeling in control of language, have usually held back, all of a sudden, with a convulsive movement, take fire, seize a chance to speak and bring something incomprehensible into the world. Indeed, having drawn the whole company's attention upon themselves, they seem then by embarrassed gestures to indicate that they themselves no longer quite know what it was they wanted to say. It is probable that such a person has thought something very apt, and very clearly. But the sudden shift of activity, the mind's transition from thinking to expression, caused the lapsing of all its excitement, which it needed both to hold on to the thought and then to utter it. In such cases it is all the more necessary that we have language readily at our disposal so that the things we have thought of all at once but have not all at once been able to utter we may as quickly as possible deliver in sequence. And in general if two men have the same clarity of thought the faster speaker will always have an advantage since he brings, so to speak, more forces to the battle than his opponent. That a certain excitement of the intelligence is necessary even to revivify ideas we have already had is amply demonstrated whenever open-minded and knowledgeable people are being examined and without any preamble are asked such questions as: What is the state? Or: What is property? Things of that kind. If these young people had been in company and for a while the subject of conversation had been the state or property they would by a process of comparison, discrimination and summary perhaps with ease have arrived at the definition. But being wholly deprived of any such preparation they are seen to falter and only an obtuse examiner will conclude from this that they do not *know*. For it is not *we* who know things but pre-eminently a certain *condition* of ours which knows.

Only very commonplace intellects, people who yesterday learned by heart what the state is and today have forgotten it again, will have their answers pat in an examination. Indeed, there may be no worse opportunity in the world for showing oneself to advantage than a public examination. Besides the fact that it offends and wounds our sense of decency and incites us to recalcitrance to have some learned horsedealer looking into how many things we know who then, depending on whether they are five or six, either buys us or dismisses us: it is so difficult to play upon a human mind and induce it to give forth its peculiar music, it so easily under clumsy hands goes out of tune, that even the most practised connoisseur of human beings, a real master in what Kant calls the midwifery of thinking,* even he, not being acquainted with the one whose labour he is assisting at, may make mistakes. And if such young people, even the most ignorant among them, do most often achieve good marks this is because the minds of the examiners, if the examination is in public, are themselves too embarrassed to deliver a true judgement. For not only do they themselves feel the indecency of the whole procedure: we should be ashamed to ask a person to tip out the contents of his purse before us, let alone his soul: but their own intelligences come under dangerous appraisal and they may count themselves lucky if they manage to leave the examination without having revealed more shameful weaknesses than the young finalist himself has whom they have been examining.

(To be continued.)*

REFLECTION
A Paradox

We are forever being told how useful it is to reflect; especially to reflect coolly and at great length before we do a thing. If I were a Spaniard, an Italian or a Frenchman that might apply. But since I am a German I have in mind to address my son one day, especially should he decide to become a soldier, as follows:

'The proper time for reflection, let me tell you, is not *before* you act, but *after*. If reflection plays a part beforehand or at the very moment of decision it seems only to confuse, inhibit and repress the power we cannot act without and which has its splendid source in the feelings; whereas afterwards, when the deed is done, our powers of reflection may serve the purpose they were actually given us for, namely to bring us to consciousness of what was wrong or unsound in how we acted and to regulate the feelings for other occasions in the future. Life itself is a struggle with Fate; and in our actions it is much as it is in a wrestling match. The wrestler, having hold of his opponent, cannot possibly at that moment proceed otherwise than according to the promptings of the moment; and a man who tried to calculate which muscles he should employ and which limbs he should set in motion in order to win would inevitably be disadvantaged and defeated. But afterwards, when he has won or is lying on the mat, it may be useful and appropriate to think by what application of force he threw his opponent or how he ought to have moved in order to trip him and stay upright himself. A man must, like that wrestler, take hold of life and feel and sense with a thousand limbs how his opponent twists and turns, resists him, comes at him, evades him and reacts: or he will never get his way in a conversation, much less in a battle.'

THE PUPPET THEATRE

In a public garden one evening in the winter of 1801, which I was spending in M.,* I met Herr C.,* recently appointed first dancer at the Opera there and enjoying an extraordinary success with the public.

I said to him that I had been surprised to see him — several times indeed — at a puppet theatre erected in the marketplace where little burlesques, into which were woven songs and dances, were being given for the entertainment of the common people.

He assured me that the puppets' silent acting gave him a great deal of pleasure, and hinted that a dancer wishing to improve his art could learn a lot from them.

Behind his words, so it seemed to me, by the way he said them, there was more than a passing thought, and I sat down beside him to question him more closely on the grounds he might have for such a strange assertion.

He asked me whether I had not in fact found the marionettes, especially the smaller ones, often very graceful in their movements as they danced.

I could not deny it. A quartet of peasants dancing a round in rapid time could not have been done more prettily by Teniers.*

I asked how these figures were worked and how it was possible, without thousands of strings on one's fingers, to govern their separate limbs and particular points in just such a way as the rhythm of the movements or the dance required.

He answered that I should not suppose that every limb at all the different moments of the dance had to be separately positioned and pulled by the puppeteer.

Every movement, he said, had a centre of gravity; it sufficed if this, inside the figure, were controlled; the limbs, which were nothing but pendula, followed without further interference, mechanically, of their own accord.

He added that this movement was a very simple one; that whenever the centre of gravity was moved *in a straight line* the limbs described a *curve*; and that often, if shaken by accident, the whole thing was brought into a kind of rhythmical activity similar to dancing.

This observation itself seemed to throw some light on the pleasure he claimed to find in the puppet theatre. But I was far from suspecting how much further he would go.

I asked him whether he thought the man working the marionettes must be a dancer himself or at least have some notion of what constitutes beauty in dancing.

He replied that though an activity might in its mechanics be a simple one it did not follow that it could be conducted wholly without feeling.

The line the centre of gravity had to describe was indeed very simple and in most cases, he believed, straight. In cases where it curved the law of its curve did not seem to be more than of the first or at most of the second degree; and even in that latter case only elliptical, and a movement of that description was altogether natural to the extremities of the human body (because of the joints) and so would not require much skill on the part of the operator to achieve it.

However, in another sense that line was something very mysterious. For it was nothing other than *the way of the dancer's soul*; and he doubted whether it could be discovered otherwise than by the operator's putting himself into the centre of gravity of the marionette; in other words, by *dancing*.

I replied that the operation had always been presented to me as something rather mindless: rather like the turning of a handle to play a barrel organ.

'Not at all,' he replied. 'In fact the relationship of the movements of his fingers to the movements of the marionette is quite a subtle one, rather like that of numbers to their logarithms or the asymptotes to the hyperbola.'

He did however think that the last remnant of intelligence, of which he had been speaking, could itself be taken out of the marionettes; that their dancing could be shifted wholly into the realm of mechanical forces and produced by turning a handle, as I had supposed.

I said how astonished I was to see him honouring this popularized version of a noble art with so much attention. Not only did he think it capable of a higher development: he even seemed to have put his own mind to it.

He smiled and said he would go so far as to assert that if he could get somebody to make a marionette to his specifications he would perform such dances with it as neither he nor any other trained dancer of the day, not even excepting Vestris* himself, would be capable of equalling.

'I wonder,' he said, as I looked down at the ground and was silent, 'whether you have heard of the mechanical limbs that craftsmen in England make for people who have lost their legs?'

I said no: such things had never come my way.

'A pity,' he replied; 'for if I tell you that those poor people can dance with them I am almost afraid you will not believe me. — Dance? What am I saying? The range of their movements is limited, I grant you; but those they are capable of they execute with an ease, grace and poise that every thinking person must be astonished by.'

I remarked, in jest, that there he had found the man he was looking for. For a craftsman capable of making such a remarkable leg would without doubt be able to construct him a whole marionette to his requirements.

'And what,' I asked, since he himself now, rather taken aback, was looking down at the ground, 'what exactly would you require of the skills of such a person?'

'Nothing,' he replied, 'that we don't see here already: balance, agility, lightness — only all to a higher degree; and particularly a more natural arrangement of the centres of gravity.'

'And the advantage that the puppet would have over living dancers?'

'The advantage? In the first place, my dear fellow, a negative one, namely this: that it would be incapable of *affectation*. — For affectation occurs, as you know, whenever the soul (*vis motrix*)* is situated in a place other than a movement's centre of gravity. Since the puppeteer, handling the wire or the string, can have no point except that one under his control all the other limbs are what they should be: dead, mere pendula, and simply obey the law of gravity; an excellent attribute which you will look for in vain among the majority of our dancers.

'Watch P.,' he went on, 'when she is playing Daphne* and, pursued by Apollo, turns to look at him: her soul is somewhere at the bottom of her spine, she bends as if she would snap, like a naiade à la Bernini.* And watch young F. when, as Paris,* he faces the three goddesses and hands Venus the apple: his soul — it is painful to see — is actually in his elbow.

'Such mistakes,' he added, breaking off, 'have been unavoidable ever since we ate from the Tree of Knowledge. But Paradise is locked and barred and the Cherub is behind us. We shall have to go all the way round the world and see whether it might be open somewhere at the back again.'

I laughed. — True enough, I thought. Your wits will not lead you astray if you have none. But I could see that he still had things to say, and begged him to go on.

'Also,' he said, 'these puppets have the advantage of being *resistant to gravity*. Of the heaviness of matter, the factor that most works against the dancer, they are entirely ignorant: because the force lifting them into the air is greater than the one attaching them to the earth. What wouldn't our friend G. give to be four or five stone lighter or to have such a weight working in her favour in her entrechats and pirouettes! Marionettes only *glance* the ground, like elves, the momentary halt lends the limbs a new impetus; but we use it to *rest* on, to recover from the exertion of the dance: a moment which clearly is not dance at all in itself and which we can do nothing with except get it over with as quickly as possible.'

I said that although he was defending his paradox very cleverly he would still never persuade me that there was more grace in a mechanical marionette than in the form and build of the human body.

He replied that it would be quite impossible for a human body even to equal the marionette. In dance, he said, only a god was a match for matter; and that was the point where the two ends of the round earth met.

I was more and more astonished, and did not know what to say to such strange assertions.

It seemed, he replied, taking a pinch of snuff, that I had not read the third chapter of Genesis* attentively; and a man not familiar with that first period of all human education could not properly discuss those following it, let alone the last.

I said that I was perfectly well aware of the damage done by consciousness to the natural grace of a human being. A young man of my acquaintance had, I said, by a chance remark lost his innocence before my very eyes and had afterwards, despite making every conceivable effort, never regained that paradise. — 'But,' I added, 'what conclusions can you draw from that?'

He asked me what had happened.

'About three years ago,' I began, 'I was bathing with a young man whose development at that time had a wonderful grace about it. He would be in his sixteenth year, I should say, and only very remotely, brought on by the kind regards of women, were the first indications of vanity discernible. As it happened we had just seen, in Paris, the youth pulling a thorn out of his foot;* the cast of the statue is well known, most German collections have it. Resting his foot on a stool, to dry it, and glancing at himself as he did so in a large mirror, he was reminded of the statue; he smiled and told me what he had seen. In fact, at precisely that moment, I had seen the same; but either because I wished to find out how securely grace dwelled in him or because I thought it would do him good if I combated his vanity a little, I laughed and answered: he must be seeing things. He blushed, and raised his foot a second time, to show me; but the attempt, very predictably, failed. In confusion he raised his foot a third time, a fourth, again and again, a dozen times: in vain. He was incapable of reproducing the movement — indeed, in the movements he made there was something so comical I could scarcely refrain from laughing at him: —

'From that day, or from that very moment, forth the young man underwent an unbelievable transformation. He began spending days in front of the mirror; and one after the other all his charms deserted him. An invisible and incomprehensible power seemed to settle like an iron net over the free play of his manners and a year later there was not a trace left in him of those qualities that had in the past so delighted the eyes of people around him. There is a person who witnessed that strange and unhappy episode and who word for word could corroborate my account of it.' —

'At this point,' said Herr C. with a smile, 'I must tell you another story. You will soon see its relevance here.

'On my journey to Russia I was staying at the country house of Herr von G., a gentleman of Livland,* whose sons were just then busily engaged in practising their fencing. Especially the elder boy, just down from university, prided himself on his skills and one morning when I was in his room offered me a rapier. We fenced; but it happened that I was better than him; he became heated, confused; almost every thrust of mine hit home and at last his rapier flew across the room. With a laugh, but also a trifle piqued, he retrieved his rapier and said that he had met his match: but everybody would one day, and now he would take me where I should meet mine. The two brothers laughed out loud and cried: "To the wood store with him!" And they took me by the hand and led me down to a bear that Herr von G., their father, was rearing in the yard.

'The bear, when I approached him in astonishment, was reared up on his hind legs and leaning back against a post to which he was fastened, his right paw lifted in readiness and his eye fixing mine. That was his stance, for fencing. I thought I must be dreaming when I saw myself confronted by such an opponent; but "Go on, go on," said Herr von G. "See if you can land a hit on him." Recovering a little from my astonishment I thrust at the bear with my rapier: he made a very slight movement with his paw and parried the thrust. I tried to mislead him with a feint; the bear made no move. I thrust at him again, swiftly and shrewdly, beyond any doubt had it been a human breast I would have hit: the bear made a very slight movement with his paw and parried the stroke. Now I was almost in the position of young Herr von G. And the bear's seriousness discomposed me. Now I tried a thrust, now a feint, the sweat was dripping off me: all in vain! Not only did the bear, like the foremost fencer in the world, parry all my thrusts; when I feinted — no fencer in the world can follow him in this — he did not even react: looking me in the eye, as though he could read my soul in it, he stood with his paw lifted in readiness and when my thrusts were not seriously intended he did not move.

'Do you believe this story?'

'Absolutely!' I cried, applauding him in delight. 'I should believe it from any stranger, it is so very likely. How much more so from you!'

'Well my good friend,' said Herr C., 'you now have everything you need if you are to understand me. We see that in the same measure as reflection in the organic world becomes darker and feebler, grace there emerges in ever greater radiance and supremacy. — But just as two lines intersecting at a point after they have passed through infinity will suddenly come together again on the other side, or the image in a concave mirror, after travelling away into infinity, suddenly comes close up to us again, so when consciousness has, as we might say, passed through an infinity, grace will return; so that grace will be most purely present in the human frame that has either no consciousness or an infinite amount of it, which is to say either in a marionette or in a god.'

'But,' I said rather distractedly, 'should we have to eat again of the Tree of Knowledge to fall back into the state of innocence?'

'Indeed,' he replied; 'that is the final chapter in the history of the world.'

LETTERS

To his aunt,* Auguste Helene von Massow, Frankfurt am Main, 13–18 March 1793 (extract).

On the journey from Gotha to Eisenach,* deep in the mountains, we encountered a man not at all unlike, as it seemed to us, a highwayman. He clung on stealthily behind and when the coachman noticed and beat at him with the whip he sat there in silence and let himself be beaten. The coachman stood up on the box while the coach was moving and lashed and lashed until the man fell off. Then in a terrible fashion the man began to scream. Imagine the mountains, us all alone in the middle of them where every sound is double, and the man screaming in that frightful fashion. It didn't seem like one voice, it seemed like 20 for the crying came back off every mountain twice as loud. The horses were frightened and bolted, and the coachman, still standing up on the box, fell down, the man continued roaring after us — until one of us caught the horses' reins. Now we drew our swords against the robber (which he certainly was) and asked him what exactly he wanted; but his only reply was screams, raging and noise. The coachman drove on fast and we could hear the man still shrieking far behind. With that pleasant music as accompaniment we arrived in *Eisenach* at midnight.

To Christian Ernst Martini,* Potsdam, 19 March 1799 (extract).

Soldiering, which I never did much like since there is in it something utterly incommensurable with my whole being, now became, in the light of these considerations, so detestable to me that I chafed more and more at having to serve its ends. The greatest wonders of military discipline, an object of amazement for all who know about such things, became the object of my heartiest contempt; I thought the officers no more than drill-masters, the soldiers no more than slaves, and when the whole regiment was showing off its tricks it seemed to me the living monument of tyranny. Added to that, I began to be keenly sensible of the bad effect my situation was having on my character. I was often obliged to punish where I should gladly have forgiven, or I forgave where I ought to have punished; and either way I thought myself culpable. At such moments, naturally enough, the desire rose in me to quit a condition in which I was perpetually tormented by two wholly opposed principles, never knowing whether I must act like an officer or like a human being; for to combine the duties of both is, in my view, given the present state of our armies, impossible.

To his sister, Ulrike von Kleist, Frankfurt an der Oder, May 1799 (extracts).

I hear a thousand people speak and see them act and it never occurs to me to ask after the why? Nor do *they* know, they follow obscure inclinations, their actions are determined by the moment. They never come of age and their fate is the plaything of chance. They feel themselves led and drawn as if by invisible forces and follow these, in the sense of their own weakness, wherever it may take them — to happiness, which they only half enjoy, or to unhappiness which then they suffer doubly.

Now it goes without saying that such slavish submission of oneself to the whim of the tyrant fate is wholly unworthy of a free and thinking human being. No free person, no thinking person, stays where chance happens to thrust him; or if he does he does so for a reason, out of choice, because it is better there. He feels that a man may rise above fate; indeed, that, viewed aright, it is actually possible to direct one's fate. He determines according to his reason what manner of happiness is the highest for him, he devises a plan for his life and strives towards his goal with all his strength and in accordance with securely founded principles. For even the bible tells us that God helps those who help themselves.

A person not in a position to draw up a plan for his own life is one not come of age, he may be a child under the guardianship of his parents or a grown man under the guardianship of fate. The first thing a man will do who has his independence is draw up such a plan. And I see now, having wasted seven years as a soldier, seven irretrievable years which I could have employed on my life's plan had I managed to devise it earlier, how necessary it is to draw up such a plan as soon as possible.

The behaviour of a man acting on secure principles is characterized by a beautiful purposefulness, connectedness and unity. In all he thinks, feels and does what drives him is the lofty object he has set himself. Every thought, feeling and intention is connected with that goal, all the forces of his body and soul strive for that common end. His words will never contradict his deeds, nor his deeds his words, he will have grounds in reason to show for every one of his utterances. Only know your goal and it will not be difficult to understand the reasons for your behaviour.

Indeed, it is so inconceivable to me that a man might live without a plan for his life, and I have in the sureness with which I use the present and in the tranquillity with which I look to the future so strong a sense of how inestimably mine benefits me, and the condition of being without such a plan, with no fixed purpose, havering perpetually among uncertain desires, the plaything of chance, a marionette worked by fate — that unworthy condition seems to me so contemptible and would make me so unhappy that death would be far preferable.

To his fiancée, Wilhelmine von Zenge, Würzburg, 13 September 1800 (extract).

Visiting the mad we saw things that were disgusting, things that were risible, but much also instructive and pitiable. Two or three persons lay in a heap, lumpish, wholly insensible, so that one almost doubted whether to call them human beings at all. But then in a cheerful and amusing manner a professor approached us who had studied too hard and began haranguing us in Latin and his questions were so rapid and fluent, his Latin was so coherent and correct, that we were seriously at a loss how to answer him, quite as though he were sane. In a cell sat a monk, in black, his look was profound, deeply serious and sombre. Slowly he raised his eyes upon us and seemed to be weighing our innermost lives. Then, in a voice that was weak but resonant and that it crushed the spirit to hear, he began to warn us against joy and to put us in mind of the life everlasting and of our devotions. We did not reply. He spoke with long pauses. Now and then he looked at us sorrowfully, as though, after all, he thought us damned. Once in the pulpit during a sermon he had made a slip of the tongue and thereafter was convinced that he had falsified the word of God. From the monk we went on to a merchant who had gone mad out of pique and pride because his father had been knighted but the honour had not passed to the son. But the most frightful thing of all was the sight of a creature driven mad by an unnatural vice — An 18-year-old youth who, it was said, had until recently been a picture of health and beauty and who bore traces of this still, hung there over the filthy opening with naked, pale, emaciated limbs, a cavernous chest, a lolling head — His dead-white countenance had over it a breath of redness, dull and veined, such as consumptives show, his lids drooped over his dying, almost extinguished eyes, a few lank hairs, like an old man's, covered his prematurely whitened head, his thirsting tongue, parched dry, hung out over his pale and shrivelled lips, his hands were behind his back, swaddled and stitched in — it was beyond his strength to move his tongue in speech, his breath hurt him, he was scarcely strong enough to draw it — the nerves of his brain were not themselves untuned but weak, wholly exhausted, incapable of obeying his soul, his whole life one paralysing everlasting debility — Oh, rather a thousand deaths than one such life as his! So terrible is nature's vengeance when her will is criminally contravened. Away with this frightful image —

To Ulrike von Kleist, Berlin, 5 February 1801 (extracts).

And I should like to tell you everything, if that were possible. But it is not possible, for this reason if for no other: that we lack the means. Language, all we have, is not adequate to the task, it cannot depict the soul and gives us only shreds and fragments. That is why I feel something like horror whenever I am to disclose my innermost self to anyone; not because that self is shy of being uncovered but because I cannot show the person *everything*, simply *cannot*, and am fearful therefore that offering only fragments I shall be misunderstood.

I still have not been able to decide to take a job, and you know the reasons. There are reasons why I should, and I do not need to tell you those either. I shall always be glad to do what is right, but what should one do not knowing what is right? This state of inner uncertainty had become unbearable and, to make up my mind, I did what the Roman did* in Porsenna's tent to force him, the King, when he was dithering over the terms for peace, to make up his mind. He drew a chalk circle around himself and the King and declared that neither would step out of it until a decision had been reached in favour of war or peace. I did much the same. I resolved not to leave my room until I had decided on a plan for my life; but 8 days passed and in the end I was obliged to leave the room still undecided. — Oh, Ulrike you do not know how often and badly I am shaken in my inner self — Please do not misunderstand me when I say this. Oh we have no means of making ourselves *wholly* understandable to other people and by his very nature the human being has no one to confide in but himself.

Meanwhile day by day it is becoming ever more obvious to me that I am quite incapable of doing a job. I have grown completely accustomed to following my own purposes and wholly unaccustomed to following anyone else's.

To Wilhelmine von Zenge, Berlin, 22 March 1801 (extract).

Even as a child (I think it was on the Rhine, reading Wieland) I had adopted as my own the idea that attaining perfection is the purpose of Creation. I believed that after death, on some other planet, we should progress from the degree of perfection we had attained on this and that there in the future we should be able to make further use of the treasury of truths we had collected here. Out of these thoughts gradually I developed a religion of my own and the determination never for a moment to stand still but always constantly to strive towards a higher stage of culture, that was soon the principle underlying everything I did. *Culture* seemed to me the only goal worth striving for and *truth* the only wealth worth having. — I don't know whether to you, my dear Wilhelmine, those two ideas *truth* and *culture* could ever be as holy as they are to me. They would have to be if you wish to understand the continuation of the story of my soul. I thought them so holy that to those two ends — collecting truth and acquiring culture — I made the *costliest* sacrifices — you know what they were. — But I must be brief.

Not long ago I became acquainted with the new, the so-called Kantian, philosophy* — and must now pass on to you one of the ideas in it, though I am not apprehensive that you will be as deeply and painfully shaken by it as I was. Nor are you familiar enough with the whole context to grasp its significance fully. But I will be as clear as I can.

If people all had green lenses instead of eyes they would be bound to think that the things they see through them *are* green — and they would never be able to decide whether the eye shows them things as they are or whether it isn't adding something to them belonging not to them but to the eye. It is the same with our minds. We cannot decide whether what we call truth is truly truth or whether it only seems so to us. If the latter then the truth we gather here *is* nothing after death — and all our striving to acquire something of our own that will go with us even into the grave, is in vain —

Oh Wilhelmine, though your own heart may not be pierced by this thought do not think me ridiculous that I feel myself wounded deep in my innermost life by it. My highest and only goal has sunk and now I have none —

Since this conviction — that no truth is discoverable here on earth — appeared before my soul I have given up reading. I have paced my room in idleness, sat down at the open window, run out of the house, in the end by the unrest in me I was driven to the cafés and tobacco houses, I went to plays and concerts, to distract myself, I even, to blot everything out, did a very silly thing that I would rather Carl told you about than me; and still in all this outer tumult the one thought working and burning in my anxious soul was this: your *highest* and *only* goal in life has sunk —

To Wilhelmine von Zenge, Paris, 15 August 1801 (extract).

Truly, considering that we need a lifetime to learn how we ought to live, that even in death we still have no idea what heaven wants with us, if nobody knows the purpose of his existence nor what he is intended for, if human reason is not adequate to comprehend us, our souls, our lives, the things around us, if even after thousands of years we are still doubtful whether there is any such thing as *right* — can God ask of such creatures that they be *responsible*? Let nobody tell me there is a voice in us that whispers clearly what is right. The same voice telling the Christian to forgive his enemies tells the South Sea Islander to roast his, and piously he devours them — Are we right to trust our convictions if they can justify such deeds? — And then what does it mean, to do something evil, judging by effect? What is *evil*? *Absolute evil*? The things of the world are connected and intertwined in a myriad ways, every act is the mother of a million more and often the worst begets the best — Tell me who on this earth has ever done anything *evil*? Anything to be counted evil *in all eternity* —? And despite what history tells us about Nero and Attila and Cartouche* and the Huns and the Crusades and the Spanish Inquisition still our planet rolls amiably through space, spring comes round again, and people live, enjoy themselves and die as they always did. —

To Ulrike von Kleist, on the island in the Aare, near Thun, 1 May 1802 (extract).

Now I am living on an island in the Aare, where it leaves Lake Thun, entirely enclosed by Alps, a mile or so from the town. I have rented a little house on the tip of the island, for six months, and, because it is so remote, very cheaply, and am living there all alone. Nobody else lives on the island except, at the other end, a little fisher family with whom I have already been out on the lake once at midnight when they haul their nets in and set them again. The father has sent over one of the two daughters to keep house for me: a sweet girl who looks like her name: Mädeli. We get up with the sun, she plants me flowers in the garden, does my cooking, whilst I work for my return to you. Then we eat together; on Sundays she wears her pretty Swiss costume, a present from me, we row across, she goes to church in Thun, I climb the Schreckhorn* and after the service we both come back. I know nothing more of the whole world than that. I should be quite without any unpleasant feelings were I not, after a lifetime's habit, compelled to create them myself. So for example now I have strange fear that I might die before I have finished my work. But as to dying of hunger, there, thank God, I have no worries though everything I earn I spend at once. As you know, I am quite incapable of saving money. I did think of it recently and told Mädeli: she had to save. But the girl didn't understand the word, I wasn't able to make the thing comprehensible to her, both of us laughed, and we shall have to go on as before. — Besides, I cannot but live cheaply here, I rarely leave the island, see nobody, read no books or newspapers, need nothing but myself. Now and then Geβner or Zschokke or Wieland* come from Bern, hear some of my work and flatter me — in brief, my only wish is to die having achieved three things: a child, a beautiful poem and a great deed. For the noblest thing in life is, after all: our ability nobly to discard it. — In a word these extraordinary circumstances are amazingly good for me and I have so unaccustomed myself to common things that I should have no desire to cross over to the other shore if you were all not living there. But I am working without respite for release from exile — You understand. Perhaps I shall be back among you in a year's time. — If I do not succeed I shall stay in Switzerland and you must come to me. For if my life is to have a worthy end it must be in your arms. —

To his cousin, Marie von Kleist, Berlin, summer 1811.

The life I lead is, since you and A. Müller left, too desolate and sad for words. Then lately I have rather lost contact with the two or three houses here that I used to frequent and am almost every day at home from morning till evening without seeing one single human being who might tell me how things are in the world. You come to your own assistance with your imagination and from all quarters summon those you love and care for into your own room. But I, do you see, cursed as I am in some incomprehensible way, I have no such comfort. Was ever another poet's case quite like mine? I doubt it. Faced with the white page my imagination is as busy as can be, the figures it brings forth are definite in outline and colour, but imagining what is real I find not only hard but actually painful. It is as if my imagination, at the very moment of its being activated, is fettered by things already so definite, articulated and wholly determined. Confused by too many *shapes* I cannot come to any inner clarity of perception; I have the constant feeling that the object is not an object of the imagination: I have a desire to penetrate and comprehend it with my senses in the true and living present. I find anyone viewing these things differently quite unintelligible; he must have had experiences wholly unlike mine. Life with its pestering, endlessly recurring demands tears one mind from another in so many ways even at the moment of their coming together, and how much more so when they are apart. We cannot hope to move any closer; and the most we ever manage is to stay where we are. But then in moments when we are sad and out of tune, and they are all too many nowadays, we are deprived of any comfort. In brief, Müller, since he went away, seems dead to me, and I feel just that sort of grief about him, and if I did not know that you will be coming back again it would be exactly the same in me with respect to you.

To Marie von Kleist, Berlin, summer 1811.

As soon as I have finished the business in hand I shall take up something thoroughly of the imagination again. Now and then reading or in the theatre I feel, as it were, a breath of air out of my earliest youth. Life, stretching before me in utter desolation, suddenly opens on a view of wonder and beauty and powers stir in me that I thought wholly dead. Then my desire is to follow my heart wherever it might lead and pay absolutely no heed to anything except my own inner satisfaction. Till now I have been too much ruled by other people's verdicts; *Das Käthchen von Heilbronn* in particular has many marks of this. It was from the outset an entirely excellent conception and only by wishing to make it suitable for the theatre was I led astray and made mistakes that I could weep at now. In brief, I shall fill myself through and through with the thought that so long as a work comes forth in utter freedom from the womb of a human mind it must also necessarily for that reason belong to the whole of humanity.

To Marie von Kleist, Berlin, 19 November 1811.

Dearest Marie, Even as my soul lifts up a song of triumph at the moment of my death my thoughts turn, as they must, your way once more and I will open myself as well as I can to you: the only person whose feelings and opinion I care anything about; for in my heart I have overcome everything else on earth, the sum of it and all particulars. Yes, it is true, I have deceived you, or rather I have deceived myself; but having told you a thousand times that this is a thing I would not survive I now give you the proof, taking leave of you. While you were in Berlin I replaced you with another friend;* but, if that is any consolation to you, not one who will live with me but who, in the feeling that I would be no more faithful to her than I was to you, will die with me. My relationship with this woman prohibits me from telling you any more. But you should know this much: that my soul, by touching hers, has become wholly ripe for death; that I have measured the whole splendour of the human spirit in hers and that I am dying because there is nothing left on earth now for me to learn or acquire. Farewell. You are the one and only woman on earth I should wish to see again in the beyond. Not Ulrike? Yes and no: let her own feeling decide. She has not, it seems to me, understood the art of sacrificing oneself, of going under utterly for the thing one loves: the greatest blessedness imaginable on earth, indeed it must be the stuff of heaven itself if it is true that in heaven we have enjoyment and happiness. Adieu! — Consider also that I have found a friend whose soul soars like a young eagle's, such as in all my life I have never encountered; who understands my sadness as the higher kind and firmly rooted and incurable, and therefore though she would have means enough at her disposal to make me happy here will die with me instead; who accords me the unprecedented joy of allowing herself, for this purpose, to be lifted, as easily as a violet from a meadow, out of a situation in which she desired nothing; who is leaving for my sake a father who adores her, a husband generous enough to cede her to me, a child as lovely and lovelier than the morning sun: and you will understand that my one triumphant concern must be to find an abyss deep enough to leap into with her. — Adieu once more! —

To Sophie Müller

Heaven knows, my dear friend, what strange feelings, half melancholy, half extravagant, have moved us at this hour as our two souls like two cheerful balloonists rise over the world to write to you once more. You see we had decided not to send out any cards among our acquaintances and friends. Probably the reason is that in a thousand happy moments we have thought of you and a thousand times imagined how you in your cheerful fashion would have laughed out loud (in delight) if you had seen us in the green room or the red. Truly, the world is a very odd set-up! — It is *right* that Jettchen and I, two unhappy and unfortunate people who have always been accused of coldness, should have fallen so utterly in love, the best proof of which is that we are now going to die together.

Dear, dear friend, farewell, and have on earth, as may indeed be possible, much happiness. We for our part desire to know nothing of the joys of this world and dream of the meadows of heaven where we shall wander in a hazy radiance with long wings on our shoulders. Adieu, a kiss from me, the writer, to Müller: say he should think of me now and then and be a valiant fighter on God's side against the devil Superstition who holds the world in chains. —

[PS from Henriette Vogel]

> *Exactly how this happened though*
> *I'll tell you all some day.*
> *I haven't time to now. —*

Farewell then, my dear friends. Remember in joy and sorrow the two strange people about to set off on their great voyage of discovery.
                                                                    Henriette.

[In Kleist's hand again]
Written in the Green Room*
[Berlin,] 20 November 1811
H. v. Kleist.*

To Ulrike von Kleist

I cannot die without having first, contented and cheerful as I am, reconciled myself with the whole world and so also and above all others with you, my dearest Ulrike. Let me take back the harsh remark contained in my letter to Marie. You did everything not just in a sister's but in any human being's power to save me: the truth is there was no help for me on earth. And now farewell; may heaven grant you a death

even half as joyous and inexpressibly cheerful as mine: I can wish you nothing more sincerely and fervently than that.
Stimming's, near Potsdam.
The ?, on the morning of my death.   Yours,
                                            Heinrich.

To Marie von Kleist, Stimming's 'Krug' near Potsdam, 21 November 1811.

Dearest Marie, If you knew how death and love take turns to garland these last moments of my life with the flowers of heaven and of earth, surely you would be content to let me die. Oh I assure you, I am blissfully happy. Morning and evening I kneel — a thing I have never been able to do before — and pray to God; now I can thank him for my life, the most tortured ever lived by any human being, since He makes it up to me with this most splendid and pleasurable of deaths. Oh if only I could do something for you to lessen the bitter grief I shall cause you. For a moment I intended having my portrait painted; but then it seemed to me that I had done you too much wrong to presume my portrait would give you much pleasure. Will it console you if I say that I would never have taken this friend in your place had she only wished to live with me? Dearest Marie, that is the truth: there have been moments when I told my dear friend so quite candidly. Oh I assure you I love you so much, you are so supremely dear to me that I can scarcely say that I love my friend (whom I idolize) more than I do you. The resolve rising in her soul to die with me drew me I cannot tell you how powerfully, irresistibly to her bosom. Do you remember that I often asked you would you die with me? — But you always said no — A whirlpool of never before experienced blissful happiness has seized hold of me and I cannot deny that her grave is dearer to me than the beds of all the empresses of the world. — Oh my dear friend, may God soon call you to that better world where we shall all with the love of angels embrace one another again.
— Adieu.

NOTES

Plays

The Broken Jug / *Der zerbrochne Krug*

As he says in his Note, Kleist was prompted to write the play by seeing an engraving at the house of his friend Heinrich Zschokke in Bern in the winter of 1801–2. Indeed, he, Zschokke and two other friends, the young Wieland and the young Geßner, all agreed to write something having that engraving as starting point. Naturally, Kleist's was best. He got on with it in Dresden in the early summer of 1803 (borrowing Aristophanes and Sophocles from the library), finished it in 1806 (by which time he was working on his other 'comedy' *Amphitryon*), published three scenes of it in his *Phöbus* in March 1808. It came out entire in 1811, when it already had some notoriety because of its disastrous staging by Goethe in Weimar 2 March 1808.

The title is that of a painting and an engraving, but also alludes to a proverb in French and in German: 'tant va la cruche à l'eau qu'à la fin elle se brise'; 'der Krug geht so lange zu Wasser, bis er bricht': roughly, 'everything has its day' or 'you'll do that once too often'. The painting by Jean-Baptiste Greuze (1725–1805), *La Cruche cassée*, shows a pretty girl holding a broken jug on her right arm and with many hints connects it with a sexual fall. In Beaumarchais's play *Le Mariage de Figaro* (1784) the proverb is altered so as to conclude 'qu'à la fin elle s'emplit' — thus not 'until it breaks' but 'until it fills'. So there is a well-established sexual innuendo in the saying itself. In the picture at Zschokke's house the cognoscenti — and doubtless Kleist was one — would recognize that the court is actually sitting outside a brothel. Kleist's play, whose subject is Judge Adam's attempted seduction of the village girl Eve, is laced with often quite coarse sexual allusion and in Scene 6 Frau Marthe makes the connection between the jug and Eve's good name explicit. Since Eve is not 'guilty' Kleist must contradict the traditional sense of his play's iconography.

p. 3 Kleist's Note: Describing the disposition and the gestures of the characters he has his own play in mind more than the engraving (whose full title was *Le Juge, ou La Cruche cassée*). The original was not Dutch but French, by Jean Philibert Debucourt (1757–1824), and harks back to Greuze. The allusion to

Oedipus and Creon sets up a paradigm which, like Adam and Eve, is suggestive but ill-fitting. Oedipus in Thebes initiates proceedings to find the murderer of Laius but, unlike Kleist's Adam, does not know that the guilty man is himself.

p. 3 Dramatis Personae: Some have 'speaking names' which actually misdirect. Walter in German suggests 'walten', 'to govern', and perhaps thus some absolute authority. His role and manner in the play don't quite bear that out. Licht means 'light'. Towards the end, fetching Frau Brigitte, he does throw light on the situation. But he is nearly as corrupt as Adam (see p. 8), serves his own interest, and we can't think things will be much better under his rule. Adam seduces Eve, or tries to. His fall is literal (from her bedroom window), and then from office. Eve is innocent (except that, deceived by Adam and fearful for Ruprecht's safety, she is prepared to connive in what would be a bending of the law, but not to pay Adam's price). Insisting heavily on the Adam and Eve story, as also on Adam the Clubfoot (Oedipus or Devil), Kleist is not so much directing us towards the main sense of his play but rather, and very characteristically, offering us familiar patterns and showing that they don't fit.

The action takes place on 1 February (see p. 39) towards the end of the seventeenth century. But Kleist is careless about the historical context and there are inconsistencies. His localities — Huisum, Holla, Hussahe — are comic inventions.

p. 4 clubfoot: The name Oedipus means 'swollen foot'.

p. 5 stove: A large tiled stove used for heating a room and here decorated with a protruding billy-goat.

p. 8 let this cup pass from thee: Matthew 26,39.

p. 8 Demosthenes: 384–322 BC, Athenian orator, was said to have been bribed by Harpalus, Alexander the Great's fugitive treasurer, to keep silent when the Athenians prosecuted him. Adam's reference to the King of Macedonia (Alexander) himself only muddles the matter. But clearly, Licht is not clean and Adam has some hold over him.

p. 14 Puffendorf: Samuel Puffendorf (1632–94), German jurist and historian.

p. 21 Batavia: Now Jakarta. Formerly the capital city of the Dutch East Indies.

p. 24 United Provinces: 'The seven northern provinces of the Netherlands, allied together principally by the Union of Utrecht in 1579, and subsequently developing into the kingdom of Holland' (*OED*).

pp. 25–7 For Frau Marthe's description of her jug Kleist used a history of the Netherlands by Jan Wagenaar published in German in 1756–66. For the comic effect it is not, I think, necessary to know exactly who everybody was. Besides, Kleist is careless or takes liberties. The Sea Beggars were Dutch freedom-fighters. They took Briel from the Spaniards in 1572.

p. 57 *praeter propter:* Roughly, more or less.

Amphitryon / *Amphitryon*

Kleist seems to have worked at *Amphitryon* and *Jug* together, beginning in the early summer of 1803. It was finished by the end of 1806. Adam Müller published it in May 1807, to raise money for Kleist, then in a French prison. It was not staged until 1899.

The essential structure of the story is very ancient. See Genesis 6,4: 'when the sons of God came in unto the daughters of men, and they bare children to them, the same became mighty men which were of old, men of renown.' Thus, in Greek mythology, Zeus fathers Heracles on Alcmene. That story is told in the *Odyssey*, Book XI; in Hesiod ('Shield of Heracles'); in Pindar's *Isthmian* VII; and there were plays, since lost, on the subject, by Aeschylus, Sophocles and Euripides. The first surviving classical version is by the Roman dramatist Plautus (*c*.254–184 BC). Molière goes back to Plautus for his comedy *Amphitryon* in 1668, and Kleist goes back to Molière. He calls his play 'a comedy after Molière' or, in a letter to Wieland of 17.12.1807, 'a reworking' of Molière.

In the story a woman is deceived into adultery. She sleeps with a man who deludes her into thinking he is her husband. Such a mistake is the stuff of scurrilous comedy and Plautus and Molière, with coarse subplots, treat it so. But because Zeus is involved and Heracles is born the story had, for the ancients at least, a serious dimension too. Plautus actually introduces his play as a *tragi*comedy. There is not much seriousness of any kind in Molière's play, but there is in Kleist's and not because a god and a prince are involved. The seriousness is all in the intensely developed character of Alcmene, and, as in *Jug*, it is incongruous in a context of coarse comedy. Again the issue is a woman's sexual integrity. It is remarkable how often Kleist locates his most radical and disturbing experiments in that issue. And he seems to enjoy — here, in *Jug*, in *Marquise*, in *Das Käthchen von Heilbronn* (not included) — situations which are thoroughly ambiguous, in which the scurrilous and the sublime coexist and where there is a continual veering between the two. In *Jug* and *Amphitryon* a woman is subjected to a severe, not to say sadistic, inquisition. She is more at risk than anybody else, has more to lose, suffers more.

p. 66 A comedy after Molière: Molière's play is a comedy of manners and a satire on the court of Louis XIV. The only issue, not a very serious one, is male honour. Alcmène, who does not even appear in Act 3, is not much more than the occasion for that issue. Kleist's consistent intention is to shift the play out of the merely social into the psychological and — some think — the metaphysical. Which means that he deepens, intensifies and complicates the character and predicament of Alcmene. Act II Scenes 4 and 5 (containing the changed initial on the diadem and the long tormenting of Alcmene by Jupiter) are entirely his, and throughout, as he translates the French text, he moves it into a language all his own. Kleist's play, though often very funny and not just in its subplot, is from Alcmene's point of view certainly not a comedy. For what she undergoes Jupiter and Amphitryon together offer no compensation at the end.

p. 68 Athenians, Labdacus, Pharissa: In the myth Amphitryon fights against a tribe in Thessaly. Labdacus and Pharissa are Kleist's inventions.

p. 69 Styx: A river of the Underworld. The gods swore by it.
   Phoebus: Here as the sun god.

p. 79 Lover or husband: The distinction is made by Molière's Jupiter too, but Kleist develops it. Note particularly the sexual uninhibitedness of Alcmene's reply.

p. 89 Juno or **p. 103 Hera:** Jupiter/Zeus's wife, whom he often deceived.

p. 93 ortolan: A small bird, a species of bunting, considered a delicacy.

p. 104 Callisto, Leda, Europa: All seduced by Zeus. The first, a companion of Artemis, gave birth to Arcas, ancestor of the Arcadians; the second, wife of the Spartan king Tyndarus, to Castor, Pollux and Helen; and the third, sister of Cadmus, was carried away by Zeus in the form of a white bull and bore him three sons, Minos, Aeacus and Rhadamanthus who became judges in the Underworld.
   Tyndarides: Castor and Pollux.

p. 109 Orcus, Eurydice: Orpheus went down into Orcus (the Underworld) to fetch back his wife Eurydice, but failed.

p. 110 Hermes: The Greek equivalent of Mercury.
   Ganymede: A beautiful youth who, minding sheep on Mount Ida, was taken up to heaven by Zeus to be his cupbearer.

p. 127 Argus: A giant with a hundred eyes, was employed by Hera to guard Io against Zeus's attentions. Hermes killed him.

p. 128 Ares: God of war.

p. 130 Peneus: A river in Elis, in the north-western Peloponnese. It and the Alpheus were diverted by Heracles to clean out the Augean stables.
   Bosporus: The straits between the Black Sea and the Sea of Marmara.
   Ida: The mountain overlooking the Plain of Troy (which extends to the
      Hellespont, the straits at the western end of the Sea of Marmara).

p. 132 Cadmus: The founder of Thebes.

p. 134 To you there will be born a son: Cf. Matthew, 1,21: 'And she shall bring forth a son.' Some commentators, among them Goethe and Adam Müller, thought of Alcmene as Mary, Amphitryon as Joseph and Jupiter as God or the Holy Spirit.

The Prince of Homburg/ *Prinz Friedrich von Homburg*

Kleist found raw material for his play — an account of the Battle of Fehrbellin, of Homburg's impetuosity and of the Elector's leniency towards him — in K. H. Krause's *Mein Vaterland unter den hohenzollerischen Regenten* (Halle, 1803). Kleist borrowed the book from the Dresden library early in 1809 and finished his play a year later on 19 March 1810. He seems to have intended it, like his *Arminius*, 1808, as a patriotic piece that might stiffen Prussian resolve against the French. He looked forward confidently to publication and performance. Neither happened. Kleist then dedicated the play to the King's sister-in-law Princess Amalie Marie Anne, who was a descendant of the historical Prince of Homburg. His cousin Marie von Kleist presented it to her on 3 September 1811. She thought it insulting to her ancestor and actually prevented a production of it in 1822. Tieck retrieved the dedication copy for its first publication in 1821.

In *Homburg*, his last play, Kleist seems no more at ease with the world than he does in any of his writings. *Homburg* is recalcitrant, it doesn't fit the patriotic purpose for which it was supposedly intended. The last lines — 'To war!' etc. — ring out very definitely in one direction, but in fact they are as uncomfortable as Alcmene's 'Oh!' The issue *looks* simple: A young man has to be taught a lesson, he is put through an education, taught that he must subordinate himself to the law. The process is severe, but he comes through the ordeal and will be reliable henceforth. *Does* he come through? He seems annihilated, like Alcmene. And the state itself, for whose service Homburg is thus educated, is from the first dreamy scene to the last a very queer place indeed, most un-Prussian. If Homburg needs educating so surely does the Elector, who does much to induce the unreliable young man into catastrophe; himself, on his white horse, acts foolishly; and, in Act IV Scene I, is astonished and confused when he learns that Homburg is not acting as an officer should. Kleist's drama is no apologia for absolute authority. On the contrary, Law and the State are upheld only because subjects and sovereign, all quirky and liable to confusion and weakness, co-operate in upholding it.

Dedicating his play to Princess Amalie, Kleist wrote eight lines of verse which I have not translated. In them he imagines himself crowned by her for his efforts.

p. 135 Dramatis Personae: The historical characters, notably Homburg, the Elector and the Electress, are much altered by Kleist for his own ends. Natalie is entirely his invention.

p. 136 Fehrbellin: Lies seventy-five miles north-west of Berlin. The battle was fought on 18 June 1675. Kleist is careless about the date (see p. 188).

p. 136 Wrangel: Count Waldemar Wrangel; he commanded the Swedish troops at Fehrbellin.

p. 140 Mamelukes: They were the ruling class in Egypt, famous for their cavalry, defeated by Napoleon in 1798. Hohenzollern is giving a facetious answer to Homburg's bewildered 'What cavalry?'

p. 140 What is this glove?: Once he knows it is Natalie's, it 'proves' his dream. No predicament could be more Romantic. See Coleridge: 'If a man could pass through Paradise in a dream, and have a flower presented to him as a pledge that his soul had really been there, and if he found that flower in his hand when he awoke — Aye! and what then?' (*Notebooks*, ed. by Stephen Potter, p. 189).

pp. 145–6 The aim of the plan ... Hennings is to get behind the Swedes, secure the bridges across the Rhyn and so cut off their retreat. Once he and Truchss have forced them into the marshes 'lying behind their right wing' then, and only then, is Homburg to charge. He charges too soon; the Swedes, though mauled, are able to withdraw over the river. The war, as the play finishes, is resumed. The historical Homburg also engaged the enemy too soon and got the forces of Brandenburg into difficulty. After the battle the Elector reprimanded him but forgave him.

p. 146 Rathenow: On the Havel, south-west of Fehrbellin. They had fought there three days before.

p. 155 the Prussian Ten Commandments: Their military code here — ironically, coming from Homburg — given the status of absolute religious authority.

p. 156 the Mark: Here all the territory of Brandenburg. The word's first sense, in English too, is boundary.

p. 159 In Natalie's fictitious family history Kleist alludes to contemporary politics. For example, by 'tyrannous Spanish armies' he means the French.

p. 161 Froben: Emanuel von Froben was master of the Elector's stables. Kleist's sources carried the story, perhaps only a legend, of his sacrificial death. Kleist elaborated it.

p. 165 *Per aspera ad astra*: 'By hard ways to the stars.'

p. 166 Brutus: Lucius Junius Brutus, founder and First Consul of the Roman republic, had his two sons executed when they conspired against the state.

p. 171 Dey of Algiers and **p. 190 Dey of Tunis:** A dey is an Arab ruler. To Kleist's audience these two would stand for cruelty and tyranny.

p. 171 Sardanapalus: Last king of Assyria, notably vicious.

p. 171 the ancient Roman tyrants: The worst of the emperors — Nero, Caligula, etc.

pp. 174–5 Homburg's abject fear of death is like Claudio's in *Measure for Measure*, Act III Scene I.

p. 176 to the nunnery: Like Hamlet to Ophelia: 'Get thee to a nunnery' (Act III Scene I).

p. 184 dervish: A Mohammedan mendicant friar.

p. 190 the silk cord: As sent by oriental despots to subjects they wished to be rid of. The recipient was supposed to strangle himself.

p. 193 Swiss: Here 'door-keeper'. Cf. French 'le suisse'. The Swiss had for centuries served as mercenaries at the courts of Europe.

Stories

Michael Kohlhaas / *Michael Kohlhaas*

Kleist's friend Ernst von Pfuel is said to have prompted him to write the story, perhaps by indicating a source. Probably he began it in Königsberg or during his sick leave in Pillau (late summer 1806). A fragment appeared in the sixth issue of *Phöbus* (November 1808). *Kohlhaas* was either finished or revised in May 1810 for publication in the first volume of the *Erzählungen* that September.

Kleist (p. 209) describes the story as coming 'from an old chronicle' — almost certainly the *Märckische Chronic* of Peter Hafftiz (c. 1525–c. 1601) — which he would have found in a work by Christian Schöttgen and George Christoph Kreysig published in Leipzig in 1731 and entitled *Diplomatische und curieuse Nachlese der Historie von Ober-Sachsen, und angrentzenden Ländern*. Through that compendium volume he had access to other documents as well, including Luther's letter to Kohlhaas. Needless to say, Kleist does what he pleases with this material.

Kafka was particularly fond of *Michael Kohlhaas* and it is easy to see why. His heroes struggle with similar jurisdictions and bureaucracies; a comic and terrifying *disproportion* rules in their world too. The ending of Kleist's story is characteristic. Its moral neatness is deliberately marred by the fact that Kohlhaas, having taken communion, does not forgive his enemy the Elector of Saxony but with his last act, swallowing the capsule, has his revenge. How else are the high and mighty to be punished?

p. 209 The Havel flows through the lakes on the west side of Berlin. There is a Kohlhasenbrück near Potsdam on the Griebnitzsee.

p. 209 He is crossing out of Brandenburg into Saxony. The Elbe is the frontier.

p. 211 Dresden: In Kleist's day, though not in Kohlhaas's, Dresden was the capital of Saxony.

p. 223 Schwerin: Far to the north-west of Berlin, out of harm's way.

p. 225 'Forgive thine enemies ...': Matthew 5,44. The verse actually reads: 'Love your enemies, bless them that curse you, do good to them that hate you ...'

p. 228 Mulde: A river between Leipzig and Wittenberg.

p. 231 St Jervis's Day: 19 June.

p. 233 Pleissenburg: A fortress of the Pleisse, defending Leipzig. The Pleisse is Leipzig's river.

p. 233 Jessen, Mühlberg, Damerow, Lützen: Within the rough triangle Wittenberg, Naumburg, Dresden.

pp. 234–5 Luther's real letter, 8 December 1534, though it takes as its text 'Vengeance is mine, saith the Lord', is by no means unfriendly. Moreover, the historical Kohlhaas seems to have approached Luther for advice.

p. 239 my two sovereigns: Kohlhaas, a native of Brandenburg but owning property in Saxony (see p. 221), is a subject of both Electors.

with your saviour, no: Notice that here Luther refuses him the sacrament.

pp. 246–7 Wilsdruf, Döbbeln, Hainichen: Between Dresden and Leipzig.

p. 253 Erzgebirge: Mountains on the border between Saxony and Bohemia.

p. 256 Lockewitz: Nowadays a suburb of Dresden.

p. 260 Altenburg: On the Pleisse, some way south of Leipzig.

p. 262–63 Dahme, Herzberg: On the long way north to Berlin. The geographical zone of Kohlhaas's career is large and itself suggests the great ramifications from a small beginning. By now the Holy Roman Emperor himself is involved.

pp. 264–5 Jüterbock, Luckau: To the west and east of Dahme respectively.

p. 277 the chronicles: This reference to historical sources is disingenuous, since Kleist has largely gone his own way. Note his casual reference to 'history' as his own fiction ends (p. 280).

p. 280 in a churchyard: Men executed, like suicides, were not normally allowed in consecrated ground.

The Marquise of O. / *Die Marquise von O …*

Probably Kleist brought back the finished story with him when he was released from his French imprisonment in July 1807. It is mentioned in two letters of 19 December 1807 as being among those of his manuscripts which were ready for publication. It was first published in the second issue (February 1808) of his *Phöbus*, then in the first collection of his stories in 1810.

Unwitting conception has quite often been treated in literature. Montaigne relates a case in his essay 'On Drunkenness'. There the woman announces her pregnancy in church and asks the culprit to come forward. Kleist's own anecdote 'Strange Occurrence, in my day, in Italy', published in the *Berliner Abendblätter* 3 January 1811, tells of female resourcefulness in the face of the world's hypocritical blame.

The Marquise, 'a lady of excellent reputation', is severely tried by Kleist. She suffers two crises: first her involuntary pregnancy; second, perhaps even worse, the realization that her knight in shining armour is her rapist. Altogether the usual safe categories are broken down in this blackly comic story. Father, jealous of the Count no doubt, swings from murderous rage to incestuous fondness. And there are lesser indecencies too: mother and daughter tittering behind Leopardo's back. The story gave offence, as Kleist hoped it would.

p. 281 Based on a real event: None has come to light. Kleist, and other storytellers at the time, commonly used such 'authenticating' notes.

p. 281 the —— War: The Second Coalition War, 1799–1802, and particularly the campaign of 1799 when the armies of Austria and Russia drove out the French from the republics they had established in Italy. Italian and Polish troops fought on the French side. With the initials M., V., etc. Kleist suggests plausible places — perhaps Mantua, Vicenza, etc.

p. 284 P.: Perhaps Piacenza. There was a battle near there, on the Trebbia, 17–19 June 1799.

p. 287 General K.: Perhaps General Korsakow.

p. 288 Z: Zürich? General Korsakow had his headquarters there.

pp. 307–8 There is a similar reconciliation between father and daughter, though not quite so extreme, in Rousseau's *La nouvelle Héloise* (Part I, letter 63).

The Chilean Earthquake / *Das Erdbeben in Chili*

Probably written in 1806, whilst Kleist was in Königsberg. It was the first of his stories to be published, appearing as 'Jeronimo and Josephe, a scene from the Chilean earthquake of 1647' in the *Morgenblatt für gebildete Stände*, in five instalments, 10–15 September 1807. Kleist's friend Rühle had sold it to that periodical, to raise money for him then still in a French prison. It was published again in the first volume of the *Erzählungen*. There for reasons of space the thirty-one paragraphs of the *Morgenblatt* edition were compressed into three. My text, following Sembdner's, restores the thirty-one.

Two earthquakes are important for Kleist's story. The first is that named in the title which wrecked Santiago in 1647 and killed about four thousand people. Eyewitness accounts had been translated into German, and Kleist very likely read one or other of them. But in some ways the Lisbon earthquake of 1755 matters more. The death and devastation caused by it were worse. Its shock waves travelled across Europe, literally; and caused thinking people to wonder whether they were, after all, living in 'the best of all possible worlds'. Kleist has his bitter say in that debate. Frequently — p. 313, for example — his irony reminds us of Voltaire's in *Candide*.

Family, Law and the Church show up especially badly in Kleist's story. But into the carnage, as an interlude, he sets an image of a better humanity, outside the city. No class distinctions have validity there, and the family is opened and extended when Josephe nurses Donna Elvire's child. Then they go back in and the Christian violence resumes. *The Chilean Earthquake* is perhaps Kleist's bleakest tale, and yet it finishes with the words 'as though he must rejoice'.

p. 312 Corpus Christi: Usually celebrated on the second Thursday after Whit.

Betrothal in San Domingo / *Die Verlobung in St Domingo*

The story is set in 1803. The blacks of San Domingo, now Haiti, first rose up against their French (and Spanish and English) overlords in August 1791. Their leader was Toussaint l'Ouverture. Slaves in the French part of the island were freed by the Convention in 1794. Toussaint declared the island independent and became its governor in 1801. But he was captured in 1802 by Napoleon's general Leclerc and jailed in France, in Fort Joux. When the French sought to re-introduce slavery the blacks rebelled again, this time under Jean-Jacques Dessalines, and drove them out.

Kleist, in 1807, was himself imprisoned for some weeks in Fort Joux, where Toussaint l'Ouverture had died three years before. That connection perhaps prompted him to write the story — which appeared first in instalments in the Berlin paper *Der Freimütige* (25 March–5 April 1811), then (July) in the Viennese *Der Sammler*, then (August) in the second volume of Kleist's *Erzählungen*.

The story is not black and white. M. Villeneuve, generous to Congo Hoango, gives Babekan sixty lashes for telling the truth against a white man who has betrayed her. The faithful Toni betrays her mother and her stepfather for Gustav — who by his foolishness has caused the death of his first betrothed and now kills his second in his want of faith. Everything happens at night, rights and wrongs are obscurely confused.

p. 324 mulatto: The child of a black and a white.

p. 325 mestiza: The child of a mulatto and a white.

p. 325 creoles: Whites born on the island (as opposed to immigrants from Europe), but on p. 331 the word seems to imply mixed race.

p. 333 old enough to marry: In C. F. Gellert's verse tale *Das junge Mädchen* when her father says she is only fourteen and too young to marry, the girl, who wants to, insists she is fourteen and seven weeks.

The Beggarwoman of Locarno / *Das Bettelweib von Locarno*

Kleist published the story first in his *Berliner Abendblätter*, 11 October 1810; then in the second volume of his *Erzählungen*. He may owe the plot of it to the family of his friend Ernst von Pfuel; though a somewhat similar tale was published by J. H. Jung-Stilling in 1778 and collected, as *Die alte Bettelfrau*, by the brothers Grimm.

Kleist's characters inhabit an unstable world. Here: a small harshness, an unhappy accident — and it collapses.

The Foundling / *Der Findling*

Probably written in the summer of 1811. It appeared that year for the first time in the second volume of Kleist's *Erzählungen*. There are some literary parallels. The narrator himself calls Nicolo 'a tartuffe' (p. 364); Elvire's debt to the young Genoese nobleman rather resembles Daja's to the templar in Lessing's *Nathan der Weise*; and her worshipping his image is prefigured in the story of Laodamia in Hyginus's *Fabulae*.

Piachi is the agent of his own destruction. Nicolo may be vicious, but he works on material — Piachi's foolishness, Elvire's fixation and repression — that almost seems to be crying out for him.

Saint Cecilia / *Die heilige Cäcilie*

Kleist published a shorter version of this story in his *Berliner Abendblätter*,

15–17 November 1810, as a christening gift for Cäcilie Müller, the daughter of his friend Adam Müller who had joined the Catholic Church in 1805. Expanded it appeared in the second volume of his *Erzählungen* in 1811. A possible source is Matthias Claudius's *Der Besuch im St Hiob zu* — (1782) which describes a lunatic asylum where four brothers were confined who sang a dirge whenever an inmate died. Kleist visited the asylum in Würzburg in September 1800 (see pp. 419–20). In a letter of 21 May 1801 he told Wilhelmine how moved he had been by Catholic church music in Dresden.

As to his story: Are the miscreants benighted by St Cecilia's punishment or enlightened?

p. 367 St Cecilia was a Roman martyr of the third century. Her life is recounted in Chaucer's *Second Nun's Tale*. Since the sixteenth century she has been best known as the patron of music.

p. 367 predicant: A minister of the Reformed Church.

p. 368 a nervous fever: This usually means typhus.

p. 369 Treaty of Westphalia: 1648, ending the Thirty Years War.

The Duel / *Der Zweikampf*

Kleist's starting point seems to have been the essay by C. Baechler 'Hildegarde von Carouge und Jakob der Graue' which appeared in a Hamburg newspaper on 21 April 1810. His own 'Account of a Remarkable Duel', which he published in the *Berliner Abendblätter*, 20–21 February 1811, draws heavily on that essay but also names the French chronicler Froissart (1338–1405) as a source. 'The Duel' itself, greatly expanded from that nucleus, was first published in the second volume of the *Erzählungen*.

The murder rather gets forgotten and, as so often in Kleist, it is a woman who is on trial and with her the institutions, premises and categories of her society. Littegarde's family behave as badly as the Marquise's. After a 'happy ending' the Emperor alters the statutes, leaving his people with one illusion less.

p. 377 St Remigius: Bishop of Reims, died 533. His feast day is 1 October.

p. 387 St Margaret's Day: 20 July. Put out of house and home and subjected to many ordeals she makes an appropriate patron for Littegarde.

p. 390 flamberg: Roland's sword, in the *Chanson de Roland*, was called 'flamberge'. The word came to mean simply 'sword', but the association with chivalry perhaps lingers here, ironically.

Anecdotes

Kleist published his anecdotes in the *Berliner Abendblätter* and it is likely that he wrote them immediately before their publication. Stylistically and in their curious, blackly comic material they are quintessential Kleist.

Hospital Incident / *Charité-Vorfall:* Published 13 October 1810. The Charité was (and is) a hospital in Berlin.

Anecdote (Capuchin and Swabian) / *Anekdote (Kapuziner):* 30 November 1810.

Anecdote (Two English boxers) / *Anekdote (Baxer):* 22 November 1810.

A Latter-day (and more fortunate) Werther / *Der neuere (glücklichere) Werther:* 7 January 1811. Goethe's Werther, hero of the novel published in 1774, shot himself for love of the married Lotte.

Strange Court Case / *Sonderbarer Rechtsfall in England:* 9 February 1811.

Essays

I have translated three of the dozen or so important essays Kleist wrote on literary and philosophical subjects.

On the Gradual Production of Thoughts / *Über die allmähliche Verfertigung der Gedanken beim Reden:* Probably written in 1805–6. It was not published till 1878.

p. 405 **Rühle von Lilienstern:** An old friend. He and Kleist were in the army together.

p. 405 **l'appétit vient en mangeant:** 'Appetite comes whilst eating.' As Kleist parodies it: 'Ideas come whilst speaking.'

p. 405 **Euler:** Leonhard Euler (1707–83), a Swiss mathematician and physicist.
        Kästner: Abraham Gotthelf Kästner (1719–1800), professor of mathematics at Leipzig and at Göttingen.

p. 406 **Molière:** He is said to have tried his jokes out on his maid to see if she found them funny.

p. 406 **Mirabeau:** Though an aristocrat he went as a representative of the Third Estate to the meeting of the Estates General in May 1789. He was a formidable orator.

p. 407 **Kleistian jar:** A condenser. It was invented almost simultaneously in the mid-eighteenth century by Ewald Georg von Kleist and by Cunaeus of Leyden (hence its commoner name: a Leyden jar).

p. 407 **Châtelet:** The ancient court and prison of Paris.

p. 407 **Les animaux malades de la peste:** 'The animals sick with the plague', La Fontaine, *Fables*, VII,i. The French, translated, reads: 'And as for the shepherd … it may be said … that he deserved all possible ill luck … being … one of those people … who imagine they have a right to rule over the animals.'

p. 409 **midwifery of thinking:** Kant (in *Metaphysik der Sitten*, 1797) says that the teacher, by skilful questioning, acts as midwife to the pupil's thoughts.

p. 409 To be continued: No continuation has been found.

Reflection / *Von der Überlegung. Eine Paradoxe*

Published in the *Berliner Abendblätter* 7 December 1810. The Prince of Homburg acts first; then in a long reflection *perhaps* regulates his feelings for other occasions in the future.

The Puppet Theatre / *Über das Marionettentheater*

Published in the *Berliner Abendblätter* 12–15 December 1810. This is Kleist's best-known and most influential essay. The argument that we cannot *return* to a state of grace but must seek to recover it (in a new form) by advancing was well established before Kleist. Schiller, Novalis, Hölderlin had all thought that way. But Kleist gives the structure a novel imagery and the tone of his essay is quite unique. Many twentieth-century authors have admired *The Puppet Theatre*. It influenced Rilke in his *Duino Elegies*, especially the fourth. Experts have found Herr C. unconvincing on the workings of marionettes and the argument, within a familiar structure, takes some odd turns; but the entirety, with its component anecdotes, is deeply intriguing.

p. 411 M.: Mainz? Metz?
    Herr C.: It is not known who, if anyone, Kleist had in mind.
    Teniers: David Teniers the Younger (1610–90), Flemish genre painter.

p. 413 Vestris: Several famous dancers had this name. Kleist probably means Marie-Jean-Augustin Vestris-Allard (1760–1842), soloist at the Paris Opera.

p. 413 *vis motrix*: The moving power.
    Daphne: Pursued by Apollo she escaped him by metamorphosing into a laurel tree.
    naiade à la Bernini: A naiade is a nymph of the water sources. Bernini (1598–1680), chief representative of Italian high Baroque. The poses and gestures of his sculptures are notably expressive (or affected).
    Paris: Son of Priam of Troy. Asked to decide who of Hera, Athene and Aphrodite was the most beautiful he chose the last and gave her the golden Apple of Discord as prize.
    Who P. and F. are is not known.

p. 414 Third chapter of Genesis: There the story of the Fall and of man's expulsion from the Garden of Eden is told.

p. 414–15 youth pulling a thorn out of his foot: The statue (a Roman bronze), was in the Louvre for a time (Napoleon stole it from Italy) and Kleist may well have seen it. The statue's pose, however — seated, the left foot drawn up — does not much resemble that of the youth in the anecdote.

p. 415 Livland: Or Livonia, a Baltic province south of Estonia.

Letters

There are two hundred and twenty-eight letters by Kleist in Sembdner's edition. But for the very last, all the letters in my small selection are from the early years. There is *some* justification for this. On the whole it may be said that Kleist wrote most interestingly to other people whilst he was still in the process of becoming a dramatist and a storyteller.

p. 417 his aunt: She became his guardian after the deaths of his father and mother.

    Gotha to Eisenach: He was travelling, after his mother's funeral, to rejoin his regiment in Frankfurt am Main.

p. 417 Martini: He was Kleist's boyhood tutor. Clearly, Kleist felt he owed him an account of himself.

p. 420 I did what the Roman did: The Roman is the ambassador Lucius Popilius Laenas who forced the Syrian king Antiochus IV (not the Tuscan Porsenna) to make up his mind.

p. 421 Kantian philosophy: Particularly the *Kritik der Urteilskraft* (1790), but the term may mean the whole line of subjective idealism as Fichte and others continued it.

p. 422 Cartouche: Louis-Dominique Cartouche (1693–1721), notorious robber-chieftain active in the environs of Paris.

p. 423 I climb the Schreckhorn: Most unlikely.

    Geβner, Zschokke, Wieland: See p. 429.

p. 425 another friend: Henriette Vogel (1777–1811). Kleist met her through Adam Müller, who had been her lover. She had cancer of the uterus and wished to die.

p. 426 the Green Room: A room in Henriette's house in Berlin.

p. 426 Having written this letter they took a cab to Stimming's 'Krug', an inn on the Wannsee, on the west side of Berlin. There they settled their affairs, wrote final letters, and on a small rise overlooking the lake committed suicide the following day, 21 November, in the late afternoon. Throughout their stay they were in very high spirits.